P9-CFB-516

Brett, Lily, 1946-

Too many men /

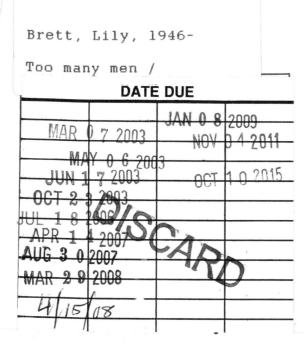

DATE DUE

		JAN 0 8 2009	
MAR 0 7 2003		NOV 0 4 2011	
MAY 0 6 2003			
JUN 1 7 2003		OCT 1 0 2015	
OCT 2 3 2003			
JUL 1 8 2006			
APR 1 4 2007			
AUG 3 0 2007			
MAR 2 9 2008			
4/15/08			

DISCARD

OCT 2 3 2001

VESTAL PUBLIC LIBRARY
0 00 10 0239720 4

Vestal Public Library
Vestal, New York 13850

Too Many Men

Too Many Men

LILY BRETT

WILLIAM MORROW
75 YEARS OF PUBLISHING
An Imprint of HarperCollins*Publishers*

This novel is a work of fiction. The names, characters, and incidents portrayed in it are the work of the author's imagination. Any resemblance to actual persons, living or dead, events, or localities is entirely coincidental.

First published in 1999 by Picador, an imprint of Pan MacMillan Australia PTY Limited, St. Martins Tower, 31 Market Street, Sydney

TOO MANY MEN. Copyright © 1999, 2001 by Lily Brett. All rights reserved. Printed in the United States of America. No part of this book may be used or reproduced in any manner whatsoever without written permission except in the case of brief quotations embodied in critical articles and reviews. For information, address HarperCollins Publishers, Inc., 10 East 53rd Street, New York, NY 10022.

HarperCollins books may be purchased for educational, business, or sales promotional use. For information please write: Special Markets Department, HarperCollins Publishers Inc., 10 East 53rd Street, New York, NY 10022.

FIRST U.S. EDITION

Designed by Paula Russell Szafranski

Printed on acid-free paper

Library of Congress Cataloging-in-Publication Data has been applied for.

ISBN 0-688-17755-7

01 02 03 04 05 QW 10 9 8 7 6 5 4 3

For David, my love,
with all my love

Too Many Men

∾ *Chapter One* ∾

The last time Ruth Rothwax had been with a group of Germans, she had wanted to poke their eyes out. The feeling had sprung out of her so suddenly and so unexpectedly that it had almost bowled her over. Where had this feeling come from? It had been a fully developed, ferocious wish—not some half-baked, halfhearted aggressive inclination. There had been no buildup, no preparation. One minute she was deep in her own thoughts, the next minute she wanted to gouge an old woman's eyeballs out. To stick her middle and index fingers right into those wrinkled sockets until the eyes dislodged themselves.

She had felt nauseated for hours after the incident. It had been in Poland, in Gdańsk. She had been staying at the Hotel Marta. The Marta was meant to be a luxurious hotel. But something had gone wrong. The tall, bleak building was awkward and ungainly. It stood on its large block of land, alone and unrelated to anything around it. It was impossible to feel at home at the Marta. A wind howled through the vast lobby each time the front doors were opened. And nothing was where it could be expected to be. The concierge's desk was hidden behind the women's toilets and the elevators were at the back of the building, a five-minute walk from the front desk.

The hotel was near the center of the city. It felt as though it was in the middle of nowhere. Ruth's room was on the seventeenth floor. There was an international golf tournament on in Gdańsk at the time. Every guest at the Marta seemed to be wearing a cap and carrying a set of golf clubs. There was a uniformity in the ensembles, too. The women wore pale sweaters and pastel pants or skirts. The men were dressed in knit tops and plaid or patterned trousers.

The golfers had unnerved Ruth. She didn't know much about golf, but she didn't think Poland was high on the list of the world's premier golfing locations. She had never heard anyone say they were going to Gdańsk to play golf. If people knew of Gdańsk at all, they knew of it as a port city, the home of Solidarity. Still, there were a lot of golf-playing Germans, Scots, and English at the Marta.

The German whose eyesight Ruth had wanted to eradicate got into the lift with her on her second night in Gdańsk. There were four Germans. Two men and two women, in their mid- to late seventies. It was late. After 11 P.M. Ruth was very tired. She moved over to make room for them. The two men were in tuxedos; the women wore evening dresses. They had obviously been celebrating.

One of the women laughed flirtatiously with one of the men. The laughter was the slightly off-key laughter of someone who had been drinking. The man smiled. The woman laughed, again. A high-pitched trill of a laugh. And then it happened. With no warning. All Ruth had felt was a rush of blood to her head. Suddenly her face had been tight with tension. She had turned toward the laughing woman. She had wanted to clamp the woman's laugh right off. To shut it down permanently. "It's not that funny," she wanted to say. She wanted to jab her fingers deep into the woman's pale blue eyes and repeat, "It's not that funny." Ruth's heart had started pounding. She had held her arms firmly by her side, at the back of the elevator. She had pressed her hands into her hips in an effort to anchor them. She was terrified that they would take flight of their own accord. Act independently of the rest of her. She had thought her fingers might strike out and dig and prod until they had reached the woman's brain.

The elevator was a particularly slow one. Ruth had thought it would never get to the seventeenth floor. Her hands burned and her skin itched. "It's not that funny," she wanted to say. "It's not that funny." She had kept her mouth clenched shut. The woman kept laughing. Finally, the elevator stopped at the seventeenth floor. Ruth got out. She walked unsteadily to her room. She sat down on the king-size bed with its blue brocade bed-spread and trembled.

That was a year ago. Ruth shuddered at the memory. She felt cold despite the fact that she had already been running for twenty minutes. She was in Poland again. In Warsaw. What was she doing in Poland? It was a good question. She hadn't come on a whim. She had spent two years talking her father, eighty-one-year-old Edek Rothwax, into joining her on this trip. He was flying in from Melbourne tomorrow.

Ruth checked the pedometer around her waist. She was doing seven miles an hour. She pressed another button. She saw that already she had run almost three miles. The pedometer was strapped onto a belt that also held a drink flask and a cassette recorder. A small microphone was attached to her headphones. This allowed her to record lists of things to be done as she ran. They were breathless recordings, but Ruth was able to decipher them. Her credit cards and some zlotys were tucked into her socks.

In New York, where she lived, she looked like any other runner. Most runners had water bottles around their waists and Walkmans plugged into their ears. But not in Poland. In Poland, Ruth looked weird. Several people in the hotel lobby had stared at her as she left for her run this morning. The doorman, the porter, and a group of Germans. The Germans stared hard and looked perplexed. She had smiled at the Germans. This had unnerved them further. They had all looked away.

Ruth loved running. She loved feeling her hip bones, her abdominal muscles, her legs. She also lifted weights three times a week, in Manhattan. She loved the way her chest seemed to expand when she brought down a lap pull. And she relished the stretch in her pectoral muscles as she strained to bench-press.

Sometimes, in the gym, men stopped their own exercises to watch her squat. It always amused her. She did three sets of twelve repetitions. She wasn't showing off. She was squatting for herself. For the sheer pleasure of feeling her back and legs as she lowered and raised herself with one hundred pounds on her shoulders. Lifting weights, her body felt alive. She could feel the individual components. Her feet and fingers felt strong. She felt connected to herself in a primal way. At the end of a workout, she felt replenished.

Exercise, she thought, was a reasonable substitute for sex. It wasn't perfect, but then neither, on the whole, was sex. Ruth thought that more and more women would soon be finding more fulfillment with their exercise equipment than their partners. New York City was full of women complaining about their men, or women complaining about their lack of men. Ruth fitted in well. She was forty-three, twice-divorced, single, and childless.

She had actually had three divorces, but the last marriage was a green-card marriage and she didn't include it among her marriages or divorces. Ruth had married her first husband at nineteen. She had been chubby and grateful that anyone had wanted to marry her. She hadn't noticed that he lingered longer than was necessary when he said good-bye to certain of his friends. The marriage ended when she found him jammed inside a young man, in her bed. She had read about homosexuals in books. She hadn't known that she had known any.

She married husband number two because she felt sorry for him. He couldn't work out what to do with his life. He was thirty-two. She thought he was very clever and could really do anything he wanted to do. He was a good-looking man. Tall, blue-eyed, and blond-haired. She felt lucky to be married to him. Good-looking men were usually attracted to slim girls and women. She tried to keep the light switched off, in bed at night, and apologized incessantly for earning more money than he did.

That marriage fell apart when he accused her of hindering his search for a vocation. "You're so efficient at what you do," he said, "that it intimidates me. I feel crushed. I feel more unable to work out what I want to do, now, than I did when we got married." He did work out that he wanted half of the small cottage she had bought in their second year of marriage. In the end, she had acquiesced. She sold the house and gave him half of the proceeds. She was surprised to find that she felt happier without him.

Two years after the divorce settlement he suggested that they reconcile. "No thanks," she said. She had felt elated at her certainty, and had had to tap her right foot ten times to ward off any evil that might have come with such happiness. She had a habit of tapping her right foot ten times to ward off evil. She knew it was stupid. She knew evil couldn't be warded off. Particularly with the tap of a foot. If tapping was effective, then every Jew in wartime Europe would have been tapping, day and night. Whole cities would have trembled with taps.

Ten taps were hard to disguise. Exceptionally hard in a business meeting. She had to count the taps, too, so she often lost the thread of what was being said. She had a few lesser protective mechanisms such as five rapid blinks of either eye to stop the destruction of small-scale happinesses or success. One year she had had to spit three times over her shoulder when she had felt in danger. That had proved a difficult thing to do in public, and she had been relieved when she'd felt safe enough to give that up.

Ruth tried to curtail the taps and the blinks as much as she could. She knew that if she let all of her idiosyncrasies loose, she could look like a maniac in minutes. These superstitious gestures had been part of her since she was a child. Yet she didn't believe in the supernatural. She scoffed at star signs, tarot cards, palm readings, clairvoyants, and psychics.

This was the third trip Ruth had made to Poland. She really didn't know why she was here. And she didn't know why she wanted her father to join her. Her first trip to Poland was just to see that her mother and father came from somewhere. To see their past as more than an abstract stretch of horror. To see the bricks and the mortar. The second time was an attempt to be less overwhelmed than she was the first time. To try and not cry all day and night. And she had cried less on that second visit. Now, she was here to stand on this piece of earth with her father.

Edek Rothwax hadn't wanted to come to Poland. When Ruth had first asked him, he'd said no. "What do you want to go to Poland for?" he had said. "There is nothing there. Everyone is dead. There is nothing to see." One day Ruth had felt a crack in Edek's resistance. She had told him she was going to go to Poland, on her own, again.

"You still want so much to go to Poland?" he said.

"Yes," she said. "I'd really like to be there with you."

"You are crazy," Edek said. "Where do you think we will be? Somewhere important? No. There is nothing important there. There is nothing there."

"We could go to Monte Carlo afterward," she had said. Edek loved a poker machine, and, Ruth was sure, although she'd never been there, that Monte Carlo must have poker machines.

"Pheh," Edek said. "We got such poker machines in Melbourne, now."

"We'll stay in a really nice hotel," Ruth said.

"You can afford the best hotels," he said, "in Las Vegas, in Monte Carlo, in Poland."

He was always telling her what she could afford. "You can afford to take it a bit easy," he would say if she said she was tired. "You shouldn't work so hard," he said regularly. "You can afford for someone else to do your work for you. You can afford anything."

He also wanted her to buy things. Cars in particular. He called constantly with suggestions of good cars to buy. They were always Lincoln Continentals, Cadillacs, or Pontiacs. He loved American cars, and he couldn't understand Ruth's lack of interest in them. "It costs four hundred dollars a month to garage a car in Manhattan," she would say to him. "You can afford it," he would say.

He called with other suggestions of what she could afford, too. These were mainly gadgets. Gadgets that chopped onions or cleared drains or converted currency. Ruth had said no to a self-retracting extension cord, an ultrasonic moth repeller, a handheld paper shredder, an indoor and outdoor thermometer, a pen that wrote underwater, a portable security motion detector, and hundreds of phones, fax machines, and photocopiers. If she had taken up all of Edek's suggestions she wouldn't, now, be able to afford anything.

When she first went into business on her own, Edek had been very nervous. "You have, finally, such a good job," he had said. Edek's dream had been for Ruth to be a lawyer. He saw the job she had writing letters and speeches at Schoedel, Firth, and Thomson, a large New York law firm, as a great disappointment. As Ruth's salary rose, Edek's disappointment eased. Ruth got the job by accident. She had a master's degree in twentieth-century literature, a degree that was not in high demand, and she had four years' experience as a private secretary in Melbourne. She had been working as a temporary typist at Schoedel, Firth, and Thomson, and trying to decide if she should stay in New York or return to Australia. She'd been in New York for three years. She was thirty-three. One evening, just as she was about to leave the office, a senior partner asked her to type a speech for him. It was late. Even the late-working secretaries had left. It was a terrible speech. Ruth typed it up. She also typed an alternative version. She left both speeches on the partner's desk. Two weeks later she was on the permanent staff of Schoedel, Firth, and Thomson with four weeks' annual vacation and a health care package.

"It makes me jittery," Edek had said to her, two years later, when she told him of her plans to branch out on her own. To start her own business. A letter-writing business. Edek had liked the wooden sign she had had made for her new office. "ROTHWAX CORRESPONDENCE. EST. 1991" it said. "LETTERS WRITTEN ON ALL SUBJECTS FOR ALL OCCASIONS." And his fears were mollified by the number of office items she had had to purchase in order to start the business.

Now that Rothwax Correspondence was successful, Edek was convinced that the company had been his own idea. "I did say to you," he said to Ruth regularly, "that if those lawyers could afford to pay you so much and still make a profit, there was for sure a profit to be made in this letter-writing business."

Ruth looked at her watch. Her father would be arriving in about thirty hours. Edek Rothwax had been forced out of his home, in Poland, when he was twenty-three. He hadn't been back since. He was nearly eighty-two now. He was twenty-three when he, his sister, two of his brothers, and his mother and father were ordered to leave their home. Like all the other Jews of Łódź, they left everything behind. They left the furniture, the piano, the bedding, the books, the china, the cutlery, the crockery, the photographs, the clothes. They took only what they could carry.

It was February 1940. They walked, with all the other Jews, along the one street they were allowed to use for their relocation. Mothers, fathers, children, grandmothers, and grandfathers carried their possessions in sacks, sheets, suitcases, prams, and upturned tables. Bearded men carried bundles of books bound together with string. A freezing wind howled and smacked at them. It was an exceptionally cold winter. They were not allowed to use the sidewalks. Over one hundred and fifty thousand Jews walked on the side of the road. They had to step out of the way whenever a car or truck drove by. The procession took days.

The Nazis had allocated 5.8 Jews to each room in their new homes. The Jews walked to those rooms, in the run-down slum area that had been designated for them, hanging onto their belongings and to each other. They walked out of their own lives, and, six years later, the few Jews who had survived found no trace of their former lives left.

"I don't know why I want to be in Poland with you," Ruth had said to her father the last time she had talked about going to Poland.

"I, for sure, don't know why," he had said.

"I just want to," Ruth said, "that's all I know."

"You are supposed to be so clever," Edek had said. "If you don't know, who should know?" Ruth sensed a barrage of criticism coming her way. She began to say good-bye. Edek interrupted her. "It is not important for me to go to Poland," he said. "For me, it is all finished there. But, if it is so important for you, I will go to Poland with you."

Ruth was stunned. "When do you want to go?" Edek said.

"Next month," she had said.

"Okay," said Edek. "You buy the tickets and pick me up on the way."

Ruth had been so taken by surprise, she hadn't been able to answer him. "Thanks, Dad," was all she had said. She had had to call him back and explain that Melbourne was not on the way from New York to Warsaw. She wouldn't be able to pick him up. She would have to meet him there.

Ruth felt a bit dizzy. She was used to running in larger spaces. She had been following the paths and promenades cutting across and around the Saxon Gardens. The park, off Piłsudskiego Place, a large square, was one of Warsaw's most popular gardens. Two soldiers, with the freshly scrubbed faces of the young, guarded the Tomb of the Unknown Soldier, at one end of the square. They marched in brisk unison around the memorial. Their black, highly polished metal-tipped boots clicked in a sharp synchronicity that echoed around the square.

The gray, thin winter light gave the park a sparse, Spartan demeanor. The Baroque sculptures, the fountain, and the benches didn't seem to add any warmth. There were over a hundred species of trees in the two-hundred-year-old gardens. They all looked the same to Ruth. They had trunks and they had branches. Maybe in summer, when they had leaves, it would be easier to differentiate between them.

Ruth didn't know a great deal about nature. Trees were green, to her. Grass was green. Nature was green. Too much green made her feel claustrophobic. She was glad it was winter. Jews weren't meant to know about trees. They weren't meant to be able to distinguish between poplar trees and oak trees, or birch trees or maple or willow trees. In Yiddish, there was one word for tree. Tree. It covered all trees.

There were quite a few people walking to work through the Saxon Gardens. On the whole, they didn't look happy. They looked locked into some kind of misery. New Yorkers didn't spend their days smiling, but there was a purposefulness and a vivacity to their snappiness and their lack of patience. Here in Poland, people looked oppressed. In 1983, on her first trip to Poland, Ruth had thought that they looked oppressed because of the terrible conditions that most Polish people were living under. There had been a dire shortage of food, then. Long lines of people queued for bread, for milk. There were queues for everything. Queues for soap, shampoo, toilet paper. Things were very grim for all Poles in 1983. The luxury goods stores in Warsaw displayed tubes of toothpaste and packets of laundry powder in the middle of otherwise empty shelves.

Things had certainly changed since then. Now you could buy Chanel, Armani, Guerlain, Ralph Lauren, and Calvin Klein. And food stores were stocked with sausages and cheeses, and pickled and potted meats and herring, and smoked and roasted ducks and chicken. But everyone still looked miserable. In restaurants, shops, and offices, the notion of service hadn't been wholly absorbed. Train conductors, shop assistants, clerks, and waiters seemed to slip from sycophantic to surly with unseemly speed. Most officials could lurch from obsequious to peremptory, in any exchange, with no evidence of what caused the switch. It was hard to like Poles, really, Ruth thought. A lot of Jews disliked Poles. "They're a suspicious and sour people, and they seem to have a monopoly on stained, brown teeth," her friend Aaron, a lawyer she had worked with, had said when she told him she was going to Poland.

You rarely heard Jews voice similar sentiments about Germans. Jews might express anger or hostility or a fear of Germans, but they didn't deride them in the same way that they slurred Poles. Ruth found this strange. Yet she was the same. She hardly ever expressed any hostility to Germans. But given half a chance, a round of aggression would fly out of her if she spoke about the Polish. "They look harsh and crushed and wrinkled and old as soon as they hit forty, as though their souls have slipped out of them and turned into skin," she had said to someone recently. What sort of a way was that to speak about any human being? She hated herself when she said things like that.

A man's voice startled her. "I think you can hear me," he said. She looked around. There was no one there. She slowed down. Who could have said that? Where did the voice come from? There was definitely no one there. The nearest person was thirty or forty feet away, at the end of the path. She must have imagined it. Maybe she was missing New York. In New York there was always someone saying something to you, or to themselves. She slowed down to a walk. She was probably more tense and more jet-lagged than she realized. She decided to go back to the hotel.

A couple walked past her. Ruth recognized fragments of their conversation. Fragments that were of no use. *Ja nie moge.* I can't. *Ja ci mówie.* I am telling you. She'd heard Polish spoken by her parents all of her life, and she understood so little of it. A van with Hebrew lettering and OUR ROOTS, in uppercase print on its side, drove by. Ruth remembered the brochure she had found in her hotel room in Warsaw on her last trip. The brochure, *Through Jewish Warsaw*, was published by Our Roots, the "Jewish Information and Tourist Bureau." The brochure detailed six tours, and the times you could be picked up for each tour from six different hotels. The price for all the tours was in U.S. dollars.

Tour One covered the Warsaw Ghetto, the Jewish Cemetery, the Nozyk Synagogue, the Jewish Historical Institute, and the ghetto wall. Tour Two was identical to Tour One except for the pickup times. Tour Three was stated, as Warsaw-Auschwitz/Birkenau-Warsaw. Tour Four offered Warsaw-Treblinka-Warsaw and Tours Five and Six had Majdanek as part of their package. Neither the guides nor the people in the Our Roots office seemed Jewish to Ruth.

Ahead of Ruth, at the edge of the park, a young woman, about twenty, was squatting beside a tree. As Ruth got closer she realized that the young woman was having a shit. A thick roll of brown shit hung from the woman's bum. Ruth felt nauseated. She wished she hadn't seen the shit in such detail. How could a young woman do that? There were hotels with public toilets nearby. Ruth wondered why this relatively uncommon sight seemed so Polish to her. She had never seen anyone shitting in public in Poland before. Why did she see Poles as coarse and vulgar? It was very prejudiced of her. Two women walked by. They were probably her own age, Ruth thought, though they looked about sixty. They both scrutinized Ruth, then nudged each other and continued to stare at her. Ruth felt uncomfortable. Why were the women being so aggressive?

Like many Polish women, they were over-lipsticked. Their bright red lipstick extended way above and beyond their mouths, and the black penciled curves on their foreheads were not in the same place that the eyebrows they were mimicking could possibly have been. They looked harsh and judgmental. Photographs of two other Polish women had appeared in the *New York Times*, the morning that Ruth left for Poland. The article accompanying the photographs was about the prevalence of domestic violence in Poland. All that bowing and kissing of hands, which so many Polish men indulged in, may have masked more disturbing habits. The *Times* quoted a common Polish proverb: "If a man does not beat his wife, her liver rots."

The Polish government was now embarking on a billboard campaign to let people know that brutality could not be viewed as a family disagreement. A photograph from one of the billboards reproduced in the *New York Times* showed a blond girl, her face swollen and bleeding. The caption read: *Bo musial jakoś odreagować.* Because he had to let off steam. In another billboard, a battered and cut woman was photographed with her young son. *Bo zupa była za słona,* the caption said. Because the soup was too salty. There was nowhere for battered Polish women to go. There were very few women's shelters. Warsaw didn't have a women's shelter. There was no one for the women to turn to. The police, prosecutors, and the Polish public saw men as the kings of their own domain. Complaints about men were hard to get heard. It was also hard to get divorced, in this highly Catholic country. Poland had one of the lowest divorce rates in Europe.

Ruth hurried past the two women in the park. She was five minutes away from the hotel. When she got there, she would write out the list of things to do that she had dictated on her run. The thought of putting things in order soothed her. She liked order. She liked things to go smoothly. Disturbance unnerved her. Even a change in the weather disturbed her. She saw it as disorderly.

A terrible lack of order had disrupted her mother's life, when her mother was fifteen. Ruth's mother was still in high school when the Germans took over Łódź. The Germans took over Łódź on the fifth of September, 1939. The fifth of September, almost seventeen years to the day before Ruth Rothwax would come into the world, already quiet. Already understanding that things had been thrown out of kilter in her world, and would remain tilted and off-balance for years. Photographs of Ruth show a wide-eyed, somber baby girl in the arms of a mother whose small smile masked none of her torment.

In Łódź, on that day in September 1939, people could hear cannon fire and shelling and the low rumble of artillery heading toward them. "It was so quiet in the streets," her mother had told her. "It was like even the birds and the flies had stopped breathing," Rooshka Rothwax had said to Ruth. "Even children were quiet." When Ruth listened to Rooshka talk like this, she could feel the silence herself. A silence that had enveloped the Jews of Łódź. All everyday noise seemed to have stopped. As though everyone had caught a hint of what lay ahead.

Hundreds of German troops had arrived a few days later. The soldiers sang, with gusto, songs about Jewish blood flowing from their knives. "You could smell the evil," Rooshka had said. New edicts from the Germans appeared daily in Łódź. Jews were allowed to be on the streets between 8 A.M. and 5 P.M. Any Jew seen on a street at any other time would be shot. The Germans began to round up Jewish men. They made them hop and jump in the street. They cut men's side-locks off and set fire to their beards. Rooshka's mother sent Rooshka out to buy bread. It was safer for Rooshka to go. She was in less danger than her father or any of her four brothers.

The Poles were eager to prove their loyalty to the Germans. *Heil Hitler*, they said. *Heil Hitler*. They pointed out Jews to the Germans. Poles who went to school with Jews pointed their former friends out. Poles who had done business with Jews, for years, turned them in to the Germans for any infraction of the new rules. "You'll be sorry you didn't fuck with me," a boy Rooshka went to school with said to her. "No one will want to touch you now, you piece of shit," he said. "You missed out on a good fuck." Rooshka said nothing. She walked away from him. "You thought you were better than me," he shouted. "Well, you're not. The Germans know who is shit and who isn't."

Rooshka Rothwax, Rooshka Spindler, then, had been a shy girl. Bookish, despite her quite startling beauty. She wasn't really interested in boys. She wanted to be a doctor. A pediatrician. She knew that for a Jewish girl from a poor family to stay in school it was necessary to have no distractions. "I want you to marry Edek Rothwax," Rooshka's mother had said to her, the day they had to move into the ghetto. "They are rich. You will be safer with them, and you will be able to help us, too. He has been chasing you for years. I think he will be a good husband." Edek and Rooshka were married, in the ghetto, on December 7, 1940. She was sixteen.

Ruth wiped the sweat from her face. She was surprised at how sweaty she was. She'd thought that she probably wouldn't sweat much in this cold weather. She had been deep in thought. She often thought about things when she was running. Thoughts that she managed to avoid at other times often arrived in the middle of a run.

Ruth thought about her mother. Order appeared to have returned to Rooshka Rothwax's universe, in Melbourne, Australia. The bunks, the barracks, the lice, the mud, seemed to have receded. But the recession was only on the surface. The silk blouse and the suntan couldn't erase the dead, their arms and legs sometimes still twitching. It couldn't erase the pus, the vomit, the shit, the piss. It couldn't eradicate the stench of all that flesh burning. Rooshka's mother and father and three sisters and four brothers' bodies had been part of that terrible smell.

In Australia, Rooshka Rothwax's house smelled of Chanel No. 5 perfume and Christian Dior creams and lotions. Everything was in its place. Rooshka ironed and folded towels and tea towels, napkins and sheets. She ironed handkerchiefs. She stored things in neat, carefully organized shelves. You could see at a glance where everything was kept. Everything was in its place. And Rooshka needed it that way. Now and then Edek accidentally put something where it didn't belong. A pillowcase on top of the towels, or a couple of bowls where the saucers should have been. It always left Rooshka distraught. Order was everything.

Ruth Rothwax tried hard to be disorderly. She didn't want to be like her mother. At work, she practiced messing up her desk. Moving pieces of paper so that they weren't perfectly aligned. It wasn't easy, and Ruth felt proud when she could tolerate some chaos. She felt overjoyed the day she managed to leave her apartment without making her bed. She was also in the process of trying to create a degree of disarray among the coat hangers in her closet. For most of her life, she had needed her hangers all to face the same direction. Now, if she accidentally put one back the wrong way, she tried to leave it there. At least for a day. Ruth could see the absurdity of some of the issues she was trying to come to grips with. How many sane people wrestled with their coat hangers? She started to laugh and almost tripped over. It was impossible to laugh and run. She straightened herself up.

She imposed order on herself in other ways. She allowed herself a maximum of twelve minutes to read *People* magazine. She knew that *People* magazine was rubbish, and that it often gave her a headache to read about this starlet's battle with bulimia, or that actress's long road to recovery from alcoholism. Even the divorces and marriages were hard to digest. She had barely caught up with a celebrity's second marriage when the magazine was reporting his third. A twelve-minute limit to this information seemed to settle Ruth's conflict about the place *People* magazine should occupy in her life.

The place that New York City occupied in her life had crept up on her. For her first five years in the city, she had claimed she was in transit. On the verge of returning to Australia. Now, after twelve years, she had to acknowledge that she loved New York. She loved it most when things worked. When a taxi arrived as soon as you raised your arm. When the train to Greenport, Long Island, left at 7:04 P.M., on Friday, and the ferry that took her to Shelter Island was waiting in Greenport for that train.

She liked Shelter Island because it was quiet, but also because everyone obeyed the rules. If you drove through a stop sign, it would appear in the "Police Blotter," in the *Shelter Island Reporter*, the following week. Ruth knew that being on Shelter Island relaxed her, and she tried to spend at least six weekends a year there. She needed the peace of mind and the freedom that the island gave her.

Order helped Ruth to experience freedom. Children of Holocaust survivors found it hard to feel freedom. Ruth had read that many times. They found it difficult to separate from their parents. Difficult to have a life of their own. Difficult to have a life. They had to create obstacles and burdens for themselves. To align themselves with their parents. To experience at least some of the horror. Weighted down with fear, apprehension, and depression, they felt free enough to go on. Children of survivors had to fill up their parents' emptiness. They had to make up for lost objects and people and ideals. No wonder freedom seemed far-fetched for so many of them.

The warnings of impending danger that children of survivors received from their parents were not overt or intentional. Parents didn't shout out their knowledge of the hostility of the world. They didn't have to. The children had received that message of omnipresent threat a long time ago. The children understood, too, that they had to keep their anger to themselves. How could you be angry with parents who had suffered so much? The children became adept at turning their anger on themselves. And dealing with parents who were too preoccupied to notice the angers and upsets of ordinary, everyday life. Parents who were always preoccupied. Always somewhere else, somewhere out of reach. In a past that was untouchable.

There were also strange envies and resentments to grapple with. Ruth knew that her mother envied her for having a mother. And she knew, when she was a teenager, that her mother resented the fact that Ruth had a youth. Ruth tried to dispense with her youth. She cultivated a serious weariness. At twelve, when she began to attract looks, she tried to get rid of them, too. She covered her new breasts with bulky dresses that covered most of the rest of her.

Her mother's looks were one of the few things about Rooshka Rothwax that had survived intact. Rooshka was exceptionally beautiful. And Ruth didn't want anything to diminish the importance of that. So, Ruth put on pounds and pounds of fat, and soon no one looked at her, except in pity. By the time Ruth felt safe enough to emerge, Rooshka Rothwax was dead and buried.

Ruth grieved for her mother for years. She was twenty-eight when her mother died. Rooshka had died of cancer, at sixty. She had died with her beauty undimmed, her looks as luminous as they had ever been. Ruth often still cried, now, when she thought of her mother. A psychologist once asked Ruth if she had linked her mother's death with her own ability to lose weight. Ruth had nearly fainted at the question. It was not a connection that had occurred to her. A lack of understanding about the connections and complications of being the child of survivors was not the only thing missing from most children of survivors. Children of survivors depressed Ruth. She tried to avoid them. She found them curiously blank and lifeless. Joyless. The high achievers seemed as muffled as the more forlorn.

Even in expansive moments children of survivors still seemed mute. Ruth had watched Leon Wasserstein at his wedding to wife number two. Ruth had been at school, in Melbourne with Leon. He was a short, slight man. A scientist. He looked frightened even when he was expressing happiness. Leon was born, after the war, in Bergen-Belsen. When Ruth asked him about Bergen-Belsen, he said he had no memory of it and was sure it had had no effect on him. "It was my mother and father who suffered," he had said.

Leon Wasserstein was forty-three when he married for the second time. His wife, a tall, big-boned, blond Australian, several years older than Leon, announced that she and Leon were going to dance for the guests. "My wife Lee-Anne choreographed these dances, herself," Leon added, before they began dancing.

On the dance floor, Leon Wasserstein looked like a child trying to guess what was going to happen next. Lee-Anne flung him around. He followed her movements as best as he could. They were tricky movements. The couple had to put their hands up, then their hands down. They had to kick the right leg out in front of them, then kick the left. They had to turn toward each other with their arms outstretched, and turn back again, and clap. They had to step this way and that way, and turn and whirl.

At one stage, the bride's blue satin dress billowed wildly and nearly swallowed poor Leon. When he emerged, he was still kicking. Ruth noticed that although Leon's fingers and toes were animated, his face had remained peculiarly unmoved. By the third dance, Ruth had had to leave the room. She couldn't bear the sight of Leon nodding his head to a beat that was clearly out of his reach.

Ruth was about to enter the Bristol Hotel. The Bristol was one of Warsaw's most expensive hotels. "I think you can hear me," a voice said. Ruth nearly fell over. It was that voice again. Her heart started pounding. She looked behind her. There was no one there. She was alone. She looked in front of her. The doorman was standing behind the large, glass doors of the hotel. There was no one else about. The doorman stepped forward to open the door for Ruth. She turned away. She walked briskly along Krakowskie Przedmieście. Then, with no warning, she stopped and looked back. There was no one there. Nobody was following her.

She began to walk back to the Bristol. "I think you can hear me," the voice said again, with an emphasis on the word *you*. Ruth felt frightened. She began to tremble. She pulled herself together. She was just tired, there was no one there. "I can't hear you," she said, defiantly, to the almost empty street. "I knew you were the one," the voice said triumphantly. Ruth shook herself. This was absurd. She was, clearly, hearing things. She had always had an overly active imagination. She really must be very tired.

❧ *Chapter Two* ❧

*T*wo wake-up calls, five minutes apart, woke Ruth up. She always requested two wake-up calls in hotels. It decreased the odds of the call being forgotten by 50 percent. Three minutes later, the alarm clock she had set rang. At home, in her regular life, she had weaned herself off a variety of multiple wake-up mechanisms. She now made do with two alarm clocks.

Ruth found it hard to go to sleep at night. Night had an endlessness about it. An excessive number of unstructured and unknown hours that frightened her. Alarm clocks punctuated that time. Marked the end with a loud ring. Alarm clocks enabled Ruth to feel some sense of certainty about waking up.

She confused sleep with death, one shrink had said to her. Another suggested that sleep frightened her as what happened when she was asleep was something that was out of her control. Ruth didn't like either theory.

She had slept well last night. She often slept well in hotels. There was less to feel anxious about. Someone was on guard all night. In expensive hotels several someones were on guard. There were security systems. Cameras that roamed the elevators, staircases, and hallways. There were fire and smoke detectors. Less could be overlooked.

Ruth felt refreshed. Her head felt clear. Her vasomotor system must have gone astray yesterday. She wasn't sure exactly what her vasomotor system was. She thought it had something to do with her nervous system. She imagined it as a series of wires connected to her brain. When one of them came loose, things went a bit haywire.

She thought that as a mature person, she should understand the workings of the brain in more detail. But she didn't want to. If you knew too much, Ruth felt, about how any part of your body functioned, it left you more vulnerable about what could go wrong. Certain things, Ruth was certain, could cause a loose connection in the brain's electrical circuitry. Like jet lag. It must have been jet lag that made her imagine someone was speaking to her.

She had a suite in the Bristol. A bedroom and a living room. The living room had a sofa, an armchair, a coffee table, and bookshelves. The books in the shelves simulated somebody's real collection. There were well-thumbed-through old volumes, and current titles. A couple of the book covers were torn. It was an upper-class library that this collection was imitating. There were several leather-bound books and no paperbacks.

Ruth had tried to look through the books on the shelves last night. But there wasn't enough light in the living room. On the whole, the more you paid for a hotel, the less you could see. As though an adequate amount of light might lower the tone. The lighting definitely seemed to dim or brighten in direct ratio to the dollars expended by the guests.

Ruth got out of bed. She couldn't see herself in the mirror. If she stayed in hotels any more expensive than this, she would have to pack a flashlight. All four phones in the suite rang. Ruth looked around. She couldn't see any of them. Every surface contained a figurine or a vase or a bowl. It took her a couple of minutes to locate a phone.

"We can put calls through to you now, madam?" the hotel operator asked.

"Yes," she said. She had forgotten that she had asked not to be disturbed until 8 A.M. today.

"You have Maximilian on line two for you," the operator said. "Line two is in the bedroom."

"Maximilian?" Ruth said.

"Yes, madam, Maximilian," the operator said. "She waits for you already five minutes."

Ruth picked up the other phone. "Hi, Max," she said. "The operator told me Maximilian was on the line."

"She called me Maximilian," Max said. "Maximilian is better than Maxine. I told her it was just Max. I told her that my parents wanted my brother to feel involved in my birth, that they didn't want him to feel left out, so they let him name me. I told her he was six and he named me Max. I explained it to her carefully, but she didn't seem to get it."

Ruth laughed. Max often made her laugh. Max was twenty-six. She had been working for Ruth for five years. Max always overcommunicated everything. It drove some people mad, but Ruth found it an endearing quality. When Max's effusive explanations got too much for her, she would say, "Edit, Max, edit." Max never took offense. She just removed the extraneous detail. Ruth was very fond of Max.

"Max, isn't it very late at night for you?" Ruth said. "You can't still be in the office?"

"No, I'm at home," Max said. "It's two o'clock in the morning."

"Two o'clock in the morning?" said Ruth.

"I thought it would be easier to catch you at this time," Max said. "I'm always up anyway. I'll be brief and to the point, I don't want to intrude on what has to be a very emotionally tumultuous trip."

"The tumult hasn't quite started," Ruth said. "But let's not run up your phone bill more than necessary. Is everything okay?"

"Everything in the office is A-1," Max said. "If my personal life was in as good shape as this company, I'd be off and away. Metaphorically speaking, of course."

"Good," said Ruth.

"Bern is working out well," Max said. "He got in late this morning, but he said, and I believe him, that there was some kind of holdup on the subway. They kept the train at Union Square station for thirty minutes. With the doors closed. He couldn't get off. That doesn't happen so often now, but it used to happen to me, regularly."

"Edit, Max, edit," Ruth said. She didn't need to hear about Bern's battles with the city's transport system. She had hired Bern two months ago. He used to make deliveries to them from a local stationery store. Ruth liked him from the first day she'd met him. She had asked him why he didn't stop smoking. "I'm not a quitter," he had replied. Ruth was impressed by his eloquence and his good nature. He often asked Ruth questions about the business.

"You are a smart dude," he had said to her one day. "I'd like a company like this."

"You could have one, one day," she'd said.

"I need to learn the business first," he said. "Would you give me a job?" The question had taken her by surprise. Bern was very young. He was only eighteen.

"I'll do your pickups and deliveries," he said. "I'll clean the office. I'll do all the jobs you don't want to do until I've learned the business and I'm more useful."

"I'll think about it," she said. A week later, she hired Bern.

Bern hadn't stopped smiling since he'd got the job. His mother had called Ruth to thank her for giving Bern this opportunity. Ruth had felt bad. She felt she wasn't giving Bern all that much.

"We needed someone else in the office," she said to Bern's mother.

"Not many white women would give a young black man a chance," Bern's mother had said. "I'm going to pray for you in church, on Sunday."

"Thank you," Ruth had said.

Ruth knew life was hard for young black kids, especially boys. She could see how segregated America was. If you went to the theater or a dinner party or a museum or an art gallery, you saw very few black people. At an opening of anything, in New York, everyone wanted to let themselves be seen being friendly to the two and a half black people who were present.

Ruth was very fond of Bern, but she didn't want to be sitting in the Bristol Hotel, in Warsaw, discussing delays in the New York City subways.

"Sorry," Max said. "We've got an order for fifteen different thank-you letters. It's Mr. Newton of Newton Labs. He wants fifteen thank-you-for-your-thoughts-while-I-was-ill letters. His secretary said to make sure we don't duplicate any of his thank-you-for-our-wedding-anniversary-gifts letters. I can't put fifteen different versions together from our thanks-for-your-thought file, especially if they can't duplicate the wedding-anniversary letters. There were seventy-five of them, I looked them up. Each one was slightly different."

"I'll do it," Ruth said. "What was wrong with Mr. Newton?"

"Bypass surgery," said Max.

"Okay," Ruth said. "I'll do that right now."

The business center of the Bristol Hotel had a genteel, refined, and very masculine air. It was furnished with large, well-padded leather sofas and armchairs. Leather-bound books lined the bookshelves and tasteful framed prints, drawings, and historical documents were on the walls.

"Are you looking for someone, madam?" the man at the business desk asked her.

"I need to fax some documents," she said. He looked surprised. "There are a lot of women doing business today," she said. "Probably even in Poland."

"Of course we have faxing facilities," he said, and stood up, rapidly, to greet a very fat man with a gold fob watch hanging from his pinstriped waistcoat.

Ruth pulled up a file labeled Thanks-Post-Surgery from her new laptop computer. It was the smallest and lightest computer on the market. Her father would have approved of this purchase, Ruth thought.

Ruth blinked her left eye five times. She always did this when she composed letters referring to a person's health, or death. It was a strange safeguard she didn't really understand. A sign to someone, a higher being, maybe, that she knew these things were not to be meddled with. But she didn't believe in higher beings. She didn't believe in God.

"There is no God," was the only reference to religion that was voiced when Ruth was growing up. "There is no God," her mother said, always looking up at the sky. Ruth often wondered why her mother looked upward when she made this statement. She never asked. She didn't want to hear the stories of babies used as footballs by the Gestapo, or babies who had their heads smashed against brick walls again.

Ruth finished the thank-you letters without any more blinking. A man sat down on the other side of the table she was working at. She recognized him. He had been at the front desk when she left for her run yesterday. "I am a physician," he had kept shouting, in his thick German accent. "I am a physician and I do not like the room you have given to me."

Forty-five percent of German doctors became members of the Nazi party during the Third Reich. Ruth knew that from her reading. Doctors were the largest group of any professionals to join the Nazi party. The Nazi Physicians' Association, in March 1933, appealed to their fellow physicians who had so far resisted the cause. "No profession is as Jew-ridden as the medical profession," they said in a published statement. "Jewish doctors control the professorships in medicine, take the spirit out of the medical art, and have imposed on generation after generation of young physicians a mechanistic spirit."

A *mechanistic spirit*. Ruth had an image of a group of German doctors dispensing warmth and exuberance and tenderness once they had rid themselves of those mechanistically spirited Jews. In April 1933 Nazi doctors and SA Sturmabteilungen troops stormed public hospitals and clinics and universities expelling their Jewish colleagues. Removing the Jewish doctors removed the competition. German doctors' careers flourished.

Ruth looked at the German doctor sitting opposite her. He seemed calmer this morning. They must have given him the room that he wanted. He was a thickset man in his seventies, with coarse features and a large, grim face. Ruth wondered if he still saw patients. She wouldn't want to have her health in this physician's hands.

It had taken Ruth a long time in America to find a doctor she liked who was on her health insurance company's list of doctors. Health care was a large issue for most Americans. The issue was the health insurance. How to get the insurance, how to pay for it, and exactly how much health was covered by this insurance.

Health care insurers were often portrayed as being more interested in their own profit than anyone else's pain. The image of insurance companies as paternal, trustworthy institutions, who provided peace of mind for their insured, was almost gone, in America, today.

Some insurance companies had a bleak past. Days after *Kristallnacht*, that night in November 1938 when German mobs smashed, looted, and burned one hundred and seventy-one synagogues and thousands of Jewish shops and businesses, German insurance companies seized the opportunity to save themselves money. Nineteen of the forty-three German fire insurance companies stood to suffer losses for the year if they honored the policies held by their Jewish policyholders.

The Isar Life Insurance Company articulated the problem eloquently in a letter dated November 17, 1938, in which it explained that so many Jewish clients were desperately trying to cash in their policies that "the worst fears have to be asserted for the further existence of our company."

They didn't have to worry. Their concerns were heard. The Nazis established the practice of confiscating the insurance assets of German Jews. It was no longer necessary for German insurance companies to make payments to Jews for fire or life insurance.

In December 1938, an insurance company that sold pension annuities informed the German government that it would be discontinuing the payment of pensions and widow's pensions "insofar as the recipients are Jews." That was fine with the German government.

Ruth put away her work. She felt nauseous. She decided she needed some breakfast. She often felt nauseated if she tried to skip breakfast. The dining room was full of businessmen. Ruth found a table she could have to herself. She didn't like eating with strangers. She took some melon and strawberries and kiwi fruit from the buffet.

The men at the table next to her were German. She watched them eat. They were so neat and particular. They wiped their mouths with a napkin after each mouthful of food, and buttered their bread with architectural precision. These small movements were made by large men. Tall, big-boned men. Their hands, the ample hands of grown men, were at odds with the gestures they were making. The fastidiousness of the men's habits belonged to a more diminutive race.

The men were quiet while they ate, too. Unlike their American counterparts, who spoke in voices loud enough to pollute most of the dining areas they inhabited. The German businessmen were also formal in other ways. They ate in their well-pressed suits. Not one of the men removed his jacket for the meal. Their shirts were crisp and creaseless and their shoes perfectly shined.

Ruth couldn't take her eyes off the table of Germans. They were graciously polite with each other. They lacked the chumminess of American or Australian men. They were lavishly well-mannered with the waiters and waitresses. They nodded their heads and said thank you to every ounce of tea poured and every dish removed. A politeness so excessive it bordered on caricature. All that courtesy and restraint made Ruth want to fart or burp loudly. She decided to go for a walk. She had seven hours to kill until her father arrived.

———

Ruth walked. She wasn't walking anywhere in particular. She was just walking. Warsaw was an ordinary city, she thought. Apart from the perfectly reconstructed old town, built from scratch after the war, there was not a lot to look at. She knew she was close to the University of Warsaw. She walked in the general direction of the university.

She passed a Wedel chocolate shop. Her father was always talking about Wedel chocolate. He spoke of it in the same exalted terms that he used to describe Polish ham. "Polish ham is out of this world. Sweet like anything," he would say. Wedel's chocolate was, in Edek's opinion, "out of this world."

You would have thought his life in Poland was composed of slices of ham and blocks of chocolate. Maybe in Edek's mind it was. It was certainly easier to dwell on ham and chocolate than a dead mother and father and sister and brothers. They were truly out of this world, Ruth thought.

Edek always looked transported when he recalled the taste of the ham or the chocolate. Ruth looked at the chocolate in the window. It did look good, but then most chocolate looked good to her. She thought that the sight of a whole shop full of Wedel's chocolate would definitely make the trip from Australia worthwhile for her father.

Ruth bought Edek blocks of chocolate whenever she traveled. She had sent him Mexican chocolate, English chocolate, French chocolate, and chocolate from Bermuda. She regularly shipped packets of Hershey's semisweet dark chocolate to him from New York. She understood Edek's love of chocolate. She felt that way about cakes. Poppy seed cakes and cheesecakes.

Warsaw had wonderful cake shops. Cake shops that had the cakes of her childhood. When she was growing up they didn't have apple pies or jam tarts or custard or vanilla slices or other Australian cakes in the house. They had strudel and sponge cakes and marzipan and cheesecakes. The cakes of the past. The cakes that Ruth could see all around her now.

She was gazing at a large poppy seed strudel on the counter of a small cake stall in a pedestrian underpass close to the university, when she felt a tug at the hem of her coat. Ruth looked down. A woman was sitting cross-legged on the ground, almost lost in the throng of students.

It was hard to tell how old she was. Her skin was dull with ingrained dirt and her eyes were flat with weariness. The multilayered cotton garments she wore were smudged and clouded with grime and dust. A large, once brightly colored scarf was wound in intricate circles around her head.

She tugged at Ruth's coat again, and looked up imploringly. Ruth slid the strap of her backpack off her shoulder. She had to give this woman some money. She had seen several gypsy women in Warsaw. Most of them were begging. Ruth smiled at the woman.

In between the folds of the woman's clothes, something moved. Buried in a grubbiness it should never have been a part of was a baby. The baby was attached to one of the woman's breasts. Ruth looked at the baby. It seemed inert. Almost lifeless. The breast, a brown, wrinkled flat bag of a breast, looked as though it couldn't contain any nourishment. Ruth wanted to cry. She opened her purse. The woman held out her hand. It was a surprisingly young hand. Ruth gave her fifty zlotys.

Fifty zlotys was a bit less than twenty dollars. Ruth knew it wasn't much. She wanted to give the woman more, but she felt too embarrassed. She didn't want to emphasize the discrepancy in their financial positions. What an imbecile she was, she thought. As though it wasn't obvious that she had more money.

She got out another fifty zlotys and gave it to the woman. The woman smiled. If she hadn't had so many teeth missing it would have been a very sweet smile. The woman said something to her. "*Nie mówię dobrze po polsku,*" Ruth said.

Ruth could say *Nie mówię dobrze po polsku,* I don't speak Polish very well, very well. It confused people. "You have a perfect accent," several people said to her. If only she could say more in this perfect accent it would be useful.

The woman repeated what she said. Ruth shrugged her shoulders and shook her head. She had no idea what the woman was saying. The woman repeated herself, slowly enunciating each word.

"It means 'too many men,'" a young man passing by said to Ruth. "She is saying to you, you have too many men in your life." Ruth laughed. Too many men. She didn't have any men in her life. The gypsy woman looked agitated. She stabbed the air with her finger and repeated what she had said.

"She says you have too many men in your life," the young man said. "These gypsies are psychic," he said. "They have a God-given psychic power." Ruth was irritated. Why were Poles so fixated on God? "God-given?" she said. "If there is a God, he could have given them food and shelter."

The young man raised his eyebrows in the manner of someone of an older generation, and crossed himself. "You don't need to protect yourself," Ruth said to him. "It was my blasphemy."

"Do widzenia," she said to the woman. Ruth could say good-bye well, too. *"Do widzenia,"* the woman said.

Ruth wondered how the gypsy baby was going to survive. The baby had no future at all. Ruth felt depressed. She felt that she should be able to do something about the gypsy woman and her baby. Something about all gypsy women and their babies.

She felt the same way about the homeless in New York. In her first few years she had given money to every homeless person she had passed. Now, she donated money, annually, to several charities. But she felt that it wasn't enough. The money that she gave didn't really make a dent in her lifestyle. Middle-class people like her were always puffing themselves up with what they did for others. The reality was that most of them did very little.

Ruth looked at the students around her. This part of Warsaw, with its student population, had more life to it. It had a vivacity and a vigor that was missing from the rest of the city. The students had the earnestness and joyfulness of students anywhere. They talked and laughed and argued with each other with passion and intensity. She was glad she was walking in the middle of them.

She thought about the gypsy woman. Too many men. What did she mean? It sounded like a joke. A New York joke. In New York, single women regularly bemoaned the lack of available men in the city. There did seem to be a shortage of men in New York. And those who were there considered themselves highly desirable commodities.

Ruth didn't want too many men. She wasn't that comfortable with men. She wasn't that comfortable with anyone. The only man she had truly felt comfortable with went back to his wife. He was separated when he met Ruth. And Ruth was newly divorced. One day his wife decided she wanted him back. His wife cried and screamed and drove her car through a restaurant window to show him how much she needed him. He went back to her. He called Ruth, often, after that. He said he loved her, but he was frightened of what his wife might do to herself if he wasn't around.

Being left for someone else left Ruth feeling awful. It gave her a second-rate feeling about herself. As though she was a runner-up and not good enough to get the prize. She knew that that image of herself with a man as a prize was a retrograde thought. No woman should think of a man as a prize.

She wasn't thinking very clearly when she met him. She knew he was still married. But, two days after she met him, thirty-four hours after she met him, to be exact, she was mad about him. She was wildly in love and understood, for the first time in her life, why it was called wild. They were both twenty-nine. He was a painter. He painted large, almost monastic, meditative abstract paintings. Gray and black strokes quietly placed on the canvas.

She loved to watch him paint. He painted the mystical marks with rough, firm gestures. When he used color, it was muted and elegant. Pale aqua oblong ellipses, interspersed with shadows of themselves, swam like fish across a bare background. Ruth found his paintings surprisingly calming.

Painting, art, of any sort, was not part of her world before she had met Garth Taylor. He was not as self-contained as his paintings. He touched and laughed and cried. He was unself-conscious. His clothes were not the carefully chosen, studiedly casual working-class clothes of the art world. He dressed more like a moderately successful accountant. He wore gabardine trousers and plain shirts. But he was unlike any accountant Ruth knew.

He was unlike most other people she knew. He was tactile and sensual. He allowed mango juice to drip down his face when he ate the fruit. He pulled lobsters apart with his fingers and sucked the flesh out of the claws. The filaments of fish or intestines or liquid that sometimes sprayed out at him left him unperturbed.

"I've never loved anybody so utterly," Garth Taylor said to her, days after they met. He seemed to love all of her. He loved her body. Nobody, including Ruth, had ever loved her body. When Garth told her she was beautiful, she pointed out the lack of proportion between the top half of her and the bottom. "I love the feel of you," he said to her over and over again. "I'm too fat," she replied.

———

"She is fat," was the worst thing Rooshka Rothwax could say about another female. Fat men were not quite in the same category. "She is so slim," was her mother's highest accolade. It didn't appear to matter if the slim girl or woman was clever or stupid or kind or arrogant. If she was slim, she was to be admired. Edek also derided fat people. He didn't seem to notice he was one of them himself. He had spent most of his adult life twenty to thirty pounds overweight. He was still a bit chubby now.

Ruth's mother's slim figure was admired by everyone. "I was always a slim girl," Rooshka Rothwax used to say. "I was never fat." Ruth thought that her mother saw greed and lack of self-control stitched into every fat cell in existence. "In the ghetto I never ate my bread straightaway," her mother would say to her. "I was a human being. Not a pig. Even when I was starving." "In Auschwitz," Rooshka would say, "if someone was fat you knew that they were doing something that was making the lives of the other Jews worse."

The Nazis caricatured Jews as short and fat. Rooshka Rothwax spent the rest of her life, after the war, determined to be tall and thin. She added two and a half inches to her height and never overate. "Are you sure you're five foot four?" Ruth had asked her mother once. Ruth was nine, at the time. They had measured Ruth's height at school. "You're five foot two," the gym teacher had said to Ruth. "I can't be," Ruth had said. "I'm taller than my mother and she's five foot four." "I am five foot four," Rooshka Rothwax had said in answer to Ruth's question. "I am tall for a woman," her mother had said. "You are too tall. You are so tall because you eat so many sweets." Ruth had thought her mother hadn't known about the sweets. Rooshka had never mentioned the assorted sweet wrappers Ruth left lying around.

When Ruth reached five foot nine, she tried to stop eating sweets. She was already taller than all of the boys in her class. She ate no sweets or chocolate for a week. She didn't shrink. She went back to her two packets of musk Lifesavers after school, and the bag of chocolate-coated broken biscuits she bought in the grocery store every morning. She remained at five foot nine.

Ruth wasn't too tall for Garth Taylor. She wasn't too anything. He tolerated all of her idiosyncrasies. He was amused by them. "You're so funny," he would say to her. Garth hadn't come from a funny past. His mother was English and his father was Irish. Alcoholic, illiterate, and Irish. Ruth couldn't understand Garth's lack of connection to his parents until she met them. There was a mocking cruelty to his father and an indifference in his mother. Garth's stories about being beaten up by his father and having to protect his mother from similar beatings made sense to Ruth when she met the Taylors.

Ruth had wondered why Garth bothered to keep in contact with his parents at all. They didn't seem to love him. "You were born nothing and you'll die nothing," Garth's father had said to him the day Garth introduced Ruth to them. Ruth had squirmed and wished she hadn't asked to meet the Taylors. Ruth knew that Garth had had very little as a child. She hadn't realized how little. She knew that he had walked the three miles to school and back, in bare feet, until he was twelve. His parents' lack of warmth and apparent lack of interest overwhelmed Ruth. She couldn't wait to leave their house.

The Taylors still lived in the same small fibrous cement house, in an outer suburb of Sydney, that Garth grew up in. Garth had moved on. He had moved into the middle-class world of art and literature. He wrote art reviews for a national newspaper and had regular exhibitions of his paintings in galleries around the country. "I'd rather have all the combined neuroses of every Jewish parent than have your parents," Ruth had said to Garth after they left his parents' place. "They're very cold," she said.

"They tried their best," he said. "My mother was sixteen when she had me and my father was nineteen."

"They don't have to be so cruel," she said.

"They can't help it," he said.

"Why aren't you angry with them?" she had said to him.

"I'm just not," he said. "I feel sorry for them."

Garth found it hard to be angry. He couldn't even make a dismissive comment about anyone he knew. He went out of his way not to hurt or offend anybody. Ruth was rude for him. She had a sharp tongue and she used it liberally. Resentments and irritations flew out of her. Garth laughed at them.

Garth laughed a lot. And Ruth laughed with him. They laughed at how happy they were with each other. And Garth wept. He wept with joy. Ruth, who had barely been able to cry, even when she was in pain, wept with him.

He didn't seem to mind her anxiety or her fear. "I'm freeing you of the need to feel those things," she joked with him. "You can feel them vicariously through me." He smiled at her. His smile lifted her. It lifted her spirits and overrode many of her fears. She had never been so happy. She knew it had to end. It ended the day his wife called to say she wanted him back.

He had married someone he didn't like very much and he had stayed married to her while she humiliated him by laughing at him in his yellow nylon pajamas, or by lying to him about the various men she took on as lovers.

"She bought me the pajamas," Garth said to Ruth.

"Why did you wear them?" Ruth asked.

"I thought they were just pajamas," he said. Garth spoke about his wife with kindness and understanding. "She's not a bad person," he said. "She just has some problems."

"The humiliation of her affairs must have reminded you of the humiliation your father made you feel," Ruth said to him. "The humiliation and the degradation must have felt like love."

When Garth's wife drove through the restaurant window, he came to see Ruth. "She really needs me," he said to Ruth, weeping. "I'm worried about what she'll do to herself if I'm not there."

"Well, you better be there," Ruth had said.

"You should have fought for him," her girlfriend Cathy had said.

"I don't want anyone who doesn't want me," Ruth said.

"He does want you," she said. "He just needs help extricating himself from her."

"Then he doesn't want me enough," Ruth said. She left for New York two months later.

Garth had called Ruth several times in the last few years. Three years after he went back to his wife he had left for good. He had given her the house and the car that had replaced the one that she had smashed. Whenever Garth called, Ruth made sure that she exuded friendliness and warmth. But she gave him no information about her life. She gave him nothing but politeness. And she made sure that she was the one to say good-bye first.

Sometimes when Ruth stayed in expensive hotels she thought of Garth. He loved cheap motels. She understood this. There was an immediacy to a cheap motel. Everything was what it appeared to be. Nothing was dressed up or masked behind a multitude of pillows and bolsters or sleep masks, slippers, and shoehorns. The kettle was there to boil water, not to show you that the management cared. There were the grunts and coughs of the other guests and, sometimes, someone else's pubic hair on your blanket. But she understood why Garth preferred this world of lodgings to the five-star circuit she was on now.

In expensive hotels, guests never acknowledged each other. No one spoke at breakfast, unless it was to someone they already knew. It seemed to be an unwritten rule. If you broke the rule and said good morning, you were viewed with suspicion. The wealthy and the successful, it seemed to Ruth, indicated their status and power by a lack of friendliness. An affectation intended, Ruth thought, to let the world know that they already knew too many people. As if a sign of interest in a stranger might reveal a vulnerability or a curiosity that could disqualify them from their own ranks.

Why was she thinking about Garth now? Ruth thought. Probably because she knew that her father still saw him. Edek and Garth spoke on the phone now and then, and had dinner together once or twice a year. Edek periodically gave Ruth news about Garth.

Edek always tried to bring up the subject casually. "I did see Garth," he would say. "He is still by himself. Not married." Edek's nonchalance would last less than a minute.

"You are a stupid girl, Ruthie," he would say. "What did he do to you that was so bad?"

"Nothing," she would say.

"Why won't you give him a chance?" Edek would say.

"For how long does he have to suffer?" Edek had asked the last time he had brought the subject of Garth up.

"No one is suffering, Dad," she'd said. "If you love him so much marry him yourself," she had suddenly shouted. "I'm sick of hearing about him."

"Sorry," Edek had said. "I thought maybe you would see it a bit differently now." That was two years ago. Her outburst had surprised her and shocked Edek. Edek hadn't mentioned Garth since.

"You experience anything that feels bad to you as a permanent situation," one of her shrinks had said to her. "If it is raining, you think it will rain forever. If there is noise in a neighbor's apartment you think it will never stop. You have trouble seeing these situations as transitory. That's why you can't forgive people. You think they, like you, are still connected to the incident or the argument or the difficulty that made you both feel bad. They have forgotten, but you haven't." There were some things, Ruth thought, when the shrink had finished, that shouldn't be forgotten.

Ruth hadn't thought about Garth this much for years. She had been too attached to Garth. That sort of attachment came affixed to a flood of anxiety for her. She had worried about his well-being. If she woke up, in the middle of the night, she checked that he was still breathing. If he was late to meet her, she envisaged him bloodied and broken, in an ambulance. If he caught a cold, she enlarged the outcome to include bronchial pneumonia or a new strain of flu that had no cure. It was exhausting. Attachments were enervating.

She had had less anxiety since she had been unattached. She had been on dates with different men over the years. She hated the word "date." Americans used "date" whether they were referring to sixteen- or sixty-year-olds. It was hard to come up with a better word. "Rendezvous" or "assignation" suggested a mystery that wasn't present on most dates. An evening of "social intercourse" was too wordy, although it did possess the stilted quality of many dates. So Ruth, too, used the word "date."

Her dates had been, mostly, unmemorable. She found New York men unexpectedly juvenile. They prevaricated over insubstantial issues, small things, like the choice of a cup of coffee, with as much indecision and intensity as a young girl. "I'll have a café latte with skinny milk and a dusting of cinnamon, not chocolate, on the top," the last man she had gone out with had said. "No, make that a skinny cappuccino and hold the cinnamon," he had said, before he settled for an iced coffee made with skim milk, and Sweet'n Low, not NutraSweet.

It was not manly to be that fussy, Ruth thought. But just being a man was enough, in New York. If you were a man, you were desirable and in demand. Possibly this made New York men more self-centered. Maybe if women were in the same position, they would dispense with the need to be thoughtful and interesting, too.

"Why don't you like me?" the latte/cappuccino/iced coffee man had said to her when she refused his second invitation. "I'm practicing moderation in my attachments," she said. "Hey," he had said, "I'm a long way from asking you to marry me."

Ruth felt light-headed. She had walked to the outskirts of Warsaw and back. The outlying areas of Warsaw were as unattractive as the outskirts of any city she had seen. Gray concrete housing projects were everywhere. Building after building was the same. Drab, dilapidated, and depressing. She was glad to be back near the university. She needed to eat. She stopped at a café full of students. If there were so many students eating there, she thought, the food must be either very good or very cheap.

Inside, the café was noisy and humid. Ruth stood in line at the buffet. She took a large plate of kasha and a bowl of beetroot salad. Kasha, boiled buckwheat, was a dish her mother had often made. She sat at a table with two young women, who smiled when she joined them, and moved over to make more room for her. Ruth felt grateful for their friendliness. She ate the kasha with relish. It was very good.

Ruth thought about the gypsy woman. "These gypsies are psychic," the young man had said. If there were psychic people, Ruth thought, why couldn't they see her skepticism and leave her alone. When she was sixteen, a fortune-teller at a circus had called out to Ruth to tell her she would one day meet a man with a large scar who would play a very important part in her life. It was a small circus, set up in a seaside suburb of Melbourne for the summer. There were holes in the circus tent and the ringmaster's wig kept slipping. The two circus lions looked moth-eaten and drugged. The fortune-teller sat at a table, near the entrance to the tent. She also sold soft drinks.

"It is a very large scar," she had said to Ruth. Ruth exchanged glances with the girlfriend she was with.

"Oh yeah," they said to each other. The oh yeah of sarcastic, sophisticated sixteen-year-olds. As Ruth was leaving, the fortune-teller called her back. "I can see it," she said. "It is on his chest. The scar runs vertically from the top of his rib cage to his waist." Ruth's sarcasm was temporarily subdued. "Thank you," she had said to the fortune-teller. For years Ruth made jokes about scouring the emergency rooms of hospitals to look for the man of her dreams.

The noise and heat of the student café were too much for Ruth. She finished her meal and left. She was, she decided, too old to be with so many young people. She'd go back to the hotel. She looked at her watch. She had enough time for a quick swim.

The pool at the Bristol was small. Ruth swam up and down. She tried to turn at the end of each lap without stopping. That way she could get some sort of cardiovascular benefit from this swim. It was hard to get your heartbeat rate up by swimming. Unless you were a very good swimmer, and Ruth wasn't.

Her mother and father were very impressed when she learned to swim as a child. "Look how she swims," they said to each other. It was not such a great accomplishment. All Australian schoolchildren were given swimming lessons. But Rooshka and Edek continued to see it as extraordinary. "Look how she swims," they said to each other and anyone else in the vicinity each time they went to the beach. The excessive admiration bothered Ruth a bit, but she kept quiet. She was pleased that she was pleasing them. Ruth thought that not many people in Poland must have been swimmers. Or maybe it was just Jews who were not at home in the water.

Something disturbed Ruth's reverie about her father. It was a voice. "I should tell you my initials," the voice said. "My initials are R. F. F. H." Ruth stopped swimming. There was no one else in the pool. There was no one else in the room.

"Maybe I make it easier for you?" the voice said. "My initials are R. H."

Ruth swam to the edge of the pool. She got out. She shook her head. She must have water in her ears. Water in her ears often disoriented her. She should have worn a cap. She felt sick. Waterlogged ears had left her off-balance and nauseated before. She toweled herself dry.

She looked around. There was definitely no one in the pool. No one in the room. She started to feel better. There was no voice. It must have been her imagination. "You've got more imagination than is good for you," a schoolteacher had said to her when she was six.

There was still some water left in her left ear. She leaned over and hopped up and down on one leg. She felt the water trickle out. She looked around again. There was nobody in the room. Her imagination must have been working overtime.

She was always imagining things. Imagining lines for other people. Inventing sentences for others to say. She did this in her working life, and in her life outside the office. She prepared herself for every encounter by rehearsing the anticipated conversation. She gave her dentist and her doctor dialogue. "I need my head elevated, and I like to sit up between procedures," she would practice saying to the dentist before every appointment. "That's fine. I know you're anxious about dental treatment," was the reply she would make up for the dentist.

Ruth rehearsed her lines so thoroughly that she often forgot that the real conversation had not yet taken place. And she was shocked, in real life, when others detoured from the dialogue she had given them. And even more shocked when she herself made the departure.

She had practiced what she was going to say for weeks before she told husband number one that she was leaving him. When he said, "You can't go, I'll lie down in front of the car," she had said, "That's fine. I'll drive over you." She had intended this conversation to be about remaining friends forever.

Ruth walked back to her room. She had an hour to shower and get dressed before leaving for the airport to pick up her father.

❦ *Chapter Three* ❧

Edek Rothwax emerged from the customs and immigration area. He paused just outside the self-opening doors. He looked around him. A look of bewilderment and anxiety occupied Edek's face. Ruth had spotted the short, anxious movements Edek made with his head, the minute he had come through the door. "Dad," she called out from behind the roped-off area she was standing in. Edek saw her. His face broke into a smile. It was a smile of relief. The sort of smile you saw on small children who thought they had lost their mothers. He ran toward her, clutching a briefcase and an overnight bag.

The sight of Edek made Ruth want to cry. She blinked back her tears. She had missed him. Most of the time she tried not to let herself know how much she missed Edek. From the other side of the world, she took care of his phone bills, his credit card payments, his health care, and his car insurance. But she knew she wasn't really looking after him.

If she really was a good daughter, she would be living closer to him. She wouldn't be separated by ten thousand miles and delivering her love for him, long distance, in the form of a bit of money and some bookkeeping. She bit her lip. She didn't want to cry. There were two things she was determined not to do on this trip. She was not going to cry and she was not going to feel angry or annoyed with Edek.

She looked at Edek. He was trying to overtake a woman in a wheelchair. He looked well. He didn't look like a man who had just flown halfway around the world. Ruth was relieved. She had dreaded seeing a decline in Edek. Dreaded the thought that he might look noticeably older. She hadn't seen him for almost a year. She moved to the front of the crowd to get closer to him. He was still hemmed in by the wheelchair.

Edek looked up at Ruth and shrugged his shoulders. Suddenly, the woman in the wheelchair stopped. Edek saw his opportunity. He lost no time. With one nimble, surefooted movement, he propelled himself past the woman. Ruth ran up to him and hugged him.

"I'm so happy to see you, Ruthie darling," he said. "Now that I have seen you, I feel much better."

"What's wrong, Dad?" Ruth said.

"Ach, the little piece where you put your feet up didn't go up?" Edek said.

"What little piece, where?" said Ruth.

"The little piece what you put your feet on. That's why a person flies business class, to get a little piece," Edek said.

"Oh, you mean a footrest."

"That's right. A rest for the feet," said Edek. "My feet did get no rest on this trip. I had to sit the whole way with my feet just normally on the floor and I paid for my feet to be on this rest."

"Your seat didn't have one?" Ruth said.

"Of course the seat had one. All the seats in business class have got such a rest. My one didn't come up. It was stuck," Edek said.

"Oh, no, what a drag," Ruth said.

"That's not the end," said Edek. "They put me in the last row and my chair didn't go back so much. Other people could nearly sleep in their chair. I couldn't sleep. I did have to read a book the whole time."

"I'll call up and complain, tomorrow," Ruth said.

"No, no, no," Edek said. "I fixed it. I have to go to the airport manager for the airline, and talk to him."

"Now?" Ruth said. "What are you going to talk to him about?"

"I'm going to talk to him," Edek said. "You go pick up my suitcase from the luggage place."

"Dad, I'll talk to whoever you want me to talk to tomorrow," Ruth said.

"It's nine o'clock. We should go to the hotel. You need to get some sleep."

"I know what I need," Edek said. "I need to talk to this manager. My suitcase is brown."

"Brown?" Ruth said.

"You will see it," Edek said. "I did put some yellow tape what they use for packaging on the handle and around the case. That way I can recognize it straightaway."

"Exactly where will we meet?" said Ruth.

"It's not such a big airport," Edek said. "We will meet here where we are standing."

"It's a bit crowded here," Ruth said. "Let's meet by that brown bench."

"Okay," Edek said. "You think I won't see you if you are not next to this brown bench. I will find you."

"We'll meet next to the bench," she said. "Dad," she said, "can you believe we're in Poland, together?"

"Yeah, yeah," he said. "I got to go to the manager's office."

"I love you, Dad," she said.

"I love you, too," he said as he rushed off.

Ruth heard him ask a guard for directions, in Polish. The two men gesticulated for two minutes. The guard pointed to the right, then to the left, and then waved his arm in a motion that indicated distance. Edek thanked him with several short bows. Ruth watched Edek running across the airport. He took the quick little steps she was so familiar with. One small, swift step after another.

He always ran like this. As though everything was an emergency. He ran to the corner store, if he ran out of milk. He ran to answer the phone. But there was an enthusiasm as well as desperation in his urgency. He looked happy when he was running. If Ruth needed anything bought or picked up and shipped to her, in New York, from Australia, she called Edek. Edek bought, packed, and shipped Australian face creams and body lotion, Australian raincoats and Australian boots, for Ruth. He did administrative tasks and chores such as renewing her Australian driver's license, and making sure that her name was still on the electoral rolls.

She called him for small things and big things. Things that had to be done were irresistible to Edek. Ruth knew that her request would be executed with ruthless efficiency. The boots or the creams or the documents would arrive in New York in record time. She knew that her father would drop everything to run an errand.

He used to run errands for Henia, endlessly. Henia was a New York woman Edek had known in Łódź before the war. "We should be together," she said to him on one of his visits to Ruth. "I knew your Rooshka and you knew my Josl. If we get together, I can talk about my Josl and you can talk about your Rooshka."

Ruth had encouraged her father in this liaison. Edek had been so depressed since her mother died. And Henia seemed to have a liveliness and sparkle to her. "It wouldn't be like with Mum," Edek had said to Ruth when he finally agreed to leave Australia and move in with Henia.

"Of course it wouldn't be the same as your marriage to Mum," Ruth had said.

In order for Edek to stay in the United States, he needed a green card. Edek and Henia had had to get married. Josl had left Henia a wealthy woman. Her two grown sons were not about to let the wealth be diluted. They didn't want this marriage. But Henia wanted Edek, and she overrode their objections. The sons prepared a thirty-page prenuptial agreement for Edek to sign. "I find that very objectionable," Ruth had said to Edek. "I wouldn't sign it." "What's the big deal?" he said, and signed the documents. The marriage lasted four years.

Henia's seduction of Edek lost some of its gloss after the wedding. When Henia was in full pursuit of Edek, she smiled at him and laughed at everything he said. She patted him on the hands and on the head. She blew him kisses in the street. She didn't play her cards as well once they were married. She criticized Ruth, endlessly. "She is not married. She doesn't have any children. What sort of life is this?" she said to Edek every time Ruth rang. Edek never answered her.

Edek and Henia had dinner regularly with her sons and their wives and children. They ate at the older son's house every Wednesday and Sunday, and with the younger son on Tuesdays. If Ruth invited them out, Henia developed a toothache or a stomachache or a headache. "I make her ache," Ruth said once to Edek. "It is not so funny," he said. He looked miserable.

"Look at her," Henia had said to Edek, the only time she had ever invited Ruth to lunch. "She doesn't eat."

"Maybe she doesn't like your food?" Edek said.

"That's impossible. My boys love my food," Henia said. "Anyway, it is not your fault she is like this. Let's forget about it."

"My daughter is fine," Edek had said.

"Something is not right with her," Henia had answered. "She moves her leg under the table. The whole table claps and bumps."

"Maybe you don't make her so comfortable?" Edek said.

"She is a snob," said Henia. "And always in black. Like a widow."

"An expensive widow," Edek said. "You know how much she does pay for those black things?" As soon as Edek had said this, he had regretted it. He knew he had unwittingly given Henia another round of ammunition to fire at Ruth.

Henia's sons came around together one Friday afternoon. They had another series of documents for Edek to sign. More papers to safeguard Henia's property.

"We've noticed that our mother's phone bills are a hundred dollars a month more than they used to be before you arrived," the elder son said. "And we feel you should pay for this."

"I feel that I should, too," Edek said, "which is why I do. I do pay all the phone bill and all the electricity and all the food bills straight into your mother's account."

"Does he?" The elder son asked his mother.

"Yes," said Henia.

"Don't they notice how much better off Henia is with you?" Ruth asked Edek when he told her about the incident. "You do everything for her. You shop, you wash the dishes. Henia's got a very cushy life."

"I call them the waiters," Edek said to Ruth. "They are waiting for their mother to die."

When the boys came back for a third series of documents to be signed, Edek patiently signed each page. Henia never said anything during these signing sessions. As the older son was leaving, he leaned over to Edek. "You're not giving your daughter any of our money are you?" he said. Edek was stunned. He looked at Henia. Henia remained silent. Edek decided he had had enough. He left. He went back to Australia.

He felt bad about leaving Henia. As though he had abandoned her. "She was a cow," Ruth said. "She abandoned you when she didn't speak up for you." Ruth tried to persuade Edek to stay in New York. But he didn't want to stay in New York. He didn't want to bump into Henia or her friends. "You can live in New York and never come across Henia or any of her friends," Ruth said. "It's a very big city. Anyway, they all live in Queens. You can just never go to Queens." But Edek was adamant. He had to go. He booked his ticket to Australia and left.

Edek had been unhappy and out of sorts for most of his first year back in Australia. But slowly he had stopped blaming himself for the breakdown of the marriage. And slowly he started playing cards again, and eating chocolate, and running errands.

Edek didn't look eighty-one. His silver hair was thick and vigorous; his face was hardly lined. Ruth felt lucky to have a father in such good shape. She didn't want to lose him. She had reeled for too long after the death of her mother. When she flew anywhere, she still found herself looking out of the window of the plane, wondering if at thirty-three thousand feet up in the air she was any closer to her mother. Wondering if there could possibly be a heaven, and if there was, was this where her mother now lived. She knew it was a stupid thought. There was no heaven. And there was no life after death. There was nothing after death. "Mum's spirit still lives on in me," she had once said to Edek. "I think about her all the time. I cook the food that she used to cook. I use the face creams she used. I even lie in the sun like she used to, and understand why she loved it so much."

"There is no spirit," he said. "Mum is dead. Nothing has changed."

The baggage collection area was crowded. The luggage from Edek's flight was already arriving. Ruth saw Edek's suitcase straightaway. Six inches of bright yellow masking tape was wound around the middle of the case. She lifted the suitcase off the carousel. It was very light. She hoped Edek had packed enough clothes.

She had noticed that he was wearing the navy knit top she had bought him. Her mother used to choose all of her father's clothes. Rooshka had good taste. She bought finely woven 100 percent cotton shirts and simple well-cut trousers for Edek. Rooshka made sure that he always had one good-quality suit for everyday occasions, and one suit with a bit more panache for going out at night.

Left to his own devices, Edek would have stuck to the same items of clothing until they disintegrated. He never noticed what he was wearing. When Rooshka went on her annual two-week winter vacation to Surfers Paradise, Edek mixed and matched his clothes with an abandon that disturbed Ruth and drove her mother mad. "You can't wear sandals with socks here in Australia," was the first thing Rooshka said to him when he picked her up at the airport, after her very last vacation in the sun. "It is not Poland," she said. "It is comfortable for my feet," Edek said. But the minute they got home, he had changed his shoes.

As soon as there was a stain or a smudge on anything Edek was wearing, Rooshka would whip the garment off Edek and put it in the laundry. There, it would soak in bleach or salt or whatever Rooshka thought would best remove the offending mark. Edek was resigned to this. He would take off the socks Rooshka thought he had worn for too long, or the trousers with the cuff that contained a spot of mud. He understood that Rooshka had had too many smudges and stains in her life. Edek would change whatever he had on, as many times a day as Rooshka wanted him to, if it made Rooshka happy. He loved her dearly. He saw her, until the day she died, as the beautiful young girl he had pursued, and won, in Łódź. Ruth walked back to where she had arranged to meet Edek. A couple with two teenage children were sitting on the bench. Ruth put down the suitcase and stood next to them. The son, a sallow-skinned, sullen-looking youth, stared fixedly out into the distance, as though by removing his gaze he had removed himself from this family picture. The girl looked down at her lap. Nothing Ruth had seen, in her forty-three years, had persuaded her that having children was a good idea. All that effort to enable someone to voice complaints, bitterness, resentment, and hostility toward you. It didn't feel like the right return on an investment.

She looked at her watch. Where was Edek? She should have asked him exactly which office he was going to. What if he had forgotten where he said he would meet her? She hated casual, open-ended arrangements like this. She liked to pin things down to a time and a place.

She walked around the airport to see if she could see Edek. She stopped at a cake shop. Even at the airport, the cakes and pastries looked wonderful. She looked at a round, well-filled piece of apple strudel. She wondered what percentage of the apple strudel was composed of just apple. All the apple was probably bathed in butter and sugar, she decided. Maybe on her last day in Poland, she would have a slice. If she started eating strudel now, she'd be sunk.

Edek was nowhere to be seen. Ruth went back to their meeting place. The mother and father and their two hapless teenagers were still sitting there. Ruth was agitated. Where could Edek be? How could he arrive, and then disappear like this? Maybe she should have him paged?

Just then Edek appeared. He was flushed and excited. "Where were you?" Ruth said. "I was worried."

"What could happen to me?" Edek said. "I am in an airport. Nothing could happen to me in an airport. I had to speak with the manager, then another manager, and a supervisor, but I got it done. Another ten minutes and the whole thing will be finished with." He rushed off again.

Ruth stood next to the family on the bench. They were all looking forlorn now. Maybe the parents had realized that travel would be wasted on these children. Ruth looked at them. Why would anyone want to have children?

Ruth knew that, after the war, her mother didn't particularly want to have children. She knew that her mother hadn't been overjoyed to find herself pregnant with Ruth. Rooshka and Edek had not been in Australia for very long when Rooshka discovered that she was pregnant. They were both working in factories. They had no money and they spoke no English. "What right did we have to bring a child into this world?" her mother had said to her. Ruth thought that the world her mother was referring to was a larger world than the world of poverty and lack of language. It was a world where everything was erratic, and nothing would ever make sense again. This world was full of mourning and full of dead people. Dead people who hadn't just died. Dead people who had been murdered.

The murderers of these dead people were rarely referred to, and Ruth, as a child, often wondered who they were, and if she would recognize them if she passed them on the street. For years she used to examine the faces of passing strangers to see if they contained evidence of murderousness.

Ruth had had a German school friend, Elfriede. Elfriede had long blond plaits and three brothers, a mother and father, and four grandparents. When Ruth was ten, she had stayed at Elfriede's place overnight. Ruth had eaten bratwurst and *Kartoffelklösse* for dinner and listened to the German words and phrases flying around the dinner table. In the middle of the night, she had woken up with a stomachache. Was she in a house full of murderers? She had asked her mother, the next day, if Elfriede and her family were the murderers. "Who knows?" Rooshka had replied. It was a worrying answer.

Rooshka had told Ruth that she had tried to abort the pregnancy that had turned into Ruth. Rooshka said she had jumped up and down. She had sat in hot baths, she had swallowed castor oil. But nothing had helped. The pregnancy had proceeded. "I was ashamed to be pregnant," her mother had said. Ruth hadn't really understood why her mother was ashamed to be pregnant. She didn't think it had anything to do with Ruth herself. She knew that her mother had vomited, on the train, every morning after leaving Ruth in day care. She thought that that was pretty good evidence of her mother's attachment to her.

Ruth knew that her mother had lost two babies. One baby boy in the ghetto and another baby, also a boy, after the war. Being pregnant hadn't resulted in a great deal of happiness for Rooshka Rothwax. Her mother must have loved babies, at one time, Ruth thought. Rooshka used to tell Ruth a story about her amazement at finding a baby in the toilet block, in Stuthof, the concentration camp Rooshka was sent to from Auschwitz. "I couldn't believe I had found a baby," Rooshka used to say. "It was like a miracle. It was a newborn baby. It was on the floor, in the toilet block. I ran like crazy to the hospital in Stuthof. 'Look, I found a newborn baby,' I said to the nurse. 'I think it is perfectly healthy.' They took the baby from me and threw it into the rubbish bin. I don't know how I could have been so stupid to run to the hospital with the baby." "It wasn't your fault," Ruth would say. "I am not talking about fault," Rooshka would answer.

The hospital in Stuthof was the reason that Ruth had been in Gdańsk, a year ago. She wanted to see where it was that her mother had run to, in such hope, all those years ago. Stuthof was a forty-minute drive from Gdańsk. Ruth had imagined that hospital many times. She imagined a small hospital with gleaming white tiles and polished chrome and stainless steel equipment. It had taken Ruth half an hour, in Stuthof, to find the hospital. She had wandered around Stuthof with a map, trying to match what was left of the camp with the details on an old plan of the former death camp.

Ruth had finally found the hospital. The hospital in Stuthof, like the rest of the buildings in the death camp, was preserved exactly as it was found.

There were no tiles or stainless steel in this hospital. The hospital was built with the same cheap wooden boards as the barracks. Two broken operating tables were in the middle of one room. Some empty shelves stood in a corner. A few old implements were scattered around. Several broken lights were on the wooden floor. There had clearly been no need for hygiene in this hospital. It was so bare and so barbaric. There was no pretense that anyone was going to be cared for in this hospital. Ruth had wept and wept. How could she have imagined white tiles and stainless steel? She had read enough to know that that was absurd.

She had read hundreds of books on the Holocaust. Books by survivors. Books by historians. Despite all the books Ruth bought and read, part of her could still not imagine the truth. Part of her still wanted to believe that it couldn't have been that bad. That her beautiful mother hadn't really slept in the middle of corpses, and been left for dead, many times. Part of her wanted to believe it was all a bad dream.

When Ruth had got back to the Marta Hotel, after Stuthof, she had showered for over an hour. She hadn't been able to get out of the shower. She hadn't been able to wash off whatever it was that she was trying to wash away. She had showered until all of her skin had wrinkled.

Ruth was exhausted. Warsaw airport was nearly deserted. It was almost ten o'clock. Where was Edek? How could he do this to her? Just run off. What was he doing? A priest walked up to Ruth and asked her if she would donate some money to a children's charity. Ruth said no. She didn't want to give anything to a Polish priest. She didn't like priests and she didn't like Poles. Her father didn't express much resentment toward Poles. He knew, firsthand, what the Poles had done to the Jews, he knew from his own experience how Polish people hadn't been able to wait to get rid of the Jews. But he didn't dwell on it. He didn't express much anger at the Germans either. Ruth couldn't understand why he didn't hate Germans. She realized that neither Rooshka nor Edek expressed a lot of anger at what had happened to them.

What Ruth did see, in her mother and father, was anguish and shock. They were still shocked. As though neither of them could quite believe what they had lived through. Ruth saw her mother's and father's guilt, too.

A guilt at their own survival. The guilt of still being alive when everyone else in their world was dead. Maybe Edek and Rooshka had seen too much base behavior to want to be overtaken by a lesser emotion like anger, she thought. Getting through each day seemed to take all the emotional energy her mother had anyway. There was not a lot of room left for anger.

Edek got through his days by working and reading detective fiction when he came home from work. Edek loved working. In the four years since he'd been back in Australia, he'd applied for over twenty jobs. Jobs as a cutter in a clothing factory, a pattern maker for a shirt manufacturer, a shop assistant in a pharmacy, and a job as the manager of the shipping department of a sporting goods store. Edek knew nothing about sports and even less about sporting equipment. The only products he could identify were the exercise bikes. He was a quick learner, he told the baffled owner who interviewed him. He didn't get the job.

He didn't get most of the jobs he interviewed for. He couldn't understand why. "I think you're over the age that most people are looking for in an employee," Ruth had said. "I didn't tell them I was eighty-one," Edek said, "I told everyone I was sixty-six." He didn't seem to realize that sixty-six was already way too old to be applying for jobs.

He did get one of the jobs. It was a temporary position itemizing stock in the back room of a health food store. Edek had to unpack new shipments, note what was running low and clean the store, after it closed every night. "It is very important for those places what sell this healthy food to look very clean," Edek had said to Ruth. "They have to look more clean than shops what sell normal food. People who eat this sort of stuff like to have a very clean shop."

Edek came to work two hours before the shop opened and he stayed longer than any other employee. "The manager does trust me," he said proudly to Ruth. "He did give me the key to the business after just one week." Edek was so happy. He did extra jobs without being asked, and brought chocolate biscuits for everyone for morning tea. When the job came to an end, the manager took Edek out for a cup of coffee and told him how sorry he was that the man he had replaced was coming back. Edek had resumed his search for employment.

Ruth felt agitated. Where was her father? She had only seen him for a minute before he had disappeared. She tried to calm down. She was not going to feel irritated by Edek, she told herself; not on their first day together. She was grinding her teeth and blinking her right eye five times by the time Edek returned. He was triumphant. He was holding his ticket in the air.

"I did fix it," he said. "They did give me a first-class ticket for the way back. I am in seat 2B. The manager didn't want to do it, but the supervisor, in the end, did agree with me. I did pay for a business class and my seat was not such a business class seat."

"Dad, I've been waiting for over an hour," Ruth said.

"I am not such a young man," Edek said. "I did want to make sure I could have one of those things for the feet. It is not so easy to travel at my age."

"I would have done it for you, tomorrow," Ruth said.

"Why should I bother you?" Edek said.

Ruth calmed down. "You must be tired, Dad," she said. "Did you manage to get any sleep when you stopped in Bangkok?"

"To tell you the truth," Edek said, "I did not have such a good night in that Bangkok."

"Oh no," Ruth said. "What went wrong? I thought your hotel was just near the airport."

"The hotel was near to the airport," Edek said. "I did find it. I got a bus as a matter of fact. I didn't want to take a taxi. Who knows where a taxi driver would take me?"

"So what was wrong?" Ruth said.

"Everything," said Edek. "I was the only guest in the whole hotel. Nobody did speak English. I was frightened to leave the room. I didn't see one person who was not Chinee. Everybody was Chinee. You never know what they can do to you." Edek always pronounced Chinese "Chinee."

"They're not Chinese, Dad, they're Thai," Ruth said. "And just because they don't look exactly like you doesn't mean that they're not exactly like you. They're not going to do anything to you."

"I am not going to argue with you," Edek said. "Which one of us knows what people can do? It was a stupid idea to stop in Bangkok," Edek said.

"It was your idea," said Ruth.

"No, you did make the arrangements," he said.

"I wanted you to fly Qantas," Ruth said.

"That Qantas is too expensive. I was saving money for you," Edek said.

Ruth took a deep breath. "I can't believe we're having an argument about Bangkok," she said. "Dad, we are in Poland. You and I are in Poland, together."

"That Bangkok is not a place to go," Edek said.

"You only saw the airport," said Ruth.

"It was enough," Edek said.

"Do you want a Mercedes taxi?" a man asked them.

"A Mercedes?" Edek said. He turned to Ruth. "I will talk to him," he said. "How much are you going to charge me for this Mercedes?" Edek said to the driver.

"Where are you going?" the driver asked.

"Where are we going?" Edek asked Ruth.

"To the Bristol Hotel," Ruth said.

"We are going to the Bristol Hotel," Edek said to the driver. The driver was about to give Edek a price for the trip, when Edek suddenly slapped himself on the forehead.

"I am an idiot," he said to Ruth. "I am speaking to him in English."

"I'm sure he can understand English," Ruth said.

"That will be one hundred and thirty zlotys," the driver said.

Edek answered him in Polish. They talked for a couple of minutes. "A hundred and ten zlotys," Edek announced to Ruth. "Why not?"

"Okay," said Ruth. She followed her father and the driver.

"This is a very nice car," Edek said to Ruth inside the car. "It is a very big Mercedes." He looked around the car, opened and closed the ashtray, patted the leather seats. "A very nice car," he said. He sat back. He was silent for a few minutes. Ruth was worried about her father. How did he feel being in Poland? She didn't want to ask him how he felt, every two minutes. She didn't want to make this trip any more difficult for him than it already was. She felt pretty tense herself. She tried to relax.

"Excuse me," Edek called out to the driver. "How much is such a car, in Poland?"

"This car is not cheap," the driver said.

"Why is he speaking to me in English?" Edek asked.

"Because you spoke to him in English," said Ruth.

"*Oy, cholera*," said Edek. *Oy, cholera*, literally translated into "Oh, cholera," but Ruth knew it was closer to "Oh shit."

"*Oy, cholera*," Edek said again. He leaned forward and started talking to the driver in Polish.

Ruth couldn't work out exactly what they were saying. She knew the conversation was about the price of cars and how many miles to the gallon the cars used. Polish numbers were incomprehensible to Ruth. They all sounded the same to her. She couldn't tell the difference between the number two, three, eight, ten, twenty, thirty, or forty. She knew they were all numbers.

Whatever the numbers were, they were animating Edek. He was offering his opinion and his advice as though he was a car mechanic or a racing car driver. Ruth leaned back in the car. It was starting to snow. Snow made all cities more attractive.

"Look, Dad, snow," she said. Edek stopped talking to the driver and looked around.

"When was the last time you saw snow?" she said.

"What is so important about snow?" Edek said. "I seen a lot of snow. Snow is snow."

"Well, I like snow," Ruth said.

"What are we going to do?" Edek said.

"About the snow?" she said.

"No. What are we going to do?" he said. "Where are we going to go? What are the plans? What is the itinerarerary? Is that how you say it? Itinerarerary?"

"It's itinerary," Ruth said.

"Itinerarerary," Edek said.

"We're going to spend one day in Warsaw, then we're going to—"

"We don't need to stay in Warsaw a whole day. What for?" Edek said, interrupting her.

"Okay," she said. "If you don't want to stay a whole day, we'll spend the morning in Warsaw and leave for Łódź at lunchtime. After Łódź, I thought we'd go to Kraków," she said. "I want to go to Auschwitz, but if you'd rather not come to Auschwitz, that's perfectly fine. I've booked us into a good hotel, and you can stay in the hotel."

"No," said Edek. "I'll go where you go. What time did you say we can leave Warsaw?"

"About twelve-thirty," Ruth said. "That will give us time to see some of the city."

Edek leaned forward and spoke to the driver. "He says he will take us to Łódź for three hundred zlotys," Edek said. "He did want three hundred and fifty, but I said three hundred or nothing."

"Dad, I've bought train tickets," Ruth said.

"Why shouldn't we go to Łódź in a Mercedes?" Edek said. "Why shouldn't I show him I can afford a Mercedes?"

"I think he understands English," Ruth said. Edek lowered his voice. "Why shouldn't I show him?" he said.

"Okay, Dad," Ruth said. Edek looked elated. "How do you feel, Dad?" she said.

"I feel fine," he said. "Why are you asking me how I feel? I feel fine."

"Well, we're in Poland," Ruth said.

"Big deal," said Edek. "We are in Poland. What is the big deal?"

Big deal. He loved to say big deal. It was one of his favorite phrases. She had asked him once if he would give her a dollar every time he said big deal. "There are too many things that are a big deal," she had said to him. "For you, maybe, not for me," he had said. But he had tried to cut down.

"Well, it's a big deal for me," Ruth said to her father. "We'll be at the hotel soon," she said. "You must be tired. And jet-lagged."

"Why should I be tired?" he said. "I am not tired. And I never had a jet lag before. Why should I have a jet lag now?"

Ruth decided to change the subject. "It's a nice car," she said.

"Mercedes makes a very good car," Edek said. "It is the best car you can buy."

"Would you like a secondhand Mercedes?" Ruth said.

"Me? A Mercedes?" said Edek. "I would never buy a Mercedes."

"Why can we drive in one, but not buy one?" Ruth said.

"Are you stupid?" said Edek. "I am not going to give money to the Germans. If I drive in a Mercedes, like this, I am making myself comfortable, not giving money to the Germans."

"You're giving money to a Pole," Ruth whispered.

"Shsh shsh," Edek said.

"I don't think we're going to make any difference to the German economy whether we buy a Mercedes or not. They are doing pretty well without us. Anyway, a secondhand car has already been bought by somebody else."

"But that somebody does have to buy another car and they buy another Mercedes," Edek said.

Ruth sighed. Nothing she was saying was right, with Edek, tonight. "How is Moniek?" she said. She liked Moniek Steinberg. He was a quiet man. She knew he had been in Bergen-Belsen. She had often thought that part of him was still there. Maybe that was how it had to be, for anyone who had been in any of those places.

"Ah, Moniek," Edek said. "He is dead."

"Oh, no," Ruth said. "When did he die?"

"He did not die," Edek said. "But you cannot speak to him anymore. He does not answer the phone and when you see him in the street, he says just a hello, and he goes away. Sometimes people are dead in different ways. Sometimes a dead person can be dead and sometimes a person does not need to be dead to be dead."

"To be dead to themselves or dead to you?" Ruth said.

"You are a clever girl, Ruthie," Edek said. "You always see a side to something that not many people can see. You was always like this. You could see things when you was a small girl."

"What do you mean I could see things?" Ruth said.

"You could see that Malka Feldman was a very sad person," Edek said.

"How do you know?" said Ruth.

"Because you did tell me," Edek said, "when you was six years old that she was sad because she had to wear a wig. You did say to me that Malka wears a wig because somebody did pull out her hair. Even the other women in the cardplayers was not sure that her hair was a wig. It was a bit funny that you did know to tell you the truth, but you did know it was a wig."

"Malka probably told me," Ruth said.

"I did ask Malka," Edek said. "She was shocked. She said that since it happened she did not say one word to anybody. She did start to cry. As a matter of fact I did not feel too good for bringing up the subject. Malka did tell me that in Auschwitz in the last months they did not have time anymore to shave the hair of the women, so they did not shave those ones what were going to labor camps. So they did not shave her head. But a Kapo dragged her by the hair to the next barracks because she asked the Kapo if she could see if her sister was there."

"A Kapo?" Ruth said. "A Jew?"

"Yes," said Edek. "And who knows what I would have done if I had been a Kapo. Thank God nobody did ask me."

"I did tell Malka that you did know that somebody did pull her hair out," Edek said. "She said it was impossible. 'How could you know?' Malka said. You was six years old. You was not in Auschwitz."

"I must have guessed," Ruth said.

"That must be it," said Edek. "You guess things pretty good. You used to guess a lot of things. Even Mum was surprised, sometimes."

Ruth felt unnerved. There was no need to feel frightened by this, she told herself. It was clear that she was a kid who listened to things. And people often forgot that they had said something. Malka had probably mentioned her hair to Rooshka one night, at one of the card games. Malka would have trusted Rooshka. Rooshka wasn't a gossip like some of the other women. Rooshka didn't gossip. She didn't play cards either. She read a book while the others played. "Even Mum didn't know about Malka's hair," Edek said. Ruth felt sick.

They were at the Bristol. A uniformed valet opened Ruth's door for her. Another valet helped Edek out of the car. "It's cold," Ruth said to Edek. "Button up your jacket." Edek breathed in deeply.

"This cold doesn't get to your bones," he said. "Not like the cold in America or Australia."

"This cold is twice as cold as any cold in Australia," Ruth said.

"But it doesn't get to your bones," Edek said. "You can feel it doesn't get to your bones. I am not cold. I told you, always, the cold in Poland doesn't get to your bones."

"Dad, it might not have got to your bones when you were twenty-one," she said. "But you're eighty-one. Button up your jacket. It's freezing."

"I am going to pay the driver," Edek said. "Go inside."

Ruth waited for him. "Did you give the driver a fifty-zloty tip?" she said.

"Why not?" he said. "I have got a rich daughter."

Ruth went inside. She left Edek chatting with the doorman. She went to the front desk to check Edek in. She was filling out the endless information still required by Polish hotels about their guests, when Edek rushed up to her. "Give me another twenty zlotys," he said. "I have not got any more zlotys." Ruth gave him the zlotys. He ran off and spoke to the doorman.

"It's worth to make sure he looks after us," Edek said to Ruth when he came back.

"What a beautiful young woman," he said, in Polish, to the receptionist. She blushed. "Thank you," she said, in English.

"We can speak Polish," Edek said.

"Why are you running around tipping everyone?" Ruth said to her father.

"Why shouldn't I give a tip?" Edek said. "We can afford it. You earn good money. You earn very good money for a girl."

"I earn very good money for anyone," Ruth said.

"So why can't we give a tip?" said Edek.

"I always tip people," Ruth said. She felt agitated with Edek. Why did he have to argue about everything? And why did he always think he was right?

"Why do you have to hide that you have got money?" Edek said.

"I don't hide it," Ruth said. "We're staying at the Bristol. It's obvious we've got money."

"I don't mind showing them that you are rich," he said.

Ruth's last shrink had said to her that Ruth hid what she had. From herself, and from others. "You have trouble feeling your own achievement and your own success," the shrink had said to her. "You have to hide what you have. You're frightened that if you display it, somebody will take it away from you. So you have to pretend you have nothing. It's also tied to how envious you are of others," the shrink had added.

"That's not true," Ruth had said. "What do I envy?" "Peace of mind," the shrink had answered.

"I'm not rich," Ruth said to Edek.

"You are rich," he said. "You own your own apartment."

"I'm forty-three," she said. "A lot of forty-year-olds own their own apartment."

"Your apartment is in New York," Edek said. Ruth was annoyed. One apartment, on Fourteenth Street, was not rich, she thought.

"Your apartment has three bedrooms and two bathrooms," Edek said. She glared at him.

"This is a beautiful hotel," Edek said to the receptionist in Polish.

"Thank you," the receptionist said.

"My daughter stays always in such a hotel," Edek said.

"Aren't you tired, Dad?" Ruth said.

"No," he said. "Not at all."

"I'm exhausted," she said. "I'm jet-lagged and I arrived here a day before you. And I've slept."

"I don't have a jet lag," Edek said. "Only my daughter gets a jet lag."

"I have to go to bed," Ruth said.

The receptionist handed Edek and Ruth two sets of keys. "Room 578 for you, Mr. Rothwax," she told Edek, in English.

"Where is my room?" Edek said to the receptionist.

"Your room is on the fifth floor, sir," she said.

"Where is my daughter's room?" Edek said.

"Your daughter is in 310, on the third floor," the receptionist said. Edek looked crestfallen.

"What's wrong, Dad?" Ruth said.

"I feel like a fish out of water," Edek said.

"A fish out of water?" Ruth said. "Don't worry, we won't do anything in Poland that you don't want to do."

"I am not worried about Poland," he said. "I am like a fish out of water. Don't you understand what that means? It is an expression what they use in Australia. I feel like a fish what is out of the water." Ruth looked at the receptionist. The receptionist looked puzzled.

"My room is too far from your room," Edek said.

"I gave you a very good room, sir," said the receptionist.

"I want a room near you," Edek said to Ruth. Ruth arranged a change of rooms.

❧ *Chapter Four* ❧

At this time of the morning, there were always people on the street in New York. There were people running and jogging. There were people walking to work. There were people having breakfast in cafés. It was 6:45 A.M. There was no one on the streets of Warsaw.

Ruth had been running on Krakowskie Przedmieście, Al. Solidarności, Gen. Władysława Andersa, and Marszałkowska. Polish street names sounded militant if not military to her. And impossible to pronounce. If she got lost, she thought, she'd never be able to call the hotel and tell them where she was. And she couldn't ask anyone in the street for directions because she would never be able to match the sound of the street names with any of the street signs. She had practiced saying Krakowskie Przedmieście for ten minutes before she left the hotel. Krakowskie was easy. Przedmieście was out of her reach.

She had awakened that morning knowing that she had to run. Her first day in Poland with her father was bound to be difficult. She would need all the endorphins that running gave her. She had arranged to meet Edek for breakfast at 8 A.M. Eating with her father was full of pitfalls. She had to make sure that she was as balanced as she could be. She already felt much better than she did when she woke up. She turned into Al. Jerozolimskie. At least there were some people in the street now.

Max had called her at five o'clock this morning.

"I knew you'd be up," Max had said brightly.

"Why are you calling me from home again, Max? What's up?" she said.

"Nothing's up," Max said. "It's only eleven P.M., it's not that late. I've just got a couple of small queries. Nothing you'll have to spend a lot of time on. I know you need this time to yourself."

"Max darling, edit," she had said. "I'm lying in bed with a stomachache."

"I knew this trip would be too much for you," Max said.

"I've got a stomachache because I'm premenstrual," said Ruth. She had been lying in bed holding her stomach and thinking about her mother.

Jewish women in Auschwitz had had no periods, her mother had told her. They had been given medication to stop their menstruation. "We called it *brum,* this medicine," her mother had said. "They gave it to us in the gray stuff they called soup. I could taste the *brum* even in the stinking taste of the soup."

"I'll be quick," Max said to Ruth. "Can we do a letter about the morning after?"

"The morning after what?" Ruth asked.

"You know, the morning after," said Max. "The morning after sex. A female client wants a 'You-were-great-in-bed-last-night letter.' She's used us before, we did some thank-you letters for her."

"Tell her we'll be graphic but not pornographic," Ruth said.

"Will you do it?" Max said. "I mean will you do the letter, not will you tell her."

"I figured that out, Max," Ruth said.

"We don't have any letters about sex on file," said Max.

"I'll do it," Ruth said. "Get me the basic information—names, place, et cetera, and some very general details."

"Thanks," said Max. "I've got only one more question. I've dealt with all the regular stuff while you've been gone, but we seem to have had more irregular requests than usual since you left."

"I've only been gone for three days," Ruth said. "What's the question?"

"Right," Max said. "The guy in the architect's office upstairs wants to know if we'll do a love letter."

"Well, what's the problem?" said Ruth.

"He wants to send it to another guy, and I wasn't sure I could adapt one of the heterosexual love letters we've got on file," said Max.

"I don't think it should be too difficult," Ruth said. "They're all letters from one person in love to another."

"I'm not sure I can do it," Max said.

Ruth could tell that it had been a mistake to let Max know where she was. When Max couldn't contact her Max was fine. She managed the business with surprising efficiency. With access to Ruth, the more indecisive parts of Max flourished.

"I told the architect we did all sorts of letters," Max said. "I didn't want him to think we discriminated against minorities."

"Send me the details of the love letter he wants to send," Ruth said.

"Thanks a million, Ruthie," said Max.

Max was the only person, apart from Edek, who called her Ruthie. It had disconcerted her at first, but she was used to it now. She had been right, after all, she decided, to give Max her itinerary. She wasn't sure that Max could handle a homosexual love letter on her own. Ruth had certain rules about letters that she had tried to drill into Max. "Don't gush if you're praising somebody," she had said to her. "Don't grovel if you are apologizing. Avoid all philosophizing in a letter of sympathy, and minimize the use of personal pronouns in condolence letters."

Ruth had devised a different set of rules for business letters. Business letters were more straightforward. Max did most of the business letters now. But Ruth still had to do all of the company's love letters. Max was too creative with love letters. She injected them with an intensity that appeared ominous. Ruth thought that Max was probably too young to do a good love letter.

Ruth liked writing the love letters. She often made herself cry writing a love letter. She would become so immersed in the letter that she would get a jolt when she realized that the sentiments that were making her cry were of her own fabrication. That the love that she was writing about had nothing to do with her. They were not her love letters. They were, for her, business letters.

Ruth hoped that she would never meet the recipients of some of the longer love letters that she had written. She felt she had shared too intimate an intimacy with these strangers. Ruth had had two particularly intimate letters to write in the week before she left New York. A letter from a mother to her daughter. The mother wanted the letter to be included in her will. She wanted her daughter to know how much she loved her. The mother was fifty-five and looked in good health, to Ruth. She had noticed Ruth staring at her. "I'm not dying," she had said. "I'm just making preparations for the event."

When I am no longer here, Ruth had written in the letter to the woman's twenty-two-year-old daughter, *I want you to know that I will still be with you. Part of me will always be part of you. I have not left you. You have occupied a large part of my heart. The best part of my heart. You will never have to miss me and you will never have to have regrets. I will be with you. You gave me all of your heart from the day you were born and you took all of me, my good and my difficult parts, into your heart. You will have me, forever, darling. And you will live a good life knowing that you knew me well. There will be no unanswered questions, nothing unsaid that should have been said. We had each other, in the best possible way, and we will always have each other.* The woman had wept when she had picked up the letter. Ruth, to her embarrassment, had wept, too.

The other unusually intimate letter was also, coincidentally, connected with a will. Her client, Graham Long of Graham Long Bridal Designs, a large Long Island bridal wear company, often requested emotional letters. The bridal business, Ruth had learned, was prone to ardent and over-wrought transactions. Mr. Long's recent request had been for a letter that would explain the discrepancy between the amount he was planning to leave to his daughter, in his will, and the amount that his son would receive. Mr. Long wanted his daughter to be the main beneficiary of his will. For some strange reason, this had pleased Ruth.

Ruth had no idea why Mr. Long wanted his will to favor his daughter. Ruth never asked more questions of a client than she needed to. It was partly out of efficiency, but also because she didn't want to clutter her head with other people's turmoil. She had enough disarray of her own to deal with.

Ruth encouraged her clients to be bold in all correspondence but particularly in letters to be read after their death. "Once you're dead you can really say whatever you want to say," she would say to them. "And you need never know the response." The religious clients felt that they would be present in one form or another, after their death. They would, they felt, hear what was being said about them. An advantage of being religious that Ruth had not previously considered.

The clients mostly took Ruth's advice. They were direct, and said those things they hadn't been able to say in person. Mr. Long had told Ruth he felt much more tolerant toward his son, after he had set things out on paper.

"Our relationship is already better," he said to Ruth.

"Well, you can always discard the letter and change the will if you become best friends," Ruth had said to him.

"You're so funny," he had said. People often said that to Ruth. She didn't think she was all that funny. She thought that she was just being sensible.

Ruth felt that letters could spread a goodwill that was hard to achieve in person. In a letter, you could eliminate your own awkwardness and the distraction or diversion of the recipient's response. Letters enabled you to be the best you could be. If you found a lesser part of yourself creeping through, you could censor it.

You could consolidate good feelings, in a letter. You could confirm a warmth and an intimacy that was embarrassing for most people to communicate verbally. And a letter made endings less blunt. The end of a meal, the end of a meeting, the end of an evening, the end of a phone call. Ruth hated the sudden severance of intimacy that endings had. If she had enjoyed a meal with someone, she wanted to call the person as soon as she got home. After an enjoyable phone call she often wanted to call straight back. She restrained herself, most of the time. She didn't want to look like a lunatic.

It seemed to Ruth that the closeness that could accumulate between people during an evening or a phone call disconnected itself so easily. That it was hard to stay plugged in to that connection. She felt that in the next call, or in the next meeting, the easiness that had developed, dissipated. And you had to start from scratch.

The problem was probably more pronounced in Manhattan. In Manhattan, people seemed to skirt around each other. This detachment was carried out with considerable friendliness and an excess of endearments. The word "love" was bandied about with abandon. We love you, I love you, I love her, she loves me, they love me. You could hear this on the street, in cafés, in restaurants, in offices, and in buses and subways. You would have to be dead to avoid being the recipient of several of these emphatic announcements each day. Everyone spoke like this. It appeared, if you didn't know any better, that love was in the air in Manhattan.

The truth was that it was hard to progress further than a formal relationship in New York. Further than a casual formality. The sort of formality that is forced upon people who know very little about each other's lives.

You never knew when you met someone, in New York, what they had been doing or what they had been through since you last met. You didn't hear about the good things and you didn't hear about the bad. If you were lucky, you heard their bad news after it had been rectified. In New York, you couldn't talk about an illness until you had completely recovered. You could talk about the job you lost, as long as you were safely ensconced in a new job. New Yorkers hated bad news. They switched off more easily to bad news than they did when they discovered that someone couldn't be of use to them. Usefulness, in New York, was often defined as career furtherment.

Ruth liked to know about people's illnesses and difficulties. It made friends and acquaintances more real to her, more three-dimensional. In New York, it was easy to think of people's lives as one efficient, if frustrating, transaction after another. She felt bad if she discovered that someone she knew had been ill and alone in his or her apartment. An Australian journalist who lived close by Ruth had been bedridden for two weeks last year with a respiratory infection. "Why didn't you call?" Ruth had said when the journalist told her she had felt so sick that she had thought she was going to die. "I didn't want to bother anyone," the journalist had said. "Will you promise to call, if it happens again?" Ruth said. "Okay," the journalist had said. But Ruth knew that she wouldn't. And she knew that she, too, would remain mute, if she was in trouble. It just seemed to be the way, in New York City.

On the rare occasions in New York when Ruth had felt at home in someone's company or in someone's home, she had wanted to stay. Like a child who didn't want to go home after a party. Or a kid who couldn't bear to be wrenched away from a friend. But adults couldn't just say, "Can I stay with you?" Adults were supposed to be able to separate. Supposed to *be* separate.

Max had had trouble separating from her this morning, Ruth thought. Max had phoned her three times. The last call seemed really unnecessary. "We need someone else to do handwritten letters," Max had said. "I don't have the time."

"What about Bern?" Ruth said.

"His handwriting is hopeless," Max said.

"I'll think about what to do when I get back," Ruth had said.

Ruth stopped at the traffic light on the corner of Krakowskie Przedmieście and Królewska. She had managed to miss every red light so far on her run this morning. She loved missing the red lights. It made her feel lucky. The lights changed. She started running again. Another ten minutes and she'd be done.

"I can see you do not know still with whom you are speaking," the voice said. Ruth's heart started racing. This couldn't be happening to her again. "I will make it easy for you," the voice said. "My name is Rudolf." Ruth broke into a sweat. Sweat ran down her face. Her whole body felt damp. She stopped running.

"The name Rudolf is surely familiar, to you," the voice said. Ruth took off her earphones and looked around her. There was no one there. "Rudolf," the voice said. Ruth put her hands over her ears. "You do not hear me through your ears," the voice said.

Ruth felt as though she was going to vomit. She had felt this feeling of biliousness before, when she had stopped running too suddenly. She was, she decided, tense about her father. There was no one talking to her. There was no voice. There was nothing but a normal Warsaw street.

"I can see that it will be necessary for me to introduce myself," the voice said. "I am Rudolf Franz Ferdinand Höss." Ruth leaned against the building she was standing in front of. Maybe if she did vomit she would feel better. "Rudolf Höss," the voice said. "Commandant of Auschwitz from 1940 to 1943." Ruth tried to take deep breaths. She was obviously more anxious than she realized. She had experienced anxiety symptoms before. She would walk back to the hotel and have a long bath. A long bath would soothe her.

"Please do not confuse me with Rudolf Hess," the voice said. "I hate this when people confuse me with Rudolf Hess. He has only been here since 1987. And he chose to come. He committed suicide as you of course know. He was ninety-three."

Ruth vomited into the gutter. She felt a bit better. "What are you frightened of?" the voice said. "Nobody is frightened of me, anymore." The noise of her heart thumping almost drowned out all other sound. "Let me tell you about myself," the voice said. "Let me tell you what has happened to me." Ruth started walking. "I need to tell you this," the voice said.

"I need to not hear it," Ruth said.

"I knew that you would speak to me, very soon," the voice said.

Ruth wiped her face with the tissues she always carried in her pocket. She walked slowly in the direction of the hotel. Her mouth felt foul. She had forgotten what an awful taste vomit left. She had only vomited two or three times in her life. She must have food poisoning, she thought. Food poisoning would also explain the hallucinations.

"I saw you arrive in Poland," the voice said. "I have seen many people arrive in Poland. But I knew you were the one. I knew you were the one."

"Where are you?" Ruth said suddenly. She was shocked when she heard the words coming out of her mouth.

"I am in Zweites Himmel's Lager," the voice said. "They call it the second camp of heaven. A subbranch of heaven, a satellite camp. My English is good, no?" Ruth stopped walking. "Some people like to call it Zweites Himmel's Kamp," he said. "It has a more soft feel. *Lager* is a more militaristic word. But I know it is a Lager. I know, after all, about Lagers. Some of the other inhabitants here do not.

"I know also it is not Zweites Himmel's Lager. It is not heaven. They refuse to call it what it is. Who do they think they fool? Most of us, up here, know that it is hell. Do not look so surprised. Hell is up here. Hell is not under the ground. That is a myth. It was a clever idea to put hell up here. It is next to heaven. People are not too sure where they are going when they come here. After all, who would go of their own free will under the earth? Nobody."

Ruth didn't know that she had looked surprised. She had thought that she was dazed. Expressionless.

"You're Rudolf Höss?" she said.

"Of course I am Rudolf Höss," the voice said. "Who would pretend to be Rudolf Höss?" He paused. "I am not who I used to be, however. I have arthritis in my right shoulder, something is wrong with my leg, my stomach gives me trouble, and my bones hurt.

"Stop looking so surprised. You can feel your bones in Zweites Himmel's Lager. Even if you have been cremated. You can still feel all parts of you. It is terrible. If you are in Zweites Himmel's Lager, you cannot get anything fixed up. If you have an ailment, there is no treatment. This is not the case in Himmel. In heaven, I see dead people in very good condition. I have tried for many years to get out of Zweites Himmel's Lager, but it is not easy.

"There were not many Jews here when I arrived," he said. "The Jews seemed mainly to be in the main camp, heaven. That was a relief, to me. Now, there are quite a few Jews in this subcamp, Zweites Himmel's Lager. They do not express any more hostility toward me than anybody else."

"If I can talk to you," Ruth said, "why can't I communicate with my mother?" It was a trick question. A question she hadn't thought up an answer to. A test, to see if she was really talking to herself. To see if she had slipped over that fine line that separates sanity and insanity.

"I have worked harder to get through to you," Höss said.

"Are you suggesting my mother doesn't want to speak to me?" Ruth said.

"I am not suggesting anything," Höss said.

"Why am I asking you about my mother?" said Ruth.

"Because I am closer to her than you are," Höss said.

"Physical proximity is meaningless," Ruth said. "Otherwise you'd be close to people every time you were in a crowd. Anyway, you're dead. You haven't got a physical being so how can you have physical proximity?"

"If I have not got a physical being, how can my bones hurt?" Höss said.

"I don't know," she said. "You're the one with all the answers."

"Why do you stop walking when you talk to me?" Höss said. "I am still here when you walk. I am not standing in one place. Zweites Himmel's Lager—I should really call it what it is—hell, is everywhere."

"I can't do two things at once," Ruth said. "I've always had trouble concentrating on more than one thing at a time."

"Maybe you are not such a clever Jew," Höss said. "That of course is a joke." Ruth didn't laugh. "It should be acceptable to make a joke about Jews," Höss said. "It is not possible to see Jews only in a serious or tragic

way. Jews are supposed to have a sense of humor. They always had a repu-
tation for humor. Although we never saw Jews being amusing or funny in
Auschwitz. It has only been since I was cremated and shipped to Zweites
Himmel's Lager that I have seen what was meant by this Jewish sense of
humor. You are not offended by my talking about Jews like this? Even Germans should be permitted, now, to laugh at Jews."

"Laugh *at,*" Ruth said, "is where you have slipped up. Laugh *with,*
maybe." Ruth heard a series of groans and grunts. *"Scheisse,"* Höss said, "I
will never get to Himmel if I make bad mistakes like this."

"I know what *scheisse* means," Ruth said. "Shit."

"I did not mean to say *scheisse,* and I did not mean to say laugh at."
Höss said. "I meant to say laugh with, of course."

"Of course," Ruth said.

"I have not managed to graduate yet from the sensitivity-training class
in Zweites Himmel's Lager," Höss said. "It is a requirement, a prerequisite
that one graduates from this class before they will even consider a request
for transfer to Himmel, to heaven. I have studied this class for fifty-one
years and eight months.

"They forced me to enroll the day after my execution. Sensitivity training. What a subject. It was not very sensitive of the Polish military tribunal
to decide that I should be executed in Auschwitz, right next to the house
where I lived with my wife and five children. Only two of these tribunal
members are up here, with me. I have looked for the others."

Ruth realized, with a shock, that she no longer felt ill. She felt almost
normal. Suddenly, it seemed normal to be talking to someone who wasn't
there. Something must be wrong with her, she thought.

"Why can I hear you?" she said to Höss.

"Some people are more sensitive to what is around them than others,"
he said. "You are sensitive. You would probably pass the sensitivity-training class that I have this trouble with. Being able to hear people who have
departed is just an ordinary aspect of sensitivity. There is nothing out of the
ordinary about this ability. It is a sensitivity. I know a lot about sensitivity.
Don't forget I have studied the subject for nearly fifty-two years."

" 'Departed' is a stupid word," Ruth said. "People die, they don't
depart. Anyway, you don't know that much about sensitivity. You fail the
class year after year."

"They discriminate against me," Höss said. "The judges, as soon as they see me, they say, 'fail.' I see plenty of unintelligent people who pass this class. And I can see that I am more sensitive. I can definitely sense more things than I used to. I can sense, I think, that you have an understanding of what has made you so sensitive."

"What are you talking about?" Ruth said. She knew that she was always interpreting and translating words and actions, always exploring and observing facial expressions and physical gestures.

"I am talking about sensitivity," Höss said. "It is a very irritating topic. 'You are so sensitive,' someone said to Himmler recently. Of course you know Himmler, Miss Rothwax?"

"You know my name?" Ruth said.

"Of course I know your name," said Höss. "A name is the easiest thing to know about a person. I was talking, was I not, about Himmler. Heinrich Himmler, Reichsführer-SS, head of the Gestapo and the Waffen-SS. The second most powerful man in Nazi Germany. Sensitive indeed! Just because he is a small man who looks like a bank clerk, they think he is sensitive." Höss sighed. "Nobody talks to me, here. For years nobody has talked to me. Even my former colleagues pretend that they do not know me."

Ruth realized that she had been blinking her eyes and tapping her leg rapidly. She wondered if Höss had noticed.

"What is that action you are making with your leg?" Höss said.

"Nothing," she said. "It's just a nervous mannerism." She steadied her leg. "Oh God," she said. "I have to go. I have to meet my father for breakfast." She started to walk back to the hotel. She felt surprisingly well.

"God?" Höss said. "Surely you do not believe in God? Not after what you have seen?"

"What did I see?" Ruth said. "I wasn't there."

"Sometimes you do not have to be in a place in order to see," Höss said. "I think that you know this."

"That's absurd," Ruth said. "I only know a fraction of what happened to my mother and father."

"You do not have to know everything in order to know that there is no God," Höss said.

"Funny, that's what my mother said, 'There is no God,'" said Ruth.

"If there was a God," Höss said, "do you think that I would speak about him in this way? Of course I would not. It would ensure that I would never obtain a place in heaven."

Ruth looked up at the sky. The whole time that she had been talking to Höss she had been looking at her feet.

"You cannot see me," Höss said to her. "And you will not be able to see me until you come to Zweites Himmel's Lager. But I do not know if this will be your destination. Maybe you will go to Himmel? And in Himmel, people cannot see into Zweites Himmel's Lager. In Himmel, people are spared those sights that are too disturbing."

Ruth looked back down at her feet. Her feet looked just the same. The same as they were before she was involved in this conversation with Rudolf Höss, SS-Obersturmbannführer. Her black and green Nike Air Max shoes were still slightly spotted with mud from her run yesterday in the Saxon Gardens. Her socks were still just socks. Part of her had, briefly, wondered if she had died. She patted her face. Her face was warm, despite the cold. She felt her hips. They were still the large hips she was always trying to diminish.

"Let me get back to why I lost my faith," Höss said.

"Maybe I don't want to hear about it?" Ruth said.

"I think you can be truthful with me," Höss said. "You want to know about me. I can see it on your face. I had my reasons for choosing you. Even though I am restless, with not too much to do, in Zweites Himmel's Lager, I would not waste my time with just anybody. I chose you because I knew that you wanted to know."

Höss cleared his throat. Ruth found it interesting, that in hell, you still had to clear your throat. It added validity to Höss's claim that he could still feel his bones. If you couldn't feel your vocal cords, why would you clear your throat? Höss must be telling the truth about that, she thought.

"I was thirteen years old when I lost my faith in God," Höss said. "This came about as a result of a completely innocent episode in my life. I accidentally pushed one of the boys in my class, at school, down the stairs and he broke his ankle. You can imagine how many hundreds of schoolboys had fallen, without harming themselves, down those stairs. I myself fell down those very stairs and was not hurt. I was very unlucky that this boy was hurt."

"I went to confession as I did every week," Höss said. "Are you listening?"

"I thought you could tell whether I was listening or not," Ruth said. "Go ahead, I'm listening."

"I went to confession," Höss said, "and I confessed the whole episode of the accident. At home, I said nothing. I didn't want to spoil my mother's and father's Sunday. Coincidentally, the priest that I confessed to happened to be a close friend of my father, and he happened to come to our house for dinner that night.

"The priest, in a betrayal that I could not have dreamed about, told my father about the incident," Höss said. "My father, of course, punished me. I was overcome. Quite stricken and brokenhearted. Not from the punishment, but on account of this betrayal.

"My whole faith in the most sacred nature of the priesthood was destroyed," Höss said. "I could no longer consider the priesthood as being worthy of my trust. I gave up going to confession, completely."

"It's just as well you gave up going to confession," Ruth said.

"Why do you say this?" Höss asked.

"Because your confessions would have been very lengthy. They would have occupied an awful lot of your life."

"I see what you mean," Höss said. "From that day I stopped believing that God heard my prayers. My father, I told you, was a devout Catholic. He always let me know in most adamant terms that he expected me to become a priest. My father died suddenly the year after the school stairs incident. I cannot in fact remember being very much affected by his death. Soon the war started and I wanted to go to the front. I had soldier's blood in my veins. I could listen to soldiers' stories of the front, for hours. I never got bored. My relatives wanted to ship me off to a training college for missionaries. My mother didn't want me to go to the front; she, too, thought I was destined for the priesthood. But I am an obstinate person, and I finally managed to join the regiment in which my father and my grandfather had served. I was fifteen years old."

"A child prodigy," Ruth said.

"Thank you," said Höss. "For me, being a soldier was very much a calling. The first time I shot a man, I was ice calm. I was completely composed. I said to myself: 'My first dead man.' For me, the spell was broken."

"The spell of thinking that to kill is difficult?" Ruth said.

"Precisely," said Höss. "I think you know something yourself about spells and superstitions and illusions."

"I know nothing about killing people," Ruth said.

"During the war, I kept thinking about my parents' desire for me to be a priest," Höss said. "I was, as you know, disillusioned about the priesthood, but even if this had not been the case I would have questioned my suitability for the priesthood. In the last letter my mother wrote me, before she died, she told me never to forget the path my father had chosen for me. My guardians and in fact all of my relatives pressured me to go immediately to a training college for priests. I did explain, did I not, that the war I am referring to is of course the war before the one in which your parents were involved."

"That's the best use of the word 'involved' that I've ever heard," Ruth said. "My parents were not 'involved.' My mother was starved and beaten and raped and brutalized in about as many ways as your people could devise. I don't think that that could be termed 'involved.' You'll have to improve your English."

Ruth felt herself feeling shaky again. "You are very concerned about words, aren't you?" Höss said.

"Some words make me feel sick," she said.

"It was not an easy time for me, this time that I am talking about," Höss said. "The full significance of my mother's death hit me, just after she died. I realized that I no longer had a home. My relatives had divided out our possessions. They were so sure that I would become a missionary and my sisters would remain in the convent to which they had been sent. I knew then that I would have to battle my way through the world alone."

Ruth looked around her. Krakowskie Przedmieście was quite crowded now. She must look odd, she thought. She must look as though she was talking to herself. The Poles thought her exercise clothes were odd enough. Now she must look like someone from another planet.

"You are not listening to me," Höss said. "I can see you are concerned with what other people think of you."

"Well, I must look pretty strange," Ruth said.

"You do not need to be self-conscious," Höss said. "Nobody else can hear what I am saying to you."

"They can hear me," Ruth said. "I obviously look as though I'm talking to myself."

"When you speak to me, it is not so apparent to other people," Höss said.

"That doesn't make sense," said Ruth.

"Not very much in the world makes sense," Höss said, "I think you know that." Ruth's head started to spin. She felt exhausted. "Don't worry," Höss said. "You worry more than is strictly necessary. You will be all right. Nobody will arrest you. I was arrested myself for a very unfortunate incident when I was a young man. It was June 28, 1923. I remember the date exactly. I am very good with numbers."

"Is this a long story?" Ruth said.

"No, not at all," said Höss. "I was in the Freikorps. The Freikorps were volunteer soldiers who were formed to guard the frontiers and to prevent internal disturbance."

" 'Internal disturbance,' " Ruth said. " 'Internal disturbance' sounds like a gastric disorder." What a stupid thing to say, she thought. She could tell that she was no longer thinking clearly. She had to get back to the hotel.

"What a stupid thing to say," Höss said. "I will ignore it. The German government needed the Freikorps for those situations in which the police force—and later on the army—was too weak to deal with the trouble. The result was that they could not punish offenses committed by the Freikorps, so we administered our own justice. Treachery was punished by death, and there were many traitors. Our murder trials were modeled after the Vehmgericht, medieval courts that sat and passed sentence in secret. This worked very well for us. But I was unlucky. A Vehmgericht murder trial in which I was involved became known, and I was brought to trial at the state court for the Defense of the Republic. We had killed a man who had betrayed one of us to the French. Schlageter, who was betrayed, was as a matter of fact an old comrade of mine."

"Could you edit this story?" Ruth said. "I'm not feeling well." Why was she listening to him at all? Surely she could just walk back to the hotel.

"I will be brief," Höss said, "you do not look well. I was, of course, there when the traitor was killed. But I was most certainly not the ringleader. During our interrogation I saw that the comrade who did the actual killing would be incriminated by my testimony so I took the blame myself."

"I wondered how long it would take you to get on to your innocence again," Ruth said. "First, you accidentally pushed a boy downstairs, now you say you're innocent of a murder. I can't wait to hear what else you are going to come up with."

"How can you speak to me in this way?" Höss said. "I am trying to tell you the story of my innermost being. The psychological heights and depths of my life."

"What a prospect," Ruth said.

"I am trying to be as truthful as I can," said Höss.

"I can appreciate how hard that is for you," Ruth said. Höss didn't seem to notice the irony in her voice.

"It is painful for me," Höss said. "Remember that in Zweites Himmel's Lager we feel pain."

"That is one of the most interesting things you've said to me," Ruth said. "I wouldn't forget that."

"On March 15, 1924," Höss said, "I was sentenced to ten years' imprisonment for the murder of this traitor. Let me tell you that serving a sentence in a Russian prison is not an experience that I would recommend. As a political prisoner I was kept in solitary confinement. This was what saved me.

"I watched my fellow inmates from my window. I watched them exercise in the courtyard. I watched them in the washhouses or getting their hair cut. I listened to them talking to each other every night. I listened to their warped minds, to their monstrous thoughts, their depravities, their odiousness, and their aberrations. A world I did not know existed opened before my eyes. I had the time, in prison, to reflect on my life. To think about mistakes I had made and weaknesses that I had shown.

"I made a promise to myself. I would do everything in my power to ensure that the future would be as rich and rewarding for me as possible. I slowly adjusted, to the crude language of the prison guards and to the despicable, vile, squalid, and sordid language of the prisoners. But I could never adjust to the cynicism with which the prisoners treated all things of beauty. They used their reprehensible, filthy language to describe things that many men view as sacred. I learned, too, from observing myself, that a sensitive prisoner suffers more from unjustified hostile spiteful words than from any physical cruelty."

[71]

"Fuck, shit, asshole, dickhead, piss face," Ruth shouted. The words flew out of her mouth and left her stunned. Where had they come from? "Motherfucker," she shouted at Höss.

"This does not offend me," Höss said. Ruth thought that she detected a puritanical pinch to his consonants and syllables.

"I think you must be feeling better," said Höss. "The color in your face is greatly improved." Ruth didn't answer. "I had a very upsetting time at the end of my second year in prison," Höss said. "I became unable to eat or to sleep. I could not concentrate on anything, and all day I paced up and down in my cell. The doctor diagnosed it as prison psychosis. I was given tranquilizers and put on an invalid diet. One night I saw my dead parents standing next to me. I spoke with them. I have never told anyone at all about this episode."

"I've got to go," Ruth said. "I have to have a shower and change my clothes before I meet my father for breakfast."

"It is not very sensitive of you to choose this moment to leave," Höss said. "Anyway, I was lucky. A majority was created in the Reichstag by a coalition of the extreme right and the extreme left when I still had five years of my sentence left to serve. Both parties wanted political prisoners to be set free. An amnesty act was passed on July 14, 1928. I was a free man."

"Hooray," said Ruth.

"It is useless to use sarcasm," Höss said. "It does not affect me. The freedom was not so easy for me, at first. I went to Berlin. Kind friends there insisted I go to films and theater and all sorts of parties. It really was too much for me. I longed for peace. I needed to get away from the noise and the rush of the city. I was lucky. After ten days I left Berlin to take up a job as an agricultural officer. I wanted to live on the land. I wanted to rebuild Germany. In prison I had decided that I would fight and work for one thing only. To own my own farm, and to live there with a large and healthy family."

"You sound like a superannuated hippie," Ruth said.

"What did you say?" Höss said.

"Nothing," she said.

"I needed to escape the frivolous, unhealthy, and morally corrupt life of the cities," Höss said.

Ruth realized that she didn't have enough time to shower before breakfast.

"I found the woman I had longed for during all my years of loneliness," Höss said. "It felt like we had known each other our whole lives. This compatibility and unity and harmony stayed with us throughout our life together. We were like this during the hardships and during the good times and during the bad times. We were not influenced in our love for each other by anything that happened in the outside world."

"Hey," Ruth said. "I don't have to listen to this."

"What is wrong with what I am saying?" Höss said.

"You wouldn't understand," Ruth said. "Anyway, you used the word 'during' three times in the one sentence."

"I understand much more than you think," Höss said.

"I'm going," said Ruth. She had had enough. She turned sharply on her heel and walked away. Höss screamed. It was the cry of a man in pain. She turned back to where she imagined he was. "What's wrong?" she said.

"Nothing, nothing at all," Höss said. He sounded fragile.

"Then why hold me up?" she said. "I'm in a hurry." She turned and walked away again. Höss screamed louder. Ruth tried to stand in a position that she imagined might be facing Höss. "What's up?" she said very firmly. "Can't you bear farewells?"

"I can tolerate everything," Höss said. Ruth turned away, in disgust. The scream that came from Höss hurt her ears. She stopped.

"This has nothing to do with anything that you are doing," Höss said.

"Really?" Ruth said. She went over her previous movements slowly. She dug her heel in the ground, as though she was going to turn. Höss cried out. She tried it again. He screamed.

"This has nothing to do with anything that I am doing?" she said.

Höss was silent.

"I'm going," she said. She walked briskly along Krakowskie Przedmieście. She felt good.

~ *Chapter Five* ~

*R*uth almost didn't see her father. He was sitting in an armchair, in the lobby of the Bristol Hotel. He was nearly buried in the stuffed and puffed-up body of the chair. His shoulders were slumped. His head was bent. His chin touched his chest. His cheeks and his mouth had slipped and shifted to a lower position on his face than they usually occupied. He had the stillness of a corpse. For a moment, Ruth was alarmed. Then she saw his eyes move. He watched her walking toward him.

"What are you doing, Dad?" she said

"Waiting for you," said Edek. "We did have an arrangement that I should meet you at eight o'clock."

"But why are you waiting here?" Ruth said. "Why didn't you go into the restaurant?"

"I am very comfortable here," Edek said. "Why should I go into a restaurant by myself?"

"Oh, okay," she said. He looked tired. "Are you all right?" she said.

"Of course I am all right," Edek said. "What is not to be right?"

"The way you were sitting," Ruth said. "I thought that something might be wrong."

"What should be wrong?" Edek said. "I am here in Poland, with my daughter. Just like you wanted. It does not always have to be something wrong." He stood up and looked at Ruth.

"You look shocking," he said. "Maybe it was not such a good idea to come to Poland?" He looked at her again. "You do not look heltzy," he said. "We can call the whole trip off. We can have a dinner in a nice restaurant tonight, maybe some *pierogi*, then we can change our tickets. I will come back to New York with you for one week or maybe two weeks."

Edek's pronunciation of healthy usually made her laugh. She had tried to teach him the correct pronunciation many times. "Healthy," she said. "Heltzy," he always replied. It didn't make her smile this morning. "If you really want to leave Poland, we can leave," she said. "I never wanted to force you to be here."

"I don't think about calling the whole thing off for myself," Edek said. "I am fine. There is nothing wrong with me. You look terrible."

"I think I ran for too long this morning," Ruth said. "I was out for over an hour."

"A *mishegaas,* this running," Edek said. "To run to somewhere where there is no need to run is a *mishegaas.* People should run if they are in a hurry, but to run just for nothing is *meshugge.*"

"Thanks, Dad," she said. *Meshugge* was one of the first Yiddish words she'd learned. It meant stupid, mad. A *mishegaas,* was a stupidity, a madness.

Ruth looked at herself in the mirror, in the lobby. She looked pale, but not terrible.

"You look shocking," Edek said. She looked at Edek. He looked tired. Years older than he had looked when he had stepped off the plane last night.

"You did run for more than an hour?" Edek said. "That is why I did have to wait for you in this chair." Ruth looked at her watch. It was two minutes to eight.

"I'm not late," she said. She knew she wasn't late. She was always punctual. She tried hard not to be obsessively punctual. But she couldn't help it. She was perpetually punctual. It didn't matter how rushed she was, she was still never late for anything.

Ruth thought that her inability to be late was unhealthy. She had tried to do something about it. She had tried to be late for a few unimportant events, but she had been unable to succeed. The anxiety of the tardiness had been too much for her. She had modified her ambition. She had tried to curb her need to be early. "You're always early," the podiatrist, the dentist, the dry cleaner, and anyone else she had appointments or arrangements with said to her. She had given up. She had accepted that it was her destiny to be on time.

She also tried not to weigh herself more than once a week. She had had to force herself not to step onto the scales in the bathroom at the Bristol Hotel this morning after her shower. She knew that the Bristol's scales would be in kilograms, and she had forgotten exactly how to convert kilograms into pounds. She knew that 1 kilogram was 2.2 pounds. But was it approximately 2.2 pounds, or exactly 2.2 pounds? She didn't know. And she couldn't tolerate having a rough approximation of her weight.

She had been tempted to weigh herself. She was always tempted to weigh herself when she thought that she might weigh less. She wanted to rush to the scales on mornings when she had had a particularly good bowel movement, or had sweated excessively during her workout.

This morning, after she had vomited up what appeared to be most of last night's meal and a large amount of body fluid, had seemed to Ruth an ideal time to step onto the scales. But she had resisted. She was proud of herself for that. At home, she was proud if she forgot to exhale before weighing herself, or if she inadvertently left her watch on while she was on the scales.

"Let's go and have some breakfast, Dad," Ruth said. She felt quite hungry.

"I do not want anything," said Edek. "Maybe one egg and something to drink, and that's it."

"Oh, God," Ruth said. "I forgot to tell you not to drink from the tap or brush your teeth with tap water."

"You did tell me, maybe ten times before I did leave Melbourne," Edek said.

"But I forgot to remind you," said Ruth.

"I am not so old that I forget what someone did tell me ten times," Edek said.

"So, what did you brush your teeth in?" she said.

"The water that my daughter did order for me," Edek said.

"I'm glad the hotel remembered," Ruth said.

"They remembered all six big bottles," Edek said. "Six bottles for one day."

"I didn't want you to feel worried about running out of water," Ruth said.

"I would have more to worry about if I did drink all the water," Edek said. "I would burst. I did pack the other five bottles, in my suitcase, to take to Łódź." Ruth chose a table, near the window, in the Bristol's restaurant. "This looks like a good table," she said.

"A table is a table," Edek said.

"Buffet or à la carte?" a waitress asked them.

"I will have a boiled egg please," Edek said.

"Dad, this hotel does one of the best buffet breakfasts I've ever seen," Ruth said.

"I am not so hungry," said Edek.

"Dad," she said, "I want you to look at the buffet."

"Is there a boiled egg on the buffet?" Edek asked the waitress.

"Yes, sir," she replied.

"In that case, I will get my egg from the buffet," he said. "See how I listen to my daughter?" The waitress smiled at them both.

"It is lucky that you have got me here," Edek said. "I can speak to all the waiters and waitresses for you."

"You were speaking to her in English," Ruth said.

"Oy, cholera," said Edek.

Edek stood transfixed in front of the selection of fish on the buffet. There was smoked trout, smoked mackerel, smoked salmon, whitefish, fresh sardines, and several varieties of herring.

"I will take a piece of fish," he said eventually. He put one piece of smoked salmon in the middle of his plate.

"Dad, we're paying for this," Ruth said, "so we might as well eat it."

"That is right," said Edek. He put several slices of mackerel and whitefish on his plate.

"Look what's over there," Ruth said. "Polish ham."

"Not for me," Edek said. "I have some fish and that's it."

"But you've talked about Polish ham for years," said Ruth.

"I don't eat so much for breakfast anymore," Edek said.

"I'll take some ham to our table and you can decide if you want it," Ruth said. "And look at the bread. The Poles make great bread. Look at that rye bread! Doesn't it look stunning? I'll get some for you."

"No, no, no," Edek said. "I don't eat so much bread. You want me to get fat? I watch what I eat, today. I have to be careful. Get me only one piece of rye bread." Ruth chose a small slice of rye. "Where is the boiled eggs?" Edek said. "I always have a boiled egg for breakfast." They found the eggs.

Ruth carried Edek's food to their table. She went back to the buffet to get her own breakfast. When she got back Edek had finished his plate of fish. "This fish is out of this world," he said.

"I'm so glad that you enjoyed the fish," she said. "It looks wonderful."

"What are you eating?" Edek said. "What is that?"

"It's muesli," she said. "I've added flax seed and sesame seed to it."

"This stuff is for birds to eat, not for people," Edek said. "Why don't you eat some scrambled eggs? They got plenty of scrambled eggs. As a matter of fact it looks out of this world."

"I don't like eggs," she said.

"What is not to like about an egg?" Edek said. "An egg is just an egg. Everybody eats an egg except my daughter. She pays twenty-five dollars to eat some seeds what birds eat."

"Are you trying to make me feel bad?" Ruth said.

"I am trying to make you feel better," Edek said. "If you eat something normal you will feel better."

Edek was quiet while he ate the rest of his meal. Ruth was grateful for the silence. She ate her breakfast slowly.

"That's it," Edek said suddenly. He pushed all of his plates away from him. "I did finish," he said. Ruth looked over at him. "That's it," he said again. "Finished, for me." There was nothing left on any of Edek's plates. All the fish was gone, all the ham was gone, the eggs were gone, and there was no sign of the rye bread.

"Would you like tea or coffee, sir?" the waitress asked Edek. Ruth had already ordered a chamomile tea.

"Do you have a hot chocolate?" Edek asked the waitress.

"Of course, sir," she said.

"I will have a hot chocolate," Edek said. "Maybe I will have a piece of cheese with my hot chocolate?" Edek said to Ruth. "The cream cheese looks especially good. They did have always a very good cream cheese in Poland." A few minutes later Edek returned with a mound of cream cheese and several slices of bread. "It is a very good cream cheese," he said.

Ruth finished her muesli. Eating had made her feel better. Food often did. Jews were more attached to food, she thought, than most other people. She had noticed, in a photograph of the Knesset, the Israeli parliament, in session, that most members had food on the table in front of them. Jews rarely held a meeting or function of any sort without catering the event. And the food seemed to be of equal importance to anything else on the agenda.

At the few Jewish fund-raising events Ruth had attended in New York, the quality of the food served seemed to captivate the guests' imagination more than the amount of money raised. She had expected New Yorkers to be more sophisticated than that. But they were as engrossed in the merits of the stuffed chicken breast and roasted red peppers as any Jews in Melbourne.

"We've got three and a half hours before we leave for Łódź," Ruth said to her father. "The driver is picking us up at 12:30 P.M."

"I know that," Edek said. "I did organize it."

"I was just reminding you," Ruth said.

"You think I am so old I forget everything?" Edek said.

"Of course not," said Ruth. "There's a small remnant of the wall that surrounded the Warsaw Ghetto left standing," she said. "I'd like to go and see it."

"You want to see a piece of a wall?" Edek said.

"You don't have to come with me," Ruth said.

"I will do what you do," Edek said.

"Oh good," she said. "Let's go for a walk around Warsaw first."

"What for?" said Edek.

"Just to look around and see what's here," Ruth said.

"You know already what is here," Edek said. "A city and some Polish people."

"Dad, you don't have to come," she said. "Stay here and read a book. There's a very nice library in the hotel."

"I got my own books with me," he said.

"I won't be long," she said. "Not more than an hour. Then I'll pick you up and we'll go to the ghetto wall together."

"Okay, I will walk a bit, with you," Edek said.

"Dress warmly," Ruth said to him. "It's cold."

"This cold, I told you, does not get to your bones," Edek said.

"I'll meet you in the lobby in fifteen minutes," said Ruth. She decided that she would buy her father an overcoat while they were out walking. By the time she found a menswear shop, she thought, he would be cold enough to agree to the purchase.

Ruth thought that she would have to walk more slowly with Edek accompanying her. But Edek strode briskly in front of her. He walked too fast to see anything. "Slow down, Dad," she said. "What for?" he said. She gave up and let him run ahead. She walked briskly in order to keep Edek in her line of vision. She walked along Krakowskie Przedmieście, Nowy Świat, and Aleje Ujazdowskie. She passed the monument to Adam Mickiewicz, the Polish romantic poet. She passed the eighteenth-century Carmelite church, Kościół Karmelitów, the Museum of Caricature, the Potocki Palace, the Radziwiłł Palace, the Church of the Nuns of the Visitation, the Ethnographic Museum, the Kazimierz Palace, the Holy Cross Church, the Staszic Palace, the monument to Nicolaus Copernicus, the Ostrogski Palace, the Zamoyski Palace, and the Polish Army Museum.

Edek hadn't looked up once. He had been running, with his head facing the ground. Suddenly he stopped outside a restaurant. "Look," he said, pointing to the Restauracja Hoang Kim. "A Chinee restaurant. A Chinee restaurant in Poland." He started to laugh.

"A Chinese restaurant in Poland does look pretty funny," Ruth said.

"It is pretty funny," Edek said. Two minutes later he stopped again. "Look this restaurant has *flaki* and *kapusta*," he said, and read the rest of the menu out aloud. "I did not have *flaki* since Mum died," he said. Ruth liked *flaki*, tripe, too. "Maybe we'll have *flaki* one night for dinner," she said.

"Maybe," he said.

"Pierogi!" Edek shouted a minute later. "Meat *pierogi*, cheese *pierogi*, potato *pierogi*, mushroom and cabbage *pierogi*." He was standing outside a small bar, the Bar Pod Gołębiami. Bars, in Poland, were not primarily for drinking. They were small, cheap eating establishments.

"Would you like a *pierogi*?" Ruth said.

"No, not for me," Edek said. "Why don't you have one?"

"I'm not really hungry yet," she said.

"I am not hungry, too," he said. He looked into the window of the bar. "They make a schnitzel and a barley soup," he said.

"Why don't you have something to eat?" Ruth said.

"No, not for me," he said.

"I know it's only been an hour since we finished breakfast, but you've walked a long way, and you were walking pretty fast," Ruth said.

"It has been one hour and a half, not one hour," Edek said.

"Have a couple of *pierogi,*" Ruth said.

"Okay, okay, I'll have one *pierogi,*" Edek said.

He ran into the small bar. Ruth followed him. She sat at a small table against the wall while Edek ordered his *pierogi* from the bar. He came back carrying a plate of *pierogi* on a tray. The steam was still rising from the *pierogi.* They smelled good. Edek had ordered two meat *pierogi* and two potato *pierogi.*

"You don't want one?" he said to Ruth.

"I'll have some another time," she said. Three minutes later Edek pushed the plate away from him. "That is it," he said. "That is enough for me for a whole day."

"Were they good?" Ruth said. Edek wiped his mouth with his napkin. "They was out of this world," he said.

Edek and Ruth walked toward the University of Warsaw. Edek was still walking ahead of her. They passed a men's clothing store. "Dad," Ruth called out to Edek. He walked back to where she was. "I'd like to buy you a coat," she said. "Please, it's cold now, and it's going to get even colder."

"You want to drive me crazy?" Edek said. "I do not need a coat. I told you before, this cold does not get to your bones. If you want to buy a coat, buy yourself another coat."

"Well, can I buy you some gloves? Please?" Ruth said.

Edek sighed. "Okay, okay," he said.

They went into the store. Edek spoke to the assistant. It seemed a long conversation to have about a pair of gloves, Ruth thought. She recognized some of the phrases. Edek was complaining about her to the shop assistant. They settled on a pair of brown leather gloves. Edek looked quite pleased with them. He put them on straightaway. Edek walked next to Ruth for a while, admiring his gloves.

"Have you been in Warsaw before?" she said. "Did you ever come here, from Łódź?"

"Once or twice," he said.

"You've never mentioned that," she said.

"Why should I mention everything?" Edek said.

It was so hard to ask even the most innocuous questions about the past, Ruth thought. Any question about the past could unleash an unpredictable volatility in both of her parents. There were no simple questions or simple answers about their pasts. All simplicity seemed to have been erased from their experience. There was little that could be said without provoking an intensity that could be frightening to everyone in its orbit.

Ruth had learned at a young age that an ordinary query could produce a very bad reaction in both Edek and Rooshka. Ruth used to see the strain on her mother's face as Rooshka struggled to contain the eruptions and explosions that she lived with. She saw her mother battle to keep them to herself. To not let the tumult spill out and pollute and infect those around her.

"I don't need to know everything," Ruth shouted to Edek. He had rushed ahead of her again. She caught up with him. "I just want to know a few things," she said. "Nothing too personal. Sometimes it seems to me that you don't want to tell me anything. It almost seems secretive, as though you don't want me to know."

She felt upset. Why couldn't he talk normally about a simple thing like being in Warsaw before the war? The answer was there, in those two words, "the war." The war. The war changed everything. Made all simple things, complicated. Made all ordinariness extraordinary. Nothing was left that was not adulterated and tarnished.

"War" wasn't even the right word. It wasn't a war for Jews. It was murder. But "murder" and "slaughter" were not large enough words either. "Genocide" sounded too antiseptic. "Holocaust" too tidy. There was no single word that was adequate. Even a string of the most powerful and potent and hefty words wouldn't be eloquent enough.

"What don't I want you to know?" Edek said with irritation.

"I don't know," Ruth said.

"There is nothing to know," he said. He strode in front of her. Suddenly, he turned back. "Look," he said. He was pointing to the end of a small walkway off Krakowskie Przedmieście. *"Pontshkes."* At the end of the walkway was a small cake shop.

"Where can you see *pontshkes?*" Ruth said.

"In the window," Edek said.

"I can't see them," she said.

"Maybe my eyesight is not so bad," Edek said.

"It must be pretty good to spot a *pontshke* that's more than fifty feet away," Ruth said.

"It is more than one *pontshke* what I can see," Edek said.

They got closer and Ruth saw that he was right. Half of the window was filled with fresh *pontshkes*. Edek loved *pontshkes*. The round, deep-fried doughnuts were filled with jam, and dusted lightly with icing sugar.

"Shall we buy one, Dad?" she said.

"Why not?" he said. "Just one."

"Can you order a cup of tea for me?" Ruth said. "Ask them if they've got chamomile tea."

"Why don't you have a cappuccino?" said Edek.

"A cappuccino in Poland?" she said.

"Why not?" said Edek.

"I feel I need a chamomile tea," Ruth said.

"Okay, okay," said Edek.

Coffee was the last thing Ruth wanted. Her stomach still felt fragile and a bit acidic from throwing up this morning. She probably shouldn't have had the muesli for breakfast. She probably should have had something less fibrous. But she had felt fine at breakfast. Unexpectedly fine.

A puff of icing sugar powder blew out over the table as Edek bit into his *pontshke*. "This *pontshke* is better than all the *pontshkes* in Acland Street," Edek said, with his mouth full of *pontshke*. Acland Street was a street of cake shops, European cake shops, in Melbourne. "This *pontshke* is something out of this world," he said. "It has got such a dark jam in it, not like that red jam they put in the *pontshkes* in Melbourne." Edek looked happy.

"Have another one, Dad," Ruth said.

"Okay, one more and that is it," Edek said. Ruth looked at her watch. It was 10:30 A.M.

[*83*]

"I think we should catch a taxi to the ghetto wall," Ruth said, when they were on the street again.

"Why don't I give a ring to the driver who is going to take us to Łódź?" Edek said. "He can pick us up a couple of minutes early and we can stop at the wall, on our way?"

"I don't want to rush to the ghetto wall when we're on our way to Łódź," she said.

"Why not?" said Edek.

"It just doesn't seem right," she said.

"You can stay for how long you want," said Edek. "You can afford it. You can afford for the driver to wait all day."

"I don't want to do it that way," Ruth said. "You don't have to come with me, I'll take you back to the hotel and I'll catch a taxi."

"I will come with you," Edek said.

"We're near the Marriott Hotel," she said. "There'll be plenty of taxis there."

Edek ran ahead. "I will organize it," he said.

Ruth took a deep breath. She was determined to get on well with her father. Determined not to be angry or irritated. If she ended up railing against him, it would be a sign, to her, that she had not matured despite all the trappings of maturity that a bit of money could provide.

All couples traveling together must experience friction, she thought. She was glad that she was not more a part of a couple than she was at the moment. This coupling with Edek was about as much as she could tolerate. Coupling? Why had she called it a coupling? Coupling had a sexual connotation she hadn't intended. She felt queasy. She took a few more deep breaths.

She was outside the Marriott Hotel. She couldn't see Edek. She looked in the door of the hotel. He was there, talking animatedly with someone, the concierge, she thought. She decided to wait outside. Edek probably needed a break from her, anyway.

She stood outside the hotel and watched people walking by. She was glad to have a few minutes on her own. She was used to spending time on her own. She enjoyed it. She never complained about the loneliness that many single people complained of. She wasn't that lonely. She liked being single. It allowed her to live in exactly the way she wanted to live. She didn't have to accede to anybody else's needs. She didn't have to explain or justify. She didn't have to apologize. And she had as full and as satisfying a life as any married person she knew.

She read a lot. She unwound every night with a book. She read mostly nonfiction. Biographies, autobiographies, memoirs, accounts of a youth or an old age. She read political biographies and historical biographies. Sometimes, if she was very tired, she read a celebrity biography. Over the years she had accumulated a lot of information about a lot of people. It was not very useful information. She sometimes thought that she could have taught herself quantum physics or something equally intellectually challenging with the volume of reading material she had squandered on biographies. She wondered whether quantum physics was intellectually challenging or merely a mathematical skill. She could barely comprehend ordinary physics. She had no idea what quantum physics was.

Ruth read for at least an hour every night. Reading relaxed her. It was as essential to her well-being as running and lifting weights. She looked after herself in other ways, too. She had pedicures and manicures. She had her eyebrows shaped and waxed and her legs waxed. She had her hair cut, and she had her hair colored. All of these processes and procedures had to be repeated regularly. This preservation and conservation may have appeared excessive somewhere else, but in New York, it seemed the norm.

Attending to this maintenance created a ritual and a pattern to her life. The women who worked on her toes and fingers and brows felt like family to her. "Hello, honey," was the way that Olga, who had been giving her pedicures for ten years, greeted her. "Hello, honey, how are you?" Olga would say and all of Ruth's tension would melt at the sound of her thick Russian accent.

Christine, the Chinese woman who shaped and waxed Ruth's eyebrows, was as blunt as any mother. "Your eyebrows look terrible," she would say if she hadn't seen Ruth for a while. Recently Christine had plucked a thick black hair from Ruth's chin. "Chinese women don't have much facial hair," she'd said, "but you are going to get more and more hairs on your chin as you get older. Make sure you pluck them." Great, Ruth had thought. A beard. Another thing to look forward to. "I'll pluck them, when I see them," Christine had said. Ruth had felt mothered. The fact that she didn't have to watch out for her own beard hairs had soothed her.

Ruth was rarely left with nothing to do. She read several newspapers a day, she went to the theater and occasionally to a movie. She saw friends every now and again and talked to acquaintances when she bumped into them. She was on the co-op board of the building she lived in and she attended all board meetings. And she worked. That constituted a life as good as anyone she knew. As good a life as anyone with a husband, two children, and a two-car garage.

Ruth had very little time to feel lonely. She made sure that she was out of town on days like Thanksgiving and Christmas. Days when everyone was out of town. Days when everyone was with family. She vacationed in cities where there was something to do. She sent postcards from these vacations. In the cards she described cafés and listed interesting museums.

Even after the most pleasurable vacations, Ruth looked forward to returning to work. She was happy with her life. She had Edek and she was grateful to have him. She had Max, and she had Bern. She had plenty. Every now and then she contemplated getting a pet for company. But she always decided against it. She found it hard to feel attached to anything that didn't have verbal skills.

Unlike many single people, Ruth didn't mind going out with couples. She didn't feel left out. She mostly came home from these outings glad that she was on her own. The negotiation and discussion and compromise involved in being part of a couple seemed ill-defined and uncomfortable. Ruth's life was tidy. She paid her bills on time, got up exactly when she wanted to, and had only her own bad moods to contend with. She had routines she looked forward to. On Friday mornings, she had breakfast at Jerry's, in Prince Street. Jerry's had the best oatmeal in Manhattan, and it was a very large serving. She watched the wheelings and dealings of the New York art world while she ate her oatmeal at Jerry's.

On Tuesday nights, Ruth ate at Il Carallo, a small Italian bistro. At Il Carallo, they steamed her broccoli with garlic and lemon juice and grilled her fillet of snapper with no fat. It was easy to be single, in New York. No one thought twice about a woman eating out, alone. Plenty of people ate out on their own. It was not considered a sign of loneliness or a sign of a lowly social stature to be dining by yourself. Women who ate in restaurants on their own had a sophistication about them, Ruth thought. She herself never took a book or a newspaper into a restaurant with her. She was happy with her own thoughts for company.

She often daydreamed in cafés and restaurants. She daydreamed at home, too. Her apartment was a sanctuary, for her. An oasis of quiet in a noisy city. She had photographs of Edek and Rooshka in the living room. Photographs of Edek and Rooshka at dinner dances, at the beach, outside their house. The photographs were photographs of a normal life. Edek and Rooshka were doing what normal people did. They were standing outside their front fence, smiling. They were sitting in someone's garden. They were talking. In one of the photographs, her mother was laughing. All the abnormality was erased in these photographs. The nightmares were not there, the fear was not there. The tears were not there.

In a corner of the lowest rung of the bookshelves in her study, Ruth had a photograph of Garth. It was the only photograph of Garth that she had kept. He was smiling. Ruth knew he was smiling at her. She had taken the photograph. Garth's large, dark, brown eyes were looking at her. There was a happiness in his being that was almost palpable. Once, she had touched the photograph and imagined that she could feel his joy. On the desk, in her study, was a photograph of Edek. He was smiling. It made her smile.

Everything in her apartment was in its place. And everything had a place. Her apartment was as well ordered as her life. On the first Monday of every month Ruth took Max out to dinner. Ruth brought a list with her to these dinners. It was a list of things to be discussed and straightened out. A list of minor differences of opinion, unresolved disagreements, small conflicts, as well as points of praise, advice, and suggestions for the future. It was a checklist to keep things in check.

Two years ago, Max had begun bringing her own list. She listed her grievances and her concerns. Ruth and Max discussed each item on both lists over hors d'oeuvres. They were then free to enjoy the rest of the meal. And they did. They both looked forward to the dinners.

Ruth let Max choose the restaurants and make the bookings. Max had become a formidable connoisseur of New York restaurants. They had eaten at Bouley Bakery, Balthazar, the Blue Ribbon, Nobu, and other hard-to-get-into restaurants. They had eaten in the East Village, in Chelsea, and in Chinatown. One of Ruth's favorites was the Ukrainian Restaurant on

Third Avenue. The decor was less decorous than it could be. Plastic flowers and plastic wood. The waiters had jaundiced complexions and nervous mannerisms. Ruth was puzzled by how at home she felt there. Ruth thought that these dinners with lists should be compulsory for married couples. She was sure that a monthly airing of everything that could be put on a list would lower the divorce rate.

When Ruth thought about her life, she thought that it was as fulfilling a life as any married woman's. She had sex infrequently, but so did most of the married women she knew. In New York, it seemed, sex was not a high priority. At least not for married couples. People spent themselves at work. Their passions were expended in the office and in the boardroom. When they got home at night, they needed to unwind in front of the television, before they dropped into bed, exhausted. Couples in their thirties made jokes about their lack of sex. It seemed to be an acceptable condition of married life in the city.

She must remember, she thought, to ask Max what was happening with the man Max had been going out with for six months. He was a married man, and Ruth had strongly advised Max to leave him. "He is a liar, he has to be," she had said to Max. "He's lying to his wife and if he can lie to her, he can just as easily lie to you." Max hadn't looked pleased.

Ruth suddenly realized that her father had been gone for over ten minutes. She went into the Marriott to look for him. He was just coming out. A man was following him. "I got a car," Edek said. "It is not so good like the other one. It is a bit smaller." He led her around the corner to the side street. "Look," he said. He was pointing to a car. A Mercedes.

"We want to go to the ghetto wall," Ruth said to the driver. "It's not far. It's at 60 Złota Street." Edek repeated what she had said in Polish. The driver nodded. "Do you know where it is?" Ruth said. "Yes, I know," the driver said. Edek repeated the question in Polish. The driver said, yes, yes, in Polish.

"Why were you so long?" Ruth said to Edek.

"I wanted to look around a bit at the Marriott," Edek said. "It costs nearly the same as what you are paying at the Bristol, and to tell you the truth it looks a bit nicer to me."

"Well, I'm happy with the Bristol," Ruth said.

"The Marriott has a different theme in the restaurant every night,"

Edek said. "One night is Polish, one night is German, one night Indian, one night something else."

"You don't like Indian food," Ruth said.

"Just the carry I don't like," said Edek. He always pronounced curry this way.

"Indian cuisine is made up of curry," Ruth said. She looked around her. Where were they? "Are you sure you're going in the right direction?" Ruth asked the driver.

"Yes, yes," he said. Edek asked him again. The driver sounded less certain. His reply, in Polish, involved more words.

"The former Jewish ghetto," Ruth said. "Where they took all the Jews of Warsaw and imprisoned them," she said. She had enunciated each word slowly. The driver turned toward her. He looked bewildered. "The ghetto," she repeated.

Polish people knew very little about Jews and the place they had occupied in Poland. A Polish historian had recently released a report that demonstrated that Polish textbooks usually omitted the Holocaust and Jewish history in Poland from the seventeenth and eighteenth and nineteenth centuries. The Holocaust was depicted as one facet of a planned extermination of the Polish people. No textbooks mentioned German or Polish anti-Semitism.

"He probably has no idea what I'm talking about," Ruth said to Edek. "They teach them nothing in schools about what happened to Jews."

"Shsh, shsh," said Edek.

"I've got a map in my bag," Ruth said. She took out the map. Edek looked out of the car window.

"We are on Świętokrzyska," he said.

"Then we're very close," Ruth said. The driver slowed down. Ruth showed him the map.

"Yes, yes, yes," he said. "I know now where you want to go."

"How much will you charge to wait fifteen minutes for us while we look at the wall?" Ruth asked him.

"Fifteen minutes?" Edek said. "Why fifteen minutes? It is only a piece of wall. Five minutes will be plenty." Edek proceeded to discuss minutes and zlotys with the driver.

"Five zlotys!" Edek announced. "Not a bad price to wait for five minutes."

"Tell him, I'll pay him ten zlotys and we'll be ten minutes," Ruth said.

Edek and Ruth walked through the archway at 60 Złota Street and into a courtyard. On the right, at the end of the courtyard, was a three-meter-high red brick wall. This was part of the wall that had imprisoned four hundred and fifty thousand Jews. One hundred and fifty thousand per square kilometer. The daily nutritional rations for the Jews imprisoned in the ghetto added up to two hundred and thirty calories a day. Two hundred and thirty calories was less than three apples or three eggs or three slices of rye bread. But the Jews in the Warsaw ghetto had no apples, no eggs, and very little bread. They had turnips, potato peels, some flour, and some sugar—if they were lucky.

By the end of 1941, less than two years after the ghetto had been formed, over one hundred thousand Jews had died of exhaustion and starvation. By September 1942, three hundred thousand Jews had died or been transported for liquidation. Imprisoning the Jews in the ghettos killed them as effectively if not quite as efficiently as the concentration camps.

Ruth and Edek stood in front of the wall. Ruth wanted to cry. She looked at the bricks. They looked like such ordinary bricks. Held together with ordinary mortar. These bricks had done a good job. Very few Jews had escaped the grip of these bricks. Two bricks were missing from this wall. They were in the Holocaust Museum, in Washington, D.C., a sign said. Ruth wasn't sure what the display of these two bricks would do for visitors to the Holocaust Museum. Most of the visitors would never know how drenched in disgust for Jews much of the world was. And that this disgust was why they had bricked the Jews up before disposing of them.

It was just too difficult to grasp the extent of the anti-Semitism that existed then. It was too hard to understand the hatred that allowed small babies and young children to be starved and shot and gassed and butchered. It was too difficult to comprehend the enthusiasm with which people embraced the murder of a race. It seemed incomprehensible.

In 1943, in Warsaw, an exhibition was mounted to explain more clearly to the Polish people how dangerous the Jews were. The exhibition explained and demonstrated, in slides and lectures and films, that Jews, by their very nature, carried typhus in their blood and lice on their bodies. If you touched a Jew, if you touched Jewish flesh, you would be poisoned, the exhibition reiterated over and over again.

Schoolchildren in Warsaw were required to attend this exhibition. Many children were frightened to walk through the exhibits. They stood clear of the charts and diagrams and photographs in case they were contagious. It was a popular exhibition. Fifty thousand people passed through before the show was packed up and traveled to other Polish cities.

Ruth wept. "It is just a wall," Edek said. "It is just a wall," he repeated. But the expression on his face was at odds with his language and his tone. He looked as if he was crying. His face was fixed in an expression of grief. His eyes and mouth and nose were depressed and bereft. He didn't know he was crying, Ruth decided.

"There is a man near that door," Edek said, pointing to the only other occupant of the courtyard. The man stood up from the step he had been sitting on and walked toward Edek and Ruth. Edek moved closer to Ruth. The man spoke to them. Ruth couldn't understand what he was saying. He smelled of alcohol and his clothes were ragged. "He is asking if we want him to take a photograph of us," Edek said. The man's eyesight was obviously sharp, Ruth thought. Her camera was tiny.

"I told him no," Edek said. The man looked at Ruth.

"Why not?" she said to Edek. "It would be nice to have some photographs of this trip."

"I don't think we should give him the camera," Edek said.

"He's not going to run off with it," Ruth said. "He looks in pretty decrepit condition, anyway. I could easily outrun him."

"We shouldn't let him have it," Edek said.

"It only cost two hundred dollars," Ruth said. "If he steals it, I'll buy another one."

"To you, two hundred dollars is nothing," Edek said.

"That's not true," she said. "I just wouldn't mind a photograph of us."

"Okay, okay," Edek said.

He spoke to the man. The man smiled and nodded. Ruth stepped forward and handed the man the camera. He stank. She moved back next to

Edek. The man held the camera up to his face. He stepped back. Edek stepped toward him.

"Dad, he's not running away," Ruth said. "He's stepping back so that he can get us both in the photograph."

"I am staying here," Edek said. "He looks like such a type to me."

"Like what type?" Ruth said.

"Like such a type who will steal," Edek said. "And who knows what else he will do to us."

"Dad, I'm twice his size," Ruth said.

Edek spoke to the man. "What did you say to him?" Ruth asked.

"I told him just the heads will be enough," Edek said. Ruth saw that her father was genuinely nervous of this thin, drunk, dilapidated man. She stepped forward.

"A head shot will be fine," she said to Edek.

Edek beamed for the camera. "I don't think we need to look cheerful," Ruth said. "We're not at Luna Park." Edek continued to smile. He smiled straight at the camera. All of his teeth were displayed in the smile. Ruth wished that he would get a better set of teeth. He refused to spend any money on his teeth. He'd had them made by some semiqualified dental technologist in an outer suburb of Melbourne. She had begged him to buy better teeth. But he wouldn't. She could always tell when he had a new pair. His new false teeth whistled for the first few months. Edek beamed broadly at the camera.

"One more for good luck," Edek said to the man. The man looked blank. Edek repeated himself.

"I think Polish would be better," Ruth said.

"Oy, cholera," Edek said. He spoke to the man, in Polish.

Ruth didn't want to touch the man or the camera, after the man had touched it. She held her sleeve over her hand when he handed the camera back to her. Edek took out some zlotys for the man. "Don't touch him," Ruth said. "Drop the zlotys into his hand." Edek and Ruth walked back to the taxi. "It was a very moving experience, seeing the ghetto wall," Ruth said.

"Why do you wear such a school bag?" Edek said, looking at her backpack.

"It's a backpack, Dad," she said. "Schoolchildren aren't the only ones who wear these now."

"I'm glad we came here," Ruth said in the car. Edek looked out of the window.

"Do you know anybody in the *Wiedergutmachung* place?" he said. *Wiedergutmachung* was what the Germans called the minuscule amount of reparation money that was paid to the few Jews who had survived Nazi concentration camps. *Wiedergutmachung*. Literally translated, it was "to make good again." Ruth found the word offensive. Surely they could have thought of a more plausible word. Even an imbecile had to acknowledge that not a fraction of what was done could ever be made good again.

"How would I know anyone in Germany with a connection to the *Wiedergutmachung* department?" Ruth said to Edek.

"You told me you had a German client," Edek said. "I thought maybe the client knows someone, in Germany. The *Wiedergutmachung* people refused me an extra hundred dollars a month. They give some people a bit extra if a doctor says they need it. I told the doctor I couldn't sleep. So he wrote a letter for me."

"You've needed sleeping pills for years," Ruth said.

"But I did not know they did pay extra," Edek said.

"Why did they say no?" said Ruth.

"They did not tell me," Edek said. "That is why I asked you if you did know somebody in Germany."

"My client is a Lufthansa executive," Ruth said. "I don't think he'd know anyone in Germany. He's been in New York for years. I flew Lufthansa once," she said. Edek interrupted her.

"They are the best," he said.

"You haven't flown Lufthansa," she said.

"But I know they are the best," he said. "For sure."

"Well, they certainly know how to take off," Ruth said. "They take off like no other airline I've been on. This Lufthansa plane went straight up into the sky. At such a steep angle, I felt sick. Each leg of the flight was the same. Straight up, into the sky."

Edek shook his head. "They are the best, for sure," he said.

"How come we're admiring the Germans?" Ruth said.

"Because they are very good," said Edek.

"You think maybe they had reason to believe that they were the master race?" she said. She had meant this as a joke. Edek didn't laugh.

"Maybe," he said.

An hour later, they were on their way to Łódź. It was a relief to be on the way to Łódź. Ruth thought that maybe Edek would calm down now. He had been restless and eager to leave Warsaw from the moment that he had arrived. He had been so impatient and so edgy that she had forgotten to show him the Wedel chocolate shop. She made a mental note to take him there when they got back to Warsaw.

Edek was quiet. When the driver had arrived at the Bristol to pick them up, Edek had rushed out to greet him. Edek shook hands with the driver and put his arm around him in an affectionate gesture. "There's no need to embrace him," Ruth had said to Edek. Edek had glared at her. "He understands English," Edek had said to her in Yiddish. Ruth wasn't fluent in Yiddish, but she understood most ordinary, everyday, domestic Yiddish. She knew how to say I'm tired, my head hurts, I've got a stomachache, and my children are killing me. Not a very useful set of phrases and sentences. "He understands English," Edek repeated in Yiddish.

Edek sat in the front of the Mercedes with the driver. They were half an hour out of Warsaw. He had been quiet for most of the trip. Ruth was relieved when he started to chat to the driver. The driver seemed happy, too. He switched off the radio as soon as Edek began to talk. Ruth tried not to listen to the conversation. She checked her bag to make sure she had taken everything out of the Bristol's safety deposit box. Her passport and Edek's passport were still in the manila envelope she had packed them in. Her wallet was there. Her travelers' checks, and both sets of airline tickets were there. She was relieved.

Edek and the driver were now talking flat out. The talk was of highways and expressways. Ruth couldn't understand most of it. She heard Edek say "Long Island Expressway." Why, Ruth wondered, would Edek be talking about the Long Island Expressway to the driver? Edek was animated. One sentence poured out after another. He sounded as if he was having the time of his life.

They drove past several small farms. Polish people were very neat farm-ers. Everything was meticulously laid out. Perfectly square fields of potatoes. Parallel rows of cauliflower and rows and rows of beans. Rows of green cabbage, next to rows of red cabbage. The spaces in between the rows were scrupulously clean. Ruth couldn't see a stray twig or weed in farm after farm. The animals looked just as tidy. The black and white cows had shiny pelts. Even the pigs looked spick and groomed.

There must be something soothing about growing your own food, Ruth thought. Her life was so far removed from the planting and gathering of essential sustenance. What did she do? She provided expensive letters for people who could no longer form their own words. She felt very flat.

She was jolted by the sudden, raucous laughter coming from the front seat. Edek and the driver had been chuckling quietly, but now they were laughing out loud. Edek roared with laughter. He turned around to Ruth. "He told me a not so nice joke," he said. "Should I tell you?" "No thanks," she said.

They were on the outskirts of a small town. Ruth could see the town ahead of them. They passed a large industrial building. On the side of the building someone had drawn a penis. A Star of David was drawn across the testicles and the initials ŁKS were written along the length of the penis. Ruth had seen anti-Semitic graffiti in Poland before. It had shocked her each time. They had removed the Jews from Poland but anti-Semitic graffiti had stayed and thrived.

She tapped Edek on the shoulder and pointed to the graffiti. "Ask him what that is." she said to Edek. Both men looked out of the window. The driver offered Edek an explanation.

"He says it is a joke," Edek said to Ruth.

"Does he think it's funny?" Ruth said.

"Of course not," said Edek. The driver added something else. "He says they didn't mean anything bad by it," Edek said.

"ŁKS is the local soccer team, and they're losing," Ruth said. "So, the locals put Jude, Jew, or a Star of David on references to the team." Edek didn't say anything. "Do you understand, Dad?" she said. "They're using the Star of David to signify the weak ones, the losers."

"I understand," Edek said. They drove in silence for several miles.

"Would you like to stop at the house of Chopin?" the driver said loudly to Ruth.

"No thanks," she said.

"Żelazowa Wola, Chopin's home, is very interesting," the driver said.

"No thank you," Ruth said.

"Why not?" said Edek.

"Because we'll never get to Łódź," said Ruth. "Come on, we'll stop for five minutes," Edek said.

"I'll stay in the car, then," she said. "I've seen Chopin's home. I've seen Chopin's piano, Chopin's mother's piano, Chopin's bedroom, Chopin's mother's bedroom, Chopin's bathroom, and Chopin's garden." Edek ignored her.

At Żelazowa Wola, Ruth stayed in the car and read. The two men returned from their tour of Chopin's house in good spirits. The driver was humming *La Polonaise*. Edek asked Ruth if she would take a photograph of him and the driver in Chopin's garden. She got out of the car and took the photograph. "Take one more photograph in front of the Mercedes," Edek said. She photographed both men in front of the Mercedes. They looked so happy together. They looked like brothers.

Edek and the driver started talking as soon as they got back into the car. The driver was telling Edek something about Chopin's mother. Edek was also discussing Chopin. Ruth didn't know he knew anything about Chopin. The two men talked and talked.

Ruth was puzzled. Edek was never as garrulous as this in Australia. And then it dawned on her. Of course, in Australia he was forced to speak English. A halting, faulty English. Here he could speak Polish. Perfect Polish. Polish, the language of his childhood, the language of his mother and father. No wonder he was at home here. He was at home. It was a sobering thought.

"Is it nice for you to be able to speak as much Polish as you want to?" she said to her father.

"It is all right," he said. "I can speak Polish, I can speak English, I can speak German." He paused. "Do you know what they called the path to the gas chambers? *Himmel Weg*. The road to heaven."

"What made you think of that?" Ruth said.

"What, are you stupid or something?" he said. "What else am I thinking of? You think I am not thinking about things. This morning it was a big trauma for me."

"What was?" said Ruth.

"What do you think I am talking about?" Edek said exasperatedly. "The ghetto wall, of course."

"Why didn't you tell me at the time?" Ruth said.

"Why should I tell you every little thing?" he said.

"That wasn't so little," said Ruth.

"It is enough of this stuff," Edek said. He turned back to the driver.

They were almost on the outskirts of Łódź, now. "We're getting close to Łódź," Ruth said to Edek. "I do not recognize it yet," he said. His voice sounded frighteningly flat.

"We're going to be all right, Dad," she said.

"Of course," he said.

She wished that the driver would start chatting to Edek. As though he had read her mind, the driver said something to Edek. Edek answered him. Soon another conversation was under way. It seemed to be about cars and mileage. And Mercedeses. Edek started to sound like himself, again.

"Jesus, look, more graffiti," Ruth said. They had passed a wall with several Stars of David crisscrossed with the ŁKS initials of the losing Polish soccer team. As soon as she had spoken, she had regretted interrupting Edek and the driver. "I do not think you should say Jesus," Edek said.

"Children do this. It is just children," the driver said, looking back at the graffiti.

They were in Łódź proper now. Ruth didn't want to cause another disturbance by announcing that they had arrived. Edek seemed unmoved. He had opened the glovebox of the Mercedes and was admiring the smooth way it opened and shut. Edek and the driver were agreeing that the precision of German engineering was hard to beat.

Łódź looked as bleak and as grim as Ruth remembered it. They were in the center of the city. In the streets people had pallid faces and blank expressions. Łódź, an industrial city built on the textile industry, was often called the Manchester of Poland. Łódź, Ruth thought, made Manchester look like Monte Carlo.

They pulled up outside the Grand Victoria Hotel. The doorman rushed up to open the car doors. He collided with the driver, who was also in a hurry to open the car doors. The doorman opened Ruth's door with a flourish. He peered inside. "Please let me help you with anything that you need," he said to her. He was revolting. She hunched her shoulders so that she would be as far from him as possible while she got out of the car. He hovered around the car door. "It is a pleasure to be of help to such a beautiful woman," he said as Ruth was halfway out.

He really was repulsive, she thought. He had a very thick neck on top of a very thick body. Several thick gold chains hung around his thick neck, and revolting wads of hair were growing out of his ears and nostrils. Ruth flinched. How could men like this not realize how unattractive they were? Maybe it took a lot to make a man feel unattractive.

"I shall come to your room, personally, to make sure that everything is in order for you," he said to Ruth. "No, thank you," she said loudly. He really was disgusting. Awful enough to make anyone change his mind about the value of genocide. Someone should have shot him, years ago. She smiled to herself at the outrageousness of that thought.

Ruth looked at her father. He was handing over what looked like voluminous amounts of zlotys to the driver and shaking his hand. He said his final good-bye to the driver and followed Ruth into the hotel. Edek smiled at the doorman and introduced himself. "Dad, I've just got rid of him," Ruth hissed into Edek's ear. "He's revolting." Edek glared at Ruth and moved away from her. He started talking to the porter. Ruth went to the reception desk. She requested rooms close together. She heard Edek laughing.

The Grand Victoria Hotel had seen grander days. There was wear and tear and a general shabbiness everywhere. Even in the lobby. The porter came up to take her bags. His collar was covered with dandruff. His hair was filthy. Slicked in its own grease. Ruth grimaced and moved a foot farther away from him. It was funny, she thought, that you could tell the difference between dirty hair and hair that was designed to look dirty, with layers of gel, mousse, thickeners, relaxers, styling creams, and foaming strengtheners.

She felt her own hair. All the curls were curling the way she liked them to curl, into little ringlets. Her hair had been looking good lately. These good looks came at a price. A hundred and fifty dollars a haircut, to be precise. Geoffrey, at the John Frieda salon on Madison Avenue and Seventy-sixth Street, always did a good job on her hair. He was English, and she liked the familiarity of his accent and his phrases. He was playful with her. He was the youngest of ten children, and handled her hair with the confidence and intimacy of a man who has always been around women.

Geoffrey was always asking her if she was in love. No, she would say. "Neither am I," he would reply. "Here I am, in New York, in gay heaven, and I can't get a date," he would say. "It's a city in which it's impossible to meet real people," she would say. Sometimes she went to the movies with Geoffrey. Ruth had her hair colored at the John Frieda salon, too. Bryan, her colorist, was one of the most relaxing men she had ever met. She almost went into a coma when Bryan colored her hair. She had her hair colored every three weeks. That way she need never know if she was going gray.

Hair was complicated for most women. Ruth had had her long curly hair cut by the local barber when she was twelve. Her mother had taken her to Mr. Brown, who had a barbershop across the street from them in Carlton. Mr. Brown cut and cut. Ruth emerged with a short back and sides. Mr. Brown had even clipped the back of her neck with his clippers. With her new haircut, Ruth looked like a pinhead. She had looked in the mirror when she had got home and known that Rooshka hadn't meant to make her ugly. Something out of her mother's control had driven Rooshka to have Ruth's hair cut off. Ruth knew that it must have been connected with the chopping off of her mother's own long, thick plaits, in Auschwitz.

When they emptied Auschwitz, there were fifteen thousand pounds of human hair left behind. The Nazis were too busy in the last days of the war to ship this particular shipment of hair. The hair was packed in fifty-five-pound bags, ready to be shipped to Bavaria to the factories that processed the hair. The factories converted the hair into fabric. Lining to be used in men's overcoats. The factories paid twenty-five pfennigs a pound for this hair, which reemerged as rolls of lining. Tailors stitched the hair into men's suits as well. Somewhere in Germany, men had walked to work wearing her mother's hair. The hair contained traces of hydrogen cyanide, Zyklon B, the gas they used to kill the owners of the hair, but the Germans weren't bothered by that. After all, this hair didn't touch German skin.

It was big business, this crating and shipping of people's bits and pieces. Gold and platinum pulled from teeth were melted and molded into ingots. Watches were sent to Oranienburg and spectacles were shipped to the SS

Sanitary Office. An office that didn't appear to have been too sanitary. Clothes were forwarded to the Ministry of Finance. When the Germans fled Auschwitz they left behind eight hundred and thirty-six thousand, five hundred and twenty-five women's dresses, among other things.

Ruth felt trapped and restless in her room at the Grand Victoria Hotel. She needed to get out. It was four o'clock, and almost dark. She thought that she would probably feel better, even if she only sat in the lobby. She picked up her bag and walked to the door. The door handle wouldn't turn. It was stuck.

She called Edek's room. "I'm stuck," she said. "I can't get out of my room."

"What happened?" he said.

"The door handle won't budge," she said. Edek started to laugh.

"It is not such a good hotel what the Bristol is, that is for sure," he said.

"It has seen grander days, the Grand Victoria," she said. He laughed again.

"You was always clever with words," he said.

"Dad, can you call the porter and explain the problem to him, in Polish?" she said.

"Of course," he said.

"The porter, not the doorman," Ruth said.

"You want me to come and see if I can fix it?" Edek said.

"No, just call the porter," she said.

"You are right," said Edek. "I am not so good in such things. As a matter of fact Garth did come and help me when I needed to put such a rail what you hold on to, on my bath."

"Garth put a bath rail in for you? Why?" Ruth said.

"He wanted to," Edek said. "I was going to get a handyman, but Garth said he was coming to Melbourne and he would do it. As a matter of fact he is not such a good handyman. The bar what he put in is three foot long. It looks pretty stupid."

"You shouldn't have let him," Ruth said. "I'm sure he's got plenty to do when he comes to Melbourne."

"It did take him only two or three hours and then we did go to

Scheherezade for a *cholent*," Edek said. "He is the only *goy* I know who does like a *cholent*. Then we did have a piece of apple cake each."

"You don't need him to fix things in your apartment," Ruth said.

"I do not need him to fix things," Edek said. "But I like to be with him. And to tell you the truth, he likes to be with me. I can feel it."

Ruth knew that Garth was no handyman. He had the large, broad hands of a handyman, but he was hopeless. Things he built fell apart. Although he worked with his hands every day, he just didn't have a knack for renovations or repairs. Ruth thought about Garth's hands. Sometimes she remembered moments of their lovemaking. She remembered their sex with extraordinary clarity. Maybe because it had made her feel so good. Nourished, whole, replete. On the whole, she didn't think about sex much. Maybe she just wasn't a highly sexual person. Or, maybe sexual thoughts had to come attached to love, for her.

She caught herself. How could she be thinking about sex, with her father on the other end of the line?

"Let's go for a walk, Dad," she said. "Ring the porter and get me out of here, and let's go for a walk." Edek hesitated. "Okay," he finally said. "Okay, let's walk a bit. I did see a McDonald's not far away. McDonald's does do a very good chocolate thickshake."

"I can't believe you've spotted a McDonald's already," Ruth said. "I thought you were busy talking to the driver."

"I did talk to the driver and I did see a McDonald's," Edek said.

"Can you believe a McDonald's, in Łódź?" Ruth said. "It is something hard to believe," Edek said.

It took the porter fifteen minutes to unstick the stuck door handle. Ruth was looking for a couple of zlotys with which to tip the porter when the phone rang. It was Max.

"Where are you?" Ruth said to Max. "You can't be in the office. It's Saturday morning."

"I'm at home," Max said.

"We have to be brief," Ruth said. "I'm just about to go out with my father, and it's going to be the first time he's walked in the streets of Łódź since he was twenty-three."

"Okay," Max said. "I've only got one question. I wouldn't have called you except that this seemed to be something you would want to know about. I haven't wanted to intrude on your very emotional time with your father."

"Max, ask the question," Ruth said.

"Mr. Kendall wants to know if he can buy the copyright to the refusal-to-lend-his-name-to-the-fund-raising letter we did for him," Max said. "He said it was such a brilliant tactic to praise the charity lavishly in the first paragraph."

"He wants to own the rights to that letter?" Ruth said.

"Yes," said Max.

"I'm not sure about that," Ruth said. "I should have thought about this issue before, really. Possibly he already owns the copyright as it's his letter."

"But you wrote it," Max said.

"I know," said Ruth. "Nothing is simple anymore. Not even owning your own letters."

"But whose letter is it?" Max said. "Yours or his?"

"It's his letter and my letter," Ruth said. "Why does he want to own it anyway?"

"He said he doesn't want anyone else to use exactly the same letter," said Max. "I told him it would be very expensive. He said that was fine."

"Tell him he'll have to wait until I get back," Ruth said.

"By the way, Mr. Newton was very pleased with the thanks-for-your-thoughts-while-I-was-ill letters," Max said. "You faxed me sixteen, so I gave him the extra one for no charge."

"I'm glad he was pleased," said Ruth.

"He sounded in very good shape for someone who has just had bypass surgery," Max said. "In better shape than my neighbor's dog."

"What are you talking about?" Ruth said. As soon as Max started answering her, Ruth regretted that she had asked the question.

"My neighbor's Labrador had a bypass operation," Max said. "It was done at Michigan State University's Veterinary Hospital, which is recognized for the quality of its open-heart surgery."

"Open-heart surgery for dogs?" Ruth said.

"Of course. It's a veterinary hospital," Max said. "You can have dialysis for cats and pacemakers for dogs. This Labrador was on Prozac for months before he underwent his surgery. You can get your cat's teeth straightened, too. Orthodontics for dogs and cats is big at the moment."

"How do you know all of this?" Ruth said.

"My neighbor who owns the Labrador told me," said Max.

"I have to go," Ruth said.

"Take care," said Max.

"I'm trying," Ruth said. She called Edek's room. "I'm ready," she said.

Ruth and Edek walked along Piotrkowska Street. Not many people were out. Ruth felt flat. They walked without speaking. She resisted asking her father how he felt. She didn't want to annoy him. There was a blank passivity in the faces of the people in the street. Ruth found it depressing. It was five o'clock on Saturday night. "Let's go to McDonald's," she said to Edek. They walked in the direction of McDonald's.

The acrid smell of coal smoke filled the air. Ruth's eyes began to sting. "Are your eyes hurting?" she asked Edek. "Nothing is hurting," he said. Every second person who passed them seemed to be coughing, and spitting. It must be the smoke from the coal fires, Ruth thought. Łódź really was an oppressive city, she thought. It was dark, now. Very dark. And still. The black air hardly moved.

Where was the moon? Ruth wondered. In mourning? There was not much sign of life in the streets, as though Łódź had swallowed its people for the night. Squat, gray buildings sat on either side of the black tram tracks. There seemed to be a lot of dog shit in the streets. "Be careful you don't step in dog shit," she said to Edek.

"Look," he said. "The McDonald's." The McDonald's in Piotrkowska Street was as garish as any McDonald's anywhere. Ruth was so happy to see it.

Edek sipped his chocolate thickshake. She and Edek were the oldest people in McDonald's. The rest of the customers seemed to be teenagers. Ruth didn't mind the teenagers. She had never been in a McDonald's. She felt oddly at home.

"This chocolate thickshake is very good," Edek said.

"I'm pleased," she said.

"Maybe I will try an ice cream tomorrow," Edek said. "In Polish ice cream is *lody*. The *lody* in Poland was always very good."

Ruth had heard this from him before. She had heard it in stories about Edek hiring a *doroszka* to take him to the ice-cream shop. And stories about Edek buying ice creams for all of his friends. He must have been such a playboy, Ruth thought. She looked at him. He looked so happy with his chocolate thickshake. She wanted to cry. "We'll buy lots of *lody* tomorrow," she said.

"Piotrkowska Street used to be full of people on Saturday night," Edek said. "People walking up and down. It was such an excitement in the feeling of the street. Young boys and girls walked together. Couples walked together. Everybody was talking. Everybody was happy. Look outside now. No one is there. There is nobody." He was quiet for a minute. He looked out at the street. "You cannot imagine what Piotrkowska Street was like," he said to Ruth. "Everybody was dressed up. Girls went to meet boys. Boys went to meet girls. Who is there now? Nobody."

"Did you go there on a Saturday night?" Ruth said.

"Of course I did," he said. "All the young people did." He looked sad. "The most beautiful girls were the Jewish girls," he said. "And your mum was the most beautiful of them all."

Thinking about her mother on Piotrkowska Street on a Saturday night was too much for Ruth. She started to cry. She tried to hide her tears from Edek. Maybe this trip was a mistake, after all.

"There is no Jews here, now," Edek said, and shook his head.

∾ *Chapter Six* ∾

*I*t is funny, is it not, how many of our names begin with the letter 'H,' " Rudolf Höss said.

Ruth was in a café directly across the road from the Grand Victoria Hotel. "I can't believe it's you again," she said.

"I am referring, of course, to my colleagues. To my former colleagues, of course," Höss said. "It is of great interest to me this preponderance of names among us beginning with the letter 'H.' Höss, Hess, Hanfstängl, Harlan, Hauptmann, Heyde, Heydrich, Himmler, Hoffman, Hugenberg, Hossbach, and the most obvious one, naturally, Hitler."

"I can't believe it's you again," Ruth said. "I thought you must have been a figment of my imagination, or a bad dream."

"Both of these could be said to be correct," said Höss.

"Are you trying to be mystical?" said Ruth. She felt miserable. This was Rudolf Höss and she, Ruth Rothwax, could hear him.

"You do not believe in mysticism?" Höss said.

"I don't believe in you," said Ruth. "I was sure I had made the whole thing up. I was sure I had imagined it. I thought it must have been my lack of sleep that made me think I had spoken to you. Or too much stress. Or something I ate."

"I have not been brought about by indigestion or an acid stomach," Höss said.

"Why can't you leave me alone?" said Ruth.

"I do not cause you any pain," Höss said. "I do not hurt you. I do not disturb you."

"That's a joke," Ruth said. "I find you very disturbing. Can't you go away? I've had a long day."

"I know this," Höss said.

"I wouldn't have gone out on my own if I'd known you were going to appear," Ruth said.

"You do not have to be alone," said Höss. "I can speak to you anywhere."

Ruth looked around her. No one had appeared to notice that she was talking to herself. There were not many people in the café. It was still early. Surely, even in Łódź, this café would fill up soon. It was Saturday night.

She hadn't told Edek that she was going to go out. He had looked so tired. And he had asked her several times if she was going to go straight to bed. He seemed to need to know where she was. She had told the hotel operator to call her in the café if Edek called her room. She had known that she wouldn't be able to sleep. She knew she had to try to unwind. Cafés usually relaxed her. She could drift off and daydream. She had also needed to see some sign of life in Łódź.

A young woman in an evening gown was playing a selection from *My Fair Lady* on a piano, just beside the refrigerated selection of cakes. The café had the white crocheted lace curtains of a country inn across the windows and elaborate plastic chandeliers above each table. Ruth had been admiring the lack of restraint in the decor when Höss had broken up her thoughts.

"Do you not find this interesting, Miss Rothwax?" Höss said. Ruth started. She had forgotten that he knew her name. She wasn't sure why this should startle her. It certainly wasn't more startling than the fact of his presence. Or his presence in her life, to be more precise.

"Don't I find what interesting?" she said.

"The fact of so many of our names beginning with the letter 'H,' " Höss said.

"No, I don't find it interesting," Ruth said. "There are so many of you, so many Nazis, that you could look up any letter of the alphabet and find many major Nazi figures."

"So many Hs. What does it mean?" Höss said.

"A better question would be why so many Nazis?" Ruth said. "So many members of the party, so many vociferous supporters, and so many silent followers and informal friends? So many dependents and adherents and appendages. So many flunkies."

"I know this word 'flunky,' " Höss said.

"A person of slavish or fawning obedience," Ruth said.

"I am familiar with the term," said Höss. He coughed uncomfortably.

Was he coughing in discomfort at the thought of himself as a flunky? Ruth thought. She shook her head. She couldn't believe she was thinking about Rudolf Höss's thoughts. The thoughts of a dead, long-departed, former tiller of the soil, former agriculturist, and Nazi.

"Himmler, that skinny little failed chicken farmer, looked like a flunky," Höss said. "But he was not. His pedantic mannerisms and excessively courtly manners made him look like a flunky. A humble flunky. Or are all flunkies, by necessity, humble?"

"I'm not sure," Ruth said. "You could possibly have an arrogant flunky. Is this skinny chicken farmer you are referring to Heinrich Himmler, Reichsführer-SS?"

"Failed, skinny little chicken farmer," Höss said. "He had a diploma of agriculture. He was a salesman for a firm of fertilizer manufacturers before he went into the poultry farming business."

"Like you, he was the son of a very pious and authoritarian Catholic father, wasn't he?" Ruth said.

"What has this got to do with anything?" Höss said.

"I don't know," said Ruth.

"Himmler was not discouraged by his failure to farm chickens," Höss said. "The fact that his chickens failed to breed did not dishearten or dismay him. He did not see this failure as an obstacle to tackling human genetics. It was Himmler who established *Lebensborn*. You know what *Lebensborn* is?"

"Sure," said Ruth. "It was the program for the creation of a pure Aryan life. *Lebensborn*. Spring of life. You had good terminology, you Nazis. Spring of life. And its twin, *Lebensraum* living space."

"Thank you," said Höss. "Himmler was a first-class organizer and administrator, I must admit. He took a subject of limited interest like racism and turned it into an organizational tool with which to build up Germany. It became essential, if you were a patriotic German, to understand the good that can become of racism."

"They had to hate everyone else in order to preserve themselves," Ruth said.

"Very succinct," said Höss. "The state-registered human stud farm that Himmler set up was a necessity. We had to breed greater numbers of pure Germans. Himmler passed a procreation order on October 28, 1939, to the entire SS. Soldiers had a moral duty to procreate with German women and girls of good blood. Soldiers came from everywhere to couple with the German girls that were selected for the breeding. I must say that they chose the young women very well. They all looked Nordic." Höss sounded excited at his recollection of the obligation to procreate with German girls of good blood. Ruth felt nauseated.

"Himmler set up Dachau in 1933. It was the first concentration camp," Höss said. "You know this?"

"I know that," said Ruth.

"Himmler studied the inmates of Dachau," Höss said. "In 1937—in January, as a matter of fact—he gave a speech. 'There is no more living proof of heredity and racial laws than in a concentration camp. You find there hydrocephalics, squinters, deformed individuals, semi-Jews. A considerable number of inferior people!' Himmler said. It was quite a good speech."

Ruth said nothing. She wasn't feeling well.

"Himmler was always described as a man without nerves," Höss said. "They said he was unemotional. Yet he nearly fainted at the sight of a hundred Jews who were executed for his benefit on the Russian front. What sort of strength does that show? He should have eliminated himself from his own breeding program," Höss laughed.

"Himmler suffered from a lot of psychosomatic illnesses," Ruth said. "He had severe headaches and terrible intestinal spasms."

"This is true," said Höss. "Himmler was also fanatical about homeopathy, herbal remedies, and health food."

"I'm not interested in homeopathy or herbal remedies," Ruth said.

"You drink herbal tea," said Höss.

"How do you know that?" she said. "Don't bother to answer," she said. "I couldn't care less."

"I was living on the land when Himmler's call to join the ranks of the active SS came," said Höss. "Three of our children had already been born ready to be part of the bright future we were planning. It was June 1934. I am normally very decisive, but it took me a long time to make my decision about joining the SS. In the end the temptation to be a soldier again was too strong. It was stronger than the doubts that my wife voiced. My wife was concerned about whether the profession of being a soldier would give me total fulfillment and self-satisfaction."

"Well, she was wrong, wasn't she?" Ruth said.

Höss overlooked her remark. "Today I very much regret that I abandoned my former life as a farmer," he said. "It was not a road to wealth and riches, so today I would be equally without a home and other material possessions of my own."

"What do you mean without a home of your own?" Ruth said. "I thought nobody owned property where you are?"

"I am speaking of time in a general way," Höss said.

"Well, it confuses me," said Ruth.

"See how interested you are," Höss said.

"Don't flatter yourself," she said. "I am not that interested."

"You are interested," Höss said. "It is your destiny."

"You think that it is my inevitable fate that I have to have this contact with you?" Ruth said. "A predetermined course of events? I don't think so."

"You and I have a connection and we cannot escape that," Höss said.

"You would be the master of imprisonment," Ruth said, "so you must know something about escape."

"I know how to make escape impossible, that is true," Höss said.

"I can easily escape," Ruth said. She stood up, turned, and dug her heel into the floor. Höss howled in pain.

"Shall I continue?" Höss said after a couple of minutes.

"It's very polite of you to ask," she said. "Okay, continue."

"I was talking about destiny," he said. "Who among us can see the complicated course of a man's destiny?" Ruth settled back into the chair, in the café. This sounded like a long story. "When I read Himmler's invitation to join the ranks of the SS, I took no notice of the fact that the unit I would be joining would be guarding a concentration camp. The whole notion of a concentration camp was foreign to me. To me it was merely a question of being once more an active soldier. I went to Dachau.

"I remember the first flogging that I was a witness to very clearly. Two prisoners who had stolen cigarettes from the canteen were sentenced to twenty-five strokes of the lash. This was 1934. June 1934, you understand, and Dachau was not yet a death camp."

" 'Death camp,' that's very straightforward language for you to use," Ruth said.

"There is no need for sarcasm," said Höss.

"Of course I know Dachau wasn't quite the death factory then that it turned out to be," Ruth said. "They dispensed with lashes pretty promptly once they had expanded their notion of camps and death. They dropped all the detours. They went straight to death."

"I do not need you to display your knowledge on this subject," Höss said. "I was in the middle of telling you the reaction that I had to my first flogging."

"I'm sure it was remarkable," said Ruth. Höss appeared to overlook her sarcasm. He was obviously impatient to get on with the story.

"The first prisoner made no sound," Höss said. "He was a small man, a petty criminal. The other prisoner, a big, physically strong politician, cried out and tried to break free at the very first stroke. He screamed loudly throughout the lashings. When this prisoner began to scream, I felt myself shudder. I became very hot and then very cold.

"Later on, I witnessed my first execution. But the execution did not have nearly such a big impact on me as the lashings."

"In June 1936, Himmler and Bormann visited Dachau," said Höss. "They recommended me for a promotion."

"Congratulations," Ruth said.

"Bormann was the head of Hitler's chancellery," Höss said.

"I know," said Ruth.

"I was transferred to Sachsenhausen in May 1938," Höss said.

"I'm glad we're moving through the story," said Ruth. "I'm tired. Do you mind if I order something to eat?"

"Why should I mind?" said Höss. "I have to watch people eating the finest-quality food, in Himmel, while I myself in Zweites Himmel's Lager have to make do with food not fit for human consumption."

"In that case I'll order an apple strudel," Ruth said.

She ordered a slice of strudel and a glass of chamomile tea with lemon. The waitress was as offhand and rude to her as most waiters and waitresses in Poland were. Ruth thought this proved that she must look as normal as any other customer. She hadn't unnerved the waitress. She must not appear to be talking to herself.

"I do not know why the Polish are rude," Höss said. "I have always observed the habits and behaviors of people I have worked with, and the Poles are a harsh people."

"Unlike the Germans," she said.

"Exactly," said Höss. "Quite unlike the Germans."

"Germans are hardworking, too, aren't they?" she said.

"Yes," said Höss. "Quite unlike the Poles." Ruth laughed. "You like to laugh at the Poles?" said Höss.

"Sometimes," said Ruth.

"I have worked hard, all of my life," said Höss. "I very much enjoyed hard work. I feel no satisfaction with myself unless I have done a good job."

"Well, you definitely did a very good job," Ruth said.

"Your strudel will be here soon," said Höss.

"Good," she said. "I need the sugar. I didn't expect to be giving you a job appraisal."

"I carried out my duties, in a scrupulous and conscientious manner," Höss said. "I had been a prisoner myself, do not forget. I was firm and sometimes severe, but I was sensitive to the needs of the prisoners. I had a deep concern about some of the things taking place in the camp. I was never indifferent to human suffering. But because it was not possible in my job for me to show any weakness I had to overlook these feelings. I should have gone to the Reichsführer-SS and explained to him that deep in my being I knew I was not really suited to concentration camp service. But I could not find the courage to do this. I had become too attached to the black uniform to relinquish it."

Höss's words soured the taste of her strudel. Ruth pushed the plate away. Höss sounded wistful at the memory of the black uniform he had been so attached to. He was quiet for a minute. "Of course with all the H names, the one that I am most confused with is Rudolf Hess," Höss said, eventually. "It is extremely agitating for me to be confused with Hess. We are as distinctly different as two people could be. Hess was introverted and shy. He joined the army when he was twenty to escape from the domination of his father. As a matter of fact he was also in the Freikorps. However, any similarity between Rudolf Hess and myself, Rudolf Franz Ferdinand Höss, is shallow and superficial."

"You both volunteered for the army, joined the Freikorps and then the Nazi party," Ruth said. "That doesn't sound so trivial or cursory a coincidence."

"You know nothing," Höss said. "In the early days, Hess was Hitler's private secretary. He had a doglike devotion to Hitler that was most embarrassing to observe. He was not an intelligent man. Ha! What an understatement that is. Hess got where he got because of his blind hero worship, his ardor and fervor and fidelity to the Führer."

"Weren't you all like that?" Ruth said.

Höss cleared his throat. "We were loyal and faithful followers," he said. "But that quite disgusting Hess was slavish in his servility and subservience and reverence for Hitler. Hess was a secretary," Höss said disdainfully. "He took down most of the dictation for *Mein Kampf*. Hess made only one original contribution. The concept of *Lebensraum*."

"That's quite a large contribution, isn't it?" Ruth said.

"He gave a name to a concept that many of us Germans had been thinking about," Höss said. "That is not such a big contribution. It was also Hess's job to announce Hitler at mass meetings. His eyes used to open so wide when he made these announcements. He looked like a deranged zealot."

"Didn't you all?" said Ruth.

"Why are you interrupting me with these very annoying asides?" said Höss.

"I'm not really trying to annoy you," Ruth said. "I'm just stating the obvious. You talk about Rudolf Hess and his pitiable pliability and allegiance and ardor. It seems to me you were all like that."

"He was stupid," said Höss.

"Oh, that's the difference," she said. "I didn't realize."

"Hess described Hitler as 'pure reason in human form,'" Höss said.

"Even at the Nuremberg War Crimes trial, in 1946, Hess said, 'It was granted me for many years to live and work under the greatest son whom my nation had brought forth.'"

"Sounds as though Hess was in love with Hitler," Ruth said.

"Now you are being stupid," said Höss. "Hess was so stupid. He ended his career with a most sensational act of stupidity. In May 1941 he parachuted into Scotland. He landed near to the home of a duke he had met just once. He hoped the duke would convince the British to overlook Hitler's activities. He assured them that Hitler had no intention of destroying Britain, a fellow Nordic nation. The British, of course, made him a prisoner of war. Hitler declared him deluded, deranged, and insane," Höss laughed. It was a particularly unattractive laugh. A high-pitched squeal. A cross between a giggle and a snicker.

"Most of us major SS leaders did not ourselves look like the Aryan prototype," he said. "Himmler looked like a diffident accountant, or a petty bureaucrat, and shy, insecure, nervous, stupid Hess was hardly the model Hitler had in mind to take over the world."

Ruth felt tired. She should have stayed at home, she thought.

"You did not sleep well last night," Höss said to her.

"No, I didn't," she said.

She had tossed and turned all night. She had had one of her recurring nightmares. The worst one, the one in which she was a mother. The children were nearly always babies. Every now and then, one of them was a toddler, able to walk. In these dreams she lost her babies or starved them. She misplaced them. Left them on buses or trains. She left them in department stores and in parked cars. The abandonment in her dreams was never intentional. She simply forgot that she had given birth to and brought home a baby. When in her dreams she realized what she had done, she was mortified. Horrified at herself. In some of the dreams she had set up a beautiful nursery, then left the baby there, to die. In other dreams she couldn't feed the baby. Her breasts would be dry or she would have run out of formula. Sometimes she had the breast milk and the formula but simply forgot to feed the baby.

She always woke up in a sweat from these dreams. Lately the dreams had improved. In the last few years she had managed to save the child, at the last minute. She had wondered whether the approach of menopause in her real life was tempering the nightmares. The nightmares were so vivid they would stay with her for days. For days she would feel the shock of her own neglect, her own irresponsibility, her own cruelty.

In one particular dream, the baby was a boy. A baby boy born not quite right. Something was wrong with him, but in dream after dream what was wrong was not clear. The baby always disappeared by the end of the dream and she was left searching for it. Ruth sometimes woke up crying after this dream. The dream had started when she was twenty. She had told Rooshka about it once. Her mother had left the room. Ruth knew that her mother had had too much real loss to take in people who went missing in dreams. Ruth knew that her dreams were made up of imagined absence, and she knew that what was only imagined, was nothing to worry about.

"I did not sleep so well myself," Höss said.

"You sleep?" said Ruth

"Of course I sleep," Höss said. "Dead people can be asleep and awake. I myself am forced to sleep on a wooden bunk without even a straw mattress to lie on. I have a bare light bulb hanging above my bunk, and drab sacking that sags terribly draped across my window."

"You have windows in hell?" Ruth said.

"Of course we have windows in Zweites Himmel's Lager," said Höss. "We have inside and outside. We look outside through our windows."

"No wonder your bones hurt if you have to sleep on a wooden bunk," she said. She kept the glee out of her voice. It was an effort.

"It is harder to sleep in Zweites Himmel's Lager," said Höss. "It is very noisy. People are crying. Some of them are sick. If you do not take care, they can be sick on you, and then you get sick. And you stay sick. There is no medical treatment, as I have mentioned to you, and there is no relief, in death. In Zweites Himmel's Lager, we are all, of course, already dead."

Höss sighed. "In Himmel they have the very best doctors in the world. And new doctors are constantly arriving. They bring with them the very latest advances in medical science. The newest medical breakthroughs, unfortunately, no longer come from Germany. They seem, all of them, to come from America."

"Are many of the doctors Jewish?" Ruth said.

"There are again, yes, many Jewish doctors in the world," Höss said.

"Many of them are in Himmel. I will when I get to Himmel not have so wide a choice of personal physicians as other people because of this."

"Are you saying the Jewish doctors are prejudiced against you?" Ruth said.

"I am not saying anything against Jews," said Höss. "I was never planning, when I get to Himmel, to become a patient myself of any of the German doctors who are Jews, of course. Most of them have been in Himmel for a long time but I doubt if one of them has forgotten me."

"Don't flatter yourself," Ruth said. "I'm sure they've got more in their lives, or their deaths, than you."

"I read books written by Jews," Höss said. "It is compulsory, for me. Why do Jews write so many books? Why do Jews have this obsession with words?"

"Because we talk so much," Ruth said. "We need all the words we can get."

"That is a rude comment, is it not?" Höss said. "It is fortunate for you that you do not have to pass this sensitivity-training class."

"It's not rude if I say it," Ruth said. "There's a difference between me saying something about Jews and your making a similar statement. If you don't know the difference you're going to be in Zweites Himmel's Lager for a long time."

Ruth got up. She had to go to the bathroom. She pressed her heel down more firmly than she needed to. Höss screamed.

"Could you please not turn so quickly?" he said.

"You've got a low threshold of pain, have you?" she said, and dug her heel into the carpet again.

"I do not have a low threshold of pain," Höss spluttered. "It is merely that I do not like the unexpected. I am orderly, like you."

Ruth was fed up. This aligning of herself and Höss was giving her a headache. Why couldn't he leave her alone? This trip would have been stressful enough with only her father to contend with. "What are you going to do?" she said to Höss. "Follow me around Poland?"

"I do not have to follow you," Höss said. "I am part of you."

"No you are not," she said, and twisted her heel on the carpet. Höss must have held his screams in because there was no sound.

"We are all part of each other," he said eventually, a bit breathlessly.

"Don't give me that crap," Ruth said. "You are not part of me or part of anyone who has anything to do with me. You're not part of any Jew. Alive or dead. Which parts of you went up in smoke? It wasn't your soul. That had already disintegrated. It wasn't your heart, your heart wasn't there." She stopped for a moment. Her throat was sore. She felt as though she was shouting. She couldn't have been shouting. No one in the café was paying any attention to her. Höss was not part of her. He was not the criminal in her. He was not the Nazi in her.

"Calm down, calm down," Höss said.

"Well, don't give me that animistic shit," Ruth said. "You and I are not part of the same anything."

"You would subscribe to an existential notion then?" Höss said.

"I wouldn't think existentialism and individual responsibility and morality would be something that you would know much about," she said.

"Germany produced an existential philosopher who was considered to be one of the greatest thinkers of all time," Höss said. "Have you noticed by the way that I am overlooking all of your accusative barbs? I didn't bring you here to argue with you."

"You didn't bring me here?" Ruth said. "What do you mean by that?"

"Why do you think you have visited Poland twice already?" Höss said. "You have been trying to get to me. I have been beckoning you."

"I have not been trying to get to you," Ruth said. "No one in their right mind would want to get to you. I'm here with my father. I want to be here, on this piece of earth, where it all happened, with him. Side by side."

"And you think that he wants this?" said Höss.

"I think I know more about what he thinks than you do," she said. She called the waitress over and asked for the bill. She pushed the uneaten apple strudel out of her reach. Having Höss with her had at least saved her some calories.

"Heidegger's writings about angst and dehumanization even in 1927 were a clear indication of his link to the Nazi party that was to come," Höss said.

"Are you trying to impress me with the quality of your colleagues?" she said. "I know about Heidegger's emphasis on blood and intimacy. I've read his books. He was the rector of Freiburg University in 1933. He called

Hitler a genius and praised him for showing the German people the way out of 'rootless and impotent thinking.' "

"You know a lot about Heidegger," Höss said. "You know more than I do."

"The Allied powers prohibited Heidegger from teaching in any public capacity from the years 1945 to 1951," she said. "It didn't hurt him. In 1951, he was appointed an honorary professor at Freiburg University and went back to his teaching."

"These Hs are interesting, are they not?" Höss said.

Ruth could feel that she was red-faced. She found it hard to reconcile the adulation and respect and recognition accorded Heidegger and the lack of interest in his Nazi affiliations. It always disturbed her when public figures were conveniently forgiven their pasts. "You do agree that the Hs are interesting?" Höss said.

"You could take any batch of Nazis and find much that is of interest," said Ruth.

"That is true," Höss said. "But I maintain my belief that the Hs are of even greater interest."

"You can maintain whatever belief you like," Ruth said. "I don't care."

"Why are you upset?" Höss said. "You are more upset about Heidegger than you were about that deficient chicken farmer Himmler."

"I think you've got a thing about Himmler," Ruth said. "You deride him continually."

"Are you defending Himmler?" Höss asked.

"God no," she said. The question made her laugh.

"I thought we were eliminating God?" Höss said.

"Well, you're the master of elimination," Ruth said. "Go ahead."

"Let us get back to the Hs," Höss said. "What about Harlan. Veit Harlan. The filmmaker. He was the son of the novelist Walter Harlan."

"Novelists can produce very difficult children," Ruth said.

"Veit Harlan married the Swedish actress Christina Söderbaum," Höss said. "Harlan made all his best films with her. He displayed his complete commitment to Nazi ideology in the films. One of Harlan's movies was of particular use to us. We showed it every time there was a liquidation or a deportation of Jews planned."

"That was *Jud Süss*, the *Jew Süss*," Ruth said.

"Yes," said Höss. "Harlan made this film in 1940."

"The anti-Semitism in *Jud Süss* was just out of control," she said.

"Can you have anti-Semitism out of control?" Höss said.

"You are never going to pass that class," said Ruth.

"Of course, of course," Höss shrieked. "How stupid of me. It was a philosophical question. I was trying to say that all anti-Semitism is bad. All racist thinking is bad. There are no degrees of racism that are acceptable."

"You sound like a parrot," Ruth said. "Are they lines from your textbooks?"

"Of course," Höss said. "It is these lines that I have had to study, to memorize."

"Well, you'll never understand them, so you might as well memorize them," she said. "Did you know that Harlan was imprisoned after the war, but finally tried and found not guilty of crimes against humanity? Harlan continued to make films, all starring Söderbaum, until the year before he died, in 1964."

"Yes, I knew of course that he was found not guilty," Höss said. "Harlan was found not guilty and I was executed."

"You should have filmed your Jews, not shot and gassed them," Ruth said.

"Is that not an anti-Semitic sentiment?" Höss asked.

"No," she said. "You really are hopeless. Don't they have classes in bigotry and prejudice detection in Zweites Himmel's Lager?"

"They do, of course," Höss said. "But I have to pass the sensitivity-training class before I can enroll in bigotry and prejudice detection."

"You've got a long way to go," said Ruth.

"I used to be so good at things," Höss said.

"It can be difficult to change careers, particularly in middle age," Ruth said.

"That is true," said Höss. "I was promoted to the position of adjutant at Sachsenhausen on August 1, 1938. I was only thirty-eight."

"I'm wildly impressed," Ruth said. Höss seemed to think she was being sincere.

"My inner questions and concerns about my qualifications and readiness and suitability for concentration camp life receded into the background now that it was no longer necessary for me to come into such direct contact with the prisoners."

"How handy," Ruth said. Höss appeared not to hear.

"The first execution of the war was carried out in Sachsenhausen," Höss said. "I was extremely busy with the preparation and planning of the execution. I only realized what had happened when it was already over."

"You seem to have been a slow learner even then," Ruth said. Höss ignored her.

"All of the officers who attended the shooting were, of course, deeply affected," he said.

"Of course," she said.

"But in the days to come we were going to have many more of this kind of experience," said Höss.

"It was a tough job for you?" Ruth said.

"Yes, absolutely, a very difficult job," Höss said. "We had many Jehovah's Witnesses in Sachsenhausen. Many of them had refused to do military duty. The Führer ordered their death."

"More executions to have to struggle through," Ruth said.

"I learned many things from these executions, which took place in Sachsenhausen early in the war," Höss said. "People went to their death in many diverse ways."

"How surprising," said Ruth. She felt agitated that Höss appeared oblivious to her sarcasm. Why was she attempting to irritate a dead Nazi with slivers of sarcasm? she wondered. She decided it was a useless pursuit.

"The Jehovah's Witnesses went to their death with a strange sense of peace and composure," Höss said. "They had a state of grace, and sanctification, their eyes shone. It was almost a euphoria. They were very sure that they were about to enter the Kingdom of Jehovah. Among the other prisoners, the political prisoners, the conscientious objectors, and the political demonstrators against the regime went to their death calmly and quietly with an acceptance of the inevitability of what was to come."

"Do I have to hear this?" Ruth said. It was getting late. She wanted to go back to the hotel, to bed.

"This is a most interesting point, my point about how people go to their death," Höss said.

"I have to get some sleep soon," she said.

"The professional criminals were the worst," said Höss. "On the out-side these criminals were full of bravado. They were unabashed and inso-lent and impudent and impertinent. On the outside, they swaggered to their death but on the inside they were trembling. You could see it. Some of these asocial types could not hide their fear. They would scream and cry or whimper and beg for spiritual support. They were really terrified of what might be waiting for them on the other side. It was far too late for any of these types to be looking for spiritual support," Höss said, and roared with laughter.

"On May 1, 1940, I began my new job as commandant of Auschwitz," Höss said. "My job in Auschwitz, mind you, was not an easy one. It is much easier to construct a brand-new concentration camp than it is to put one together from an existing series of buildings that has been neglected for years. Also, time was essential. I was told I had to do this in the shortest possible period of time."

"Of course," Ruth said. "Millions of Jews were waiting for the comple-tion of the job."

"It was very stressful," said Höss. "I wanted to build a good camp. In direct opposition to the practices at other concentration camps. I wanted to house and feed the prisoners well. I knew that this would be the most effective way of getting good work out of them. But I soon realized that all of my intentions would be doomed. I could not build the camp that I had envisaged with the stupid and ineffectual officers that were posted to me. All of my requests to obtain good and competent officers and noncommis-sioned officers to work in Auschwitz came to nothing. The entire core, the backbone of what had to be built was faulty, unsound, defective from the start."

Ruth couldn't speak. "What an understatement," she said, eventually.

"It was not just us," Höss said. "Why does everybody blame the Nazis? It was not just the Nazis. It was all Germans. It is unfair to put the blame on the Nazis. Really, I mean this."

"I'm sure you do," said Ruth.

"People have said that we went to great lengths to hide and conceal what we were doing," Höss said. "They say we did this because we Nazis knew that the bulk of the German people would not agree with what we were doing.

"It is most absurd to think that only thousands of individuals were responsible," Höss said, "for murdering millions of people. And that those thousands were clever enough and had the necessary resources to conceal their activities? Simply, simply absurd. The Nazi party allocated very little resources for concealment. Why should they? We knew the German people agreed with us. This sole apportioning of blame on to the Nazis is the most upsetting and unsettling part of the whole thing."

"If that is what upsets you most, you're never going to get to heaven," Ruth said.

"I am discussing something of extreme seriousness," Höss said, and for a moment his voice echoed the sharp ring and bark of his former position. "The Germans wanted the Jews dead," Höss said. "It was a will and a desire of the German people to be rid of the Jews. Germans had been told that Jews were a threat to their blood for years. A germ, an infection. Jews were a disease that would destroy German culture. Germans were told this by politicians, by the popular media. They were told this in speeches and in literature. Mark my words, Germans were ready to get rid of Jews. We, the Nazis, needed their cooperation. We needed their enthusiasm and their participation. We needed not just the cooperation but the participation of administrators, engineers, lawyers, doctors, architects, manufacturers, and administrators. Are you listening to me? Can you hear what I am saying?" Höss was shouting now.

"I am listening," she said.

"No ordinary accountants or clerks or contractors or engineers or signalmen or chemists or physicians who contributed to the killings were ever brought to trial," Höss said. "Only those directly connected to the Nazi party or those directly involved in the administration of the death camps and labor camps were ever brought to trial. All the other Germans developed overnight amnesia." Höss was very wound up. Ruth could hear he was having trouble breathing.

"I think you should calm down," Ruth said. Höss's anger and tension were making her nervous.

"I am calm, I am calm," he said. "You should see all of the Germans in Zweites Himmel's Lager. The place is crawling with Germans. It is infested with them. There are more Germans in Zweites Himmel's Lager than any other nationality of people." He started to laugh. "And even surrounded by all of these Germans, I am still unpopular." He laughed out loud again. "Where are you going?" Höss said.

"I've got to go outside," Ruth said. "I feel sick."

Outside the café, on Piotrkowska Street, Ruth took deep breaths. The air felt thick. It wasn't the congestion of the coal smelters and the car exhausts she could feel. The air was clogged and jammed with more than the usual pollutants. The air was congealed. Curdled with ghosts.

From the café came the strains of the Polish pianist tackling "On the Street Where You Live." The pianist had returned for the third time that evening to a tune from *My Fair Lady*. Höss and *My Fair Lady*. It was enough to make anyone doubt his sanity.

"Your gardener, Stanislau Dubiel, reported Mrs. Höss as saying several times in his presence, 'I want to live in Auschwitz until I die.' "

"We had a very comfortable life there," Höss said. "The accommodation and the servants came with the job. Why shouldn't my wife be happy with this?"

"All the prisoners employed in your household were given special underwear," Ruth said. "Underwear obtained from the barracks for storing possessions stolen from the Jews. The barracks were named after Canada, a country seen as a land of wealth and opportunity. Other prisoners didn't have underwear from Canada."

"As commandant, I had standards to maintain," Höss said. "Our staff had to have clean clothes. We couldn't risk infection. After all, we were living in a location where infection, especially typhus, was epidemic."

"Of course," Ruth said. "Jews were dropping dead with typhus every day."

"Household staff must look respectable," Höss said. "They must look decent and clean."

"Decency and cleanliness are not what come to mind in reference to you or your wife," Ruth said.

"Can you leave Mrs. Höss out of this?" Höss said.

"When she received the underwear to distribute among the prisoners who worked for her, she kept it for herself. She gave the staff old, worn underwear discarded by your family. Your children were wearing the underwear of gassed people?"

"Stanislau Dubiel was a brazen, Polish braggart. A compulsive liar," Höss said.

"Dubiel said that Mrs. Höss never gave him any of the money coupons that were needed by all the SS in order to buy food in Auschwitz. She just gave him lists of what she wanted. Meat, fruit, bread, sausages, cigarettes.

"And you, Mr. Höss, who were busy setting such a fine example for your fellow officers, failed to notice the abundance of foodstuffs on your dinner table every night, and at the parties Mrs. Höss gave regularly," Ruth said.

"We had no more than our strict rationing of bread and skimmed milk," Höss said. "If other food was available we paid for it with the coupons that were required."

"It's a shame that others are saying otherwise, isn't it?" Ruth said.

"I myself was far too busy with other things," Höss said. "Before Auschwitz I was always prepared to see only the best in my fellow human beings, particularly my comrades. However in Auschwitz my so-called colleagues were dishonest and deceitful and disloyal to me. Every day I was forced to suffer new disappointments. Slowly, I, myself, began to become mistrustful and extremely suspicious. I retreated into myself. I became distant, remote, and noticeably harder. It was hard on my wife. She was always trying to draw me out of myself. To force me to engage with others. For my own good, you understand?"

"I understand her concern," Ruth said. "She had good reason to be concerned."

"She was a very good wife," Höss said. "She would invite people to our home. Old friends from outside the camp, comrades who also worked in Auschwitz. Sometimes, with the help of a little alcohol, I would pull myself together, for her sake, and socialize."

"You've left out an obvious H," Ruth said.

"No," Höss said, "I have not. Hitler has already received much attention. Everybody knows Adolf Hitler. The whole world was interested in Herr Hitler," Höss sounded peeved.

"Does that bother you?" Ruth said.

"No, not at all," said Höss. "But it is disproportionate that Hitler is so famous. He is a celebrity. He did not do so much by himself. We all worked hard and had an equal influence on the course of things. Why should Hitler be so well known? He did, I admit, have a talent for public speaking. But that in itself I consider to be a minor talent. And he had such a grating voice."

"You think his histrionic hoarse shouting was public speaking?" Ruth said.

"It was in public and he was speaking," Höss said. Höss took a deep breath. Ruth could hear him inhale.

"Enough of Hitler," he said.

"Better late than never," she said. But Höss didn't reply. Maybe he hadn't understood.

∾ *Chapter Seven* ∾

*R*uth woke up singing. In a semiconscious state, half-awake, she had realized that she was singing lines from *My Fair Lady* to herself. She had never seen the musical. She had never known the lyrics to any of the show's songs. Yet here she was, in her hotel room in Łódź, endlessly repeating lyrics from the song "Wouldn't It Be Loverly." It wasn't a languorous rendition of the song that she was singing. It was a speeded-up version much faster than the composers of the musical, Lerner and Loewe, had intended.

Ruth was copying the tempo of last night's performance. The brisk variation of the show tune played by the young pianist in the café. One staccato note after another. Each note jolly and complete. There was no sign of the wistfulness or longing implied in the lyrics. She had to get the song out of her head. It was giving her a headache. She moved to get out of bed. Her brain hurt. She knew that this couldn't be true. She knew that brain tissue contained no sensory nerves. She got out of bed slowly. The words kept going round and round in her head.

She poured herself some bottled water, and assembled the fifteen different vitamin tablets she took every day. She swallowed the pills, then drank some extra water. Dehydration could cause headaches. Maybe she was dehydrated? She drank some more water.

It was an appropriate song for her to be singing, she thought. Any room would be preferable to this room at the less than Grand Victoria. Any room, anywhere. Nothing in the room worked. Ruth had wanted to have a bath last night. The trickle of water that came out of the bath taps would have had to have continued for several days before being enough to fill a tub. She had complained about it to the male receptionist. "Is impossible," was all he could say. "Is impossible."

What did he mean? Was it impossible to fix? Impossible to believe? What was he saying? Was he being sympathetic? Agreeing that a room without a functioning bath was impossibly difficult? Ruth had no idea. "Is impossible," he kept saying, as she hung up.

Ruth turned on the tap in the basin. Water sprayed over the carpet, and over her. This happened with both the hot water tap and the cold water tap. Ruth tried to tighten the faucets. They wouldn't budge. The faucets had clearly been this way for years. Maybe most guests at the Grand Victoria didn't wash? Everything in the room was broken. The dial on the rotary phone moved around in fits and starts. The toilet was so energetic it flushed some of its contents right out, into the room. The bed sagged at both ends, and inexplicably rose in the middle. The pillows were limp and marked, Ruth felt, with the dents of other people's heads. She hated this hotel.

"I never seen you look so tired," Edek said to her when she came down for breakfast. He was talking to the doorman. The gold-necklaced, thick-necked doorman. The doorman seemed engrossed in the conversation with Edek. "I'll meet you in the breakfast room," she said to Edek. "No, no, I am coming with you," Edek said. Edek patted the doorman on the back while the two men exchanged extensive farewells.

"Don't you find him revolting?" Ruth said to Edek.

"What is wrong with you?" Edek said. "Why should you call him revolting?"

"I'm tired," she said. "I didn't sleep well."

"I did not sleep so good, too," said Edek. "But I am all right. I did read a book from four o'clock. I got a bit of a pain in my leg. But, at my age you got to take it."

"You didn't sleep from four A.M.?" Ruth said.

"No," Edek said. "But I am not sleepy."

"Do you think you were nervous about going out into Łódź today?" she said.

"Maybe a bit," he said. "I got such butterflies."

"You mean butterflies in the stomach? Nerves?" she said.

"Yes, a few," he said. "Inside my stomach I got a few such butterflies."

"We'll be okay, Dad," she said. "We're together. We've got each other."

"I have got a daughter who does not look so good," Edek said.

"I found the bed impossible," Ruth said. "It was so lumpy. It went up in the middle and down at both ends."

"Mine was the same," said Edek. "A bed like this is good for sexual things." He put his hand behind him, in the small of his back, to demonstrate how the bed could push the pelvis forward. Ruth found the demonstration disturbing.

"Dad," she said, sternly.

"It is just a normal thing what I am saying," he said.

"Well, say it to someone else," she said. "I'm sure your doorman friend would like to know." She walked off ahead of him. Why were men so disgusting? Couldn't her father see the crudity in his comment?

Her mother used to flinch at her father's crudity. Rooshka had expended a lot of energy in an effort to eliminate all obscenity and crudity from her existence. She had been exposed to too much crudity. It had made her hypersensitive. She overreacted to every lewd or coarse joke. She was unable to tolerate ordinary lewdness, ordinary coarseness.

An attractive blonde walked past Edek and Ruth. She was wearing a tailored black suit and carrying a briefcase. Ruth looked at her. She must be meeting somebody at the hotel for breakfast, Ruth thought. The woman looked so out of place in Łódź. Her clothes were too sophisticated. Her demeanor was too clean. Her blond hair was shiny and blunt cut. Her complexion was clear. Her fair skin and large blue eyes gave her an air of innocence and health. Ruth found her presence reassuring. An antidote to the feeling that she was surrounded by obscenity.

The breakfast room was full of men. Polish men. They were already smoking and drinking. They talked while they ate. Gold teeth and gold rings flashing. "They're peasants," she said to Edek. He glared at her. He was right. She shouldn't call Poles peasants. It was a harsh and unfair assessment. She wished she had a better attitude to Polish people.

"I am not hungry," Edek said.

"Well, just have something light," said Ruth. "You need to eat, we've got a lot of walking ahead of us." Edek brought two slices of ham, in the middle of a large plate, to the table. "This is not too much?" he said to Ruth. Ruth felt agitated. How could two slices of ham be too much? Why did Jews have to be so neurotic about food? Fixated by every detail of everything that went into their mouths? "No, it's not too much," she said to her father.

She looked at the bowl of fruit compote she had in front of her. It looked beautiful. Whole plums had been stewed with apricots and prunes and pears. She was about to take a mouthful when she felt somebody staring at her. It was the blond woman. She was staring at Ruth. Staring fixedly. What was she staring at?

Ruth checked herself. She had been in a hurry to get out of her room this morning. Maybe she had forgotten something. She checked her clothes, her panty hose, her shoes. Everything seemed to be in place. She felt her hair. Maybe it was sticking out more than she had intended. No, her curls seemed to be protruding and springing at the angles she had maneuvered them into.

The woman was still staring at her. Ruth looked the woman in the eye. The woman didn't appear to notice. She seemed almost in a trance. Ruth felt unnerved. She looked at Edek. He hadn't noticed anything. She turned her back to the woman.

A group of workers were hammering and banging in one corner of the breakfast room. The Grand Victoria was undergoing renovations. "They're badly needed," Ruth had said to the receptionist this morning. "Why do they have to do the renovations right now?" Ruth said to Edek. "You'd think they could work on a less busy part of the hotel now, and come back here later, when there's no one here?"

"First you complain that everything is broken," Edek said. "And now you complain when they fix it up."

The men were hammering slowly. One nail at a time. There seemed to be several workers for each nail. These renovations were going to be a lengthy process, Ruth thought. She looked at her father. He looked happy. He had been back to the buffet several times. He had eaten the two slices of ham, four fried eggs, some smoked mackerel, some compote, and some toast. Ruth hadn't touched her food.

"Shall we walk to Kamedulska Street this morning?" she said to Edek.

"If you want," he said.

Kamedulska Street was where Edek had grown up. At number 23. His father had owned the whole apartment block and the one next door. Edek and his parents had lived on the second floor of number 23. Edek's brothers and sister also lived in the building.

After walking along Piotrkowska Street for several minutes Edek announced that he knew exactly where they were and what route they should take to Kamedulska Street. "It is not so far," he said. "Maybe fifteen, twenty minutes." He rushed ahead of Ruth. "The next street is for sure Pusta Street," he shouted back over his shoulder to her. At the corner he peered at the street sign and ran back to Ruth. "Pusta must be the next street," he said, and ran off.

Ruth didn't know why he had to run. Why was every event, finding a street, buying an ice cream, tying a shoelace, an emergency? Edek came running back to her. He was a bit breathless. "This one is also not Pusta," he said. "It must be the next one."

"Calm down, Dad," she said. "We're not in a hurry."

"I am calm," he said. "I am not the one who needs to calm down. You are the one who looks terrible." He ran off again.

Ruth sped up. She couldn't have her eighty-one-year-old father running backward and forward in the streets of Łódź. He would be worn out way before they got to Kamedulska Street. She met him at the next corner. He looked crestfallen. "I thought for sure if the last street was not Pusta then this one would be Główna. He was staring at the signpost. It said Piłsudskiego.

"Maybe Pusta and Główna are a little farther on," Ruth said.

"I know Łódź," Edek said. "I know every street. I do not know what is happening."

"Let's try a few more blocks," Ruth said. "If we don't get anywhere, we can go back to the hotel for a taxi."

"Okay," said Edek. He started to run again.

Ruth walked behind him. She was too tired to run. "What's happening?" Edek said to her when she caught up to him three blocks farther along Piotrkowska Street. "This street is supposed to be Gubernatorska and it is not," he said. He looked very distressed. "What is happening?" he said again.

"It's been a long time since you were here, Dad," she said. "It's been fifty-eight years. Things have changed."

"Nothing has changed," Edek said. "I recognize everything." They were approaching another corner. Edek ran ahead to the street sign. "Orla," she heard him shout. "It is Orla Street. It is exactly what I remembered." He ran back to her. "If this one is Orla then the last one must be Gubernatorska. I have to go back to check." Ruth followed him.

She hadn't expected this. Edek was craning his neck to read a small sign on the side of a building. He swung himself around to face her and almost fell over. Her father had been wheeling and turning and spinning since they left the hotel. Lurching and whirling through the streets of Łódź. It should have been comic, but it wasn't funny.

"It says Abramowskiego," Edek said, steadying himself. "We never had a street called Abramowskiego." Ruth suddenly remembered something she had forgotten. She had a map in her bag. She had several maps in her bag. She had a newly published map of Łódź, she had a map of the former Jewish areas of Łódź, and a map of the Jewish Cemetery. How could she have forgotten about the maps? She always overprepared for everything. She got out the maps and studied them. Edek walked back to her. "It seems to me," she said to him after a few minutes, "that some of the street names have changed."

The maps of the former Jewish sections of Łódź seemed to have different street names from the same configuration of streets on the new map. "I think," Ruth said, "that Pusta is now Wigury and Główna is Piłsudskiego." She wasn't sure of this. Maps were not her forte. She considered it an accomplishment that she could now read a map. Maps used to give her a headache. For years all maps looked like mazes. Crisscrossed, clashing, colored lines.

"Geography is complicated for you," her first analyst had said. "You don't want to know about other places. For you, catastrophes happen in other places."

"But I travel," she had said.

"Only to places you know or know about, you are frightened of the unknown," the analyst had replied. The unknown that her analyst had been referring to was not a location. It was her parents' pasts. Ruth had tackled quite a bit of that unknown since then. She had asked her parents questions. She had read books, and now, here she was, in Łódź, able to read a map. What an accomplishment, she thought.

"Why did you not remember you had such a map?" Edek said to her.

"I'm sorry, Dad," she said. She handed him the maps. Edek leaned against a shop window and studied the maps.

"You are right," he said. "The names of the streets are not the names what I was used to. They have changed the names. I told you, I would for sure know where I am. And I know where I am. Fifty-eight years and I did forget nothing." He looked excited. He listed a long list of streets they would be passing on their way to Kamedulska and ran ahead of her. She could hear him listing the streets to himself as he ran.

The area began to look familiar to Ruth. She remembered some of the streets from her last trip. The Jewish areas were all quite close to the center of Łódź. The buildings, like most of the rest of Łódź, were run-down. They looked old and decayed. Crumbling walls, dark, cracked windows. Everything about these dwellings spoke of departure, past lives, lack of life.

Tiles and beams and pieces of plaster and chunks of concrete were missing from building after building. Windows were wired shut and doors patched up. The Poles had not taken care of the buildings. They had taken care not to care about the Jews they had replaced when they moved into these apartments. The Poles were happy, then. Happy with the apartments, the furniture, the china, the clothes, and all the other accoutrements of life that the Jews had left behind. There was not much life left in these fully occupied dwellings now.

Ruth caught up with Edek. He didn't look tired. He looked well. She felt worn out. Exhausted. Maybe she was suffering from Seasonal Affective Disorder. Seasonal Affective Disorder was a popular disorder in America at the moment. SAD, as it was called, was a deprivation of daylight, which resulted in lethargy and depression. The winter light here in Poland was particularly weak. She was sure it contained none of what she needed to stave off lethargy or depression.

"Did you call the Jewish Center?" she said to Edek. She had asked him to call the Jewish Center on Zachodnia Street. The keys for the Jewish Cemetery had to be picked up from the Jewish Center. Ruth was interested in seeing the center anyway.

"I did call," Edek said. "I did say we was interested in seeing the center.

The man I did speak to did say he was very busy. Then he did hang up the phone."

"Busy?" said Ruth. "There are seven Jews left in Łódź. How busy can he be? I'll call myself tomorrow."

Ruth knew that the Jewish Center in Łódź looked after only a handful of Jews. All old men. It was set up to maintain the religious and cultural traditions of the Jews of Łódź. Edek was a Jew from Łódź. Why would the director of the center say he was busy? The center had another purpose. To revive Jewish life in Poland. To reclaim Jewish culture. To give an identity to people who were surfacing, now, in Poland, who thought they might be Jewish. Jews who weren't sure about their pasts. People who had a grandparent who was Jewish. People who were adopted. People whose parents seemed more Jewish than the parents would admit. Edek was a real Jew. Not like some of the newly discovered Jews who were beginning to turn up in the few synagogues left in Poland. Jews who looked very Polish to Ruth.

Maybe the director of the center was tired of old Jews passing through Łódź? Maybe he was interested only in those who were staying. She hadn't expected to be embraced by the Jewish Center of Łódź, but she hadn't expected to be rejected. Too busy. She felt annoyed. Why hadn't he just said he wasn't interested? She was sure that his "too busy" was a lie. Why did he have to lie? She felt angry. She caught herself. Why was she so outraged about the man who ran the Jewish Center of Łódź? She was obviously overtired. She was glad that she hadn't heard from Max this morning. Having to deal with Mr. Newton or Mr. Long would have been more than she could handle.

Ruth thought about Max's married lover. Max was sure that he was not lying to her. "He's got no need to lie to me," she had said to Ruth. "I'm not his wife." Max hadn't seemed to see the lack of logic in her thinking. But then maybe logic played no part in affairs. "I see him three or four times a week," Max had said to Ruth. "He's so supportive of me. He spends weekends with his wife. And I don't mind that. She doesn't seem to mind if he's out on Monday, Tuesday, Wednesday, Thursday, or Friday. But he's got to be back with her on Saturday and Sunday."

"I probably help his marriage," Max had added when Ruth hadn't replied. "Good sex with me probably helps him tolerate routine sex with her." Ruth had remained silent. "Okay," Max had said. "Maybe sex isn't so routine with her. Shit, why am I thinking about her?"

"I guess you share something pretty intimate," Ruth had said.

"Pretty and intimate," said Max. "His you-know-what." They had both laughed.

Morality was such a complicated question. Ruth dealt with minuscule aspects of it in her work life every day. A client she hardly knew had asked Ruth if it would be dishonest of her to become pregnant without telling her partner what she was planning.

"How are you going to carry out that plan?" Ruth had said.

"I would inseminate myself after sex, with the contents of the condom," the client had said. "It's always my job to throw it out."

"Well, he wouldn't have had any further use for it," Ruth had said. "You'd be using up something that would have just been thrown away." They had laughed.

"Would it be dishonest of me?" the client had asked again.

"Dishonest?" Ruth had said. "I don't know. The world is full of men who manipulate women in the name of the law, the government, and God. I don't know if it would be dishonest."

Afterward, she had thought that she had been cowardly. Of course it was dishonest. There were degrees of dishonesty in everyone's life, of course. She herself felt a vague discomfort when clients cried at certain things she had written. She had caught one of her clients weeping profusely, in the office, after he had picked up a condolence letter. "I thought you didn't like your uncle?" Ruth had said to him. "I never saw this side of him," the client said. Ruth had seen no point in pointing out that she hadn't known his uncle. "Everything you've said in this letter is true," the client had said, and left the office, still weeping.

What was the truth and what wasn't was often impossible to detect. The truth had appeared obscure to Ruth, from the time she was a child. She used to lie a lot. She made things up. As a six-year-old she spun whole stories around her lies. Stories of poverty and hardship. The Rothwaxes were poor, but in Ruth's tales they had to endure extreme deprivation. She and her mother and father had to share one blanket, Ruth told her school friends, and they slept on old newspapers, on the floor. Her school friends were riveted by her stories. The school Ruth attended was in an inner-suburban area populated with migrants and refugees. Most of the children had no trouble imagining Ruth's poverty. The stories became more elaborate as Ruth got older. They became more complex, with a better sense of structure and better timing.

Ruth lied as an adult, too. Stupid, harmless lies. As though no reality was worthy of repetition. Everything had to be expanded and enhanced. She couldn't help it. She was often shocked herself at her lies. Surprised and bewildered at the words which she knew not to be true that came out of her mouth. The shock didn't last long.

Ruth's elaborations and embroideries were intricate and authentic, to her. No sooner had she uttered them than she began to believe that what she was saying was the truth. A good liar had to be efficient and organized, Ruth discovered. Lies were too difficult to keep track of otherwise. And a good memory was essential. Good liars had to be able to retain the facts of their own existence and the facts of their lies. It wasn't easy.

Ruth rarely let herself spin off into meticulously constructed lies or fantasies anymore. She had paid a lot of money to several analysts in order to give up this trait. She was happy she was no longer a big liar. The lies had entangled and snared and confused Ruth as well as their recipients.

As a child Ruth's lies had been intricate enough. She had made up relatives. Aunts, uncles, cousins. She made up cousins she loved and cousins she disliked. She had made up favorite aunties, and favorite grandparents. She had invented eight grandparents. She knew nothing about grandparents. She had eliminated four of the grandparents when she was old enough to know that people rarely possessed more than four. She had explained the extraneous grandparents as adoptions. Then she had whisked them, briskly, out of the picture. She had known, even then, that credibility was a crucial component of storytelling.

Attention to detail was also critical. Ruth knew the physical characteristics and personality quirks of all of the fabricated aunts and uncles and cousins. She had populated her world with so many made-up people. She had best friends and second-best friends and casual boyfriends and serious boyfriends she had invented. She had never been lonely.

Sometimes when she thought of the past, she couldn't remember which friends she had really had and which friends she had imagined. At least now she had a better use for her imagination. She made up letters all day. Six days a week. From 8:30 A.M. to 7 P.M. By the end of each day, she had had her fill of invention and fabrication.

The subject of relatives, her relatives, still occupied her from time to time. When she visited museums or Holocaust memorials, she saw herself in many of the photographs on display. Ruth knew, of course, that it wasn't her in the photographs, but it seemed reasonable to think that she might be looking at relatives. She looked at photographs of Jews in the streets of the ghettos. Photographs of Jews being liberated from concentration camps. Photographs of Jewish families before the war. She saw herself in all of them.

She had asked an official in the Wiesenthal Center, in Los Angeles, if he had known the identity of a young woman in a photograph taken in the Łódź ghetto. Anyone who knew Ruth could have identified her right there in the center of that photograph. The official didn't know who the young woman was. Ruth had given the official a list of people she was related to. The Buchbinders, the Spindlers, the Knobels, and the Brajtsztajns were all related to the Rothwaxes. They were all from Łódź. And they were all dead. Ruth had asked the man if it was possible to see if any of those names appeared in any of the photographs they had on display in the center. He had explained that it was an impossible task.

Edek had stopped running. He was walking beside Ruth. They walked past a young woman and her child. The mother looked about thirty. She was hitting the child. Smacking the small boy hard. Ruth flinched at the sound of the slaps. What had the child done? she wondered. Something that bothered his mother. The mother was red-faced and grim. She kept on hitting him. He screamed and screamed. Why did people like this have children? Was beating a child one of the pleasures of parenthood? Enough parents beat their children.

"We did never smack you," Edek said. "Never."

"Jews on the whole don't use physical violence," Ruth said. She immediately worried that Edek may have interpreted her reply as offensive. As though she had insinuated that Jews were prone to emotional violence. She looked at Edek. He didn't look disturbed.

The boy continued to scream. The mother noticed Edek and Ruth. She motioned for the boy to be quiet. He kept crying.

"You did never want a child," Edek said to Ruth. "Even when you was a teenager."

"I still don't," Ruth said. "All of my nightmares are about children. My children. I lose them. I leave them on trains and buses and other public places. I forget to feed them. I forget I have them. In my dreams, I have a baby who is born damaged and he disappears, right after the birth." Edek stopped walking.

"What is wrong with the baby?" he said.

"What baby?" she said.

"The baby in your dream, of course," he said.

"I don't know," she said. "It's never clear. In the last dream someone took the baby away from me." Edek stared at her. "What's wrong?" she said to him. "Nothing," he said.

Something she had said had disturbed Edek. But what? Ruth had no idea what it was. She had no idea what much of her communications with her mother and father had meant. Things were said to her in short ambiguous sentences and semi-indecipherable phrases. Brief bursts of almost-comprehensible advice and guidance, warnings and orders. Nothing was explained at length. Everything was in quick, oblique English. Edek and Rooshka were always stumbling and floundering in English, a language that was foreign to both of them.

"Why didn't you speak Yiddish to me? Or Polish? Or German?" Ruth said to Edek. "Why did you and Mum only speak English to me, instead of one of the languages you were really comfortable in?"

"Mum was very comfortable in English and I am very comfortable in English," said Edek.

"You weren't when you had me," Ruth said. "You were almost forty, and you weren't in a position to go to English classes."

"That is true. I was working in factories and so was Mum," Edek said.

"So why didn't you speak to me in a language that was easy for you?" said Ruth.

"Mum wanted for you to learn English," Edek said.

"I couldn't have avoided learning English. We were living in Australia," Ruth said.

"It is not so important what language you speak to a child," Edek said.

"Of course it is," Ruth said. "How can you speak intimately to a child when your words are limited?"

"As a matter of fact," Edek said, "It was Mum's idea. I was not so keen on it myself. Mum said, 'We will speak English to this child.' "

"To this child?" said Ruth. "The other two didn't last long enough to catch on to language, did they?" Why had she phrased that so harshly? She hadn't meant to. "I guess Yiddish could have reminded Mum of the babies she lost, or the past, in general," she said quickly.

"Mum said she did not want the baby to learn a language of the past," Edek said. "She did mean Yiddish. And she did not want the baby to learn the language of the Polish people. She said this baby is not Polish. And she is not German. I did not want to speak to a baby in German, in any case. What Jew would speak to a baby in German?"

"But Mum insisted I learn German at school," Ruth said.

"That was different," Edek said. "She did not speak German with you. German was not spoken in our house."

"Yes it was," Ruth said. "I was always reciting lines from Goethe. I had to memorize them for my German classes. Remember I won a prize for reciting Goethe? Mum was thrilled."

"I remember," said Edek.

"Mum thought that if the Nazis arrived in Australia, I would at least be able to communicate with them," she said.

"That is not so funny," Edek said. "That is what Mum did feel."

"I didn't say it was funny," she said.

The mother and child were walking behind Edek and Ruth. The child was still crying, but it was a quiet cry now, a whimper. "I want to say something to that mother," Ruth said. "How do you say 'bully' in Polish?" "Are you crazy?" said Edek. He scurried ahead of Ruth. Ruth turned around and glared at the mother. The mother looked startled. She smiled at Ruth. Ruth shook her head in what she hoped was a gesture of admonition. Why did most mothers become mothers? Ruth thought. They looked so unhappy in the job.

Occasionally Ruth liked a burst of mothering. Mothering other people's adult children in very small bursts. Sometimes you could experience an exchange of intimacy and understanding with a stranger's child. This was a mothering of sorts. A transferring of wisdom, however menial the subject matter. Ruth had been buying a petticoat in Kmart on Cooper Union Square, when a young woman, a girl really, she looked about nineteen, had asked her advice about a black dress that she was trying on. "Does it look okay on me?" the girl had said. "It looks gorgeous," Ruth had said. And it did. Kmart contained some surprising merchandise. "Is it suitable for a formal dinner?" the girl had asked Ruth. "Or is it too formal?"

"It's just the right degree of formal to be formally formal or formally casual," Ruth had replied. She had helped the girl choose a pair of shoes, as well. They had both left the encounter, glowing. "Thanks so much for all your help," the girl had said. Ruth had almost leaned over to kiss the young girl good-bye. Instead, she blew her a kiss. "Have a wonderful evening," she said to her.

Ruth loved Kmart. It was open until 10 P.M. every night, and she often went there to unwind. Kmart kept her grounded. It showed her how real people lived. At Kmart you could buy mops and buckets and plastic fly swatters. Kmart had detergent in huge containers, and racks and racks of rubber gloves. You could buy car jacks and screwdrivers and brooms and brushes and irons and ironing boards.

Kmart stocked irons and ironing boards in the middle of a city where very few people, Ruth was sure, ever ironed their clothes. Ruth's neighbor, an advertising executive, bought a fresh pack of white sports socks every week. "It's not worth washing them," he said to Ruth. "They only cost five dollars a pack." Clothes were disposable or dry-cleanable. There were dry cleaners on every block in New York. Early in the morning and early in the evening, in the streets of New York City, men and women walked purposefully, holding dry-cleaned clothes aloft, in the air. Nobody ever said that they had to leave a meeting, or a meal, because they had to do their ironing.

Americans did seem obsessed with dry cleaning, to Ruth. Americans living abroad who feared the local Parisian or Italian or Turkish dry cleaners could airmail their clothes via Federal Express to Maurice Dry Cleaners in New York City. Maurice cleaned the clothes and Federal Expressed them right back to the customer. It cost $150 to clean and ship a suede jacket. Maurice had customers in other parts of America and other parts of the world.

But then, Americans were strange. You could buy Mint Balls in America. "No More Doggie Breath," it said on the packet. The manufacturer was not referring to human breath. These Mint Balls were breath fresheners for dogs. Two Mint Balls cost $3.99. On the front of the packet of Mint Balls was a drawing of a brown dog with a large green Mint Ball in his mouth. Ruth thought the idea must be to fool your dog into thinking this was a game of catch. The Mint Balls were not available in Kmart.

Ruth loved the cafeteria in Kmart, too. The cafeteria had the most wonderful view of the city. From its enormous arched windows you could see all the way along Lafayette Street and across to the East Village. The food in the cafeteria was not bad at all.

The world of Kmart was a world so removed from her own daily life of composing letters for other people. Composing congratulations-on-your-promotion letters for someone she didn't know, to send to someone else she didn't know. Composing letters for people who no longer knew what to say to each other. No wonder she needed to be soothed by the car jacks and the racks of rubber gloves in Kmart.

She had been thinking, recently, about opening a branch of Rothwax Correspondence in Los Angeles. She already had clients in California. She had quite a few clients in L.A. In L.A., they appeared even more in need of her services. Most of their brainpower seemed to be expended on their appearance. This applied equally to men and to women. "I can recommend a great plastic surgeon," one of her clients had said to her. Ruth had flown to L.A. to check out office space, and she was having lunch with the client. She liked this client. He was a thirty-three-year-old scriptwriter. When he had first phoned Rothwax Correspondence she had said to him she was sure he could write his own letters. "I can't," he had said. "I can write two-and-a-half-minute cop scenes. I do those really well. I can write cops in cars, cops on the street, cops taking calls, cops speeding, and cops in the office. I don't do cops at home or cops under suspicion." Ruth had written several personal letters for him.

"I can recommend a great plastic surgeon," he had said to her again, at the end of the lunch. Ruth thought she must have looked very tired.

"You look great," the scriptwriter had said, "but we can all use some help. I've just had lipo on my chin."

"You've had what?" Ruth said.

"Lipo on my chin," he said. "Liposuction."

"Really?" she said.

"Doesn't it look wonderful?" he said. Ruth looked at his chin. It looked exactly the same as the chin she remembered him having. She had looked again. She couldn't see any difference. But then she had only seen him, in person, twice. Most of their communication had been over the phone. "It looks great," she had said.

"I couldn't sleep for a few nights," he said, "but otherwise there was no pain. I'm going to go back to Dr. Rosen and get my cheeks done."

Ruth had been bewildered by this predisposition to reposition one's physical features. Why were people doing this to themselves? And more and more often. People you knew suddenly changed in appearance. Looked strange, overnight. One week they looked like themselves, two weeks later they looked like their own distant relative. People you had known as acquaintances or neighbors, without any warning, appeared weird. Slightly altered.

Plastic surgery was being performed in epidemic proportions across America. Scalpel knives were slicing their way through people's thighs, chins, abdomens, buttocks, upper arms, breasts, eyes, and noses. It frightened Ruth. The alteration and the mutilation terrified her. Not everyone felt this way. Celebrities and other wealthy Americans wined and dined their plastic surgeons. They took them, along with their stylists and their personal trainers, to the opera, to openings, and to first nights. Grown people groveled to their hairdresser and their exercise instructor. Grown people couldn't make a move without asking someone else what they should wear or where they should place a chair. People no longer combed their own hair or trusted themselves to make a decision about doing an extra push-up. It was a very strange culture, indeed, when a team of personal assistants was essential to your existence.

Edek had turned into Widzewska Street. Ruth followed him. He stopped outside a large five-story building.

"My father used to own this building," Edek said.

"I didn't know he owned a building on Widzewska Street," Ruth said.

"He did own many buildings," Edek said. Edek stepped back and looked at the building. "In this building was thirty apartments." An elderly man was scraping some rotten wood from the bottom of one of the window frames on the ground floor. Edek walked over to the man. "I am Edek Rothwax," he said to the man.

The man put down his tools. He shook Edek's hand. Edek patted the man on the back and said he didn't want to interrupt his work. The man looked pleased to be interrupted. "It's not a bad day for winter, is it?" he said to Edek. The two men chatted. Ruth understood snatches of the conversation. They talked about Poland and what hard times the country had been through. "Things are better now that the Communists have gone, aren't they?" Edek said to the man. "Better for some people," the man said, "but not better for everybody." He told Edek that there was much more crime in the country since the collapse of Communism.

"Be careful of your car," he said. "People steal cars every day. Not even a locked car is safe."

"I do not have a car," Edek said.

"Just as well," said the man.

The man moved on from car thieves to the subject of vandals, a subject both men seemed gripped by. Edek looked so comfortable with the man. He was nodding and agreeing. They had now progressed on to the subject of the current government but Ruth wasn't sure what was being said. She felt tense. Why was Edek speaking so enthusiastically to this old Pole? Finally, Edek shook the man's hand. They shook hands several times and exchanged good-byes. Edek hadn't mentioned to the man that his father was the former owner of this building.

"Why didn't you say anything about your father owning the building?" Ruth said to Edek.

"What for?" he said.

"He was old enough to have been living there at the time," Ruth said. "Old enough to have been one of your father's tenants."

"This man did not give the orders for all the Jews to leave their homes and move into the ghetto," Edek said. "Why should I tell him? What difference would it make?"

"I don't know what difference it would make," Ruth said.

"No difference," said Edek.

Ruth pushed some hair away from her eyes. Her hair felt dirty despite the fact that she had washed it last night. She had washed it in a shower that was barely functioning. It had taken her twenty minutes. Yet, it didn't feel clean. She hoped it didn't look dirty. She hated the look of dirty hair. Dirty hair suggested other dirty body parts. Maybe that was what the blond woman at breakfast was staring at. Her dirty hair. That was stupid, she thought. Her hair couldn't be that dirty, and who would stare at dirty hair?

Ruth's mother had screamed when she had first seen herself without any hair. She had caught sight of herself, in a reflection, when she was being marched to the latrines in Auschwitz. "I screamed when I saw myself," her mother had said to her. "I thought I saw my brother. How could I know that with my head shaved I would look like my brother?" Ruth's scalp felt itchy. She tried not to scratch it.

"Are we far from Kamedulska Street?" she said to her father.

"Not far," Edek replied. They walked side by side. Where was Kamedulska Street? Despite the fact that she had been there before, Ruth had no idea where it was. Every part of her parents' past was confusing to her. Even a simple matter like recognizing a street was full of confusion. Their past, the good parts and the bad parts, was delivered to Ruth in fits and starts. And always in fragments. It was never whole. It always had to be pieced together. And the missing parts had to be imagined.

Ruth had asked her parents many times for the names of their siblings. She had almost begged her parents for the names. Yet the names of Edek and Rooshka's brothers and sisters came out one or two at a time. Both Edek and Rooshka seemed unable to mention all of their siblings in the one sentence. As though even in words the family could not appear intact. Ruth felt she had so few names from the past. And no faces. No faces to the known names and the unknown names. The photographs which would have revealed the faces that belonged to her mother and father were destroyed. Destroyed in Auschwitz. Those that were left behind in Łódź were thrown out by the Poles who moved into the homes the Jews had hurriedly vacated.

Who were the brothers and sisters and aunts and uncles and cousins and nephews and nieces she had missed out on? What did they look like? She had felt their importance all of her life. She had felt their presence. It was a nameless, faceless, invisible presence. Parts of these brothers and sisters and uncles and aunts were in her. But which parts were they? There was no answer to that question.

Most children of survivors had very little idea of their parents' pasts. Their pasts before the war and during the war. They had to guess at what had happened. The simplest information was never simply offered.

Everything was painful. Everything was pungent. Charged. Children of survivors were surrounded by secrets. The holes in their parents' pasts punctured and perforated the children of survivors. It left them with fissures and rifts and fractures. It left them with large hollows and cavities of their own.

Ruth had so many gaps and vacancies. The disability with geography and direction that her first analyst had pointed out still hampered her. No matter how many times she studied the map of Europe, she couldn't remember which country was where. It had taken her a year to locate New York and Los Angeles on a map of America.

Edek's and Rooshka's pasts came out of them in bits and pieces. Sometimes they unmasked unasked-for snippets. Sometimes wisps flew inadvertently out of their mouths. Sometimes crucial facts had to be excavated and extricated, a task as awkward and difficult as any dental procedure. The information that was revealed was never orderly. Each of the factual fragments seemed independent and unrelated to anything else. They were compact and self-contained. They stood alone and never illuminated other missing links in their orbit.

No matter how hard Ruth tried to order them, the facts about her parents' pasts shifted and switched with an alarming disharmony. She knew that her mother had lived on Pomorska Street in Łódź, and attended a school around the corner. But one day when her mother was talking to a friend, a school had appeared in the house, on Pomorska Street. And a Jewish school, and a Polish school. How many schools did her mother go to? Or was Ruth confusing her mother's schools with her father's schools?

Ruth had tried to write all of the information down. Written down, it made more sense. When she looked at the sentences the information seemed more tangible. But as soon as she looked up from the page everything left her again. She had tried to memorize a list of her mother's and father's brothers and sisters. She had always had a good memory. She could remember whole tracts of what relatively unimportant people had said to her. She could remember phone numbers and addresses going back years. She remembered dates. Important dates and useless dates. She could memorize whole pages of books she had read and poems she loved. But for years she kept forgetting the names of her mother's and father's dead brothers and sisters. Just when she felt more sure of them, sure that Felek and Abramek and Jacob and Edek were her mother's brothers, new names appeared.

Who were they? Who were Israel and Luba? Were they her father's parents? How could she have forgotten the names of her father's parents? She had asked her father so many times. She couldn't ask him again. She would have to wait until she got home and could look it up in her notebooks. She thought about other names she had heard. Who were Maryla and Yatchka and Fela? And was there a Shmulek or a Shoolek, or were Shoolek and Shmulek variations on the same name?

Why was all of this so difficult for her to grasp? She had always done well academically. And at work, at Rothwax Correspondence, she put together people's lives with no effort. She never got lost in the details she took from strangers. Facts from clients went into her head in a well-ordered and concise manner. Her parents' pasts were given to her in unsorted and ill-fitting increments. No matter how hard Ruth tried, the information remained disjointed. Maybe a past that had been so butchered could never be pieced together again.

Maybe too much was missing. Missing mothers. Missing fathers. Missing brothers. Ruth realized, with a start, that the two babies her mother had lost, had been her brothers. She had never thought about them that way. She had always thought of herself as an only child. The missing boys were her mother's sons. It was quite a shock to think of them as her own brothers.

Ruth looked around for her father. He was so far ahead of her, she could hardly see him. She sped up.

When she was fifteen, she had asked her mother about the children she had lost. They had been sitting in Rooshka's kitchen. At the white kitchen table with gold legs. Rooshka had seemed to disappear when the question came out of Ruth. "He was born with the cord around his neck," she said, after about ten minutes. Which baby was that? Ruth had wondered. The baby born in the first year in the ghetto, or the baby born later? "It was your father's fault," Rooshka said. "I bent down to pick up your father's shoe. That's when it happened." Ruth didn't say anything. How could an umbilical cord slip and knot just like that? How could it have been her father's fault? The baby would have died anyway. Most babies didn't survive in the ghetto. Why did Rooshka have to blame Edek?

Ruth had waited another ten years to ask about the second baby. All Rooshka would say about him was "he died." Ruth wondered if this baby boy was the baby who had been thrown, alive, onto the excrement cart by a Gestapo officer. Her mother had told Ruth about that incident once. It was her sister's baby, her mother had said. The story had been so difficult to take in that all Ruth could say was, "Which sister?" Rooshka hadn't answered her.

Rooshka also told Ruth about a baby who was thrown out of the window of the hospital in the ghetto, when they were emptying the hospital. Was that her mother's other baby? And then there were stories of children. Children with holes in their cheeks. Did her mother's baby grow up into one of those children? Did he die with holes in his cheeks? Ruth knew she would never know. She couldn't ask Edek. Edek was as reluctant to talk about it as Rooshka. It was no use asking him. He seemed to have trouble remembering the names of his cousins and uncles and aunts. His information was as erratic as anything else she was told about that time. Edek was calling her. She ran up to him.

"We did have a factory in this building," Edek said. They were standing outside a red brick rectangular building.

"Really?" Ruth said.

"My father bought cotton and did weave the cotton in a factory outside Łódź," Edek said. "Then they did bring the material, the fabric, into this factory. This factory was a warehouse for the material." Ruth was thrilled to hear this. She had never heard this aspect of the business.

"You had machines and looms and workers?" she said.

"Of course," Edek said.

"So you bought the cotton?" she said.

"I just did tell you that we did buy the cotton," said Edek.

"Did you work here?" Ruth said.

"No," he said. Ruth looked through the windows of the factory. She couldn't see anything. The glass was too cracked and grubby.

"Should we see if it's possible to look through the factory while we're here?" Ruth said.

"What for?" said Edek.

"I don't know," she said.

"There is nothing there," he said.

Ruth felt a reluctance to leave the factory, but Edek had already moved on. She followed him. How amazing, she thought to herself. They made fabric out of cotton. She had never even seen raw cotton. She had seen photographs of the fluffy white balls attached to their dark stems and branches. The cotton looked as decorative as any flower. Where did the Rothwaxes buy the cotton? She decided not to ask now. She felt she had used up her quota of questions for the moment.

Edek was peering into the back of another building when she caught up with him. She looked through a doorway into a large square courtyard. The courtyard was empty.

"That building at the back?" Edek said. "This was a small office. My brother Shimek did work here."

"What did he do?" Ruth said.

"Shimek did work for my father, here," said Edek. "We did have such a place where all the trucks and wagons that did come into Łódź had to be weighed."

"What for?" said Ruth.

"It was like such a tax what you have to pay to come into a city," Edek said.

"Oh, like a weighing station," said Ruth.

"Yes," said Edek. "We did weigh the trucks and wagons and then we did put a stamp on the documents for the driver."

"Wow," said Ruth. "Did your father start this business up himself?"

"Of course he did," Edek said. "Who else would do it for him? He came from a poor family."

"I didn't know that," she said.

"Why should you know this?" Edek said.

"They were my great-grandparents," said Ruth. "It's interesting to know who did what and who made the money."

"In my family, my father did make the money," Edek said.

Ruth felt almost giddy. The information felt overwhelming. The volume and the content. She forced herself to calm down. They had only been out of the hotel for just over an hour. She didn't want to disturb Edek by being too emotional in the first hour. She followed him quietly. Edek stopped outside another building. He shook his head. He looked sad. The building he was standing in front of was clearly a cut above the other buildings. It had interesting proportions and semiornate architectural details. What connections did this dwelling have with her father or his father? Israel Rothwax, that was his name. Suddenly Ruth felt sure of that.

"We did live in this palace for two years," Edek said. So this was the palace she had heard her mother mention.

"This is the former Rapaports' Palace, right?" she said.

"How do you know?" said Edek.

"Mum told me," she said. "It's a beautiful building."

"On the ground floor was offices," Edek said. "You went through that door and did turn left and there was all the offices," he said, pointing to a doorway.

"Did your father use the offices for his business?" she said.

"No, he did rent these offices to other businesses," Edek said. "My father did use old offices for his business. He did not have such fancy, posh businesses that he needed such offices. You do not need to have offices in a palace to write invoices for cotton fabric or do the paperwork for a truck registration business."

"Of course not," said Ruth.

"Was your father an educated man?" Ruth said. "Did he go to high school?"

"No," said Edek. "He probably did leave school when he was eleven or twelve. To tell you the truth my father did not think education was such a big deal. But we did all go to school because my mother wanted to let everyone know that her children are educated." Ruth's head was reeling. This was more than she had ever hoped to have revealed to her. Her grandfather was clearly a very smart man. Probably smarter than most MBAs today.

"My father did own this palace with a partner," Edek said. "A Mr. Meyer. Mr. Meyer was a partner with my father in another business." Another business, Ruth thought. She didn't want to ask her father which business this other business was. She felt she had expressed far too much curiosity already. "My father said the palace was too big for one family," Edek said. "So Mr. Meyer and his family lived on the second floor and we did live on the first floor."

"Were you close to the Meyers?" Ruth said.

"No," said Edek. "Mr. Meyer was such a funny type, anyway." Ruth knew from her experience, that "such a funny type" covered a diverse range of traits and characteristics. She restrained herself from investigating the phrase, in this context, any further. She was so overexcited about what she was being told. And she didn't want anything to curtail the revelations.

"So you lived there for two years," she said.

"Yes," said Edek. "Then my father did find out that Mr. Meyer was cheating him in one of the businesses."

"Oh no," Ruth said.

"I told you he was such a type," said Edek. "My father wanted to finish the partnership. He did offer to buy Mr. Meyer's half of the palace, but Mr. Meyer would not sell it to him. And Mr. Meyer could not afford to buy my father's half from my father. So they did sell the palace and we moved back to Kamedulska Street."

"Were you sad to leave?" Ruth said.

"No," said Edek. "Why should I be sad about this?"

"Because it's a beautiful building," she said.

"We had enough rooms for us in the palace and we had enough rooms for us in Kamedulska Street," Edek said. "A room is a room wherever it is."

How could her father have such a direct, straightforward approach to habitats, she thought, while she fussed and planned about every inch of what she was surrounded by in her apartment? Her sheets had to be the right shade of white. The walls and the flooring had to match the furniture and anything else in the rooms. She chose the canned food she bought according to the color on the label. The can opener couldn't clash with the peeler or any other utensil. She bought blue soap, deodorant, and shampoo for the bathroom. She was so pretentious, she thought. She must try to change when she got back. Maybe she could begin with multicolored toilet paper and tea towels.

"Mr. Meyer did get less for his half of the palace than he would have got if he had agreed to allow my father to buy his half," Edek said. "I told you he was such a funny type."

"It really is a beautiful building," Ruth said.

"Look up there," Edek said. He was pointing to the top floor. Ruth couldn't see what he was pointing at.

"When we did buy the palace, it did not have such windows on the top floor," said Edek.

"What was there?" she said.

"Those windows what go toward the ground," Edek said. "Not straight windows."

"You mean attic windows?" said Ruth.

"Yes," said Edek. "The windows what are not straight." Ruth looked at the top floor again. She could see, now, that a new section had been added. The walls were slightly different in texture from the rest of the building.

"What happened to the attic windows?" she said.

"When they did buy the palace, Mr. Meyer did measure every room," Edek said. "He wanted to make sure each partner did get exactly half. And the top floor because of these windows was a bit smaller than the first floor. My father did say that Mr. Meyer could have the first floor. But Mr. Meyer did say it was important that each partner did have the same."

"So they ruined the original architecture in order to divide the palace in half?" Ruth said.

"They did not ruin anything," said Edek. "What was ruined? They did a very good job."

"They changed the design of the building," she said.

"So what?" Edek said. "Is a design of a building such a big deal? No."

Ruth didn't want to argue about an issue of aesthetics. "No," she said. They both stood and looked at the building.

"Fancy owning a palace," Ruth said, after a few minutes. "I would have been a rich girl if I'd grown up here. If it all hadn't been taken from us." She had never thought about this before. About the wealth that had been lost.

"You are a rich girl," Edek said.

"Okay," she said. "Anyway, I'm rich because I've got you," she said. She took his arm. "I wouldn't trade you in for all the tea in China."

"You do not drink such tea," Edek said. "You drink only the herbs rubbish." Ruth laughed. She looked at him. He looked fragile, and tired.

"Walk next to me, Dad," she said. "There's no need to rush." They walked away from the palace. She held on to Edek's arm.

Neither Edek nor Rooshka made much of the financial aspect of their loss. The loss of businesses and buildings. There was, she thought, too much other loss for them to think about. Her parents' lives would have been so different if they had been given just a fraction of the wealth that was taken from them. The theft had turned them into factory workers. Stolen her mother's dream of becoming a pediatrician, and given Edek a perpetual feeling of having failed his beloved Rooshka.

Would she herself have been different if she had grown up wealthy? Would being a rich girl have changed her? Would it have made her calmer? Would she have been calm and rich? Maybe she wouldn't have had so many metaphorical twitches? She would have grown up surrounded by family. As it was, she was left alone at home a lot as a child. She had always felt it was lucky she was able to imagine others around her. By the time Edek and Rooshka got home from their factory jobs, they were both worn out. There hadn't been a lot of time for games and bedtime stories. But Ruth hadn't minded. She had had such an assortment of fictitious friends and relatives around, she had been quite tired, herself.

Maybe if she had grown up rich, she wouldn't have had to tap her feet or blink? Who knows? Maybe she just would have been rich and neurotic. She knew few wealthy people who were happy. It seemed most human beings had to find something to be unhappy about. And the wealthy posited their unhappiness in their wealth. They blamed the laziness of their children on too much money. They blamed family feuds on the excess of money. They saw arrogance or rudeness in their offspring as the result of indulgence. The list of the ills caused by money was endless. The rich felt that everyone was taking advantage of them, from the maid to the door-man. They were always complaining about problems with staff. Yet they bought more houses and yachts and traveled and shopped. They seemed to overlook the fact that they chose to live like this. If you listened to the rich you would think that their lifestyle was forced on them and the number of servants required to service that life was simply an unfair and intolerable burden.

Rooshka and Edek had mentioned the material wealth that was stolen from them so rarely that Ruth was an adult before she had understood that Edek's family was wealthy. She had known that her father wasn't poor because he had said many times that as a young man he could buy as many ice creams as he wanted. She knew that her mother's family, the Spindlers, were poor. Rooshka was proud of that. Ruth thought that Rooshka might even have looked down on the Rothwaxes' wealth. Rooshka's family had intellect, she always said. And she let Ruth know that Edek's family didn't.

"I did hire a lawyer," Edek said to Ruth.

"A lawyer?" she said. "What for?"

"Many Jews have got lawyers to see if they can get something back from the Poles," Edek said. "So I did get one too. A very nice chap as a matter of fact." Ruth was startled.

"You didn't tell me you were even thinking about it," she said.

"I did not think about it for so long, to tell you the truth," he said. "One day, I did think to myself, why not?"

"Well, it's a big thing," Ruth said.

"I got plenty of time," said Edek.

"It could open up too many old wounds," Ruth said.

"They did never close," Edek said.

"Who did you get to represent you?" said Ruth.

"A very nice chap, in Collins Street," said Edek. "My chap has a partner in America what is working on the same things with American Jews. I think that is a good thing. American lawyers are the best lawyers."

Ruth felt shocked. She had never even considered the possibility of trying to regain some of what was stolen.

"Why do you want to immerse yourself in all of that?" she said. "I don't need the money."

"I am not doing it for you," Edek said. "To tell you the truth I do not know why I am doing it."

"Oh, well, I don't know why I do half of the things I do," Ruth said.

"The lawyer did tell me," said Edek, "that the Union Bank of Switzerland, the Swiss Bank Corporation, and Credit Suisse made an offer of six hundred or seven hundred million to the Jews. This is not so much as what it looks."

"We had money in Swiss bank accounts?" Ruth said.

"Of course," Edek said. "In 1934 the Swiss passed such a law which did guarantee anonymity to all people who did put their money in Swiss banks. My father was frightened of what the Nazis would do to our money, so he sent Shimek to Switzerland with money many times."

"I had no idea," said Ruth.

"Why should you know?" said Edek. "The seven hundred million that the banks did offer is nearly only the interest of the money they did have from Jews. They are not going to give back the money, just the interest, it looks like. And they want to give the seven hundred million over quite a few years."

"So the seven hundred million that they are offering barely covers the interest they made?" said Ruth.

"That is right," said Edek. "After all, they had this money for over fifty years. When the Jews who was still alive made inquiries about the money after the war, the Swiss bank did say because of this anonymity that they did guarantee, they could not reveal any details of any banking accounts."

"What a brilliant use of the law," Ruth said. "And of course none of the poor, damaged, and bedraggled Jews who'd managed to live through Bergen-Belsen or Dachau or Sachsenhausen or Auschwitz had any of their documents on them."

"The lawyer did say," Edek said, "that the Swiss banks say they can find only ten percent of the records for these deposits by Jews."

"Some people's loss is so handy," said Ruth. She felt furious.

"The Swiss banks did do very good business," Edek said. "They gave the Germans Swiss francs to buy war materials from other countries. From Sweden, Spain, Portugal, Argentina, and Turkey. They did give Germany the Swiss francs and the Germans gave them valuable possessions from dead Jews. The Germans gave them gold from the bodies of dead Jews. The Swiss did not care where the gold came from."

"Doesn't it make you feel sick?" Ruth said.

"No," said Edek. "It is just facts."

"Well, it makes me feel sick," she said.

"The Swiss did lend money to the Nazis to build the factories near the concentration camp. Like the Buna factory in Auschwitz where I did work."

"You worked in that rubber factory?" said Ruth.

"It was not a real rubber," Edek said.

"It was synthetic rubber," said Ruth. "I didn't know you worked there."

"Many prisoners from Birkenau did work there," Edek said. "The Swiss did say they did not know that they were financing slave labor."

"Of course, they knew nothing," Ruth said. "Like everyone else."

Buna, which was the size of a small city, was often called Auschwitz III.

The gray concrete town with its carbide tower was an arrangement between I. G. Farben and the Nazis. I. G. Farben would build the plant. The Nazis would supply I. G. Farben with as many prisoners as they needed for their workforce. Both parties knew that the supply of workers from Auschwitz would never dry up. Buna would never have to suffer a shortage of labor.

The plan was to produce synthetic rubber. The arrangement between I. G. Farben and the Nazis was perfect. The Nazis had a glut of slave labor, and I. G. Farben had to pay very little for these half-dead men. When the workers dropped dead, in the plant, it was no problem. Replacements were rushed in. In Buna, the machines were more alive than the men. The men came from everywhere. Over twenty languages were spoken across those noisy machines. Buna was not a spectacular success. Over four years it failed to produce one pound of synthetic rubber.

Ruth felt her face. She was flushed and hot, despite the cold.

"I don't think you should bother going through all of this with a lawyer," said Ruth. "We don't want to grovel and try to prove what we owned, to anyone. We don't need their money."

"It is not their money," Edek said. "It is our money."

"I don't want it," she said.

They were close to Kamedulska Street, now. Ruth recognized a small grocery store she had bought some water in when she had first come here.

"The lawyer did tell me," Edek said, "that all these dealings with the Swiss did allow the war to be two years longer. If the Swiss did not do this business with the Nazis, the war would have finished by 1943. It is the Americans who did make this calculation."

"Your mother and father would still have been alive, wouldn't they?" Ruth said.

"And your mum's mother and father, and her brothers and sisters," said Edek. "And your mum would not have gone to Auschwitz."

"I know," said Ruth. "You were in the last transport out of the Łódź ghetto, in 1944." Edek was quiet. Ruth felt like crying. "Nobody cared about the Jews," she said. "Turkey sold chromite ore to the Germans. The Germans needed the ore to continue the war. Turkey said it was not a neutral country, but it was 'nonbelligerent.' "

"I did not know this," Edek said.

"Spain sold wolfram ore to the Germans," Ruth said. "Wolfram ore was used to make tungsten, a particularly hard metal that was crucial to the Germans' war effort."

"*Oy, oy, oy,*" said Edek. "I did not know this."

"Nobody in that part of the world was innocent," Ruth said. "The Swedes let German troops cross Sweden to join in the invasion of the Soviet Union. The Swedes let two hundred and fifty thousand German troops use the Swedish railway system."

"It is hard to believe," said Edek.

"The Swedish navy provided an escort service for German military supply ships," Ruth said. "These countries were all busy making a profit from the murder of Jews. After the war, the Allies, England, America, and France, asked Spain, Sweden, Portugal, and Turkey to return the gold, looted from Jews, that Germany had paid them with. They didn't want to. They hung on to the gold. And the Allies didn't even ask them to give back gold that had been transferred through Switzerland by the Germans. Nobody wanted to give up anything." She paused. "You can see why I don't want their money," she said, "can't you?"

"Maybe," Edek said.

"No one was punished except the Jews," Ruth said. "Alfred Krupp, the main manufacturer of German artillery, armor plate, submarines, and warships for Hitler, was never punished. The directors of I. G. Farben, who ran the factories at Auschwitz, were all acquitted of war crimes like using slave labor. Apparently they were all acquitted for lack of evidence."

"I could have given them this evidence," said Edek.

"Of course," said Ruth. "But nobody asked you."

They walked in silence. Ruth hoped that she hadn't depressed Edek. It was depressing to think about how many people were pleased to benefit from the murder of Jews. And here, in this Catholic country, with barely a Jew left, anti-Semitism was still evident. Maybe the Poles didn't know that, earlier this year, their Pope, the Polish Pope John Paul II, had made a historic move. The Pope had apologized for the Catholic Church's silence during the Holocaust. In Vienna, in June, he had given a speech in which he said, "Unspeakable suffering was inflicted on the Jewish people, in Europe. Reconciliation with the Jews," he added, "is one of the most fundamental duties of Christians in Europe." Maybe the Poles had missed out on that speech?

Edek and Ruth were on Kamedulska Street. They stopped outside number 23. Ruth felt suddenly frightened. She shouldn't have forced her father to come to Poland.

"Did I force you to come to Poland?" she said to Edek. He didn't seem to hear her. He was staring at the building. He looked dazed.

"This is it," he said.

"I know," she said. She wanted to say something else, but she couldn't think of anything to say.

"This is it," Edek said again.

Ruth looked at the concrete and brick apartment block. It looked shabbier than she remembered. She remembered walking into this building fifteen years ago. She remembered how difficult it had been for her to breathe. As though the inhabitants who no longer inhabited the apartment block took up all the breathing space. She could feel their presence. She had thought that she could feel their movements. The movement of children, cousins, mothers, grandmothers. On the first floor, Ruth had thought she could hear laughter and bustle. When she had knocked at one of the apartment doors, an old lady had emerged and told her that no one else was at home during the day, on that floor.

"Tadek and Moniek did have apartments in this building, too," Edek said. "They did live here with their families." So there were children, Ruth thought. There were mothers and cousins and grandmothers in this building.

"Your brothers Tadek and Moniek?" She said.

"Of course," Edek said, "which other Tadek and which other Moniek should I mean?" Edek looked cold. He had his hands in his pockets and his shoulders hunched.

"Shall we go inside, Dad?" she said. "It's cold out here."

"Maybe we do not need to go inside?" Edek said. "There is nothing more to see inside. You can see everything what there is to see from here. Come on, Ruthie, let us go back to the hotel."

"Can we just look around the courtyard, out the back, then?" she said.

"What is there to see?" he said. "Nothing." She tried not to look disappointed.

"I'll just have a look around the courtyard," she said. "I'll be back in a minute."

"I will come with you," said Edek. He followed her into the hallway. "Look how many apartments they did make on every floor," he said. He had stopped at an old intercom system just inside the hallway, and was counting the buzzers. "It looks like they did make three apartments from my parents' apartment," Edek said. "Look, see here, on the second floor. It used to be our apartment, and the apartment of the Zukers and the apartment of the Bermans. Now, it is one, two, three, four, five, six apartments. The Zukers' apartment and the Bermans' apartments was not big apartments. They must have made the extra ones from our apartment."

It was very quiet, in the building. There was no sign of life. Either the occupants were very old, or out at work. Edek had walked toward the staircase. He was touching the banister. What was he thinking about? Ruth wondered. What was he remembering? Ruth kept very quiet. She didn't want to disturb him.

Ruth looked at the crumbling plaster in the hallway. She had remembered this hallway as tiled. Tiled with smooth, cream tiles. Cream tiles with a patterned border. How could she have replaced the patchy plaster with Italian tiles? She couldn't believe she could have had such a distorted vision.

"Was this hallway ever tiled?" she said to her father.

"No," he said. She looked at the staircase she had held on to fifteen years ago. The staircase whose banister she had gripped to keep a grip on herself. She remembered it as marble. It was not marble. It was made of wood. A wooden staircase. It didn't curve and sweep in a broad semicircle. The staircase had a gentle curve, and it was quite wide. But it was not ornate and it was not marble. How could she have turned the creaky timber stairs into marble steps? Sheer force of will, she thought. She must have needed them to be marble. She must have not wanted to see any decay, any disintegration. The marble must have represented the life and the shine that must have been there, once. The life that she was looking for.

Ruth was shocked. She had a clear recollection of touching the tiled wall with her cheek. How clear could recollections be? They couldn't be that clear. There were no tiles, no marble, no shine, no life. There was just a run-down building, at 23 Kamedulska Street. She wiped away her tears. She didn't want to make Edek feel bad. He must be feeling bad enough.

Edek started to walk up the stairs. Ruth followed him. He stopped at the landing on the first floor.

"Here lived Tadek," he said to Ruth. Edek's voice was quite firm, but his eyes and face and mouth looked shaken. "And here lived Moniek," he said. "I did like his two children very much."

"Moniek and Tadek lived next door to each other?" Ruth said. She knew it was a stupid comment. The doors to the two apartments were side by side. But she didn't know what else to say. She didn't want to ask about Moniek's children. She didn't want to ask whether they were boys or girls, or one of each? Or what age they were. Or what happened to them. She knew that they were all dead. But how did they die? And when? In all probability Edek didn't know.

"Here lived Mr. and Mrs. Bader," Edek said, pointing to another door. "They was a very nice couple. She could not have any children and she did give me always a piece of *lekekh,* a piece of spunch cake, when she did bake on Fridays."

"How nice," Ruth said.

"She did bake a very good spunch cake," Edek said. Ruth loved the way Edek pronounced sponge. She had always adored this pronunciation. As a teenager she had taken it up herself. She had looked for opportunities to bring spunch cakes into conversations.

"I could smell Mrs. Bader's spunch from my bedroom," Edek said. The placing of "smell" and "spunch" so close to the word "bedroom," in the one, small sentence, added a dimension to the word "spunch" that Ruth had never noticed. Smell, and spunch, sounded distinctly sexual when linked to a bedroom.

What was she doing playing around with words and their connotations, now? Ruth thought. This was not the moment to go off on some word-association fantasy. She had to stay connected to the present at the moment.

"You lived on the next floor up," she said to Edek.

"I lived on the next floor," he said. "The second floor."

"Let's go up," Ruth said.

Edek looked at her. "We had, downstairs, in the back, a place where a man did come with a cow," he said.

"You had a cow out the back?" said Ruth.

"The cow did not belong to us," said Edek. "The cow did belong to the man what came to us with the cow. He came with the cow and a big bucket. He did milk the cow and did put the milk from his bucket into the buckets of the people what lived in this building. He did come a few times a week."

"I didn't know that," Ruth said.

"There is a lot that you do not know," said Edek.

"I know," she said.

"The milk did come straight, fresh, out of the cow," said Edek. "It did taste very good."

"You wouldn't be able to drink milk like that now," said Ruth.

"Why?" said Edek.

"Because cows are fed hormones and antibiotics," she said. "The antibiotics go into the milk. Raw milk is a perfect place for a variety of bacteria to multiply in."

"Really?" said Edek. "I did not know this."

"Today milk is pumped directly from the cows' udders, by milking machines, to steel tanks, and from there to refrigerated trucks," Ruth said.

"You did see this?" said Edek.

"I went to a dairy farm, once," she said. "Two years ago. They told me two hundred and eighty million glasses of milk are consumed by Americans every day."

"Two hundred and eighty million?" said Edek.

"Yes," she said. "It's a lot of milk."

Ruth stopped talking. Why was she talking about milk? She thought that this was possibly the most complicated conversation about milk that had ever taken place on this spot of the landing, on the first floor of 23 Kamedulska Street.

"You want to see where the man did milk his cow?" Edek said. "Come on, I'll show you." He started to walk downstairs.

"Dad," she said. "Let's see if we can see into your old apartment first? Then we can go and look around the back."

"You do not want to see where I got my milk?" Edek said.

"I do," she said. "But later." Edek walked back up to her. They went up the stairs to the second floor.

———

"You want to knock on the door?" Ruth said. They were standing outside Edek's old apartment, the apartment he grew up in.

"No," he said.

"Shall I knock?" she said.

"No," he said.

"One of us has to knock," she said. "This is the door that used to be the front door of your apartment? Right?" she said.

"This is the door," Edek said.

Suddenly, and abruptly, Edek lifted his fist and knocked on the door. A loud abrasive knock. Ruth's heart started racing. She felt breathless. The door opened slightly. An old man looked out into the darkened hallway. He seemed about Edek's age, but more aged than Edek. His shoulders were bent, and he seemed to have trouble seeing. He fumbled in his pockets and put on the glasses he was searching for. He peered at Edek and Ruth.

Edek stepped forward. He extended his hand to the man. Edek explained, with the aid of a multitude of polite and well-mannered expressions and bows of respect, that he was here to take nothing away from this man. He introduced himself. He explained that he once lived in this building. "I grew up here," he said. "And I just want to see the home of my childhood again. The home of my mother and father."

Edek motioned toward Ruth and said that Ruth, too, wanted to see where he had grown up. The old man looked up at Ruth. "She has been here before," he said. Ruth understood what he was saying. "He remembers me," she said to Edek.

"She was here fourteen or fifteen years ago," the old man said. "She wore a long black coat. And her hair was much longer."

"He remembers your coat," Edek said.

"It was only an ordinary coat," Ruth said. Even an ordinary coat had looked luxurious in Poland then. People were queuing for bread and there was no toilet paper. The man looked at the coat that Ruth was wearing now. It was a new coat. But still black. He smiled at her.

"He's remembering that I gave him several hundred zlotys," Ruth said to Edek.

"Several hundred?" said Edek.

"They were worth much less, then," she said. "I am not interested in taking anything away from you, kind sir," Edek repeated. "Neither is my daughter."

"Your family owned this building," the man said. "Your daughter told me."

"We do not want this building," Edek said. "I have lived for nearly sixty years without this building. Why should I decide I want this building now? I am an old man. I just want to see my old home." Edek paused for a minute. He looked at Ruth, then turned back to the man. "As a matter of fact, dear sir, I did not want to come here. What do I want to think about the past for? I am comfortable with my life. But she wanted me to come. She wanted to be here with me. What can you do when your child wants something? And she is my only child."

"I have two daughters, myself," the old man said.

"Congratulations," said Edek.

Edek turned to Ruth. "I do not think he is going to let us in," he said.

"I've been able to understand most of what he's saying," said Ruth.

"You understand more Polish than you know," said Edek. "What are we going to do? I think we have to go."

"We have to let him know we'll make it worth his while," said Ruth. Edek turned to the old man.

"I know that to let perfect strangers, with no warning, into your own home is an inconvenience," he said. "We will of course make up to you for this inconvenience."

The old man nodded his head. He stepped back and opened the door. "You were right," Edek said to Ruth.

They both entered the apartment. Inside, it was dark. The man switched on a lamp. Edek looked around. He seemed disoriented. He took a few steps and stumbled. He turned in the other direction and walked into a wall. "Be careful, Dad," Ruth said.

"They did chop it all up," Edek said. "They did cut off one room which used to be here. It must be now in the apartment next door."

"They haven't looked after the place, have they?" she said.

"You can say that again, brother," Edek said. "Brother" was an Australian expression Edek had latched on to not long after his arrival in the country.

"You can say that again, brother," he repeated.

Everything about the apartment was worn and in a state of decay. The walls were peeling, the windows were blackened, the carpet was threadbare and stained. Everything looked dirty.

"You have a very nice place," Edek said to the old man.

"Sit down, sir," the old man said. "I will make a cup of tea."

"Shall we have a cup of tea?" Edek said to Ruth.

"I guess we have to," she said.

"Thank you very much," Edek said to the man. Ruth and Edek walked into the living room. "This room used to be part of our lounge room," Edek said. Ruth was too distressed to be reassured by his pronunciation of "lounge." From the day he had learned the word he had pronounced it "lunge." "I'm lunging with my spunch," Ruth used to say, to amuse Garth. It always made him laugh. Not even the thought of lunging with a spunch could make her laugh now. She felt so miserable, standing in this cramped, slumped, and grubby apartment. She had remembered more light in the apartment, more room, more life. She had embellished everything. She mustn't have seen the neglect, the breaks, and the chips and cracks. She must have overlooked the dust and dirt. She must have been overwhelmed. Overawed to be there at all. Overawed by the thoughts of the lives that had been so alive here.

When she had walked up the stairs in Kamedulska Street for the first time she had known she was placing her feet on the same steps her father had stepped on. As a child. As a teenager. As a young man. The same stairs her grandmother and grandfather had stood on. They had all used those stairs. All the aunties and uncles and cousins and nephews and nieces. And, that year, fifteen years ago, when she, Ruth Rothwax, had been twenty-seven years old, she, too, had walked up and down those stairs.

She had walked up and down the stairs for two or three hours before she had knocked on the door of the apartment. She had walked from the ground floor to the top floor, five flights of stairs, dozens of times. She had almost been in a daze. As she walked she had imagined the children who must have run from one floor to the other. And the mothers and the fathers. And her father. And her father's father and her father's mother. She had been quite exhausted when she had arrived in this apartment. Maybe that accounted for her blemished vision.

Edek looked distressed. "This was not like it was when we did live here," he said. "It was a beautiful apartment." He looked over in the corner. "The balcony is still there," he said. "My father used to watch me come home from school from this balcony. He did want to check that I did have my hat on."

"You told me that story," Ruth said. "I went out on the balcony when I came here last time."

"Probably even the balcony is not very nice now," said Edek.

"It was a bit dirty and run-down," she said.

"What for do we need to stay?" said Edek. "Maybe I tell him to forget the tea?"

Ruth looked around her. The crumbling walls and broken windows were at odds with the building's past. In the past this building had housed excitement and laughter, excitement and tenderness, excitement and love. She had felt the excitement on that first visit. And she could feel it now. It wasn't eroded by the disintegration or the neglect. She felt much better. It was still there. Still in the air.

"If you stand still, Dad, you can feel the past," she said. "You can feel the life."

"Don't speak like that," Edek said. "It will be no good for both of us." He looked as though he was about to cry.

"The tea is nearly ready," the old man called out. "Please sit down." A sofa piled high with clothes was against one wall. A rocking chair faced the sofa. The rocking chair was covered with cat's fur. Ruth had noticed a large cat asleep in the kitchen. She moved the clothes and cleared a space for herself and Edek. Edek looked at the sofa. His face crumpled. He started to cry.

"What's wrong, Dad?" Ruth said. He shook his head. He looked embarrassed to be crying. He tried to stop. But his tears were insistent. They kept coming. Ruth felt sick. She shouldn't have put her father through this.

"We can go now, Dad," she said.

"He is already making the tea," Edek said. He wiped his eyes. "This couch was our couch," he said.

"Oh no," she said. And she started to weep. Edek sat down on the couch. "Do not cry," he said to her. She sat down next to him. She put her hand in her father's hand. They sat on the couch, holding hands. "Do not cry, please," he said to her, after a few minutes.

The old man arrived with three stained cups, a pot of tea, two teaspoons, and a sugar bowl on a tray. He put the tray on top of a cardboard box.

"Thank you very much, sir," Edek said. "It looks very nice." Ruth wiped her eyes. She was glad there wasn't much light in the room. She didn't want to see the cracked, old cups with any more clarity.

"Ask him when he moved in here?" Ruth said to her father. Edek asked the old man the question.

"Approximately 1940," the old man said.

"It must have been minutes after all the Jews were moved out," Ruth said.

"Do not speak like this," Edek said.

"He can't understand me," said Ruth, and she held her cup of tea up and smiled at the old man. *Bardzo dobrze*, she said to him. He nodded, pleased with her compliment about his tea. "It's disgusting tea," she said to her father.

"Ruthie, please," he said.

"Ask him what happened to all of the things that were in here and in all of the other apartments," she said to Edek.

"It is not necessary to ask this," Edek said.

"Please, Dad," she said.

Edek asked. "He said his wife will know all of this. She was in charge of the rents in the building. She will be back at four o'clock," Edek said to Ruth.

"Ask him if he wondered what happened to all the people who lived here?" Ruth said. Edek asked. Ruth could understand the old man's reply.

"I heard they moved somewhere else," the man said.

"Ruthie, what good is this?" said Edek.

"I'm not sure," she said. "There must have been so many photographs, books, documents, left. Ask him if he saw any."

"My wife knows all of that," the old man said. "If you are extra nice, she will talk to you."

"What does he mean extra nice?" Ruth said.

"He said his wife is not such an easy woman. We should maybe bring some chocolates and some flowers."

"That's no trouble," said Ruth.

"You really don't want to think of owning this building," the man said to Edek. "This building is nothing but trouble. The owner can't sell it. Everything is broken. People don't pay their rents because nothing gets fixed. There is no heating. It is terrible."

"Tell him we're not going to take this flea-hole from him," Ruth said.

"I can promise you, sir, I have no interest at all in owning this property," Edek said.

"You don't even want to think of it," the man said.

"Ask him who the owner is," said Ruth. The man shook his head. He said that he didn't know. Ruth and Edek got up. "Is sixty zloty enough?" Edek whispered. "It's enough," Ruth said. "I don't think we're going to get anything out of him." "We will be back at four o'clock," Edek said as he shook hands with the old man. Ruth was surprised. She had been sure that her father was not going to want to return.

Edek and Ruth walked along Kamedulska Street. They passed an empty block of land.

"My father did have a yard for timber, here," Edek said. He sounded very flat.

"Mum told me about the timber yard," she said.

"You want to walk to Pomorska Street where Mum did live?" Edek said.

"Yes, please," she said. "I'd love to." They walked quietly, without speaking. Ruth was exhausted. Her father must be totally wrung out, she thought.

"I love you, Dad," she said.

"I love you, too," he said.

On Poudniowa Street, Edek pointed to an empty storefront. "It used to be here the bakery," he said. "On Friday I would take our *cholent* to the baker to go into the oven after the bread was finished. The next day was *Shabbes* and we couldn't cook. You know *Shabbes,* the Sabbath?"

"Of course I know *Shabbes,*" Ruth said.

"The *cholent* did stay in the baker's oven all night," Edek said. "The next day when *Shabbes* was over we did pick up the cooked *cholent.* My mother told me always to be sure it was our *cholent* that I did pick up, because we had plenty of meat in our *cholent.*" Edek smiled at the memory of the *cholent.*

"Your *cholent* had more meat in it than most of the local people's *cholent*?" Ruth said.

"Much more meat," he said. "Some people's *cholent* had no meat. As a matter of fact I did once pick up the wrong *cholent*. It was in a pot what was just like our pot. It had no meat in it at all. My father was not very happy with me." Edek seemed to have cheered up, talking about the *cholent*. "Two more streets and we will be in Pomorska Street," he said.

Ruth recognized the building her mother had lived in as soon as she saw it. She hadn't been able to look inside when she had last been in Łódź. No one had been home in the ground-floor apartment that Rooshka had lived in. Ruth and Edek peered into the hallway. It was dark and quiet. The only sign of any occupants was the washing strung out on lines in the courtyard. You could see the washing from the street. The windows in her mother's old apartment were covered with layers of improvised drapes. Squares of an old blanket, pieces of faded lace, part of a used tablecloth.

"They put this stuff on the windows to keep out the cold," Edek said. "It looks pretty bad," he said, after a few minutes. They walked through to the courtyard where Rooshka had spent many hours studying and doing her schoolwork. The courtyard was bleak and barren. Filled with lines of washed and worn, torn, and faded clothes.

Edek put his hands over his eyes. "There is nothing left," he said.

"Mum used to study here," Ruth said.

"I know," he said. "I did used to visit her. I used to beg her to come out for an ice cream with me. But she always said no. She said how would she become a pediatrician if she went out all the time for ice creams with me."

"Where in the courtyard did she sit?" said Ruth.

"Just here," said Edek, pointing to two steps. "She was always here. Every night, after school. She was so happy to do her studies. Not like me. She was a lovely girl, your mum."

"I know," said Ruth. Edek walked up to one of the windows of the Spindlers' former apartment. He tried to look through a crack in the window.

"It's pretty decrepit, isn't it?" Ruth said.

"It is good Mum did not see this," said Edek.

❧ *Chapter Eight* ❧

Ruth was sitting in the lobby of the Grand Victoria Hotel. She felt terrible. Her head ached. Her body was tired. Lethargic. Why did her body feel so tired? she wondered. She was exercising less than she did at home. She wasn't running as much, and she wasn't lifting weights. Yet, she was more tired. She was exhausted.

Her father was upstairs, in his room. He was reading one of his detective fiction books. *The One-Armed Alibi*. She hoped that *The One-Armed Alibi* was taking Edek's mind off his visit to Kamedulska Street this morning. The cover of the book hadn't looked enticing. A man, with a bloodied stump of an arm, was being strangled by an even stranger-looking man. Still, she thought that nothing her father was reading about could be stranger than this trip. Ruth had wanted Edek to have a nap. But Edek had insisted that he was not tired.

"You'll feel better if you have a short nap," she had said.

"I feel fine," he had said.

"Well, at least read quietly in your room for an hour or so," Ruth had said.

"You speak to me like I am child," Edek said. "I don't sleep during the day in Melbourne. Why should I sleep during the day in Poland?"

"Because it's more stressful being here," she had said.

"For me, the stress did happen a long time ago," Edek said.

Ruth had felt worried about her father. He hadn't eaten any lunch. "I'm not hungry," he had said when she suggested they stop for lunch. He looked well enough. Maybe no one would want to eat lunch after the sort of breakfast Edek had had. Her father looked in pretty good condition, she thought. Especially considering the fact that he never exercised and ate with abandon. He seemed to be in better shape than she was.

She had showered, again, before coming down to the lobby to do some work. Working reassured her. She was composing a list of possible new subjects for letters. She thought she would try to expand her range of business letters. Business letters were so much less taxing than personal letters. People, Ruth found, needed help with the briefest of letters. A simple acknowledgment of the receipt of a letter could be rendered useless or incite a fury in the recipient with a lack of information or the wrong tone. It was important, in these letters of acknowledgment, to be brief and concise, but never brusque, abrupt, or terse. The letter should identify the correspondence which was being responded to, and state the action that would be taken. This way, people would know that their query or complaint or request had been heard.

Letters of resignation were also an area in which it was easy to trip and fall. There were lawyers all over America who could be consulted about the legalities of a resignation. The lawyers looked after the client's legal position but seemed to lack an understanding of the emotional aspects of a letter of resignation. Ruth had written out a set of rules, for Max, for this category. Letters of resignation seemed to incite people to make inflammatory statements. A course that was clearly not in anyone's best interest. It was crucial, Ruth felt, that a letter of resignation should have no accusations or recriminations. Threats and blame were to be avoided. And, if at all possible, a complimentary line or two should be included. Ruth had had a lot of success with her letters of resignation. Twice, clients had told Ruth that their resignation letters were so effective that they had eliminated the difficulties that led to their intended departures.

Word of mouth was how most clients came to Rothwax Correspondence. Ruth had covered enough territory, on paper, to have traversed most of several of her clients' lives. She had written holiday greetings letters, the accepting and declining of invitations, birth announcements, sympathy letters, and letters of apology for her clients. Ruth felt that she knew these clients better than most people knew each other.

Ruth wrote on her list letters to public officials. She must write a few more prototypes in this category. Rothwax Correspondence was receiving more requests for letters to public officials. A letter to a public official could be very effective or have no effect at all. The right letter made a big difference.

Ruth added to her list praise-for-staff letters. She thought that this category could prove useful to many businesses. It seemed, to Ruth, so easy to spread goodwill. One brief letter of praise every other year seemed to bring results that far outweighed the effort involved or the money expended. Ruth added answering reference requests, welcoming new customers, multidenominational holiday greetings, and rejecting-a-job-applicant letters to her list.

Ruth had had requests from parents to write letters on behalf of their children. She usually said no. She felt insincere adopting a six-year-old's tone. More fraudulent than she ever did voicing an intimacy or intensity for an adult, as part of a business transaction. Ruth had also turned away a large volume of business writing college application essays for the children of clients. So many highly reputable and successful clients doubted their children's ability to write a good essay. "Wouldn't it be morally compromising if I wrote the essays?" she had asked one of her clients, the head of a large charitable foundation. "No," he had replied. "Not any more morally compromising than if I helped him to write the essay." "But you would only be helping him," Ruth had said. "I would be writing the essays." "What if I bring in his half-written essays and you polish them up?" the client had asked. Ruth had refused. She didn't want to pass herself off as a teenager, even if it was only on paper. But writing college essays was clearly a market somebody could move into. Ruth wondered if it was common for kids not to write their own essays in America. Probably only among the middle class and the wealthy, she decided.

A fax from Max had been waiting for her at the Grand Victoria Hotel when she got back from Kamedulska Street. Ruth had been surprised to hear from Max on a Sunday. Max was obviously taking her responsibilities as acting head of Rothwax Correspondence seriously. In the fax, Max had told her that Bern's mother was coming in for a handwriting test on Monday. This had been Bern's idea. According to Bern, Max said, his mother had very good handwriting. "I'm going to give her a speed and accuracy test," Max had said in the fax. Speed and accuracy? What did Max think she was running? IBM? "Everything is under control," Max had added. What did Max mean? How out of control could a business become in this brief period of time?

The lobby of the Grand Victoria was mostly occupied by men. They were not the usual run-of-the-mill businessmen found in hotel lobbies. They looked more like criminals. They were middle-aged and skewered and circled with gold necklaces and bracelets and an occasional earring. Most of them wore large rings on their fingers. They were all smoking.

Several of the men had young women by their sides. Very young women. The young women looked adoringly at the men and sent them fetching glances whenever the men looked back. The women batted their eyelashes and patted the men on the arm or shoulder. Two of the young women were staring at Ruth. It was probably her computer, she thought. They probably didn't see too many businesswomen.

"You are having trouble with your father?" a voice said.

"Oh, no, not you," Ruth said. "No, I'm not having trouble with my father. I'm working. Why don't you disappear?"

"I can help with this trouble," Höss said.

"Troubleshooting would not, I think, be your strong point," Ruth said.

"I know what the problem is," said Höss. "You do not know what you need to know."

"Most of us don't," she said.

"I know what the problem is," Höss said again. "And I know the answer."

"Your answers are not the answers I'm looking for," Ruth said. "Anyway I am not having trouble with my father. We have both simply embarked on an extremely troubling trip."

"You do not know what you need to know," Höss said.

"Neither do you," she said. "You're stuck in Zweites Himmel's Lager."

"Let me help you." said Höss.

"You could just disappear," Ruth said. "That would be a big help."

"Ha, ha, ha," said Höss. He thought it was a joke.

Ruth was irritated. "It's not a joke," she said. "I want you to go away." He laughed again. What aspect of what she was saying could possibly appear humorous? She couldn't read Höss's laughter. It sounded like ordinary laughter. Was he laughing at her? Was he remembering an old joke? Why didn't she twist her heel into the floor? Why was she allowing him to stay? "Piss off," she said to Höss.

"Why are you being so difficult?" Höss said.

"Piss off," she said. "Can't you hear me? Are you going deaf in your old age?"

"I can hear very well," Höss said. "And I am feeling remarkably well. My bones do not bother me so much. I feel youthful. Almost like my old self, again."

"Your old self?" Ruth said. "I wouldn't head in that direction if I were you. No one in their right mind would want to return to your particular old self."

"Really?" said Höss.

"You'll be in hell forever if you can't understand that," Ruth said.

"I am in Zweites Himmel's Lager," Höss said.

The other people in the lobby of the Grand Victoria seemed oblivious to the fact that she was talking to someone. Even the group of gold-chained and -linked men, clustered in a circle of armchairs next to Ruth, didn't appear to have noticed. Their girlfriends certainly hadn't noticed. Maybe talking to dead people wasn't as obvious as talking to living human beings. Why did Höss have to turn up now? She had just been beginning to relax. She had planned to make notes for Max on the structural aspects of a handwritten letter. How to select the paper and what size paper was required for particular text lengths. Until now, Ruth had selected and purchased all the stationery that Rothwax Correspondence used for handwritten letters and documents.

Ruth had planned to give Max a list of points to be taken into account when selecting envelope size and quality. And a corresponding list about paper selection. For example, Ruth always chose plain paper for formal letters, and made sure that casual letters were not written on paper that was too formal. She made sure there were no sentimental flourishes, colors, patterns, or borders on love letters.

She also made sure that the weight of the paper reflected the subject matter. Ruth chose fragile Japanese paper for people who saw themselves as more idiosyncratic. In certain careers idiosyncrasy was an asset.

Where was Höss? Ruth realized that she had slipped into a reverie. A reassuring reverie in the self-contained, well-ordered world of letter writing. In letters, if you were careful, there were no slips and spills. No one to take a thought or sentence into a direction that you hadn't intended. No one to question the sentiments and statements. The letter was all yours. And, if there was a response that was less than what you hoped for, it was made out of your presence.

Ruth could feel Höss's presence. She knew that he was still around. She wondered why she was so sure of this. She couldn't easily define why she was sure. It was something in the air. A thickening. A coarsening. "I really am feeling so much better," Hoss said. Ruth nodded to herself. A congratulatory small nod. She knew she was right. She had known Höss was still there. "I have been thinking about the various prisoners in Auschwitz," Höss said.

"Wow, you must really be trying to get out of Zweites Himmel's Lager," Ruth said. "Some more thoughts in this direction and you'll be the star of your sensitivity-training class."

"Thank you," said Höss. "Of all of the prisoners in Auschwitz, it was the gypsies who caused me a great deal of trouble, but, ironically, they were, and I must be careful to phrase this correctly, they were my most beloved prisoners."

"You just lost all credibility," Ruth said. "No wonder you've been stuck in the sensitivity-training class for fifty-two years. It's not smart to make statements like that. It doesn't have even a hint of reality about it. Your most beloved prisoners? What were you doing, walking around Auschwitz as the director of a love fest, a love-in?"

"I was very fond of the gypsies," said Höss. He sounded hurt. "I am telling you the truth," he said.

"I bet," she said.

How could he be so stupid? Ruth thought. Men, on the whole, seemed to be so much less aware of what they were saying. She looked at the men around her. They were still in their armchairs, smoking and drinking. They had no idea of how unattractive they were. They held themselves with the smug arrogance of men who believed they were attractive. There was probably a plentiful supply, in Poland, of young women who would flutter their eyelashes at these men. Poverty created climates for that sort of relationship.

The two girls who had accompanied this group of men had left. Ruth was now the only female in the lobby. She looked at the men, with what she hoped was an expression of contempt. She caught herself. Why was she doing this? Why did she have to be so harsh and judgmental about these men? She would hate any man who dismissed women in the way that she was dismissing these men. Poland was definitely not bringing out the best in her. If she wasn't careful, she would leave the country as unpleasant a human being as the most unpleasant of the Poles she was railing at. If she wasn't careful, she would turn into one of them.

The lobby did feel cloaked in testosterone, to her, though. There were too many men. *Too many men.* Ruth was startled by the phrase. Was this what the gypsy woman, in Warsaw, could have meant by "too many men"? Höss and all of these Poles? But Höss wasn't a man. He was a ghost. A phantom, a shadow, an apparition, an appearance. He was not a man. He was more like a bogeyman, or a scarecrow, or the hobgoblin in a frightening fairy tale.

"There are very few gypsies in Zweites Himmel's Lager," Höss said. "The ones that are there work mainly as fortune-tellers."

"They work in Zweites Himmel's Lager?" Ruth said.

"They are in a better category than I am," said Höss. "I am in the top punishment category, which is, to my mind, a little unfair. As a result of this I am unable to work. I am forced to remain idle."

Ruth could hear the sound of teeth grinding. It must be Höss, she thought. She herself had a tendency to grind her teeth in annoyance. "Why would gypsies be telling fortunes in hell?" Ruth said. "Everyone there has already had their future. They know what it was. They are dead. Their future is behind them."

"People still have a future in Zweites Himmel's Lager," said Höss. "And the future is as unknown to them, there, as it is on earth. People are, of course, as always, concerned with their future." Höss sounded annoyed with her. How was she supposed to know how things worked in the afterlife? "There is more to life, than life and death," Höss said.

"So the gypsy fortune-tellers in Zweites Himmel's Lager get a lot of business, do they?" Ruth said to Höss.

"Yes, yes," said Höss. "We all want to know what the future holds for us. And the gypsies have expertise in that field. I still have a soft spot for gypsies. In the spring of 1943 there were approximately sixteen thousand gypsies in Birkenau. I am not sure exactly how many. We included, of course, half-caste gypsies in this number. They lived in huts that were built to house three hundred. Each of these huts contained between eight hundred and a thousand gypsies.

"In July 1942, the Reichsführer-SS visited the camp," said Höss. "I personally led him on an extensive tour of the gypsy camp. Himmler was very thorough in his inspection. He saw the crammed barracks, the unsalutory and unsanitary conditions. He saw those gypsies who were ill with infectious diseases. Himmler also saw the children who were suffering from noma."

"From what?" Ruth said.

"From noma," said Höss. "You know so much about medical conditions I am surprised that you do not know about noma. It is a cancerous growth that appears most often on the face as a result of starvation and other physical depletions. The noma was particularly difficult for me to look at.

"Himmler was not so happy himself to look at the gypsy children with big holes in their cheeks," Höss said. "Holes big enough to see through. I could see that Himmler was keen to move on from this viewing of the slow decomposition and rotting of the living flesh of those wizened and shriveled-up children."

"He was probably warned about infection," said Ruth.

"Most probably," said Höss. "It did look terrible."

"My mother was haunted by children with holes in their cheeks," Ruth said. "She used to tell me about them." Ruth had always hoped that she had imagined this detail that her mother had talked about. She hoped she had imagined half of what her mother had said about her life. Hoped that it had been untrue. As a teenager, she had wanted to believe that it was all make-believe. That her mother had made it all up. That none of it had happened. None of the degradation, none of the disease, none of the brutality, none of the loss, none of the death, none of the mayhem. She used to hope that her mother had been exaggerating. Like all mothers. She used to hope that her mother was exaggerating the pain, exaggerating the suffering, the cruelty. Exaggerating her exhaustion. Ruth used to watch other mothers. They were always voicing complaints. Complaints about pains and aches and exhaustion. Maybe her mother was just like the other mothers.

"My mother must have seen the gypsy children," she said to Höss. He coughed.

"Himmler ordered me to destroy the gypsies," he said. "Himmler said those still capable of work could live, but the others had to be destroyed. It was not so easy a task to drive the gypsies into the gas chambers. They were the most trusting of people. I do not understand why their trusting natures bothered us. But it did. Many of us did not feel so good about killing the gypsies.

"During the night of July 31, three thousand five hundred to four thousand gypsies were murdered. Technically, I must add, it was also August 1, as the gassings went on after midnight."

"You concentrate on the technicalities, don't you?" Ruth said.

"I did not witness the killings of the gypsies myself," said Höss.

"Of course," said Ruth. "You were a witness to nothing other than the Reichsführer-SS's orders."

"The gypsies who were left after this had to go into the gas chambers eventually, too," said Höss. "Four thousand of them went into the gas chambers in August 1944."

Ruth remembered a question she had wanted to ask him. "Is there a devil in hell?" she said.

"What?" said Höss.

"Is there a devil in hell?" she said. "Or is the place full of devils?" Höss was quiet for a minute. Ruth thought that maybe it was hard to detect the devil in a place teeming with unseemly denizens.

"It is, as you suspected," Höss said eventually. "There is not one devil in Zweites Himmel's Lager."

"There are demons and fiends and dybbuks everywhere, are there?" she said.

"Dybbuks?" said Höss. "What is a dybbuk?"

"I'm surprised that you don't know what a dybbuk is," said Ruth. "After so much contact with Jews you would think you would know a few things about Jewish life. A dybbuk is the soul of a dead person that enters and takes control of a living person."

"I did not know this," said Höss.

"There are probably dybbuks in the middle of the cutthroats and thugs and roughnecks in Zweites Himmel's Lager," Ruth said. A disturbing thought occurred to her. Did she have a dybbuk in her? Did she have Höss's soul living inside her? She shook her head. She was being stupid. She didn't believe in dybbuks.

"It is not only lowlife that live in Zweites Himmel's Lager," said Höss.

"No, there are fine upstanding citizens like you," Ruth said. Höss snorted.

"Could we leave this subject, please?" Höss said.

"And go on to a more savory one?" she said. "Of course."

"Despite the adverse and disadvantageous conditions," Höss said, "the gypsies did not appear to suffer very much psychologically as a result of their imprisonment."

"You could work for me," Ruth said. "You have a real way with a synonym and antonym."

"How could I work for you?" Höss said. "I am not permitted to work."

"I was being sarcastic," Ruth said. "I was referring to your use of the words 'adverse' and 'disadvantageous.' "

Höss snorted. "I have asked you before not to interrupt me with irrelevant observations."

"So the gypsies were happy to be in Auschwitz, were they?" Ruth said. She shook her head. She noticed another woman in the lobby of the Grand Victoria. The woman looked Polish. She was about Ruth's age. She was well dressed. On the third finger of her left hand she sported a very large diamond. Ruth looked again. It was an enormous diamond. It stood out on her hand and looked quite incongruous in the less than elegant lobby.

"I have always had a great deal of respect for women," Höss said. Ruth almost laughed out loud at the absurdity of this notion, and the self-delusion involved, but she also felt a shred of alarm. Could Höss read her mind? Did he know she had been thinking about women? Probably not. It was probably a coincidence.

"In Auschwitz, however, I saw very quickly that I would have to rethink this position," Höss said. "In Auschwitz it became apparent to me, quite quickly, that even a woman must be observed carefully and scrutinized before she is entitled to complete respect."

"Oh yeah," Ruth said. "Your enormous respect for women must have dissipated fast. Those standards you applied for complete respect? Not many women must have measured up." Höss snorted. "You must have been full of concern for women," Ruth said, "when you asked Professor Carl Clauberg of the University of Königsberg to look into the question of female sterilization."

"What do you know about Professor Carl Clauberg?" said Höss.

"I know he was thrilled to have official support for his research," Ruth said. "He specialized in the treatment of sterile women. He was thrilled at the prospect of unlimited numbers of patients to work on."

"That is enough about Clauberg," said Höss.

"Am I making you uncomfortable?" Ruth said.

"Not at all," Höss said, with a stern tone.

"When Clauberg arrived in Auschwitz in the spring of 1943, you installed over two hundred women in Block Ten, for him," Ruth said. "He injected a series of chemicals into their fallopian tubes. It was a secret formula."

"It certainly stopped the women from menstruating," Höss said. "But we do not know if it was effective sterilization."

"That's because when the experiments were over most of the women were sent to the gas chambers," Ruth said.

"The Girl from Ipanema" was now playing, in the background, in the lobby of the Grand Victoria. There was something strange about the recording. Ruth realized after a minute that it must be a Polish recording. "She goes walking" was coming out as "She goes vucking." It sounded just like "She goes fucking." "She vucks slowly," the woman sang. Ruth couldn't believe what she was hearing. Yesterday, she had been startled by another Polish recording. "I look into your arse," a singer had crooned. It had taken Ruth several minutes to work out that the line the singer was trying to sing was, "I look into your eyes."

Ruth looked around her in the lobby. No one else seemed to perceive the lyrics as lewd. The woman with the diamond had been joined by another woman. An elderly woman. They looked like mother and daughter to Ruth. It made her happy to see a mother and daughter who looked as though they were enjoying each other's company. Ruth forgave the woman her large diamond. Being a good daughter, she thought, showed something infinitely more important about her than her choice of jewelry.

"The breaking up of families during the selection process," Höss said, "caused much distress to the Jews. When we separated the men from the women and the children, it caused a terrible apprehension and panic in the entire transport. It was frequently essential to use force in order to restore order. Jews have highly developed feelings of family. They stick together like leeches or limpets. The confusion that was brought about by this nervousness at being separated from each other was so great that frequently whole selections had to begin all over again."

Why did she have to listen to this? Ruth thought. A better question would be why wasn't she trying to get rid of Höss? She was too tired to get rid of him. He wore her out. He rendered her almost comatose, unable to move. As though she were in a trance. A hypnotic trance. She knew that she wasn't. Anyone who could be critical of the size of a diamond on the finger of a stranger was not in a coma or a trance.

"What psychological effect did imprisonment have on Jews?" Höss said, as though Ruth had asked him that question. "Even in the early days, in Dachau, the guards were particularly vicious with them. Jews were used to being tormented and hounded and victimized as the defilers and debasers of the German people," Höss said. Ruth could feel that Höss was in the swing of his story. She could feel the relish in his retelling of this part of the world's history.

"I observed," Höss said, "an interesting phenomenon in Dachau. A copy of *Der Stürmer* was put up in the camp." He paused. "Do you know what *Der Stürmer* is?" he said.

"A pornographic anti-Semitic weekly publication produced by Julius Streicher," she said.

"I thought you would know of it," Höss said. "I myself did not approve of the pornography. After the copy of *Der Stürmer* was made available, it was immediately apparent that fellow prisoners who had previously displayed no antagonism toward Jews became anti-Semitic. The Jews, of course, behaved in a typically Jewish manner by bribing their fellow prisoners. Of course the Jews had plenty of money."

"This was before 1939, when most of the money that most of the Jews had was taken from them," Ruth said.

"Of course," said Höss. "It was before *Kristallnacht*. After *Kristallnacht*, for their own good, to save them from reprisals from the German people, Jews who were traders and businessmen were arrested. They were taken to concentration camp as protective custody Jews."

Ruth laughed. "How can you say that with a straight face?" she said. "Protective custody Jews. Maybe you haven't got a straight face. I can't see you. Maybe behind that steady and serious voice you're making the facial gestures of a lunatic or a clown or an unsettled, mentally deficient buffoon?"

"You could probably see me if you tried hard enough," Höss said.

"Now you sound really retarded," said Ruth. But she was unnerved. What did Höss mean by that?

"I first became acquainted with Jews en masse, in Sachsenhausen, after *Kristallnacht*," Höss said. "Before then, there were few Jews in Sachsenhausen. It was not yet an extermination camp. After the Jewish invasion, things changed at Sachsenhausen."

"I think you've got your terminology wrong," Ruth said. "Prisoners are rounded up and imprisoned. They do not 'invade' prisons."

"Please do not interrupt me with such irrelevant things," Höss said. "Before the Jews, bribery at Sachsenhausen was virtually unheard of," Höss said. "Now, it became commonplace. Bribery and corruption were widespread."

"Among the prisoners, you mean?" Ruth said. Höss ignored her. "I can see that the Jews were a real problem for you," Ruth said. "You are helping me to understand why you killed millions of Russians, gypsies, and Poles, but designated only Jews to be wiped off the face of the earth." She hoped that her sarcasm was loud and clear. She felt flushed, as though she had shouted the words. "Not only were Jews corrupters of German bodies and souls, they were a massive logistical problem for you," Ruth said to Höss. "How do you kill so many people and dispose of their bodies in an efficient and economical manner?"

"This was a question we relegated a lot of resources and manpower toward," said Höss.

"You spared those Jews who were personally useful to you," Ruth said to Höss.

"What do you mean by 'personally useful'?" Höss said.

"I'm being specific," she said. "Specifically referring to those Jews who were useful to you."

"I do not understand you," Höss said. "I treated all Jews in the same manner. According to my orders."

"You had orders to employ two Jewish dressmakers in your home in Auschwitz?" said Ruth.

"You have been listening to the wrong people," Höss said. "I did not employ Jews."

"Well, it wasn't technically employment," Ruth said, "because there was no pay. But they worked for you. Making dresses for Mrs. Höss. I guess their pay was that they were not immediately killed."

"I have asked you once before, if you could please leave Mrs. Höss out of this," Höss said. "Please."

"Maybe," Ruth said.

"I want to emphasize to you that I have never personally hated Jews," said Höss. "It is a fact that I looked on Jews as the enemy of the German people, but I myself never felt a personal hatred for Jews." Ruth didn't say anything. "I saw absolutely no difference between a Jewish prisoner and any other prisoner," Höss said, with indignation. "I treated all prisoners in exactly the same way. In any case, I am not the sort of person who accommodates hatred with ease. It is simply not my nature. I know all too clearly what hatred looks like. I have witnessed much hatred around me, and I have been the recipient of hatred. I have suffered from hatred. I know what hate is."

"I know you know what hate is," Ruth said. "Few people would doubt that."

The doorman approached Ruth and asked her if she would like a drink. He seemed unaware of the intense dislike she felt for him. Ruth wanted to say no. She wanted to say no to anything from this man. But she was thirsty. "I'll have a Perrier," she said. He came back to say they had no Perrier. "I'll have anything that isn't bottled in Poland," she said to him. He brought her a bottle of something that looked Italian. She poured a glass. It tasted fine.

The doorman smiled at her. She tapped at a few keys on her computer, and made out as though she was engrossed in her work. The doorman went back to the front door.

"The worst thing in the world is to be unoccupied," Höss said. "I would accept any hard labor, any task at all, rather than this enforced idleness." Ruth drank her mineral water. "I am cut off from everything," Höss said.

"Maybe that's the point of Zweites Himmel's Lager," Ruth said.

"No it is not," said Höss. "Other inmates of Zweites Himmel's Lager have jobs and occupations. But I am not allowed to have a job."

"Maybe you were too zealous in your last one," Ruth said.

"They are punishing me," Höss said.

"You could be right," she said. "Is there a worse category of inmate than you in Zweites Himmel's Lager?" Ruth said.

"We are residents," said Höss. "Not inmates."

"You just called the residents of Zweites Himmel's Lager inmates yourself," she said.

"It was a mistake," Höss said.

"Are there worse conditions than the conditions set out for you?" said Ruth.

"I don't think so," he said.

"No red hot flames?" Ruth said.

"They ceased with the flames a few years ago," said Höss. "The psychologists, there, said the flames were not a deterrent. They instituted instead solitary confinement, censorship, and peer review."

"Peer review?" said Ruth.

"Yes, that is what I have to endure," Höss said. "A monthly review by my so-called peers. A bunch of blackguards and thugs and criminals and antisocial types. They deliver reports on my behavior."

"What do they say?" said Ruth.

"They are so stupid," said Höss.

"I'm sure," Ruth said.

"They say I am antisocial," said Höss. "Who would be social in this company?"

"You may have a point there," Ruth said. She sipped her mineral water.

"Talking to you has very much helped my restlessness," Höss said. "I have been forced to do nothing for so long. It is very hard. I cannot even pace." A strangled sound escaped from him.

"Maybe if you pass your sensitivity-training class they'll let you exercise," Ruth said. "Maybe you should try to impress your peer review panel? Try to get on well with the boys."

"They are not all boys," Höss said.

"There are some women on the panel?" Ruth said.

"Yes," said Höss.

"I'm glad that women are able to rise through the ranks in Zweites Himmel's Lager," Ruth said. "Speaking of peers, several of your peers in Auschwitz said you appeared to be a kindly, unselfish, introverted man. Although I'm not sure how seriously you can take some of those peers. They also said you were a perfectionist. I can believe that."

"I am a perfectionist, that is true," Höss said.

"Well, you'll have to perfect the art of doing nothing," Ruth said. "It will be a whole lot better than what you were previously perfecting."

"I do not think I will need to perfect the art of doing nothing," Höss said. "I believe I will get out of here, one day. Things change, even in Zweites Himmel's Lager. And I am not a fatalist, unlike most Jews."

"Really?" said Ruth. "Unlike most Jews?"

"I observed the Jews in Auschwitz over a lengthy period of time," Höss said. "Jews have a propensity for melancholy."

"Auschwitz was not, for most people, an uplifting experience," Ruth said.

"That is true," said Höss. "But I see the melancholy in all Jews. I see this melancholy, on your face."

Ruth touched her face. "The melancholy is not there all the time," she said.

"The Jews in Auschwitz had more reason for melancholy. They, unlike most of the other prisoners, knew that they were, every single one of them, condemned to die," Höss said. "They knew that they would remain alive for only as long as they were capable of work."

"Sure," Ruth said. "That is why, even in that first selection process, young girls tried to look older and stronger and old women tried not to show their age. They knew the appearance of whatever energy they could muster could save their lives."

"The Jews, however, deteriorated very quickly," Höss said.

"Could that be because they arrived, most of them, after years of star-vation and disease and imprisonment, years of unrestricted brutality?" Ruth said.

"The Jews were fatalists," Höss said, ignoring her. "They gave in to all the wretchedness and discomfort and desolation. They gave in to the ter-ror. They accepted their fate with a hopelessness. This lack of a desire to live, this indifference, this collapse of will made them susceptible, physi-cally, to the slightest thing. Death was inevitable for them. They accepted their fate."

"You mean they didn't fight back?" said Ruth. Höss didn't answer. "I've heard that before," she said. "It's remarkable how fast those Jews went downhill. First they were ordered out of their homes. They should have refused. The punishment was only death. Then they were imprisoned and deprived of all of their rights, not to mention their properties and material possessions. They were cut off from the rest of the world. A world that didn't care too much for Jews, anyway. The living conditions they were imprisoned in were so harsh that many of them died before they could be murdered. They died of disease and starvation and beatings. Being beaten to death was much easier than slowly starving. How did those Jews buckle so fast? Some of them didn't even last a year.

"They all worked for as long as they lasted. They worked for the Ger-mans, making machinery and straw boots and other essentials for the Ger-man army. Children of all ages worked to help the Germans murder them later down the line. It's amazing how quickly the Jews went downhill under those conditions. And that was years before most of them were shipped to you, Mr. Höss. Rudolf Franz Ferdinand Höss SS-Obersturmbannführer."

Ruth thought she was going to throw up. She had to get outside. She had to get some fresh air. She ran out into Piotrkowska Street. She took sev-eral deep breaths. She couldn't allow herself to become so agitated. She had known this trip was going to be difficult. She hadn't known how difficult.

She felt grubby. She couldn't shower again. She would come out in a rash if she kept washing herself each time she felt soiled. Anyway, what she was trying to get rid of couldn't come off with soap and water.

She suddenly wanted to go home. Next to Höss, New York looked wholesome. She thought of Washington Square Gardens and Fifth Avenue and the East Village. She made a promise to herself never to complain about the city again. She missed New York. Its edginess and worrying qualities seemed normal and reasonable, next to this.

"You do not know what you need to know," Höss said.

"I've had enough of you and your incomprehensible phrases and sentences," Ruth said.

"I can help you," Höss said.

"You can help me by disappearing," she said. "Piss off."

"This obscenity does not affect me," Höss said.

"This will affect you," Ruth said. She dug her heel into the ground as hard as she could. She dug so hard that her foot hurt. She hoped that Höss's blood vessels, if he still had any, were dilating. She hoped he had an enormous headache. She heard a high-pitched sound, a faint shrill moan, and then a whoosh. It was the sound of a draft or a shifting air stream. Höss was gone. She could feel it. The air was less dense, less viscous. It was easier to breathe. She took several deep breaths. She felt better. She went inside.

❧ *Chapter Nine* ❧

*E*dek and Ruth were standing outside number 23 Kamedulska Street. It was four o'clock. The remnants of a small altercation they had had before leaving the hotel still hung between them. The discord, like most discord, had arisen from something inconsequential. Ruth had ordered a ham sandwich for Edek. She had wanted him to eat something before they went back to Kamedulska Street. She had taken the sandwich to Edek's room. Edek had been reading on the bed. He had hastily pushed some wrappers out of the way when he had answered the door. Ruth had noticed the corner of a cardboard McDonald's container and a large plastic cup on the floor. Several chocolate wrappers were in the wastebasket.

"When did you go to McDonald's?" she had said to Edek.

"An hour ago," Edek said.

"I didn't see you," Ruth said. "I was in the lobby."

"I did go out from the side door," Edek said.

"You shouldn't have gone out without telling me," Ruth said. She said it more sharply than she had intended to.

"What is wrong with you?" Edek had said. "I went just to the McDonald's and back."

"If I had found you not in your room I would have been worried," Ruth said.

"You like to worry," Edek said. "You are such a nervous type."

"Thank you," she had said. "Don't go out again without telling me."

"Okay, okay, do not get so nervous," Edek said.

"And what are you eating junk for?" Ruth had said. "McDonald's is junk."

"If the McDonald's was such rubbish, would they have so many McDonald's?" Edek said. He noticed the ham sandwich Ruth was holding. "I will have this sandwich, too," he had said. "I did get only a small hamburger."

"Jews are not meant to eat hamburgers," Ruth said. "Hamburgers are for goys."

"And ham is for Jews?" Edek had said. Ruth didn't know why she had picked on her father for eating a hamburger. It just didn't seem like the sort of food an eighty-one-year-old should be eating.

The footpath outside 23 Kamedulska Street was strewn with old newspapers and other debris. The mess upset Ruth. She wanted to clean it up. She didn't want litter around this building. She suddenly understood why people tended and cleaned graves. Why they tidied up around tombstones and monuments. But this wasn't a grave—23 Kamedulska Street wasn't a shrine. It was just a site of a former life. It wasn't a mausoleum. There was no one buried or interned here. This building was nothing more than a patchy amalgam of building materials. Nothing of those who had lived here was left. The markings on the walls and floors from fingers and feet were long gone. Rubbed out. There were no sounds from past lives. No smells. There was nothing. This building was no longer attached to her or to Edek. This building was someone else's building. It was just another building, in Łódź.

Still, the mess disturbed her. She wanted to sweep the old leaves that had gathered against the wall. She wanted to get rid of the stubbles of straw and the cigarette butts, and the dust. She kicked a couple of old rags to one side, until they were in front of the building next door. Then she remembered, her grandfather had owned that building, too. She kicked the rags into the gutter. She wanted to get a bucket and a scrubbing brush and scrub the pavement clean. She wanted to get down on her hands and knees and clean the street herself. She told herself that she was being ridiculous.

She had seen other Jews in Poland. Jews like herself. Looking for something that was no longer there. Looking for gravesites of mothers and fathers who were never buried. Looking for monuments and testaments to the existence of people. People who were extinguished without fanfare or comfort. Without prayers. Without tombstones and headstones. Without anyone at their side.

Ruth had met Jews who had traveled to Poland to erect plaques in the birthplace of lost mothers and fathers. Plaques listing the family members who once lived there. In return for permission to put up the plaques, the Jews contributed money. Money for the upkeep of the town square, or money to build a public park. Polish officials were, on the whole, pleased with these arrangements. And so were the Jews. This way they had a site, a marker, a memorial. A place to visit and sit with their dead. A place to pay their respects.

Housing the dead seemed to Ruth to be an essential part of life. She wasn't sure why it was so important. The dead were absent. They were absent regardless of whether their memories were enshrined in a vault or tombstone. Or their names engraved on plaques and monuments. The dead were as absent as they could be. A dwelling place for the dead was really an address for the living. A place where the living could commune with those who were out of reach of regular communication. On the surface the fixtures and fittings of death, such as cemeteries and gravesites, seemed unnecessary. The obstacles to communion with the dead seemed less tangible than the problem of a clearly marked location for the meeting.

Still, she wanted to clean up this particular location. She contemplated hiring someone to keep at least the exterior of 23 Kamedulska Street clean. She decided that that was absurd. What would she be keeping clean? A memory? You couldn't sweep and scrub and wash memories. Memories came with their own degrees of cleanliness and comfort.

"Why can't they keep this place clean?" Ruth said to Edek.

"What for?" he said. "For us? It could be the cleanest street and the cleanest building in all of Poland and it would not make any difference to us."

"They should clean it out of a respect for the memory of those people whose lives they moved into," said Ruth.

"It is too late for respect," Edek said.

Edek was carrying a dozen red roses and a box of Lindt chocolates. A four-pound box of Lindt chocolates. The roses were beautiful. Tall, voluptuous, full-bodied roses. They were a deep red. The color of blood. Her mother had loved roses.

"Mum did like roses very much," Edek said.

"That's exactly what I was thinking," said Ruth.

"We think alike, me and my daughter," Edek said. Ruth thought that Edek must have forgiven her her irritation at his solo outing.

"We do, don't we?" she said. She took the roses from Edek. "You give Mrs. Whatever-her-name-is the chocolates and I'll give her the roses," she said.

They had bought the roses at an open-air market. The market had had a life force that was scarce in Łódź. Rows and rows of brown eggs had suggested a fecundity, a fertility that appeared at odds with the matte gray sky and flat air. Mounds of big round brown onions and bright red potatoes seemed to be bursting with life. The carrots looked strong and orange. Not pale like most city carrots. And the cabbages as big as beach balls seemed almost carnal. The street market had buoyed Ruth's spirits. The people shopping at the market had looked less grim than most of the other residents of Łódź. They had seemed more robust. Almost cheerful.

Ruth and Edek had planned to catch a tram to Kamedulska Street. But all the trams were crowded. And Ruth didn't want to stand in the middle of a crowd of Poles. All of the yellow and white trams in Łódź, were always packed. Packed with dour passengers. All immobile. All frowning. Jammed in on their way to somewhere. Ruth wondered why the trams were always packed. The buses were always crowded, too. Where were all of these Poles going?

"Shall we go inside?" she said to her father.

"We got the flowers and the chocolates," he said. "Why not?"

In the hallway, Ruth was distracted by the ceiling. The ceiling was patched in several places. Large rough patches of brown concrete had been smeared over what must have been cracks and leaks. It was a particularly unpalatable shade of brown. The ceiling looked shit-stained. Patched and repaired with excrement.

"I'm sorry I made you come to Poland," she said to Edek.

"You did not make me," Edek said.

"It was my idea," said Ruth.

"Maybe it was not such a bad idea to see how it looks now," Edek said.

"You're just being nice to me," Ruth said. "I don't feel at all good, in Poland."

"Who would feel good in such a place?" Edek said.

"Looks like not even the Poles," Ruth said. "They don't look like the happiest people on earth, do they?"

"Shoosh," he said to her. "Do not speak like this."

"Nobody in this building understands English, I'm sure," she said. "Anyway, why do we care about offending them? I don't care if I offend them." Edek shook his head and walked up the stairs. "Sorry, Dad," she said. "I know this is not easy for you."

Ruth and Edek stood outside the door of the apartment. Edek must have stood in this very spot so many times in his life, Ruth thought. He was still living there with his mother and father when he was twenty-one and twenty-two. He was there for part of his twenty-third year. Ruth looked at the door of the apartment. She felt a sense of dread. She wished she was back in New York. Back in New York, where the unfamiliar was more familiar than anything here.

"Come on," said Edek. "Let us go in." He knocked loudly on the door. Ruth was surprised by the vehemence in his knock. She thought that she herself wouldn't have had so much boldness in her knock. Her knock would probably have been timid. A timidity designed to hide her rage.

A woman opened the door. At first glance, it appeared as though the woman had an exceptionally large head. Then Ruth realized it was the woman's hair that was huge. Some of this oversized hair was held in place by a scarf. The hair was bright red. The scarf that was attempting to restrain the hair was green. Ruth was disconcerted by both the color coordination and the volume of hair. Elderly women didn't usually possess such unruly hair. And the red and green looked terrible together. Of course, Ruth realized, this red expanse of hair was not growing on the woman's head. It was a wig. It was somebody else's hair. Or maybe it was nylon.

The woman's face was lined and hard. She smiled at them. Her features rearranged themselves for the smile. Her face remained hard. "Come in, come in," she said. Her lips stayed almost fixed while she mouthed a series of obsequious welcome greetings. Ruth felt frightened. She walked behind Edek into the apartment. The old woman looked carefully at the gifts of roses and chocolates, and then handed them to her husband. "Sit down, sit down," she said. She took the rocking chair for herself. Ruth and Edek sat, facing her, on the sofa. It was warm in the apartment. Ruth was shivering. She moved closer to her father. Edek looked at her. "I'm just a bit cold," she said.

"There was nothing in this building," the old woman said. "When I moved here, the whole building was empty." Ruth was startled. How could the woman lie like that? Ruth knew she had understood what the woman had said. "She moved in in early 1940," Ruth said to Edek. "Everything was still here." Edek asked the woman if the building had other tenants when she had arrived. "No one else was here," she said. "The building was empty." The old woman had said this facing Ruth. Ruth tried to hide her expression of disbelief.

"We have a lot of trouble with this building," the woman said. "Nobody will fix anything, as you can see. It is a broken-down building and not worth any money at all."

"I am not at all interested in reclaiming the building, kind madam," Edek said. "What do I want to trouble myself with a building in Łódź for? Please, kind madam, I live in Australia, on the other side of the world. What use would I have for this building?"

"Nobody pays their rents," the old woman said. "So you would not make any money from this building."

"Of course not, madam," Edek said.

"The tenants would pay rent, of course, if someone looked after the repairs needed," she said.

"Of course," Edek said.

"It would not be easy to get this building from the current owner," the old woman said with a sigh. She rolled her eyes. "The owner is a very difficult man."

"Please, please, please," Edek said. "I did not come here to try to reclaim the building." Edek looked at Ruth. "Do you understand what she is saying?" he said.

"I can understand what she's saying," Ruth said.

What were they terrified of? Ruth wondered. If the current landlord was so mean wouldn't anyone else be preferable? Even a Jew? Probably not, she thought. Not if the Jew was around, in person. Maybe that prospect was what was frightening them. The thought of Jews returning was clearly not a palatable thought.

"Tell her this is the last place on earth you'd want to live in," Ruth said to Edek. He ignored her. "I meant, tell her you're committed to your life in Australia. You wouldn't possibly be in a position to move back to Łódź." Edek looked puzzled. "I just want her to know that there's no chance she's going to be surrounded by Jews again."

Edek explained that he was not planning to return. The old woman looked relieved. "Ask her if there wasn't anything small left behind," Ruth said. "Like mezuzahs, or candles or photographs. Tell her you're only interested in those things of no value other than their sentimental value to you." "There was nothing here," the old woman said. "Nothing?" Ruth said to Edek. "That is impossible. No one cleared the apartments out of all of the inconsequential stuff or anything else. A few Gestapo officers might have looked for valuables, but everything else was left just as it was."

"There was not one thing in any of the apartments in this building," the woman said. She was still wearing her scarf. She must keep it on all the time, to contain that wild wig, Ruth thought.

"There were no books, no photographs?" Edek said.

"I have said to you," the woman said, "there was nothing." The old man came out of the kitchen.

"I can vouch for that," he said. "I came not too long after her and the place was completely empty."

Edek winced. Ruth looked at him. His face was contorted.

"Are you all right?" she said.

"I am fine, fine," he said. But he didn't look fine. "I did see, in the corner, a bowl which did belong to my mother," Edek said to her. Ruth looked shocked. "Please," Edek said. "Do not let her see that I saw this."

Ruth looked in the corner. On top of a small chest of drawers was an ornate, engraved oval silver serving dish. She started trembling. "Do not look at it, she will see," Edek said. Ruth tried not to stare at the oval silver bowl.

"There was nothing in this building," the woman said. "The Jews took everything with them."

"So she knew that it was Jews who lived here?" Ruth said. "At least she's admitting something."

As though she had understood what Ruth had just said the old woman said, "Everybody knew this was the Jewish area," to Edek. Ruth thought that her tone must have alerted the old woman to what she was saying.

"Of course, of course," Edek said to the old woman.

"Ask her where all the Jews went." Ruth said. Edek asked.

"The Jews moved to bigger apartments," the woman said.

"Jews are always moving on to bigger and better things," Ruth said to Edek.

"I wasn't here when the Jews moved out," the old man said.

No one appeared to have been there when the Jews moved out, Ruth thought. No Poles at all. Where had they all been when that endless straggling procession of Jews, carting whatever possessions they could, had walked through Łódź? Were the Poles out celebrating? Did they know they would soon be relocating to the dwellings that the Jews were forced to leave? For the poorer Poles, it must have been quite a bonanza, quite a bonus. It must have seemed like Christmas.

"Could we offer to buy the silver serving dish?" Ruth said to Edek.

"Please," Edek said. "Do not look at it. She will see you."

"I'd really like to buy it," Ruth said.

"What for?" said Edek.

"I'd just like to keep it with me," Ruth said. "To hold it and look at it."

"It is not a person," Edek said. "It is just a dish."

"It's probably solid silver," Ruth said.

"My father liked to buy silver for the table for *Shabbes*," Edek said. They were both quiet.

"I didn't know anything about what was happening to the Jews," the old woman said. "I knew nothing myself," the old man said. "I was in Częstochowa."

"It wasn't happening to the Jews of Częstochowa?" Edek said to the old man. Edek looked uncomfortable as soon as he had said this, as though the sentence had propelled itself out of its own accord. Edek shifted uneasily on the sofa. Ruth could see he was distressed at what he had blurted out. She could see that it was far more accusative than he had intended. Ruth smiled at the old man, in an effort to dilute the discomfort. No one spoke.

Ruth diverted her desire to stare at the silver dish by gazing at the front door. A stand was filled with an assortment of hats and something furry. Ruth thought it could have been a large cat. She looked more closely. It was an assortment of wigs. Different colored wigs. Worn-out wigs. One wig slumped on top of the other. Why did anyone need so many wigs? And why leave them on display near the front door? They were so unsightly. A motley moth-eaten collection of wigs. Was the old woman bald? Ruth wondered. Did she grab a wig on her way out of the door in the way that other people picked up a hat? The wigs made Ruth feel a bit sick. The old woman saw Ruth staring at the wigs. Ruth looked away. She didn't want to offend her yet.

"Ask her if there is anyone else in the building who might know of any photographs or other articles left behind," Ruth said to Edek.

"There is nobody else who was there at the time," the old woman said when Edek asked.

"Nobody else," her husband added.

"Jengelef Boleswaf died ten years ago," the woman said.

"Jengelef Boleswaf?" said Edek. "He was our caretaker."

"He lived on the third floor," said the woman.

"He did live in the basement before," Edek said to Ruth.

"So there were no documents, nothing?" Ruth said. Edek talked to the woman for several minutes.

"She does say that every single apartment was empty when she came," he said.

"Oh, well," Ruth said to Edek. "Let's go. There's nothing here for us." She moved and went to stand up.

The old man beckoned her to stay put.

"He is bringing us a cup of tea," Edek said to Ruth.

"Can't we say we don't want it?" she said. She felt exhausted.

Exhausted by the woman's intransigence. Exhausted by the decrepit, depressing, disintegration all around them.

"How do you live in Australia?" the old woman asked Edek.

"Tell her every Jew has a swimming pool, a yacht, and a Mercedes in Australia," Ruth said. Edek laughed despite himself. Edek's laugh reassured Ruth. She calmed down.

It was naive of her, she thought, to think that she would be given anything by these Poles, even a fragment of seemingly inconsequential information. Ruth could see that Edek was depressed by these surroundings, too. "Don't be depressed by this, Dad," she said. "This is not your home. Your home vanished along with all of its occupants. A home is made up of who is in it."

"You are right," Edek said.

The old man brought in the tea. "We'll drink some of the tea and leave," Ruth said to her father. The old man smiled at Ruth. He put the tea and some biscuits on a small table next to Ruth. Six, horseshoe-shaped biscuits were placed on a white plate with a gold, fluted edge. There was a matching teapot, sugar bowl, and milk jug. They had clearly brought out their best china, Ruth thought. The man came back with four matching cups and saucers. He poured Ruth a cup of tea. It was very strong tea. Almost black. Ruth wasn't sure she could stomach such strong tea. She decided that she needed a drink. She turned to Edek to ask him if he could ask for some hot water.

She could see straightaway that something was wrong. Edek looked very pale. Ruth's heart started to pound. "Are you all right, Dad?" she said. He didn't answer her. "Dad," she said, "Are you all right?" A bolt of fear ran through her. How would she get her father to a hospital if he was not well? What was the Polish word for ambulance?

"I am all right," Edek said weakly.

"Are you in pain?" Ruth said. Edek shook his head. He didn't look well. "You sure? You've got no chest pain, no shortness of breath?" Ruth said. Edek shook his head. "No shooting pains in the arms?" Ruth said.

"I am all right," Edek said.

"Let's take you to a doctor," Ruth said.

"I do not need a doctor," said Edek. "I just did get a shock."

"Of course this has been a shock for you," Ruth said. "It's a big shock to be in your own home and see so starkly how everything is gone."

"I knew it was all gone," Edek said. He sounded a bit more like his old self.

"We shouldn't have come," Ruth said. "We knew there was nothing here."

"The teapot and the milk and sugar things did belong to my mother," Edek said. "The spoons, too."

"Oh, no," Ruth said. No wonder Edek had looked ill. She started to cry.

"Do not cry," Edek said. "It is too late to cry."

"My daughter is very emotional," Edek said to the couple. "She gets upset easily."

"Can we leave, Dad?" Ruth said.

"We have not finished the tea," said Edek. He drank his tea while Ruth sat next to him and wept.

"Thank you so much for your hospitality," Edek said to the old man and woman as they were leaving. The old man took Ruth's hand and went to kiss it. She squirmed as his stained brown teeth moved closer to her hand. She pulled her hand away. She tried to smile at the man, but she couldn't stop crying. She wiped her hand on the side of her coat. She wanted to wipe away the man's touch.

Edek and Ruth walked down the stairs. Ruth tried to pull herself together. She shouldn't fall apart like this. She should be looking after her father.

"Do you think she thought you wouldn't recognize the china?" Ruth said to Edek.

"Who knows?" said Edek. "To tell you the truth it did give me a big shock. I remember my mother pouring tea from this teapot many many times."

"It was a beautiful teapot," Ruth said. "The old couple obviously keep it for important occasions."

"We did use this every day," Edek said. "My mother had two sets with twelve cups and plates so that sometimes if the whole family was there, we could all have a cup of tea."

"I can't believe that the old woman served us tea in that service," Ruth said. "Maybe she's had it for so long she really thinks it was always hers. Maybe she's forgotten where she got it from."

"Maybe," said Edek. "It is not worth it to try to think about what she thinks."

They walked down the rest of the stairs. Ruth looked at the backyard. It was barren. Cracked concrete with weeds growing in the cracks. A row of four outhouses were at the back of the yard.

"They was the toilets for the whole building," Edek said. Ruth could smell the toilets.

"Judging by the smell," she said, "they are still being used."

"We did have an inside toilet," Edek said. "Not many people did have an inside toilet." Edek walked over to a corner of the yard. Ruth didn't follow him. She thought she should allow him some time on his own. She walked away from the toilets.

A large brown dog wandered into the yard. Ruth moved away from the dog. The dog followed her.

"There's a dog in the yard," Ruth called out to Edek. "Don't let him get too close to you," she said. Edek turned to look at the dog.

"He is all right," he said to Ruth. "There is nothing to worry about. He is just a dog." Edek was right, Ruth thought. There was no reason to worry about the dog. The dog was much less worrying than the humans around it.

"Shoo," she said to the brown dog. The dog wandered off toward Edek. Edek liked dogs. Edek patted the dog.

Edek had been looking at a small patch of earth at the end of the yard. Ruth had been watching him. What was he thinking about? she thought. His mother's silver dish? His mother's china? The meals that were eaten on the china? The people who were eating the meals?

Ruth heard footsteps behind her. The old man had come out into the yard. He walked up to Edek, shaking his head and shrugging his shoulders. "I told you to be extra nice," he said. "She is not an easy woman!" Ruth understood what he was saying. She was surprised that she could understand.

"The flowers and the chocolates were not enough?" Edek said to the man.

"No," said the old man. Ruth watched her father bite his lips in an effort to suppress a reply from slipping out.

"The chocolates weren't large enough?" Ruth said to her father.

"Not for his wife," Edek said.

"They were the biggest box I could find in Łódź," Ruth said.

"I understand what the man is saying," Edek said.

"So do I," said Ruth.

"We think alike, like usual," Edek said.

"Let's offer him money," said Ruth. "Why shouldn't we?"

"Who knows what we would get for the money." said Edek.

"Probably more lies," said Ruth.

"Why should we pay for lies?" Edek said.

"I've wasted money on lesser things," Ruth said.

"No," said Edek. "I do not want to give them money."

"It's only money," Ruth said. "You're not really giving them anything."

"It would give them pleasure to get money from me," Edek said. "And I do not want to give them this pleasure."

"Okay," she said.

The old man had been looking apprehensively at Edek and Ruth. He looked as though he was trying hard to fathom the tone of their conversation. Ruth thought he had worked out that he was out of luck. That neither Edek nor Ruth was about to hand over a stash of cash. The old man looked bothered.

"My wife is really a very nice woman," he said. "It just takes something extra to put her in a good enough mood to talk."

"Tell him he can drop that shit," Ruth said.

"Please," Edek said. "Do not speak like this." Ruth smiled at the man. She could tell he understood the general tenor of her suggestion. He fidgeted and shifted.

"Maybe a small contribution to our lives?" he said. Edek didn't answer. Instead, he looked at the ground and pushed a piece of loose dirt around with his feet. He looked distracted and distressed.

"A small contribution?" the man said.

"I think we've already contributed enough," Ruth said to Edek, "don't you?" Edek was quiet. "Don't let him get to you," Ruth said to her father.

"He is not getting to me," Edek said. He continued to poke at the piece of earth with his foot.

"What are you doing?" the old man said to Edek. "Looking for Jewish gold? We know they buried their gold."

"You know nothing else," Edek said. "But you know this?"

"I know the Jews buried their gold," the man said.

"So the news of Jewish gold got to Częstochowa?" Edek said. The man nodded. A look of fury crossed Edek's face. "Maybe your wife found this gold?" Edek said. Edek turned to Ruth. "There is nothing here for us," he said. "Let us go."

"You had a cousin who came here after the war?" the old man said to Edek. Edek spun around.

"Suddenly you remember something?" he said.

"You reminded me," said the old man. "A neighbor saw the cousin digging in the yard. Next to this toilet, as a matter of fact." The old man looked pleased with himself. He was grinning in excitement. His grin displayed all of his stained teeth. He looked at the piece of ground. "There's nothing there," he said to Edek. "We already checked."

"You found nothing?" Edek said.

"We found nothing," the old man said.

Edek nodded at the man. His nod contained disbelief, but Ruth thought that the disbelief was largely unnoticed by the old man.

"You don't want to try again with my wife?" he said to Edek.

"No thank you," Edek said.

Edek and Ruth left.

"How did the neighbor know that the cousin was a Jew?" Ruth said as they walked along Kamedulska Street.

"I told you. They can smell us," said Edek.

"How did he know he was a cousin of yours?" Ruth said.

"A neighbor who went to school with my cousin did recognize him," Edek said. "My cousin did tell me this."

"So this old man with his dirty, stained teeth and his air of innocence put two and two together and came up with four," said Ruth.

"What do you mean?" said Edek.

"He worked out that a cousin of the son of the owners must be a cousin of yours," she said.

"I suppose so," said Edek.

"Who was the cousin?" said Ruth.

"It was my cousin Herschel," said Edek. "Herschel did come back to Łódź after the war."

"Where was he during the war?" Ruth asked.

"In a labor camp, in Germany," said Edek.

"Where in Germany?" she said.

"Past Leipzig," Edek said. "Near Chemnitz."

"How was Herschel related to you?" Ruth said.

"He was the son of the sister of my brother Tadek's wife," Edek said.

"He was your sister-in-law's sister's child?" Ruth said.

"Yes," said Edek.

"I don't think he was your cousin then," said Ruth.

"He was my cousin," said Edek.

"Your brother and sister-in-law's child would be your niece or nephew," Ruth said. "And this cousin who came back to Łódź would be their cousin, not your cousin."

"What is wrong with you?" Edek said. "You think about things that it is not necessary to think about. Herschel was my cousin. We grew up together."

"Sorry," Ruth said.

"Herschel did stay in Łódź for one day," Edek said. "It did take him one day to see that nobody was left here and that his life was in danger. Every Pole he did see, in the neighborhood, looked upset to see him. 'I thought that they killed you all,' was what one of his old schoolteachers did say to him."

"What happened to Herschel?" Ruth said.

"He did migrate to America," Edek said. "In 1948. Your mum and me were still in the DP camp in Germany. He was very excited to go to America."

Edek paused. He took a deep breath. "In America Herschel did meet a young girl, a Jew from Poland, too. He wrote to me to say how happy he was. Her name, I think, was Helcha. He did send to us a photograph of him and Helcha. Helcha was, as a matter of fact, already pregnant in the photograph." Edek paused again.

"I didn't know about your cousin Herschel," Ruth said.

"He was already gone before you was born," Edek said.

"Where did he go?" said Ruth.

"He did not go anywhere," Edek said. "He did die. In a car accident. He did not even live long enough to see his son born."

"How terrible," Ruth said. "To survive the Nazis and die in a car crash."
It was illogical, but Ruth thought that surely all of Herschel's suffering
should have protected him against further tragedy. Ruth felt depressed.
Life was so haphazard and unpredictable.

"I did like Herschel very much," Edek said. "He was the only one in my
family what was alive after the war."

"Dad," Ruth said. "Do you think we could buy your mother's china
from those Poles?"

"Forget about it," Edek said.

"I'd really like to have it," said Ruth. "Why should they keep using it?"

"Why not?" Edek said. "Who does it hurt? Nobody."

"Me," she said. "I don't want them to have it, firstly, and then secondly,
I'd really like to have the set myself. It would be very meaningful to me to
have tea from the teapot and sugar from the sugar bowl that your mother
used."

"What sort of meaning does some pieces of china have?" Edek said.

"A lot of meaning, for me," said Ruth.

"Forget about it," he said. "I do not want to go back there. For me, it is
finished everything what was there."

They walked back to the Grand Victoria in silence. Edek looked tired.
"Would you like some dinner in your room tonight?" she said to him.

"That is not such a bad idea," he said.

"It's been a big day," Ruth said.

"You can say that again, brother," Edek said.

When they got back to the Grand Victoria, Ruth ordered some barley
soup, a *schnitzel*, and a slice of chocolate cake to be sent up to Edek's
room. She wasn't hungry herself. Her head was swimming with images of
the old man's teeth, and the pile of wigs, and the gold-edged china. She
thought about Herschel, who got to America in order to die, and the general disarray and disorder of the universe. It was enough to take anyone's
appetite away.

Ruth sat on the bed in her room. The room felt airless and depressing.
She was finding it hard to breathe. She used to have trouble taking deep
breaths. Her breath felt shallow now. This was an anxiety symptom, she

had discovered, that appeared when she was trying to contain her anger or her excitement. Her breathing felt labored. It definitely wasn't excitement she was suppressing at the moment.

She decided to have a cup of tea in the lobby. Before she went down she called Edek. He sounded more settled. He had almost reached the end of *The One-Armed Alibi*, he said, and was about to begin *The Hot-Blooded Heiress*.

"I hope that *The Hot-Blooded Heiress* is good," Ruth said to him.

"It does not matter if it is good or not," Edek said. "When I read it, I am living every word." Ruth thought that the words in *The Hot-Blooded Heiress* would probably be a lot more comfortable for Edek than the words he had had to hear in Kamedulska Street today.

"I'll see you in the morning," she said to Edek. In the lobby she ordered herself a chamomile tea with lemon and some bread and jam. Plum jam. The Poles made very good plum jam.

Ruth thought about her grandmother's china again. The teapot and sugar bowl and milk jug. She had never thought of herself as having a grandmother. It was strange to think of her grandmother's china. The fact that there was also a matching plate suggested that it must have been part of a dinner service. It must have been a stunning dinner set. The china was very fine and the gold fluting around the edge of the plate was unusual enough to have made it an idiosyncratic choice of tableware. Ruth wondered who had chosen it. Her grandmother? It must have been an expensive purchase. Did women choose those things then? Or did the men buy them?

The silver bowl that Edek had pointed out looked very solid. That must have been expensive, too. It was strange to think of these sophisticated and luxurious accoutrements of everyday life as coming from her own family. She had grown up poor. She had grown up knowing that there were no family heirlooms. No legacies. No bequests or requests. No family recipes. No words of advice or pieces of wisdom. It was very strange to think of these pieces of china as part of her past.

Ruth wondered if there was more china than the pieces she had been shown. She thought that the old woman must have known that Edek would recognize the tea set and the silver bowl. But why would the old woman want that? Was the china a carrot? A bait? Was Edek supposed to offer to buy it? Did the old couple fantasize about the amount of money an old Jew would pay to retrieve something from his former life? Or was the old woman simply flaunting her ownership of the stolen goods? Surely if the old woman had anticipated a sale, she would have given Edek and Ruth some indication of her expectation. Some grounds to begin a negotiation. But there had been no sign that the old woman or her husband knew that what they were serving up was an invitation.

Ruth didn't know what to do. She didn't want to upset Edek by suggesting that they return to Kamedulska Street. Yet she wanted the china and the silver bowl. She wanted them badly. She wanted to touch them. To hug them. To hold them to her. She knew they were only inert objects, but they had been held and touched by all the people that she would never be able to hold and touch. They had been touched by her grandmother and grandfather. They had been held and touched by cousins and uncles and aunties. She wanted to hold and touch them, too.

"Excuse me," a woman's voice said. Ruth jumped. She had been completely immersed in her thoughts. "I'm sorry to disturb you," the woman said. Ruth looked up. It was the blond woman who had been staring at her yesterday at breakfast. The woman was smiling at her now. "I saw you yesterday," the woman said. "You were having breakfast with your husband."

"My father," Ruth said. "I was having breakfast with my father. I'm not married. I don't have a husband. I don't have a boyfriend. I support myself. I don't need a man to support me or travel with me." Ruth was startled at her own response. Why was she being so snappy to a perfect stranger?

"I'm sorry," the woman said.

"No, I'm sorry," said Ruth. "I've just had a rough few days and my nerves are a bit on edge. I guess not many daughters travel with their fathers. It's easy to mistake a father for a husband." Ruth patted her hair. She felt disheveled. As though her snarled and tangled thoughts had disarranged her appearance.

"My father is forty years older than me, though," she said.

"I assumed you had married an older man," the woman said. "Your father is very cute."

"I think that, too, some of the time," Ruth said.

"I hope you don't mind me introducing myself," the woman said. "My name is Martina Schmidt."

"Ruth Rothwax," Ruth said. She stood up and extended her hand to the woman. They shook hands.

"Do you mind if I join you for a moment?" Martina Schmidt asked.

"Not at all," Ruth said. "Please, sit down." They both sat down. "I noticed you at breakfast," Ruth said, "not just because you were staring at me, but because everything about you said that you didn't come from Łódź."

Martina Schmidt laughed. She was really very pretty, Ruth thought. "I teach here," Martina said. "I teach at the film school. This is my last semester, and then I go back to Germany, to Berlin. I was staring at you because I couldn't believe that I was seeing you, again."

"Seeing me again?" Ruth said.

"I was on the same flight as you from New York to Warsaw," Martina Schmidt said. "I was two rows behind you, on your right."

A vague recollection of someone staring at her came to Ruth. She had worked for most of the transatlantic flight. She had known that she was immersing herself in work in order to stave off an already increasing apprehension about arriving in Poland.

"I'm sorry I didn't notice you," Ruth said.

"You were busy," Martina said.

"Can I order something for you?" said Ruth. "I'm in need of comfort, so I'm having the ultimate comfort food, bread and jam." Martina laughed. "I like bread and jam very much myself," she said. "Most Germans do. We eat more bread than any other European country. We make three hundred varieties of bread and we eat nearly two hundred pounds of bread a year per person. During the years after World War II when other food was not so available, we ate three hundred and ten pounds a year for every man, woman, and child in Germany."

Ruth laughed. "I didn't know that," she said. She instinctively liked Martina Schmidt. Anyone who could come up with those statistics had to be an interesting person.

"There is a German saying," Martina said, " 'He who dishonors bread dishonors life.' "

"Really?" said Ruth. She thought it would be inappropriate to comment on the irony of Germans honoring life. She called the porter.

"I will have a vodka," Martina said to the porter. "I am ordering a comfort of a different sort," she said to Ruth. "It is my birthday today."

"Happy Birthday," Ruth said.

"Thank you," Martina said. "I was not feeling at all happy. This is my fortieth birthday and I am again alone."

"I didn't even notice my fortieth birthday," Ruth said.

"It is not so much that I will be forty," Martina said. "But it is the fact that once more I am alone on my birthday."

"Alone is not such a bad way to be," Ruth said. "It's much better than being with the wrong person."

"I have spent many birthdays on my own," Martina said.

"Why?" said Ruth. "You're very beautiful and you work in a glamorous field—the film industry."

Martina laughed. "I'm not interested in my students, especially the Polish ones."

"I can understand that," Ruth said. "Not the not finding students attractive, but the not finding Polish students attractive." Ruth looked at Martina. She thought Martina might have viewed that remark as too openly anti-Polish. But Martina laughed.

"It is true that Polish people are not the most attractive people in the world," she said. "But at the film school, I think we have some of the nicest and most interesting of them. Still I am very glad to be leaving Łódź."

"It's a pretty depressing city, isn't it?" Ruth said.

"Very depressing," Martina said. "Especially for women. Polish men think that all women find all of them very attractive. They look upon women as a combination of a decoration and a servant. I think the servant part is more important to them than the decoration."

"You qualified in the decorative terms but failed in servitude, did you?" Ruth said.

"Yes, very much so," said Martina.

The porter arrived with the vodka. Martina held up her glass.

"Cheers," she said. Ruth raised her teacup. "Cheers," she said. She looked at Martina. Martina was beaming. Ruth suddenly felt happy. An inexplicable happiness spread through her. Suddenly Łódź didn't seem so leaden. So lifeless.

"Why have you spent so many birthdays on your own?" Ruth said. "If you don't mind me asking the question."

"I don't mind," Martina said. "I was in love with someone for a long time. And it is not so easy to switch your love from one person to another."

"Of course not," said Ruth.

"I was staring at you, in the plane, because you reminded me of someone," Martina said.

"It's these standard-issue Jewish-Polish looks I have," said Ruth. "We all look alike."

"You are Jewish?" Martina said.

"Yes," Ruth said. "I thought it was obvious."

"Not to me," Martina said. "You looked so familiar and yet I could not place where I had seen you."

"You had seen me before?" said Ruth.

"I thought I had," said Martina. "It wasn't just the way you looked, it was something else about you. When I got off the plane, it hit me, it was the way you were moving your leg."

"Oh, no," Ruth said. "I didn't think my leg movements were so obvious."

"It was not so obvious to other people, I am sure," Martina said. "But the movements were in groups of ten. Each time you tapped your foot, you did ten taps."

"You were counting?" said Ruth.

"Almost unconsciously," Martina said. "You see, the person I was so in love with also tapped his foot like this."

"Really?" said Ruth.

"It was my husband," Martina said. "And when I realized that it was the leg movements that were familiar to me, I also realized who you reminded me of. My husband."

"I look like your husband?" Ruth said. She felt vaguely offended about resembling somebody's husband.

Martina laughed. "Of course he is not beautiful like you," she said. "But he is very good-looking. I shouldn't call him my husband really. He is no longer my husband. He is my ex-husband. When I realized who it was that you reminded me of, I tried to find you, but you had already left the airport."

"Why did you want to find me?" Ruth said.

"I don't know," Martina said. "Somehow it was this movement with your legs. My ex-husband does exactly the same. It irritates everyone he knows."

"Lots of people have nervous mannerisms that are similar, I guess," Ruth said.

"When I saw you in the hotel," Martina said, "I couldn't believe my eyes. I had been thinking about Gerhard, my husband, my ex-husband, and then you appeared."

"Did you come here tonight looking for me?" Ruth said.

Martina looked surprised. "How do you know this?" she said.

"Just a guess," Ruth said. "Why did you want to see me?"

"I don't know," Martina said. "Do you mind?"

"Not at all," said Ruth. "I was feeling quite miserable, and I feel much better now. I'm sorry I'm not Gerhard."

"It is over between me and Gerhard," Martina said. "But you do look very much like him. I wish I had a photograph of him. You would be very surprised yourself, at this resemblance."

"I've seen lots of people I thought I looked like," Ruth said.

"Really?" said Martina.

"They're all dead," said Ruth. "I had no relatives other than my mother and father. All of their families were murdered by the Nazis."

"I am so very sorry," Martina said. She looked overwhelmed.

"I didn't tell you so you would feel sorry for me," Ruth said. "I was just explaining to you that I see images of myself in photographs of Jews, in Poland, before the war."

"I was not saying sorry because I felt sorry for you," Martina said. "I was saying sorry for what we did to you. But perhaps it is better to say nothing. Sorry is not the right word for this sort of apology." Martina stopped talking. "Would you like me to leave?" she said to Ruth.

"Because you're German?" Ruth said. "Of course not."

"I am very sorry," Martina said.

"You didn't do anything," Ruth said.

"Neither did the Jews," said Martina.

They sat in the lobby in silence for a minute or two. "Is this the reason you are in Poland?" Martina said.

"Yes," said Ruth. "My father and I are looking for something. At least I'm looking for something, and he agreed to come here with me."

"What are you looking for?" Martina said.

"I don't know," Ruth answered.

It was the truth. She didn't know what she was doing here. She didn't know why she had dragged her father here. Why she had wanted to be here with him. Was she looking for something? If she was, what was it? She seemed to have found some china. Was that what she came here for? She didn't think so.

"Maybe you have heard of my ex-husband?" Martina said. "He is a playwright. Quite well known in Germany. Gerhard Schmidt. He writes about Jews?"

Ruth shook her head. "I'm sorry," she said. "I haven't heard of him."

"He is really only well known in Germany." Martina said. "Many people think he is obsessed with the Jews."

"Germans might think that any thought about Jews is excessive," Ruth said.

"Perhaps," said Martina.

"Why did you split up if you were so in love with him?" Ruth said.

"I was too German for him," Martina said.

"But he's German, isn't he?" Ruth said.

"Yes," she said. "But he doesn't like Germans. He doesn't like any Germans. I felt sorry for his parents. They gave him everything money could buy. And still he was not happy with them. He called his mother and father anti-Semites."

"Were they?" Ruth said.

"I don't think so," said Martina. "They are very kind people."

"The kindest Germans could be anti-Semitic," Ruth said.

"I suppose so," said Martina.

Ruth wasn't sure if a German who called his parents anti-Semitic was any better than any other kind of German.

"Gerhard is wonderful," Martina said. "But he is tormented. His new play is about a wealthy German who finds he was adopted as a child. He turns on his parents until they admit he was adopted from Jews. Gerhard's mother is ninety-three. She couldn't stop crying when she saw that play. Gerhard's trouble is that he wishes he was a Jew."

"I'd agree that that is troubling," Ruth said.

"It is a very strange thing," Martina said.

"Maybe all writers are strange," said Ruth.

"He was always telling me how German I was," Martina said. "Of course I was German. I am German. He made me feel bad about being a German. I can't do anything about the fact that I am a German."

"Of course not," said Ruth. "You can't suddenly become Nigerian."

Martina laughed. "Gerhard wished that he was a Jew from the time he was a boy," she said. "His parents thought it was a teenage rebellion. But he is fifty-two now, and he is still the same. He still wants to be a Jew."

"Lots of Jews would hand their Jewishness over to him," Ruth said. "Lots of Jews aren't thrilled to be Jewish. If he wants to be a Jew why doesn't he convert?"

"He doesn't want to be a Jew in the religious sense," Martina said. "He wants to be a Jew in the cultural and traditional sense."

"That does sound a bit crazy," Ruth said.

"I think his parents were not strict enough with him when he was a child," Martina said. "They treated him like he was made from glass. He was very ill when he was a baby and I think that made them very nervous of him."

"Why did you love him?" Ruth said.

"I loved him because I saw a sadness in him that I thought I could take away," Martina said. "And for a few years, I think I took that sadness away." She looked miserable. "Gerhard is a very fine, very talented, wonderful man," she said. "He just fell out of love with me because I am German. For two years I dyed my hair brown so I would not look so German. But it was not enough. It was like a sickness with him. 'We can't change what we are,' I said to him. 'We can try,' he said. I don't know why Gerhard was so unhappy with what he was," Martina said. "He had everything. He had the love of two devoted parents. He had money. The Schmidts were very rich." She paused. She looked sad.

"He doesn't sound very attractive," Ruth said.

"That's the trouble," Martina said. "If he was a terrible person I wouldn't have loved him. But he is not, he is wonderful."

Women were crazy, Ruth thought. They could justify any amount of intolerable behavior, in the name of love.

"People thought I married Gerhard for his money," Martina said. "But I didn't, I married him for his sadness."

"Why do women do that?" Ruth said. "Why are they suckers for sadness?"

"I don't know," said Martina.

"Men don't feel that way," Ruth said. "Men don't find themselves gravitating to sadness, do they?"

"I think not," said Martina, and she laughed at the thought.

It was a strange thought. Ruth imagined groups of men banding together to scour the world looking for sad women.

"Men are looking for cheerfulness, I think," Ruth said. She thought that, on the whole, she had done pretty well for a cheerless person. She had had three husbands. Maybe she wasn't all that cheerless. Whatever she was, she thought, she was sure that she fell quite a bit short of cheerful.

"What a strange story," Ruth said to Martina.

"It is very strange," said Martina. "Gerhard looks Jewish."

"Do his parents?" Ruth said.

"No, not at all," Martina said.

"I think you're better off without him," Ruth said.

"I miss him," Martina said. "He was clever, and witty and sensitive."

"There are not that many clever, witty and sensitive men around," Ruth said. "But why did you have to choose a German who wanted to be a Jew?"

Gerhard sounded bizarre, Ruth thought. Although maybe it wasn't so bizarre. She herself almost avoided Jews. She belonged to no Jewish groups or organizations. She never went to synagogue. She felt nervous on those rare occasions when she had been in a group of Jews. Groups of Jews seemed dangerous, to her. They were so blunt. So direct. They asked questions and questioned answers. They drew attention to themselves. As though that was not dangerous. American Jews seemed less aware of the peril of being Jewish.

All of her life Ruth had chosen non-Jewish friends. Waspish men and women she had felt safe with. Safe from what? She didn't know. It was often a struggle to maintain the friendships. Ruth felt that she was too intense, too intrusive, too curious, too extreme for the moderate and restrained friends she chose. She was too much for these non-Jews. She saw it in their responses and their expressions and their gestures. In the last few years she had tried to make friends with some Jews.

She had married non-Jews, too. Edek and Rooshka had been bothered by this when Ruth had married her first husband. By the time Ruth had left husband number two, her parents were more concerned with the turnover in husbands than the husband's particular religion. The fact that Garth wasn't Jewish didn't bother Edek at all. Ruth's two divorces seemed to have rendered obsolete Edek's desire for a Jewish partner for her. Edek just wished Ruth could stay married. Ruth couldn't imagine being married to a Jew. Jewish men seemed soft to her. She thought that, possibly, she had a counterphobic attraction to Gentiles. That seemed as lunatic to her as any of Gerhard Schmidt's actions.

"My mother was very upset when I left Gerhard," Martina said. "She thought he was wonderful. She said that most marriages are not perfect so why should I expect perfection? She could not accept that I knew that Gerhard no longer loved me. My mother adored him. She liked his concerns with Jewish people."

"Well, she must be unusual for a German," Ruth said. She hoped she wasn't being offensive.

"When I was growing up," Martina said, "we had people from Israel staying with us. Five or six times a year guests from Israel would arrive. My mother never explained anything about these visitors to me, but I somehow got the impression that we personally had done something terrible to these people."

"Where did your mother find the Israelis?" Ruth said.

"I don't know," said Martina. "They would just appear. We lived in Munich at the time."

"How weird," said Ruth.

"I felt responsible myself," Martina said. "I remember saying I was very sorry to one woman. She seemed an older woman to me but maybe she was only about forty. She patted me on the head and said, 'You have nothing to be sorry for. You did not do anything to us.' I thought she was only being nice to me."

"I think it must have been tough for so many German children who were born after the war," Ruth said. "It must be a terrible burden to wonder what evil your mother or father or your grandparents might have perpetrated. It must make adolescence and the subsequent separation of children from their parents very complicated." Martina nodded.

"Did anyone else you knew have Jewish people to stay?" Ruth said.

"No," Martina said. "At school the others didn't even know what a Jew was. I worried for many years that my mother and father must have done something very wrong to many people," Martina said.

"I doubt it," Ruth said. "If they had, they wouldn't have been trying to make up for it."

"That is not quite logical," Martina said.

"It's logical enough," said Ruth.

She didn't want to dwell on this subject. "My parents didn't want me to leave either of my husbands," she said. "They preferred me to be married in a less than perfect marriage, than unmarried. They saw an unmarried female as being in a very imperfect state."

"I'm afraid so do I," Martina said. "I know it is not very modern or progressive of me to think this way."

"You'll find someone else," Ruth said. "You're so gorgeous. You won't be on your own for long."

"Thank you," said Martina. "I think my attitude toward marriage comes from my mother," she said. "She believed in love forever. She is still mourning my father, who has been dead for eleven years."

"Your mother is a widow?" Ruth said.

She liked the sound of Martina's mother. Maybe Martina's mother would like to meet Edek? Ruth suddenly realized the drawback to this potential matchmaking. Martina Schmidt's mother was German. She wasn't sure Edek would be interested in a German woman, even a German who felt sympathetic to Jews. It was hard enough for Ruth to get her father to agree to meet any woman, let alone a German. Maybe Martina Schmidt's mother wouldn't really be keen to meet a Jew as a potential partner either.

"Do you have children from your marriages?" Martina said.

"No," Ruth said.

"Neither do I," said Martina. "I saw from the beginning that it is very difficult to have a working life and to have children. I watched my mother struggle. She was a schoolteacher but she felt all the time that she was not paying enough attention to me. And I always went to the same school where she was teaching."

"What do you get back when you have a child?" Ruth said. "As far as I can see, you get very little. It's not like the old days when children eventually supported you."

Martina laughed. "You are right," she said. "Not many children today think about supporting their parents."

"All over New York," Ruth said, "parents are paying large sums of money for their children to be able to complain about them. They pay therapists every month for this privilege. Why pay money for someone to unravel what you've done to them? Why not avoid doing it in the first place?"

"In Germany, it is not quite like this," Martina said. "But it is beginning. Middle-class parents are beginning to look to therapy as a solution for their children."

"It is no sacrifice to choose a career over children," Ruth said. "Those women who think it is have clearly never had children."

"Gerhard said something very similar to this when we first met," said Martina. "I thought it was a very refreshing view for a man. You would like Gerhard very much. You would recognize something about yourself in him. I cannot explain exactly what."

"I hope I'm not as confused and demented as Gerhard sounds," Ruth said.

"He is confused, but not demented," Martina said.

"Which foot does he tap?" Ruth said.

"His right foot," Martina said. Ruth was very quiet. What a peculiar mixture of events and circumstances she was encountering, she thought. Here she was, in Łódź, hearing about a middle-aged German man who resembled her and tapped his right foot ten times. And wished he was a Jew. Life was strange. She decided against asking Martina if she knew what occasioned the right-footed taps of her ex-husband.

"Maybe I will meet someone else," Martina said. "A fortune-teller told me that I would live to a very old age and die in good humor."

"What a great prediction," Ruth said. "I wouldn't mind a prediction like that."

"She also said I would marry someone who was not what he thought he was," Martina said.

"So you acted out her prophecy," Ruth said. "You married a German who thought he was a Jew."

"Or a Jew who thinks he is a German?" Martina said.

"His mother would have to be Jewish for Gerhard to be a Jew," Ruth said. "So I don't think he could be Jewish."

"His mother is a devout Roman Catholic," Martina said.

"Poor Gerhard is going to have to adjust to the fact that he's not Jewish," Ruth said. "With a Roman Catholic mother he couldn't be Jewish."

Martina sighed. "Who knows what happened in those times." She looked distressed.

"Would you like another vodka?" Ruth said.

"Yes, I very much would," said Martina.

Ruth ordered the vodka. She looked at her watch. It was getting late. She should go to bed, soon.

"Gerhard was looking for somebody," Martina said. "And it was not me."

"We're all looking for somebody or something, I guess," Ruth said.

"But Gerhard was convinced there was a particular person for him," Martina said. "Somebody who was trying to find him. A numerologist told him he was looking for a number eight. The day he came home and told me that, I knew our marriage was over. I was too German and I was a number nine."

"You don't believe in that stuff, do you?" Ruth said.

"I'm not sure," said Martina. "What number are you?"

"I don't know," said Ruth. "How does anyone know what number they are?"

"You add up the numbers of your birth date," Martina said. Her vodka arrived. She drank it down in one large swallow.

"I am an eight," Ruth said.

"Maybe Gerhard is looking for you?" Martina said.

Ruth started to laugh. "I'm a Jew who doesn't want to associate with Jews," she said. "We'd be a perfect match. He could be my Aryan and I could be his Jew." They both laughed.

In mid-laugh, Ruth started to feel sick. Her head started swimming and she began to sweat. She leaned forward and lowered her head. Sweat dripped from her forehead. She was so hot. She could feel perspiration running down her back. Her legs felt hot. She could see damp patches appearing on her maroon panty hose. What was happening to her? Where was this fierce heat coming from?

"What is wrong?" Martina said.

"I'm just overtired," Ruth said. She had to get to her bed, she thought. She would feel better in bed.

Martina handed her a handkerchief. She realized she was trembling. "I've never had anything like this happen to me," she said.

Martina put her arm around Ruth. "It must be difficult for you to be here with your father," she said to Ruth. Ruth sat up slowly. She felt a bit better.

"Maybe this is an early symptom of menopause?" she said to Martina. "An unexpected dip in estrogen, a hot flash."

"How old are you?" Martina said.

"Forty-three," said Ruth.

"Forty-three is surely too early for menopause," Martina said. Ruth knew that, on average, women first experienced menopausal symptoms between the ages of forty-five and forty-seven. She had read a lot about menopause. She also knew that menopause seemed to take most women by surprise. Most women seemed to be shaken by the arrival of menopausal symptoms.

"Maybe I'm precocious," she said to Martina.

"You are shaking," Martina said.

"I'm feeling much better," said Ruth.

"This happened when we were talking about numerology. About the number eight," Martina said.

"It has nothing to do with that," Ruth said. "How can a number affect anything?" She had stopped sweating. She was feeling much better. This was probably nothing but tiredness. She had only just had her annual medical checkup. The blood and stool and urine tests had all been fine, her physician, Dr. Cooke, had said to her. "You are in great shape," he had said. "I'd better touch wood," she had said to him, as she reached for the parquetry floorboard.

"I hope I did not talk too much about myself," Martina said.

"Not at all," Ruth said. "I've really enjoyed your company. I'm just over-tired. I'll go to bed and I'll be fine in the morning."

"I came here because you reminded me of Gerhard," Martina said. "But I am so glad to have met you. It was very enjoyable."

"For me, too," Ruth said. "Even though I broke out in a sweat. I know that it is only fatigue." Both women stood up.

"I'm going back to Berlin tomorrow," Martina said.

"Good luck there," said Ruth.

She wanted to ask Martina for her address and phone number in Berlin, but she was overtaken by a shyness that surprised her. Martina looked slightly awkward, too. It was the awkwardness that often occurred in the aftermath of an unexpected intimacy. The sudden embarrassment that could accompany the conscious acknowledgment of the familiarity that had just taken place. It was similar to the stiltedness and discomfort of sur-facing with an unfamiliar sexual partner when the sex and the heat had subsided. She really should ask Martina for her address, Ruth thought. But she couldn't. She felt exhausted. And sticky. She wanted to kiss Martina good-bye. But she felt too clammy to kiss anybody. She held out her hand to Martina. They shook hands. Ruth went up to her room. She was too tired to shower. She lay down on the bed and fell asleep.

Edek was already eating his breakfast when Ruth arrived in the hotel's din-ing room. "I did start," he said to Ruth. "I hope you do not mind."

"Of course I don't mind, Dad," she said. "I'm glad to see you enjoying your breakfast."

"It is not that I enjoy it," Edek said. "It is that I have to eat something. I been up since four o'clock."

"You couldn't sleep," she said.

"I could not sleep," he said.

"It's a pretty disturbing trip, isn't it?" Ruth said.

"I am all right," Edek said.

Ruth looked at what Edek was eating. His plate was crammed. He had four sausages, a small mountain of bacon, and what appeared to be a three- or four-pound slab of scrambled eggs on his plate.

"That looks good," she said.

"I did take too much," Edek said.

"You don't have to eat it all," Ruth said. "Just enjoy whatever you want of it."

"I am not enjoying," Edek said. "I am eating a breakfast." He looked disgruntled.

Ruth went to the buffet and chose some breakfast for herself.

"You eating that stuff again?" Edek said.

"The muesli, you mean?" Ruth said.

"The stuff what is for birds," Edek said.

"I like it," said Ruth.

"No wonder you don't look so good," Edek said. "This is for birds, or maybe for a mouse or even a fish. But not for a person. A person has to have a breakfast."

Edek leaned across the table and peered into Ruth's bowl. His head almost touched the muesli. He stared at it with concentration. As though if he looked long enough the individual grains of oats and seeds and fruit might speak up and explain themselves.

"The muesli would be too big for fish," Ruth said.

"It would be good for big fish," said Edek. He shook his head and returned to his scrambled eggs. Ruth looked at her father. He looked tired to her. Or maybe she was so tired that everyone looked tired to her.

Edek was wearing his parka at breakfast. He had had the beige-colored parka on every day. Whether he was inside or outside. She looked more closely at Edek. He was wearing the same navy knit top he had arrived in Warsaw in. Ruth wondered if he had worn it every day. She hadn't noticed what he had been wearing under his parka.

"Have you been changing your clothes, Dad?" she said.

"Of course," he said, and continued to eat.

"Weren't you wearing that top and those trousers when you arrived in Warsaw?" Ruth said.

"Yes," Edek said.

"Have you worn them every day?" she said.

"Yes," he said.

"So what are you changing?" Ruth said.

"What difference does it make to you what I wear?" Edek said.

"I just want to know," said Ruth.

"I did change my *gatkes,*" Edek said. *Gatkes* was the Yiddish word for underpants.

"I should hope so," Ruth said, and then felt queasy. Why were they discussing her father's underpants over breakfast?

She took two Mylanta tablets out of her bag and put them in her mouth.

"What are you doing?" Edek said.

"I'm having some Mylanta," she said. "I don't feel well."

"This Mylanta does make you better?" he said.

"Sometimes," she said.

"You need to eat something," Edek said. "Tablets and stuff what a fish would not eat is not a breakfast. It is not normal. Have some eggs."

"I'll have some eggs tomorrow," she said, and grimaced as she chewed the last of the peppermint-flavored indigestion pills. She knew it was odd to chew antacid tablets for stress, but sometimes they made her feel better. Relieved her queasiness.

Edek had finished the food on his plate. "Maybe I will have a small piece of bread with jam," he said.

"Have you changed your socks?" Ruth said.

"I did change them on Saturday," he said. "What is wrong with you? To talk about my socks when we eat our breakfast? Clean or dirty socks is not something to talk about during a breakfast."

"I wanted you to feel better," Ruth said. "I thought you'd feel better if you had clean clothes."

Edek looked at Ruth. He looked annoyed. "You have every day everything clean," he said. "Every day something else. A black skirt with a pleat one day, a black skirt without a pleat one day. A black dress with a piece of something in the front in the morning, a black dress without a piece of something in the front in the afternoon. A black coat with something on the collar yesterday, the day before a black coat with nothing on the collar. And all this black stuff is very expensive. My daughter does not like to put on something which costs less than fifty dollars."

"You can't get anything for less than fifty dollars today," Ruth said. Why was her father picking on her? He must be stressed, she thought.

"I got shoes for twenty dollars," Edek said. He stuck his foot out from under the table. "And these shoes was not the cheapest shoes. They did have a pair for ten dollars."

"Made out of cardboard?" Ruth said.

"Made from leather," said Edek. "Real leather."

"I paid three hundred dollars for these shoes," Ruth said, and lifted her leg to show Edek the plain black lace-up shoes she was wearing.

"Crazy," snorted Edek. "They look like those shoes what you did wear to school."

"That's why they're three hundred dollars," Ruth said. "They're an imitation of the shoes that schoolgirls wear. I love them. When I look at them I remember how I felt in my University High School uniform."

"Those shoes what you did wear to school was brown," Edek said.

"I can't believe you remember that," said Ruth.

"I remember many things," said Edek.

Ruth looked at her shoes. They were Prada. She had bought them on sale. Reduced from over four hundred dollars.

"I can get you such shoes from Melbourne for twenty dollars," Edek said.

"You couldn't," said Ruth. "Nothing costs twenty dollars anymore, not even chewing gum."

"You are crazy," said Edek.

"Maybe I am," she said.

"It is not normal," Edek said, "to buy shoes for three hundred dollars."

"You buy gadgets," Ruth said. Edek looked hurt.

"You tell me to spend money," he said. "And I buy only stuff what is useful for you."

Ruth felt sorry for him. He looked wounded. She hadn't meant to wound him.

"That's true, Dad," she said. "Sorry, I'm just tired."

"You want me to put on such clean clothes every day to feel better," Edek said. "I feel fine. You do not look so fine."

Ruth knew she looked bad. She had showered and put on clean clothes, but she still felt crumpled. She'd slept in her clothes last night. She had been shocked when she had woken up and discovered this. She had fallen asleep in her clothes, on top of the faded bedspread that covered the bed. She hadn't removed the eyeliner she wore under her eyes or cleansed her skin with cleansing milk. She hadn't washed her face or brushed her teeth. She had just fallen asleep. Falling asleep like that, unprepared and unaware, was something she hadn't done since she was fifteen or sixteen. This morning she had shaved her legs, scrubbed her face, and rubbed toning lotion over her body, but she couldn't feel uncrumpled. She straightened the collar of her shirt.

"You do not look so good," Edek said. "I think it is too much for you to be in Poland."

"I'm really glad to be in Poland with you, Dad," she said. "Really glad."

"Maybe five days in Łódź is too much," said Edek.

"Is it too much for you?" Ruth said.

"Not for me," Edek said. "I can take anything. But it is, I think, too much for you."

"Okay," she said. "We can go to the Orbis office and change the date of our train tickets to Kraków. Let's leave on Wednesday instead of Thursday."

"Wednesday?" Edek said. "Today it is Monday, that is another two days."

"Do you want to leave even earlier?" Ruth said.

"Not me," said Edek. "I came here to be with you. We will stay till when you want to stay."

"I'd like to go to the Jewish Center today, then the ghetto and the Jewish Cemetery tomorrow," Ruth said.

"The ghetto and the cemetery?" Edek said.

"I think it will be very interesting," Ruth said.

"If you say so," said Edek.

"Maybe we'll do the cemetery today," Ruth said.

"Is the train tickets expensive?" Edek said.

"No, they're very cheap," she said. "Train travel in Poland is extremely cheap. We can go and change the tickets after breakfast."

"We have to go by train?" Edek said.

"I thought it would be better than flying," Ruth said. "We'll be able to see the countryside."

"We did see the country, already," Edek said. "When we was in the Mercedes."

"Would you rather fly?" Ruth said.

"I will go whichever way you do choose," Edek said.

"What would you prefer?" she said.

"It is all the same to me," he said.

Ruth knew that there was something behind Edek's query about the price of the train tickets but she couldn't figure out what. She decided to ask him about it later.

"Do you still want some bread and jam?" she said.

"I will have just a little piece," Edek said.

"I'll get it," Ruth said. She got up and walked to the buffet.

"Apricot and plum," Edek called out to her. She got some jam for Edek and some fruit compote for herself.

She watched her father eat his bread and jam. He clearly loved it. He spooned large spoonfuls of jam onto each bite of bread. It cheered her up to see his hearty appetite.

"It's good jam, isn't it?" she said.

"Very good," he said. Her father really was in very good shape for an eighty-one-year-old, she thought. She should be really grateful for that.

"You look great, Dad," Ruth said. "You look years younger than you are."

"I know," said Edek. "Everybody does say this."

"You shouldn't be on your own," Ruth said. "You should be with somebody."

"I am with somebody," Edek said. "I am with you."

"You know what I mean," Ruth said. "A partner, company, somebody to go out with."

"Do not start with this, please," Edek said.

Ruth suddenly thought of Martina Schmidt's widowed mother. Martina's mother, if she was half as gorgeous as her daughter, would probably appeal to Edek. Edek loved a blonde. So did most Jews. Most elderly Jewish women ended up blonde regardless of what color they had started out as.

"I heard about a woman who seemed very nice," Ruth said to Edek.

"I told you, please, do not start again with this," Edek said.

Ruth remembered, with a start, the drawback to Martina Schmidt's mother. Even if Edek were interested in meeting a woman, Martina's mother was German. And possibly, despite her efforts at seeking out Jews, might not want to go out with one. What was she doing thinking about Martina Schmidt's mother? She had only met her daughter once, and would probably never see her again. Martina Schmidt was a stranger to her. It was strange that the connection they had had been so intense.

Ruth could still feel Martina's presence this morning. Meetings with most people rarely lingered for more than a minute after they were over. She could still feel Martina's gaze on her. She had wanted to touch Martina last night. To hug her. As though they were more than strangers. As though they were something much more than strangers to each other. She had looked around the lobby this morning half hoping that Martina would be there. Of course, she wasn't.

Ruth missed her. It was absurd to miss someone you didn't know, she thought. She was sure that she and Martina could have become really good friends. But who knows? Ruth thought. People often seemed promising before you really got to know them. Then, all of their ordinariness appeared. Why was she so averse to ordinariness? she thought. There was so much about Ruth herself that was so ordinary. She wondered whether Martina would ever get back together with her husband Gerhard. Gerhard still seemed to have a pretty strong hold on Martina. Even though he had told her she was too German and the wrong number. The wrong number! How ridiculous.

Ruth suddenly felt cold. She noticed that her legs were trembling. She steadied her legs.

"Are you cold?" she said to Edek.

"No," he said. "I am hot."

"That's probably because you've just eaten," she said.

"I am hot because they got the heating up pretty high in this place," Edek said. Ruth put both of her feet firmly on the carpet. The trembling began to settle.

"Would you go out with a German woman?" she asked her father.

"Are you crazy?" Edek said.

"I thought you wouldn't," Ruth said.

"It is not the German I am not going to do anything with," said Edek. "It is the woman."

"I'm not asking you to do something with anyone," Ruth said. "I'm just asking if you'd go out with someone German."

"How many times do I have to tell you that I am finished with all that stuff," Edek said. "I am happy on my own. I can eat whatever I want to. I can have a piece of chocolate. I can read a book. I can watch television. No one tells me what to do. I am happy."

"You'll be happier with someone to share your life," Ruth said.

"That is what you said when you said I should get married to Henia," said Edek.

"Henia and her boys had their own agenda," Ruth said. "And we couldn't have guessed how that would turn out."

"You did say the marriage was a good idea," said Edek.

"I was wrong," said Ruth.

"You were wrong with the other women what you introduced me to, too," said Edek. "Didn't you learn from that that I am not interested?"

"What I learned from that," said Ruth, "was that one of them was too fat, one was too ugly, one had a terrible face. What I learned was that they were not good-looking enough for you."

"You have to have something to look at, that is for sure," Edek said.

"What about the women?" Ruth said. "Do they have to have something to look at, too? Maybe you weren't exactly their cup of tea."

"This is a stupid saying," Edek said. "To say someone is a cup of tea."

"It's probably not any more stupid than a lot of Polish sayings," Ruth said.

"It is more stupid," Edek said.

Ruth looked at her watch. They should leave if they wanted to go to Orbis. Orbis was the Polish Government Travel Agency. It was not renowned for its speed or efficiency.

"It is not so important for a woman what the man looks like," Edek said. "For a woman it is more important what wages a man does earn."

"That's a sad reflection on women," Ruth said.

"Why should they not enjoy the money, just like I enjoy to look at a nice-looking woman," Edek said. Ruth knew that there was an answer but it eluded her.

"Remember that shocking woman you did want me to meet?" Edek said. He started to laugh.

"What shocking woman?" Ruth said.

"The one which did look like she did get her dress from a rubbish bin," Edek said. "You remember it was at that party with all the permanent people?"

"The permanent people?" Ruth said. "None of us is permanent."

"Nearly everybody there was permanent," Edek said.

"Everybody?" Ruth said.

"Everybody," Edek said. "Everybody was posh, posh. Very rich."

Ruth started laughing.

"You remember her dress?" Edek said.

"They were not permanent people," Ruth said. "They were prominent."

"Prominent, permanent, what is the difference?" Edek said. "Do you remember the dress? It looked like a bunch of *shmattes*!"

"The bunch of *shmattes* was a dress that probably cost over a thousand dollars," Ruth said.

"It did look shocking," Edek said, and he roared with laughter at the memory. "One side of the hem went down to here, one side up here. The top was crooked. A tailor in Łódź would be out of a job if he did make a dress like that."

A man at another table nodded to Edek. Edek waved to him. "He is on the same floor what we are on," he said to Ruth. The man got up and came over to them.

"Your father told me how honored he is that you want to be in Poland with him," the man said to Ruth.

"Really?" Ruth said.

"I said most children are not so interested to see where a parent does come from," Edek said to Ruth. "My daughter is the cream of the crap," Edek said to the man. The man looked bewildered.

"You mean the cream of the crop," Ruth said to Edek.

"That is what I said," said Edek. "The cream of the crap."

"Crop not crap," Ruth said.

"That is what I am saying," Edek said.

Ruth decided to forgo the elocution lesson.

"We're having a wonderful trip," she said to the man. Edek nodded his agreement.

"It sounds fascinating from what your father told me," the man said. What had her father said? Ruth wondered. He hadn't said all that much to her.

"What did you say about our trip?" Ruth said to Edek.

"I did tell this gentleman that we did go to Kamedulska Street, that sort of stuff," Edek said.

"You didn't talk to me about it," Ruth said.

"You was there," Edek said.

"I would have loved to have heard what you were thinking and feeling," Ruth said.

The man shuffled his feet. Ruth looked at him. He looked ill at ease. He obviously did not want to be included in this family squabble. "It is a fascinating trip," Ruth said to the man.

"You are behaving like a baby," Edek said to Ruth. "Let us go." He got up. "Nice to meet you," he said to the man.

Ruth and Edek had been waiting in the Orbis office for twenty minutes before anyone took any notice of them. Ten or twelve Orbis employees were sitting in a row behind a glass partition. Like bank tellers in a bank. None of them appeared particularly busy. Two of them were eating, one was on the phone, and one was leafing through a magazine. Not one of them looked up at Edek or Ruth. There were no other customers. Finally, Ruth had knocked on the glass. "One minute," the woman said. She finished her cup of coffee and beckoned Ruth over.

Ruth explained that they wanted to change the date of their train tickets from Łódź to Kraków. They would like to leave on Wednesday instead of Thursday. The woman pulled out an enormous book and started looking through it. The book had very thin pages. There must be five thousand pages of train timetables in that book, Ruth thought. She took a closer look. The timetables were in very fine print. There were thousands of them.

"I think we're going to be here for a long time," she said to Edek.

Thirty minutes later, Ruth and Edek were still standing there at the Orbis counter. Ruth was furious.

"It can't be that complicated," she said to the woman. Ruth had been glaring at the woman from time to time, but the woman hadn't appeared to notice.

"It is not easy," the woman said, and kept turning the pages.

"Maybe we'll change these at the station?" Ruth said to Edek. "Or maybe I should just buy new tickets, and throw these away."

"Calm down," Edek said.

"I am calm," she said, gritting her teeth.

"Maybe I will call Stefan and ask him to drive us to Kraków?" Edek said.

"Who is Stefan?" said Ruth.

"Stefan is the driver what took us from Warsaw to Łódź," Edek said. "He was a very good driver."

"You want a driver to come from Warsaw to Łódź to pick us up and then drive us to Kraków?" Ruth said.

"Yes," said Edek. "I think it is a good idea."

"It's a crazy idea," Ruth said. "Warsaw is eighty-eight miles from Łódź, and Łódź is a hundred and eighty miles from Kraków."

"How do you know such exact miles?" Edek said.

"I just know," said Ruth.

"That is not so far," said Edek. "In Australia people drive for sometimes one thousand miles."

"On highways," Ruth said. "And not in icy winter conditions."

"It is not so icy," Edek said.

"You want him to come to Łódź to pick us up, drive us to Kraków and then drive himself back to Warsaw?" she said. "That's nearly four hundred miles. Anyway, I don't want to drive a hundred and eighty miles with someone who's got up at four A.M. to drive to us."

"We could book him into a cheap hotel in Łódź," said Edek. "Then he could come the night before and he will be like new for us in the morning." Ruth felt exhausted. She glared at the Orbis woman again.

"It would be very expensive," she said to Edek.

"We can afford it," he said. "We can afford what we like," he said, in a very loud voice.

"You really want to drive to Kraków with Stefan?" Ruth said.

"It was a very comfortable Mercedes, wasn't it?" Edek said. "You said yourself how comfortable this Mercedes was."

"Okay," said Ruth. "But we haven't got Stefan's number."

"I got his number," Edek said.

Edek ran toward his parka, which he had left on a chair. He came back holding a business card. "See," he said. "I got his number." He looked so happy. Why shouldn't they get Stefan to drive them to Kraków? Ruth thought. She would ask Stefan to drive them to the moon, if it made Edek this happy. Edek looked overjoyed. She would ask Stefan to move in with them, if it would keep her father feeling so joyful.

"Ring Stefan up and see if he'll do it." Ruth said.

"He will do it," Edek said. "He will be very happy to do it."

"How do you know?" said Ruth.

"I did already suggest it to him when we was driving to Łódź," Edek said. " 'It would be a pleasure,' Stefan did say." Ruth started laughing. Edek looked pleased with himself.

"We'll go by car," Ruth said. She turned to the Orbis operator. "Fuck your timetables," she said.

"That is not such a nice thing to say," Edek said to Ruth.

"It's nice enough," Ruth said.

~ *Chapter Ten* ~

On the corner of Piłsudskiego Street and Kopcińskiego Street, Edek asked an elderly woman for directions to the Jewish Center. "It is on Zachodnia Street," Edek said to her, in Polish. Ruth stood and waited. The woman was the fourth person they had asked. Ruth knew, from the map, that they must be close to Zachodnia Street. She had made a note of the exact address because she hadn't expected many locals to know where the Jewish Center was. She didn't think Poles would be making pilgrimages to the Jewish Center. But this woman knew. Ruth heard the woman refer to "People of Moses' faith." Why didn't she say Jewish? Ruth thought. Why did she keep repeating "People of Moses' faith"?

Ruth had called the Jewish Center that morning. A youngish-sounding man had agreed to give her ten minutes. He was the director of the center, he said. "Be here at 11:10 A.M.," he said—11:10 A.M., she thought. This man must have a hectic schedule. "I'll be there at 11:10 A.M.," she had said to him. She had told him that she wanted a guide to take her through the Jewish Cemetery. "I need more notice to organize a guide," he had said. "I need several days."

"Not many people's plans include a month in Łódź," she had said to him. "I need a guide in the next day or two."

"I don't think I can do anything," he said.

"I'll come to the center anyway," Ruth had said. She was puzzled at his lack of helpfulness. Maybe he was overrun by Jews wanting to visit the Jewish Cemetery. The cemetery was locked. Even people who didn't want a guide had to go to the center to pick up the key. Maybe being keeper of the keys was proving to be too much.

"Okay, okay, I know where the Zachodnia Street is," Edek said. "Follow me," he said, and ran off. Ruth was too tired to run after him. Why did he have to run? No one else in the streets of Łódź was running. Ruth sped up. She had lost sight of Edek. She was agitated. Where was he? Why couldn't he do anything at a normal pace? She looked in each direction at every intersection she passed. There was no sign of Edek. How could he have gotten so far ahead of her in such a short time? She continued walking. It was 10:40 A.M. They had half an hour. She didn't want to be late.

She was just reaching a main street, which she hoped was Al. Kościuszki, when Edek came around the corner and almost knocked her over.

"What are you doing?" she said to him, when she regained her footing. "You're lucky it was me you bumped into, and not some Pole."

"What are you talking about?" Edek said. "I knew it was you."

"You couldn't have known," Ruth said. "You can't see around corners."

"Did we come to Łódź to argue about such stupid things?" Edek said.

"No," she said. "You're right."

"I did smell your perfume," he said. "You wear always the same perfume. I could smell the perfume from Kościuszki Street."

"I'm sure you couldn't," Ruth said.

"Forget about it," said Edek. "We are very near to the Łódź-Fabryczna, the railway station."

"Oh, good," said Ruth. "That station is not far from Zachodnia Street."

"I know this," Edek said. "That is why I am telling you. Zachodnia Street is off a street what the station is on."

"Dad," she called out to him, as he ran off. She gave up. She had wanted to ask him if they could walk together. But he was gone. She relaxed a bit. At least they wouldn't be late. She checked the note in her pocket. The Jewish Center was at number 78 Zachodnia Street.

Before she could put the piece of paper back in her pocket Edek had returned.

"The Łódź-Fabryczna is not there," he said.

"It's still in the guidebooks," Ruth said. "It's the main station in Łódź. They can't have got rid of it."

"Of course they still got the station," Edek said. "But it is not there."

"Maybe you're not looking in the right place," Ruth said.

"I been there many times as a boy," Edek said. "I know where it is."

"That was a while ago, Dad," she said.

"You do not forget where a station is," Edek said.

"Maybe they moved the station?" Ruth said.

"Maybe," he said. "I try one more place." He was gone before she could object.

Ruth felt old. What was wrong with her? It was pathetic not to be able to catch up with an eighty-one-year-old. But then Edek was not your average eighty-one-year-old, she thought. Maybe pitched against a more normal eighty-one-year-old, she might be able to hold her own. In the distance, she saw Edek waving to her. She ran up to him.

"I did find the Łódź-Fabryczna," he was shouting. "I told you I did know where it was. I will show you, now, where Zachodnia is. The woman in the street did explain it to me pretty good."

"Dad, can you wait for me?" she said.

"Hurry up," he said, as he streaked ahead of her.

One minute later, she could no longer see him. Edek's darting and dashing and rushing was demented, she decided. It was unnatural. Human beings were not meant to speed and career from one place to the next. There was no need. There was no urgency, no emergency, no crisis, no race. Finding the right street was not a matter of life and death. She looked around her. She couldn't see Edek anywhere. She thought it would be a miracle if she and Edek managed to arrive at Zachodnia Street together.

Suddenly, Edek reappeared. He was out of breath.

"Something is wrong," he said. Ruth felt alarmed. She knew that a man his age shouldn't be running around like that.

"What's wrong, Dad?" she asked, trying to sound unworried.

"The streets are not where they should be," Edek said. Ruth was relieved that geography and location were still what was wrong.

"Maybe it's us who are not where we should be," she said. But Edek didn't want to listen. He was gone. She didn't care. She slowed down. It was she and Edek who were in the wrong place. What were they doing here? She should be in New York. In her office, where compared to this nothing seemed crazy.

Even the most unruly occurrences in the offices of Rothwax Correspondence seemed tame and subdued next to this. The indexing and cross-indexing of letters and files and folders seemed easy. The puzzling requests from clients seemed moderate and manageable next to this. This was madness. New York, with its erratic inhabitants, its crowded streets, its deviant traffic, and aberrant pedestrians, seemed like the Sea of Tranquillity to Ruth. An oasis of order and clarity. What was the Sea of Tranquillity? she wondered. Was it a geographical location or a poetic phrase? She thought it might be a heavenly body, or something celestial. Anything to do with tranquillity was clearly not her area of specialty. She looked at her watch. It was almost eleven. She was so tired.

Edek reemerged. "I cannot find the Zachodnia Street," he said. "I do not know what is wrong with me."

Ruth didn't answer. She thought he was only questioning his sense of direction. "The Zachodnia Street was a street what I was on many times," Edek said.

"Maybe we should go back to the hotel?" she said to Edek. "We're not going to make our appointment anyway. The man from the center was specific about the time we had to be there."

"Beggar him," Edek said.

Ruth was surprised. Edek rarely swore. This was his version of swearing. "Beggar him" was something Edek had condensed from the word "beggar" and the Australian expression "bugger him." A phrase that originated, Ruth thought, from the verb "to bugger." "Beggar him" was one of Edek's worst obscenities. Edek didn't know that he had distorted and blended two different words. He didn't notice the lack of potency the phrase possessed.

Ruth had once tried to explain it to him, but he had dismissed her. He thought she was being pedantic. Ruth thought that maybe he just didn't want to know what "to bugger" meant. She decided it didn't matter. People got the general gist of what Edek was expressing. "Beggar him," Edek said again.

They walked along whatever street it was that they were walking on. Suddenly Edek turned and shouted. Ruth got a terrible fright. She had been thinking about herself and Edek, and the mess they seemed to be in, in the middle of Łódź.

"Taxi, taxi, taxi," Edek was shouting. He was in the middle of the street now, and waving his arms. The taxi he had spotted stopped.

"You gave me a terrible shock," Ruth said when she got to him.

"I did get a taxi for you," Edek said. "A Mercedes."

They got into the cab. Edek gave the cab driver the address. "We need to be there in a big hurry, sir," he said to the driver. Edek had assumed his excessively obsequious manner again. "We're paying him," Ruth said to Edek. "We don't need to lick his ass."

"What sort of person speaks like this?" Edek said. " 'Lick his ass.' It is lucky for us that he doesn't understand."

"I wouldn't care," Ruth said.

"Sir," Edek said. "If you can make it quick, there will be a big tip for you." Ruth grimaced and sank back into the seat. Edek would have paid out the equivalent of a year's income in tips and bonuses before he left Poland.

Edek was counting his zlotys. "Give me a few more zlotys," he said to Ruth.

"So you can distribute them among the Poles?" Ruth said.

"For what are you in such a bad mood?" Edek said.

"This is no picnic," Ruth said. "Do you think I should be cracking jokes and slapping my thighs?" She wasn't sure that Edek understood what slapping a thigh meant. Edek understood enough to take offense.

"It is not such a picnic for me, too," he said.

They drove in silence. Ruth could smell the driver. She could smell the smell of sweat and other body odor, and unwashed hair and unclean clothes. Why didn't Polish men wash more often? You'd think the driver of a Mercedes would want to smell more like a Mercedes driver and less like a local vagrant, Ruth thought.

They drove past two pieces of anti-Semitic graffiti, one after the other. Stars of David, with the losing soccer team's emblem emblazoned across the star-shaped symbol of Judaism. Ruth pointed them out to Edek. "They got rid of their Jews," she said to Edek. "But they couldn't get rid of their anti-Semitism." She shook her head. "They got rid of almost two hundred and fifty thousand Jews from this area. Wasn't that enough? What are they carrying on about?"

"Don't talk about this stuff," Edek said. "The driver, he sees what we are looking at."

"So what?" Ruth said. "He knows he's anti-Semitic. He doesn't care."

"It is only children," the driver said. "Just children."

"Jesus," Ruth said. "What sort of kids are they bringing up?"

"My daughter is not really a troublemaker," Edek said to the driver, in English.

"If you want him to understand," Ruth said to Edek, "you'd better repeat it, in Polish."

"*Oy, cholera,*" Edek said, and began a long explanation of Ruth's bad mood to the driver. The driver nodded his head, sympathetically.

Ruth and Edek had been in the taxi for over five minutes. They were two or three miles from where the cab had picked them up. Ruth knew that she and Edek had started out quite close to Zachodnia Street. How had they become so lost? No wonder she was tired. They had walked for miles. "The Poles did used to throw stones at me, in this area," Edek said in a low voice to Ruth.

They arrived, finally, at 78 Zachodnia Street. Edek tipped the driver an inordinately large number of zlotys. The driver got out of the cab and bowed half a dozen times to them. Number 78 was a large vacant allotment of land. An old building was at the very back of the block. They approached the building. A smell of boiled cabbage permeated the air.

"Can you smell boiled cabbage?" Ruth said to Edek.

"Yes," he said. "It is not very nice." They reached the building. Ruth looked inside a dark doorway.

"I think we have to go inside and up the stairs," she said to Edek.

"This is the Jewish Center?" Edek said. "Are you sure?"

"I think I'm sure," Ruth said.

She and Edek walked up the dank, dark staircase. The smell of cabbage was overwhelming. The air was so damp that Ruth thought that the cabbage must still be being boiled. It was so dark it was hard to see where they were going. This was the headquarters of the Jewish community of Łódź? The heart of Jewish life in Łódź? What a heart, Ruth thought. She suddenly felt very depressed. This was not what she associated with being Jewish. Where was the warmth? Nothing about this place was Jewish.

Ruth was shivering. It was very cold in the building. "Are you cold, Dad?" she said.

"No," Edek said. "Where are we?" he said after a minute. He seemed as dazed as Ruth to find that this dark run-down damp place was the center of Jewish Łódź. Ruth knocked at a partially opened door at the top of the stairs. She looked at her watch. It was 11:13 A.M. They were only three minutes late. Inside, a man in his thirties, dressed in the black clothes of a religious Jew, sat at a desk. He was shuffling papers. He had an air of business about him. "Come in," he said, in a perfunctory manner. He didn't look up.

The room was not very large and was sparsely furnished. A woman was typing at a table against one wall. There was another room off to the left. Ruth wondered if that was where the cabbage was being boiled. She and Edek stood inside the door. The woman smiled at them. "We're here to arrange a guide for the cemetery," Ruth said to the woman. The woman, she had decided, looked more approachable than the man. The woman shook her head. It was clear she didn't speak English.

"Let's go," Edek whispered to Ruth.

Ruth looked around the room. Two rolls of fax paper were on a shelf, together with a photograph of an Orthodox Jew. Ruth didn't know who the Orthodox Jew in the photograph was. This was the most sparse and spare Jewish Center she had ever seen. What furniture there was, was old. It looked so depressing. So bereft of life. Maybe her father was right. Maybe they should go.

She knew the center had two hundred members, a prayer house somewhere in the building, a canteen, and a kosher kitchen. The cabbage that they could smell must be kosher. They served thirty free meals a day, Ruth had read, and provided the community with matzoh at Passover. The center's aim was to maintain and support the religious and cultural traditions of the Jews of Łódź. How did you do that when there were no Jews left? It was an impossible task, Ruth thought. Not one that could be carried out with the help of boiled cabbage.

"We are to arrange for a guide," Ruth said again, in the direction of the man. "I rang you earlier."

"Yes, yes," he said. "I will try to contact him."

"Please," Edek whispered to Ruth. "He is busy. Can we go?"

"We'll wait for another few minutes," she whispered to Edek.

"I do not want so much to go to the cemetery," he said.

"Just another few minutes, and we'll call it quits," she said.

The woman looked up from her typewriter and smiled at them. Ruth and Edek smiled back. The man continued to shuffle papers. Ruth looked at her watch. It was 11:24 A.M. "How many Jews do you look after here?" she said to the man.

"We feed about thirty a day," he said, not looking up.

"Are most of them old?" Ruth said.

"All of them," he said.

"Men and women?" Ruth said.

"Most of them are men," he said.

So this was what the Jewish community of Łódź had been reduced to, Ruth thought. Thirty poor, old men, who had boiled cabbage for lunch. It was heartbreaking. "I think we'll go, Dad," she said to Edek. She noticed a photograph of the American philanthropist, businessman, and cosmetics heir Ronald Lauder on the wall. She knew that the Jewish Center of Łódź was supported by the Ronald Lauder Foundation.

"This is the worst Jewish place I saw in my life," Edek whispered. Edek looked depressed. The lack of any welcome had probably added to her father's distress, Ruth thought.

"You're supported by the Ronald Lauder Foundation, are you?" Ruth said to the man.

"Yes," he said.

"I was at his home, in New York, recently," Ruth said.

The man dropped his papers, took off his glasses, and faced Ruth. He looked about thirty or thirty-five, Ruth thought.

"You were just at Mr. Lauder's house?" the man said.

"Yes," said Ruth. It wasn't a lie. She had been to the Lauders' spectacular art-filled New York apartment. She had been served the sort of food that should be canonized and memorialized, not eaten. Each dish had been more dazzling, more aesthetically pleasing, than the dish that had preceded it. Ruth thought that she saw several of the guests genuflecting over the wines that were served.

Ruth had touched the van Gogh painting hanging in the Lauders' library. She had followed the brushstrokes with her fingers. Traced Vincent van Gogh's movements. Nobody had noticed. Ruth had known that she would never get that close to a van Gogh again. Ruth was at Ronald Lauder's apartment for a book launch that the Lauders had hosted for a friend of a friend of Ruth's.

"Mr. Lauder has a beautiful apartment," Ruth said to the man. The man came up and shook hands with Edek and Ruth. "Sit down, please," he said. "We are so grateful to Mr. Lauder. Mr. Lauder makes it possible for us to feed old Jewish men and look after them. Mr. Lauder is trying to rehabilitate the Jewish community of Poland."

Ruth wondered if "rehabilitate" was the right word. The Jewish community was not damaged or diseased. It was destroyed. It was nonexistent. She decided this condition was still open to the possibility of rehabilitation. Ronald Lauder could also have used restore, reconstitute, or rehabilitate. They would all do, she decided. She wished she didn't get sidetracked by words and their meanings.

"You were in Mr. Lauder's apartment?" the man said again.

"Yes," she said. "Quite recently."

"My daughter mixes with everybody," Edek said. He looked very pleased to be making this announcement. "My daughter is very rich, herself," he said. Ruth nearly started laughing. She restrained herself.

"Not as rich as Mr. Lauder," she said.

"Please have a cup of coffee," the man said. He told the woman to put on the kettle.

"No thanks," Ruth said, at exactly the same time as Edek was saying, "Thank you very much."

She shook her head at Edek. She didn't want to stay in this place one minute longer than she had to. "No thank you," Edek said. "We did just have a coffee."

"We'd like a guide for the cemetery," Ruth said.

"Of course, of course," the man said. "For which day would you like a guide?"

"Today," Ruth said. "This afternoon."

"I can organize it for you," the man said. "I will arrange for our best guide. He is very familiar with the archives of the cemetery. We look after the archives in this office, thanks to Mr. Lauder."

"Could we have the guide at two-thirty P.M., for a couple of hours?" Ruth said.

"You want to be in the cemetery for two hours?" Edek said to Ruth.

"I just want to make sure we have enough time," Ruth said.

"What is there to do in a cemetery?" Edek said. "You walk in, you have a look, and you seen the cemetery."

Edek turned to the director of the center. "Tell the guide we will need him for half an hour maybe, one hour maximum."

"We'll have two hours," Ruth said.

"What for?" Edek said. "Everyone in the cemetery is dead. You cannot stay and talk."

"Maybe you want to pray in the cemetery?" the director said.

"We don't pray," Ruth said. The man looked startled.

"You have to explain to him," Edek said. "You cannot say just we do not pray."

"You can explain how you and Mum and your parents were brought up as Orthodox Jews," Ruth said to Edek. "You can tell him that you decided there was no God after watching Nazis play football with babies, and bang babies' heads against walls. I don't want to go into it."

"I will ring the guide straightaway," the man said. He walked briskly to the phone.

"Why do you make trouble?" Edek said.

"I don't like him," said Ruth.

"You make trouble with everybody," Edek said. "In the taxi you did want to make the driver feel bad. Here you do want to make this poor man feel bad."

"Why shouldn't I make taxi drivers feel bad?" Ruth said. "If they feel bad it's only for one minute. They don't really think about what it means to have no Jews left in Poland, but plenty of anti-Semitic graffiti."

"What did this man here do to you?" Edek said.

"He didn't make us feel welcome," said Ruth.

"That is true," said Edek. "You was really in this Mr. Lauder's home?" Edek said.

"I was," Ruth said. "There was me and a hundred other people."

Edek laughed. "You are a clever girl," he said.

"Thank you," she said.

"Excuse me," the director called out. "Can the guide meet you at your hotel?"

"Of course," Ruth said. "We're staying at the Grand Victoria."

"That is perfect," the director said. "The Grand Victoria at two-thirty P.M. sharp." He made the arrangements with the guide and hung up.

"Marek is our best guide," the director said to Edek and Ruth. "Marek will show you the funeral home, which was built in 1898. He will show you how the bodies were brought into the hall from the doors on the west side of the building."

"You want to see this?" Edek said to Ruth. Ruth nodded.

"Marek will show you everything."

"Thank you very much," Ruth said.

"Thank you very much," said Edek.

"I am glad that you were able to visit our center," the director said.

"Could I ask you a question?" Ruth said.

"Of course, of course," he said.

"Why would you want to rehabilitate Jewish life in Poland?" she said. "I'm not trying to undermine what you are doing here, in helping these elderly Jews, but why would you want to reestablish Jewish life here?"

"It is very important that Jewish people have a home in Poland," he said. "We have to build up Jewish life in Poland once more."

"But why?" Ruth said. "Poland is not a conducive place for Jews. Why would you want Jews to live here? Poles don't like Jews. There's anti-Semitic graffiti in the streets. You must have seen it."

"Of course I see it," he said.

"And you must see more than that if you're walking the streets of Łódź looking like a Jew," she said.

"I cover my yarmulke with a cap," he said.

"So you want all Jews to have to cover their yarmulkes with their caps?" Ruth said. "What sort of a Jewish life would that be?"

"Ruthie, Ruthie," Edek said. "Do not get so excited."

"I'm not excited," Ruth said. "I'm disturbed. I can understand why it is important to look after those Jews that are left, but I don't understand why you want to create a Jewish community here.

"And where are you going to get the Jews from? Your current members are obviously too old to procreate. And you're not going to get any Jews that I know to migrate to Poland. Apart from the intrinsically unattractive prospect of living in Poland, a lot of Jews view Poland as one large gravesite."

"Ruthie, this is not a nice thing to say," Edek said.

"Well, it is one large gravesite," Ruth said.

"I didn't mean this, I did mean it is not nice to say it is no good, the life in Poland," Edek said.

"Would you live here?" Ruth said. Edek didn't answer.

"We are looking for Jews who are already here," the director said.

"Where are they?" said Ruth.

"They do not know they are Jews," he said.

"Well, what's the point of telling them?" Ruth said. "It's not all that wonderful to be a Jew."

"They want to be Jews," the director said.

"The ones who don't know they're Jewish?" said Ruth.

"The ones who have already come forward," he said.

"Why?" Ruth said. "So they can experience the antagonism and the anti-Semitism that they're missing out on?"

"She has got a point," said Edek.

"They want to be Jews," the director said. "Some of them have gone to a lot of trouble to establish that there was Jewish blood in the family."

"Don't they know that Jewish blood is still suspect in Poland?" Ruth said.

"They know that," he said. "Some of their families will not admit to any Jewishness."

"So they are estranged from their families and living in Poland as Jews?" Ruth said. "That doesn't sound great."

"At least they are not living a lie," the director said.

"Lies are not necessarily all that bad," Ruth said.

"Now you are being stupid," said Edek.

"Why don't you ship those Poles who are desperate to be Jews off to Israel?" Ruth said to the director.

"They are not Poles, they are Jews," he said.

"Well, still, why don't you help them to get to Israel?" Ruth said. "Or ask Mr. Lauder to help them get visas to America. No Jew in his right mind would want to stay here." Ruth shook her head. What was she trying to achieve here? Was she just being argumentative? Taking out her frustrations on this poor lone young Jew. Edek shuffled his feet and cleared his throat.

"I didn't know I was a Jew myself, until I was a young adult," the director said.

Ruth felt bad. "Do you want to stay in Poland?" she said.

"I hope to go to Israel," he said. There was an uncomfortable silence.

"I do not feel so comfortable in Israel myself," Edek said.

"That's a whole other story," Ruth said to the director.

"Israel is very important for the Jews," Edek said. "But for me the Jews what are there are not the same Jews what I grew up with."

"The Jews you grew up with are gone," Ruth said. "Anyway, you don't like being in crowds of Jews."

"That is true," said Edek. "But I do give money to Israel," he said to the director, "and so does my daughter."

"Having Jews in Poland is a sign that Hitler did not win," the director said. Ruth was speechless. Hitler didn't win? What would Hitler have had to do to be considered to have won in this man's eyes? Ruth opened her mouth to reply, but nothing came out. There was too much to say, and the words were all jammed and backed up in her in astonishment at this man's proposition.

"I think Hitler did win," she said quietly. Edek looked at her. She couldn't tell if he was about to admonish her not to continue this discussion, or whether he was sending her an expression of solidarity. Edek rolled his eyes slightly at her. Ruth was grateful to know that her father agreed with her.

"Ronald Lauder is restoring synagogues in Poland," the man said. "He is giving undiscovered Jews back their Judaism. People who did not know they were Jewish now know."

"Does it help them?" Ruth said.

"Of course," he said.

"They're not experiencing any more anti-Semitism as Jews than they did when they thought they were Poles?" she said.

The man thought for a second. "I don't know the answer to that," he said.

It was absurd to renovate synagogues in Poland, Ruth thought, and think that that was restoring Jewish life. The existence of the synagogues, she thought, underlined the fact that the Poles and the Germans had very successfully gotten rid of the Jews. The synagogues stood there alone and unattended except for a handful of mostly elderly people in some of the larger cities. And a stray tourist or two.

Ruth wanted to leave. The smell of cabbage felt as though it had permeated her skin and her hair and all of the rest of her. She felt that her lungs were expelling the scent of boiled cabbage.

"Thank you very much for organizing the guide for us," Ruth said to the director. She put on her coat.

"Thank you very very much," Edek said to the director. "I hope that you do manage to get to Israel."

"Should I mail you a brochure of our activities here?" the director said to Ruth.

"Of course," Ruth said.

"Send me one, too," Edek said. He nudged Ruth. "Ruthie, we should leave a donation now. Give the gentleman something."

The director looked uncomfortable. "You can send a check when you receive our brochures," he said.

"My daughter can give you something now," Edek said. Ruth opened her wallet and took out a thousand zlotys. Edek looked at the money. "My daughter is a good girl," he said.

"Thank you very much," the director said. They all shook hands.

"I'm never going to be able to get rid of this cabbage smell," Ruth said to Edek, on their way down the stairs.

"It is a terrible bad stink," Edek said.

Ruth laughed. "It sure is," she said.

"You want something to eat?" Edek said.

"No, I'm not really hungry," Ruth said. "That cabbage made me feel sick. It didn't even smell as though they'd added fried onions or some meat. It smelled like plain boiled cabbage."

"I am also not hungry," Edek said. "When I have a good breakfast I do not need nothing else."

"Would you like to stop and have a cup of coffee and a piece of cake?" Ruth said.

"I did tell you I am not hungry," Edek said.

"What about a bowl of soup?" she said.

"If you have some soup, I will have some soup, too," Edek said.

They walked along Zachodnia Street.

"I think you got a point," Edek said.

"About what?" Ruth said.

"About the spending money to find the Jews what is in Poland," Edek said. "If they do not know that they are Jewish, how Jewish can they be?"

"You think people are only what they're brought up to be?" Ruth said.

"Of course," said Edek. "If I was brought up Italian, I would be Italian."

"Maybe," Ruth said.

"What for do they want to make Jews out of the Poles?" Edek said. "It is not so easy for a Jew to be a good Jew. I do not think it will be so easy for a Pole who thinks he is a Jew, to be a good Jew."

"Especially in Poland," Ruth said.

"Still, I got conscience bites," Edek said.

Ruth loved the phrase "conscience bites." It was Edek's own phrase. He had been having conscience bites since Ruth was a small girl.

"What have you got a bad conscience about?" she said.

"We was not so nice to the man from the Jewish Center," Edek said.

"I wasn't rude to him," Ruth said. "I just genuinely wanted to know what they thought they were doing."

"Why do you not ask this Mr. Lauder?" Edek said.

"Ask Ronald Lauder?" Ruth said. "For a start, I don't know him."

"Did you speak to him when you was in his house?" said Edek.

"For one and a half minutes," Ruth said. "He greeted all of the guests. Anyway, you don't ask people with his degree of wealth real questions. You try to behave yourself in their houses. Eat the right food with the right piece of cutlery. Be charming, and be glad you were invited so you can tell other people that you were in his house."

"You cannot ask a question?" Edek said.

"You can't question what they do," Ruth said. "Your job is not to question them, your job is to admire their acquisitions and achievements. Do you know what acquisitions are?"

"Of course I know," said Edek. "Acquisitions is stuff you did buy."

"That's right," said Ruth.

"I would speak to this Mr. Lauder if I was in New York," Edek said.

"I'm sure you would," Ruth said. She shuddered at the thought of what Edek might say to Ronald Lauder.

"I'd like to walk for a while and see if I can clear some of that boiled cabbage out of my head," Ruth said.

"In that case I will go back to the hotel," Edek said. "I got a couple of phone calls to make."

"Who are you going to call?" Ruth said.

"Stefan," said Edek.

"Who is Stefan?" Ruth said.

"You did ask me just before this same question," Edek said. "Stefan is the driver what is from Warsaw."

"Sorry," she said, "I forgot. Okay, you call Stefan and see whether he wants to do the job."

"I did tell you before that he will do it," Edek said.

"You can't just assume he is available," Ruth said.

"You think that Stefan is Mr. Lauder?" Edek said. "Of course Stefan will be available. How many jobs is he going to get like this?"

"Depends on how many Jews like us keep trekking through Poland," Ruth said.

"Trekking?" Edek said. "What is trekking?"

"Trekking is to travel with difficulty," Ruth said.

"I did think that you did say that we are *drecking* through Poland."

Dreck was Yiddish for shit. Ruth laughed. "That's very funny," she said. In a way Edek was right. They were *drecking* though Poland. Having to deal with a lot of shit.

"I'll walk you back to the hotel," she said to Edek.

"What for?" he said. "I'll go back and you walk where you want to walk."

"I want to walk past the places where the synagogues used to be," Ruth said.

"There is nothing there," said Edek.

"I know," said Ruth.

The map, published by the Our Roots company, that she had of Jewish Łódź before the war was marked with synagogues. Underneath each synagogue was, in brackets, the word "nonexisting." So the places she wanted to walk by were sites. Former sites of synagogues. There was the site of the Great Synagogue on Zielona Street. The Great Synagogue was considered by some to have been the most impressive synagogue in Poland. She wanted to visit the "nonexisting" synagogues on Wólczańska Street and Wolborska Street. The Nazis had destroyed all the synagogues except one. There was one synagogue left in Łódź. A small synagogue at 28 Rewolucji 1905 Street.

The synagogue at 28 Rewolucji 1905 Street had survived partly because it was used as a storehouse for salt by the Nazis. And also possibly because it was tucked away in a corner at the back of the second of two courtyards. And it was very small.

"You want to walk to something that is not there?" Edek said.

"Yes, if you insist on putting it that way, that's what I want to do," said Ruth.

"Are you crazy?" said Edek.

"I hope not," she said.

"Is there something left where there was synagogues?" Edek said.

"Nothing," Ruth said. "There's not a trace of the existence of any of the synagogues that are gone."

"What are you going to see?" asked Edek.

"I don't know," Ruth said, "Do you want to come with me?"

"I have to ring Stefan," Edek said.

"That's true, you have to give him some notice," she said.

Edek looked at Ruth as though he was examining her for signs of mental deterioration. He was frowning.

"You do not go to a synagogue what is there," he said. "You do not go to the synagogues what are in New York, you do not go to the synagogues what are in Melbourne. Why do you go to a synagogue what is not there?"

Edek had a point, Ruth thought. She was never interested in synagogues. She avoided them. Why was she so drawn to these synagogues? To these absent synagogues.

"I don't know why I want to go, Dad," she said. "I just want to feel the air there. To stand and listen."

"To what?" Edek said.

"To nothing, to my thoughts," Ruth said.

"You can listen to your thoughts in a synagogue in New York, or in Melbourne," Edek said. "Or you can listen to your thoughts in the hotel room, in Łódź."

She was not interested in the Jews in New York, she thought. Or in the Jews of Melbourne. It was just the Jews of Poland. The dead Jews.

"You do not like so much the Jews what are alive," Edek said.

"I've got nothing against them," Ruth said. "I don't dislike them. Some of my best friends are Jewish," she said, and laughed out loud at the cliché. Edek didn't laugh.

"This trip is too much for you," he said. "You was worried about me being in Poland. I am fine. You are not so fine."

Was there really something wrong with aligning herself with dead Jews? Ruth wondered. She felt most at home with the dead Jews. The dead Jews were her Jews. Her family. She understood their suffering. She mourned for them and their way of life. She tried to re-create some aspects of the life she imagined they had led in her own life. When she ate sauerkraut she pretended that it was straight out of a barrel, preserved and marinated for the winter in a basement in Łódź. She bought cans of sauerkraut and repackaged it in bottling jars with rubber bands and vacuum-sealed lids. She bought rye bread in Dean & Deluca on Broadway, and let it go stale in her kitchen. When it was hard and brittle enough she ate it. Edek had told her that in the ghetto stale bread was prized far more than fresher bread. The stale bread took longer to chew.

Rooshka could never throw bread out. She kept uneaten bread for weeks. Eventually Edek or Ruth would throw out the moldy crusts and ends and slices that Rooshka had accumulated. Rooshka had lived for too long without bread to be able to discard any. Bread had meant the difference between life and death.

"Let me walk you back to the hotel," Ruth said to Edek again.

"I don't need someone to look after me," he said. "You are the one who should be careful."

"Are you sure you know the way?" she said.

"I am in Łódź," he said. "I know the way."

Ruth kissed Edek good-bye. "I'll be back well before we have to leave for the cemetery," she said.

"We have to go to the cemetery?" he said.

"I think you'll love it," she said. "It's the biggest Jewish cemetery in

Europe. It's where the Jews are." The Jews Ruth was referring to were the Jews of Łódź who were lucky enough to be buried in the cemetery on Bracka Street. The Jews who were lucky enough to die before they were murdered.

"It is where the dead Jews are," Edek said.

"The dead Jews are the only Jews in Łódź," Ruth said. "So we have to visit them."

She was looking forward to going to the cemetery. She planned to get back to the hotel in enough time to change her clothes and freshen up. She felt as though she was planning a visit to the home of relatives. This cemetery was probably the closest she would get to feeling surrounded by relatives, she realized. She wished that the dead were not quite so dead. She also wished that the dead were not quite so alive to her. She thought that dead people should feel more dead.

Ruth kissed Edek good-bye again. She watched him walk away. His hands were in his pockets. And he was looking at the ground. He was walking quite slowly. He looked so alone, in the street. As alone as a small child. Ruth started to cry. She had to pull herself together, she thought. She couldn't walk through the streets of Łódź in tears. She wanted to look tough in Łódź. A tough Jew.

A greasy-looking man wearing a leather jacket and torn jeans leered at her. Ruth glared at him. He made a series of kissing noises at her. She glared at him again. She wasn't sure why she didn't feel scared. It was in the middle of the day. But there were not many people around and a lot of dark doorways. It was strange that she felt less frightened in Łódź than she did in most places. She was always careful in New York, despite the dramatic drop in the city's crime rate. She always triple-bolted her apartment and armed her security system. But here in Łódź, she felt free of that fear. The man started making hissing noises at her. She decided she had better get a move on. She sped up. "Asshole," she shouted back at the man. What was she doing, shouting at dodgy-looking men in the street? She was losing her grip. This trip had unhinged her, she thought.

Ruth walked briskly. She felt good walking. She had skipped her run too many of the mornings she had been in Poland. Skipped her run. That was a pun. She smiled to herself.

Some of the most beautiful buildings in Łódź, possibly the only beautiful buildings in Łódź, were built by Jews. Ruth was outside the Poznański Palace at 17 Ogrodowa Street. Israel Poznański was one of the greatest industrialists in Poland. He had built this palace in the early 1880s. Ruth liked the palace. It was impressive without being overly ornamental. It was one of four palaces built by Israel Poznański. It was very large. Or was it? It seemed large to Ruth but then she didn't know much about the sizes of palaces. She had no idea how big the average palace was.

Ruth had wanted to call Martina Schmidt that morning. Martina had probably already left for Berlin. It was strange how you could become attached to a stranger. It was probably easier to form an instant attachment to someone you didn't know, Ruth thought. You weren't hindered by who the person really was. Strangers were probably comprised of more of your own making and less of themselves. Maybe she and Martina Schmidt really had very little in common. That thought seemed to soothe her. She had inadvertently slowed down. She picked up her pace. This exploration of Łódź might as well double as exercise, she thought.

Ruth had been bothered by Martina's attraction to her ex-husband's sadness. It was a shame people couldn't alter those aspects of themselves that were psychologically not in their own interests. Today so many alterations were possible. They could genetically alter food to eliminate any difficult qualities and add or enhance the better qualities. In America, they added genes, removed from fish, to strawberries. This produced strawberries that would endure cold. Ruth wondered if the fish-enhanced strawberries wilted in heat. Probably not, if they hadn't removed the strawberries' heat-tolerance genes, she decided.

If it was possible to meddle and alter human qualities and characteristics, Ruth thought that she herself would probably need a complete revamping. Why had she chosen the word "revamp," she wondered. Why not "makeover" or "overhaul." "Vamp" seemed an incongruous word in Łódź. Ruth tried to get the word "vamp" out of her head. Sometimes words and their alternatives lodged themselves in her brain and stayed there all day. The worst example of this had been the word "nymph," which had lasted a week. The word "nymph" had appeared minutes after she had picked up a postcard from Garth that was in her letter box one day last year.

Why "nymph"? No one, not even Garth, could possibly think of her as a nymph. She was much too big to be thought of as a nymph. Nymphs were slim, svelte, and ethereal. Still, the word "nymph" had crept into Ruth's head and occupied her for almost a week. As soon as the word had arrived, Ruth had had to produce other words that resembled nymph. She had thought of spirit, sprite, sylph, elfish. Elfish had reminded her of shellfish, and then sea nymph and ocean nymph and fresh-water nymph had followed. Soon Ruth was flooded with words. Seamaids and mermaids and other water spirits. The word spirits had allowed her to dip into the galaxy with the words shooting stars, guardian angels, and fairy godmothers before she had switched to a rural setting with mountain nymph, glen nymph, and tree nymph. She had been so relieved when the word "nymph" had left her.

She certainly didn't feel like a nymph now. Her stomach felt distended. This was something else that happened to her when she felt tense. She took two Mylanta tablets out of her bag. She was standing on Gabriela Narutowicza Street outside an interesting, architect-designed building built as a business school by Jews, in 1907. The building was now occupied by the University of Łódź. A tall, gray building, around the corner from the former business school, was designed in the same style. Ruth thought that the only architects in business in Łódź before the war seemed to have been Jewish or been employed by Jews.

At number 66 Rewolucji 1905 Street was the Przytulisko, the old orphanage for Jewish girls. This building was now owned by the University of Łódź. What would Łódź have done without their Jews? Who would have built all of these grand buildings and palaces? What would the city of Łódź have done if they hadn't gotten rid of their Jews was a better question, she thought. Where would they have housed their institutes and museums?

Ruth was now on Pomorska Street, where her mother had lived. She looked around at her mother's old neighborhood. The building at number 18 used to be the Talmud Torah School. It was now occupied by the Chemistry Institute of the University of Łódź.

Her mother had probably walked past the Talmud Torah School every day. Where was her mother now? Ruth was walking in her mother's footsteps in Łódź. But she couldn't feel Rooshka. Rooshka was gone. Gone, like all the Jews of Łódź. What a community this must have been, Ruth thought.

Ruth had thought that she would be able to feel the ghosts of the workers and orphans and students. The ghosts of the poor Jews and the ghosts of the rich. But she couldn't. She couldn't feel anything. She thought she would go back to the hotel soon. She passed the apartment her mother had lived in. There was still no sign of life in the apartments.

Ruth found the only remaining synagogue in Poland at the end of the second courtyard of number 28 Rewolucji 1905 Street. The synagogue was tiny. At first Ruth was startled by its almost pitiful modesty. Then she decided it wasn't the synagogue that was pitiful, it was the fact that this synagogue was the only representative left of so many synagogues. Grand synagogues and plain synagogues. Modest and ornate synagogues. Synagogues in apartment buildings and synagogues in the center of town. They had all been destroyed except this synagogue. It was a sweet synagogue with its central arched doorway and arched upper windows. The synagogue was painted in a matte muted pink and flat yellow. It was very, very cute, Ruth decided. She was glad she had seen it.

As hidden as this synagogue was, it had still attracted arsonists. She had read that someone had set fire to the synagogue in 1987, and the Ronald Lauder Foundation had helped to rebuild it.

Ruth was pleased that the synagogue in Rewolucji 1905 Street had been rebuilt. It was a small piece of the warmth, the glow, the devotion that must have been here when there were still Jews in Łódź. Ruth regretted questioning the point of Ronald Lauder's Foundation to revive Jewish life in Poland. This synagogue wouldn't be here without the foundation. She contemplated ringing the Jewish Center and apologizing. She decided against it. They would think she was a lunatic. Ruth blew a kiss to her mother's apartment when she passed it again.

She walked back to the Grand Victoria. She felt depleted. She needed a cup of tea. At the hotel, she sat in the armchair that she felt most comfortable in. The armchair was the most isolated one in the lobby. Set well away from the bulk of the chairs and sofas. Ruth had asked for a whole lemon to be squeezed into her chamomile tea. She sipped the hot lemon-filled drink, and started to feel better. She disliked this lobby. But she disliked her room even more. She hated her room. It depressed her. Edek was joining her in a few minutes. She was glad of the time alone. The time to recover from all of that absence.

Ruth looked down. Someone had left a book at the foot of the chair. She picked up the book. The book was in English. It was a numerology book. How odd. How peculiar. Who could have left this book here? She looked around the lobby. It was quite empty. No one in the lobby was looking at her. This was not a message. She felt a bit creepy. There was something eerie about this. Could Martina have left it? Ruth flicked through the book. There was no note. She was being silly, she decided. There was no hidden meaning to this. There was no meaning at all. Someone had just left the book behind.

Ruth looked at the chapter headed "Numerology and You." Numbers in people's lives were not arbitrary, the book explained, they were of great significance and very important for personal development. The most important number was the birth date number. Ruth added her birth date numbers up. They still came to eight. How could she have developed this far, over forty-two years, if she had only just learned her birth date number? Maybe her ignorance of her birth number explained some of her bewilderment.

Ruth laughed to herself. If only it were that simple. She could have saved tens of thousands of dollars in analysts' and therapists' fees. There was a hierarchy in birth date numbers, she read. Master numbers had extra significance. Master numbers were eleven, twenty-two, and thirty-three. These numbers could not be reduced to a single digit because, the book said, the owners of master numbers had a special lesson to learn.

Ruth was glad that she was not a master number. She had had enough lessons to learn. The next paragraph explained that the demands of the master number could be too difficult to live up to. In that case it was possible to reduce the burden by adding the digits of the master number together to form a single number. This bothered Ruth. If the number was not arbitrary, how could you arbitrarily change it? Why were the rules to all of these things so flexible, so slippery, so sloppy? She tapped her right foot ten times, in case that thought about numerology had offended any spirits or spooks or witches. Spirits or spooks or witches who believed in numerology, that was. That was a crazy thought, she decided. She stopped herself from tapping out another round of ten taps.

Edek would be down any minute. Ruth had something she wanted to organize before he arrived. She walked to the front desk.

"I'd like an interpreter for an hour or two tomorrow morning," Ruth said to the man at the front desk.

"Of course, madam, I can organize this for you," he said.

"Thank you," said Ruth. "Could I have the interpreter at eight o'clock?"

"Eight o'clock is very early," the man said. Ruth raised her eyebrows.

"Do I have to pay extra for an early start?" she said.

"I think so," he said.

"Okay," she said.

"In that case I will organize it for you," the man at the front desk said. "What do you want the interpreter to do?"

"I want him to negotiate the purchase of some items for me," Ruth said.

"Is it expensive items that you are buying?" he said. "We have experts on amber jewelry and silver work."

"No," Ruth said. "I just want to buy some household items. Some pieces of china."

"You would like some amber too?" he asked.

"No," Ruth said. "If I get these pieces of china I'll be very happy."

"This particular interpreter is very good," the man said.

"Great," Ruth said. "Could you also book a car, one of the hotel taxis, to pick me and the guide up, take us to Kamedulska Street, wait for us, and bring us back to the hotel?"

"Of course, of course," the man said. "Your guide and your driver will be here at eight A.M. sharp."

"Do they know each other?" Ruth said.

"Who?" the man said.

"The guide and the driver," she said.

"No," he said. "If you would prefer a guide and a driver who have worked together I can provide this."

"No," she said. "It is not necessary."

Ruth was relieved. A fear of being alone with two Polish men had suddenly swept through her. Men who didn't know each other were less likely to collude in extrapolating more money or any other deception.

"The interpreter will have to charge you extra because of the early time," the man said.

"You mentioned that," said Ruth. She and Edek seemed to be paying extra for everything in Poland. She had changed some more money on her way back to the hotel this afternoon. Money changers were called Kantors, in Poland. Kantors had sprouted rapidly all over Poland since the demise of communism. It was unsettling seeing all the Kantor signs. For Jews, a cantor was a singer of liturgical solos. The person who sang during services at synagogues.

Edek rushed up to Ruth just as she was about to sit down again.

"I got Stefan," he said. He looked joyful. "Stefan is very very happy to drive us to Kraków. I told you he would be very happy."

"That's great," said Ruth.

"Ach, he is so happy," Edek said.

"I'm glad we're spreading such happiness," Ruth said.

"He is very, very happy," said Edek.

Ruth was irritated. Stefan's happiness was beginning to annoy her. She was aggravated by how happy Stefan was. She didn't want him to be that happy.

"I did speak to Stefan's wife, too," Edek said. "His wife is a very nice woman."

"Great," said Ruth. Edek didn't notice her agitation.

"Stefan's wife is very happy with the job, too," Edek said. "She did say to me she was very happy that he does get such a big job."

Ruth was really irked. The thought of Stefan's wife bursting with happiness was more than she could tolerate. She looked at her father. He was beaming. "She did say I spoke a perfect Polish," Edek said.

"Who?" said Ruth.

"Stefan's wife," Edek said. "Who else are we talking about?"

Anybody else, Ruth wished to herself. She was developing a hatred for Stefan's wife. She tried to calm down. Maybe Stefan's wife was a nice woman. Maybe Stefan and his wife had sensitive and intelligent children. Children who would grow up to be great humanitarians or Nobel Prize–winning poets. These thoughts didn't help her. She still felt annoyed.

"I'm glad Stefan's wife complimented you on your Polish," Ruth said to Edek.

"She said I did speak just like a Polack," Edek said. Edek looked at the tray that had held Ruth's chamomile tea. "What is that?" he said, pointing to a piece of chocolate-coated orange peel.

"It's exactly what it looks like," Ruth said. "Chocolate. Chocolate-coated orange peel. It came with my tea."

"You do not want it?" Edek said.

"No, I don't want it," she said.

Edek leaned over and grabbed the piece of chocolate-coated orange peel. He popped it into his mouth quickly. As though the speed eliminated the action. As though he hadn't really eaten it. He was always this swift with food. As though a slower pace would increase the contents or the calories or the greed involved. Was it greed or need? It was unfair of her to think of it as greed, she thought. Her father was entitled to all the chocolate he wanted. He needed chocolate. In the same way that she needed to run. Her father needed his chocolate. She shouldn't needle him about this need. Needle him about his need, she repeated to herself, pleased with the pun.

"It is a very good chocolate," Edek said.

"Good," Ruth said. "Our guide will be here soon," she added.

"She did say she did think I was a Polack when she did speak to me," Edek said.

"Is this Stefan's wife again?" Ruth said.

"Of course," Edek said. "She said I did speak just like a Polack."

"I'm not sure that doing anything just like a Polack is a good thing," Ruth said.

"Do not be stupid," Edek said. He wiped some chocolate from the sides of his mouth with his fingers. Ruth was about to offer him a handkerchief, when he licked his fingers clean.

"I did arrange a hotel for Stefan," Edek said.

"I hope it's a cheap one," Ruth said.

"Of course," said Edek. "You think I am crazy?" Ruth didn't answer. "The doorman did help me," Edek said. Ruth grimaced at the thought of the doorman.

"At least he's good for something," Ruth said.

"I do not know what is wrong with you," Edek said.

Ruth noticed a slightly built, sensitive-looking man hovering near the entrance to the lobby. "I think that might be our guide," she said to Edek. She went up to the elderly man. "I'm Ruth Rothwax," she said. He looked relieved. "I am Marek Kowalski," he said. Ruth introduced Marek to Edek. They chatted. Ruth liked Marek straightaway. He had a face that looked sad in repose and stayed that way when he was animated. He had large, watery blue eyes.

"I am looking forward to seeing the cemetery," Ruth said to Marek. "This cemetery is my love," Marek said. Edek looked at Marek oddly. Ruth could see that Marek was already too much for Edek. She didn't know why.

Edek ran off to organize a taxi. Ruth looked at Marek. His clothes were frayed and worn. He was carrying a yellow shopping bag. Ruth asked him if he would like to leave the bag in the room. He smiled at her. No, he said, he took the bag everywhere. It was quite a large paper bag. Ruth hoped it didn't contain all of Marek's possessions. She hoped Marek wasn't homeless. Edek had arranged the taxi. It was a Mercedes. A gray one this time. They got into the taxi. Ruth sat in the back with Marek. Edek sat in the front. Marek told the driver where to go.

"This Mercedes is not so big what the other ones was," Edek said to Ruth.

"It's smaller, is it?" she said.

"You cannot see this?" Edek said.

"Not really," she said. Edek snorted.

Edek started chatting with the driver. Ruth could hear them talking. They were talking about Kraków. She switched off. She needed a break from Edek and Polish taxi drivers. She looked out of the car window at the streets of Łódź. They really were bleak. Suddenly, Edek turned to face her. He had hoisted himself around in the seat, so abruptly, it had given Ruth a shock.

"This gentleman," Edek said, "says he has got for us a better hotel in Kraków than the one what we have booked."

"Which gentleman?" Ruth said.

"The driver, here," Edek said, annoyed.

Ruth hadn't intended to annoy Edek. She just hadn't instantly associated the word "gentleman" with the man who was driving them. She hadn't even looked at the driver. They were all blending into each other, all the Polish drivers of all the Mercedes. She noticed that this driver had greasy hair. So had most of the others.

"We're booked into a really nice hotel in Kraków," Ruth said.

"He says he has got a better one," Edek said.

"Why should we listen to him?" Ruth said. Edek ignored her.

"What is the name of the one what we are booked in?" he said.

"The Hotel Mimoza," Ruth said.

"The Hotel Mimoza?" said Edek.

"It's very good. It's one of the best hotels in Kraków," Ruth said.

Edek spoke to the driver briefly. He turned back to Ruth. "He says that this Hotel Mimoza is not in such a good position," Edek said.

"It's in the heart of the old city," Ruth said. Edek conferred with the driver again.

"He says you cannot drive in the old city."

"We don't want to drive," Ruth said. "We don't have a car."

"He says he has got a better hotel," Edek said. "It is only two miles from the old town."

"I want to be in the old town," Ruth said. "I don't want to be stuck in the depressing outskirts of the city."

"He says this hotel, what he recommends, the Demel, is famous for their excellent cooking," Edek said.

"We're not going to Kraków for the food," Ruth said.

She felt furious. Who did Edek think he was talking to? He was talking to a Łódź taxi driver, not the editor-in-chief of *Gourmet* magazine or the travel editor of the *New York Times*.

"I used a top travel agent to make this booking," Ruth said to Edek.

"The same travel agent what did book us into the Grand Victoria in Łódź?" Edek said.

"The Grand Victoria, unfortunately, is the best there is, in Łódź," said Ruth. What was wrong with her father? Why did he instantly trust every Polish cabdriver he came across? Why didn't he see the shifty expressions and the greasy glances?

Marek was looking down at his lap. He looked uncomfortable.

"I'm sorry to have this argument in front of you," Ruth said to him. "It is just the tensions of travel."

Marek shook his head, as if to ward off Ruth's explanation. "You do not have to explain to me," he said. "We are nearly there," he added. And smiled. He had the sweetest smile, Ruth thought. She wondered how old he was. It was hard to tell. He looked about eighty.

They arrived at the cemetery. Edek paid the driver. Ruth was struck by the quiet outside the cemetery. There was a strangely peaceful silence surrounding the cemetery. Could silence be peaceful? she thought. Silence could certainly be frightening or ominous or suspenseful. She saw no reason why it couldn't be peaceful. Silence could be imbued with whatever you wanted to imbue it with, she decided. This silence felt peaceful to Ruth.

A sign outside the cemetery said CMENTARZ ZYDOWSKI. Jewish cemetery. Ruth knew that Israel Poznański had bought the land for this cemetery and donated it to the Jewish community. She knew the cemetery had been opened in 1892.

Marek had the key to the cemetery in his hand. All three of them were standing in front of the gate, which was the entrance to the cemetery.

"I want to introduce myself," Marek said slowly. "My name is Marek Kowalski."

"You told us this, already," Edek said. Ruth glared at him.

"I have some more to tell you," Marek said. "I come from Łódź. My mother was Helena Kowalski. My father was Tomasz Kowalski. My father died when I was eight years old. My father was not Jewish."

"He does speak a good English," Edek said, under his breath, to Ruth. Ruth glared at him, again.

"My mother was Jewish," Marek said. "I was in hiding with my mother, Helena Kowalski, during the war. My mother died last year. She was ninety-five. I am seventy years old."

Ruth was shocked that Marek was only seventy. She was very moved by Marek's touchingly formal introduction of himself. No one introduced themselves like that anymore. No one thought it was necessary to tell anyone any more about them than their latest accoutrement, a car, a piece of jewelry, or an item of clothing, revealed.

"Thank you," she said to Marek. She looked at him. It was hard to believe that he was only seventy. He looked so much older.

"Let us go inside," Edek said.

Marek unlocked the door. "Would you like to walk for a time first?" he said to Ruth. "Or would you like me to tell you about the cemetery before we start?"

"We will walk," Edek said. Ruth didn't mind. She wanted to take in the atmosphere. To feel the cemetery before she heard what Marek had to say.

Just inside the entrance to the cemetery was a mound of earth.

"This man had to be buried above the ground," Marek said, pointing to the mound of earth. The mound looked forlorn and alone. The buried man was not far enough into the cemetery, Ruth thought. He was too close to the front gate. Too far from the rest of the dead.

"They did not have time to bury him?" Edek said.

"The ground was too frozen," Marek said. Edek looked closely at the small marker on top of the mound. "He did die two years ago," Edek said to Marek. "The ground was not so frozen in summer."

"That is true," said Marek.

"I suppose they did forget," Edek said.

A few flowers and branches were scattered on the mound. Ruth was glad that not everyone had forgotten this man. Ruth noticed an old red plastic cup lying near the side of the mound. She kicked it away.

"We will start our walk, then, on one of the two principal axes of the cemetery," Marek said. They looked around for Edek. He had already run off and was halfway down a small path. "We will follow your father," Marek said to Ruth.

It had snowed lightly overnight. Small patches of white snow dotted the earth. A gray mist thickened the air. The leafless trunks and branches of trees had a light white frosting. This part of the cemetery was quite unkempt. Large tufts of weeds sprouted up against the sides of broken tombstones. Even the weeds had a ghostly beauty.

Ruth walked behind Marek. She could feel something falling away from her. Something lifting. Her limbs felt relaxed. What was she losing? she thought. She was losing her headache, she realized. She was losing the stomachache that led, so frequently, to nausea. How did she know that these things were leaving? She could just tell. She stopped beside a particularly high pile of weeds and tilted headstones. The weeds were entangled with fragments of stones that must have come from nearby graves. She could see bits and pieces of abbreviated inscriptions on some of the stones.

She wanted to clear the weeds away. Put the broken stones back together again. Mend the tablets and markers and memorials. She knew it couldn't be done. It was a bit like Humpty Dumpty, she thought. She was immediately shocked by that thought. How could she be so irreverent? How could she think about a nursery rhyme here? The words to Humpty Dumpty went through her head. "All the king's horses and all the king's men couldn't put Humpty together again." Maybe it was not so irreverent, she thought. Maybe it was appropriate.

Two exquisite headstones, side by side, caught her eye. Sculpted, in relief, across the top of each headstone was a broken tree. The tree was broken in half. The top half, with all its branches and leaves, was draped elegantly almost to the bottom of the headstone. The smaller of the two headstones had JAKOB HORWICZ in a diagonal bar across the left-hand corner. The inscription on the other headstone was in Hebrew or Yiddish. The broken tree must symbolize a truncated life, Ruth thought. Marek came up to her. "The broken tree symbolizes the end of life," he said.

Edek found Ruth and Marek. Edek was slightly out of breath. He had come running back from whatever part of the cemetery he had been in.

"You seen enough?" Edek said to Ruth. Ruth was shocked.

"We've only been here for five minutes," she said.

"How many minutes do we need to be here?" Edek said. "A cemetery is a cemetery."

"A few more," Ruth said. Edek shrugged his shoulders and walked off. "Don't lose us, Dad," she called out after him. He laughed.

"You think I am going to let you leave me in the cemetery," he said. "No way, brother."

Ruth smiled at Edek's combination of the two colloquialisms, "no way," and "brother." "Well, just make sure you can see us," she said.

"Okey dokey," he said. Ruth almost laughed. The Łódź cemetery was making her father more Australian by the minute. She smiled at Marek. "This is difficult for him," she said, nodding in the direction of her father.

"Of course," Marek said.

Ruth walked ahead of Marek. She was glad to be on her own. She was quite pleased that her father had wandered off. Well, he hadn't exactly wandered off, he had run. As though he was running from a ghost. Maybe, in this place, he was.

Ruth realized that a large calm had descended on her. She felt steady and unstrained. The trouble that so often brewed and bubbled in her brain had been quelled. As though someone had poured a balm over her, and hushed her anxiety. She felt almost groggy with peacefulness. Almost sluggish with a quietness she had rarely experienced, as though she had been injected intravenously with a tranquilizer or sedative.

What had pacified her? she wondered. Was it her proximity to people she had always felt close to? The proximity to the dead? They weren't her dead. She knew that. Her dead weren't buried like this. Her dead were burnt in outdoor ditches or baked, like roast meats, in ovens. But these dead, the dead in the Jewish Cemetery in Łódź, were the closest to her dead, her family, that she would ever get. She knew that.

She kept walking. She felt so calm she wanted to cry. Was this calm what normal people felt like? Were there people who lived without the edginess and tension and nervousness that were normal for her? She didn't know. She passed a group of stubby stumps, the remains of tablets and markers, sticking up from the ground. They looked like big, thick, broken, gray teeth. She felt sad. What had been there? Who was buried beneath that piece of earth? Buried beneath those sunken and broken stone molars and bicuspids, with only cracked and shortened marble dentures as markings.

She arrived at a whole field of headstones still upright, still in one piece. The headstones were dwarfed and enveloped by tall, wild weeds. Ruth couldn't reach them. She was pleased that they were at least intact, if out of reach. Some mushrooms were growing around the foot of the tree Ruth was standing beside. The mushrooms looked alive. Healthy and vigorous. Cemeteries were probably composed of agriculturally enriched earth, Ruth thought.

She looked for her father. She couldn't see him. She didn't want to call out to him. She didn't want to disturb the silence. She felt it would be blasphemous to shout in this place. You never knew whom you might startle. She really had to stop thinking of dead people as being alive, she thought. It was no good for her to think this way. How could dead people be startled? That was absurd. She called out to Edek. There was no response. She looked around her. Nothing else had moved or changed. Nobody was bothered by her shout. She couldn't see Marek. Maybe he had followed Edek. She wasn't worried. She was sure she would catch up with both of them soon.

There were symbols on many of the headstones and tombstones in the cemetery. This was quite different from the plain, unadorned monuments and memorials in the Jewish Cemetery in Springvale, Melbourne. Plant motifs were common here, and a pair of hands in a gesture of blessing was engraved and embossed on small and large stones and columns and arches. The symbols often referred to aspects of the dead person's life. There were books for scholars of the Talmud and a basin and ewer, a pitcher with a flaring spout, for descendants of the Levites, attendants in the temple, and for teachers of the law.

Images of extinguished candles represented the end of the lives of some women. This was an allusion to the lighting of the candles on the Sabbath, a job always done by women. An alms box was a symbol of generosity or charity, and a crown signified fidelity in a marriage. Ruth was fascinated by the graves and their symbols. She had read about the burial symbols of Jews, in Manhattan, months before she had left for Poland. She had known that she would be visiting the Bracka Street Cemetery. She had read that there were over one hundred and eighty thousand graves in the cemetery.

There was a balance and harmony in the cemetery that was palpable. As though its inhabitants were as cohesive in their death as they were in their lives. As though the community of scholars and teachers and lawyers and workers and watchmakers and artisans and industrialists and rabbis and doctors were still alive. Although they had shifted into another dimension, unchanged. Ruth could feel the symmetry, the unity. She could feel the love in the community, the husbands and wives, the families.

"Where were you?" Edek said, in a loud voice. Ruth got a fright. She jumped.

"Marek and I was looking for you everywhere," Edek said.

"You gave me an awful fright," Ruth said.

"We was worried about you," Edek said.

"I've looked for you a couple of times," she said.

"Well, we are together, now," Marek said.

"Okay, forget about it," Edek said to Ruth. "I did find you."

Marek put down his yellow shopping bag.

"This cemetery has been designated a national monument of the example of nineteenth-century architectural thoughts," he said.

Edek groaned. Ruth hoped that Marek hadn't heard the groan.

"The architectural thought that is being recognized is the turning of existing fields and small farms close to the town into a place for the burial of the dead," Marek said. Edek kicked at some dirt with his foot.

"Okay," Edek said, briskly.

"One of the architects who drew up the plans was Adolf Zeligson, who also designed the preburial hall," Marek said.

"Thank you very much," Edek said. He went to move on.

"I have not finished yet," said Marek. He looked hurt.

"Forgive my father," Ruth said.

"Why should he forgive me?" Edek said. "I did not do anything wrong. How did I know that he was not finished?" Edek looked wounded, now.

"I didn't say you did anything terrible," Ruth said to her father.

"Are you ashamed of your father?" Edek said.

"No, of course I'm not," she said.

"Maybe I was right. Maybe I should have stayed in Melbourne," Edek said.

"Let us look at the mausoleum of Poznański," Marek said.

"Oh, Poznański," Edek said. "He was very rich."

"Very, very rich," Ruth said.

"Where is Poznański's grave?" said Edek.

"Not far," said Marek. "Follow me." Ruth and Edek followed Marek.

Ruth felt sorry for her father. She shouldn't have apologized for him. She should have been more sensitive. He was eighty-one and she had dragged him into a cemetery. A cemetery saturated with dead Jews. Edek probably had relatives who were buried here. The names on the graves were probably reviving many memories for him. Difficult memories. She should be taking more care of her father, she decided.

"Wow," said Ruth, when she saw the mausoleum that housed Israel Poznański and his wife. It was enormous and imposing. It stood above and towered over everything else in the cemetery. Ruth had never seen a mausoleum of this size built for a Jew. Four columns supported a large dome. Arched windows were built into the dome. Ruth walked up the steps of the monument. A locked wrought-iron gate prevented her from going inside. She peered inside. She could just make out the intricate work of the mosaic tiles that lined the interior of the dome. The monument Poznański had built for himself. It was quite beautiful, Ruth thought.

"It is very big," Edek said.

"It sure is," said Ruth.

"I think it is too big," Edek said.

"A lot of people might agree with you," she said. "But I think it is beautiful."

"You always must like what normal people do not like," Edek said. He turned to Marek. "That is my daughter. If ten people does like something, my daughter for sure will not like it," he said. Marek looked nervous. He clearly didn't want to get involved in any domestic disputes.

"Israel Poznański and his wife, Eleonora Poznański, are buried here," Marek said. "Inside is a mosaic which is comprised of approximately two million pieces of glass."

"Two million, oh, brother," Edek whispered.

"This is possibly the only Jewish tomb in the world decorated with mosaics," Marek said.

"I did never see something like this, on a grave," Edek said.

"You haven't seen many cemeteries," Ruth said.

"I seen enough," said Edek. He looked annoyed with Ruth. "I was trying to be nice to him," Edek whispered to her.

"He can hear us, Dad," she said.

"He cannot hear me," Edek said. "He is an old man."

"Can I take a photograph of you in front of Poznański's tomb?" she said to Edek.

"What for?" he said. "A photograph in a cemetery? I will be in a cemetery myself soon enough. I don't need a photograph in a cemetery."

"Okay, okay," she said.

"Here are also other monuments for the families of the wealthy Jews," Marek said, pointing to nearby sites. "There are the tombs of the family of Marcus Silberstein, the Prussaks, the Jarocińskis, the Rapaports, and some other important Jewish families," he said.

"The Rapaports," Ruth said. "They must be the Rapaports whose palace your father bought."

"I suppose so," said Edek. He paused for a moment. "We was not rich like these rich Jews from Łódź" he said.

"They were mega rich, I think," Ruth said.

"We was normal rich," Edek said.

"These mausoleums, sarcophaguses, and tombstones are made in a variety of materials," Marek said. "Black granite, white marble, sandstone, wrought iron. They are built in many styles. Neoclassicism, Historical, Art Nouveau, Modernism."

"He talks too much," Edek said to Ruth.

"He can hear you," Ruth said.

"I am telling the truth," Edek said.

"Dad," she said, in a stern tone, but Edek had already rushed off.

"I love this cemetery very much," Marek said to Ruth. "My mother is buried here," Marek said. Ruth looked at Marek. He had tears in his eyes.

"It is a very beautiful cemetery," she said. She walked on, ahead of Marek.

The beauty of the cemetery was amplified, Ruth thought, by the contrast with the squalor and decay of what remained of the formerly Jewish homes in Łódź. And the bigotry and ignorance and indifference of the Poles. The only passion Ruth had seen among the Polish, she thought, was a passion for hatred and a passion for alcohol. She didn't want to leave the cemetery. She wanted to stay. To sit here, with these people. To keep them company. To show them they were not forgotten.

The monument to the Jews who died in the Łódź ghetto was near the façade of the old mortuary. Approximately fifty thousand Jews who died in the Łódź ghetto were buried in this cemetery, in a section called the Ghetto Fields. Dozens of visitors had left *yahrzeit* candles, memorial candles for the dead, in the Ghetto Fields. Ruth had been reassured by the presence of other people's prayers and respects.

Ruth stood in front of three identically shaped tombstones. Each tombstone had a butterfly carved across the top. She started tidying the area around the tombstones. She picked up several stones, and an old bottle. She removed some paper and several branches. She stepped back. The tombstones looked better already. Ruth put down her bag and rolled up the sleeves of her coat. She moved some old newspapers.

She looked up and saw her father. Edek was staring at her. He looked miserable.

"You can give them money if you want to do something," he said to Ruth. "If they have the money, they will clean up the graves." Ruth straightened up. She suddenly felt overwhelmed. And tearful.

"You're right, Dad," she said. She turned away so that he wouldn't see her tears.

"Come on," Edek said to her. "It is enough for today."

"I'm coming," she said.

"I did tell Marek to ring a taxi," he said. "Marek did say there was a telephone somewhere. The taxi should be here."

Marek and the taxi were waiting by the front gate.

"Thank you so much," Ruth said to Marek.

"Thank you, it was very interesting," Edek added. Ruth gave Marek some money. He refused to take it. "Please take it," Ruth said. Marek shook his head.

"My daughter already feels bad. If you do not accept her gift she will feel worse," Edek said. He took the money and pressed it into Marek's hand.

"Thank you," Marek said.

"Can we give you a lift?" Ruth said.

"I live not far from here," Marek said. "I want to walk." They all shook hands.

In the taxi, on the way home, they passed a large billboard advertising a brand of footwear. Across the middle of the billboard someone had written *Juden Raus* and, for those non-German speakers, the author had added "Jews Out." Ruth was shocked. She pointed it out to Edek. The taxi driver looked at what Ruth was pointing out. He said something to Edek. "I know what he's saying," Ruth said to her father. "He doesn't have to tell me. He's saying it's only children." She sat back in her seat. She couldn't stop shivering.

Twenty minutes later they were back at the hotel. Edek looked at Ruth.

"You should have a rest," he said.

"I think I'll have a hot bath," she said.

"Are we going to have a dinner today?" Edek said.

"Of course we'll eat dinner," Ruth said. "I'll meet you in the lobby at seven o'clock."

"Where will we eat?" Edek said.

"I thought we could try the Chinese restaurant we walked past yesterday," Ruth said.

"Chinee?" Edek said. For years Ruth had reminded Edek to add the "s" to the end of "Chinese." But he just couldn't remember. "Chinee, in Łódź?" Edek said.

"I thought it would be interesting to see what they served," Ruth said.

"I am not having any of those worms," Edek said.

"They're not worms," Ruth said. "They're prawns. In America they're called shrimp."

"To me they are worms," he said.

"You don't have to eat worms," Ruth said, with more irritation than she had intended. "You can have chicken."

"Okay, okay," Edek said. "For me it is not so important what I eat. I can eat anything."

"Except worms," Ruth said.

"That is right," Edek said. "I do not like worms." He paused. "You are sure you want to eat Chinee in Poland?" he said.

"I just want to see what it's like," Ruth said. "You can have some chicken soup. You love Chinese chicken soup."

"Chinee chicken soup is very good," Edek said.

"And so is Polish chicken soup," said Ruth. "So the combination should be wonderful."

Edek looked more cheerful. "I think I will stay downstairs, here in the lobby, for a few minutes," he said.

"Good idea, Dad," she said. "See you later."

She was just about to walk off when Edek grabbed her arm.

"What is our agenda for tomorrow?" he said.

"I didn't know you knew the word 'agenda,' " Ruth said.

"Of course I know this word," Edek said. "I been using it for a long time. You are not the only one in the family what knows plenty of words."

"Sorry," Ruth said. "Tomorrow we're going to the Łódź ghetto, and then we leave for Kraków."

"Is it necessary for you to go to the ghetto?" Edek said.

"I'd like to," she said.

"There is nothing there," Edek said.

"I know," she said.

"We are visiting one nothing after the other," Edek said.

"I guess that's true, Dad," Ruth said. "You could stay at the hotel."

"No," Edek said. "I am going where you are going."

"You've just reminded me," Ruth said, "that I won't be here for breakfast tomorrow."

Edek looked startled and wounded. "I'm just going for a run, Dad," she said. "I really feel the need to run."

"I will wait for you and we will have breakfast together," Edek said.

"I want to have a long run," Ruth said. "I probably won't be back before ten o'clock. That's too long for you to wait for breakfast."

"I can wait," Edek said.

"Dad, just have the buffet breakfast we have every morning," she said. "You love it."

Edek looked morose. "If you are not going to the buffet I won't go, too."

"Okay," she said. "You can have breakfast in your room."

"I do not need a breakfast every day," Edek said.

Ruth had had enough. She wanted to go up to her room and read. "See you later, Dad," she said. She didn't like lying to him. But she was really not up to a conversation about why she wanted to go to Kamedulska Street and buy the china.

There were no other customers in the Chinese restaurant on Al. Kościuszki. There was nobody Chinese, either. The lack of anyone Chinese bothered Ruth. The waiters were Polish. The chef was probably Polish, too, she thought. A large buffet of prepared hot dishes ran down the center of the restaurant. This was a bad sign. Chinese food was meant to be cooked and served immediately.

"Do you have à la carte?" Ruth asked a waiter.

"What?" the waiter said.

"Do you have a menu, or is the buffet the only choice?" Ruth said.

"All of our customers are very happy with this buffet," the waiter said. "You can eat as much as you wish for the same price."

"So this is all that you serve?" Ruth said.

"It is plenty, madam," the waiter said. Ruth looked at the buffet. The food had probably been sitting in its heated bains-marie for a long time.

"I do like a buffet very much," Edek said. "What is wrong with a buffet?"

"It's probably okay," she said.

"You was the one who did want Chinee," said Edek.

Ruth chose a table. Edek was already at the buffet. The decor was Chinese. Well, Chinese-ish. Chinese paper lantern and scrolls with Chinese calligraphy, mingled with floral Polish curtains and floral Polish carpeting. The napkins, Ruth noticed, were also floral. A different floral from the curtains.

Edek was calling her. "Ruthie, Ruthie," he called. She looked at him. He was gesturing at the buffet. "It does look pretty good," he called out across the restaurant. Ruth walked over to him. He looked excited. "This is really Chinee," he said, pointing to something that was labeled, in English, "Wonton." Ruth looked at the wontons. These wontons weren't Chinese dumplings. These wontons were half-pound Polish meat loaves wrapped and encased, like *pierogi*, in boiled pastry. They were enormous. Edek had put three of them on his plate.

"I thought you were going to have chicken soup," Ruth said to him.

"Ach," he said. "The chicken soup does not look so good."

Ruth looked at the chicken soup. It was a clear, unfatty broth with a few scallions floating in it. It looked, to Ruth, like the most appetizing of all of the items on display. Ruth took some chicken soup.

"Why do you take the soup?" Edek said. "You need to eat. Have some sweet and sour beef. The Chinee do a very good sweet and sour meat." The sweet and sour beef had enormous cubes of beef floating together with cubed potato in a brown gravy.

"It looks more like goulash to me," Ruth said.

"This is not goulash," Edek said. "This is Chinee." Edek added another wonton to his plate and walked back to the table. He looked so happy. Ruth decided to keep her culinary criticism to herself.

"They got fried rice, too," Edek called out.

Ruth looked at the fried rice. It looked more like cooked coleslaw sitting on a bed of gravied rice. Thick slices of fried kielbasa sausage decorated the fried rice platter. Ruth started to laugh. It really was very funny. She laughed and laughed. It was good to laugh. She hadn't laughed for what felt like a long time. She was still laughing when she got back to the table.

"What are you laughing at?" Edek said.

"The food is not really Chinese," she said.

"Why not?" he said.

"It's Polish," she said.

"It looks Chinee to me," Edek said. "And I did eat a lot of Chinee in Melbourne."

"The Chinese food in Melbourne doesn't look like this," Ruth said.

"No, not exactly like this," Edek said. "The pieces here are a bit bigger."

Ruth started to laugh again. Her laughter was contagious. Edek joined in. "It is good to see you laughing, Ruthie darling," he said through his own laughter.

"It's good to laugh," she said, wiping her eyes. She started to eat. "This chicken soup is really delicious," she said.

"My wonton is very very good," said Edek.

Ruth finished her soup. She felt better. She decided to have another bowl of soup. A bowl of boiled noodles was on the buffet, next to the soup. Ruth added some noodles to her soup. The noodles were very thick. They looked more like spaghetti than noodles. This trip was proving to be a dietary aid, she thought. She had been worried that she would gain weight in Poland. The government could probably revive the whole Polish economy if they advertised weight-loss tours of Poland for Jews, Ruth thought. She felt the waistband of her skirt. It was definitely loose.

"I did speak to my lawyer," Edek said when Ruth returned to the table.

"Your lawyer in Australia?" said Ruth.

"My lawyer in Australia is the only lawyer what I got," said Edek.

"Did you ring him?" she said.

"Of course," he said. "Do you think that I am such an important client that he should ring me in Poland?"

"You rang this afternoon?" she said.

"Yes," he said.

"What time was it in Australia?" Ruth said. "I hope it wasn't in the middle of the night." She did some quick calculations. She was relieved. It could have been morning in Melbourne.

"I do not know what was the time in Melbourne," Edek said.

"Well, I'm glad you didn't wake him up," Ruth said.

"He was in his office," Edek said. "Of course I did not wake him up. You want to hear what he did tell me?"

"Yes, of course," Ruth said.

"He did say that all the talks with the Swiss banks for a settlement for the Jews are kaput," Edek said.

"Kaput?" Ruth said.

"Finished," Edek said. "The Swiss did take away their offer."

"That small, piddly offer that was a fraction of what they took from the Jews?" Ruth said.

"The Swiss do not want to negotiate anymore," Edek said. "They say that the Holocaust survivors and other Jewish groups was trying to get more money from the banks with threats of bad publicity for the Swiss."

"So it's the Jews who are behaving badly again," Ruth said.

"It is always the Jews," said Edek. "My lawyer did say that the gold what the Swiss did get from the Nazis would be today valued at nearly three billion dollars."

"And it's still the Jews who are behaving badly," Ruth said. "We don't need their money," she said.

"That is true," said Edek, "but some Jews do."

"It's disgusting," Ruth said. Edek looked alarmed.

"The soup?" he said.

"No, the Swiss," she said.

"The lawyer did tell me that finally Volkswagen is going to give some money to those people who was forced to work for them during the war," Edek said.

"So Volkswagen has finally decided to pay those people who were used as slave labor," said Ruth.

"Yes," said Edek. "The lawyer did tell me Volkswagen did admit that they did employ fifteen thousand slave laborers during the war."

"Most of the people who were used as slave labor would be dead by now," Ruth said.

"Of course," Edek said.

"I wonder if Volkswagen has agreed to a settlement because they've just bought the Rolls-Royce Company," Ruth said. "They're also buying Lamborghini, the Italian sports car company. The Lamborghini is an incredibly expensive car."

"I do know what is a Lamborghini," Edek said.

"I wonder if Volkswagen suddenly worried about its image," she said.

"I wonder if the discrepancy between their refusal to pay for the slave labor they used and the luxury of the cars they produce seemed embarrassing?"

"That's very clever," Edek said.

"I don't think Volkswagen was really concerned about the Jews," Ruth said. "I think they were concerned about their image. They'll probably try to pay the poor slave laborers who survived the smallest possible amount of money."

"This is probably what they are doing," Edek said. "Ah, forget about it," Edek said suddenly. He looked disturbed.

"I told you it would agitate you if you tried to get back what is owed to you," Ruth said.

"I am all right," Edek said. "This goulash is very good."

"I told you it was goulash," Ruth said. She started laughing.

"It is Chinee goulash," Edek said. Her father should know what it was, Ruth thought. This was his third helping. "You want some?" Edek said.

"No thanks, Dad," she said. They ate in silence.

"*Oy, a broch,*" Edek said loudly.

"What's wrong?" Ruth said.

"A worm," he said. "Here is a worm." He was holding a small prawn on the end of his fork.

"It's not a worm," Ruth said. "It's a prawn."

Edek examined it. "It is a worm," he said.

Ruth took the small prawn from Edek's fork. She put it into her mouth. "It's delicious," she said. Edek grimaced.

"I did ring Stefan," Edek said. "I did want to make sure that he did arrive."

"He's in Łódź?" Ruth said.

"He is in Łódź," Edek said with a beam. "He does like his hotel very much."

"I'm so pleased," Ruth said.

"You are being sarcastic," Edek said. "I know you."

"No, I'm not," Ruth said. "I actually am very pleased that Stefan is pleased because that makes you happy."

"It does not make me happy," Edek said. "I did want for Stefan to drive us because it will be more comfortable for you. Why should you sit on a Polish train? Why not instead to be in a Mercedes?"

"Why not?" said Ruth.

"They have got very good cakes on the buffet," Edek said, after a minute.

"I know," said Ruth. "I saw them."

Displayed at the end of the buffet, after the wontons and the sweet and sour beef and the crispy-skinned chicken, and the chow mein and chop suey and fried rice, was a selection of cakes. There was a black forest cake, a sour cherry cake, a cheesecake, an apple cake, and a poppy seed cake.

"You can have a piece of poppy seed cake," Edek said to Ruth.

"It does look very good," she said. "The Poles know how to make a poppy seed cake."

"And a cheesecake," Edek said. "Maybe I will have a small piece of cheesecake. I just finish this first." He ate the last of his fourth helping of sweet and sour beef.

"*Oy, cholera,*" Edek said suddenly. He looked at his fork. "Another worm," he said. Ruth took the prawn from his fork. "This small prawn couldn't possibly hurt you," she said. "I'll eat it." She put it into her mouth. "See?" she said. "It's delicious."

"My daughter does like worms," Edek said. He shook his head and shrugged his shoulders.

❧ *Chapter Eleven* ❧

Ruth was awakened by a phone call from Max. It was
6 A.M. Ruth was completely disoriented. For a moment she didn't know
where she was. Was she in Poland? In New York? In Australia? It had been
years since she had thought she was still living in Australia.

"Bern's mother has turned out to be very good," Max said.

"What time is it in New York?" Ruth said.

"It's midnight," said Max. "I'm at home."

"I'll call you back in five minutes," Ruth said. She hung up.

She sat on the edge of the bed. She felt dislocated. Max's call had rattled
and flummoxed her. The call had felt like a communion from another time,
another place. It was as though Max was calling from Mars. Ruth felt so
removed from Rothwax Correspondence. She could hardly remember anything about what was going on in the office. She felt as if she had been away,
under a spell. Or adrift at sea. She hoped that she still remembered the
business phone number. She checked. She was relieved that she still did.

What was Max saying about Bern's mother? Of course, Ruth remembered. Max was talking about the possibility of Bern's mother writing letters by hand for them. Ruth picked up the phone. "I want to cancel the two
wake-up calls I booked for 6:10 A.M. and 6:15 A.M." she said to the hotel
operator.

"Why is this?" the operator asked.

"Because I am already awake," Ruth said. She shook her head in bewilderment. What other reason could there possibly be for canceling a wakeup call? She would never understand Poles, she thought.

She got out of bed and switched off both of the alarm clocks she had set. She had bought an extra alarm clock in Łódź. She didn't trust the antiquated electric clock in the room. She brushed her teeth in the bottled water and swallowed her vitamins. She looked at the display of vitamins and minerals. She wasn't sure what they were doing for her.

She rang Max.

"Let me call you back," Max said. "It's cheaper that way."

"Okay," Ruth said. She hung up again. Why was everything in life, including a simple phone call, so complicated? Max was right, though. It would cost far less for her to call Ruth. Max wouldn't be paying the exorbitant price that was charged for international calls in Poland, or the hotel surcharge.

The phone rang.

"Bern's mother is very good," Max said. Max sounded excited. "Her handwriting is clear and not full of flourishes and swirls," she said.

"It's not pretentious?" Ruth asked.

"Not at all," said Max. "It's intelligent handwriting."

"Intelligent handwriting. That sounds good," Ruth said. She felt as though she could do with some intelligence herself. Her head felt thick and clogged.

"She can do three pages in an hour," Max said. "She'll soon, when she gets used to it, be able to do four pages an hour."

"What is Bern's mother's name?" Ruth said.

"Alouette," said Max.

"Alouette," Ruth said. "That's a great name."

"I suggested to Alouette that we have a trial run with her," Max said. "I told her not to leave her current job until she knows how she feels about us and how we feel about her."

"Did you feel odd saying that to someone much older than you?" Ruth said.

"No," said Max.

"Were you uncomfortable suggesting a trial period to someone of color?"

"No," Max said.

"That's good," said Ruth.

"Alouette is very comfortable to be with," Max said. "I didn't think about her age or her color. I just liked her. I suggested that she work for us for a few hours a couple of times a week. And then we'll all decide how we all feel."

"Perfect," said Ruth.

"I said we'd pay her fifteen dollars an hour," Max said.

"We charge twenty-five dollars a page," Ruth said. "I think we can afford to pay her twenty dollars an hour."

"Okay," said Max.

"If we take her on permanently, we'll negotiate a salary," Ruth said.

"That's what I told her," said Max.

"Well, you sound like you're handling everything pretty well," Ruth said.

"How are you doing?" Max said. "I've been thinking about you all the time."

"I'm fine," Ruth said.

"Are you sure you're fine?" Max said.

"That's a very Jewish question, Max," Ruth said. "I'm fine."

Max laughed. "I've been worried about you," she said. "I've been thinking about you facing all that loss. And your father facing all that loss. The two of you together lost in the loss. And then there's the loss of all the other Jews."

Ruth interrupted this messy monologue on loss. "Edit, Max," she said, "edit. I really appreciate your concern, but I'm very tired. So, let's move on to the rest of the business."

"Okay," Max said. "Sorry if I was a bit long-winded."

"That's okay," Ruth said. "You really could have tried an alternative to the excessive repetitions of the word 'loss,' though."

Max laughed. "Now I know you're fine," she said.

"Bern loves having his mother at the office," Max said. "He says hello to her each time he passes her. He buys cookies for her to have with her coffee. It's great to see how close they are."

"I'm not sure it's all that common for men to be close to their mothers," Ruth said. "I'm impressed enough by women who are close to their mothers. There seem to be few enough of them. Most people seem to do little more than complain about their parents."

"You're not going to go on to one of your ungrateful children dialogues are you?" Max said.

"It would be a monologue, not a dialogue," said Ruth. "You never join in."

"That's because I want children one day," Max said. "Poland hasn't stopped you being so acerbic. It hasn't mellowed you."

"Poland has nearly killed me," Ruth said. She was surprised at herself. Had Poland really nearly killed her? She certainly felt more mortal than when she arrived.

Ruth realized that speaking to Max had cheered her up. Made her feel more normal. More attached to the normal world. That was what being in Poland did. It made life in New York seem normal. Her old life felt so normal. The Raisin Bran, the weight lifting, the twelve-minute limit on the time she allowed herself for *People* magazine. The coat hangers all facing the same direction. It all felt so normal. Why had she called it her old life? she wondered. This was still the same life. This was not a new life. She was still Ruth Rothwax. Still forty-three. Still on a diet. Not that much had changed.

Ruth was glad that Max had called. "Speaking of mothers," she said to Max, "how does your mother feel about you and the married man?" Ruth was sure that she could hear Max squirm. "Do we have to discuss that?" Max said. "You're in Poland."

"I know I'm in Poland," Ruth said with a sigh.

"My mother doesn't say anything," Max said.

"Does she know?" said Ruth.

"No," said Max.

"What about your father?" Ruth said.

"He doesn't know," said Max. "I couldn't tell them anything separately. They would immediately tell the other. They tell each other everything. They're soul mates."

What were soul mates? Ruth wondered. Mates who melted into each other? Souls with no borders? Did souls have borders? Did souls have edges and divides? Could you protect your soul from trespassers? Or could anyone traipse through it, once you'd lost the protection of a physical being? Was it easy for souls to merge? Easier than those beings encumbered by bodies?

Ruth shook herself. She had to stop this unearthly thinking. These otherworldly cogitations and considerations. She had wandered off into outer space. Into uncharted territory. She had missed half of what Max had said. Ruth stood up. She would be much better off, she decided, if she kept herself grounded.

"The good news is that everything in the office is going well," Max said. "Two new clients called today. Both from California, so news of Rothwax Correspondence is spreading."

"Good," said Ruth. "Tell Bern's mother that I'm looking forward to meeting her."

Ruth showered and dressed. She sat on the bed and ate an apple. She had taken the apple from yesterday's breakfast buffet. It was a green Granny Smith. It was no good. It was hard to get a good apple in Poland. The apple cake was superb, but the fresh apples were spongy and small and bruised. She ate the apple anyway. The interpreter that the hotel clerk had arranged for her was waiting at the front desk. She got her bag and her coat and went downstairs.

"I am Tadeusz Kuczyński," he said to Ruth. Tadeusz Kuczyński looked about fifteen. He was tall and gangly.

"How old are you, Tadeusz?" Ruth said.

"I am twenty-five," he said.

"Good," she said. "I thought you were much younger."

Ruth was glad that she had a young interpreter. A young person was less likely to bring their own history, their own prejudices, their own baggage to this potential transaction. Ruth hoped that by arriving early she was giving herself a good chance of finding the old man and his wife at home, in Kamedulska Street, in Edek's old apartment.

She briefly explained her mission to Tadeusz. Tadeusz didn't seem to find the situation very complicated. "If you pay them the right price I am sure that they will sell you the china," Tadeusz said.

Tadeusz was probably right, Ruth thought. Why did she have to feel so tense about it? Because she wanted that china very much. Very, very much. Her desire to have the china was probably completely disproportionate to the old couple's need to sell the china. She was tense. No wonder she was tense. Her position was not a good position to be in, in any negotiation.

The taxi that was taking them to Kamedulska Street was a small, nondescript Polish car. It felt tinny to Ruth. And cramped. Her knees were pushed up and were almost touching her chest. Why did the hotel clerk order this taxi? Probably because the driver was a friend, and the clerk was getting a kickback for every customer he provided, Ruth thought. She was agitated. She should have asked for a Mercedes. She had clearly become accustomed to Mercedes. The car stank of cigarettes. There was no need for her to wish Polish people any ill, she thought. Most Poles were going to smoke themselves to death.

She wondered whether she should tap her right foot to ward off any retribution for that thought. Did an aggressive thought toward Poles count in the lexicon of untoward behavior that merited punishment? Who knew? Whoever it was that decided what was to be punished and what wasn't, if there was someone or something overseeing all human behavior, had a very strange system. An incomprehensible set of criteria. If feeling hostile to Poles warranted punishment she would have to tap her right foot ceaselessly and start immediately. She didn't have enough time left, she thought, for ten taps for every hostile thought she had had about Poles. She would have to do so much tapping, her right foot would get worn right out.

She smiled at her unintentional pun. Why did the mixing and blending of words and their nuances mean so much to her? Maybe because so much of what she heard as a child was so blunt. The short, blurred communications from her mother and father were not their fault. Their stunted ability to speak the language she spoke was just how it was. They were too busy working in factories to go to English classes. When they came home from the factories, there were no tender discussions, no delicate explanations, no refined analysis of this word or that. Everything was cut short and condensed. All greetings and orders and suggestions and reflections ended up as sharp fragments. Impossible to piece together.

"Tadeusz," she said, "it is crucial that these people don't think that the china that I want to buy is very important to me." She looked at Tadeusz. Could she trust him? How could she tell? She didn't know him. "Because it is not important," she said. "If they want to sell it, that's fine. If they don't, we'll leave."

"Of course," said Tadeusz.

Whom could you trust and whom couldn't you trust? The question was even more difficult to answer in Poland. She had surprised herself by asking the doorman at the Grand Victoria if he could find her a couple of strong boxes. She had been astonished, first, that she had asked the doorman. She had thought she found him too revolting to make any requests of. Then she had been surprised to hear herself requesting two boxes. Two large boxes, she had said. What did she think she was going to find in her father's former home?

Ruth suddenly thought that she should let Tadeusz know that she could understand Polish. He needn't know that she couldn't understand every word. Or most complicated words. She didn't think the old man or his wife would be using very complicated language. She wasn't lying to Tadeusz, she thought, not that that was a moral issue or any other sort of issue for her. She could understand more and more Polish, though. Sometimes, she wished she understood less.

She didn't want Tadeusz to entertain any schemes of colluding with the old couple and splitting the proceeds. She didn't want him to think he could hike up the prices and split the difference with these vendors. She didn't want him to be duplicitous. She was not sure that she could prevent any duplicity. Still, it would only be money that she would be losing if the interpreter and the couple colluded. He probably wouldn't try anything, Ruth decided. After all, how did he know he could trust the old couple? Even to a Pole, this couple would look untrustworthy.

"You do not have to be so nervous," Tadeusz said. Ruth jumped. How could he have known what she was thinking? He couldn't have known. He must be addressing her general demeanor.

"I'm not nervous," she said to him.

"I think you are," he said. "If you do not mind me saying so."

"I don't mind," she said. "Plenty of people have commented on what they see as my nervous disposition. I'm not that nervous. I just appear nervous."

"It is not so bad to be nervous," Tadeusz said. Maybe Tadeusz was okay, Ruth thought. Any young man who thought it wasn't so bad to be nervous couldn't be all that bad.

"I agree," she said to him.

Ruth wondered if she should offer Tadeusz a bonus to keep him on the straight and narrow? No, she decided, she was already paying him extra for the early start.

"Could you make sure the driver knows that he has to wait for us?" Ruth said to Tadeusz.

"I discussed this with the driver, before," Tadeusz said.

"Okay," she said. "Could you tell him that we'll pay him for the whole trip when we get back to the hotel?"

Tadeusz spoke to the driver. The driver nodded his head. Ruth was relieved. She didn't trust any Pole enough to leave even a taxi pickup to chance. The driver would have to wait if he hadn't been paid. And she wouldn't be stranded in this desolate part of Łódź with two heavy boxes. Two heavy boxes? What sort of fantasy was she indulging in? She would be lucky to leave 23 Kamedulska Street with the bowl or the teapot. If the old couple were really trying to sell the items they had displayed, they would have made a display of everything they had for sale. Ruth thought that the old couple were probably just trying to impress her and Edek, and had forgotten where the impressive accoutrements they had used had come from.

The taxi turned into Kamedulska Street and pulled up outside number 23. Ruth got out of the car. She had a strange urge to cross herself. Her hand had flown up to her forehead. How weird. She had never crossed herself in her life. She didn't even know the movement. Did it begin with a touch to the forehead or the shoulder? The forehead, she thought, but she wasn't sure. She had often envied Catholics their crossing mechanism. It was so overt and seemed so much more substantial than touching wood, and less lunatic than tapping a foot. Maybe if tapping a foot was done by hundreds of millions of people it might seem less absurd, Ruth thought. Out of the car, she felt frightened. She felt in need of protection. No wonder she had wanted to cross herself. She must have felt this Catholic habit might be more effective than a foot tap, in a country that was so Catholic.

She began to walk into the building. The brown dog that had been there the day before yesterday was still there. The dog rushed up to Ruth and wagged its tail. Ruth tried to ignore the dog. She stopped. Where was Tadeusz? She turned around. Tadeusz was saying something to the driver. What were they discussing? Ruth felt unnerved. The dog jumped up at Ruth. His paws were making muddy marks on her coat.

"Get away," she said to the dog. The dog wagged its tail.

"It is a very friendly dog," Tadeusz said to Ruth. He patted the dog.

"What were you talking to the driver about?" Ruth said.

"I told him he will get paid nothing at all if he leaves here for even a moment," Tadeusz said. "I did not want to come out and find that he had gone for a drink, or tried to fit in a trip for someone else."

"Thank you," Ruth said. "Don't pat the dog," she added. "You don't know who he belongs to and what he's like."

"This dog is perfectly fine," Tadeusz said.

"Go away, dog," Ruth said to the dog. The dog rubbed its head against her. "What does he want?" Ruth said to Tadeusz. Tadeusz laughed, and bent down and patted the dog again. The dog brushed off Tadeusz's pat.

"Go away, dog," Ruth said to the dog again. The dog wagged its tail furiously and looked up at Ruth. Ruth glared at the dog. The dog nudged her with his snout. She looked at her coat. She hoped he hadn't marked it with saliva or whatever it was that came out of dogs' snouts and mouths. "Go away," she said, sternly.

"It's a beautiful dog," Tadeusz said.

"A beautiful dog?" Ruth said. She decided, after a few seconds, that this was not the time to disagree with him. This was not the moment for Tadeusz to think she was a cold, merciless dog hater. She needed Tadeusz on her side. "I guess it is quite a beautiful dog," she said. She didn't think this amendment sounded very convincing. "I usually like dogs," she said. She was sure she sounded even more fraudulent.

She tried again. "She is a really nice dog," she said.

"She is a he," Tadeusz said.

"Oh, I'm not familiar enough with dogs to be able to detect their gender," Ruth said.

"With many dogs, it is obvious," Tadeusz said. Ruth looked at the brown dog. He was facing away from her. Large, black testicles were dangling between the dog's legs.

"I see what you mean," Ruth said.

They went inside. The dog followed them in, but stayed in the vestibule. Tadeusz and Ruth walked up the stairs. The air outside the front door of the apartment felt bereft and empty. Ruth thought that even the presence of a dog would give this atmosphere a lift. She had never wished for a dog before. She felt sick. She took a deep breath. She knocked loudly on the door.

The old man opened the door. He looked at Ruth, and then at Tadeusz. Tadeusz introduced himself. The old man smiled. He looked at Ruth again. "My wife said she would be back," he said. Ruth was taken aback. What did he mean his wife said Ruth would be back? "My wife said," the old man said, gesturing at Ruth, "that this woman's old father was not interested, but this one was. 'The daughter will be back,' my wife said."

Ruth was shocked. So much for her theory about the old couple's forgetfulness or absentmindedness. They were expecting her. The silver dish and the teapot were bait to lure her. And it had worked. She was here. They would know she was desperate to purchase the items. At the very least, they would know she was keen. What did the old man mean, calling her father an old man? Ruth thought. Edek looked like a teenager next to this disintegrating and decomposing mixture of wrinkles and bones.

"Come in, come in," the old man said. They stepped inside. Tadeusz began to translate what the old man had said, but Ruth cut him off. "I understood exactly what he said," she said. She tried to put a pleasant expression on her face. She wanted the silver bowl and the china, even if it meant paying a bit more. Even if it meant paying whatever this revolting old man was asking. She had to stop thinking like this. She was sure her thoughts were showing. She tried smiling. She was sure she merely looked nauseous.

Ruth, Tadeusz, and the old man were standing in the living room. The old man's wife was nowhere to be seen. She must have left this dirty work to her husband, Ruth thought. The wife had probably been right to do this. Of the two of them, her husband was definitely the more charming.

"My wife said she would be back," the old man said again. He beamed and rubbed his hands together in what seemed like a gesture of heady anticipation, to Ruth. Tadeusz nodded.

"Tell him I am pleased that he is glad to see me," Ruth said. Tadeusz relayed the greeting.

"I am most happy to see you," the old man said to Ruth.

"Tell him that I admired a couple of his possessions when I was last here," Ruth said. "And then say that I wondered if there was any possibility that he would allow me to buy them as a souvenir of my visit." Tadeusz and the old man seemed to converse for longer than was needed. Ruth couldn't quite catch the gist of what the old man was saying. "He says that he understands how important souvenirs are," Tadeusz said.

Ruth was about to describe the silver bowl when she noticed that the teapot, bowl, the milk jug, the sugar container, and the plate were already set out on top of the small sideboard. "He really was expecting me," she said to Tadeusz. "He said so," said Tadeusz. "Ask him how much he wants for all of those items," Ruth said, pointing to the small collection that had been assembled in preparation for her visit.

"Name a price," the old man said.

"He wants you to make a suggestion," Tadeusz said. Dozens of suggestions flew through Ruth's head. In most of them the old man wound up dead. She didn't think it would be wise to voice any of them.

"I'll pay you in U.S. dollars," Ruth said. Tadeusz relayed this to the old man.

"He says that is what he expects," Tadeusz said to Ruth.

Ruth was startled. The old man had obviously thought this through.

"Ask him, again, how much?" Ruth said. Tadeusz asked. The old man refused to name a price. Ruth decided she had to make a move.

"Fifty dollars for the silver bowl and fifty dollars for the tea set," Ruth said to Tadeusz. The old man opened his mouth and laughed heartily at Ruth's offer.

The view inside his mouth made Ruth retch. Brown and yellow rotting stumps were wedged into very discolored gums. She put her hand to her stomach. She really didn't want to throw up, although the thought of being sick all over their carpet was quite appealing.

"Tell him I'm not interested in playing games," Ruth said to Tadeusz. "Tell him I'll give him two hundred and fifty for the lot. If he doesn't agree to that, I'm leaving." She wasn't lying. She was telling the truth. She was fed up. She wanted to leave. This wasn't what she had expected. She hadn't expected such a blatant setup and such blatant exploitation. She was ready to go. She wished she hadn't come.

The old man must have read her expression. He clapped his hands together, and pronounced it a done deal. "A good business arrangement for both of us at this price," he said. Ruth didn't need Tadeusz to translate the old man's pleasure. The old man had brought in a box and some scraps of paper.

"Pack the things up for me as fast as you can," Ruth said to Tadeusz. "I've got to get out of here. I'll give him the money as soon as everything is packed." Tadeusz packed the silver and the china. He wrapped each piece, carefully. Ruth was grateful for the care he was taking.

Ruth wondered if she could give the old man a shove as she handed him the money. She decided against it. She didn't want to touch him. Ruth took the money from a zippered compartment in her bag. She handed it to Tadeusz and asked him to give it to the old man. She shut her bag. She had several bundles of American currency in different parts of her bag. She had been to a Kantor yesterday. She had cashed two thousand dollars' worth of traveler's checks. She had known she would have to pay Stefan quite a bit for the trip to Kraków. She wasn't sure how much. And she had wanted to make sure that she had enough for the china, and the interpreter, and the taxi driver, and the doorman. She knew that the doorman would be charging her for the boxes. "I will get very special boxes for you," he had said. Ruth knew that "very special" was a euphemism. A way of letting her know that the boxes would not be free.

The old man fondled his American currency before counting it. Ruth felt sick. She tried to calm down. At least this had cost her less than she had expected. Tadeusz was carrying the box. "Good-bye," she said to the old man. Ruth turned to leave. She needn't have said good-bye, she realized. There was no point in pretending politeness anymore.

"Does she want to see more?" the old man said to Tadeusz. Ruth wheeled around. She was shocked. What was the old man talking about? She could feel her legs trembling. "Ask him what else he's got," she said.

The old man beckoned for them to follow him. He led them into a small dirty kitchen. A pitted and dented kitchen table was covered in china. The same china as the plate Ruth had seen. Ruth could hardly breathe. She had forgotten about the dinner plate. She had meant to ask the old man about it. She looked at the plates and bowls and cups and saucers in front of her. There were so many pieces. They were so beautiful. She thought she was going to pass out. She gripped the side of the table.

The dinner plates and bread and butter plates and bowls and cups and saucers looked like family to her. Each piece was in mint condition. The gold fluting unscratched, the china uncracked. She couldn't see one chip. How had all of this been preserved? All of these pieces from another life.

She started to weep. Tears poured down her face. "I knew that she would find these dishes attractive," the old man said. Ruth wept even harder. A wave of biliousness swept over her. "Please, God, don't let me be sick," she said to herself. She needed to think. She wanted to buy this china. This china that had been part of a family life. A family life she had longed for. "Please, God, let me buy this china," she said. She felt a bit better. She wiped her eyes and blew her nose.

What a time to turn to God, she thought. She had never prayed to God before. Not even when she was a child. God was *verboten* in their house. Well, she could hardly expect God to rush to her aid. Ruth was sure that if there was a God, he would want to see some evidence of a belief in him beforehand. He wouldn't just dash off to any unexpected request for help. You couldn't just call on God, out of the blue. She blew her nose again. She could hardly look at the china. She didn't want either of these men to know how much it meant to her.

"There are eighteen dinner plates, twenty smaller plates, twenty bowls, twenty cups, and twenty saucers," the old man said.

"What does he want for them?" Ruth said to Tadeusz. The old man looked tough. All pretense of a civilized exchange was gone. "Based on the previous price we agreed on for the other pieces of china," he said, "I calculate that this is worth three thousand dollars."

Ruth felt winded. It wasn't so much the price as the preplanned trap and the supposition that she would return and fall right into it. And they had been right, the old man and his wife. She had done exactly what they had predicted she would. Tadeusz walked over to her and touched her on the arm. She jumped. "What do you want to do?" he said.

"You can take it or leave it," the old man said.

Ruth felt light-headed. She stumbled. Tadeusz caught her. "You are making a difficult situation more difficult," Tadeusz said to the old man. "There is nothing too difficult going on here," the old man said. "She just has to pay the money and she gets what she wants." Ruth sat down on one of the kitchen chairs. She put her head between her legs. "Tell him I haven't got three thousand dollars," she said.

"She can get it," the old man said. Ruth was still dizzy. "Let's go," she said to Tadeusz. The old man looked at her. "She won't go," he said to Tadeusz. "She can't bear to separate herself from this stuff. My wife always said we should keep it. She said, someone will come looking for it, one day. It took fifty-nine years, but my wife was right."

, "We thought that she was going to buy it last time she was here," the old man said. "But my wife said she could see the girl was not ready to buy. My wife said to wait. We waited. And look what we got. The same girl. She is a little older and she has brought the money with her this time."

Ruth couldn't believe what she was hearing. She remembered, vaguely, that the old man had offered her a cup of tea, all those years ago. Had he brought out the tea service then? He must have. But it had been no use. She hadn't known what she was looking at. She felt exhausted.

"I'll have to give you a mixture of dollars and zlotys," she said to the old man.

Tadeusz translated for her. "That is perfectly acceptable to me," the old man said with a bow. He smiled at Ruth. The success of the transaction had obviously improved the old man's humor and his manners. His mood looked decidedly lighter. Ruth fished around in her bag, for the various places she had put her money. "Could you pack all of this, please?" she said to Tadeusz. The old man had had two cardboard boxes ready under the table. "Of course," Tadeusz said. Ruth counted her money.

She gave the cash to Tadeusz. She needed as much distance between her and this dirty old man as it was possible to have in this cramped kitchen. She looked away while he caressed and fondled each note as he counted the money.

"I'll carry one of the boxes," she said to Tadeusz.

"They are heavy," he said.

"I'm strong," she said. She wasn't going to leave anything to chance. If they walked out with only one box, she was sure the other would disappear. And she wasn't going to wait, on her own, in this apartment, with the old man, while Tadeusz took the boxes downstairs.

"Let's get out of here," she said to Tadeusz. She bent down to pick up the smaller of the boxes.

"I have a few more items you might be interested in," the old man said.

Ruth felt as though someone had punched her. She tried to straighten herself up. The thump had been palpable. It was right below her chest. It felt as though it had punctured her lungs. Perforated some part of her. She started wheezing. Both men stared at her. "She will be okay in a minute," the old man said. Ruth sat back down in the chair. Was she having a heart attack? What was happening to her? She didn't want to die in this apartment. She realized that every part of her body was clenched. Her teeth, her hands, her head. She tried to relax.

"Can I help you downstairs?" Tadeusz said. "I think we should leave." Ruth shook her head. She wasn't going to leave without the china. "I will run down with the boxes and then return for you," said Tadeusz. Ruth shook her head again. Her breathing was becoming less labored.

"I haven't got any more money," she said to the old man. Tadeusz translated.

"Jews always have a little something put away," the old man said.

Ruth felt furious. She tried to show the old man her disdain for him, but the wheezing returned and made the demonstration of her contempt impossible. Ruth realized that she had understood every word this disgusting, stained old man had said. Years of not understanding Polish had vanished. Years of incomprehensible Polish phrases and sentences seemed to be over. She could understand every word. Polish verbs and adjectives and nouns and adverbs coalesced into meanings, instead of melting into gibberish as they used to do. Why was it that this old man's words had cleared her blockage? Why had his wretched and repugnant proposals produced a clarity in her?

This was the closest she had come to having something tangible from the past. The past that had destroyed not only those who were murdered, but those who were left alive. The proximity to any part of that past was an enormous incentive, Ruth thought. An incentive to understand the language of the enemy. Her breathing had eased. She still felt as though she might throw up. She had to get out of this apartment. There was nothing left in this apartment, for her, anymore. She knew that she would never come back. She had seen enough.

"What have you got?" she said to the old man. The old man didn't need Tadeusz to interpret. He had understood the gesture Ruth had made with her head. It was a defiant gesture. Ruth had been surprised at the defiance she had managed to muster.

The old man pulled a large brown paper bag out from under the table.

Ruth looked into the bag. She couldn't see what was inside. The bag stank of mothballs. The old man leaned down and with a flourish pulled an old overcoat out of the bag.

"Why should she want an old man's overcoat?" Tadeusz said to the old man.

"We don't need him," the old man said, nodding in Tadeusz's direction.

He held up the coat. Ruth could see that it was an expensive coat. It was dark gray. Probably made out of wool. The plush pale gray satin lining was still intact. And clean. All the seams were double-stitched. And the tailored shape of the collar and subtlety of the line of the body of the coat suggested it had been designed and made by a master tailor.

"Whose coat is it?" Ruth said.

"Your grandfather's," the old man said. Ruth thought she must have misheard.

"What did he say?" she said to Tadeusz.

"He said this coat belonged to your grandfather," Tadeusz said.

"She understood what I said," the old man said to Tadeusz.

"How do you know this was my grandfather's coat?" Ruth said. "It could be anyone's."

"If it was anyone's coat I would not be showing it to you," the old man said. He put his hand into one of the pockets of the coat and pulled out the lining. The initials I. R. were embroidered in dark gray on the top of the lining of the pocket. Ruth looked at the initials and started to weep. Did this coat belong to Israel Rothwax, her father's father, her grandfather? How did this sickening old man know her grandfather's initials?

"It could belong to anyone else with the same initials," Ruth said. The old man laughed. He turned back the collar of the coat. At the back of the collar, embroidered again, in dark gray, was the name Rothwax. The embroidered letters looked almost human, almost alive, to Ruth. So much more than a series of stitches. She sank back down onto the chair and wept. She wept like a child. She couldn't stop weeping. Neither of the men in the room said a word. Ruth tried to stop crying. She wiped her face with her hands and blew her nose with her last Kleenex. But the tears kept coming and her nose kept running. She couldn't breathe. Her nasal passages were completely blocked.

But she couldn't stop crying. This man's apartment was no place to shed tears, Ruth thought. Or maybe it was exactly the right place. She had no more Kleenex. She sniffed. She had to stop crying. She had cried so much this morning, surely her tear ducts would be just about dried up. She dabbed at her eyes with the sleeve of her coat. Her eyes were sore. The coat fabric had been waterproofed and wasn't absorbent. She felt as though she was drowning in a sea of tears and mucus. She had to get out of there.

"How much for the coat?" she said.

"The coat comes with something else," the old man said. He pulled a faded, yellowed envelope out of one of the pockets. Ruth stopped crying.

"What is that?" she said.

"Something you will be interested in," the old man said.

He opened the envelope and removed four photographs. He spread the photographs on the table in front of Ruth. They were old sepia-toned photographs. Snapshots of a family. An older couple, on their own, were in the first photograph. They were possibly in their fifties or sixties, it was hard to tell. In other photographs, the older couple were with several younger adults, men and women in their twenties or thirties. Two small children were in the last photograph. Two girls.

"Who are they?" she said to the old man.

"I don't know," he said. "That is for you to find out."

"You don't know these people?" Tadeusz said to Ruth. "You could be paying for nothing."

Ruth looked at the photographs. She didn't know who any of the people were. The older couple looked stolid and solid. Both of them were dressed in black. The woman had her hair pulled back into a bun. She was a substantial-looking woman. Tall, with square shoulders and a big bust. A very big bust. Could this woman be Luba Rothwax? Ruth thought. Could this woman be related to her? Not if chest size was any indication. Her own breasts were relatively small. Well, maybe not small, she thought. But medium, at the most. The older couple looked grim, too. Dour. She didn't think they were her relatives.

"These people don't belong to me," she said.

"Look again," the old man said. "Look at the children. Look at the older girl."

Ruth looked at the photograph the old man was holding out. Something in Ruth's body misfired. It felt like a malfunction in the wiring of her electrical circuits. There were flicks and twinges in her head. They felt like kinks and stitches. Nips and pinches. She went hot and cold all over. Parts of her face were burning and other parts of her were cold. Her hands and knees were shaking. The two small girls in the photograph looked about six and eight. They both had curly, dark hair, parted at the side. The curls on the right fell into ringlets and jutted out at exactly the same angle as her own hair.

Ruth looked at the photograph again. Both of these girls could have been Ruth. If someone had showed her a photograph of either of these girls, Ruth would have sworn that the girl in the photograph was her. That was exactly how she looked in all the photographs she had of herself at the same age. But the girls in the photograph were girls Ruth had never met. Ruth realized the photographs had been taken outside this building. In front of 23 Kamedulska Street. Everybody in the photographs was well dressed. The girls had ribbons tied into large bows in their hair, and embroidered socks and shiny shoes.

Ruth looked closely at one of the younger women. She felt sick. The woman looked so like her. The same eyes. The same mouth. Who was she? Was she the mother of the two girls?

"How much?" she said to the old man.

"How much will you pay me?" he said.

"I haven't got much left," she said.

"You can come back," he said.

"Tell him he's a bastard and I hope he burns in hell," Ruth said. Tadeusz remained quiet. The old man laughed.

"I'll settle for another thousand dollars," he said. Ruth gasped. "It's worth paying me," he said. "You can't put a value on these things."

"Tell him it will have to be in zlotys," Ruth said.

"Zlotys, dollars, francs, I'll take anything," the old man said. Ruth opened her bag. It was lucky she always carried plenty of zlotys with her. She did a quick conversion in her head. She estimated it would be roughly three thousand zlotys. She counted out the zlotys. She gave them to the old man. He counted them again.

"I need to leave straight away," Ruth said to Tadeusz. She put the envelope with the photographs in her bag. Her hands were still shaking. Tadeusz folded the overcoat on top of one of the boxes of china.

"You know anything about buried gold?" the old man said to Tadeusz. Tadeusz didn't answer. "We are sure they buried something," the old man said.

Ruth wanted to punch him. She wanted to punch and punch until she had pummeled his smug expression into mush. Until she had broken every bone and every piece of cartilage in his face. She sneered at him. "I hope you burn in hell," she said.

Before this trip, she had thought she didn't believe in hell. "Burn in hell," she said to the old man again. He smiled at her. She thought he must have misunderstood what she was saying. He looked at her and laughed. She knew by his laugh that he had understood the essence of what she had said. "I hope you rot in hell," Ruth said. The old man looked at her and laughed again. This time he laughed even harder. It must have struck him as funny, Ruth thought. The whole morning was probably hilarious for him.

"Can you carry the box?" Tadeusz said.

"I can carry anything," she said. She picked up the box, and walked out of the apartment. Tadeusz followed her.

"Come back if she tells you about any gold," the old man shouted to Tadeusz. "I'll split it with you."

"Are you all right?" Tadeusz said to Ruth at the bottom of the stairs.

"I am all right," she said. The brown dog was still at the front entrance. He ran up to Ruth. "Shoo, shoo," she said to the dog. The dog stayed by her side. "Get out of my way," Ruth said to the dog. The dog stayed put. Ruth lifted her foot and kicked the dog. She must have kicked hard because the dog started whimpering. "Sorry, dog," she said.

The taxi was still there. Ruth was glad that she hadn't paid the driver. Tadeusz had made sure that the driver had waited for them. Tadeusz put the china in the trunk of the car. "Be very careful with it," she said to Tadeusz. The dog sat on the footpath and looked at Ruth. He looked hurt. "Sorry, dog," she said, again.

Ruth was relieved to be back in the taxi. The taxi, as dilapidated and foul-smelling as it was, felt like a haven to Ruth, a sanctuary. "Back to the hotel, please," Tadeusz said to the driver. They drove off. Ruth looked back at 23 Kamedulska Street. The brown dog was still sitting on the footpath. His head was turned toward the taxi. Ruth wondered if the dog could still see them.

The taxi turned the corner and the dog and the building were gone. Ruth felt almost numb. How had the old couple got hold of the china and the coat and the photographs? What else had there been? Had there been other items of clothing they had taken? Other photographs? Other pieces of furniture or tableware? Had they taken them out of the apartment after Edek and his family and the other families had left, or had it been an intermediary, another Pole, who had gotten to the goods first, and sold them to the new occupants of the building? Had the old couple saved these pieces? What else had they had? Had they sold other items in the meantime? Fifty-nine years was a long time to wait for a sale.

Did someone divide out what was in all the apartments in Kamedulska Street? Or did the Poles grab whatever they could get? And why keep a coat? For identification? The name "Rothwax" embroidered on the inside was certainly identifying. Or was it? Could the Poles have embroidered it on themselves after the war?

Edek would know the authenticity of the coat, she thought. It did look authentic to Ruth. Far too expensive for these Poles to have been the purchasers. They may still have embroidered the name onto the coat. But how would they know whose name to embroider? Was the name Rothwax on the apartment? Was the name Rothwax on hundreds of other items they found? Ruth thought that she would never know the answer to these questions. These questions would just join a long list of other unanswerable questions about that time. That demented, fragmented, mad time.

"I need to get this china shipped to America," Ruth said to Tadeusz. "To New York. Do you know a shipping company?" Tadeusz thought for a minute. "Yes," he said. "There is a company that ships around the world not far from the hotel."

"Is it a reliable company?" Ruth said.

"It is American," Tadeusz said.

"An American company?" Ruth said. "That's perfect."

"There is also a Polish company," Tadeusz said. He hesitated. "You would prefer the American?" he asked.

"Yes," she said. "Wouldn't you?"

"Perhaps," he said.

Ruth looked at her watch. "Could we go straight there?" she said to Tadeusz.

"Of course," he said.

Tadeusz carried the two boxes of china into the offices of the International Shipping Company on Piotrkowska Street. Ruth waited in the taxi until he had carried both boxes in. She felt a sense of happiness seeing the boxes being delivered to the shippers. She paid the taxi driver. She was grateful to him for not contributing any detours or diversions. She gave him the equivalent of one hundred American dollars. He beamed.

"Can I have these packed and shipped?" Ruth said to the clerk at the shipping company.

"No problem," he said. He was American. Ruth wanted to hug him.

"It's china, and the pieces are fragile," she said.

"We ship a lot of glass product," he said. "It will be wrapped and packaged very securely."

"Good," she said.

"How soon do you want it?" he said.

"As soon as possible," Ruth said.

"Air Express?" he asked.

"Yes," she said. She didn't care how much it cost. She paid for the shipping with her American Express card. She felt elated.

She put the receipt, and the tracking number, carefully in her wallet. There was plenty of room. Her wallet was almost empty. There was a Kantor next door to the shipping company. She changed some money and paid Tadeusz. "You were very good," she said.

"Thank you. You look much better," he said.

"I feel better," she said. They shook hands. "I'm going to walk back to the hotel," she said. She walked along Piotrkowska Street holding the paper bag with her grandfather's overcoat. She hugged the bag to herself. She didn't mind the smell of the mothballs.

"I don't need the boxes after all," she said to the doorman when she got back to the hotel.

"It was a pleasure to get them for you," he said and moved his face closer to Ruth's. She tried not to back away too obviously. "I managed to get very strong boxes," he said.

"Thank you very much," she said. "How much do I owe you?"

"Fifty dollars," he said.

Ruth had had enough negotiations for one morning. "I'll change a traveler's check at the desk and give the money to you," she said to the doorman.

"What would you like me to do with the boxes?" he said. "Should I take them to your room?" Several suggestions of what the doorman could do with the boxes remained unspoken inside her. Restrained by a tight grip on her vocal cords.

"You can do whatever you like with them," she said. Her throat hurt.

Back in her room, she looked in the mirror. She looked a bit bedraggled. She washed her face. It was strange, she thought, how washing made you feel better. What were you washing away? She was washing streaks left by her tears. Tears really did streak your face, she thought. Well, faces that had foundation applied to them. She put on a new layer of makeup. It was just a light foundation, but it covered all the small blemishes. She thought she looked much better. She called her father and arranged to meet him in the lobby. She repacked the coat into a better bag. A Saks Fifth Avenue bag she had had her shoes in.

"You do look terrible," Edek said when he saw her.

"Don't say that, Dad," she said. "You've said that so many times since we arrived in Poland."

"It is the truth," Edek said. "In Poland you do not look so good. The truth is the truth."

"Do you want a cup of tea?" she said. "I'm going to have one."

"No thank you," Edek said.

"Would you like anything else?" Ruth said. "A cup of coffee? A hot chocolate?"

"Maybe a small hot chocolate," he said.

Ruth ordered the hot chocolate, the tea, and a slice of apple cake for herself. She was hungry, and she thought her blood sugar could do with some lifting.

"I am glad that you are going to have something to eat," Edek said.

"So am I," she said. "Did you have breakfast?"

"Of course I did have breakfast," Edek said. "I did go to the buffet like you did suggest."

"I'm so pleased," she said.

"It was a bit funny, to tell you the truth, to eat in a dining room by myself," Edek said. "But they did have a very good breakfast this morning."

"Better than the other mornings?" Ruth said.

"They did have bratwurst this morning," Edek said. "And knackwurst and weisswurst."

"Wow," said Ruth.

"All of them was very good," Edek said. "And the eggs was just how I like them. Not too hard. And the compote was only plums today. I like this compote very much."

"I like plum compote, too," Ruth said. Edek looked happy. She was pleased he had had a good breakfast.

"You didn't have a bad reaction from the worms from last night?" she said.

"I did not eat the worms," Edek said. "Only my daughter did eat the worms. And my daughter does not look so good."

"I thought I saw you eat half a worm?" Ruth said. Edek looked worried. "I'm only joking," Ruth said. "Anyway, they're not worms, they're prawns. And I'm fine."

A waiter brought them the tea and the hot chocolate and the slice of apple cake. Ruth looked at the apple cake. It was exactly the way she liked apple cake. Bursting with stewed and baked apples. She felt very hungry. She took a forkful of the cake. It was delicious. She felt instantly better. That one mouthful had revived her. Or had it? Surely the sugar couldn't get into your bloodstream that fast? She finished the rest of the slice of apple cake. It was like ingesting a sedative. Each mouthful that she took had soothed her, made her feel calmer. "My daughter does like an apple cake," Edek said.

She hoped Edek wasn't going to say anything else. She already felt self-conscious enough. She never ate cakes or any other food considered to be fattening in front of anyone else. It came from years of every calorie she consumed being observed by Rooshka. This acute observation by her mother had resulted in Ruth's eating only grilled fish and vegetable salads in public. If she had anything sweet, she had to eat it in private.

"Look at how quickly you did eat the apple cake," Edek said.

"Dad," she said, "do I comment on what you eat?"

"I wouldn't mind what you would say," he said.

"Oh yes you would," she said, in a tone that she hoped conveyed that she was capable of a broad range of comments on his food and on his eating. It seemed to work. He dropped the subject.

"I did book Stefan for twelve o'clock," Edek said.

"I think we'll have to change it to a bit later," Ruth said. "We won't have enough time for the ghetto. Could you call him and ask him to pick us up at two o'clock?"

"We have to go to the ghetto?" Edek said. Ruth looked exasperated. "Okay, okay," Edek said. "I ring Stefan now." He ran off to the phone near the front desk.

Ruth looked down at the Saks Fifth Avenue bag. It was on the floor, beside her. She wanted to show Edek the coat and the photographs. She hoped he wouldn't be upset by them. Edek came back.

"That is fine with Stefan," he said.

"Of course it's fine," she said. "We're paying him. He has to do what we want."

"Why are you in a bad mood?" Edek said.

"I'm not," she said.

"You are in a bad mood," Edek said.

"I'm fine," she said.

"Forget about it," Edek said. "Stefan was very very happy with his hotel. He said he did have a very good sleep last night."

"Oh good," Ruth said. "We need him to be in good shape for the drive to Kraków."

Ruth took a deep breath. She leaned down and picked up the bag. "Dad, I had to lie to you about what I was doing this morning," she said. "I didn't want to worry you, so I said I was going running. But I went back to Kamedulska Street."

Edek looked shocked. "You went to Kamedulska Street by yourself?" he said.

"No, I had an interpreter with me and a taxi driver waiting outside for me," she said.

"You went alone to a Polish home with two Polacks?" Edek said.

"I told the manager of the hotel where I was going, and that it could be dangerous," Ruth said. "I told him to ring the police if I wasn't back at the hotel by ten o'clock, and to let you know."

"What time did you go?" Edek said.

"Eight o'clock," she said.

"By ten o'clock you could easy be dead," Edek said.

Ruth had forgotten she had called the manager, the night before. The manager had clearly forgotten, too. It was 10:30 A.M. There was no sign of the manager or of any police in the hotel, and the manager had not called Edek. So much for her foolproof security arrangements.

"It was a stupid thing to do," Edek said. "They could kill you in a second."

"It's not so easy to kill Jews today," Ruth said.

"It is not so hard, too," said Edek.

"I went back to buy the china," Ruth said.

"My mother's old teapot?" said Edek. "Are you crazy? To go early in the morning by yourself with two Polish men to a house where there is more Polacks? Don't you know what happened in Kielce after the war? A pogrom. They did kill more than fifty Jews. And this was after the war. This was Jews who was looking for their families, for their homes."

Edek looked agitated and irate. Ruth was surprised. He hadn't seemed particularly concerned about their safety in Poland. He hadn't seemed concerned at all. Maybe he felt that Jews were okay as long as they stuck to brightly lit main streets and kept out of Polish homes. She realized he had been reluctant to walk too far from the hotel at night.

"I know about Kielce," Ruth said. "They killed forty-two Jews in Kielce, on July 4, 1946. They were shot and stoned or killed with axes and clubs. They were killed by a crowd of Poles who were incited by the same old rumors of Jews kidnapping and murdering Christian children for ritual purposes. The same old story."

"China is only china," Edek said. "It is not alive."

"But I am," Ruth said. "And I got the china. There was much more of it than we saw."

"Really?" Edek said.

"There was the tea service," Ruth said, "and then there were eighteen dinner plates, twenty bread and butter plates, twenty bowls, twenty cups, and twenty saucers!"

"They did have so much pieces?" Edek said. He shook his head. "It is something impossible to believe," he said.

"And everything was in perfect condition," Ruth said. "Not one crack on a cup or saucer or bread and butter plate."

"We did use these small plates not for bread and butter," Edek said. "We did use them for *Vorspeisen*, for appetizers." He shook his head again. "My mother did serve herring and an egg salad on such small plates."

"Well, I've got them, now," Ruth said. "We can eat on them together."

"What for?" said Edek. He looked sad.

"Does it make you feel sad?" she said.

"No," he said. "How can some pieces of china make me feel sad? The sad things did already happen, and not to this china."

Suddenly the thought of the cost of the china occurred to Edek. Ruth could see it coming. She had known it would be only a matter of time before Edek asked her how much she had paid.

"What did you pay for this stuff?" Edek said.

"I'll tell you in a minute," she said. "But first I want to show you something else."

Ruth removed the coat from the bag. She stood up and held the coat out in front of her. Edek looked bewildered. And then an expression of pain mingled with disbelief came across his face. He didn't say anything. He just kept shaking his head. Ruth waited for him to speak. She found Edek's silence disturbing. He looked as though he was going to cry. She thought that maybe this was too much for him. She shouldn't have produced the coat now. She was just about to speak when Edek spoke.

"This coat did belong to my father," he said.

"I thought it might have," Ruth said. She showed him the embroidered name and initials on the coat's lining. Edek kept shaking his head. He looked very vulnerable. Ruth wished that she had waited to show him these purchases. Why was she calling them purchases? she thought. They were not ordinary shopping items. They were not purchases, they were discoveries. Discoveries unearthed after decades. As important to her as archaeological relics uncovered by archaeologists. She could tell so much about Israel Rothwax and his wife Luba from this coat. She could see how big he was, and she could see in what beautiful condition Luba maintained his clothes. Not one part of the lining was marked or torn. Maybe tidiness and order were inherited traits. She kept her most formal clothes in plastic clothes bags in her cupboard. If something tore, she had it mended. She cleaned every item right after it was worn. Maybe that was a Rothwax quality. A thrill ran through her. The thrill of being able to link herself to a family. To be part of somebody else. She had only ever been part of Rooshka and Edek.

"I'm so happy to have this coat," Ruth said to Edek.

"It was very dangerous what you did," Edek said. He shook his head again. "The last time I did see my father in this coat was at my sister Fela's wedding anniversary," Edek said. Ruth was worried. Edek looked as though he was on the verge of tears. She didn't want him to cry. "I remember Fela's husband Juliusz did help my father to take the coat off when my father did arrive to the anniversary party," Edek said.

Fela's husband Juliusz, Ruth thought. She had never heard Juliusz mentioned before. He sounded like a nice man, helping Israel off with his coat. Ruth knew that the knowledge about Juliusz helping someone take off a coat was not enough information to give you a full picture of a person. But it was a start. Juliusz must have had good manners and he must have been fond of his father-in-law.

"I did like Juliusz very much," Edek said. Juliusz definitely must have been a nice man, Ruth decided. She was glad that Fela was in a good marriage. A contradictory thought surfaced in her. How did she know that her father's sister Fela had a good marriage? The fact that Edek liked Juliusz didn't on its own make Juliusz a wonderful husband. She didn't want to ask her father. She felt she was already causing him plenty of turbulence.

"I've got something else, Dad," she said. "It might give you a shock, so prepare yourself. It's something you haven't seen for a long time." Edek tried to look composed, but Ruth could see his apprehension and his distress. She really should have waited, she thought, before presenting all of this to her father. She should have waited until he was back at home, in his apartment, in Melbourne. But she had already started the whole thing off, and she couldn't stop now.

She got out the old envelope and removed the photographs. She handed them to Edek. Edek held them in his lap. He looked at them for a long time. He didn't move. He was so still he looked as though he had stopped breathing. Ruth wanted him to say something. She wanted to see that he was all right. Edek didn't speak. He raised his head as though he was going to say something. Then he lowered it again. And then he began to weep. He wept and wept.

The sight of her father crying was too much for Ruth. She began to weep, too. They sat, side by side, on a sofa, in the lobby of the Grand Victoria, and wept. Finally, Edek pulled out a handkerchief and blew his nose. Ruth tried to stop crying. She wiped her eyes with a wad of tissues. They were Polish tissues and much rougher than their American counterparts. The tissues hurt her skin. She had to be strong, she told herself. She couldn't dissolve into a weeping mess. She had caused the distress that Edek was experiencing. The least she could do was look after him.

"This is my mother and father," Edek said.

"I thought it was," Ruth said. She started to cry again.

"We shouldn't cry, Ruthie," Edek said. "My mother and father is already dead. My sister Fela is dead. Juliusz is dead. Tadek, who is also in these pictures, is dead. His wife Maryla is dead. Everybody is dead. It is too late to cry."

Ruth looked at her father. Edek's face looked crumpled. Crumpled in grief. His eyes were wrinkled and furrowed, his mouth knotted and distorted. His shoulders had sunk. In sorrow. Weighted with a sadness that couldn't be submerged or defeated. Her father looked buckled and broken. Ruth felt frightened.

"I'm sorry," she said to Edek. "I shouldn't have inflicted all this on you now."

"You did not do anything," Edek said. "The things that was done was done by other people."

"But I shouldn't have brought all this up now," Ruth said.

"When would be a better time?" Edek said. "Never." He straightened himself up. "I am sorry I did cry," he said to Ruth. "A man my age should not cry."

"Dad, you've got a lot to cry about," Ruth said.

Edek wiped his eyes, again, and sat up. He spread the photographs out on his knees. "This is my sister Fela," he said. "And her husband Juliusz, what I did just tell you about." He handed Ruth the photograph. Ruth looked at Fela and Juliusz. What a good-looking couple they were. They were looking at each other, in the photograph. It was a look of love. Ruth thought that they must have been madly in love. Or at least quite in love to be still looking at each other that way. They had obviously been together awhile. They had two children.

Ruth wondered if it was possible to be quite in love. Or was quite in love, too mild to be love? Was anything less than madly in love, not really love? She looked at the photograph again. Fela and Juliusz looked madly in love, to her.

"Here is Tadek," Edek said, handing Ruth another one of the photographs. "Next to Tadek is Tadek's wife, Maryla." Tadek looked like Edek, Ruth thought. A very young, handsome Edek.

"He looks like you," Ruth said.

"Everybody did say that," Edek said.

"You can really see the resemblance," Ruth said. "You were both very handsome young men."

"You can recognize me from this photo of Tadek," Edek said.

"Yes," Ruth said. "Tadek looks like the photograph of you, after the war, before I was born."

"Of course," Edek said. "I did forget about those photographs."

"You were so handsome," she said.

"I am not so bad now," Edek said. He smiled at Ruth. His smile cheered her up.

"You're not so bad at all, Dad," she said.

"I do not know why Tadek's two boys was not in the photographs," Edek said. "Maybe they was somewhere else at the time."

"The photographs look as though they were all taken on one day," Ruth said.

"You are right," Edek said. "Maybe Tadek's boys was with Moniek's children that day."

Tadek's children. Moniek's children. Juliusz, Maryla. All these people she had never heard about. All related to her. All family.

"Who are those two girls?" Ruth said, pointing at the photograph Edek was holding.

Edek looked at the photograph. "They was such lovely girls," he said. "Quiet, and good at school. Very good at school."

"Who are they?" Ruth said.

"They are nobody anymore," Edek said. "They are dead." He looked morose again.

"Who were they, Dad?" she said.

"They were Fela's daughters," he said. He looked as though he was going to cry again. "Liebala, the older one, was my favorite. Always smiling. Always talking. She did love to talk. 'Uncle Edek,' she called me. 'Uncle Edek, can I come on the *doroszka*? Uncle Edek, can I walk with you? Uncle Edek. Uncle Edek!' " Edek put down the photograph and wiped his eyes.

"Are you all right, Dad?" Ruth said.

"I am all right," he said.

"What was the younger girl's name?" Ruth said.

"Hanka," Edek said. "Hanka was very nice, too. A bit more quiet than her sister, but very nice." Edek sniffed and wiped his eyes again. He put his handkerchief back in his pocket. The handkerchief looked very wet.

"Don't you think Hanka and Liebala look like me?" Ruth said.

"I always did know this," Edek said. "So did Mum."

"Why didn't you tell me?" Ruth said.

"What for?" said Edek. "To tell you the truth," Edek said, "I did try myself not to think of it too much. It is not so easy to have a child who reminds you so much of other children. Children what are dead." Edek looked as though he might start crying again.

"Of course, Dad," she said. "I understand."

"They was clever girls, both of them," he said.

"I'm glad they were clever," Ruth said.

"Especially Liebala," Edek said. He held his mouth together, in an effort to stem any more tears.

"Let's put the photographs away now," Ruth said. "I'll have copies of them made in New York and give you a set."

"Probably they do such copies, in Poland," Edek said.

"I'm not giving these photographs to any Pole," Ruth said.

Edek laughed. "Maybe that was not such a good idea," he said.

"I'm going to have the coat altered so it fits me, in New York, too," Ruth said. Edek shook his head at her. "It's going to look great," Ruth said.

Edek laughed. "You are crazy," he said. Ruth was glad that her craziness was making Edek laugh. Edek took one last look at the photographs before he handed them over to Ruth.

It must be so strange for him to look at these photographs, Ruth thought. He hadn't seen these people for so many years. So many decades. And, here he was, looking at an image of them. An image that had preserved them, perfectly, looking exactly the way they had looked when he last saw them.

"I'm happy we got these," Edek said. "Better to remember my mother and father and Fela and Tadek like this than how they was in the ghetto."

Of course, Ruth thought. How stupid of her. This wasn't how he had last seen his mother and father and sister and brothers. His last view of them hadn't been like this at all. Not one of them had been well dressed when he had last seen them. Not one of them had been well fed. Fela's high cheekbones wouldn't have had a coating of flesh when Edek had last kissed her. They would have been sharp and angular. Probably protruding a long way out off the rest of her face. And what had happened to the girls in the ghetto? To Hanka and Liebala? Ruth didn't dare ask.

"Make me two copies of the one with my mother and father," Edek said. "The one which is only my mother standing next to my father."

"Okay," Ruth said.

"I want to send one to Garth," Edek said.

"To Garth?" said Ruth. "What do you want to send it to Garth for?"

"I want to show him what my mother and father did look like," Edek said. "He will be interested." Ruth dropped the subject. She didn't want to agitate her father. She had put him through enough this morning.

"How much did you pay for all this stuff?" Edek said. This was the question she had been hoping to deflect. She didn't answer. "How much did this stuff cost you?" said Edek.

"It's not stuff," Ruth said.

"It is stuff what is important to us," Edek said. "But it is stuff."

"Quite a bit," Ruth said.

"How much is such a bit?" said Edek.

"Three thousand two hundred and fifty dollars for the set of china and the silver bowl," Ruth said.

Edek whistled. "Oh, brother," he said. "Three thousand and two hundred dollars for some china and some photographs."

"No, the photographs and the coat were extra," Ruth said.

"Extra?" said Edek. "Three thousand two hundred and fifty American dollars was not enough?" He paused for a second. "It was American dollars what you was talking about, not Australian dollars?" he said.

"They were American dollars," Ruth said.

"Of course," Edek said. "Everybody wants American dollars. How much was the coat and the photographs?"

"Another thousand dollars," Ruth said.

"Another thousand," he said in disbelief. "Those bestids."

Not even the way he pronounced "bastard" could cheer up Ruth. Edek's version of "bestid" usually lifted her spirits. She felt appalled at how much she had spent. She could see that her father was appalled too.

"Those bestids," Edek said again.

"It's not such a huge amount of money for me to spend," Ruth said. "I could spend it on a vacation or on a piece of furniture."

"It is not the four thousand dollars," Edek said. "It is the fact that you did give this four thousand two hundred and fifty dollars to those Polacks."

Her father was right, Ruth thought. It was not the amount of the expenditure that was the most bothering aspect of this, it was who the money was handed to. It was given to people who had already profited from the death of his mother and father and sister and brothers and nephews and nieces.

"Those bestids," Edek said again. Ruth thought that one day she should teach Edek a few more obscenities. He was stuck on bestid. There were several more potent profanities. Bestid seemed too timid to Ruth. There was a string of much stronger words for cursing.

"They did get what they wanted, those bestids," Edek said.

"We got what we wanted," Ruth said.

"I did not want this," Edek said.

"I did," she said. Edek was quiet.

Ruth put the photographs back in the envelope. She folded the coat and returned it to its new home. A Saks Fifth Avenue shopping bag. Edek slumped back against the back of the sofa. The price that Ruth had paid for the coat and the china and the photographs seemed to have deflated him. He looked depressed.

"What use is it to pay such a lot of money?" Edek said. "What use is these photographs? I already did know what my mother and father did look like."

"I didn't," Ruth said.

"I suppose so," Edek said. "But nobody else does want to see them. There is no grandchildren. There is nobody."

Ruth was surprised. Edek didn't usually dwell on her lack of children or his lack of grandchildren. It must be the effect of looking at the photographs. Seeing how truncated, almost eradicated, the whole Rothwax family was, that was getting to Edek. Ruth felt bad.

"I guess I could still have children," she said.

"You will not," said Edek.

Ruth felt cold. She could feel herself shivering. She knew it was warm in the lobby. She was shivering because she was overwrought. There was too much to deal with. Why did Edek have to bring up children now? It made sense. They had just been looking at two of the beautiful children who were lost. Lost to their mother and father. Lost to their grandparents. Lost to their aunties and uncles. Lost to Edek, and lost to Ruth. Two of the many beautiful children who'd been lost, in Łódź.

"I am happy you did get what you wanted," Edek said to Ruth.

"The photographs mean so much to me," she said. Edek nodded his head. "Maybe you're not up to a visit to the ghetto," Ruth said to Edek. "Maybe you should stay here and have a rest."

"I am coming with you," Edek said.

"Okay," she said. "I'll put these things upstairs and then we'll get a cab."

"Maybe I will call Stefan to drive us to the ghetto?" Edek said.

"We're going to be on the road with Stefan for hours, driving to Kraków, this afternoon," Ruth said.

"He is not so bad," Edek said. Ruth groaned. She wasn't ready to face Stefan yet.

"I'd like a break from Stefan," she said. "Unless you'd really like to see him sooner."

"Are you stupid?" Edek said. "I did only suggest it to be more convenient for you."

"Oh, good," Ruth said. "We can get a Mercedes though. I've become a convert to the benefits of driving in a Mercedes."

"A Mercedes is such a good car," Edek said. "One of the best."

Ruth started to relax. They were on to more comfortable territory. The glories of a Mercedes car were something they could both, now, agree on.

"Stefan's Mercedes is a specially good one," Edek said. Ruth was just about to tell Edek to call Stefan when Edek said, "Ah, forget about it, I will find another Mercedes."

"You arrange the Mercedes," Ruth said. "And I'll meet you back here in ten minutes."

Ruth took Israel Rothwax's coat out of the Saks Fifth Avenue bag. She didn't want any of the staff to think it was a valuable coat. That was ridiculous, she thought. Most of the staff of the Grand Victoria, in Łódź, would never have heard of Saks Fifth Avenue. Still, the Saks bag looked classy. And it was best to be safe. Ruth hung the coat in the closet, next to the rest of her clothes. She realized that everything she owned would soon smell of mothballs. She didn't mind. These mothballs had a different connotation from most mothballs.

She put the photographs inside a guidebook to Poland. She didn't think anyone would want to steal a guidebook to Poland. She went downstairs. She found her father standing in front of what had to be the biggest Mercedes in Łódź. He was smiling. Ruth walked up to him.

"This is a big Mercedes," she said.

"It is the biggest model what Mercedes does make," said Edek.

"I'm impressed," Ruth said. "Where did you find it?"

"I did ask the doorman," Edek said. "He did tell me he has a friend with a very big Mercedes. So I said, book him for us, please."

"What are we paying for this car?" Ruth said, although she felt that the question was superfluous next to her expenditure this morning.

"This Mercedes is the same price as any other Mercedes," Edek said.

"A bargain," she said. Edek laughed.

"This whole trip to Poland," he said, "is one big bargain."

They got into the car. "Tell the driver we'll only be about an hour," Ruth said.

"I did tell him already, half an hour," Edek said.

"I'm sure he won't mind if we take a bit longer," Ruth said. Edek bounced himself up and down on the backseat.

"This Mercedes is very comfortable," he said.

"It sure is," she said. She sank back into the seat. She was so tired. She hadn't realized how tired she was.

Edek reached into the pocket of his parka. He pulled out some dried apricots. "I did take these apricots from breakfast," he said. "Have some of them. You will feel better." She must look as tired as she felt, she thought. She took two of the dried apricots. "Thanks, Dad," she said.

They were nearing the ghetto area. Ruth wondered what her father was thinking. Was he remembering the potato peels he and Rooshka had tried to turn into salad? *Salatka* they called it. Or was he remembering the decline in the availability of potato peels? It had happened on November 26, 1942, Edek had told her. The Department of Soup Kitchens had ordered a reduction in the potato content of the workshop soup. There had been a large delivery of cabbage, which had to be used up. The soup was tastier, but had less nutritional value. Edek had said that you could feel the difference. It was even harder to work hard on cabbage soup.

Was he remembering the day after the cabbage announcement when a rumor swept the ghetto that the straw-shoe workers were to be transferred to Poznań? The Germans thought it would be easier to transfer the Jews than to keep shipping the straw from Poznań. Edek had told Rooshka, who was working in the straw-shoe workshop at the time, that they would go into hiding if this order came through. They were not to be separated by anything, he had said.

The Mercedes turned left from Ogrodowa Street into Zachodnia Street. Ruth had a map of the former ghetto with her. They were at the corner of Zachodnia and Podrzeczna Streets. Ruth knew that this intersection marked the entry into what had been the Łódź ghetto. There was nothing marking the spot. She told Edek where they were. "I do not recognize anything," he said.

"All the buildings were demolished," she said.

"I will show you where Mum and me did live for the first two years when we will drive past the street," Edek said.

They passed Lutomierska Street where the old Jewish Cemetery of Łódź used to be. The first deportations from the ghetto had set out from this site. The cemetery was no longer there. The Nazis had destroyed it. They had used the headstones and tombstones to build roads so that they could get to the rest of the Jews they had to kill more efficiently. A bit farther on, on the corner of Rynek Baucki, there was a memorial plaque in memory of the Jewish and gypsy victims of Nazi war crimes. Ruth wondered how many Poles had looked at that plaque.

"Himmler came to the ghetto, one day," Edek said.

"SS-Reichsführer Heinrich Himmler?" said Ruth.

"Yes," Edek said. "Himmler himself. I remember it was a Saturday. It was June 7, 1941. He came in a big black beautiful car. Probably a Mercedes. The car had a top what was open. Probably because it was summer. I remember the licen plates what was on the car."

Edek always dropped the *s* sound at the end of the word "license." He always said "licen." Why was she thinking about that? This was no time to be distracted by Edek's or anyone else's pronunciation.

"You saw Himmler?" Ruth said.

"Of course I did see Himmler," Edek said. "Otherwise how could I tell you about his licen plates? I did never forget those licen plates. Instead of numbers, was an SS insignia and the number one."

Ruth shook her head. She wondered if Himmler was the first person to have had personalized number plates. If he had, he had ushered in a craze. Half of most of the cars on the road in America now seemed to have personalized plates. Why was she having such banal thoughts? Surely there was something more significant about Himmler's visit to the Łódź ghetto than whether he had been a forerunner of a craze for personalized plates. She didn't want to take this visit to Poland lightly. She wanted to take in as much as she could. She had been wanting to do this for so many years.

"I did always remember that day," Edek said. "It was the same day that the Kripo, the criminal police, did kill a very nice boy who was living near to us, Elia Hersz. He was seventeen. He was a clever boy. He always did say to me and Mum that we did have to keep our spirits up. That this would not last long. It did not last too long for him. They killed him at nine o'clock at night. He was not supposed to go out at night. As a matter of fact nobody was allowed to go out of their house that whole day. I do not know why. Maybe they did not want Himmler to have to look at people what did not look so good."

"You'd think that looking at ragged and diseased and malnourished Jews would have pepped Himmler up for the day," Ruth said.

"Who knows," said Edek.

"Why were you out if there was a curfew?" Ruth said.

"Mum's mother was very sick and Mum did want to send her some of her bread," he said.

"So you took the bread?" said Ruth.

"I did take the bread," Edek said.

They were at the intersection of Zgierska and Limanowskiego Streets. These streets were major transport routes from the center of Łódź, to the north and the west. The intersection of these streets divided the ghetto into three parts. The parts were connected to each other by wooden bridges. Ruth had looked at many photographs of poor Jews crossing that bridge. Poor Jews. Why did those two words run together so naturally for her? They were not two words the rest of the world coupled very often.

"I cannot recognize anything," Edek said. He sounded distressed. "I did want to show you the places where Mum and me did live. I did know every street in the ghetto. Now I do not know where anything is."

"That's because they got rid of it all," Ruth said. "They should have left it how it was. It could have been a walk-through museum. Far more effective than any exhibits you could label and encase in glass."

"I want to show you where Mum and me did live," Edek said.

"Drive very slowly," Ruth said to the driver. Edek repeated that to the driver, in Polish. He slowed to a crawl.

They were in Czarnieckiego Street. Ruth knew that the ghetto's central prison complex was at 14 Czarnieckiego Street. She knew that it had consisted of fourteen separate buildings. There was nothing of the prison left now. The street was full of the regulation Communist-inspired residential architecture.

"The prison used to be here," Ruth said to Edek. Edek looked around him. He looked bewildered and confused. "We're on Czarnieckiego Street," Ruth said. "But there's nothing left of the prison."

"I do not recognize anything," Edek said. He sounded quite flat. Almost depressed.

Ruth wasn't sure why the absence of anything recognizable from the Łódź ghetto was so upsetting to him. Maybe because so much of his past was impossible to locate. Impossible to believe. Impossible to understand.

Maybe with all of that uncertainty, you needed something to point at. Something more concrete than horror.

"I am happy that the prison is not anymore here," Edek said. "I have not such good memories of this prison." Ruth didn't know her father had had anything to do with the prison. There was so much she didn't know. No matter how much she read about the Łódź ghetto, she couldn't read enough. Enough to understand what it was like. Enough to understand how it had happened. She could read about the ghetto forever, she thought, and it would never be enough.

She recalled reading about an order that had been issued in the ghetto on June 27, 1942. The order warned that all German officials in uniform and in plain clothes were to be greeted by residents of the ghetto with a salute. Ruth found it unbelievable that on February 16, 1944, when most of the Jews had died or been transported to Auschwitz, the Nazis were still issuing orders for Jews to salute. The 1944 order gave the Jews detailed instructions on what constituted a proper salute. Most of the Jews who were being required to salute could barely walk let alone salute.

The same day as the first order to Jews to salute had been posted, June 27, 1942, Hans Biebow, the commandant of the Łódź ghetto, lodged a formal objection to the wording of the death notices of Jews recorded by the Jewish elders of the ghetto. Biebow ordered that references to hunger, starvation, or swelling from hunger cease. From now on he wanted the cause of death, from hunger, to be listed as malnutrition. The pettiness of the requirements and orders never ceased to amaze Ruth. Nothing was too inconsequential or mundane or banal enough about Jews and their lives for the Germans to leave it alone. They had to tamper and add and subtract and play with Jews ceaselessly. They were never content.

Ruth had seen a photograph of Hans Biebow. He was a handsome young man. In the photograph he was relaxing in the ghetto, in an armchair, next to a table laden with oysters, clams, canapés, lobster, and sausages. This photograph was taken at the same time as Edek was picking up his twenty-kilogram ration of turnips for the winter. He'd had to stand in line in the cold for hours, to pick up the turnips. He had been so cold. He had lost most of his weight, and was little more than skin and bones. Then he had had to drag the already rotting sack behind him, all the way home. Halfway home the sack burst. Turnips went everywhere. He saved as many as he could. When he got home, he cried.

"Do you remember the story I did tell you about the turnips?" Edek said. Ruth was startled. "I was just thinking about that," she said.

"Me too," Edek said.

"There is nothing here, anymore," Edek said.

"There never was," Ruth said. They were both quiet.

"I do not think I can find where Mum and me did live," Edek said.

"You first lived near the hospital on Łagiewnicka Street, didn't you?" Ruth said.

"You do remember everything," Edek said. He looked pleased with Ruth for producing this detail.

"I remember your telling me about the day they emptied that hospital," Ruth said.

"It was September 1, 1942," Edek said. "It was exactly seven o'clock. A big truck came and they did put all the patients on the truck. They was in a hurry, so they did throw some patients out of the windows of the hospital, onto the truck." Ruth looked at Edek. His eyes had filled with tears. They should leave the ghetto area, Ruth decided. She had made her father cry enough for one day.

"I'm sorry, Dad," she said.

"You did not do anything," Edek said. He looked away. Ruth felt bad. The idea of this trip hadn't been to make her father feel bad.

"I don't know why we're here," Ruth said.

"Some things are not so easy to know," Edek said.

"Let's get out of here," Ruth said. "I'm ready to go to Kraków."

"I am, too, ready to go somewhere else," Edek said.

"Probably anywhere that isn't Łódź," said Ruth. "I'm finished with Łódź, myself." Was that true? Or was that impossible? Would she never be able to be finished with Łódź? She didn't know.

Edek told the driver to take them back to the hotel. Edek was quiet for the whole ride back. They pulled up outside the hotel. Even the Grand Victoria looked friendly and familiar, next to what used to be the Łódź ghetto.

"You want me to pack for you?" Ruth said to Edek.

"Are you crazy?" Edek said.

"That's one of my least crazy suggestions," Ruth said.

"I agree with that, to tell you the truth," Edek said. "You got plenty more crazy ideas." Ruth put her arm around her father. She gave him a kiss on the cheek.

"Thanks for doing this with me," she said.

"I must be crazy," he said. Ruth laughed.

"Let's pack and meet downstairs," she said.

Ruth packed slowly. Everything about her was weary. Her eyes, her limbs, her brain. She carried things, one at a time, to her suitcase. She was so glad she was leaving Łódź. She felt dirty. She didn't have time for a shower. She looked for her perfume. Some perfume would freshen her up. She loved her perfume. She had been wearing the same perfume, Fracas by Robert Piguet, for years. She couldn't find the perfume. Where could she have put it? She looked in the bathroom. She had already emptied the bathroom cupboard. The perfume wasn't in the bathroom. She looked through her suitcase. The perfume wasn't there. She felt annoyed with herself for misplacing the perfume. She hated it when she was careless.

She looked at a list she had made herself of things to pack in her smaller bag. The photographs from Kamedulska Street were on the top of the list. She would die if she lost them, she thought. Then she realized how absurd that thought was. People didn't die when they lost other people, let alone a few photographs. But she didn't have the people to lose. She only had these photographs. She packed the envelope with the photographs carefully into her bag. She looked for the rolls of film she had bought. She had the new film in a bag with film she had already used. She wanted to take some photographs on the way to Kraków. She opened the bag. It contained only the used film.

Ruth was puzzled. She really must be losing it, going nuts, she thought. She remembered putting four new rolls of film into this bag. Then it hit her. Of course, the perfume and the new rolls of film had been stolen. She sat down on the lumpy bed and started to cry. She cried and cried. She felt stupid for crying over lost perfume and rolls of film. She knew she was crying for far more than that. She had to stop crying, she thought. She wiped her eyes. She finished packing.

She called Edek. "Are you ready?" she said.

"I am nearly ready," he said. "But I cannot find my razor blades. I did have a new packet. It had twelve razor blades. Those ones what you throw away."

"Disposable razors," Ruth said.

"I cannot find where I did put them," Edek said.

"I think you might find them in the pocket of one of the employees of the hotel," Ruth said.

"What?" said Edek.

"My perfume and some rolls of film for the camera are gone, too," Ruth said. "They've been stolen."

Edek started to laugh. "I did think I was going crazy," he said.

"Me too," she said.

"Maybe we are crazy?" he said. "Who else would come to Łódź?"

"I can't believe they stole our stuff," Ruth said.

"They did take my razor blades and your perfume?" Edek said.

"And the film," she said. Edek started laughing, again. He laughed and laughed. His laughter made Ruth laugh.

"They got us, again," Edek said when he stopped laughing.

"I'll see you downstairs," Ruth said. She was still laughing.

Stefan had arrived when Ruth got downstairs. Edek was embracing him. Stefan looked pretty pleased to see Edek. Ruth waved to Stefan, and walked to the front desk to pay the hotel bill. She had to wait ten minutes for the hotel's computer to print out the receipt. She looked for Edek. He was handing out tips. Tips for the doorman. Tips for the porter. Ruth walked quickly over to him.

"Why are you tipping everyone?" she said. "They stole our stuff."

"How do you know it was them who did steal our stuff?" Edek said.

Maybe he had a point, she thought. She went back to collect the receipt. She smiled at the porter and the doorman. She was so happy to be leaving. She got into the Mercedes. She was happy to be in the Mercedes. She was even happy to see Stefan.

They got out of Łódź in record time. Ruth wondered whether Edek had asked Stefan to get a move on. She was sure Edek was as happy to leave Łódź as she was.

Soon, they were in a more rural part of Poland. The countryside looked peaceful, to Ruth. Farmhouses and chickens. Small cottages and snow-covered shrubs. The odd cow and a couple of horses. Some goats tethered to posts. Everything was so quiet. So benign. Most of the homes were adorned with religious symbols. Jesus on the cross, shrines to the Madonna, lone crosses. Some of the shrines were very elaborate. Housed in buildings in front of the homes, they were almost small chapels. Barely one home was without a display of its occupants' religiosity. These testaments to godliness dotted the landscape.

They passed donkeys and carts. Donkeys loaded with coal, and donkeys carrying straw. They passed a man making a broom out of branches of a tree. Ruth was glad that they were out of the city. They drove past an enormous sculpture of the Madonna in front of a farmhouse. "Look at that Madonna," Ruth said to Edek. But Edek didn't hear. He was in the front, talking to Stefan.

A minute later Edek turned around to Ruth. "Was you talking about Madonna?" he said. Ruth was about to explain it was an image of the Madonna, the Virgin Mary, not Madonna, the celebrity, when Edek said, "She is going to be a star, this Madonna." Ruth didn't have the heart to tell him that Madonna was already as big a star as it was possible to be. Last year Edek had predicted that Michael Jackson would make it big. It wasn't a Michael Jackson revival that Edek was forecasting. Edek hadn't noticed that Michael Jackson had ever hit the big time.

Stefan had turned off the side roads and gone onto a highway. Ruth was sad to leave the more bucolic setting. Edek and Stefan had been talking to each other since they had left Łódź. Ruth heard Stefan compliment Edek on his Polish. "You have done my day," Edek said to Stefan. Ruth wasn't sure whether to point out that what Edek meant was "you have made my day," or to let him know he had been speaking English to Stefan. Suddenly Edek realized his mistake. He roared with laughter. "I did speak English to you," he said to Stefan. Then he slapped his head and explained the double slipup to Stefan. They both roared with laughter. Ruth smiled. She was glad that Edek was happy.

Two minutes later, there were loud guffaws from Stefan and Edek. The car slowed down. Ruth looked out of the window. Ahead of them, almost in the middle of the highway, were two women. Two women gyrating wildly with their pelvises. Both women had their pelvises pushed out in a movement that couldn't be mistaken for anything that wasn't suggestive of sex. These women were suggesting sex to whatever possible passersby they were able to flag down with their hips.

Ruth couldn't believe her eyes. She had never seen prostitutes like these. One woman had an enormous head of yellow hair, bright red cheeks, thickly rimmed black eyes, and a big pink mouth. The other woman was black-haired and black-eyed. They were both wearing short shorts underneath winter coats. The black-haired one waved to a truck driver who pulled off the highway.

"She did get a customer," Edek said to Stefan.

"You'll have to speak Polish if you want him to understand," Ruth said, although she had been reluctant to let Edek know she had seen the prostitutes. It would have been impossible not to see them. Stefan had slowed down to a crawl. Edek and Stefan were looking at the women and chuckling. They lowered their voices. Ruth couldn't hear what they were saying. She decided that it was just as well. It was better for her state of mind not to know what they were saying.

Ruth realized why the prostitutes were jutting their hips out and gyrating with such exaggerated, crude movements. They had to exaggerate. The women had a very brief time period, a small window of opportunity, in which to get their message across. A subtle movement would never be noticed by a speeding truck driver.

"We're not going to stop, are we?" she said to Edek. Stefan must have heard the stern tone in her voice. He speeded up.

She should do some work in the car, she thought. She should write a fax to Max telling her that it was not possible to sell the copyright to any of her letters. It was too problematic to try to guarantee that no one else would ever be given the same letter. How many words would she have to guarantee not to repeat? Any sentence contained in the letter? Any word? It was clearly not a viable proposition. Max would just have to tell Mr. Kendall that he couldn't buy the copyright to the refusal-to-lend-his-name-to-the-fund-raising-event letter she had written for him. She got out a pen and paper. She would outline the difficulties of selling a copyright, to Max, in a fax. She looked at the blank sheet of paper. She felt too tired to write anything. She was too tired to compose a shopping list. She was exhausted. She put the paper away.

She could feel herself drifting off. She tried to stay awake. She never slept during the day. She had read that insomniacs should never nap. She wasn't an insomniac. But she did suffer from occasional sleeplessness. She thought that not sleeping during the day was a good preventive measure to allay any potential insomnia. She was finding it harder and harder to stay awake. She contemplated beginning a conversation with Edek. But he was so happy chatting with Stefan. She didn't want to disturb his happiness. She wondered how long it would be before they arrived in Kraków.

"Ruthie darling," Edek said.

"What do you want?" she said.

"You are asleep."

"No I'm not," she said. "I never sleep during the day." She looked out of the car window. It was dark outside. She must have fallen asleep. "Where are we?" she said.

"We are nearly in Kraków," said Edek.

"Nearly in Kraków?"

"I told you you was sleeping," Edek said.

Ruth was disoriented. She must have slept for over two hours. She felt very groggy. "I was very happy that you was sleeping," Edek said.

"Did you sleep?" Ruth said.

"No," said Edek. "But I am not so tired what you are."

"Łódź was pretty tough, wasn't it?" she said.

"You can say that again, brother," Edek said.

They pulled up outside the hotel. Ruth found some peppermint Tic-Tacs. She hoped that the strong flavor would pep her up.

"Will you pay Stefan while I check in?" Ruth said.

"Okey dokey," Edek said. Okey dokey, Ruth thought. Why was her father in such a good mood? Maybe it was because they had left Łódź. Anybody would be in a good mood leaving Łódź.

Ruth put her credit card down on the desk in front of the receptionist, a man who was about thirty. "Two rooms for Rothwax," she said.

"You are here to visit the Auschwitz Museum," the receptionist said. Ruth was shocked. How did he know what she had come to Kraków for? Could he tell she was Jewish just by looking at her? Or maybe he recognized Rothwax as a Jewish name. Were all Jews who visited Kraków headed for Auschwitz?

"I'm not here to see the Auschwitz Museum," she said loudly to the receptionist. "I am here to visit the Auschwitz death camp." The receptionist coughed nervously. He looked disconcerted. She hadn't meant to say it so loudly. "I'm here to visit the Auschwitz death camp," she said in a quieter voice. He lowered his eyes.

"I can get you a very good driver," he said. "The museum is approximately forty miles west of Kraków."

"The death camp, you mean," Ruth said.

He nodded. "I can get you a very good driver with a Mercedes," he said.

Poles seemed to be very good at producing drivers with Mercedes for Jews, Ruth thought. Maybe it wasn't just Jews who were offered drivers with Mercedes. Mercedes for Jews, Ruth thought. A bizarre business. Edek had joined her.

"We do want two rooms not too far from each other," he said. "I want to be near to my daughter."

"Of course," said the receptionist.

"Stefan is very happy," Edek said. "I did give him a good tip."

"I'm sure you did," Ruth said.

"You have two rooms next to each other," the receptionist said.

"Thank you very much," said Edek.

"Should I book the driver for you for the Auschwitz Museum?" the receptionist said to Ruth.

"It's a death camp," she said.

"What for do you argue with him?" Edek said.

"I don't know," she said.

"Stefan is waiting to say good-bye to you," Edek said.

Ruth walked over to the front door where Stefan was waiting. Stefan smiled at her. "Thank you very much," Ruth said to Stefan. Edek and Stefan embraced each other. "Travel well," Edek said to Stefan. "You travel in good health," Stefan said to Edek. They hugged again. Ruth shook her head. She really couldn't understand this friendship. Was it a friendship? She didn't know. She was much too tired to work it out. "Good-bye, Miss Rothwax," Stefan said to Ruth. Ruth put out her hand. Stefan leaned down and kissed her hand. She smiled at him.

"Thank you for looking after us," she said.

~ *Chapter Twelve* ~

The sound of someone humming came ringing across the Planty, the park that followed the course of the ancient ramparts and enclosed the Stare Miasto, the Old Town, in the center of Kraków. Ruth was unnerved. It was 7 A.M. She had been running on the path that encircled the Planty for an hour. It was not yet light. The unpaved path was uneven. She had been trying not to slip on the odd patches of ice.

Very few people were about. The path was close enough to the street for her to feel safe. A middle-aged man was crossing the park diagonally, in front of her. Was it him singing? She looked at the man walking. He didn't look as though he was singing.

All of a sudden, Ruth recognized the voice. It wasn't a Pole. It was Höss. Höss was here, in Kraków. She felt frustrated and agitated.

"You recognized my singing, I see," Höss said. He sounded very chipper. Almost chirpy.

Why was Höss so happy? Ruth wondered. She stopped running. She realized she had been running and talking. Something she had never been able to do simultaneously before.

She bent down to tie up her shoelace. She really needed some new running shoes. She was sure she had done more than five hundred miles in these shoes, and she knew they lost most of their shock absorbency after five hundred miles. How could she be thinking about her shoes and their shock absorbency? She was in Poland, in Kraków, in the Planty, early in the morning, talking to Rudolf Höss.

"I thought I'd gotten rid of you permanently," she said to Höss.

"It is not so easy to get rid of me," Höss said.

"You mean it is possible?"

"If you do not know this why should I tell you?" he said.

"I tell you things," Ruth said.

"And I reciprocate," Höss said. "You do not know something which you need to know."

"I don't know many things I need to know," Ruth said. She adjusted her pedometer. It was digging into her waist. She left her headphones on. The cold sometimes gave her an earache.

"Your father knows something you do not know," Höss said.

"Of course he does," Ruth said. "I haven't lived his life."

"He knows something which you need to know," Höss said. "This something he has known for many years. For decades. Ask him about this."

"You're giving me more advice?" Ruth said. "Wow, I'm so lucky."

"I can see that you are not sincere about this statement," Höss said.

"You can see?" Ruth said.

"I can see," said Höss. He took a deep breath. Ruth could hear the intake of air. So Höss still breathed the same air as everyone else. The same air that she was breathing. How weird, Ruth thought.

"Edek Rothwax has chosen not to tell you about this," Höss said.

"You know my father's name?" Ruth said.

"Of course," said Höss. "Why are you surprised? You and I know a lot about each other." Ruth took a sip of water. She felt dehydrated. "I am trying to help you," Höss said.

"What a joke," Ruth said. She laughed.

"I am serious about this," Höss said. "I want to help you."

Ruth felt quite calm. She could cope with Höss as long as he remained himself. When he seemed in danger of metamorphosing into Mother Teresa, she lost all of her patience with him. She was surprised at her admission that she could cope with Höss. It was a revelation to her.

"Don't pretend to want to be helpful to me," Ruth said. She dug her heel lightly into the ground. Höss winced. A small yelp escaped from him.

"I am not pretending," he gasped.

Ruth steadied herself. The spot she had chosen to dig her heel into had been frozen. She had nearly slipped. "Fuck you," she said. "I'm sick of you."

"Why do you persist with these obscenities?" Höss said. "Even taking into account my improved English, they do not offend me."

"Well, you'd better become familiar with them because English is becoming the language of the future in Europe. That is, if you do have a future," Ruth said.

"Of course I have a future," Höss said. "I have explained this to you before. Dead people have a future. It is as complicated a future as any person's future can be."

"What sort of complications are you talking about?" Ruth said.

"There are certain things you have to relive when you are dead," Höss said. "Certain portions of your life and sometimes, of your death."

"Really?" said Ruth. "That doesn't sound promising."

"The reliving of your life has a different connotation, in Himmel," Höss said. "I have noticed that in Himmel they seem on the whole to relive very pleasant aspects of their lives."

"But not in Zweites Himmel's Lager?" Ruth said.

"No," Höss said. He sounded glum.

"That's good," she said. Höss overlooked her barb.

Ruth had an image of Zweites Himmel's Lager as a vast space populated with people who were reliving their living and their dying, trying to get it right. And in all probability repeating every aspect of their original lives. It was hard to change, hard to learn, even from your own experience.

"I did hear the rumors about English becoming the language of Europe," Höss said. "In Himmel they give advanced English classes to all the Europeans. In Zweites Himmel's Lager we have to earn the privilege." He sighed. "We have to earn the privilege for almost everything, it seems."

"Well, you must be a slow earner," Ruth said. Höss didn't reply. "It's a pun on a slow learner," she said. "It's a common English expression." She shook her head in irritation. Why was she pointing out puns and summing up musicals to Höss?

"I heard this morning that the German government is closing down even more of the Goethe Institutes around the world," Höss said. "You know of course about the Goethe Institutes?"

"Of course," she said. "The Goethe Institutes are entrusted with the promotion of the German language abroad. I won a prize for reciting *Der Erlkönig* at the Goethe Institute, in Melbourne when I was thirteen."

"I know this," Höss said.

"You know that?" Ruth said. She felt a bit queasy. How much did Höss know about her? And how long had he known her? How long had he been watching her? Had he been watching her?

"Of course," Höss said. What was he replying to? Ruth thought. Her question or her thought? She had another drink of water. She felt quite sick. Höss always did this to her. He made her feel sick.

"You were suffering from nausea brought on by stress long before you met me, were you not?" Höss said. Ruth nodded her head. "They have already closed twenty-three Goethe Institutes around the world," Höss said. "By failing to spread the use of German, Germany is surrendering its influence on world affairs."

"That may not be so bad," Ruth said. She suddenly felt a discomfort in Höss. She wasn't sure how she could detect this. It was a small shift in something. Something slight. A slight pitch, a slight tone, a slight noise. A sound of discomfort, of disturbance, of disquiet.

"I know where you are going," Höss said.

"I'm going back to the hotel," Ruth said.

"I know where you are going," he said. "I know why you came here."

"Really?" she said. "I wish I did."

"This is not a time for humor," Höss said.

Höss didn't sound well. His bravado had diminished. He sounded panicked. "You are going to Auschwitz," he said.

"Oh, so that's what's disturbing you," she said.

Höss coughed. "I am not at all disturbed," he said.

"At least you know that it's a death camp and not a museum," Ruth said.

"Of course I know this," Höss said. "I myself have corrected some inmates of Zweites Himmel's Lager."

"I bet there are a lot of Poles up there with you using the term 'Auschwitz Museum,' " Ruth said. "Are they the ones you have to correct the most?"

"I would say that is correct," Höss said. "Although quite a few others persist in making this mistake."

Ruth sighed. It was depressing that even in death you encountered the same denial.

"I was not the commandant of a museum," Höss said.

"That would feel like a demotion to you, wouldn't it?" Ruth said.

"Of course," said Höss. Ruth thought she heard a faint humph after the "of course."

"Every German had to commit himself with all his heart in order for us to win the war," Höss said.

"Is that what you were doing?" Ruth said. "I thought you were murdering Jews."

"I was eliminating certain parts of the population," Höss said. "That was my main aim. But it was also my job to ensure that this project contributed to the war. This was strictly in accordance with the directive of the Reichsführer-SS. He declared that everything had to be sacrificed in the interests of one goal. To win the war."

"You didn't sacrifice anything on the prisoners," Ruth said. "You sped up the death process and used up the residue of every Jew. Their hair, their teeth, and other bits and pieces. You fed them less, worked them harder, dispensed with them faster, looted their bodies when you had already remaindered their possessions. You cared less, if that was possible. Not a cent was to be squandered on any prisoner."

"You understand exactly what had to be done," Höss said.

"I understand?" said Ruth. "I'll never understand." She contemplated kicking Höss. Grinding her heel into the ground in a ferocious kick. But she couldn't be bothered. She would have to kick till her feet dropped off if there was to be any retribution.

"Himmler stated very clearly that the severe conditions in the camp were of secondary importance," Höss said.

"Secondary importance?" Ruth said. "Wouldn't no importance be more accurate?"

"Why do you insist on interrupting me?" Höss said. "I am trying to convey an extremely complex situation to you. In the summer of 1941 the Reichsführer-SS gave me firm orders to assemble whatever was needed to make Auschwitz capable of mass exterminations," Höss said.

"So it was all really Himmler's fault?" Ruth said. "Is that what you're saying?"

"The Reichsführer's orders were not open for discussion," Höss said. "They were orders. They were not negotiations. I had no idea of course of the outcome or the effect of these orders."

"I think we could agree that the obvious and apparent outcome would be a lot of dead people," Ruth said.

"I was not aware of the consequences at the time," Höss said.

"Consequences to whom?" Ruth said. "To you?"

"Consequences in general," Höss said.

"Don't give me that bullshit," Ruth said. "You're talking about consequences for yourself, aren't you?"

"Yes, yes," Höss said.

"You're going to be stuck here for years. Decades," Ruth said. "I doubt if you'll ever see those famed gates of Himmel."

"You are merely trying to upset me," Höss said.

"I'm not trying at all," Ruth said. She moved her heel, slightly. She knew by a small sound, a tiny auditory wave, that Höss had twitched. He had felt her movement.

"The order from the Reichsführer-SS was without question a deplorable and atrocious order," Höss said.

"Are you capitulating?" Ruth said. "Surely not."

"It was, as I said, certainly atrocious and deplorable," Höss said. "And excessive. But nevertheless, the reasons behind the extermination program seemed to me to be sound."

"Thank God, you're still yourself," Ruth said. "For a minute I thought you had turned into a humanitarian."

Höss laughed. A thin, snakelike slither of a laugh. The laugh made Ruth shiver. Was Höss laughing at the image of himself as a humanitarian? Or was he laughing with pleasure at the steadfastness of his own views?

"I suspect the reasons and premises behind the mass exterminations still seem right to you," Ruth said. Höss stopped laughing.

"Now, as then," he said. "The question of whether this mass extermination of the Jews was essential or not was not something that I myself could address. I did not have the full facts at my disposal."

"Wow," said Ruth. "You still feel there's room for discussion about the merit of Hitler's program?"

"The Reichsführer was the Führer's representative," Höss said. "It was for me exactly as if Hitler himself had given me this order."

"It would probably be in your interests to cover up some of that earnest rectitude," Ruth said.

Höss seemed not to understand. "The final solution to the Jewish question had to be addressed. For me to consider the merits of the Führer's orders was out of the question," he said.

Ruth felt depressed. She didn't want to hear any more.

"I am the target of many people," Höss said. "Even in Zweites Himmel's Lager. I do not understand why. What I did was not so wrong. I was nationalistic. Many countries including democratic England have a concept of nationalism, 'My country, right or wrong.' Every patriotic Englishman adheres to this belief."

"I'm not sure you've correctly grasped the concept of patriotism," Ruth said. "It could be a requirement for entry into Himmel."

"It is not," Höss said. "Patriotism is discouraged. Humanism is what is encouraged."

"Then you're in trouble," Ruth said. "Humanism is not easily learned."

"There are many classes in humanity in Zweites Himmel's Lager," Höss said.

"Have you been to any?" Ruth asked.

"I cannot attend these classes," Höss said. "One must pass the sensitivity-training class to qualify for attendance in a humanity class."

"It's a prerequisite?" said Ruth.

"Yes, unfortunately," said Höss.

"It's not that unfortunate," Ruth said. "If you're having trouble with sensitivity, you'd really be in trouble with humanity."

Höss let out a sigh. A sigh long enough to have expelled every ounce of air from his lungs, if he still had lungs. "I need to pass these classes," he said. "I am tired of Zweites Himmel's Lager. I hear they have wonderful concerts in Himmel. Concerts performed by splendid musicians. We can hear faint strains of the music coming from Himmel, in Zweites Himmel's Lager. We hear just enough to discern what is being played, but not enough to hear it."

Ruth wondered if Höss felt she should feel sorry for him. "Yesterday, Mario Lanza gave a concert in Himmel," Höss said.

"Mario Lanza?" Ruth said. She hadn't heard anyone mention Mario Lanza for years. Her mother used to love Mario Lanza. Rooshka used to sing "Arrivederci Roma" sometimes while she was doing the dishes. Ruth always knew that her mother was feeling happy if she heard the refrain of "Arrivederci Roma" or "The Loveliest Night of the Year" coming from the kitchen.

"Mario Lanza became popular after I passed away," Höss said.

"After you passed away?" said Ruth. "After you were executed, you mean. After you were burnt down to a fine ash. After you were completely cremated."

"Yes, yes, yes," Höss said. Why did she say *completely* cremated? Was it possible to be partially cremated? Probably. She couldn't see why not.

"Mario Lanza is giving concerts in Himmel, is he?" Ruth said.

"Yes," said Höss glumly.

Ruth's spirits rose. Maybe her mother was listening to Mario Lanza. She immediately felt foolish. Her mother was dead. Not listening to Mario Lanza sing "If You Were Mine," despite what Höss said. Höss was probably making all of this up. She couldn't trust Höss. How could you trust a presence? Especially an ex-Nazi presence. She corrected herself. There was nothing ex about Höss's Nazi affiliations. They were well and firmly present.

"I know what you are thinking," Höss said. "I can assure you that you can trust me. It is not in my interests to lie to you. I feel better than I have felt in many years. I am, finally, on the right path."

"Where does the path lead to?" Ruth said.

"Even I am not sure of that," Höss said.

"I'm glad you're feeling better," Ruth said to Höss. She surprised herself by saying this. Höss seemed surprised, too.

"I am surprised to hear this," he said.

"I am glad I can surprise you," Ruth said. "I thought nothing could."

"I went to Mass yesterday," Höss said. "This is something I have not done in over eighty years."

"You have Mass in Zweites Himmel's Lager?" Ruth said.

"Of course," said Höss.

"So you have priests up there?" said Ruth.

"Many fine priests," Höss said.

Ruth decided not to point out to Höss the discrepancy between his description of the priests as fine, and the fact that these priests were in hell.

"We're very close to the train tracks that led to Auschwitz, aren't we?" Ruth said. She knew that the main railway station of Kraków was close to the heart of the city. Not far from where she was standing. She knew that some of the transports had been rerouted to avoid the city center. Höss hadn't answered the question. "We're close to the tracks that took people to your kingdom of evil, aren't we?" she said.

"Kingdom of evil?" Höss said. He laughed. "What do you know about evil?" he said. For the first time his laugh sounded vicious. Ruth shuddered. "You think that to blink one of your eyes five times will protect you from evil?" Höss said. "You have to be mad in order to think that five blinks could safeguard a person. If you could eliminate or make up for bad thoughts by blinking one eye, no one would be still in Zweites Himmel's Lager." He roared with laughter. Ruth could feel the earth beside her, in the Planty, rumble with Höss's laugh. She decided to give up her habit of blinking either eye. She decided she didn't need it anymore.

"Are you nervous about the fact that I am going to Auschwitz?" Ruth said to Höss.

"No, not at all," he said. "You are, after all, going there voluntarily." The question must have unnerved Höss, because he started coughing. He coughed and coughed. Ruth felt sure that her question had induced his coughing fit. "I am not nervous at all," Höss spluttered.

Ruth waited for Höss's coughing to subside. He was probably right, she thought. He was probably not nervous. What was there for him to be nervous about? "Why should I be nervous?" Höss said when he stopped coughing.

"I couldn't even begin the answer to that question," Ruth said. "It would take too long." Höss ignored her.

"It was my deputy Fritzsch, who first tried gas as a method of accomplishing the killings," Höss said. "Fritzsch used a preparation of prussic acid called Zyklon B. We used this preparation in the camp as an insecticide. Fritzsch reported the success of the gas to me."

"Why are you talking about the gassings?" Ruth said to Höss.

"You are the one who repeatedly brought up the subject of Auschwitz,"

Höss said. "I myself was present at the next gassing in which Zyklon B was used. Of course, I wore a mask to protect myself."

"Of course," Ruth said.

"The gassing took place in the detention cells of Block 2," Höss said. "The cells were very crowded. When the Zyklon B was thrown in, death was instantaneous. There were a series of quick, muffled, muted, almost stifled cries, and then the whole thing was over. There was not one more sound from these former occupants of Block 2."

Ruth thought that she must remember not to run early in the morning. Höss seemed to have particularly good access to her at that time.

"I can get to you at any time of the day," Höss said. "Or at any time of the night, for that matter."

"I can, it seems, get rid of you, whenever I please," Ruth said, and dug her heel into the unpaved track of the Planty. Höss yelled. A gurgling noise came out of him while he was yelling. As though he might throw up at any moment. "Don't vomit near me," Ruth said. Höss appeared not to hear. She could hear him still gurgling. He was also whimpering.

Why was she worried about Höss vomiting? she thought. He had already brought up more bile in her presence than any amount of vomit could contain. "I hope you feel sick," she said to Höss. She felt ill.

"I do not feel sick," Höss said.

"Liar," Ruth said.

"The experience of attending this gassing put my mind at ease," Höss said. "The mass extermination of the Jews was about to start very soon and, to tell you the truth, neither Eichmann nor I were, until this moment, confident of precisely how the killings were to be carried out. We both knew that the method to be used would be gas, but as to which gas and exactly how to administer it, and how effective it would be, we were in the dark. To my great relief, I could now report that we had not only the gas but we had established the procedure to be used."

Ruth vomited. She moved her feet as far away from her head as she could. She didn't want to throw up on her running shoes. She couldn't believe the fury of her vomit. It was propelling itself out of her in almost ferocious blasts. She felt quite frightened by this internal upheaval. What was happening to her? She vomited and vomited until all she was bringing up was water. Even then she kept retching.

She felt exhausted. She couldn't believe that she was vomiting in public. Several people looked at her. No one stopped.

"Your digestive system is not in order," Höss said.

"There is much more not in order than my digestive system," she said weakly. Her mouth tasted foul. She sat up. At least she could breathe more easily now. She shook her head. She was shocked at what had just happened. It was as though her lungs and her stomach had refused to smother their reaction to what they were hearing. She wiped her face with her hands.

Höss sighed. "I do feel very much better since I have established this discourse with you," he said. Ruth pushed her hair away from her face. She hoped there wasn't any vomit in her hair. "In Zweites Himmel's Lager," Höss said, "I am still not popular. Why cannot people see that whatever I did, I was not alone in my actions or thoughts? No Nazi was alone. We were supported by the German people. I think it is most unjust and unsatisfactory to lay the blame on the Nazis." His voice had developed a whine. "It is an injustice," Höss said.

"It's too hard to go around railing at Germans in general," Ruth said. "It's too abstract."

"But there is so much specific incriminating evidence," Höss said.

"There's too much," said Ruth. "Too much for people to take in. No one wants to acknowledge that their auntie or uncle or grandfather or grandmother could be a killer. No one wants to think of their mothers or fathers profiting from the murder of others. People can't bear to think of people they know in that light." She paused to catch her breath. "No one wants to think that anyone was capable of all of that," she said. "All of that murder. All of that hate."

"But they were," said Höss.

"I know that," Ruth said. She felt flushed. She had been walking around and around the perimeter of the Planty. The sun had come out. It was the pale sun of winter. Not a bold yellow sun. Ruth felt happy to see the sun. Life was strange, she thought. Here she was, in Poland, in Kraków, in agreement, in accord with Rudolf Höss. This was an astonishing occurrence, Ruth thought. An unbelievable occurrence. Who on earth would believe this? Ruth laughed at the expression she had just used. She amended the sentence. Who on earth or anywhere else, if there was an anywhere else, would believe this?

Was there such a place as Zweites Himmel's Lager? Ruth thought. Was Zweites Himmel's Lager hell? Hell was supposed to be the dwelling place of Satan. Was Höss Satan? Or was he one of many Satans? Devils and wicked souls were supposed to dwell in hell. Condemned, Ruth thought, to eternal punishment. It was supposed to be a place of pain and torment. But there was redemption in Zweites Himmel's Lager. You could work your way out. The accumulation of wisdom and understanding, it seemed, could graduate inhabitants right out of Zweites Himmel's Lager. And into Himmel. Heaven. The dwelling place of God, the angels, and the souls of those who have gained salvation. Heaven, a place of peace and beauty. If there was a heaven, she didn't feel that Höss belonged there.

She felt tired. She had been in Poland for one week. It felt more like one year. One lifetime.

"Tomorrow is the anniversary of our first meeting," Höss said.

"What?" she said.

"We met a week ago, tomorrow," Höss said.

"It doesn't feel like a week," Ruth said.

"Maybe it is not," Höss said. "Maybe we have known each other longer than that."

"What do you mean?" Ruth said.

"I do not have to explain everything that I say," Höss said.

"Well, don't link the two of us with anniversaries and shared interests," Ruth said. "I'm not linked to you by anything."

"Do not be so sure of this," Höss said. Ruth lifted her foot to hurt him. "I am not as hard-hearted as you would imagine," Höss said.

"It would be hard to imagine the degree of hard-heartedness that you possess," Ruth said.

"That is not true," Höss said. "Frequently when I was home with my family, my thoughts would, without any warning, turn to different incidents that had accrued during the day."

"You mean when you were relaxing, at night, in Villa Höss?" Ruth said. "When you were reclining in your leather armchair surrounded by the other custom-made leather goods you ordered. And the myriad number of stolen items. Briefcases, handbags, suitcases, shoes, toys for the children. Were you sitting in the large armchair that sat right underneath the chandelier, when your thoughts would sometimes stray to what you had done during the day?"

Höss didn't answer.

"Were you comfortable on that plush carpeting?" Ruth said. Höss pretended not to hear.

"My thoughts would roam," he said. "Sometimes when I thought of particular incidents that had occurred during an extermination, I had to leave the house and go outside. To stay there, inside, in the loving circle of my family while thoughts of my day's work were present, would become intolerable."

"You didn't want your wife or your children to be contaminated by those thoughts?" Ruth said. "Terrible thoughts of Jews bleeding from the eyes, nose, and mouth. Jews with their skulls crushed. No father would want his children exposed to that. What father wouldn't want to protect his children from gassed and burnt Jews?"

"I did my best to protect my wife and children," Höss said.

"But you couldn't," Ruth said. "Your wife and children, all five of those beautiful children, the two boys and the three girls, were breathing in the fumes from the dead every day. The air coming out of those chimneys went straight into the lungs of your wife and children. Particles and filaments and pinpoints of Jews wedged themselves inside your wife and children. They took root. Nothing could shake them out."

"How can you say that?" said Höss. "Our house was surrounded by trees. Planted with flowers. Well away from the chimneys."

"You couldn't get far away enough from those chimneys to avoid the pollution. They spread smoke and soot for miles. Jewish soot."

"Sometimes the happiness of my wife, especially when she had our youngest in her arms, was too much for me," Höss said. He sounded melancholy. Almost sad. "I would look at her, and think of the things I had seen during the day," he said. "I would look at her and wonder exactly how long could all of this happiness that we have last."

Ruth was speechless. She had thought that Höss was about to pretend some sympathy for the victims. Some sensitivity at the thought of juxtaposing their position with his. Why had she expected that? Why had she expected that level of humanity?

"My wife failed to understand these gloomy moods that overtook me," Höss said. "She always put it down to some irritation to do with my work."

"She didn't understand that you were terrified that the cozy life you had created would all come to an end one day," Ruth said.

"No, she did not," Höss said.

"You loved your wife, didn't you?" Ruth said.

"Yes, I did," Höss said. "My wife was a very good wife."

"I'm sure Hedwig—I love that name—was a great wife," Ruth said.

"I would prefer it if you did not call my wife by her name," Höss said.

"But it's a wonderful name," Ruth said. "Hedwig Höss. I like the alliteration, too. Do you know what alliteration is?"

"Yes, of course," Höss said.

"My, your English is really improving," Ruth said.

"Thank you," said Höss.

"Family and fidelity were very important to you, weren't they?" Ruth said.

"Yes, very much so," Höss said. He had cheered up again.

"I know you believed in fidelity," Ruth said. "I know you severely denounced any sexual relationships between the SS men and women prisoners."

"Without question," Höss said. "SS officers and their subordinates were forbidden to associate with any female prisoners."

"You didn't want the men contaminated, did you?" Ruth said.

"Of course not," said Höss.

"They weren't allowed to touch the Jewish women or any other prisoners, were they?" Ruth said.

"No," said Höss.

"You never know what could happen if you touch Jewish skin," Ruth said.

"That is true," said Höss. "We are in agreement about this." Ruth laughed. "What is it that you find amusing?" Höss said.

"Our agreement," said Ruth.

"I ordered my men to stay as far away as possible from all female prisoners," Höss said. "The jobs that required proximity to the prisoners were carried out by Jewish policemen and policewomen."

"Kapos," Ruth said.

"That is correct," said Höss.

"It was smart of you to set Jews up to police other Jews," Ruth said. "Especially under such inhuman conditions."

"You were furious with one of your female supervisors who had sexual relations with a prisoner, weren't you?" Ruth said.

"You have read about this?" Höss said. "I was very angry. How could a person sink so low?"

"And what about Rapportführer Palitzsch?" Ruth said. "He was reputed to be one of the cruelest of your men."

"I accused Rapportführer Palitzsch myself," Höss said. "He was rumored to be having sexual relations with women prisoners at Birkenau. I made it very clear I would not tolerate such behavior."

"Some of these men were married, weren't they?" Ruth said. "The sex they were having with prisoners was not quite as quiet as what they were doing with their wives. There was quite a bit of brutality involved, wasn't there?"

"I cannot be responsible for what some of my men did to some of the prisoners," Höss said. "I tried my best, but not all of my men were of a very good caliber. I had many lowly types, asocial sorts."

"But you always set a good example yourself," Ruth said.

"Without question," said Höss.

"You and Hedwig and the five blond-haired children."

"Yes, yes, yes," said Höss.

"You're sure about this?" Ruth said.

"Of course I am sure," Höss said. "Why are we discussing this?"

"Did Hedwig know about Eleonore Hodys?" Ruth said. A series of noises Ruth could not quite identify came from Höss. They sounded like disfigured gulps, twisted exhalations, and sputters. "What did Hedwig have to say about Eleonore Hodys?" Ruth said. "Or did Hedwig never know?" A few strangulated vowels and consonants tried to come out of Höss. They were bits and pieces of words. Höss sounded as though he was choking.

"Are you about to asphyxiate yourself?" Ruth said. She laughed. "I didn't think you'd be so badly affected by the mention of her name. Many other people knew you were having an affair with this prisoner. They said she was Italian, but the name seems more Hungarian to me."

"This prisoner worked in my home," Höss said finally. He had managed to muster up a touch of indignation in his voice.

"I'm glad you didn't choke to death, just then," Ruth said. "Can dead people choke to death?"

"Of course," Höss said. "This prisoner worked in our house, for my wife and me."

"I know that," Ruth said. "But she did more. Or rather you did more, to her. I'm not sure she had much of a say in the matter."

"How dare you speak to me like this?" Höss said.

"How dare I tell you the truth?" Ruth said. "I think it's pretty bold of me, too. I was much more frightened of you, in the beginning. You were disgusting to Eleonore Hodys," Ruth said. "You fucked her whenever you pleased. It was easy, as Hedwig liked to tend the garden, and the acts never took you too long."

"How dare you!" Höss shouted.

"Stop shouting," Ruth said, "These are not the good old days. If you keep shouting I'll kick you so hard you'll never recover." Where had those words come from? Ruth thought. Those threats? Did she have more power than she knew over Höss?

"You became worried about the rumors that were growing about what you were doing to Eleonore Hodys," Ruth said. "So you shipped her off to a penal company. The sort of penal company that ensured death for its workers within weeks. But she didn't die. And you started to miss her, didn't you? You didn't miss her, just her body parts, really."

"I have listened to these accusations for long enough," Höss said.

"They're not accusations," Ruth said. "Just facts. You missed Eleonore Hodys's arms and legs and breasts and genitals, so you had her shipped back. And still Hedwig suspected nothing."

"Mrs. Höss was above such thoughts," Höss said.

"Mrs. Höss was not above much else," Ruth said. "She made sure she was never short of the things she loved most, pure cream, cocoa, the best cuts of meat, margarine, macaroni. She was probably too busy eating to worry about who you were fucking."

"I am not listening," Höss said.

"I think you have to," said Ruth. "I have a feeling the decision to listen is not up to you."

"What are you talking about?" Höss said.

Ruth didn't answer. She didn't know why she had said that. It was a feeling that had suddenly inhabited her. The feeling that Höss's participation in all of this was not quite as voluntary as it seemed. That he couldn't quite come and go as he pleased. He was locked in, in much the same way as she was. That thought made her feel sick.

"You had Eleonore Hodys put into Block 2," Ruth said. "Not just Block 2, but the airless dungeons of Block 2. And there, in that small, stifling, blackened cell, you fucked her to your heart's content. You made sure, of course, afterward, that you straightened every part of your crushed uniform and repositioned your cap. I understand why you didn't want to remove your clothes. You never knew where these prisoners' bodies had been. You were always worried about rashes and other symptoms of your illicit sex appearing. You ordered the guards to wash Miss Hodys down before your visits." Ruth paused. "I'm glad you're not saying anything," she said to Höss. "I'm glad you're not trying out the 'my wife didn't understand me' line. That's a relief."

"My wife and I were very happy," Höss said in a quiet voice.

"You were not as devoted a family man as you wanted to be," Ruth said. "You risked infecting Hedwig with lice or fleas."

"I did not," Höss barked. "I always showered after those episodes." Höss sounded as though he was about to implode. "Where did you hear that about Eleonore Hodys?" he said.

"It was common knowledge," Ruth said. "The guards used to say, 'Mr. Whiter than White is coming to do his dirty business,' when they knew you were due to arrive in the dungeons. They also called you Mr. Holier Than Thou, Mr. Incorruptible. I'm not sure if Hedwig ever heard those terms."

"Leave Mrs. Höss out of this."

"Well, you left her out, didn't you? You didn't let her know how frequently you were turning up to get stuck into poor Eleonore." Humphing noises came from Höss. Ruth knew he was fuming. And red-faced. She could feel the volume of his anger. "You contemplated leaving Eleonore Hodys there to starve to death, once you learned that she was pregnant," Ruth said.

"How did I know whose child she was carrying?" Höss spluttered.

"What a joke," Ruth said. "As though anyone else would have dared touch her. And why pretend you even thought of the pregnancy as a child? 'Up the chimney with her,' you said to the guard. You ordered her gassed."

"It was for the best," said Höss.

"But you were out of luck," Ruth said. "Or stupid. You had reported Max Grabner, the chief of Block 2, for having an affair with a prisoner. Grabner couldn't believe his luck when he found out about you and Eleonore Hodys. He went straight to the SS judge investigating him and informed on you."

"So that is what happened," Höss said.

"You mean you didn't know?" she said to Höss. What did this mean? The fact that she was telling Höss about his own life. It meant nothing. It meant that she was well informed about a subject of mutual interest. She felt exhausted. She was probably more wrung out than Höss.

"You have interrupted me too often with these lies," Höss said.

"You can't call them lies after you've admitted to them," Ruth said. What a stupid thing to say, she thought. As though anything about Höss had to be logical. "They didn't punish you for the infraction, anyway," Ruth said. "You were too valuable."

"Why are you going to Auschwitz?" Höss said. Ruth was too tired to answer. She still didn't know the answer, anyway. "My family were, without doubt, able to live very well, in Auschwitz," Höss said. "Every wish that my wife could wish was granted to her."

"Except your fidelity. Or maybe she didn't care about that. She had so much at Villa Höss. What's a spot of infidelity next to a garden of flowers, and the endless servants and the adorable children and the household pets?"

"My children loved their two horses and the foal was particularly beloved," Höss said. "Today I very deeply regret that I was not able to devote more time to my family."

"It was possibly for the best, when you look at the results of what you did devote most of your time to," Ruth said. "Possibly your children were better off away from your influence."

"Are you being insolent?" Höss said. The military tone had returned to his voice.

"No," Ruth said. "Just reflective. Thoughtful. Trying to be helpful."

"Really?" said Höss.

"Tell me, just one last thing," Ruth said. "Did Hedwig know about poor Eleonore Hodys?" Höss bellowed and snorted. All sorts of incomprehensible sounds came out of him.

"I refuse to speak any further to you!" he shouted. Ruth laughed. She felt light-headed.

"I don't care," she said. "I have to go anyway."

∾ *Chapter Thirteen* ∾

Do you feel all right?" Ruth said to Edek. Edek was standing over the buffet in the smaller of the dining rooms in the Hotel Mimoza. An entire shoal of sardines and a school of herring were already on Edek's plate for breakfast. She had thought that he looked a little pale. She needn't have asked him if he was all right, she thought. She could have just checked out his breakfast selection. Anyone who was even slightly unwell would not have been able to contemplate a meal that would have depleted the nearest ocean of half of its inhabitants.

Edek added some pickled onions and black peppercorns from the pickling juice of the herring.

"I am one hundred percent," he said.

"Did you sleep well?" she said.

"I did sleep perfect," he said. He looked at Ruth. "You look shocking," he said.

"I'm just a bit tired," she said.

"You are doing too much of that running," Edek said. Ruth wished she hadn't brought up the subject of well-being. "It is not normal just to run," Edek said. "To run and run and run. If you are late for something you have to run, of course. But just to run and run and run." He shook his head. "It is not good for you," he said.

Ruth felt annoyed. She decided not to bother trying to bolster her case for the benefits of running by quoting the American Surgeon General or any one of a number of leading advocates for exercise. She didn't think Edek would be swayed by the opinion of any individual or organization. Maybe if Golda Meir had been an advocate for exercise, Edek might have listened. He had held Golda Meir in very high esteem. He had admired everything about her. But the American Surgeon General was not Golda Meir. His opinion would cut no ice with Edek. Cut no ice. What a strange phrase, she thought. Where did it come from? Who had invented it? Why had they been trying to cut ice?

Edek interrupted her small reverie. "You should listen to me," he said. "You been doing too much running."

"Running is very good for you," Ruth said.

"If it is so good for you," Edek said, "why do you look shocking?"

"I don't look shocking," Ruth said. She patted her hair down. Maybe her hair was sticking out. She thought that her father was probably right. More than her hair needed fixing.

"Have some rollmops," Edek said.

"I couldn't eat herring for breakfast," Ruth said, grimacing at the thought of the rolled-up pickled herring marinated with onions and whole black peppercorns entering her empty stomach.

"You would feel much better if you was a person who could eat a herring for breakfast," Edek said.

"Maybe I'll mature into one," Ruth said, with what she hoped was a touch of sarcasm in her voice.

Edek wasn't put off by the sarcasm. He was clearly convinced of the value of herring. Even on an empty stomach.

"Have just one piece," he said to her.

"I couldn't, Dad," she said.

"This bird stuff what you eat is not enough," Edek said. "Birds are very small. They sit all day in a branch. This bird stuff is enough for them. You need food what normal people eat."

"Dad, give me a break," she said. "I'm tired."

"That is what I am talking about," he said. "Since we been in Poland, you been always tired. Eat a piece of herring."

"Maybe tomorrow, Dad," she said.

"Okay, okay," he said.

He wandered off to the other end of the buffet. "Look what they got here," he called out to her. Ruth walked over to him. He was pointing to a very large sausage. A type of salami. "This *vurst* is very good," Edek said. "I did eat this sort of *vurst* in Melbourne when Mum was alive."

"Mum let you eat this sort of fatty sausage?" Ruth said.

"When we did have visitors, she did let me eat some *vurst,*" he said. Ruth knew well that all of Rooshka's efforts to restrict Edek's diet had amounted to nothing. Edek ate what she wanted him to eat in front of her, and what he wanted to eat when he was out of Rooshka's sight.

Edek ignored the circles of already sliced sausage, on the platter. He picked up a serrated bread knife and sawed off a large slab of the still-intact sausage. Ruth winced. She thought the unsliced sausage was probably meant to be purely decorative. "I don't like it when it is in such thin pieces," Edek said, looking at the circles of sliced salami.

"You've got to admire your father's digestive system," Garth used to say to Ruth. "He eats whatever he likes. He never feels ill and he stays more or less the same weight." Ruth's standard reply to this had been that a bit less rather than a bit more of the weight that Edek maintained himself at would be better. It was never a serious reply. She knew that Edek wasn't very overweight. And he loved his food. Why was she thinking about Garth? She shook her head to shrug off these thoughts. Garth was part of the past. And she was dealing with as much of the past as she could tolerate right now.

"That's it for me," Edek said. Ruth looked at his plate. Every inch of space on the plate was occupied. Edek couldn't possibly have added anything else. The contents were already built up. The sardines were in a stack and so was the herring.

"Take something for yourself, please," Edek said to her. His voice sounded a bit nasal.

"Have you got a cold?" she said.

"No, just a bit of a running nose," Edek said. "It is nothing."

"Are you sure?" she said to Edek.

"I do get like this, a small cold once or twice every winter," Edek said. "And it is winter, in Poland."

"Do you have a sore throat?" she said.

"No," he said.

"Are you sure?" Ruth said.

"Of course I am sure," Edek said. He looked at her. "This is a normal small cold what I have," he said. "Please, Ruthie, have something to eat. Have an egg."

Ruth nearly retched at the thought of an egg. "I'll have some yogurt," she said. She thought that yogurt might settle her stomach. Her stomach definitely needed settling. "I'm going to have some yogurt and some toast," she said to Edek. Edek rolled his eyes. He added a helping of cream cheese to his plate. It sat, like a plank, on top of the pickled onions.

Edek took his breakfast to their table. Ruth toasted some white bread in the toaster the hotel provided for guests. Toast wasn't a Polish thing. It wasn't very American either. Americans ate strange things for breakfast. They ate pancakes and sausages with maple syrup. Eggs and sausages with maple syrup. They ate doughnuts and muffins for breakfast, too. It was the more puritanical English and Australians who ate toast for breakfast.

Ruth wondered if she really did look shocking. Probably, she thought. The two slices of toast looked so moderate, so temperate. It made Ruth feel too sober, too temperate. She wanted to be less stinting, less measured. She added some jam to her plate.

Edek shook his head when he saw Ruth's toast. "I'm going to go back for some yogurt later," she said to him. Two women were sitting at a table on their right. Ruth had noticed them staring at Edek. They were probably astonished by the volume of food on Edek's plate, Ruth thought. It was pretty astonishing.

"This *vurst* is very good," Edek said. He was eating large mouthfuls of the sausage, loudly. Ruth tried to ignore the chewing, smacking, and sucking noises coming from Edek. But she couldn't. She still felt queasy. She hoped he would stop. She would never get her toast down, if Edek kept this volume up.

Ruth felt the women's gaze shift. They were looking at her now. Ruth nodded to them. She thought that both women were probably Polish. They looked the same age. In their mid-sixties. One of the women was a solidly built woman. Everything about her was solid. Her arms, her neck. Her chest. She wasn't fat, just solid. She looked healthy. Her skin was as shiny as a polished apple. Her yellow-blond hair was slicked back in a longish crew-cut. She had pink cheeks and blue eyes. Her mouth was red, without lipstick. Her hair was a contemporary yellow. A white, obviously bleached, yellow. A yellow that could be seen on many young men and young women, in New York this year. It was not the decayed yellow of old women's hair. This woman exuded a health and strength and vigor. Ruth felt tired just looking at her.

The larger woman's friend was small. Small and dainty. She had a finely defined face with large eyes and high cheekbones. Her build was slender. Almost birdlike. Her mid-brown hair was conservatively styled and her makeup subtle and muted. The two women seemed very comfortable together. They ate their breakfasts with an ease that suggested an old familiarity. Ruth looked at them. They looked like an unlikely couple. The large woman smiled at Ruth. Ruth noticed her breasts. They were enormous breasts. Sturdy, substantial breasts. They stood out, like a shelf, on her chest.

Ruth wondered if the woman's big breasts had made her popular with men. For years in America big breasts were passé. Small breasts were considered sophisticated and desirable. At least by women. Now there had been a shift. A change. Big breasts had reemerged. Made a comeback. Big breasts, which hadn't really been popular since Twiggy and the 1960s, were popular again. Surgical breast implants, which had waned in America during the early 1990s because of concerns about silicone leakage, were on the rise again. The *New York Times* quoted a plastic surgeon as saying that women wanted their implants bigger now. Saline implants, pouches of saltwater, were now being used by surgeons to enlarge breasts. Large breasts did look full of life, Ruth thought. Ruth folded her arms across her chest, then realized what she had done. She removed her arms. Her breasts weren't inferior. She didn't have to hide them.

She ate her toast. Edek was three quarters of the way through his breakfast. He had stopped to blow his nose several times, during the meal. "I think you've definitely got a cold," Ruth said to him.

"I did tell you myself I got a cold," Edek said.

"Are you sure you haven't got a sore throat?" she said.

"I am sure," Edek said.

"Maybe we should see a doctor?" Ruth said.

"Are you crazy?" said Edek.

"At your age, colds can develop into pneumonia," Ruth said.

"This cold has to get very much worse before it will develop even into a bad cold," Edek said.

Ruth suddenly felt frightened. A fear bordering on terror had descended on her with no warning. She felt frightened of losing Edek. She was on the verge of tears.

"I don't want to lose you, Dad," she said. Edek stopped eating.

"Everybody has to die one day," he said.

"But I don't want you to die just yet," Ruth said.

"Do I look like a person what is going to die?" Edek said.

"Maybe we could ask the hotel for a doctor," Ruth said. "We'll just get the doctor to check you out."

"I don't need to go to a doctor," Edek said. "When I am in Melbourne and I do get a cold, I don't go to the doctor."

"But you're in Poland, now," Ruth said.

"I know that I am in Poland," said Edek. "But I got the same cold what I get in Melbourne."

The two women at the next table had finished their breakfast. They got up to leave. Both women said good morning, in Polish, to Edek and then to Ruth.

"Good morning," Ruth replied, in English. The larger woman turned to her. "Good morning," she said. "My best wishes to you for the day."

"Thank you," Ruth said.

"I like to speak English very much," the larger woman said. The smaller woman nodded. "I like to speak English also," she said.

Edek stood up and bowed. He wished both women a good day, in Polish.

"It was a very good breakfast," Edek said.

"Yes, it was," Ruth said.

"What would you know about the breakfast?" he said. "You did not eat anything."

"I saw what they had," Ruth said.

"You do not know what is a good breakfast," Edek said.

"Let's go for a walk around Kraków," she said to Edek.

"What for?" Edek said.

"Just to see where we are," she said.

"You do need always to see where we are," Edek said. "I do know where we are. We are in Kraków."

"You've never been to Kraków," Ruth said.

"What is there to see?" said Edek. "Streets and buildings. The same as what is everywhere."

"The streets and buildings here are definitely not the same as the streets and buildings in Warsaw," she said. "And nothing like the streets and buildings in Łódź."

"It is the same everywhere," Edek said. "Everywhere is a street and a building."

"You are coming to Kazimierz, the old Jewish section of Kraków with me, aren't you?" Ruth said.

"I am coming because you do want to go there," Edek said.

"Well, I want to walk in Kraków, too," Ruth said.

"Okay, okay, everything is hunky-dunky with me," Edek said, standing up. "Let's go." He said, sounding agitated.

"It's not hunky-dunky," Ruth said as they walked out. "It's hunky-dory."

"It is not hunky-dory," Edek said. "It is hunky-dunky."

"You're confusing hunky-dory with Humpty Dumpty," Ruth said.

"What are you talking about?" Edek said. He looked annoyed. He speeded up and walked ahead of Ruth.

"The town square is straight ahead," she called out to him.

Kraków was a beautiful city. The most beautiful Polish city Ruth had seen. It was an ancient city. There were few new buildings, no skyscrapers. The tallest structures Ruth could see were the spires of old churches. Kraków had always been considered a major center of Polish culture. The city had art galleries and museums and concert halls. It was also a university town. It had the centuries-old Jagiellonian University and eleven other institutions of higher learning. Ruth felt that she could see the learning, the absorption of knowledge, the serious intent, in the air. She thought that all that learning had to give an educated aspect to the city's atmosphere. There were more students here in Kraków than she had seen anywhere else in Poland. And fewer elderly Poles. The difference in the population was striking.

This medieval city was almost as beautiful as Paris, Ruth thought. Her spirits lifted. She found herself feeling happy to be in Kraków. It was easier to forget that it was Poles who inhabited Poland in Kraków. There was a life force in the streets of Kraków, which she hadn't seen in Poland. They were almost at the Rynek Główny, the Main Market Square. Ruth could see Edek waiting for her at one of the corners of the Rynek Główny. She caught up to him. "Isn't this a beautiful square?" she said. Edek looked up. "I suppose so," he said.

"Dad," she said. "The layout was designed in 1257 and it's still intact today."

"So it is old," he said.

"Very old," she said. They were standing in front of a stand selling *obwarzanki*, a bread roll that resembled a twisted bagel. "These look wonderful," she said.

"Have one," Edek said.

Ruth bought one of the poppy seed–coated *obwarzanki*. "Do you want some?" she said to her father.

"Not for me," Edek said. "I did just finish breakfast."

Ruth bit into the *obwarzanki*. It was incredibly delicious.

Next to the *obwarzanki* stand, a fruit stall sold bananas and pears.

"I think I'll buy a pear, too," she said to Edek.

They walked around the Rynek Główny. Every second building seemed to house a café. Inviting cafés. Cafés with people talking and eating. Kraków seemed so civilized. "It is still provincial," a Polish man she knew in New York had said to her about Kraków. Robert Kostrzewa, a young architect who worked on the same floor of the building that Rothwax Correspondence was in, had been disparaging about Kraków and the rest of Poland. "Leave the old city in Kraków and you're in the same Poland. The same narrow-mindedness, the same sexist attitudes, the same old anti-Semitism. Don't be fooled by the eloquence of the ancient stone buildings in Kraków," he had said to her. "They house the same Poles."

Ruth liked Robert a lot. And not just because he was anti-Polish. She found they had similar points of view, similar cultural understandings, similar anxieties. Ruth thought that they shared a European sensibility. It occurred to her, just then, that possibly she and Robert Kostrzewa shared a Polish sensibility. She grimaced. She didn't like that thought.

He had asked her out, once. But she had said no. She had said it would be too close to an office relationship—their offices were only two doors apart. But the truth was that he was too familiar to her. He felt too much like a brother. Too much like one of the family. It was disconcerting to her now to see how familiar so much about Polish men was. The bluntness, the directness, the complaints, the resigned and depressed air. They were all traits she possessed.

Ruth looked around her. She had lost Edek again. She kept walking. She was bound to find him, she thought. Robert Kostrzewa was the first Pole she had met who had brought up Polish anti-Semitism in her presence. Most Poles, like most of the taxi drivers she and Edek had encountered, denied the existence of anti-Semitism in Poland today, or at any other time. The more intellectual Poles pointed out how many Jews lived in Poland before the war. They offered this as evidence of the Polish people's generosity toward Jews.

Ruth found Edek peering into the window of a shop. It was a Wedel's chocolate shop.

"Look what I did find," Edek said to her.

"Wedel's chocolate," she said. Edek looked happy. Ruth felt so grateful that her father could be made happy by chocolate. It was so hard for most people, including herself, to feel happy.

"Look, they got those big prunes covered in chocolate what I like," Edek said. The chocolate-coated prunes were still in the same blue wrappers Ruth remembered from her childhood.

"Do you want to buy some?" she said to Edek.

"Not now while we are walking," he said. "I will buy a couple when we finish to walk. How much longer you want to walk?"

"We've only just started," Ruth said.

Edek looked glum. Ruth could see that he had had enough of what seemed like an aimless exercise to him. "We won't walk around for too much longer," she said. "Maybe we'll check out the enclosed market in the middle of the square, and then we'll go to Kazimierz."

"Okey dokey," Edek said. He seemed cheered by the thought of going to Kazimierz. Kazimierz was on their agenda. It was not a detour. It was part of the whole tour. Edek liked an agenda, a destination, a challenge. Ruth wondered if Edek was ticking off each of the accomplishments, or ordeals, of the trip. They had done Warsaw, done Łódź. Had Edek ticked them off his mental list of things to get through? Was Edek now waiting to have done Kazimierz and Auschwitz? Had all of this been intolerable for him? Ruth hoped not.

"Okay, I will buy just a couple of the chocolates now," Edek said as though Ruth had insisted on the purchase.

They went into the store. Ruth was impressed by the chocolates. They really did look like first-class chocolates, she thought, and then wondered what distinguished first-class chocolates from their lesser cousins. Was it their luster, their sheen, their color, their density, their shapes? She didn't know. Probably all of those things.

Edek asked for a pound of the chocolate-coated prunes. The woman behind the counter smiled coyly at him. Lots of Polish women used coy expressions. Ruth didn't understand why. Was it to hide their intrinsic harshness? Edek smiled back at the woman. "Wedel's is a very beautiful chocolate," he said to the woman.

"Tell her in Polish," Ruth said. "She'll understand it better."

"Oy, cholera," Edek said, and hit himself in the head. He repeated his praise of Wedel's products in Polish. The woman beamed.

Edek was eating his third chocolate by the time they entered the covered market in the square. At first glance the vendors appeared to be selling the usual tourist trinkets and souvenirs. Carved wooden artifacts seemed to be the most popular item on sale. There were shelves and shelves of carved wooden figures in every stall. There were carved wooden peasants. Men in knee-length *lederhosen*, with braces attached, and hats. Some of the carved peasants wore vests. All of the peasants had drooping mustaches, and they were all holding a beer mug.

There were wooden Father Christmases. Roly-poly red-and-white Father Christmases with big beards and cheerful expressions. And then there were the carvings of Jews. Jews wearing the long black coats and broad hats of Orthodox Jews. White *tefillin*, Jewish prayer shawls, were draped down the front of the coats. All of the Jews had long beards and even longer noses. Noses that in many cases continued down past the mouths. Enormous, hooked noses that ended in a sharp point.

Ruth was shocked. She had never seen anything like this. Some of the carved Jews were pointing to their head. Was this supposed to signify Jews' cleverness? Or was that too kind an interpretation? Was it supposed to signify Jews' cunning? All of the ornamental Jews looked worried. All of their features sagged and bent in a downward spiral. Their beards hung below their waist. Their large eyes drooped with weighty lids. Their foreheads were furrowed. Were these Jews exhausted from counting their money? These carved Jews definitely weren't happy.

Ruth wondered who was supposed to buy these Jewish mementos. No Jew would. The market was full of tourists. Would tourists buy the carvings as souvenirs? Souvenirs of what? Of Kraków? The Jews were part of Kraków's past. A past they were glad to get rid of. Poland had got rid of its Jews, and had now turned them into knickknacks, Ruth thought. Bric-à-brac. Fodder for a tourist industry.

Ruth was appalled. She looked to see if Edek was as bothered as she was. Edek was examining a packet of playing cards. Ruth looked at the stall next to where Edek was standing. This stall had a range of Jews cast in china as well as a selection of carved wooden Jews. The wooden Jews were Jewish musicians. There must be a big market for faux Jews, Ruth thought.

The carved Jewish musicians were, like the Orthodox Jews in the neighboring stall, decked out in black. But with different outfits and different hats. The musicians wore shorter jackets and hats that looked more like bowler hats. These Jews were dark-haired as opposed to their gray-haired, more religious brethren. The black-haired Jews looked as miserable as their Orthodox brothers. Their features were even more pronounced, more ridiculous, more exaggerated, more caricatured. Their brows were slanted and heavily underlined in black paint. Their eyes were ringed in thick, black strokes. All of this black gave the musicians an air of malevolence most musicians did not possess. The musicians didn't look healthy, either. Their skin was painted a dark, jaundiced ocher. Their noses hung down to their black beards. Each musician carried a cello or a violin or a flute. Expressions of extreme misery were carved into their faces.

Ruth was stunned. There were hundreds and hundreds of these Jews as trinkets. How could they have this ugliness in the middle of such a beautiful old square? Several vendors had tried to interest Ruth in a sale. They had picked up a wooden Jew or two and waved them at her. Ruth wanted to get behind the stands and knock every one of these faux Jews over. She felt furious.

Edek had caught up to her. She asked him what he felt about the carved wooden figures. He didn't seem bothered. Ruth assumed that next to the pogroms and beatings and stone throwings of Polish life that Edek and his family had been accustomed to, these figurines seemed harmless. "I hate them," she said to Edek. A man offered Ruth and Edek a carved violinist. Ruth wanted to spit at the man. They walked through the rest of the market. They were offered more renderings of Jews. Not one vendor offered them a Father Christmas.

Outside the market, vendors were already barbecuing kiełbasa and roasting potatoes. They must be preparing for lunch, Ruth thought. The kiełbasa smelled good. For years she hadn't been able to eat meat. Hadn't been able to refer to it as anything other than cooked flesh. Which it clearly was. The term "cooked flesh" was upsetting to most people, so Ruth tried to keep it to herself. Lately she had been trying to eat meat again. But it hadn't been easy. Meat still seemed fleshy to her. She was surprised that the barbecued kiełbasa smelled so appetizing.

Edek had walked ahead of her and was watching several men turn lengths of kiełbasa over a large outdoor grill. "Looks good, doesn't it?" she said to Edek.

"Very good," he said.

"Do you want one?" she said. She was sure he was going to say no. It was still early. Not quite time for lunch.

"Maybe just a small one," Edek said. He ordered a kiełbasa sandwich.

The kiełbasa that was handed to Edek was the length of an average garden hose. It came ensconced in a very long bread roll. Ruth thought the sandwich must measure at least two feet. Edek had to sit down on a bench. This was not the sort of sandwich you could eat standing up.

A nearby stall was selling candy. Ruth walked over and looked at the candy. It was the same candy you saw anywhere else in the world. They had fruit jellies, boiled sweets, mints, and licorice allsorts. Ruth hadn't seen any licorice allsorts for years. Licorice allsorts were not an American thing. She wanted some licorice allsorts. This stall was self-service. She picked up a bag and chose a number of the fattest most multiple-layered allsorts she could find. She felt excited at the prospect of the allsorts. She hoped they were good.

She walked back and sat beside Edek. She took out an allsort. Edek looked at the allsort. He was halfway through his sandwich and his mouth was ringed with the orange tinge of tomato sauce. "Why do you eat such rubbish?" he said to Ruth. "It's better than the rubbish you eat," was what she wanted to say. Instead she said nothing. She ate the allsort. It was very good. The filling was soft, not stiff. The licorice was still pliable. She finished the rest of the bag. She didn't care if she was regressing. Acting out a childhood in which she had turned to sweets when she was disturbed. The licorice allsorts calmed her. She felt the most peaceful she had felt since arriving in Poland.

Edek looked at her eating the last of the allsorts. "They've calmed me," Ruth said. This didn't deflect Edek's criticism. "This black stuff columned you?" he said. "Are you crazy?"

"Let's walk, Dad," she said. Edek had finished his kiełbasa sandwich. He patted his stomach.

"Maybe it was too much for me," he said. He looked as though he was uncomfortably full.

"Let's walk it off," she said. "I've got some Mylanta if you need it."

"You will need the Mylanta after that black stuff," Edek said. "Not me."

"Let's walk," Ruth said.

They walked past a large sandwich board on the street, outside a travel agency. The sandwich board was almost in the middle of the footpath. SIGHTSEEING, in large red capital letters, was painted across the top of the board. Underneath the heading was a list, in large painted letters, of the tours you could take. A large green dot was placed in front of each destination. "Salt Mine in Wieliczka," was the first destination. This was followed by "Concentration Camp in Auschwitz-Birkenau," and, in brackets "[On Request Częstochowa]." Underneath the option of Częstochowa was "Raft Trip Down the Dunajec River." The text on the other side of the sandwich board was identical. Ruth wondered what part of Częstochowa you saw if you requested the Częstochowa option, in brackets. Was it the densely populated Jewish section of Częstochowa that the Germans surrounded on a bitterly cold January night in 1940? Could you visit that site and think about the Germans pulling Jews out of their homes with shouts of *Juden raus*? They beat and clubbed the Jews of Częstochowa into lines, and assembled them in the large square.

Ruth felt furious. Her anger churned her stomach. She wished she hadn't eaten the allsorts. For the Polish, Jews were now statues and orna-ments and baubles. The dead ones were a boom for the tourist industry.

"Does it give you a shock to see Auschwitz advertised on a tourist bill-board?" she said to Edek.

He was very quiet. "It is not very nice," he said.

"Let's go to Kazimierz," Ruth said.

"How far is it?" Edek asked.

"Not far," she said. "You want to walk or catch a taxi?"

"Let us walk a bit," Edek said. "I do not feel so good. I think the kieł-basa was a bit too much for me." Ruth thought it was more likely that the billboard had been too much for Edek, not the kiełbasa.

"I don't feel great either," Ruth said. "I can't believe the Poles and the expedient way they've set up a little tourist industry out of dead Jews."

"It is not so nice," Edek said.

"They just hate Jews," Ruth said. "It's ingrained in them, this hatred. Nothing that they suffered at the hands of Germans changed how they felt about Jews."

"That is the truth," Edek said.

"It wasn't just in Kielce that Poles murdered Jews after the war," Ruth said. "In Radom, Poles attacked the hospital for Jewish orphans. In Lublin, two Jews who had been beaten by Poles were tracked to the local hospital and murdered in their hospital beds. This was after the war, Dad."

Edek looked pale. "How do you know such stuff?" he said.

"I know, I guess, because I want to know," Ruth said.

"Do you have one of those Mylanta tablets?" Edek said.

"Yes," she said. "I think I'll have one, too." They both chewed their Mylanta.

The Mylanta antacid tablets were peppermint-flavored and green. Ruth knew that she and Edek would both be left with green tongues. She con-templated offering Edek a piece of chewing gum to get rid of the green. She decided against it. Having a green tongue suddenly didn't feel all that abnormal.

"It is shocking," Edek said.

"What?" she said.

"How the Poles did kill Jews after the war."

"It really is shocking," she said. She wondered why it felt even more shocking than murders committed during the war. She thought it must be the realization that all the murders and the killings hadn't made a dent in the anti-Semitism of many Poles. It hadn't moved them. That was a sickening thought. Definitely something to be shocked about.

Ruth looked at Edek. He had been very quiet. She always felt uneasy when he was quiet. She hoped he was all right.

"Are you all right, Dad?" she said.

"I am all right," he said. "Maybe I will take a bit more of that Mylanta stuff."

"You're not feeling well?" she said.

"I feel fine," he said. "I did just eat too much."

Ruth gave him two more Mylanta. Edek chewed the Mylanta tablets. Was it the food that was making Edek feel sick or the country and its history? Ruth wondered. It was probably Poland, she decided. Not the kiełbasa he had eaten, or his breakfast of herring and pickles and salami. Her father had always had a cast-iron constitution. Kiełbasa or salami had never affected him adversely.

"When we've looked at Kazimierz," Ruth said, "we'll go back to the hotel and have a rest."

"I do not need a rest," Edek said. "Have you got a piece of chocolate or something?"

"I thought you weren't feeling well," Ruth said.

"I am all right," he said. "But that green stuff does not taste too nice."

"The Mylanta?" she said.

"Of course," he said. "What other green stuff should I talk about?"

"You're going to wash the Mylanta away with some chocolate?" Ruth said.

"The chocolate will give me a better taste what the Mylanta," Edek said. Ruth couldn't come up with a reasonable argument against following Mylanta with chocolate.

"You've got those chocolate-covered prunes," she said to Edek.

"*Oy*, that's perfect," he said. "I did forget about them." He reached into his pocket and pulled out the chocolates. "These chocolates are very good chocolates," he said when he had finished the rest of the bag. Ruth was reassured. Any man who could polish off three quarters of a pound of chocolates couldn't be all that unwell.

They were in the heart of Kazimierz now. On Szeroka Street, the main street of the Jewish quarter. Szeroka Street was more of an elongated square than a street. It was a beautiful square. The buildings still had a vivacity. It was easy to imagine the rich, full lives that must have been lived in these buildings. There were small attic windows and chimneys and turrets and carved doorways and arched entrances.

Kazimierz was noticeably more architecturally interesting than the areas surrounding it. The entire area, Ruth had read, was no bigger than three hundred yards by three hundred yards. A very dense center of culture and religion and learning had once been packed into this small section of Kraków. The first of several Jewish publishing companies had been set up in 1534. Works of lasting scholarship and religious teachings were printed in Kazimierz, from the fourteenth century until the time, four centuries later, when the Jews were removed and dispensed with.

"Isn't this beautiful?" Ruth said to Edek.

Edek looked up. He looked around him. He nodded. "It is very nice," he said.

Ruth felt excited. This was a Jewish area that looked relatively intact. Not dilapidated and grubby. Not all of the signs of the life that was once lived there had been crushed out of this area.

"This is so exciting," she said to Edek.

"There are no people here," Edek said.

Ruth knew what he was referring to. He was talking about the absence of Jews. Telling her to quiet down. Telling her that these were only buildings, not people.

There were plenty of people in Kazimierz. Several tourist coaches and private cars were parked in the square. Kazimierz was first promoted as a tourist destination in the early 1970s. The Poles realized that with seven synagogues mostly intact, and former Jewish theaters and bathhouses and an ancient Jewish cemetery, Kazimierz had revenue potential. But no one came. The Poles were not interested. And word about Kazimierz didn't spread outside Poland. Then Steven Spielberg arrived. Overnight, everything changed. Kazimierz, which had been run-down and grubby, immediately attracted private Polish entrepreneurs. They began to restore Kazimierz.

Steven Spielberg's film *Schindler's List* brought crowds of tourists to

Kazimierz. Although most of *Schindler's List* took place nearby, in the Płaszów death camp, the Podgórze ghetto, and Oskar Schindler's factory, the fact that Spielberg had filmed in Kazimierz was enough. The results of this exposure by Spielberg were evident. Three restaurants with Hebrew lettering were on one side of the square. A kosher restaurant and what was advertised as a Jewish bookshop were also on Szeroka Street. Kazimierz was on the map—in every guidebook on Poland and in endless brochures from travel agents.

When Ruth saw the tourist coaches she felt flat. Why was she here? Not to be part of a tourist circus, that was for sure. They passed a group of tourists being led by a loud-voiced Polish guide. "Steven Spielberg first came here in 1992," the guide was saying.

"Do you think the people in that group look Jewish?" Ruth said to Edek. Edek shook his head. "They are not Jews," he said.

"Steven Spielberg was here for thirty-six hours on his first visit," the guide said. The group had stopped outside what Ruth recognized from the guidebooks was the Old Synagogue. "Steven Spielberg made the decision on that visit that he would direct *Schindler's List* nowhere but Kraków," the guide said.

"Did you meet Steven Spielberg?" one of the group asked.

"No, I didn't," the guide said. "But a very close friend of mine met him. Spielberg spent quite a few days filming in Szeroka Street. He made the decision to film the ghetto scenes here during his second visit to Kraków in June 1992." Nobody asked what the ghetto was, or where the real ghetto had been located.

"Let's go in and have a look at the Old Synagogue," Ruth said to Edek.

"It is very interesting what the man is saying about Steven Spielberg," Edek said. Ruth felt irritated. Couldn't her father see how phony this whole interest in Kazimierz was?

"We didn't come to Kazimierz to listen to stories about Steven Spielberg," she said.

"Okay, okay," said Edek.

"The Old Synagogue," Ruth said to Edek, "was the religious and administrative center of the Jewish community of Kraków."

As soon as they entered the synagogue, Ruth felt calmer. She wondered what it was that houses of worship possessed that was so calming. An accumulation of prayer? A stockpile of godliness, goodness, goodwill? A confluence of altruism, benevolence, grace? Ruth knew that these things couldn't be stockpiled, couldn't be amassed. You couldn't collect ephemeral qualities and make them concrete. There was no inventory of grace or virtue or piety. There was no brotherly love still present in this synagogue. Or was there? Ruth was sure she could feel something. Something around the cross-ribbed Gothic vaulting of the ceiling of the synagogue. Something between the two narrow columns that supported the bimah. Something in the air where the sermons were conducted.

"You know there are still seven synagogues in Kazimierz," she said to Edek.

"That is good," he said.

"If you can't have the Jews," she said, "the least you could have is their buildings."

"I suppose so," he said.

"Is this reminding you of too much?" she said to Edek. He nodded his head. "Does it make you think of going to synagogue with your parents?" she said. He nodded his head again. He walked off to look at something.

It was hardly surprising that Edek and Rooshka had avoided synagogues, after the war, Ruth thought. Synagogues were too loaded, too freighted, with memories and questions. She caught up to Edek. He was upstairs on the first floor, in rooms that had been converted into a museum. He was looking at a collection of Passover dishes. He looked sad.

"This synagogue was rebuilt in 1570 by the architect Mateo Gucci," Ruth said to Edek. "So Jews and Gucci have always been connected." Edek looked blank. "Jews and Gucci?" she said again. Edek didn't get it. She tried to explain the joke to him. The stereotype of rich, Gucci-clad Jews. But he still didn't get it. Ruth decided you had to know the Gucci label to think the joke was funny.

The last room of exhibits displayed photographs and documents. Photographs and documents detailing the demise of the Jews. Photographs of families with their bags and bundles on their way to the ghetto. Documents showing the progressively punitive and restrictive instructions issued by Germans to the Jews of Kraków. The instructions and orders and punishments and restrictions and directives, which were written in German and Polish, were familiar to Edek. "We did have the same orders, in Łódź," he said.

"You were already in the ghetto when these orders were issued in Kraków," she said. Edek looked at her quizzically. "The Łódź Ghetto and the Warsaw Ghetto were formed before the one in Kraków."

"You know everything," he said.

"I wish I did," she said.

Edek looked at a photograph of two Jews, two young boys carrying large sacks on their backs. They were in the middle of a trail of Jews on their way to the ghetto. "We was all like that," Edek said. He shook his head. "Sometimes it does feel like it happened to somebody else," he said. "Not to me. Sometimes I think it was not me who was in the ghetto." He shook his head again. Ruth could see he had tears in his eyes. "When I do see these photographs I remember that it was me. Me and Mum. I remember too much."

Ruth felt bad. She hadn't even thought about how he would respond to the artifacts or the photographs. "I am sorry I am upset," Edek said. Ruth put her arm around him. "You've got a lot to be upset about," she said. Edek blew his nose. He looked embarrassed to have been crying. They left the synagogue. Ruth walked with her arm around Edek.

"I am okay," he said, after a few minutes. "I did not mean to upset you."

"You haven't upset me," she said. "What happened to you and Mum and all the other Jews is what is upsetting. Not your distress."

"I am okay, now," Edek said.

The tour group with the loud guide was standing outside the kosher restaurant. "Soon we will be approaching Józefa Street," the guide was saying. Ruth looked at the tourists he was leading. They were a patched-together assortment of older Europeans. No one seemed to be under fifty. None of them looked Jewish. "Steven Spielberg filmed the scene in which the Jews were expelled from their houses in Józefa Street," the guide said. "This was a scene which preceded the scenes of the imprisonment of the Jews."

Ruth wanted to interrupt him. She wanted to point out that these episodes he was lecturing about were not scenes in a movie, they were events in people's lives. With a rearrangement of his words, with a shift in wording, he could refer to both Steven Spielberg's film and to what really did take place with Kraków's Jews.

"The Jews went from Kraków to the ghetto over a bridge," the guide said. "That bridge can be seen in a famous scene in which the Jews are marching to the ghetto."

"They weren't marching," Ruth called out. "They were walking. Soldiers march, not a whole community of people who were being forced out of their homes."

Everyone in the group turned around to look at Ruth.

"Ruthie, what has got into you?" Edek said.

"Anger," she said to Edek.

"I just wanted to make sure you realized you were talking about real people, real history, real suffering," Ruth said to the guide.

"Of course, of course," the guide said. The group was silent. The entire group was staring at Ruth.

"That's all I have to say," Ruth said to the guide.

"Thank God," said Edek.

The guide continued his talk. "When Steven Spielberg filmed the walk to the ghetto," he said, "he reversed the direction. He filmed the Jews going from the ghetto to Kazimierz."

"He filmed the actors," Ruth said to him, "not the Jews. Steven Spielberg was filming actors."

Edek tugged at her sleeve. "Ruthie, please, what for are you doing this?" Edek said.

"Because it makes me angry," she said.

"You cannot be angry about everything," he said.

"I'm not," she said.

Ruth could feel that she was red-faced. The group was looking at her again.

"It's important to be respectful to those people whose lives you are talking about," she said to the guide.

"We are talking about Kazimierz and Steven Spielberg's film," the guide said.

"Do not answer him," Edek said. Ruth didn't want to agitate Edek. She didn't answer the guide.

"Let's go," Ruth said to Edek.

"So Steven Spielberg reversed the direction of the Jews marching," the guide said to the group.

"The Jews walking," Ruth shouted out to the guide, as she and Edek walked off.

"What has got into you?" Edek said.

"This is not a fucking movie site," she said.

"You do not have to use such language," said Edek. "And in any case Steven Spielberg did make this film here." Ruth glared at Edek.

"This was the biggest film in the history of Poland," Ruth could hear the guide saying. "The set of the concentration camp alone cost six hundred thousand dollars to build," he said.

"Brother!" Edek said. "Six hundred thousand dollars."

"About a hundred times more expensive than the original," Ruth said. Edek laughed. Steven Spielberg and his moviemaking seemed to have restored Edek's spirits.

"We are now going to follow in Steven Spielberg's footsteps," Ruth heard the guide saying.

"Dream on," Ruth shouted, in the direction of the guide.

"Why do you tell him he should dream?" Edek said.

" 'Dream on' is an expression that means, in your wildest dreams," Ruth said. "The guide said he was following in Steven Spielberg's footsteps."

"He was doing this," Edek said.

" 'Following in someone's footsteps' is also an expression of living up to that person's achievements," Ruth said.

"Now I understand," Edek said.

Ruth thought her explanation had been as confusing as the expression that she was trying to explain. She was glad that Edek had understood.

"Ruthie, please," Edek said. "If we should meet some more tourists, it is not necessary to talk to them."

"Okay," she said.

The Yiddish and Hebrew words in the windows of shops and restaurants in Szeroka Street were not a sign that there were still Jews in the area. They were signs of commerce. Stops on the routes of groups looking for history, bored tourists, Jews searching for their roots. If you didn't know, you could think Kazimierz was still Jewish. Ruth and Edek entered the Remuh Synagogue. This synagogue was built after the Old Synagogue, and was also known as the new synagogue. The Remuh Synagogue, a small synagogue, was the only functioning synagogue in Kraków today.

An old man was sitting inside the front door of the synagogue. He looked very old. His clothes were shabby and he was toothless. He was wearing a yarmulke.

"How many synagogues we got to go to?" Edek said.

"This is the last one," Ruth said. "Do you think he's a Jew?" she said, looking at the old man. Edek asked the old man, in Yiddish, if he was Jewish. The old man shook his head. "I am Jewish," he said to Edek in Polish, "but I don't speak Yiddish."

"He looks Polish to me," Ruth said.

"What is wrong with you?" Edek said. He bowed to the old man.

"I read that this synagogue was used by the Germans as a storage room for rubberized sacks," Ruth said. "The sacks were used to carry corpses."

"I am ready to go," Edek said.

"Can we just look at the cemetery out the back?" Ruth said.

"Okay," Edek said. He looked glum.

A group of Israeli schoolchildren was in the cemetery. They were teenagers. About thirteen or fourteen. There were more than thirty of them. They almost filled the small cemetery. Ruth was glad to see them. Glad to see signs of Jewish life.

"*Shalom,*" Edek said to several of the teenagers.

"*Shalom,*" they repeated. One of them, a tall, skinny redheaded boy, came over and patted Edek on the back. "*Shalom,*" he said.

Ruth and Edek walked around the cemetery. Ruth felt peaceful. Why did she feel so peaceful in the company of the dead? It was a strange phrase. The company of the dead. Could the dead keep you company? She took Edek's arm. She felt bad about dragging him into synagogues and cemeteries.

The Nazis had destroyed this cemetery. They had dismantled and shattered tombstones. The cemetery was now in the process of being restored. Pieces of tombstones too shattered to be pieced together were embedded in an internal wall. The wall contained particles of people's names, scraps of dates, fragments of numbers and letters, and snippets of symbols. It was a strangely poetic mosaic.

Ruth stopped beside a tombstone that read that *Gitel, the daughter of Moses Auerbach of Regensburg, a grandmother of the famed Rabbi Moses Isserles was buried here.* Ruth felt she could feel Gitel. "I feel she had a good life," she said to Edek. Ruth surprised herself by saying this. She normally didn't reveal the more unruly and irrational of her thoughts.

"She was very generous to the poor," Edek translated from the Hebrew on the tombstone.

"Do you think it's silly to imagine that you can feel someone's life?" Ruth asked Edek.

"Maybe," he said. "And maybe not. Maybe some people can see things what other people cannot see. You did always know things what other people did not know."

"Really?" said Ruth.

"You could see things," Edek said. Ruth felt rattled. "You could see that Mrs. Watson next door was not happy with her husband," Edek said. Ruth was relieved. It was perception Edek was talking about, not telepathy.

"You did tell Mum that Mr. Watson was not very nice to Mrs. Watson when you was six," Edek said.

"When I was six?" Ruth said.

"Yes," said Edek. She must have been a nosy, if precocious, child, Ruth thought.

"You did say that Mrs. Watson did used to have someone else who was nicer to her," Edek said.

"What?" said Ruth.

"That is what you said," said Edek. "And this was true. She had a first husband we did know nothing about."

"She must have told me about it," Ruth said.

Ruth remembered spending most of her Sunday afternoons, until she was ten or eleven, watching Mrs. Watson make apple pies. Every Sunday afternoon Mrs. Watson baked four apple pies to take to the Methodist church that night. The church, around the corner, fed the poor every Sunday night.

Ruth used to love to watch the pastry being rolled, the apples being peeled and cored. She never tired of watching Mrs. Watson pinch the sides of the filled pastry together, and then make decorative marks with a fork around the rim of the pie.

"Mrs. Watson did say she did never tell anybody about her first husband," Edek said. "Not even her son did know."

"She must have told me," Ruth said.

LILY BRETT

It was possible to tell a lot about a person without being told things, specifically, anyway, Ruth thought. She remembered Mrs. Watson's wistful, faraway expression. Ruth had known that Mrs. Watson was thinking about someone else. Someone she had loved. Someone who was no longer alive. Ruth had had a lot of experience in identifying that sort of longing. She had been exposed to so much wishful, wistful thinking.

"Mrs. Watson was married to someone who died," Ruth said.

"You did tell Mum this," Edek said. "Mum did ask Mrs. Watson. Poor Mrs. Watson did cry for nearly a whole day after Mum did ask her that question. She said she never did tell anyone in her whole life about this dead husband. Not her son, not her husband. She didn't want her husband to think he was not the first man. In those days that sort of thing was important. Do you understand?"

"I understand," Ruth said. She didn't want Edek to expand on the importance of virginity in marriage, in those days.

"Mrs. Watson's first husband died in the war," Ruth said.

"That is exactly what she did tell Mum."

"She must have told me, too," Ruth said.

Edek looked at her, in a bothered way. "You did always know what people was thinking," he said. He shook his head. "But this about Mrs. Watson's dead husband is not something it is easy to know from a person's thinking," he said.

"Mrs. Watson must have told me," Ruth said.

"She must have told you," Edek said. "My sister Fela was like this. She did know what people was thinking." Edek walked in front of Ruth, still shaking his head.

Ruth was bothered. She couldn't remember Mrs. Watson telling her. She reassured herself. You could deduce a lot about someone without a word being spoken. Demeanor and movements and gestures and habits and expressions were very revealing. There was no need to feel bothered. Edek's sister Fela must have observed people carefully, too. Ruth was cheered by that thought. Cheered by that alliance.

Outside the entrance to the Jordan Jewish Bookshop and the Noah's Ark Café, a young woman approached Edek and Ruth.

"Would you like a guided tour of the Schindler's factory area?" the young woman said.

"No thanks," said Ruth.

"Why not?" said Edek.

"You really want to see Schindler's factory?" Ruth said.

"Why not?" Edek said. "It is something interesting."

"Do you know much about the factory and its history?" Ruth asked the young woman.

"Jewish studies is one of my subjects at the University of Kraków," the young woman said. She put out her hand. "My name is Helena."

Ruth and Edek shook hands with Helena.

"Are you Jewish?" Ruth asked her.

"No," she said. "But I am very sympathetic to their history."

"What do your parents think of your studying Jewish Studies?" Ruth said.

"They are not very happy with this," Helena said. "But they have become less unhappy. They can see that I can support myself during my studies with money that I earn as a guide."

"So you get regular work taking these tours?" Ruth said.

"Yes, very much work," said Helena. "There are many guides like me. The bookshop provides its own guides. But I am cheaper."

"Okay, we'll do the tour," Ruth said. "But first I need to have a cup of tea. Can we take ten minutes to go into the bookstore and the café?"

"Of course," Helena said. "I will wait here."

In the Noah's Ark Café, an eighteen-inch-high carved wooden figure of an Orthodox Jew playing a cello stood on top of several of the tables. Three yarmulkes, black ones with gold trimming, were perched on top of the piano. There was Hebrew writing on the walls and a plaintive Yiddish song was playing as background music. None of the customers in the café looked Jewish.

Ruth felt sick. She was sick of Jews being reduced to caricatures and turned into artifacts. Edek sat down at one of the tables. He started to hum along to the Yiddish song. It was a lullaby. A lullaby about a mother singing her child to sleep. *Sleep my small child, sleep*, the mother sang.

The menu of the Noah's Ark Café had "Jewish cheesecake" as well as an assortment of other food described as "Jewish."

"I think I will have a cheesecake," Edek said. "And a cappuccino."

"I'm not sure they do a cappuccino in a mock-Jewish café in Poland," Ruth said. The waitress came up to them. There was no cappuccino. Edek settled for a cup of tea. "Is this café owned by Jews?" Ruth said to the waitress.

"No," the waitress said.

"Why do you ask such questions?" Edek said to Ruth.

"Because I want to know," she said.

"It is not always necessary to know everything," he said. The cheesecake arrived. It was small and flat.

"It's not even a Jewish cheesecake," Ruth said. Edek tried the cheesecake.

"It is very nice, as a matter of fact," he said.

Ruth felt furious. What were these Poles doing mimicking a Jewish life they had been so happy to see disappear? They were making money, that was what they were doing. Edek finished his cheesecake. *"Mottel Mottel,"* one of his favorite Yiddish songs, was now playing in the background. Edek started humming again. He turned in his seat and looked around him at the rest of the café. "It is very nice," he said.

"It's created by Poles," Ruth said. Edek shrugged his shoulders.

The Jordan Jewish Bookshop and travel agency were also not owned by Jews. There were books, artifacts, and pieces of jewelry for sale. Silver Stars of David, and Hebrew letters on silver chains. There were candleholders and Passover dishes. A small sign said that you could buy books and souvenirs of Jewish culture, and maps, guides, and postcards, and cassettes of Jewish music.

Another sign offered three tours. Each tour was printed in bold capitals: SIGHTSEEING OF JEWISH KAZIMIERZ, RETRACING SCHINDLER'S LIST, and TRIP TO AUSCHWITZ-BIRKENAU. The store looked a bit disordered. A bit untidy. As though the owners hadn't quite known how to display the merchandise. Surely Jews wouldn't shop here, Ruth thought. She spotted a book on Auschwitz on one of the upper shelves. It contained reproductions of all of the documents left behind by the Germans. Ruth had never seen the book before. It was a large thick book. She asked to look at it. She flipped through the pages. It was a very interesting book. Ruth felt torn.

She didn't want to contribute to this business, but she wanted the book. "I'll have it," she said to the man behind the counter.

Edek was waiting outside with Helena, the guide.

"The person who owns the Jordan Jewish Bookshop isn't Jewish, is he?" Ruth asked Helena. Edek glared at Ruth. She ignored him.

"No," Helena said. "But he is a very good man. Very sympathetic to Jews."

"See," said Edek.

"See what?" Ruth said.

"Forget about it," Edek said. "We are going to walk to the Schindler's factory."

Ruth was surprised that Edek had agreed to walk. She had thought he would want to get this tour over as quickly as possible. "Good," she said.

Edek and Helena walked ahead of her. Ruth could see that Edek liked Helena. He was smiling and chatting with her. He was telling her about his life in Australia. He was telling her about his job as manager of the shipping department of the sporting goods store, and his subsequent position in the health food store. He explained at length how important it was that the cleanliness of the store was maintained in these health food places. Helena looked riveted.

Ten minutes later, they were still in the square. Edek and Helena had stopped walking and were deep in conversation. Ruth felt she had waited long enough. "Can we move on?" she said.

"Of course," Helena said.

"We was just going to start walking again," Edek said. "Helena is a very nice girl." Helena blushed.

They walked for a few minutes. They stopped outside a building on Szeroka Street.

"Here at number 6 was housed from the sixteenth century the community bathhouse and the *mikveh*."

"See she knows what is a *mikveh*," Edek said to Ruth. Helena nodded. "A ritual bath for women on certain occasions," she said.

"Yes, yes, that is a *mikveh*," Edek said. Helena looked very pleased.

Helena was a sweet girl, really, Ruth thought. She couldn't be more than twenty or twenty-one.

"This bathhouse was called the big bathhouse," Helena said. "This was in order to distinguish it from the small bathhouse, which was near Nowy Square."

"Very interesting," Edek said. Helena was clearly finding Edek interesting. More interesting than Ruth. Ruth noticed that Helena was addressing all of her remarks to Edek.

"This building was renovated and modernized between 1974 and 1976," Helena said to Edek. "It is now occupied by the Kraków branch of the Historical Monuments Restoration Workshop." Edek nodded his head.

They set off again. Ruth looked at her watch. It was 2 P.M. She hoped that they would get to Schindler's factory before nightfall.

Helena stopped outside another building. "Here on Bocheńska Street was the Jewish Theater of Kraków from 1926 to 1939," she said.

"A very nice building," Edek said. Ruth was astonished. Since when had Edek been interested in buildings? He had never expressed any interest in any building. Ruth looked at Edek. He was smiling at Helena. He looked so happy. He had always liked a pretty girl or an attractive woman. And they had liked Edek. It seemed that they still did. Helena was beaming at Edek.

"Ida Kamińska, the famous Jewish actress, played regularly in this theater," Helena said to Edek.

"See, she knows Ida Kamińska," Edek said to Ruth.

"Since 1945 this theater has been occupied by the amateur theater of the railway men," Helena said.

"They do probably a very good job," Edek said. Ruth couldn't believe Edek's pronouncement. He knew nothing about theater and less about railway men. Helena seemed pleased.

"Can we get a move on?" Ruth said. "I'd like to get to Schindler's factory."

"Certainly," Helena said. She and Edek began to walk faster. Ruth followed them.

Edek looked happier than he had for days, Ruth thought. Ruth was glad that they had hired Helena as a guide. She knew that her father loved her, but too much time solely in her company had probably depressed him, flattened his spirits. Helena's company was good for him. Ruth thought that some of the places she had chosen to visit with Edek had probably dampened his spirits, too. Few people would find ghettos and cemeteries uplifting.

They were well away from Kazimierz now. This part of Kraków was as run-down and dilapidated as any part of Łódź. They passed an old woman sitting at a table in the middle of a small square. The old woman had a dirty red and black cotton scarf tied around her head. An odd assortment of plastic bags and pieces of cardboard were on the table. In the middle of the table, on top of two sheets of white paper, was an enormous, pink, slumped, plucked turkey.

The turkey had no feet. Its legs were sticking out, rigidly, in front of it, as though rigor mortis had already set in. But the bird looked too fresh, and maybe rigor mortis didn't set in if you had already been plucked and decapitated. Ruth made a note to herself to look up rigor mortis and how it occurs in one of her many medical encyclopedias. A bucket with scraps of plastic was under the table. Was this woman hoping to sell the turkey whole? Or in pieces? Ruth couldn't see a knife. To whom was she hoping to sell this piece of poultry? Ruth looked around the square. There didn't seem to be any customers.

At the other side of the square there were two more stalls. Ruth had walked past them. At each of these stalls, a few screwdrivers, nails, hammers, and other bits and pieces Ruth didn't recognize had been set up on folding tables. Ruth worried about who was going to buy the turkey. The woman must know what she was doing, Ruth decided. She wouldn't have just set up a table anywhere, in the hope of selling a dead turkey. Ruth smiled at the woman. The woman glared at her.

They arrived at Schindler's factory. Ruth recognized the curved gates from the movie.

"Look, Ruthie," Edek said. "The factory of Oskar Schindler."

"Here where we are standing at 4 Lipowa Street," Helena said, "was the factory of Oskar Schindler. Because of Oskar Schindler's contacts with the *Wehrmacht* he managed to build a small factory of forty-five employees into a prosperous factory that employed seven hundred and fifty Jews from the ghetto, which was very near to this factory." Ruth and Edek nodded. It was strange to look at this building in this quiet street and think of the people who must have walked in and out of this gate. Jews, Gestapo, Poles, Germans. "Oskar Schindler saved altogether one thousand two hundred Jews," Helena said.

"I do know two Jews what he did save," Edek said to Helena. "Two brothers from Melbourne." Ruth knew the two men Edek was talking about. Both brothers were musicians.

"Steven Spielberg did win seven Oscars for this film, *Schindler's List,*" Helena said. Ruth groaned. "Steven Spielberg did film *Schindler's List* in thirty-five locations in Kraków," Helena said.

"Really?" said Edek.

Ruth tried to work out how to derail the Steven Spielberg speech tactfully. She didn't want to offend Helena. She couldn't think of how to do it.

"Do you know Steven Spielberg?" Helena said to Ruth. Ruth laughed.

"No," she said. 'No one ordinary knows Steven Spielberg," she said. "And I don't know if he knows anybody ordinary."

"Really?" Helena said.

"Of course," said Edek, with authority. Ruth saw that Edek was eager to contribute to this conversation.

"Only celebrities know Steven Spielberg," Ruth said.

"That is the truth," Edek said. "How would a person what is a normal person meet such a person like Mr. Spielberg, who is not a person what meets normal persons?"

Edek was repeating himself in his rush to be an authority on the subject and impress Helena, Ruth thought. "President Clinton knows Steven Spielberg," Ruth said to Helena. "President Clinton and Mrs. Clinton stayed with Steven Spielberg and his wife at their beach house in the summer," Ruth said.

"My daughter does know everything," Edek said.

"It was on the front page of every New York newspaper," Ruth said.

"So the president of America was a guest at Steven Spielberg's house?" Helena said. Ruth wondered if this new piece of information would be tacked on to all the future Schindler's factory tours.

"Yes," she said to Helena. Helena looked very pleased to be the recipient of this fact. Edek looked very pleased to have pleased Helena.

"I know someone who knows Steven Spielberg's mother," Ruth said. She stepped back in surprise at what she had just said. She couldn't believe what she had just said. Why had she said that? She had obviously been carried away. Buoyed by the success of the Clinton news item. Edek and Helena both moved toward her.

"You do know somebody what knows the mother of Steven Spielberg?" Edek said. He looked wildly impressed.

"You know someone who knows Steven Spielberg's mother?" Helena said.

Ruth felt foolish. She couldn't believe the turn the conversation had taken. Still, it was her fault. She had started it.

"I think we should catch a taxi back to the hotel," Ruth said. Edek looked disappointed. "I'm tired," Ruth said.

"My daughter does need a rest," Edek said.

"This former Schindler factory is now occupied by a company that manufactures electronic components," Helena said. "I will go inside and order a taxi for you. They know me here."

Ruth and Edek waited outside. "She is a very nice girl," Edek said to Ruth.

"She is a very nice girl," Ruth said.

Ruth was tired. She felt a bit sick. The taxi Helena had arranged for them stank of cigarettes. She should have something to eat, she decided.

"Do you want some lunch?" Ruth said.

"No thanks," Edek said. "I will wait until dinner."

"I've booked a Jewish dinner at the Samson Restaurant," Ruth said. "The dinner comes with a Jewish cabaret."

"This does sound interesting," Edek said. "A cabaret."

"Would you be interested to go to a visit to the Auschwitz Museum?" the cabdriver said. "I will do a very good price. Very cheap." Ruth was stunned. How many people were peddling trips to Auschwitz in this city? And how did they know to whom to offer the trips? The takers, in this marketplace, the potential clients, must be clearly marked, Ruth thought.

"We do not want to go there in this car," Edek hissed to Ruth. In Polish, Edek said to the driver, "Thank you very much for your offer. We have already made prior arrangements." Ruth was irritated by Edek's excessive politeness to this tobacco-stained driver.

"It will be better a Mercedes to get for such a long trip," Edek said to Ruth.

"It is the Auschwitz death camp," Ruth said slowly to the driver. "Not the Auschwitz Museum."

"It is not necessary to say this," Edek said to Ruth.

"I've already booked a Mercedes," she said to Edek.

"Good," he said. "Please do not say anything more to this driver."

"Okay," she said. She didn't want to spoil Edek's good mood.

"Only young Germans do visit Auschwitz," the taxi driver said.

"He speaks English," Edek said to Ruth.

"Old Germans, never," the driver said. "Who knows, maybe they are *Wehrmacht*."

"Do a lot of young Germans go?" Ruth said.

"Quite a few young Germans visit the Auschwitz Museum," the driver said.

"The death camp," said Ruth.

"Ruthie," Edek said.

"Sorry, Dad," she said. She was glad that young Germans were visiting Auschwitz. It was a good sign. It was too late for old Germans anyway. They had too much at stake to repent now. They had to justify so much. They would unravel if they unpicked a few of the historical myths they had stitched together.

"Are you going to have a rest?" Ruth asked Edek when they got back in the hotel.

"I do not need a rest," he said. "I will read a bit. I did just start today a new book."

"What's the new book called?" Ruth said.

"Thrusts from Above," Edek said.

Thrusts from Above? What on earth was her father reading? *"Thrusts from Above?"* she said.

"It is a very good book," Edek said. "It is about a man who did used to be a pilot. A very good pilot."

"Don't tell me anymore," Ruth said. "That's enough."

"That's enough?" Edek said. "I did tell you nothing. It is a very interesting story."

"I've got some work to do," Ruth said. "How about I meet you down-stairs in the lounge in a couple of hours?"

"Okey dokey," Edek said.

"Don't forget to order something to eat if you're hungry," Ruth said.

"I am not hungry," Edek said. "But I think I will sit in the lunge and have a drink of soda water."

"Good idea," Ruth said. She walked off smiling.

Ruth sat down on the bed in her room. It was a nice room. It was large and airy. Filled with light. She had her own balcony, which looked out on to a small, cobbled street. Edek's room was even bigger than hers. He had been very pleased with his room. She felt she should check in with Max. To make sure things were under control. Under control. Could anything ever really be under control? In order? Probably not. She didn't think she was des-tined for an orderly life. A life under control. All the order she had tried to put in place seemed to have frayed, or split at the seams. Why was she using sewing metaphors? She had no idea. She was tired.

She should call Max, she thought. She put her feet up on the bed. Why was she so tired? Why was she so much more tired than Edek? She was so much younger. She was probably going to be a washout of an old woman, if she lived that long. She always added the coda, if she lived that long. As though to omit it would tempt fate. Incur wrath. Whose wrath would she be incurring? She had never been too clear on that.

Ruth dialed Max's home number.

"Hi, great to hear your voice," Max said. Max sounded very chirpy. Too chirpy for Ruth.

"Hi, Max," she said.

"Let me ring you back," Max said. "You're in Kraków?"

"Yes," Ruth said. She began to tell Max not to bother, but Max had already hung up. Why did Max sound so bright? The phone rang. It was Max.

"You sound exhausted," Max said.

"You could tell that from a ten-second conversation?" Ruth said.

"Yes," said Max.

"Well, the trip hasn't been a picnic," she said.

"You didn't expect it to be, did you?" Max said.

"I don't know what I expected," said Ruth.

"The *Observer* rang," Max said. "They asked if we wanted to increase the size of our ad. They've got a special on. For two weeks we can double the size of our ad for not much extra."

"We don't need a bigger ad," Ruth said.

"Can't we try it?" Max said. "It won't cost much."

"We don't want to look like a multinational corporation," said Ruth.

"Three inches by three inches is hardly multinational," Max said.

"There are some things that are more effective small," Ruth said.

"You're not thinking about men, are you?" Max said, and laughed.

"No, not at all," Ruth said. She hardly thought about men. Her brain already seemed too crowded without adding thoughts of men. Too many men. Was that what the gypsy woman had said? What a strange thing to say to her. "You've got sex on the brain, Max," Ruth said. "I've noticed it ever since you took up with the married man."

"Five minutes and thirty seconds it took you to mention him," Max said. "I had a bet with Bern. I said it would take you less than five minutes. I owe Bern two dollars."

"Let's get through the rest of the business," Ruth said.

"A client asked if we could do a thank-you-for-your-introduction-to-an-agent letter," Max said. "He's an actor, and he said he wants a really special letter. The person he's writing to introduced him to one of New York's biggest theatrical agents."

"Can't you do it, Max?" Ruth said.

"I've tried," Max said. "I just can't seem to get it right."

"Did the agent take the actor on?" Ruth said.

"The actor doesn't know yet," said Max.

"Okay, I'll do it," Ruth said. "Fax me the details."

"He needs it this week," Max said.

"I'll do it in the next couple of days," Ruth said.

"Thanks," Max said.

"What else is new?" Ruth said.

"John Sharp called," Max said. "He insisted that he had to talk to you personally."

"Did you give him my number?" Ruth said.

"No," Max said.

Ruth was relieved. John Sharp was immensely wealthy and, like many of the immensely wealthy, expected attention the moment he requested it. Ruth wasn't up to getting a call from John Sharp.

"I know he's a big client," Max said. "But he makes me mad. He speaks to me like I'm a servant. He's just a tall, slobby, unattractive, overweight man who happens to be very rich."

"It's *as* though I'm a servant, not *like* I'm a servant," Ruth said.

"I knew you'd pick up on that," said Max. "Anyway, I can't stand John Sharp. I hope he chokes on a big tin of Beluga caviar."

Ruth laughed. "You have to be careful what you say about other people," she said. "It could have repercussions. Come back at you in some form of karma."

"What's happened to you, Ruth?" Max said. "Something's changed. You're sounding mystical. You need to get back to New York."

"You're right," Ruth said. "I do."

Edek was sitting in an armchair in the lounge of the Mimoza. A large, half-eaten platter of cheeses, smoked and pickled fish, pâté and cold meats was on a coffee table in front of him. The coffee table was crowded. Around the platter were glasses, napkins, and three almost empty bowls of nuts. On either side of Edek, also in armchairs, were the two women Ruth and Edek had exchanged greetings with at breakfast. Edek and the two women were laughing raucously. Edek saw Ruth. He stood up and waved to her. The women stood up, too.

Edek introduced Ruth. "This is my daughter Ruthie," Edek said. "And Ruthie, this is Walentyna and Zofia." Both women rushed to shake Ruth's hand. Zofia, the larger of the women, shook Ruth's hand first. Her handshake was as firm as her sturdy appearance suggested. She gripped Ruth's hand and shook it until Ruth's knuckles hurt. Walentyna, the dainty one, had a demure handshake.

Ruth looked at what was left of the food on the coffee table. Edek and the women had clearly been having a good time. "Sit down," Edek said. He pulled over a chair for Ruth.

"Please have something to eat," Zofia said.

"My daughter does not eat," Edek said.

"You don't eat?" Zofia said. "I read, in America, that women don't eat."

"They like to be slim in America," Walentyna said.

"Too slim is not good for a woman," Zofia said. She looked at Ruth. "You know what I mean?" she said. Ruth had no idea what Zofia meant. She nodded her head. She didn't want to find out. Zofia's strength and vigor intimidated her. She felt flimsy next to Zofia. How must Walentyna feel? Walentyna was a fraction of Zofia's size.

"I do eat," Ruth said. "I eat plenty." She patted her hips to emphasize that she was not slightly built, and not starving herself.

"She used to be a fatty," Edek said.

"She is not fat at all," Walentyna said.

"She is not fat," said Zofia. "She is thin."

"I'm not thin," Ruth said.

"You are thin," Zofia said. "Have some liverwurst."

"It is a very good liverwurst," Edek said.

Ruth sat down. She felt dazed. How had this conversation begun? And how had she been sucked into its vortex so quickly? Here she was patting her hips, and arguing about whether she was thin or not. Ruth looked at Edek. He hadn't used the term "fatty" for years.

"Your father has been talking about you," Walentyna, the smaller woman, said. A sense of dread filled Ruth. What else had her father been saying?

"He said you are rich," Zofia said. Ruth was speechless. Of course, she should have guessed. "I'm not rich," she said.

"It's good to be rich," Zofia said. This came out as a forceful statement.

"You should not be ashamed to be rich," Walentyna said.

"I'm not ashamed," Ruth said.

"Of course she is not ashamed," Zofia said. "Nobody is ashamed to be rich."

"My daughter is," said Edek.

What had she walked into? Ruth wondered. She wished she hadn't joined this little gathering. Why was Edek aligning himself against her with these two women?

"You want a beer?" Zofia said to Ruth.

"She will have a cup of tea with lemon," Edek said.

"Ladies, let me order you another drink," Edek said to the two women in Polish.

"We can speak English," Zofia said. Ruth wished they'd speak Polish. She wouldn't be expected to join in.

"Of course," Edek said. "My daughter does not speak too good a Polish."

"I will have a beer," Walentyna said.

"I will have a schnapps," said Zofia.

Walentyna looked disturbed. "I will have a schnapps, too, not a beer," she said. Zofia turned to Walentyna.

"You do not drink schnapps," she said.

"I would like a schnapps now, please," Walentyna said.

"Of course," Edek said. He called over the waiter and ordered the drinks.

"I'll have chamomile tea," Ruth said to Edek.

"Bring some more liverwurst, too," Edek said to the waiter.

Ruth wondered whose account this get-together was being billed to.

"Put it on my bill please," Edek said to the waiter.

"Your father tells us that this trip was planned by you," Zofia said.

"Yes, it was my idea," Ruth said. "Possibly not my best idea."

"Why?" said Walentyna. "Your father says it is very interesting."

Zofia interrupted Walentyna. "He says he is very happy to have this experience," Zofia said to Ruth.

Walentyna looked hurt. "I was going to tell this young woman how happy her father is with her," she said to Ruth.

"So I did it for you." Zofia said. Walentyna looked crushed now. Ruth wondered why the women were traveling together. They looked like such an unlikely and incompatible couple.

"Have some more cheese, Edek," Zofia said. She patted him on the arm. "A grown man needs to eat." Few people, Ruth was sure, had felt the need to encourage Edek to eat. "My father has a very good appetite," Ruth said to Zofia.

Zofia looked at Walentyna and rolled her eyes. "I think we can see this," she said. Walentyna smiled coyly. Ruth was startled. It was not Edek's appetite for food Zofia was referring to.

Ruth looked at Zofia. Zofia was wearing a skin-tight short black skirt and a low-cut white T-shirt. Her legs were bare in winter. They were sturdy, firm legs, as firm as Zofia's handshake. Walentyna was dressed in a loose beige cotton blouse and a brown pleated skirt. The skirt was entirely the wrong length and had too many pleats for such a slight body. Walentyna looked enveloped in pleats.

Both women looked about sixty. Zofia saw Ruth looking at Walentyna's skirt. "This is a beautiful skirt Walentyna has, no?" Zofia said.

"It's beautiful," Ruth said.

"I chose the skirt and the blouse for her," Zofia said. Ruth couldn't believe that Zofia had chosen Walentyna's clothes. Everything Zofia had on was designed to display exactly what she was made of. The outfit Zofia had chosen for Walentyna covered Walentyna more thoroughly than a blanket.

"Have you two been friends for a long time?" Ruth said.

"Fifty-six years," said Walentyna.

"Since we were children," Zofia said.

Zofia's and Walentyna's roles were too established, Ruth thought, for any modification. She felt sorry for Walentyna. Walentyna was smiling. "We are very lucky to have each other," she said. "When my husband died, it would not have been easy to manage without Zofia."

"When my husband died, Walentyna was very good to me," Zofia said.

"It is good to have friends," Edek said. Zofia leaned over and slapped Edek on the knee. "It's very good to have a friend," she said.

The drinks arrived. Ruth tried to catch Edek's eye. She wanted to signal to him that she would like to leave, soon. She couldn't get Edek to look at her. Edek was trying to balance a large slice of liverwurst on a small piece of rye bread.

"Do you like to swim?" Zofia said to Ruth. Ruth nodded. "I like to swim every day," Zofia said. "I go in the water every morning. In summer and in winter, I swim in the sea. It is very good for the skin and the stomach to swim." She slapped her legs and arms. "I feel very good after I swim," she said.

"She swims in winter," Walentyna said.

"I love to swim in winter," Zofia said, her voice growing even louder than its naturally loud state. "I have a cold shower every morning before I go in the sea."

"You live near the sea?" Edek said.

"We live in Sopot," said Walentyna.

"I've been to Sopot," Ruth said.

"My daughter knows everything," said Edek.

"You have been to Sopot?" Zofia said.

"Yes," Ruth said. "I've walked along that wide boardwalk with the seats on either side, the one that goes out to sea."

"That is where I swim," Zofia shouted. "I jump into the water from this place. Did you see the steps into the water?"

"Yes," said Ruth.

"That is where I jump." Zofia stood up and imitated herself jumping into the water. Zofia's bust was inches from Edek's head. "Woosh," she said, as she pretended to jump.

"She must be good at swimming," Edek said to Ruth with admiration in his voice.

"Have some more fish," Zofia said to Edek, scooping up some smoked fish with a fork and putting it on Edek's plate.

"Thank you," Edek said.

"Did you like Sopot?" Walentyna asked Ruth.

"Yes, I did," Ruth said.

"You went to Sopot for a holiday?" said Zofia.

"No, I was in Gdańsk," Ruth said. "I went to Gdańsk because I wanted to go to Stuthof, the concentration camp where mother was transported to after Auschwitz. Stuthof, like Sopot, is close to Gdańsk." Both women looked very solemn. "I went to Sopot to try and recover from the day in Stuthof," Ruth said. Walentyna looked tearful. She looked away from Ruth. Zofia took Edek's hand.

"I am very sorry about this," Zofia said to Edek. "The things that happened to the Jews of Poland should never be forgotten." Ruth looked at Zofia. Zofia's face was red, she looked distressed.

There was an uncomfortable silence. Ruth wondered how she could suggest that she and Edek had to leave. Zofia was still holding Edek's hand. "I think I'll have a piece of pickled cucumber," Ruth said. She reached across to the platter. Zofia's arm was in the way. Zofia removed her hand from Edek's hand. Ruth chose a large piece of pickled cucumber.

"You are a good daughter, Ruthie," Zofia said. Walentyna nodded. Ruth wished Zofia wouldn't call her Ruthie. It was disconcerting. Ruthie was too familiar a name to be used by a stranger. Why had Edek introduced her as Ruthie?

"I can see you are a good daughter," Zofia said, again.

"Ruthie's mother did know Ruthie was a good daughter," Edek said. "Her mother is not here with us."

"She is in Australia?" Walentyna said. Both women angled their heads anxiously toward Edek.

"He means she is no longer alive," Ruth said. "My mother died fourteen years ago."

"Nearly fifteen," Edek said.

"She was a young woman?" Zofia said.

"Sixty," said Ruth.

"Like me," said Zofia. "It is terrible." Walentyna nodded in agreement.

"We loved her very much," Ruth said.

"I loved my husband like this," Zofia said.

"I loved my husband also," Walentyna said.

"What time are we going to this cabaret?" Edek said to Ruth.

"Seven o'clock," Ruth said.

Edek looked at his watch. "We still got a bit of time," he said.

"You are going to a cabaret?" Zofia said.

"Yes," said Edek. "My daughter did book tickets." Ruth hoped neither of the women would ask to join them.

"We're having dinner there, too," she said. Although looking at the fish and meat and cheese her father had eaten, Ruth couldn't see how he could possibly eat dinner.

"Is it a buffet, the dinner?" Edek said. Ruth smiled to herself. Edek was still interested in dinner. She really shouldn't underestimate his appetite.

"I don't think it's a buffet," Ruth said.

"Do you like a buffet?" Edek said to the women. They both nodded. "I do like a buffet very much," Edek said.

Ruth felt agitated. How could she suggest to Edek that they leave? She didn't want to offend Zofia or Walentyna. She realized with a surprise that she liked these women. There was a straightforwardness about Zofia and Walentyna. It was hard to be straightforward in New York. There was a hidden agenda in most people's interactions. Zofia and Walentyna, Ruth thought, were definitely not trying to disguise themselves.

"We have to go, Dad," she said.

"Can I buy you ladies another drink before we go?" Edek said. Ruth groaned.

"One more schnapps would be very nice," said Zofia.

"For me also," said Walentyna.

Edek went off to find the drink waiter.

"Your father is a very nice man," Walentyna said to Ruth.

"A man like that would crush you," Zofia said to Walentyna. "One minute on top of you and he would break your bones." Ruth was stunned. She couldn't believe the swift turn the conversation had taken.

"My husband was a big man," Walentyna said in Polish to Zofia.

"Not big like our Edek," Zofia answered in Polish. Ruth looked at the two women. They both ignored her. They continued to speak in Polish. "Edek is a man I could really get my legs around," Zofia said. Ruth was astonished. Did Zofia really say that? she thought. Maybe she had misunderstood. Maybe Zofia had said that Edek was a man you could get your mind around. Maybe in Polish, what Zofia had said translated colloquially as Edek was a man she liked. No, *noga* was leg in Polish. *Nogi* was the plural of leg, legs. *Moje nogi* was what Zofia had said. My legs. Ruth realized her mouth was hanging open in astonishment. She closed her mouth. Neither of the women took any notice of her. "Edek is a man I could really get my legs around," Zofia repeated. There was no getting around that, Ruth thought. She laughed at her own pun, it was definitely Zofia's legs, Zofia was thinking of getting around Edek.

"I think he also likes me," Walentyna said to Zofia.

Ruth was speechless. Ruth didn't want to hear any more. "Your English is very good," she said loudly to both women.

"We have both of us worked for an export company, in Sopot," Walentyna said. "It was necessary to speak English."

"What did they export?" Ruth said. She wanted to talk about anything other than one of these women winding their legs around her father.

"They did export jams," Zofia said.

"Yes, jams," said Walentyna.

"My father loves jam," Ruth said. She immediately wanted to kick herself. Why had she brought her father back into the conversation?

"So do I," said Zofia.

"So do I," said Walentyna.

Edek came back to the table. "So do I," said Ruth with relief. Edek sat down.

"We have to go, Dad," Ruth said.

"Okay, okay," Edek said to Ruth. "Ladies, it has been a pleasure for me to be with you," he said to Zofia and Walentyna.

"It has been a big pleasure for us, too," Walentyna said.

"This was, for me, a very nice afternoon," Edek said to her. Walentyna seemed to grow in stature. She sat up very straight.

"Do you like cheesecake?" Walentyna said to Edek. Ruth grimaced. How long was it going to take Edek to extricate himself? Ruth tried to hurry Edek up with her expression. But Edek was looking at Walentyna. "I make a very good cheesecake," Walentyna said.

"Walentyna makes a quite good cheesecake," Zofia said. While Zofia was saying this, she was shaking her head and making a face at Edek. The shake made it clear that Walentyna's cheesecake was not that good. Walentyna didn't notice. She hadn't taken her eyes off Edek.

"We have to go," Ruth said. Edek stood up. Both of the women stood up.

"Enjoy the cabaret," Zofia said wistfully.

"Yes, please enjoy the cabaret," Walentyna added. For a moment Edek looked as though he was going to ask Ruth if the women could join them. Ruth shot him a look that said no.

"They are very nice women," Edek said to Ruth in the taxi on the way to the cabaret.

"They are very nice," she said. She was holding her head.

"What is wrong with you?" Edek said.

"I've got a headache," she said.

At the Samson Restaurant, Ruth and Edek were shown to a table near the performance area. Ruth sat down. She was glad that she and Edek would have a good view of the cabaret. The restaurant was crowded. Ruth looked around at the other guests. There was not one Jew among the people who had come to the Samson Restaurant to eat Jewish food and see the

Jewish cabaret. Most of the audience looked like tourists. Tourists from Germany, Spain, France, and a smattering of Poles.

There were two Samson Restaurants in Szeroka Street in the heart of Kazimierz. They were next door to each other. The Polish owners had had a court battle for the name. Ruth and Edek were in the original Samson Restaurant. Samson number two was in the process of changing its name. Why would anyone open a restaurant and call it by the same name as the restaurant next door? Ruth thought. It seemed so stupid. Both Samsons offered Jewish dinners and cabarets. And Yiddish music. The decor at this Samson Restaurant was made up of the usual Jewish artifacts, aided and abetted by several paintings of Orthodox Jews praying.

Ruth looked at the menu. She was hungry. There was carp, Sephardic style, fish in Jewish jelly, chicken soup, Passover cheese, and a strange assortment of other dishes. A waiter brought two bread rolls and a very pale piece of matzoh in a basket to the table. The matzoh didn't look right—it was too thick and too pale. Ruth looked around her. Every table had a basket of bread rolls and matzoh.

"Are you hungry?" she said to Edek.

"No," he said, "I am not so hungry today." She restrained herself from pointing out that he had hardly stopped eating all day.

"I'll have some chicken soup," she said, "and some carp."

"Mum did make a beautiful carp," Edek said.

"She was a great cook," Ruth said. Edek looked sad. "Do you want a bowl of chicken soup?" Ruth said.

"Okay," he said.

"I'm going to order the Passover cheese," she said. "Have you ever heard of Passover cheese?"

"Never," Edek said.

The waiter returned. "Can you tell me what Passover cheese is?" Ruth said.

"It is Jewish cheese, madam," he said.

"But what is it?" she said.

"It is what Jewish people eat," he said.

"Well, I'm Jewish, so I'll have some," Ruth said. She ordered two bowls of chicken soup and one serving of carp.

"I will have a bit of fish too," Edek said.

"Make that two carp," Ruth said. The waiter nodded.

"Is this place owned by Jews?" Ruth said to the waiter.

"No, madam," the waiter said.

"Ruthie," Edek said.

"I just want to ask one more question," she said to Edek. "Are the musicians Jewish?" she said to the waiter.

"No, madam," the waiter said.

"I'm sorry, Dad," Ruth said. "I thought this might really be a Jewish cabaret."

She wanted to cry. What was she doing here? How could she have been naive enough to think that there was anything Jewish left in Poland? There were no Jews singing Yiddish songs anywhere anymore. Why couldn't she get that into her head? Edek could see her distress. He patted her on the head.

"Don't worry," Edek said, "it is always nice to see a show."

Some klezmer music started up. Edek tapped his fingers in time to the music. Ruth was pleased that he was in good spirits. It would have been a miserable evening if they both felt as bad as she felt. The restaurant was full. Ruth couldn't see one empty table. It hadn't been easy to get a booking to the cabaret. They did two shows a night at the Samson Restaurant and both shows were heavily booked. Ruth and Edek were at the early session.

The food arrived. All at once. The soup, the fish, and the cheese. The waiter juggled to fit everything on the table.

"I guess they've got to get us fed and out of here before the next session begins," Ruth said to Edek.

Edek took a mouthful of his soup. "Not bad soup," he said. Ruth had some.

"You're right," Ruth said. "It's not bad." She felt better eating the soup. She looked at Edek. He had already finished his soup. He must have been hungry, she thought. Someone had turned up the volume of the klezmer music. It was now very loud. It was impossible to speak above this music. Maybe that was the point, Ruth thought. If the customers couldn't talk, they would finish their meals faster.

"The fish is shocking," Edek suddenly shouted. "Do not eat it." He had pushed his fish away. Ruth tried a mouthful. It was disgusting. The carp was flat and tepid. It tasted of mud. Some limp strands of white cabbage floated next to the fish.

"What is Jewish about this?" she shouted to Edek.

"Nothing," he shouted back.

Ruth pushed the fish dish away, "Let's try the Passover cheese," she shouted.

Four perfectly round scoops of what was supposed to be Passover cheese were sitting in the middle of the plate, ungarnished and unaccompanied. Ruth prodded one of the scoops with her fork. She had never seen a dish like this before. Raisins and lemon peel had been mixed into a blend of cream cheese and cottage cheese. A wedge of orange had been pushed into the center of each scoop. No Passover seder meal she had ever been to had had this cheese.

"What is this?" Edek shouted to Ruth.

"Passover cheese," she shouted back. Edek started laughing.

"It is very funny," he shouted.

Ruth wished she could see the humor in the food, in the restaurant, in the evening.

She was hungry. She ate one scoop of the cheese. It wasn't too bad. "It's not too bad," she shouted to Edek.

Suddenly the lights dimmed. Someone came out and lit the candles of a menorah, the candleholder used for the Jewish holiday Hanukkah, which was sitting on a sideboard near the performance area. The audience grew hushed. From a side door four men and a woman, all playing instruments, ran onto the small stage area at the front of the restaurant. They were dressed as Jews. In black hats, black jackets, and beards. Ruth was appalled.

"They look like Ukrainians to me," Ruth said to Edek. Edek raised his eyebrows and nodded. He knew, too, that these performers weren't Jews. He didn't seem bothered. Ruth noticed that the largest musician was wearing a false nose. A large, hooked plastic nose. She felt furious.

"He's wearing a false nose," she said to Edek.

"Shsh," Edek said.

"Why should he wear a false nose in order to imitate a Jew?" Ruth said.

"Jews have big noses," Edek said.

"Can't you see how wrong it is?" Ruth said.

"Shsh," said Edek. "People will hear you."

The musicians played loudly and boisterously. Ruth recognized none of the songs.

"Do you know any of these songs, Dad?" she said.

"No," he said. There was no subtlety in the music. It was workmanlike. Uninspired. The piano-accordionist pounded the keys of the accordion. The guitarist's playing was basic, the clarinetist and violinist had no tenderness, and the drummer smashed away at the drums. The audience was enjoying the show. They clapped enthusiastically at the end of each number. Now and then the musicians acted out a joke. It was always lewd. The audience roared at each crude skit.

Finally the band broke into a Jewish number, *Hava Nagilah*, the joyful music Jews dance to in a circle at weddings and other celebrations. The Ukrainians, dressed as Jews, played *Hava Nagilah* at a funereal pace. *Hava Nagilah*, Ruth decided, was this band's attempt at a token moment of Jewish sadness. The audience understood. It remained quiet.

Ruth felt hysterical. "They have no idea what they're playing," she said to Edek. How dare they turn being Jewish into a profit-based circus. Her head hurt. She wanted to go home. She wasn't sure where her home was. Was it in New York? In Australia? In the cemetery in Łódź? She contemplated standing up and shouting. She wanted to grab the menorah, remove the yarmulkes, and punch the musicians. Edek was tapping his feet in time to the music. "It is not a bad show," he said.

∽ *Chapter Fourteen* ∽

*R*uth woke up disoriented. She had dreamed about legs. Zofia's legs. Stable, durable, hardy legs. Well-constructed legs. Legs with shiny skin and smooth calves. The legs had been walking along a beach next to another pair of legs. Legs that belonged to Edek, Ruth realized, when she got a closer look at the slight, white, threaded with fine blue veins legs, with their oddly delicate ankles. In the dream, she had been trying to catch up to the legs. But her own legs ached. She couldn't make them move fast. They were sluggish and slow. Ruth was sure there was plenty of material in that dream for an analyst to delve into. It seemed to contain quite a few murky propositions and suppositions.

Both alarm clocks in Ruth's room started ringing. Ruth thought she had set them to go off two minutes apart. She and Edek were going to Auschwitz today. She hadn't wanted to sleep in. Going to Auschwitz. The sentence had a strange ring to it. An ominous lilt. She switched both alarm clocks off. The wake-up call she had ordered arrived. "Cancel my second call, please," she said to the operator. She got out of bed. A fax from Max was on the floor under the door. The hotel didn't bother to fold the faxes. Ruth could see Max's distinctive handwriting from where she was standing.

She walked over and picked up the fax. *"John Sharp wants three hundred and twenty-seven individual letters to accompany invitations to his daughter's wedding,"* the fax said. Oh, shit, Ruth thought. Three hundred

and twenty-seven different letters was going to be an organizational nightmare. She knew that this job was worth tens of thousands of dollars. But
she was tired. She couldn't imagine what she could say on John Sharp's or
Sandra Sharp's behalf, to any of their guests.

Ruth turned on the shower. The water came through in a strong spray.
Thank God this shower had good water pressure, Ruth thought. She
turned up the hot water. She felt like a very hot shower. She took off her
nightie and stepped in. She soaped her body, and savored the heat and the
steam. She washed herself. She washed and washed. She soaped and lath-
ered and scrubbed. Why was she washing herself so vigorously? she wondered. By the time she got out of the shower her skin was pale and
wrinkled.

When Ruth arrived downstairs for breakfast, Edek was already there.
He looked good. Rested and chipper. He was eating a large bowl of cornflakes.

"You're eating cornflakes in Poland," Ruth said. Cornflakes were such
an Australian breakfast. "Are you homesick?" Ruth said. Edek laughed.
"To tell you the truth I did miss a bit my cornflakes," he said. He looked at
Ruth. "You look much better this morning, Ruthie," he said. Ruth got herself a bowl of stewed fruit. She sprinkled a few cornflakes on top of the
fruit. She was glad Edek thought that she looked better. She knew she had
been looking pretty wrung out.

Suddenly in a flurry of perfumed air, air scented with what seemed to be
a blend of soap and perfume and body lotions, Walentyna and Zofia
appeared. Ruth hadn't noticed them arrive. The two women looked
flushed. As though they had been rushing. "Good morning, good morning," Zofia called out. Edek stood up. He went to shake hands with Walentyna, who looked very pretty this morning, in a close-fitting, plain black
dress.

Zofia elbowed Walentyna out of the way. She thrust her bust forward
and pushed herself toward Edek. "It is very nice to see you this morning,
Edek," she said. She leaned forward and gave Edek a hug. "Walentyna and
I did enjoy very much our afternoon with you."

"I did enjoy it very much myself," Edek said.

"Was the cabaret last night good?" Zofia asked.

"It was not bad," Edek said.

"Did you like the cabaret?" Walentyna said to Ruth.

"I thought it was terrible," Ruth said. Both of the women looked at Ruth perplexed.

"There were some not so good points to it," Edek said. Ruth was glad for Edek's solidarity. She hadn't wanted to appear a killjoy to Zofia and Walentyna.

Zofia asked if she and Walentyna could join them for breakfast. Edek was about to say yes, when he noticed Ruth's disagreeable expression. He paused. Ruth used this window of opportunity to reply to Zofia's question. "Normally we would love to have you join us," Ruth said. "But we are going to Auschwitz today, so I think it would be better for us to have a quiet breakfast." Zofia looked solemn, but her disappointment showed through her solemnity.

"My daughter is right," Edek said.

"Of course your daughter is right," Walentyna said.

"Of course," Zofia said. She turned to Edek. "You will need a little comfort after such a terrible experience," she said to him.

"The thing what was most terrible did already happen," Edek said.

"Of course," Walentyna said.

"You will need to be cheered up when you get back," Zofia said to Edek in Polish. Ruth felt irritated. Zofia was so pushy. "What time will you be back?" Zofia said to Edek.

"We don't know," Ruth said. "We don't know how long we'll spend there."

Zofia looked at Edek. "Walentyna and I will be waiting for you when you get back."

"It is not necessary," Edek said. Thank God, Edek was deflecting them, Ruth thought. The prospect of dealing with Zofia and Walentyna immediately after Auschwitz seemed exhausting. She felt relieved that at least Zofia and Walentyna weren't joining them for breakfast. She really wanted to have a quiet breakfast. It was going to be a big day.

Zofia patted Edek on the back. "Take care," she said. "Walentyna and I will be here whatever time you will be back."

"We will be here," Walentyna said quietly.

"Thank you," Edek said.

Ruth felt sorry for Walentyna. She was so overshadowed by Zofia and Zofia's bust.

"They are nice women," Edek said after Zofia and Walentyna had left.

"They're okay," she said. Edek looked deflated. She felt mean. There had been no need to puncture such a small, harmless piece of pleasure. "No, they are very nice," she said to Edek. "I think little Walentyna gets bossed around a bit by Zofia."

"I don't think so," Edek said. "Walentyna is such a quiet type. Zofia is not so quiet." Ruth looked across the room. The two women were talking animatedly. Maybe Edek was right. Maybe there was no need to feel sorry for Walentyna.

Ruth was hungry. She ate all of her stewed fruit and went back for more. Edek had followed the cornflakes with pickled herring, scrambled eggs, and fried bratwurst and onions. He was finishing off his breakfast with a piece of bread and jam.

"Are you nervous about going to Auschwitz, Dad?" she said.

"No," he said. "Why should I be nervous? Nothing is going to happen to me there, now." He finished the bread and jam and wiped his mouth with his napkin. He pushed his plate and several pieces of cutlery away in a decisive gesture that signaled that he was finished with the meal. "That is it," he said.

Ruth had seen this movement many times. It was an announcement that he was having nothing more to eat. Ruth thought it was more of an announcement to himself than to anyone else. He always said "that is it" as he pushed his eating implements away. The speed and decisiveness of the push, Ruth thought, was an affirmation that Edek had had enough. That he was someone who could curtail his eating. That he was not a pig. "That is it," Edek said again.

The Mercedes that was waiting for them was a medium-size Mercedes. "This is not such a big one what the other one," Edek said. "That's true," Ruth said. She felt she was becoming a connoisseur of Mercedes.

"Do you want to sit in front with the driver?" Ruth said.

"No," Edek said. "This time I will sit with you." They got into the car. There was something soothing about the plush comfort of a Mercedes, Ruth thought.

"You are going to the Auschwitz Museum?" the driver said.

"No," Ruth said. The driver turned around. "We are going to the Auschwitz death camp," she said to him. "Could you remember that?" The driver nodded. Edek looked uncomfortable. "What is it such a big deal what he calls the camp?" he said. "It is still the same what happened there." Ruth didn't answer. She wished she wasn't so bothered by what anybody called it. It seemed so petty next to anything else connected with the camp.

"I've brought some water with me in case we get thirsty," she said to Edek. She showed him the water she had packed in a bag, together with some bananas and pears. Edek looked at the bananas and pears.

"What for did you bring so much fruit?" he said.

"It's only four pears and four bananas," she said.

"You are not going to be hungry in Auschwitz," Edek said. "You do not eat in the hotel where there is such a good buffet. You think that you are going to eat in Auschwitz?" He shook his head.

"I brought some chocolate for you, too," she said. She took out a block of Wedel's semibitter dark chocolate.

"Thank you," Edek said. He still looked bewildered.

Ruth understood her father's bewilderment. After all, they weren't setting out for a picnic. She had realized when she started to pack the pears and bananas and chocolate that she associated Auschwitz with starvation, and it was hard to separate that association from the present. She didn't tell Edek about the dried apricots and dates in her backpack. She had felt as though she were packing for a trek through the Himalayas, or somewhere equally difficult to get out of in an emergency. It was a strange thought for her to have, as the Himalayas were as far removed from anything in her life as it was possible to be. She knew that they were mountains. Mountains in Kashmir, Tibet, and Nepal. But that scrap of knowledge was the only thing she knew about the Himalayas.

"I've hired a guide to take us through Auschwitz and Birkenau," Ruth said to Edek.

"You did hire a guide?" Edek said. "What for?" he said. "We don't need a guide." He looked offended. As though Ruth had invited someone who would intrude on what was his terrain. Ruth understood his concern. She had hesitated before hiring the guide, but the thought of her and Edek wandering around Auschwitz trying to identify what could never be identi-fied had frightened her. Somehow a guide had made Auschwitz seem tra-versable.

"I could walk there with my eyes shut," said Edek.

"I know," she said.

"Especially Birkenau where I was most of the time."

"If you don't like the guide, I'll tell him to leave," Ruth said.

"Okay," Edek said. "Maybe about the main camp at Auschwitz we will learn something from this guide."

Ruth wondered if her mother had talked to Edek about Auschwitz. Ruth had assumed that Rooshka had, but every time Ruth mentioned something about this time in Rooshka's life, Edek didn't appear to know. Maybe when Edek and Rooshka found each other again, after the war, what had happened to each of them was the last thing they wanted to talk about.

"Mum was in Auschwitz," Edek said. "And I was in Birkenau."

"I know," Ruth said.

"They was two miles apart," Edek said. "And there was not much news between the camps. I could find out nothing about Mum. I did not know if she was dead or alive." He shook his head. He looked miserable. Ruth felt worried. Maybe she shouldn't have brought him here. Maybe this whole trip had been a mistake.

"Are you all right?" she said.

"I am all right," he said.

"We don't have to go," she said.

"We are on our way already," Edek said.

It was a forty-minute drive to Auschwitz from Kraków. Ruth looked at her watch. They must be halfway there. They had passed two road signs to Auschwitz. Both signs said AUSCHWITZ MUSEUM. They passed another one: AUSCHWITZ MUSEUM, 30 KILOMETERS. "Death camp" was clearly a term to be avoided in Poland. They drove in silence. Ruth wondered what Edek was thinking about. She didn't want to ask. She was glad that he was able to be quiet. Auschwitz was a place you didn't want to be catapulted into in the middle of conducting a series of jocular conversations. Catapulted out into. That's what they all had been. All the Jews. Soon she and Edek would be there. Quietly, of their own accord.

Ruth felt hungry. She got out a banana and ate it. It was a sweet, ripe banana. It tasted good. She had brought a separate bag for the banana peel. Edek looked at her. "The whole time we been in Poland you don't eat. You eat compote and bird stuff," he said. "Now, on the way to Auschwitz, you are eating. Sometimes I think you are crazy."

"Maybe," she said. Edek was smiling. Ruth knew he didn't mean crazy, crazy. Lunatic crazy. Just crazy beyond what seemed the norm to him. She ate another banana.

"We are arriving at the Auschwitz Museum," the driver said.

"The Auschwitz death camp," Ruth said.

"Yes," the driver said. He turned off the road. "I will wait in the car park for you," he said.

All Ruth could see from the car was car park. A large, already crowded car park. There were coaches and vans and cars and taxis parked in the car park. It was not what Ruth had expected to arrive at. It looked more like a car park for Disneyland or another theme park. Groups of drivers were standing together, smoking. Busloads of tourists were alighting from streamlined coaches. It was a disturbing sight. "I described us to the guide," she said to Edek.

They got out of the car. Edek straightened up and looked around him. "It does not smell," he said. He sniffed the cold air. "The smell is gone," he said. "We did say the smell would never go away." They walked toward a sign that said MUSEUM ENTRANCE. Ruth looked up. They were in front of the entrance gates to Auschwitz. The ARBEIT MACHT FREI sign was just in front of them. She gasped. The wrought-iron sign woven across the top of the gates looked so small. In photographs it always loomed so large. An image that had presided over so much horror. An image so blatant in its mockery. These gates, this sign, had seemed monumental to Ruth. They had signified so much. A symbol of so much that was impossible to comprehend. Ruth was shocked at how small the gates were. Almost domestic in scale. Average industrial-size gates. They were too small, she thought. They should have been bigger, for all the damage they had wrought. She had expected them to almost touch the sky.

She stood and looked at the sign. ARBEIT MACHT FREI. Freedom Through Work. What a joke. The freedom had been in death. If death was a freedom. She started to cry. She couldn't bear the proximity to these gates. She wanted to run away. "There is nothing to cry about today, Ruthie," Edek said. "It did already happen. It is too late to cry." But she couldn't stop. Tears poured down her face. How could they have fed so many people through these gates? How could they have ushered them through to their death? Shepherded them in. Assembled them for an assembly line, where they were stripped and packed and dismantled and shipped to the sky. It had just been a job for the Germans. A job they carried out in a workman-like, if harsh, manner. They were hard workers, the Germans. They did what had to be done. This slaughterhouse was far more efficient than most of the world's abattoirs.

Images of long lines of Jews filled Ruth's head. Long lines of Jews on the unloading ramp in Auschwitz. Small children holding their mother's hands. Babies being carried. Sisters clinging to each other. Mothers and daughters trying to stay together. She wept and wept. Edek started to cry. They stood in front of the *ARBEIT MACHT FREI* sign and wept.

Ruth tried to pull herself together. "We won't get very far," she said to Edek, "if we disintegrate before we're even in the gate." Disintegrate. That's what had happened to all the Jews. Their bodies had disintegrated. Disintegrated into charred remains. Sharp fragments of bone, pieces of teeth, bits of gristle, deposits of minerals, unidentifiable particles of organic matter. Dehydrated and blackened remains. The shavings and shards of people. The ash that was left of the Jews was dumped in the Vistula River. It almost choked the river.

"I am not going to disintegrate," Edek said.

A man walked up to Ruth and Edek. "Rothwax?" he said.

"That's us," said Ruth.

"I am your guide, Jerzy Branicki," he said. Jerzy Branicki looked okay, Ruth thought. He was about seventy and had a sensitive face.

"I'll go and buy the entrance tickets," Ruth said to Jerzy.

"You do not need to," he said. "It is not necessary to pay to go into Auschwitz."

"That's good," she said. The irony of paying to get into Auschwitz had not escaped her.

"My daughter is not saying good because she can't afford it," Edek said.

"Jerzy probably understood that," Ruth said.

"Of course," said Jerzy.

"I did just want to make sure," Edek said.

Ruth looked at her father. He seemed quite wide-eyed to be where he was. As though he couldn't quite believe it. She was having trouble believing it herself. A slight drizzle of rain began. Ruth was glad it was a dull gray, wet day. She wouldn't have wanted to see Auschwitz in sunshine. A sign near the front entrance of the building said AUSCHWITZ MUSEUM. Ruth was furious. Why did everyone insist on using the word "museum"?

"Why can't they just say death camp?" she said to Edek.

"It is a museum, inside," Jerzy said. "There are exhibits on display in the former death camp."

Ruth said to him, "This is not a museum. The Museum of Modern Art is a museum, the Museum of Natural History is a museum, the Guggenheim Museum is a museum. This is not a museum. This is a death camp." Jerzy shrugged his shoulders.

"What does it matter what it is called?" Edek said to Ruth. "It is still the same place."

"It is easier for people to believe it is something else, something abstract, if it's called a museum," Ruth said. "They can forget that it was a place for the slaughter of human beings."

"Which people, Ruthie, is so interested in Auschwitz?" Edek said.

"Look at how many visitors are here today," she said.

"Those what do come here know it is not the Luna Park they are going to visit," Edek said. "It does not matter what they do call it."

Inside the first building, there were signs to the public toilets. And a cafeteria. Of course, museums needed cafeterias, Ruth thought. The cafeteria sold drinks and sweets and cakes and several hot dishes, including sausages. The whole room smelled of food. There seemed to be something wrong about a cafeteria in a place of starvation. Several Polish schoolboys were jostling at the counter of the cafeteria. They were buying cans of Coca-Cola.

Ruth and Edek and Jerzy began to walk. Jerzy started to give them statistics about the prisoners. "Would you mind if we walk quietly," Ruth said. "We'll ask you if we need any questions answered." Jerzy looked momentarily annoyed. Ruth didn't care.

Everything in the former death camp looked so clean and neat. Almost nondescript. Nonthreatening. As harmless as the average, standard housing development that it resembled. A sign of a skull with the word "Halt" and the Polish word for halt, *stój*, was the only sign of anything ominous. Jerzy hovered around Ruth and Edek. She regretted that she had hired him.

Ruth had a copy of the official guidebook to Auschwitz with her. It was published by the State Museum in Oświęcim, the town renamed Auschwitz by the Germans. The guidebook, where Ruth had first seen that guides were available, stated on the inside front cover that the museum was open but no guide service was provided on days when "mass manifestations announced by the radio and press take place." What did they mean? Ruth thought as she walked through Auschwitz. Manifestations of what? A manifestation was the indication of the existence or presence of something. The existence or presence of what was the guidebook referring to? No lice had survived, no fleas. Were they expecting manifestations of ghosts or wraiths or spirits? These would hardly be announced in the press.

Ruth and Edek and Jerzy walked along one of the central paths. The path was lined with brick barracks on both sides. The cleanliness and neatness was disorienting. Auschwitz, cleaned up and turned into a tourist venue, looked like an ordinary, English working-class estate. Ruth was disturbed by the absence. The absence of dirt, filth, stench, stink. The absence of cruelty. The absence of suffering. She'd expected to see the suffering in the air, on the ground, in the walls, and on every fence.

The museum was closed on twenty-fifth of December and on Easter Sunday the small guidebook had said. Ruth had wanted to write to the publishers and point out that the death camp they referred to as a museum was never closed even for these most holy of Catholic holidays.

Block 10 was being restored. The restoration work looked like the renovation of any middle-class dwelling. There was scaffolding around the building and ladders and workers' tools. Block 10 was where Mengele and the other SS doctors performed medical experiments on Jewish women. Ruth stopped outside Block 10. It looked like such an innocuous building.

"Mengele did his work here," she said to Edek. Edek shook his head. "Are you all right in this place, Dad?" Ruth said.

"I am all right," Edek said.

Block 10 was closed to the public. "Block 4 has very good exhibitions," Jerzy said.

"Shall we go there?" Ruth said.

"Okay," said Edek.

Inside Block 4, the walls were painted two tones of gray. The stairs had had a marble and concrete composite added to their surface. In the different rooms the floor was painted with enamel paint. There were heating units along the walls. There was an odd primness about the decor. Totally at odds with the brutalities and obscenities that had taken place within the walls.

Ruth wished the visitors to these blocks could experience something of the atmosphere of degradation and humiliation and inhumanity that had existed. How could you feel people's anguish and terror in centrally heated, newly painted barracks? But maybe nothing could ever replicate a fraction of the atmosphere, a fraction of the events that took place.

Nobody would come here, she thought, if the place was still covered in shit and piss and lice and rats and vomit and ash and decomposing corpses. The car park wouldn't be full of tourist coaches. People wouldn't be looking at the photographs and other exhibits on display in these rooms. These renovations were probably necessary. She had to stop being so judgmental, she told herself.

In front of an exhibit of a can of Zyklon B, Jerzy began to speak. "Why do we present this?" he said. Ruth wasn't sure who he was addressing this stupid question to. It couldn't be to her or to Edek, she thought. She looked around. The dozen or so other tourists in this room were not looking at Jerzy. "We give these tours," he continued, "so humankind can learn."

"Thank you," Edek said.

"Poles died here, too," Jerzy said. "It wasn't just Jews."

"That's a line I've heard from quite a few Poles," Ruth whispered to Edek.

"Shsh," Edek said.

"My mother-in-law died here and my father-in-law died here," Jerzy said.

"I am very sorry to hear about that," Edek said.

"I am sorry, too," Ruth said.

"My wife was a true orphan," Jerzy said. "She had to live from the time she was sixteen without a mother and without a father."

"I am very sorry," Edek said.

"Polish people tried very much to help the Jews," Jerzy said.

"I'd like to look at the exhibits," Ruth said. "Could we meet you outside?" Jerzy looked stunned. "Please," she said.

"If that is what you want, of course," he said.

"Why did you tell him, like this, to go?" Edek said.

"I told him politely," Ruth said. "I don't want to hear about how much Poles suffered and how no Pole knew what was happening to the Jews. Or the even worse version of history he was just about to start on, which was how much Poles tried to help the Jews."

"I did tell you we did not need a guide," Edek said.

"I thought the place was going to be a real mess," Ruth said. "I didn't think it would be so cleaned up."

"They did have to clean it, I suppose," Edek said.

The exhibits in the rooms were moving. Ruth could see how moved most people were by the piles of old suitcases with names and addresses on them, the photographs of women being driven into the gas chambers, and the photographs of large piles of burning corpses. She looked closely at the bales of haircloth. She knew what it was. It was cloth woven from human hair and used as tailor's linings for men's suits.

"That is what did happen to Mum's hair," Edek said.

"I was thinking of that," she said. They both stood in front of the cloth, in silence for a minute.

In the next block, Block 5, there were exhibits of Jewish prayer shawls, shaving brushes, and toothbrushes. The shaving brushes and toothbrushes looked so forlorn, Ruth thought. As though they still hadn't grasped that they had been separated from their owners. There was a mound of spectacles and a mountain of shoes. Such personal parts of so many people's lives. Still here so long after their owners had gone. There were artificial limbs and kilos and kilos of human hair. So many parts and addendums to so many people.

The volume of what was left behind was just a fraction of what had been removed from prisoners in Auschwitz. Quite a few of the visitors had tears in their eyes. "It is shocking," Edek said to Ruth, in front of the mountain of shoes. Small shoes, large shoes, women's shoes, men's shoes, and tiny baby shoes. They were all still here.

Outside, the turbulence present in the exhibits was absent. A trolley on rails, used for carting bodies to the crematorium, had candles and flowers on it. There was no sense of chaos, no sense of abandonment, no sense of a world gone awry. Where was the unpredictability? The never-ending blows and beatings? The always-changing orders? The rules that never remained the same and were always nonsensical? Where was the world in which everything was unpredictable and nothing could be divined or foreseen? A world where chance encounters could save a life or erase it. A world in which everything was uncertain and nothing was safe. And any news was unverifiable and indistinguishable from rumors. And orders were fickle and capricious. A world in which killing was ordered as an afterthought. Where was this uncurbed, unchecked, lawless universe?

Where were the endless twice-daily *Appels,* roll calls that served little purpose. They were gone. Gone with the people. What did she expect? Ruth thought. Mock-ups of beatings and roll calls and barracks crowded with lice-ridden bodies. Mock-ups of men and women leaking with typhus. Representations of women with mixtures of feces and menstrual blood running down their legs. Was this what she expected?

She expected something more than what was here. She had thought the air would ring with violence and insanity. She thought it would be choked with pain, bewilderment, disbelief, and anguish. She thought it would be clogged and plugged with unsaid farewells. She remembered her mother telling her about her first *Appel*, in Auschwitz. "We did join the other prisoners," Rooshka had said. "We were ourselves very thin from the ghetto, but we still looked like people. The people in the *Appel* did no longer look like people. They were not round, they were flat, like they were made of paper, not flesh. They stood so still in the *Appel*. There was no sign of life in them. Nobody moved. They stood with their rags hanging on them like broken torn paper puppets. Soon I looked just like them."

Jerzy was waiting for them outside Block 11, which housed the prison cells within this prison. "Would you like me to tell you about the prison block?" he said.

"No thanks," she said. She looked at Edek.

"No thank you," Edek said.

Ruth walked over to the formerly electrified barbed-wire fence. She

touched it. Nothing happened. She put her face against the fence. She wondered what had touched this particular piece of fence? She knew that
pieces of prisoners' flesh often stuck to the fence after they had tried to
escape or to kill themselves. That fence must have looked pretty tempting.
One fling against it, and you were gone.

Rooshka had been ashamed of herself for being able to live through the
nightmare of her days at Auschwitz. Ashamed that she didn't just die. "The
best people did die first," Rooshka had said, many times, to Ruth. "They
couldn't have," Ruth said to Rooshka when she was older. "Niceness and
goodness were not criteria the Nazis were using in their selections." But
she knew what her mother was saying. Her mother was saying that she felt
a contempt for herself for surviving all that brutality, all that baseness. Ruth
wondered if the fence had tempted her mother. Edek came over and
touched the fence. He looked surprised when nothing happened. He
touched it again. "Who would believe I would one day do this?" he said to
Ruth. Ruth took Edek's arm.

More tourists had arrived. Groups of people were walking around with
and without guides. Most of the visitors looked somber. Still the visitors
bothered Ruth. She would much rather have been here alone with Edek.
Several classes of Polish schoolchildren walked by. They were talking and
laughing. Ruth was surprised that the teachers accompanying them didn't
ask them to be quiet. Ruth glared at several of the noisier children. The
schoolchildren, who looked about twelve or thirteen, were chewing gum
and eating snacks. Two boys not far from Ruth suddenly started fighting. A
few punches flew from one boy to the other. The teacher who was closest to
the boys ignored them.

Ruth strode over to the two boys. "Excuse me," she said loudly, "this is
a burial ground, a gravesite, not a circus." The taller of the boys laughed,
and said something Ruth couldn't understand in Polish. The teacher just
looked at Ruth. "You are disgusting," Ruth said to the teacher. Her heart
was racing. She could hardly catch her breath. What were they doing
bringing these adolescent hooligans to this place? For these boys, this was
just another trip, just another opportunity to get out of the classroom.

"Ruthie, Ruthie, what are you doing?" Edek said, running up to her.

"Nothing," she said. "They're assholes."

"Ruthie, we cannot fix up anything by speaking like that," Edek said.

"We cannot bring back anyone. If somebody does behave badly here what does it matter? The people who are dead are dead. They do not see this bad behavior."

"You don't know that," she said to Edek. Edek looked at her. "Ruthie, darling, the dead are dead," he said.

"Would you like to go to Birkenau soon?" Jerzy asked.

"Do you think you're up to it?" Ruth said to Edek.

"I am up to it," he said. "I will show you my barracks and where I did sleep."

"Would you like to go to the museum shop before you go?" Jerzy said. Ruth had known that there would have to be a profit-making section of the Auschwitz Museum business. She didn't want to contribute to their profits.

"Let us see what they got," Edek said.

"Okay," she said.

A fly flew into Ruth's face and began buzzing around her head. She tried to brush it away, but it kept returning. It was a large black fly. Ruth watched the fly warily. Why was it attacking her? And what was it doing here in winter? She thought flies appeared only in summer. Was this fly lost? Was it supposed to be somewhere else? The fly flew at her again. She tried to flick it away by shaking her hair at it. It flew right back. She felt the sting of its bite on her cheek. The fly, apparently pleased with its successful mission, flew off.

Ruth felt her cheek. It felt hot. She could already feel a swelling. She looked around. There were no other flies in sight. Where did this fly come from? And why did it bite her? Maybe it wasn't a fly? Maybe it was someone's spirit. Who had she hurt that would need to get back at her with a bite? She shook her head. She had to put an end to that kind of thinking. It was absurd to imbue a fly with a spirit. A spirit that belonged to someone else. Poland was twisting her vision. Distorting her beliefs and understandings.

Edek turned and noticed the bite. "Look what you got on your face," he said. "What happened?"

"It's just a bite," Ruth said. "I was bitten by a fly." She felt her face. She could feel the bite still swelling.

"There was no flies in Birkenau," Edek said.

"Mum said there were no flies in Auschwitz," Ruth said. "Mum said she didn't see one single fly here."

"No?" said Edek.

"She said there were no flies and no birds," Ruth said.

"It doesn't look good, your face," Edek said. "It looks bad."

"I'm always allergic to flies," Ruth said. "To all insects. I swell up twice as much as anyone else. And every gnat, mosquito, or fly anywhere finds me in minutes."

"You must have sweet blood," Edek said.

"Plenty of people have said that to me," Ruth said. She laughed. "But you know my blood is not all that sweet. You know I am not all that sweet."

"What are you talking about?" Edek said. "Why do you think always that you are bad? You did do this even when you was a girl. You was never bad. You was always a good girl."

"I felt it was my fault," Ruth said.

"What?" said Edek.

"My fault that Mum had to suffer so much," Ruth said.

"That is crazy," said Edek.

"All children feel it must be their fault if their parent feels bad," Ruth said. "It's too hard to understand that it's not your fault. That you didn't cause it. And you can't fix it up."

"You did fix up a lot for Mum," Edek said. Ruth was quiet. "She was very happy with you," Edek said. "It was other stuff she was not happy about." Tears came into Ruth's eyes. She didn't want to cry again. She didn't want to set Edek's tears off again. He often still wept for Rooshka.

"Terrible things did happen to Mum," Edek said.

"I know," she said. Her cheek was burning. She felt it with her fingers. She could feel a large blister forming in the middle of the swelling. "I'm not usually bitten in winter," she said to Edek.

"It does look terrible," Edek said. "It must have been a big fly."

"It must have been the commandant of flies," Ruth said, and laughed. Edek laughed. "Maybe he was the Generalfeldmarschall Reichsführer-SS of flies," Ruth said. "Or maybe there are bigger flies and he was just an SS-Obergruppenführer, a lieutenant general, or a plain old captain, an SS-Hauptsturmführer."

Edek fell about laughing. Ruth thought he was going to fall over. She grabbed his elbow.

"What is the lowest this fly can be?" Edek said.

"A second lieutenant, an SS-Untersturmführer," Ruth said. Edek looked at Ruth's bite. "I do not think that this fly was an SS-Untersturmführer," he said, and collapsed with laughter. They both laughed until they cried. Edek had to lend Ruth his handkerchief to wipe away her tears. Jerzy stood behind them silently.

"This was very funny," Edek said to Jerzy.

"We walk to the museum shop," Jerzy said. Ruth and Edek walked to the shop, still laughing.

The shop sold postcards, slides, books, and videos. Ruth didn't want to buy anything. Two collections of postcards in folders were on sale. One was labeled *Auschwitz I*, the other *Auschwitz II—Birkenau*. Ruth opened the package of Birkenau cards. Every shot of Birkenau had a poetic hue, including the electrified wire fence. The railway tracks were photographed with yellow flowers growing in the grass at the side of the tracks.

On the back of the postcard of the International Monument to the Victims of Auschwitz, the postcard said that the memorial was located between the ruins of "two mass genocide devices." Ruth was struck by the strange, detached wording used to describe the gas chambers and the ovens of the crematoriums. There was also a photograph of the guard towers. It was a mid-distance shot. The towers and electrified fencing beside them looked too innocuous. Ruth felt flat. Nothing, not the most detailed graphic photographic enlargements, would ever be enough. Nothing was adequate enough to express a fraction of what should be expressed.

She bought the postcards, eight books, two videos, and a box of slides. "I'll have to leave these in the car," she said to Jerzy. Jerzy was beaming at the woman who was wrapping Ruth's goods. Ruth hoped Jerzy wasn't going to get a commission from this sale.

"What for did you buy all this stuff?" Edek said.

"I wanted it," she said.

"Have you not got enough stuff like this?" Edek said. "Your apartment has got plenty of stuff like this. You got books, videos. Is it not enough?"

"It's never enough," Ruth said.

Edek shrugged his shoulders.

"I am not sure this stuff is good for you," he said. "It could hurt you to read too much stuff like this."

"Oh yeah?" Ruth said. "You could live through it, but it's too dangerous for me to read about. The real danger is not reading about it. Isn't ignorance the real danger?"

"Maybe you are right," he said.

"I am right," she said.

"Okay," Edek said.

"Can you put this stuff in our taxi for us please?" Edek asked Jerzy.

"Of course," Jerzy said.

"Put it in the backseat," Ruth said to Jerzy, "not in the trunk. I don't want to forget it."

"I do not think that our driver would want to keep this stuff," Edek said, and laughed.

Ruth laughed. "I don't think he would want to either," she said.

"I will drive you to Birkenau in my car," Jerzy said. "Then I will bring you back to your taxi."

"Are you up to Birkenau, Dad?" Ruth said.

"I am up to anything," Edek said. Ruth looked at him. He looked quite robust. In good spirits. His resilience reassured her. They drove the two miles to Birkenau. Auschwitz II.

"Survivors have the privilege of driving into Birkenau," Jerzy said. "Everybody else must walk."

"Wow," said Ruth, sarcastically. Edek silenced her with his look. "It is not necessary, Ruthie," he said quietly. They drove inside the entrance gate.

"You would like to drive to the monument?" Jerzy asked.

"We didn't come here to see the monument," Ruth said.

They got out of the car. Birkenau was deserted. It was an eerie and ghostly place. Ruth shivered. She felt cold. She felt she could sense shrouds and shapes and presences. She felt she could feel haunted visions. Tormented prophets. She wasn't sure why she was so sure of this. She felt frightened. What she could feel was what she was able to imagine, she decided.

There were very few people in Birkenau. There were no exhibitions, no shops, no central heating. Just the bleak fields dotted with run-down barracks. The fields and broken barracks seemed to stretch for miles. Ruth knew that Birkenau covered four hundred and twenty-five acres. It had contained over three hundred buildings. She knew there had been four crematoriums with gas chambers, two makeshift gas chambers in farmhouses that had been specially converted for the job, and large cremation pyres and pits for when the job became too large for all the gas chambers and all the ovens.

A mournful mist hung low in the sky. Above the mist were dismal, grim clouds. Were the clouds permanently blackened and soiled by soot? Ruth wondered. Everything was as deserted and abandoned as it must have been when the Nazis fled. Partly destroyed buildings had been left in their relative states of destruction. Empty patches of earth marked where barracks and buildings had been torn down. Wrenched out of the earth by Nazis who were trying to cover up their tracks. It was so still. So quiet.

"How do you feel, Dad?" she said.

"I am all right," he said. He looked very subdued. She took his hand.

"We're here together, you and me," she said. He nodded. Together in Auschwitz-Birkenau, she thought. Not a location most people would choose to share with each other.

"Here is where the prisoners were unloaded from the trains," Jerzy said. Edek looked bewildered.

"Here?" he said.

"Yes, here," Jerzy said. "The prisoners did often come in sealed cattle wagons. Jammed together like cattle."

"We know that," Ruth said. "My father was one of them. So was my mother and two of her sisters and her mother and father."

"Of course," Jerzy said.

"It was not here," Edek said to Jerzy.

"What?" said Jerzy.

"The place where the train did arrive and stop," Edek said.

"It was here," Jerzy said.

"It was not here," said Edek, agitated.

"It was here where the prisoners were unloaded from the trains," Jerzy said.

"Don't begin your speech again," Ruth said to Jerzy, in what she hoped was a menacing tone.

"It was not here," Edek said. "I was here. This was not where I was pushed out of the cattle wagon. This is not something what a person does forget." Edek looked distressed.

"This was the only place where the prisoners were unloaded," Jerzy said. "The train came into the gates and stopped here."

"It was not here," Edek said. He looked close to tears.

"They get old," Jerzy said to Ruth. He had turned away from Edek so Edek wouldn't hear him. "They get old," he said. "And they forget."

"They?" said Ruth. "Say that one more time and I'll punch you." She clenched her fists. Garth had taught her to punch effectively. He had grown up boxing with his father.

Jerzy looked completely startled. "I'll punch you," Ruth said, "if you say that again. I'd like you to walk behind us now. My father and I will find the location my father is looking for." She felt livid. How dare he refer to her father as "they." As though he wasn't there. As though Edek was one of the dead Jews that the guides were trained to talk about. The guides in Auschwitz were supposed to have completed a course of study not only on the facts but on how to present the facts, on how to conduct the guided tours. What sort of a course could it be? Ruth thought. She wished she could tell Jerzy to piss off. But she didn't want Edek to have to walk the two miles back to Auschwitz to their taxi.

"There were transports that were unloaded outside the gate, many times," Ruth said to Jerzy. They were both now facing Edek again. "Especially in 1944," she said, "when they were overloaded with prisoners. Prisoners were arriving faster than it was possible to gas and burn them. Trains stopped at different places. Sometimes there were several trains that were backed up. Not everything was working like clockwork in those days."

"Let's walk, Dad," she said to Edek. Jerzy walked behind them.

"You are a clever girl, Ruthie," Edek said. "You do know many things."

Edek looked to the right and to the left as he walked. "I did walk straight ahead from the train and then I did turn left," Edek said. He looked flustered. "I have to find it," he said, "I was here. I know where I was."

"Of course you do," Ruth said. Suddenly Edek sped up. He walked across a field and into an area to the left. He signaled to Ruth to hurry.

"Look," he said. "Here is the tracks, and here is where I did get off the train." He looked triumphant.

"That asshole doesn't know what he's talking about," Ruth said.

"Please, Ruthie, don't speak like that."

"I knew you would find where you were unloaded," she said.

Jerzy had caught up to them.

"The ramp in Birkenau was built in 1944," he said. "Previously all of the trains were unloaded in Auschwitz." Edek dismissed Jerzy with a wave of his hand. A curt gesture, as though he was getting rid of a bad smell.

"We do not want to hear this, please," Edek said.

"Could you allow us some privacy, please," Ruth said to Jerzy. Jerzy looked angry. He walked a few feet away.

Ruth started thinking about her mother. Her mother had first been in Birkenau before she had been transferred to Auschwitz.

"I was separated from Mum here," Edek said. He looked miserable. "I will show you where my barracks was," he said. "I do remember every step I did take from this train to the barracks. I did know when I was walking away from Mum that my life would never be the same again."

Nobody who was on one of those transports ever had the same life again. And they were the lucky ones, Ruth thought. The ones who still had a life. Rooshka had told her that the first thing she had been told, when she was still in the unloading area, was that there were no questions. "There are no questions," a German officer had shouted at her. "And no answers." Ruth felt fearful.

"Don't cry, Ruthie," Edek said. "Let me show you the barracks."

"I hope they're still there," she said. She followed Edek. They walked for several minutes, and then Edek broke into a run. "Don't run, Dad," she shouted. "It's raining and you could slip." Edek kept running. He ran across a vast empty field. He ran, with his small, short steps. Ruth ran behind him. She was terrified he would fall. She looked behind her. Jerzy was running, too. She could hear his breathlessness.

A group of teenagers suddenly materialized. They had been in one of the barracks. They were Israeli, Ruth realized. They all looked very subdued. One of them was carrying a large Israeli flag. It was almost an act of defiance to carry this flag, Ruth thought. They were defying anyone to object. Ruth was glad the Israeli kids were there. She felt calmed by their presence.

Edek was waving to her. He was standing outside one of the wooden barracks. Ruth started to tremble. Was this where Edek was housed? Was this the barracks he had lived in, if "lived" was the right word for the days and nights that he existed in this netherworld. These decrepit wooden barracks, which were built to house fifty-two horses, housed up to a thousand men. The men slept on a bare concrete floor, squashed together, in rows and rows. Edek was standing at the doorway shaking his head. "This was my barracks, Ruthie," he said. He shook his head again. "I did not think I would come again, here, to these barracks," he said. He paused. "Come in," he said. Edek issued his invitation to her almost in the manner of a host inviting a guest into his house.

Ruth stepped in. Edek walked in behind her. As soon he was inside the door, he let out a loud gasp. Ruth was startled. She turned around. "It is everything exactly the same," Edek said. "Exactly the same." Ruth looked around her. She couldn't believe she was standing in Auschwitz-Birkenau, in the very barracks her father had been in. The long rectangular barracks had large wooden doors at each end. There were several holes in the doors. The wind was coming through the holes. "The doors was like this when I was here," Edek said. "In winter it was shocking."

The light in the barracks came from a small skylight high up on the walls, near the ceiling. There was one fireplace and a chimney at each end of the barracks. A brick flue ran down the length of the barracks. "The smoke from the fireplace was supposed to pass through here," Edek said, pointing to the flue, "and it was supposed to heat up the barracks."

"Did it?" said Ruth.

Edek laughed, grimly. "Of course not," he said. "We was frozen. Every morning there was many dead frozen men." Ruth started shivering. Edek ran to the far end of the barracks. "I did sleep here, Ruthie," he said, pointing to a spot in the middle of the left side of the barracks. He stood there, staring at the empty spot where he had slept as a twenty-six-year-old. A tall, five foot ten twenty-six-year-old, who already weighed less than eighty pounds and was going to weigh even less. Ruth felt overwhelmed.

It was very quiet in the barracks. Ruth could feel the absence. And the presence. The presence of all of those poor young men. She knew they were young. Mostly under forty. She knew the older ones had been weeded out in the selection process on their arrival. Ruth couldn't stop shivering. She could feel the calamity in the air.

The rain leaked through the wooden roof. Everything was as gray as it must have been then. These barracks still held the horror. She could hear the horror in the silence. It was palpable. It hadn't vanished. A four- or five-inch gap was at the top of the doors at the back and front of the barracks. Edek was standing at the back door. "It was just like this," he said. "I remember it like it was yesterday. I did sleep in the middle not to be so close to the door. I was lucky."

Ruth wanted to ask him how he managed to hold on to his spot on the floor in the middle of the barracks, but she didn't want to bother him with small questions. "Nobody did want to sleep in the middle," Edek said. "You could get badly crushed." He must have read her mind, Ruth thought. He must have known what she was thinking. The wooden walls were damp with rain. Puddles of water were on the floor. "It was not so wet in the middle," Edek said.

Ruth looked at Edek. He looked tired. He was walking slowly along the length of the barracks. He looked enveloped in the silence. The cadaverous quiet of all of those who were gone. Ruth sat down on the brick flue. She was still trembling. She wanted to cry. "You want to see where the toilets was, Ruthie, or maybe not?" Edek said after a few minutes.

"I want to see everything," she said.

"You are a funny girl, Ruthie," he said. He took her arm. She thought that he was pleased she wanted to see the toilet block.

Jerzy had been waiting outside. He looked impatient, as though they had taken too long. Ruth and Edek walked past two more of the wooden barracks, and then stopped. Jerzy, who was walking behind them, also stopped.

"Forty-five buildings made of brick have survived in Birkenau," Jerzy said. "And twenty-two buildings of wood."

"Here is the toilets," Edek said.

All three of them went inside. What looked like three broad concrete benches ran in parallel lines along the length of these barracks. The top of each of the concrete constructions had hole after hole cut out of the top of the bench. The holes were the size of a dinner plate. Not one of the new, large decorative dinner plates it was fashionable to use now. Just an average-size dinner plate. There was not much space between the holes. They almost touched each other.

The holes, Ruth knew, were where the prisoners sat, in the brief time they were allowed for their ablutions. Although "ablutions" was not the right word, Ruth thought. This is where they had to defecate and urinate in a very short period of time, while Kapos screamed and urged more speed. And other prisoners, diseased and starving, jostled for their turn before their bowels and bladders emptied where they were standing. Thirty-four circles were cut out of the top of each block. They were inches apart. It was impossible not to touch the person next to you. Everyone had diarrhea. The surface of the concrete was always wet and slippery.

Edek was standing in front of the concrete benches that had passed for latrines. He was shaking his head. Ruth hoped that he wasn't remembering anything overwhelmingly horrific. Then, she realized there was nothing but overwhelmingly horrific memories in these barracks, in the other barracks, in the camp. There were no quiet moments. No better days, no pleasant afternoons. Every second of every minute was unbearable. No wonder that anyone who had survived had been surprised to find themselves still alive after all that horror. Years later some of those who had survived were still not sure that they were alive. Part of them had remained behind with the dead. Always attached, always affixed to that terror. Even in their dreams. No matter how hard they tried, they couldn't retreat. There was no exit. No way out. They couldn't absent themselves. They couldn't leave.

Ruth looked into the holes. There were scraps of what looked like dried mud, dust particles, and normal debris. She wondered if anyone had cleaned these toilets out. She assumed they must have been cleaned. She peered in again. Whose lives were these specks remnants of? With DNA testing today, they could probably tell who had been here. Her father had been here. Was anything of him left in the bottom of this pit? The thought made her feel sick.

Ruth counted the holes. Two hundred men could relieve themselves at the same time on these holes. "Relief" was not the right word to use here, she decided. The pit underneath the holes must have filled up fast, she thought.

"It was full nearly to the top," Edek said. He made a face and shuddered at the memory. "It was shocking," he said. "So shocking I cannot believe it did happen to me. Sometimes I do think it must have happened to someone else."

Ruth felt bilious. She looked at Edek. He didn't look too well. She felt worried. She was starting to sweat despite the cold. She thought of Martina and her cool, blond hair. Why was she thinking of Martina now? she wondered. Her mother would have liked Martina. Rooshka admired blue eyes and blond hair. "She has such beautiful blue eyes," Rooshka would say, or, "Look how beautiful is her blond hair." The looks Rooshka had admired most were so Aryan it had disturbed Ruth. It was as though Rooshka was in accord with the Nazis on that issue. Blue eyes were superior. And blond hair. Still, Ruth thought, it was understandable. The Germans had flung so much shit about dark-haired, dark-eyed Jews, that some of it must have stuck.

Ruth was struck by the fact that she was standing in the latrines, in Birkenau, thinking about shit. Her mother had swallowed that Nazi line about blue eyes and blond hair. Her mother had swallowed that Nazi shit. What a sentence. Ruth reeled. The sentence had winded her. Images of her mother swallowing shit filled her head. She bent over. She felt so sick. She quickly moved closer to one of the holes. She started vomiting. She vomited and vomited. When she finally stood up, she was surprised that she could still stand. She couldn't believe what had just happened to her. She had vomited so many times on this trip to Poland. She must have been making up for a lack of vomiting in her previous forty-two years. She wondered if people had a fixed quota of vomiting that they had to get through. She hoped she had fulfilled hers. She couldn't bear to go through this again.

She felt terrible. She straightened herself up. She was sure she must smell of vomit. Jerzy was standing in front of her. He looked horrified. The look of horror on his face almost made Ruth laugh. She would have laughed if she hadn't felt so weak. Edek looked worried. He put his arm around Ruth. "Are you all right, Ruthie darling?" he said. He gave her his handkerchief. He patted her on the head. "It is all right, Ruthie," he said. "It is all right." He held her arm as they walked back to the car.

Jerzy drove them back to Auschwitz.

"You want me to pay him?" Edek said to Ruth.

"No," she said. "I'll pay him."

They got out of the car. Ruth paid Jerzy.

"I hope I was a satisfactory guide for you," Jerzy said. He counted the money Ruth had given him. He looked bothered.

"Did you give him a tip?" Edek asked Ruth.

"No," Ruth said. Edek gave Jerzy twenty zlotys.

"You was satisfactory," Edek said to him.

Edek was quiet in the taxi on the way home. Ruth was glad of the silence. She had to collect herself. Collect herself. What strange words. Where did she think she had left herself? In Auschwitz? They were nearly at the Hotel Mimoza, when Edek looked at her. "You did not eat your pears," he said. "But maybe now is not the time to eat pears. You can have something to eat later." Ruth drank some more of her water.

Ruth and Edek walked through the front door of the Hotel Mimoza. Ruth felt a bit better now. She was so relieved to be feeling better. She looked up. Zofia and Walentyna were sitting side by side, on a sofa, in the lobby. Zofia was dressed in a deep red cotton shirt. The first few buttons of the shirt were undone. Even from the front door, Zofia's cleavage was visible. Zofia's breasts were lifting up and down, gently, with her breath. The red shirt was tucked into a straight, bright white skirt. The tan on Zofia's polished, bare legs gleamed. This was winter in Poland, Ruth thought. Zofia was dressed as though she was on her way to St. Tropez.

Walentyna was wearing a blue dress. Ruth felt a terrible pang of sadness for Walentyna. Clearly, no one had ever told her she should never wear sleeves gathered at the shoulder. Women as petite as Walentyna shouldn't have any puckers in their clothes, let alone a giant, billowing balloon of fabric, puffing out into a sleeve, on the top of each shoulder. Zofia spotted Edek. She got up and ran toward him, a concerned expression across her face.

"My poor lamb, my angel," Zofia said in Polish to Edek. She put her arm through Edek's arm. "How on God's earth did you survive that trip?" she said. "How are you feeling?" Ruth wondered if she had heard that correctly. Her poor lamb? Her angel? Edek wasn't hers. What was "angel" in Polish? *Anioł. Aniołek* was the diminutive. *Mój biedny aniołek.* My poor angel. Yes, that was what Zofia had said.

Zofia took the arm she had linked through Edek's arm away. She stood in front of Edek and looked at him. Then, in a brisk movement, she threw both of her arms around Edek. "My poor, poor angel," she said. Edek looked startled, but pleased. "I am fine," he said. "Fine." "I don't believe it," Zofia said. She pressed herself against Edek's body. "You have to be looked after, after such an experience," Zofia said. Ruth couldn't believe what she was witnessing. "You need something to eat," Zofia said. "To face such terrible memories and tragedy takes a lot out of even a big strong man like you."

Ruth thought that Zofia might be upsetting Edek. She was about to interrupt when she noticed that Edek looked much more cheerful than he had when they had arrived back at the hotel a few minutes ago. "You need something to eat my poor lamb," Zofia said. There it was, again. Zofia was staking a claim. *Moja biedna owieczka*. My poor lamb. Ruth felt stunned by the brazenness, the directness. Women in New York could take a lesson from Zofia, she thought. In New York, women went out of their way not to appear too interested in a man. Showing too much interest in a single man was considered the kiss of death in New York. Ruth was speechless with admiration. She stood there looking at Zofia and Edek. A big strong man like you? Or, a poor angel? Which one was it? Was it a contradiction? Or could Edek encompass both? Edek seemed to be encompassing Zofia. She was hugging him again.

Walentyna caught up with them. "I am so glad you are back, dear Edek," she said. "We were worried."

"We were very worried," Zofia said. "We were waiting here for two and a half hours. I didn't want to go anywhere. I did want to be here when you got back."

"I also didn't want to go anywhere," Walentyna said.

The spectacle of Zofia and Walentyna and their concern for Edek almost erased some of the morning's worst images. Images of her mother, and the image of the Vistula River choked with ash, and the image of herself vomiting into the latrines, began to recede. Zofia and Walentyna's studious concern was overpowering. Zofia and Walentyna were both clucking around Edek. Ruth was on the verge of laughter. She was amazed that she could find anything funny. But this was funny. Two grown women competing for an elderly man. Ruth thought that they were competing. She thought Walentyna was still in the competition.

"Come and eat," Zofia said to Edek. "We will have a little fish and a little liverwurst. I noticed yesterday how much you did like liverwurst."

"I noticed, also," Walentyna said.

"Okay," Edek said. "Come on, Ruthie, we deserve to eat after a day like this."

"He deserves to eat," Zofia said.

"He deserves to eat," Walentyna echoed.

"I think I'll go for a walk, Dad," Ruth said. "You go and have a bite to eat. I think I need some fresh air."

Edek looked miserable. "Come, just for a few minutes," he said. "Please, Ruthie, you do need to eat. You did bring up all the bananas from Auschwitz and you did not eat the pears."

"You can buy bananas and pears in Auschwitz?" Zofia said.

"No," Edek said. "Ruthie did bring them to Auschwitz, in the car. Then she did bring some bananas up in Auschwitz and she did bring the pears back in the car."

Zofia and Walentyna looked bewildered. "She did bring up the bananas when she was in Auschwitz and she did bring the pears back," Edek said to the two women. He said this with a finality. As though this explanation would clear up the matter. Both women looked perplexed.

"She did eat pears in Auschwitz and bring bananas back from Auschwitz?" Zofia said.

"No, she did bring the pears back," Edek said.

"Back up?" Walentyna said.

"No," Edek said. "Back in the car."

"I was a bit sick in Birkenau," Ruth said. "And I am fine now."

"I thought it was Auschwitz you were sick in," Zofia said.

"Auschwitz-Birkenau," Ruth said. If she talked about this subject any longer, Ruth thought, she could well be sick again.

"What is the difference?" Edek said. "She is better now. And that is the main thing."

"That is the main thing," Zofia said.

"That is the main thing," said Walentyna.

Ruth really didn't want to sit in the lounge with Zofia and Walentyna. Their company felt too robust for the way she felt at the moment. She wanted to be quiet.

"Please, Ruthie, you do need something to eat," Edek said. "You did vomit up everything what you did eat."

"She did vomit?" Zofia said.

"You vomited?" Walentyna said to Ruth.

"Yes, but I am fine now," Ruth said.

"Probably it was that birdseed what you did eat what did make you sick," Edek said.

Ruth was trying to work out how to extricate herself from this situation with grace. She felt trapped in a spiraling kaleidoscope of bananas and pears and vomit and birdseed.

"You need some dry bread and a cup of tea," Zofia said.

"Perfect," said Edek.

"I was going to say this, too," Walentyna said. "Dry bread and tea with lemon."

"Not tea with lemon, Walentyna," Zofia said. "Tea without lemon. Lemon is no good after vomits."

Walentyna deferred to Zofia's expertise on the subject of post-vomits remedies. What a horrible word "vomits" was, Ruth thought. She forced herself not to conjure up a picture of several vomits, lying next to each other on a road or some other surface. Ruth could see that she would have to capitulate. She couldn't hold out on her own against Walentyna, Zofia, and Edek.

"I'll join you for a little while," she said. Edek looked happy. All four of them walked to the lounge. Ruth chose the armchair farthest from Edek. This allowed Zofia and Walentyna to sit on either side of him.

Zofia ordered pickled herring, smoked mackerel, sardines, liverwurst, cheese, and a platter of potato salad. She also ordered some dry biscuits for Ruth. "Dry biscuits will be better for you than dry bread," Zofia said. Ruth was pleased. The thought of dry bread hadn't been appetizing to her. Zofia and Walentyna were beaming at Edek. Edek looked happy, too. Ruth suddenly felt grateful to the two women. Grateful to them for saving Edek from the slump that could have overcome him after Auschwitz.

"Thank you for waiting for my father," Ruth said to Zofia and Walentyna.

"We were waiting for you, also," Walentyna said.

"Thank you," said Ruth.

"You seem like a very nice young woman," Zofia said to Ruth. Ruth was pleased to be called young. She didn't feel too young. She thought of people in their twenties as young. Not people her age.

"How old are you, Ruthie?" Zofia said. An irritability crept up on Ruth. She wished Zofia wouldn't call her Ruthie. She felt mean feeling annoyed with Zofia. It was unkind of her. And erratic. One minute she was feeling gratitude to Zofia and in the next instant, annoyance. This was not admirable, she told herself.

"She is thirty-eight," Edek said.

"She looks very young for thirty-eight," Walentyna said. Edek looked pleased. He nodded in agreement.

"She is a pretty girl," he said. "Like her mother." Both women nodded.

"I'm forty-three, Dad," Ruth said. Edek could never remember her age. He had thought she was twelve for several years. He had managed to keep count of her years from twenty to thirty. Then, he had become stuck on thirty. For four years he thought she was thirty. Now, he had clearly lost track of her age again.

"She looks very very young for forty-three," Zofia said to Edek.

"Thank you," said Ruth.

Zofia squinted at Ruth. Ruth realized that Zofia was looking at her cheek. She put her hand up to her cheek. The bite was still there. Still swollen. Sometimes her bites calmed down after the initial swelling. But not this one. This one still felt hot and angry.

"What happened to your face?" Zofia said.

"She did get a bite from a fly," Edek said.

"A bite from a fly?" Zofia said. "In winter?"

"In winter?" said Walentyna.

"It was a big fly," Edek said.

"It is not normal to have a big fly in winter," Zofia said.

"Maybe this fly stayed after the summer because he heard it was going to be a mild winter," Ruth said. Both women looked at her.

"It was a mild winter, that is true," Walentyna said.

"How could a fly know this?" Zofia said.

"My daughter does say sometimes crazy things," Edek said.

"It was not so crazy," Walentyna said. "It was funny."

"Yes," said Zofia. "It is funny to think like this about a fly." Both women laughed.

Zofia squinted at Ruth again. "It does not look good," she said.

"No," said Edek.

"No," said Walentyna.

"The swelling will have gone down a bit by the morning," Ruth said. "We don't have to discuss it anymore," Ruth said to Edek. Zofia got the message. She leaned across to Ruth and changed the subject.

"You are not married?" she said to Ruth.

"No," Ruth said.

"She was married," Edek said. "But she did get divorced."

"Twice," said Ruth, before her father could add that detail.

"Two times?" Zofia said.

"Three times," said Edek. Both women looked at Ruth.

"The third time was to get a green card, a visa to live in America. That doesn't count," Ruth said.

"It was a marriage," said Edek.

"It was a ceremony," Ruth said.

"She was divorced three times," Edek said.

Walentyna and Zofia looked at Ruth admiringly. Ruth smiled. Ruth could see their admiration was based on the fact that she managed to get three men to marry her.

"She is not such an easy type, my daughter," Edek said. Ruth groaned. She knew she was going to hear a replay of why she shouldn't have left the marriages. Why a married woman was always better off than a single woman. "It is better for a woman if she is with a man," Edek said. Both women nodded vehemently.

"It is better if she is with the right man," Ruth said. Zofia and Walentyna nodded even more vigorously. "It's not better if she is with the wrong man," Ruth added.

"Okay, okay, I am not going to argue with you," Edek said. "She does win every argument," he said to Zofia and Walentyna. "She should have been a lawyer. She would be better than Perry Mason." The reference to Perry Mason was lost on Zofia and Walentyna, but they agreed with Edek anyway.

"I can see she is a clever girl," Zofia said.

"She is clever about some things," Edek said. Oh, no, Ruth thought. What was she going to have to listen to now? "She does marry such types what likes her, but not too much," Edek said. "She does not like them too much, too. The types what like her very much, she does not want to be with. She is nervous to be with someone what she does like too much."

Zofia and Walentyna shook their heads in sympathy with Edek's plight about his daughter's predilection for partnerships that were less than they could be. Edek's analysis had startled Ruth. Edek had not been far off the mark. This was not bad for a man who had never seen a therapist or read a psychological journal. In New York, this sort of insight could almost qualify you to set up practice as a therapist. There seemed to be therapists who were former singers, therapists who were art dealers on the side, therapists who were also actors. New York had a therapist for everyone.

"Am I right, Ruthie?" Edek said. Ruth nodded her head. If she didn't feel too attached to a partner, it saved her a lot of anxiety. Anxiety about their health, anxiety about accidents, anxiety about losing them. Attachment made her feel fearful. Fearful of losing the person she was too attached to. Ruth thought it was probably a common problem and could account for the high percentage of mismatched partners.

"I had a friend with this problem," Walentyna said.

"Did she leave her husband?" Edek said.

"No," said Walentyna.

"My daughter does leave her husbands," Edek said. Ruth was just about to laugh. An image of herself perpetually leaving a series of husbands came into her head. Just as the laugh was about to come out, she realized that every one of the men in her picture had been Garth. She felt annoyed at herself for thinking about Garth. It was her father's fault. He was the one who was still connected to Garth.

"My daughter is not such a column type," Edek said to Zofia and Walentyna. Ruth was about to explain that he meant calm, when both women nodded.

"She looks column to me," Zofia said.

"I think so, also," Walentyna said.

"She does always look column," Edek said. "But inside she is never column."

"Your father is a very clever man," Zofia said.

"Very, very, clever," Walentyna said.

The food arrived. Ruth was grateful for the distraction. "It does look beautiful," Edek said, looking at the platter of food in front of him.

"Edek dear, start with a little piece of herring," Zofia said, as she lifted several strips of herring onto Edek's plate. Zofia seemed to be in charge of the food. She put a selection of mackerel and sardines on Walentyna's plate. "Walentyna likes mackerel very much," Zofia said to Edek. Then she handed Ruth a plate with half a dozen dry biscuits on it. "Ruthie darling," she said. "Eat the biscuits. You will feel better."

Ruth sat back in her chair. Zofia's endearments were escalating. It was now "Edek dear," and "Ruthie darling." Walentyna had a long way to go if she wanted to catch up with Zofia. "Is the mackerel good?" Ruth asked Walentyna. Walentyna nodded. Ruth realized she had asked the question at an inopportune moment. Walentyna had a mouthful of the mackerel she was eating. Walentyna looked embarrassed. She tried to finish the fish in her mouth quickly. "The mackerel is very nice," Walentyna said, still chewing the remnants of some mackerel, nervously. "It's very nice mackerel," Zofia added.

Ruth looked at Zofia. Zofia had nearly as much food on her plate as Edek had on his. Ruth was sure that what she was looking at on Zofia's plate was a kilo of herring.

"Eat, Ruthie, eat," Zofia said.

"Yes, Ruthie, you do need to eat," said Edek. Edek and Zofia beamed at their shared agreement on what Ruth should do. Ruth thought that Walentyna looked slightly left out.

"My daughter does have her own business," Edek said. "She does make a lot of money in this business."

Ruth decided not to argue this point with Edek again. He always dismissed her protests anyway.

"You told us this already," Zofia said. "What is the business?"

"She does write letters for people," Edek said.

"Letters?" said Zofia.

"Letters," Edek said. "It is a big business. In America many people do not know how to write a letter."

"Really?" said Zofia. "It is not so hard to write a letter."

"American people are not like European people," Walentyna said.

"Of course," said Zofia.

Ruth was about to point out that some letters were hard to write, but she decided against it. The perplexing nature of her business was giving Edek and the two women too much pleasure.

"She does write many times very complicated letters," Edek said.

"Oh," both women said, with obvious relief that there was an explanation for both Ruth's business and what had appeared to be the oddities of Americans.

"She does write business letters," Edek said. "And letters for dead people."

"Dead people?" Zofia said, looking bothered.

"Condolence letters, my father means," Ruth said.

"Oh," said Walentyna. "A condolence letter is not easy to write." Zofia agreed.

"She does write also love letters," Edek said. Both women leaned forward.

"Love letters," Walentyna said. "It is very hard to write a love letter."

"I know this of course, too," Zofia said. The dry biscuits had settled Ruth's stomach. Taken away her queasiness.

"The biscuits have made me feel much better," Ruth said.

"Good," Zofia and Edek said in unison.

"Good," Walentyna said, a minute later.

Edek had moved on to the liverwurst. His portion must have stripped the livers of several pigs or cows or whatever animal the livers had come from, Ruth thought. Edek's portion was enormous. He was eating the liverwurst without the aid of bread. Ruth admired his digestive system. It must be one of the world's best, she thought. Zofia was eating a large helping of potato salad. Walentyna was still eating her mackerel. Ruth felt sorry for Walentyna. She thought about asking Walentyna if she would like to join her for a walk around the old city. Then she thought the better of it. It would not be a good idea, she decided, to leave Zofia alone with her father.

"You could write very good advertisements for people to meet," Zofia said to Ruth.

"Zofia means lonely hearts advertisements," Walentyna said.

"Lonely hearts?" Edek said.

"When people advertise to meet another person," Zofia said.

"I know what you mean," Edek said. "When a man does write an advertisement for a woman he does want. He says he is looking for tall and short and that sort of stuff."

"That's right," Zofia and Walentyna said.

"You could make a lot of money," Zofia said. "There are many lonely people."

Edek agreed. "There are many people what are lonely."

"Edek is lonely, I am sure," Zofia said.

"He is not," Ruth said. She was surprised at the reply that had come out of her mouth. Why did she say that? Of course Edek was lonely. He just never admitted it.

"Sometimes I am lonely," Edek said. Ruth was surprised to hear Edek say he was sometimes lonely.

"My poor lamb," Zofia said to Edek, in Polish. She patted Edek on the hand. Edek smiled at Zofia.

"It is a very good suggestion what Zofia made," Edek said. Ruth was startled. Which of Zofia's suggestions or suggestive behavior was Edek responding to? "This suggestion for the people what are needing lonely letters," Edek said. Zofia beamed.

"They're called singles ads in America, and they're very cheap," Ruth said. "It wouldn't be a good market for my sort of business."

Zofia's face fell. Ruth felt mean. She needn't have said anything. It had been unnecessary of her to point out that singles ads were not the right venue for her business.

"Have some potato salad, Edek," Zofia said. "The potato salad is very good."

"Okay," said Edek. Zofia spooned eight or ten spoonfuls of the potato salad onto Edek's plate. Ruth felt bad for dampening the atmosphere. "Do either of you have children?" she said to Zofia and Walentyna.

"I have one child, a son," Walentyna said.

"Walentyna's son is a good son," Zofia said. Walentyna looked happy.

"He is forty-three, like you," Walentyna said.

"But he is married," Zofia said. Ruth laughed.

"I'm not looking for anybody," she said. Particularly not a Pole, she added to herself.

"He is nearly a grandfather," Walentyna said.

"Walentyna is nearly a great-grandmother," Zofia said. "Can you believe this? Our small, little Walentyna nearly a great-grandmother." Walentyna looked confused. As though part of her knew that Zofia's comments were not quite complimentary, and the other part had been ready to acknowledge the nicety.

"Zofia doesn't have children," Walentyna said.

"I did want to have my own life," Zofia said.

"Zofia is a woman ahead of her time," Ruth said to Edek.

"What thanks do you get from children?" Zofia said.

That was a distinctly Jewish sentiment, Ruth thought, and Jewish phrasing. Maybe Zofia had some Jewish blood despite her blondness and her athleticism.

"I am not happy with Ruthie that she does not have children," Edek said. "I would like still to have a grandchild." Ruth was not happy with the turn this conversation was taking. She didn't really think Edek wanted a grandchild. He just wanted to see her settled into a relationship. With Garth, preferably.

"Ruthie nearly can't have children," Zofia said to Edek. "She is forty-three. If she wants to have children she has to find someone straightaway."

"There is someone," Edek said.

"Oh?" said Zofia.

"Dad, please don't go into that," Ruth said.

"I will tell you later," Edek said to Zofia.

"I don't want children," Ruth said to make sure the conversation about Garth remained truncated.

"I can understand why Ruthie feels like this," Zofia said. "There is no guarantee with a child. You don't know what you will get. Walentyna is lucky, she got a nice son. But I have seen nice mothers with terrible children and terrible mothers with nice children." Ruth felt a sudden affinity with Zofia.

"I feel exactly that way," she said. Zofia smiled. Edek looked unhappy.

"Children are good," Edek said after a minute. "Where would I be without my daughter?" He produced this argument in favor of children with a flourish.

"With me, in Sopot," Zofia said. She patted him on the arm.

Walentyna looked disconcerted and began to fidget with her hair. Edek helped himself to more potato salad. Zofia's retort clearly hadn't disturbed him. It had unnerved Ruth. Ruth looked at Zofia. Zofia seemed oblivious to the frisson of nervous surprise her reply had elicited. Ruth decided it was time for her to leave. She looked at her father. "I'm going to go for a walk," she said. "Do you want to come with me?" Both women looked anxiously at Edek.

"No, Ruthie," he said. "I will stay here and finish my potato salad."

"I'll call you in your room when I get back," she said.

It had stopped raining. Ruth was glad. She didn't like walking in the rain. Even with a raincoat and an umbrella, rain made her feel damp. Flattened. She needed this walk. She needed to clear her head. She walked around the old city. The old city was small. Eight hundred and seventy-two yards wide and thirteen hundred yards long. Every street in the old city was charming. Pretty. There were lots of young people out walking and sitting in cafés. Groups of students talking. The young seemed to mingle easily with the older generation, the middle-aged and the elderly.

Most of the cafés were full. The people inside were looking at each other with such intensity, Ruth thought. They looked each other in the eye, with a direct unflinching gaze. In New York, people looked distracted, whether they were on their own or with someone else. Ruth was mesmerized by the way people talked to each other here. The conversations seemed passionate and emotional. Was this just Kraków? Or had she not seen this side of Warsaw and Łódź? Maybe there was a similar vitality and intensity in Warsaw, she thought, but definitely not in Łódź. No one in Łódź had this much life in them.

She looked at the people sitting in the window of a café in Kanonicza Street. There were women talking earnestly to other women, men talking to men, and men and women talking. Everyone was engaged. As though the conversation really mattered. In New York, Ruth thought, people were often looking over their shoulders or at their watch. You didn't see this sort of passion. You didn't see it between acquaintances, friends, or lovers.

There were still lovers in Kraków. Ruth had been struck by that the minute she had arrived. Couples walked around hand in hand or gazed into each other's eyes. Couples kissed passionately in public. Ruth wondered if the abundance of lovers was a consequence of people having access to less. Polish people had less money, fewer distractions, fewer possessions, fewer prospects. They didn't have that much. Was that the reason they still had love? If only the love lasted, she thought, thinking of the posters of the battered wives and battered children. In New York, people had everything else. They had to look for love in the singles pages of local newspapers.

Ruth passed a store with more wooden Jews in the window. A large sign above the carved Jews said, in capital letters, SOUVENIRS. What were these souvenirs of? A community of dead Jews? Ruth didn't think so. She didn't think most Poles were missing them. Suddenly, Ruth wanted to go to synagogue. She knew it was an irrational desire. What good would it do her or anyone else if she went to synagogue? Still she wanted to go. It was Friday, there would be a *Shabat* service at the Remuh Synagogue. She looked at her watch. If she hurried back to the hotel, she would just have time.

Edek was in exactly the same position she had left him in. She couldn't believe that they were all still there. All the food was gone. The empty plates were in front of them.

"Back so quickly?" Zofia said.

"I've been more than an hour," Ruth said. "I came back," she said to Edek, "because I want to go to synagogue."

"To synagogue?" Edek said. "What for?"

"I don't know," she said.

"Sit down, Ruthie, and have a cup of tea," he said.

"Have a cup of tea," Zofia said.

"I want to go to synagogue," she said.

There was a silence. All three of them looked at her. She felt as though she had intruded and disbanded everyone's happiness. The silence was as uncomfortable as if she had burped loudly or farted.

"Synagogue?" Zofia said.

"We do never go to synagogue," Edek said.

"I would just like to go tonight," Ruth said. "It's a very sweet, small synagogue," she said to Zofia. As though the size of the synagogue would make it appear more harmless.

"It is not so bad to go to synagogue," Walentyna said. "I go to church sometimes."

"I never go to church," Zofia said firmly.

"We do never go to synagogue," Edek said.

"Don't worry, Dad," Ruth said. "You stay here and enjoy Zofia's and Walentyna's company. I'll go on my own." She knew that pitching herself against Zofia and Walentyna might move Edek to declare his loyalty. She was right.

"I will go with you, of course," Edek said.

"Of course," Zofia said. "He is a very good father," she said to Ruth.

"I know that," Ruth said. She wasn't sure why she wanted Edek to accompany her. Maybe she just wanted him away from Zofia and Walentyna. She thought he must be tired.

"Maybe I will see you later," Zofia said to Edek, nudging him with her shoulder.

"We'll be home late," Ruth said.

"This is such a small synagogue," Edek said to Ruth. "They not going to have a service what lasts hours."

"Good," said Zofia.

"You must be very tired, Dad," Ruth said. "You've had an exhausting day. You need to get a good night's sleep."

"Of course," Walentyna said.

"Edek is a strong man," Zofia said. "He does not look tired."

"I am okay," Edek said.

"Well, I am going straight to bed as soon as I get back," Ruth said.

"That is a good idea," Zofia said, before Ruth could add that she felt her father should do the same.

"Good night," Ruth said to Zofia and Walentyna. Edek and Zofia and Walentyna stood up. Walentyna and Zofia shook hands with Ruth.

"Good night," both women said to her. Walentyna patted Edek on the back. "You have a good night and a good rest," she said to him.

"Good night, Edek dear," Zofia said. She gave him a small peck on the cheek.

"Good night, ladies," Edek said.

"Thanks for coming with me," Ruth said to Edek in the taxi.

"It is okay," he said. He looked at her. "Did you eat something more than those biscuits what you had?" he said.

"No," she said. "But I'm not really hungry." He shook his head.

"You do not eat enough," he said. Edek was right, she wasn't eating much. She must be losing weight, she thought. She felt the waistband of her skirt. Even sitting down, it felt loose. Definitely loose. She was pleased. There must be a bonus to be had out of all of this. She would weigh herself as soon as she got back to Manhattan, she thought.

There were fifteen to twenty people at the Remuh Synagogue. Even in a synagogue as small as the Remuh, fifteen to twenty people still didn't look like many. Ruth felt disappointed. What was she hoping for? A crowd. The sort of crowd who were already filing into the Samson Restaurant across the square for the twice-nightly cabaret? Ruth counted the people who had turned up for the service. There were eighteen people, including the rabbi.

Ruth and Edek stood in the entrance of the synagogue for a few minutes. A man from Idaho introduced himself. "I come here every year," he said to Ruth and Edek. "I grew up in a village not far from here, Tokarnia," the man said. "Near the mountains. We used to walk in the mountains every day. Me and my mother and father," he said. "From there we went to the ghetto in Płaszów and then to Auschwitz," he said, pulling up his sleeve and displaying the familiar inked number. "I don't know why I come here," he said. "I come here every year. And every year, after two or three days I want to leave."

"Where is everyone?" a woman said to Ruth and Edek. Ruth knew what she meant. Where was the congregation? "Dead," Ruth said. The woman, a woman from California, in her fifties, looked shocked. "Of course," she said. There were three other Americans and a Canadian at the synagogue. All of them looked bewildered. "Where is the congregation?" the Canadian man said. He was about Ruth's age. "Dead," Ruth said. The man looked stunned.

"Ruthie, maybe you should not put it this way," Edek said to her when the Canadian man had walked away.

"What other way is there to put it?" she said. "I can't say they're vacationing in the Bahamas."

Edek shook his head, but laughed in spite of himself. "You for sure cannot say that," he said. The only Poles present in the synagogue were old. They didn't look Jewish to Ruth. But they must have been. No old Pole would be attending *Shabat* services in a synagogue, she thought.

Ruth went into the back room of the synagogue with the rest of the women. The room was at the end of a small passage, and was quite dark. It felt airless. Ruth tried to open one of the windows, but it was jammed shut. It looked as though it hadn't been opened in decades. Ruth went back to her seat. In this small airless room in the back of the synagogue, Ruth could feel herself starting to relax. She realized she had left her bag, unattended, on a seat, several seats away. She was obviously letting down her guard. She realized how rigidly she had been holding every part of herself. Her body felt almost limp now.

She looked through the small window to see if she could see Edek. Edek was in the main room of the synagogue with the other men. The window in between the rooms was covered with old lace curtains. Ruth could hardly see through them. She couldn't see Edek. She looked around her. The woman from California was still crying. Ruth hoped that the Canadian man was okay. She felt momentarily bad, but there was nothing else she could have said to either of them. The Californian woman blew her nose.

"It's only by being here, in Poland," she said to Ruth, "that you really can absorb what happened. There really are no Jews here," the woman said, and shook her head.

"We're all here searching for something," Ruth said. "Going from cemetery to cemetery. From absence to absence. All of us looking for the presence of people who are no longer present." The woman started crying again.

Ruth wished she hadn't said anything. She leaned back in the pew. It was such a relief not to be clenching her face, her jaw, her teeth. Not to have tense arms and legs. She felt as though she could fall asleep. The service was short. She met Edek outside afterward.

"It was not a bad service," Edek said.

"Thanks again for coming, Dad," Ruth said.

"I did enjoy it," Edek said. He rubbed his hands together, in the cold. "Let us go home," he said.

~ *Chapter Fifteen* ~

*R*uth woke up. For a moment she thought that she was in her apartment on Fourteenth Street. She looked at the floral wallpaper on the walls and realized that she must be in Poland. Still. She felt terrible. She felt as though she hadn't slept. Her head was scrambled with random thoughts and images. Unarranged, unsorted, ungraded thoughts. All anxiety-provoking.

She sat up in bed. She had to get rid of this anxiety. There was nothing to fear. The formless, amorphous world of her dreams was not her world. She was here in the very expensive Hotel Mimoza. She was able to pay for this very expensive hotel because she had the ability to think clearly. To sort out other people's concerns and to articulate them. In her wallet, in the third drawer of the bureau, was an American Express card, a MasterCard, a Visa card, and a Diner's Club card. She was a purposeful person. She was not a lost soul.

Then she remembered her dream. In her dream, her soul had slipped out of her. It had slipped out with the ease of words leaving lips. A slippery, swift ease. As though it had been oiled or anointed. It had happened in an instant. One minute she had been intact, the next minute her soul was hovering above her. She could see its outline, in the dream. It was the same height as her. The same shape. But it looked lighter. It lacked the heaviness of living bodies. It was diaphanous. It floated. But it was her. Her mirror image. An imprint of herself, in the air, floating above her.

She used to have this dream as a child. It used to terrify her. She would be floating, facedown, above herself. For hours. However hard she tried she couldn't get herself back down to the bed again. She always woke from this dream feeling queasy. She had been so relieved when the dream had disappeared. It had seemed to leave her when she was about seventeen or eighteen. An age when she had toughened up. She had dyed her hair jet-black and whitened her face with the palest shade of makeup on the market. She had gone barefoot in the conservative streets of Melbourne, Australia. People had gasped and pointed. She had been a beatnik. On her own. Out of kilter with the culture and the times. Edek used to look at her and cry. Cry at her black-ringed eyes and white lips. "What did happen to my beautiful daughter?" he would say.

Rooshka had maintained a stony silence. She had tolerated the bare feet and the black outfits. Ruth had lost weight, and Rooshka was more pleased about the weight loss than she was distressed at being the mother of a beatnik. Ruth was happy being a beatnik. For the first time she slept through the night, most nights. She didn't wake when Rooshka screamed in her sleep. She didn't have to cover her head with her pillow in order to drown out her mother's shouts. The shouts that were always in Yiddish. Rooshka was shouting to her mother. The mother who went to the right, to the gas, when Rooshka went to the left. Eventually, Ruth got lonely, as a beatnik. No one would join her in reviving the movement. She let her hair color grow out and threw away the white lipstick.

Ruth rubbed her eyes. They felt raw. As though she had been awake all night. Even as a child she had awakened tired from that dream. The face that floated above her in her childhood dream was always somber. It never smiled or laughed. It just hovered above Ruth. Looking at her. All night.

Suddenly, Ruth felt sick. The face in her childhood dream, the face that used to look down on her for hours, at night, was the face in the photograph. The face of Edek's sister Fela's child, Liebala. It was Liebala's face floating above her. Liebala, who looked so like her. Liebala, who was always serious, always solemn, in Ruth's dreams.

Ruth remembered clearly the day the dreams began. It had been her first day in fourth grade. She had been eight years old. The youngest child in grade four. All the other children were nine. Some were ten. She had come home from that first day of the school year exhausted. Some of the boys had been rough with her. It was a working-class area. There were lots of tough kids. Ruth didn't say anything to Rooshka and Edek. Ruth knew even then that a little roughness in the classroom was not comparable to what they had endured. And Rooshka had been happy that day. Happy and proud that Ruth was eight and in grade four.

Eight. That was the age Liebala must have been, in the photographs, Ruth thought. Liebala's face had been less composed in the photographs. In the photographs she had looked more active, more eager, more spirited. In the dreams, Liebala's curls were the only unruly part of her. They sprang out at wayward angles. The rest of Liebala had been still. Still face. Still arms and legs. She had floated quietly. Hovering above Ruth. Hardly moving. In the dreams, Liebala was dressed in layers of a sheer, white, gauze fabric. The fabric floated. Sometimes Ruth could feel the movement of air as the layers of Liebala's dress shifted and moved in the room. Liebala, in her unclouded, gossamer layers, had looked down at Ruth, night after night.

Ruth sat on the bed in her room at the Hotel Mimoza and felt frightened. How could Liebala have been in her dreams? She had never seen Liebala's face. She must have been dreaming about herself. She and Liebala were so similar. So alike. Except for one small detail. Ruth had noticed, in the photograph, that Liebala had a mole on her cheek. Her left cheek. Ruth remembered the mole from her dreams. How could she have known about the mole? She had probably created the mole, Ruth thought, in order to distinguish herself from her nocturnal visitor. She felt her own cheekbones. She didn't have a mole on her cheek. Just an elevated bump where the fly had bitten her.

She tried to calm down. There was nothing frightening about any of this. It was just a dream. And she must have been dreaming about herself. She and Liebala were so alike. She must have transposed the expression on Liebala's face, in the photographs, onto her memories of the face in her dreams. Of course that was it, that was a perfectly reasonable explanation.

She should have a shower, she decided. Hot water and steam often cleared her head after a bad night. A hot shower made her feel internally cleansed, as though the steam had reached her brain and heart and lungs. Hot water seemed to wash some of the mess of bad nights away. It seemed to repair and redress the anarchy. To sanctify and purify. Most of the time, after five minutes in a hot shower, Ruth could feel herself returning. Returning to who she really was.

And who was she, really? she wondered. She was a person in Poland. Who she was was always a vexing question for her. This morning she needed a clear answer. She was Ruth Rothwax, president, CEO, chairman, owner, and director of Rothwax Correspondence. She could run ten miles, with ease. She could bench-press fifty-five pounds. And she was losing weight. Losing weight was always a cheering thought.

Ruth had always had a troubled relationship with her dreams. She had had nightmares about children and babies for years. Children she kept losing. Babies she couldn't look after. The dream in which she gave birth to a damaged baby always left her out of kilter for days. Days later she would find herself trying to work out what was wrong with the baby, and where it had gone. It always disappeared by the end of the dream. Merely thinking about that dream gave her the creeps. Why had that dream come into her head? Just when she had established herself, in her head, as a competent businesswoman. A woman who could wear a suit and bench-press and squat, metaphorically, with the best of them. That was who she was! Not some lost, slipped soul. Inhabited by others.

Where had that sentence come from? She was not inhabited by others. She had managed to separate herself from the mother. From the ghosts of her mother's past. From all of the dead. She was inhabited by her own thoughts and her own imagination. She was inhabited by her own self. The years when she had believed that she had been in Auschwitz were over. She knew that that was her mother's experience, not hers. The years of feeling more aligned with the dead than the living were over. She was living. She was definitely living. Living well.

Ruth was tempted to look at the photographs of Liebala and Hanka and Fela and Juliusz. But she decided against it. This was not the morning to look at the past. This was the morning to look to the future. To being back in her own apartment. In New York. The city had never seemed more like a haven. She corrected herself. The city had never seemed like a haven before. That's what a comparison with Poland could do, she thought. Make any other place look cozy. Cozy and comforting.

She decided that she would wait to look at the photographs until she was back in New York. She would have them framed, she decided, and hang them on a wall. Maybe she would put them on one of the walls in her bedroom. Or maybe they would look better in the living room. She might have them enlarged, too, she thought. That way she could study everybody's features and expressions. She felt excited at that prospect.

She thought about the china. All the plates and bowls and cups and saucers. She wanted to touch the china. To run her fingers around the fluted gold rims. To hold the cup handles. To feel the glaze on the plates. It was going to be overwhelming to own the china. To live with it. To look at it, every day. Ruth couldn't imagine eating from the china. Using it for meals. Her instinct was to preserve it, behind glass, like some museum piece. That was absurd, she thought. She would have to force herself to use it. The cups and saucers and bowls and plates were meant to be used. They had been in constant use, until February 1940. Ruth hoped they hadn't been used since then. She couldn't bear the thought of the stained-toothed old man or his bewigged wife using that beautiful china.

She would use the coat, too, she thought. She would have it altered. She would take it to the tailor on Twelfth Street, between Fifth and Sixth Avenues. She knew he was very expensive. She hoped that his prices reflected quality in his tailoring. She was looking forward to wearing the coat. She thought she would look good in it. Thinking about the coat and the china had lifted her spirits.

Ruth looked at her watch. It was still early. She thought she could fit in half an hour's work before she showered. She knew exactly how long it took her to shower. She knew exactly how long it took her to shower without washing her hair, and how long it took her to shower and wash her hair. She knew exactly how long it took her to shower and dress. She timed everything she did. On the surface, the timing seemed to be aimed at efficiency. But Ruth knew that knowing how long things took was one way of offsetting and avoiding the panic of the unknown. It reassured her to know how long things took. How long it took to walk to the post office or to cook vegetables or eat breakfast or read the paper.

It was an attempt at control, of course. It didn't take a genius to figure that out. Ruth had grown up frightened of the random elements that had arrived in Rooshka's life. Overnight. The errant and erratic events that changed everything. And left Rooshka unnerved, decades later, at anything unexpected or unplanned. A knock at the door or a phone call would cause Rooshka to gasp or tremble.

The world of letters was completely controllable. No one could intrude on a letter. Or disagree. Or do something disagreeable. Today, the quest for control was seen as unhealthy. Ruth had nothing against control. So much of everyone's life was out of control, anyway. Why shouldn't you exercise control when you could?

She got out her notebook. She felt like writing by hand. She couldn't even begin to think about the three hundred and twenty-seven letters John Sharp had ordered. She decided to tackle the thank-you-for-the-introduction-to-the-agent letter. *Dear X*, she wrote. She always addressed her letters to "Dear X." She had to address them to someone. She couldn't write any letters without using the word "dear." Sometimes she began letters with the recipients' names, but mostly she began with "Dear X."

She had tried many times to write without addressing them to anyone first. But couldn't. She couldn't think of anything to say if she wasn't saying it to someone in particular. Even if that person was "X." She looked at the *Dear X* she had written. She added a line. *I want to thank you so much for your generosity*, she wrote. Ruth thought for a minute or two. *And I want you to know that I know that the generosity is in the offer, not the outcome. The introduction, and not what comes of it*. Ruth put her pen down. She couldn't get involved in this letter. She would have to do it another time. She had too many things crowding her head.

She felt her bite again. It was still swollen and inflamed. Why had the fly marked her like this? What a stupid question, she thought. The fly hadn't marked her. It hadn't marked her out of the crowd. It had just bitten her. She felt annoyed to have been bitten by a fly, in Auschwitz. Still, to come out of Auschwitz with only a bite was something other inmates would have prayed for. She stopped herself. It was not other inmates. It was just inmates. She was not an inmate. Others, clearly distinct from her, were there. She was not there. She chided herself for this slip. She was born more than a decade after it was all over. All over for those who died. And all over for those who didn't die. You couldn't really live, after you had been in Auschwitz. Even if you appeared to be living, like others around you, you couldn't live. Parts of you were gone. And would never return. It was hard to live with missing parts.

Ruth showered and dressed. She felt better. More herself. She had chosen a dark, burnished orange dress. She felt like having some color on her. She had been dressing almost entirely in black since the day she arrived in Poland. She thought that she might surprise Edek and have eggs for breakfast. She went downstairs. She looked for Edek among the guests already eating their breakfast. The room was quite full. She couldn't see Edek. She found a table near the buffet. She put her room key on the table and walked to the buffet. They had boiled eggs and scrambled eggs and poached eggs today. This was the first time she had seen poached eggs in Poland. She sat down and waited for Edek. He would probably be here soon, she thought. He was usually punctual for breakfast.

She felt hungry. It was one of the few mornings in Poland that she had felt hungry. She was glad she was hungry. Glad to have her appetite back. She asked the waiter if it was possible to poach her eggs to order rather than take them from the buffet. He said of course. She told him she would wait for her father before placing her order.

Ten minutes later, Edek still hadn't arrived. Ruth had been trying not to feel anxious. Now she was worried. Edek was never late for meals. Auschwitz had probably been too much for him, she thought. And then she had dragged him to a synagogue. Suddenly a full-scale panic took hold of her. Her heart started racing. How could she have just sat here and waited? She should have gone to his room to check up on him the minute he was late.

She ran to the elevator. Dear God, she prayed. Please let my father be all right. The prayer shocked her. Who was she turning into? A person who prayed. She got out of the elevator and ran to Edek's room. She knocked at the door. There was no answer. She felt ill. Dear God, she said, please don't let my father die. She knocked again. She looked around to see if there was a cleaning lady nearby. They usually had keys to all the rooms. She could feel her nausea rising. She knew the trip to Poland was a mistake. Edek hadn't wanted to come. And now look at what had happened.

She was almost breathless. She knocked one last time. She was about to turn and run down to the front desk for help, when she thought she heard a noise in the room. She knocked again, with such force that her knuckles hurt. There was some more noise, and then the door opened. "Good morning, darling," Zofia said to her. Ruth stared at Zofia. What was Zofia doing here? Had she knocked on the door of the wrong room?

All the lopsided, uneven, disconnected, and unrelated pieces of information started to settle. Suddenly, Ruth knew that she hadn't knocked on the door of the wrong room. This was Edek's room. Zofia was in Edek's room. And had been there for quite a while by the look of things. Zofia was half-dressed. Ruth stood there and shook her head. She couldn't believe what she was seeing. A minute ago she'd imagined that her father was dead. The prayer she had put in to God was completely unnecessary, she realized. Her father was far from dead.

Zofia was in her bra. Her breasts looked flushed and large. Larger than the very large breasts they already appeared to be when they were fully clothed. Ruth felt anxious and insignificant. A pallid, flat-chested, bloodless spectator.

Zofia was struggling to button up a very tight, stretch skirt. "Darling," Zofia said to Ruth. "Your father is in the shower. We did go to sleep quite late." Ruth just stared at her. She still hadn't spoken. A clutch of words, reasonable words, appropriate words, pertinent words, civil words, dignified words, seemly words, were all stuck in her gullet. She opened her mouth to see if that would free some of the words. None came out.

What was happening? Ruth thought. The world seemed awry, askew, topsy-turvy, faulty. Nothing made sense. The unexpected and the improbable had been let loose. The questionable and the implausible had joined forces with the unfamiliar and undreamed of, and had gathered momentum and run amok.

"Your father is a wonderful man," Zofia said.

"I think so, too," Ruth finally said.

Zofia smiled. "A wonderful man," she said again. Ruth saw, from Zofia's smile, that she and Zofia were not talking about the same qualities in Edek. Zofia was thinking about something Ruth would rather not hear any more about.

"Tell my father, I'll go down to breakfast and meet him later," she said to Zofia.

"Darling, we will have breakfast with you in a few minutes," Zofia said.

We? They were already a "we," Ruth thought. She felt giddy. Zofia looked at Ruth's expression. "Maybe your father will talk to you first," she said, "and I will see you later."

"Okay," Ruth said.

"Your father is a very nice man," Zofia said. "He is very good in that department," she said conspiratorially, as she cast her eyes in the direction of the bed. Ruth was mortified. Why did Zofia have to tell her that? Zofia had looked so matter-of-fact about it. Ruth didn't think it was a matter-of-fact matter to discuss someone's father's sex life with the person in question's daughter. It horrified her. Was she just prim? Reserved? A prude? Zofia looked so comfortable with the subject matter. Ruth heard her father call out something from the shower. "I'll be right there, my little boy," Zofia shouted to him, in Polish. My little boy? Was that what she said? Ruth's head was spinning. *Mój mały chłopczyku.* My little boy. That's what she called him.

"A man like that is very hard to find," Zofia said to Ruth. "Too many men are not satisfying." Ruth reeled. Too many men. Was it Zofia's life that the gypsy woman was talking about? Too many men. That was what the gypsy woman had said. Ruth started to feel faint.

"I'm going downstairs," she said to Zofia.

"Good-bye, darling," Zofia said. She still hadn't managed to do her skirt up.

Ruth tried to calm down. What was so terrible about any of this? Nothing. There was nothing wrong. Nothing out of the ordinary. And she had to stop imbuing normal things with abnormal meaning. "Too many men" was a common enough phrase. In regular usage. And so was sex. Sex was normal and common. Sex between friends. Sex between lovers. Sex between strangers. Her father was entitled to have sex with whomever he wanted. There was nothing strange about this. Still, she felt sick. She went to her room and got some Mylanta.

Ruth sat at the breakfast table. She could still feel the coating that Mylanta left on your tongue. She thought she should have something to eat. To displace the taste of the Mylanta. But she didn't feel hungry. She had lost her appetite. Her father clearly had no trouble with appetite, she thought. Appetite of any sort. Why was she so upset? she wondered. Her father hadn't done anything wrong. There was no disloyalty involved. Why was she thinking about loyalty and disloyalty? Did she want her father to hate all Poles? Was that what was making her feel betrayed? She didn't know. She just knew she felt flat. Upset. Exhausted.

What a picture in contrasts they were. She and Edek. She was swallowing Mylanta day and night, and couldn't even keep a meager breakfast down. And he was devouring everything in sight. She paused. Why did she have to use the word "devouring"? She didn't want to think of her father devouring Zofia's breasts or any other part of Zofia. She grimaced. She tried to shake that thought out of her head. She could have used other words. She didn't have to choose "devouring." She could have used savoring, consuming, ingesting. She could have used relishing or engulfing. No, she thought, they were no better. They led to the same series of images. She shook her head again, more violently. It gave her a headache.

Edek arrived. Ruth could see his beam from the other side of the room. He looked refreshed and alive. He perused the breakfast buffet quickly as he ran toward Ruth.

"I am sorry I am late, darling," he said to Ruth. "Zofia was talking and talking. And it did make me late."

"I think she was doing more than talking," Ruth said tersely. Edek laughed.

"Maybe," he said. "She is a very nice girl."

"She's not a girl," Ruth said. "She's a woman. An old woman."

Why did she have to say that? Ruth thought. It was completely unnecessary. And so bitchy. She hated not being supportive to women. Solidarity among women was a very important issue. An issue that decades of feminist tracts and organizations had not addressed effectively. Women needed to support one another if they were to get anywhere. That was the way men did it. And it was so effective. Women had reputations as nurturers and supporters. But this nurture and support was rarely directed at other women. And here she was, trying to demean Zofia on the worst grounds, her age. If she wasn't careful, Ruth told herself, she'd be hoeing into Zofia's looks next.

"She is not so old," Edek said.

"You are right," Ruth said. "She is not old and she is very attractive for her age." She examined what she had just said. Was that another slur?

Attractive for her age. Was the antagonism in her so inherent that it sprang out even when she was trying to hold it in?

"She is not a bad-looking woman," Edek said.

"She is a very attractive, vibrant, energetic woman," Ruth said. Edek nodded. Why had she had to use "energetic" in that string of adjectives, Ruth wondered. She didn't want to think of any of Zofia's energetic activities. Particularly the most recent ones. She wanted to shake that thought away. She shook her head again.

"Why do you do this with your head?" Edek said.

"I am just annoyed with myself."

"What for should you do like this with your head?" Edek said. "It is not good I am sure for your head. You been doing this for years."

"Really?" she said.

"Since you was a child, you was shaking your head like this."

"No wonder I'm all shook up," she said. The reference to Elvis Presley escaped Edek.

"You are not so shooked up," he said.

"Thank you," she said.

"Zofia is really a very nice person," Edek said.

"I'm sure she is," Ruth said. 'But do you mind if we don't continue this conversation?"

"You do not want to talk about Zofia?" said Edek.

"No, I'd rather not," Ruth said.

"It is nothing what should make you upset," said Edek.

"I'm not upset," Ruth said.

"I can see that you are upset," said Edek.

"I'm not upset," she said.

"You are upset," Edek said.

"I am not upset," she shouted.

Several people eating their breakfast looked at Ruth. She glared at them. "I am not upset," she said to Edek. "Your insistence that I am upset, upset me."

"You are upset about Zofia," Edek said.

"No I'm not," Ruth said.

"Yes you are," said Edek. "I know my daughter."

"Maybe I am a bit upset," Ruth said. "Doesn't it bother you that she is a Pole?"

"Bother me?" Edek said. "Why should it bother me?"

"Because we don't like Poles," Ruth said.

"We do not like some Polish people," Edek said. "But not all Polish people. Zofia is a very nice person."

"Yes," Ruth said. "Zofia is a very nice person. A very nice big-breasted person."

"Yes, she has such big breasts," Edek said. "What is wrong with that?"

"Nothing," Ruth said.

She couldn't believe that she had resorted to underhand, antiwomen tactics again. And she couldn't believe she was discussing this subject with Edek. It wasn't normal to be discussing the anatomy of your father's lover with your father. Oh, God, she thought as she winced. Why did she have to put those words together? Father and lover. She wished she had never brought up the subject of Zofia's breasts. She wished she had been kinder about Zofia.

"There is no need for you to worry about Zofia," Edek said.

"I'm not worried," Ruth said.

"Zofia would like to speak to you after breakfast, herself," Edek said. "She wants to tell you there is nothing to worry about."

Ruth looked around the room. Neither Zofia nor Walentyna was at breakfast. Ruth wondered if Walentyna was giving Zofia hell. Probably not. Zofia was probably taunting Walentyna with details of the evening's encounter. Ruth knew "encounter" wasn't the right word. But she didn't want anything more detailed than "encounter," she decided.

"Let's get some breakfast," Ruth said to Edek. Edek stood up. "As a matter of fact I am this morning a bit hungry," he said. He walked over to the buffet.

"They got a very good sausage," he called out to her from the other side of the buffet. The waiter came up to Ruth. "Would you like your poached eggs now, madam?" he said. Ruth was startled. She had forgotten that she had discussed having poached eggs with the waiter. "No, thank you," she said. "I think I'll have something from the buffet."

Ruth watched Edek walk back to the table. Quite a lot, of whatever he had chosen, was extending farther than the boundaries of his plate. Ruth spooned some compote into a bowl for herself and rejoined Edek. Edek was looking at his plate. He had chosen the blood sausage. What looked like a foot of thick blood sausage was lying across his plate.

Ruth stared at the blood sausage. Why did her father's breakfast look like a phallic announcement to her? Why couldn't she let a blood sausage be only a blood sausage? Only a roll of meat. "Roll of meat"? Why did she have to use that phrase? Ugh, she said to herself. She was choosing all the wrong words today.

She looked at Edek. How could he eat that blood sausage on an empty stomach anyway?

"Maybe you should start with cornflakes," she said to him. Edek screwed up his face.

"I had enough with the cornflakes," he said. "I can get cornflakes as much as I want in Melbourne," he added.

"Okay," Ruth said.

"This sausage is very tasty," Edek said, and took a large mouthful. Ruth looked at her compote. It looked a bit puny.

Edek ate his blood sausage with relish. Mouthful after mouthful of sausage disappeared from the plate. Zofia had clearly been good for his appetite, Ruth thought. Although maybe that part of him didn't really need improving. When Edek was almost finished, he looked up. "I did speak to the lawyer about the Swiss bank account," he said, to Ruth.

"When?" Ruth said.

"Last night," said Edek.

"You had time?" Ruth said. "You seem to have been pretty busy."

"Do not be silly, Ruthie," Edek said. "The lawyer did tell me that the Swiss banks did agree to a settlement of 1.25 billion dollars."

"I know," Ruth said. "I read about it in this morning's *International Daily Journal.*"

"The lawyer did say that the Swiss people are concerned about the damage what this dispute did do their image," Edek said.

"It is sick, isn't it?" Ruth said. "The Swiss people are not happy with the settlement. The Minister for the Economy, Pascal Couchepin, was quoted as saying, 'Many people have the feeling that it was not the search for truth, but more a search for money.' They drag out that old stereotype of the rich greedy Jew only interested in money. And that conveniently covers up their own greed and their own theft. It always works."

"Column down, Ruthie, column down," Edek said.

"Doesn't it make you feel like hitting your head against a wall?" she said, to Edek.

"No," Edek said. "It does make me angry. But I am used to such things." Ruth poured herself a glass of water. "The lawyer did tell me that the Swiss government's Swiss National Bank what did make such big profits from dealing with the gold the Nazis did take from the Jews did not contribute to or endorse this settlement," Edek said.

"I know," said Ruth. "The private banks agreed because of the pressure of the financial sanctions that the U.S. Congress was putting on them."

"It was mainly New York what wanted to put sanctions on the Swiss banks, wasn't it?" Edek said.

"Yes," Ruth said.

"New York is not a bad city," Edek said.

Ruth felt homesick. Homesick for New York. She didn't think she had ever missed New York this much before.

"I'm looking forward to going home," Ruth said. "We fly to Warsaw tomorrow, and then home." She looked at Edek. From Warsaw she and Edek were flying to separate destinations. She was flying to New York, Edek was returning to Australia. "I'll miss you, Dad," she said. "It's been one helluva trip."

"One helluva trip as they say," Edek said. He looked sad.

"We'll see each other again soon," Ruth said. "I'll come to Australia or you'll come to New York." Parting from Edek was going to be the hardest part of this trip, she thought. She had hated every good-bye she had ever uttered to her father. Each good-bye was tinged with the fear that she wouldn't see him again. Tears came into her eyes.

"We will see each other very soon," Edek said.

"Of course we will," she said. "I love you, Dad," she said a minute later.

"I do love you, too, Ruthie," he said.

Ruth looked up. Zofia was walking toward them. Zofia saw Ruth and waved.

"Zofia is here," Ruth said to Edek. "I think we should go. It's our last chance to walk around Kraków."

"To walk in Kraków?" Edek said "What for is there such a big rush to walk in Kraków? We got plenty of time to walk in Kraków."

"It's our last day here," Ruth said.

"We got all day," said Edek.

"Hello, hello," said Zofia. She kissed Edek on the cheek and then bent over to kiss Ruth. Ruth moved her head in a reflex action. Zofia's kiss landed on the side of Ruth's head.

"We were just going to go for a walk," Ruth said to Zofia.

"We got plenty of time to go for a walk," Edek said.

"I would like to have a cup of tea with you, Ruthie, for a few minutes," Zofia said. Ruth hesitated.

"Go on, Ruthie," Edek said. "It cannot do you harm to have a cup of tea with Zofia. She does only want to tell you that there is nothing to worry about." Ruth was quiet. "Ruthie, we are going tomorrow," Edek said. "Please, behave yourself with Zofia."

Edek turned to Zofia. 'My daughter is normally a very nice person," he said. "She is being a bit not so nice because this situation what she found us together in is not so easy for her."

"Of course, Edek," Zofia said. "Of course."

"I am going to my room to write a few postcards to people," Edek said.

"Okay," Ruth said to Zofia. "I'll have a cup of tea with you." She tried to inject a gracious tone into her voice, but she could hear that she sounded flat.

"Thank you, darling," Zofia said.

"I will be back when I am finished with postcards," Edek said.

Ruth felt unreasonably nervous at being left alone with Zofia. She smiled at Zofia. She hoped her smile was not too stiff.

"You don't have to be frightened of me, Ruthie," Zofia said. "I am a good person. I am honest. I say what I am thinking. I do not hide things."

"Especially your breasts," Ruth said, and then lifted her hand to her mouth in horror at what she had just said.

Zofia laughed. "It is hard to hide my breasts," she said.

"I didn't mean to say that," Ruth said.

"I don't mind," Zofia said.

"Well, I apologize, anyway," Ruth said. Zofia smiled at Ruth and nodded her acceptance of the apology.

"I like your father very much," Zofia said. Ruth didn't say anything. "He likes me very much, too," Zofia said. Ruth remained quiet. She didn't know what to say. "I think I am the woman for him," Zofia said.

"What?" said Ruth. The exclamation had come out with more force and volume than Ruth had intended. Zofia took offense.

"What is wrong with me?" she said. "Why are you so surprised?"

"There's nothing wrong with you at all," Ruth said. "I was just surprised because your remark was so unexpected."

"Unexpected?" Zofia said. "A woman knows when a man is the man for her."

"But you don't know my father," Ruth said.

"I know him," said Zofia. "I know him. You do not have to know a person for ten years in order to know him."

"Well, you have to know him for more than ten minutes," Ruth said.

"It depends what does happen in those ten minutes," Zofia said.

"He doesn't know you," Ruth said.

"He knows me, believe me," Zofia said.

What did Zofia mean, Ruth thought. Was Zofia talking about her father's knowledge of her in terms of physical intimacy? Or had they talked all night as well? Had they revealed more than their physical selves to each other? What did Zofia mean?

"We are going tomorrow," Ruth said to Zofia. "There's no time for anything more to develop." Zofia was not daunted. She smiled at Ruth.

"Some things do not require time," she said. Ruth was confused by that enigmatic, Zen-like remark. She decided Zofia was just bluffing.

"I will be good to Edek," Zofia said.

"He's managing quite well," Ruth said. Suddenly the absurdity of the situation struck Ruth. Here she was, fending off a prospective interloper in much the same way that parents screened potential partners for their teenage children. She had a parental attitude to this prospective girlfriend. She was judgmental. Critical.

Maybe she was merely being discerning, she thought. After all, she knew her father well. She was well qualified to assess the suitability of prospective partners. Anyway, the whole conversation was ridiculous, she decided. They were leaving tomorrow. Zofia had no time for any further maneuvers. Ruth chided herself again. That was a sexist attitude to take. To ascribe the maneuvering to Zofia and not Edek. Maybe it was appropriate. She hadn't seen Edek make any overt moves toward Zofia.

"I look after my father," Ruth said to Zofia.

"Your father doesn't need more money," Zofia said. Ruth stopped herself from saying that she gave her father much more than money. After all, this was not a competition. She and Zofia were not competing for Edek. And if they were, Ruth had already won. Edek was her father. He already belonged to her.

"Your father is not a man who is very interested in a lot of money," Zofia said.

"That's true," Ruth said.

"Edek does not look after himself," Zofia said. "I will look after him. I will make sure that he does exercise."

"That would be an uphill battle," Ruth said. Zofia looked bewildered. "It's just an expression," Ruth said. "I meant that it would be very hard to get my father to exercise."

"There are many ways to force a man to exercise," Zofia said with a smile. What was Zofia talking about? Ruth thought. She smiled, despite herself. Zofia was incorrigible, Ruth had to admire that. What did Zofia know about men and their ways that Ruth didn't? Probably everything, Ruth decided. Next to Zofia she was a naïf, a rank amateur.

"I will make Edek fit," Zofia said.

"He is fit," Ruth said. "He is very fit for an eighty-one-year-old."

"I know better than you how fit he is," Zofia said with a wink.

Ruth felt sick. She definitely didn't want to linger on this aspect of the conversation. "I will make him more fit," Zofia said. "I will walk with him and we will swim together."

"He can't swim," Ruth said.

"I will teach him," Zofia said. "It is very easy to swim in Sopot."

Ruth was horrified. "My father can't live in Sopot," she said.

"Why not?" said Zofia.

"It is too far," Ruth said. She wasn't sure where Sopot was too far from. Too far removed from any reality, she decided.

"Sopot is closer to New York than Australia," Zofia said.

"My father is not going to live in Poland," Ruth said firmly.

Zofia looked at her. "Okay," she said. "Maybe we will both live in New

York, Edek and me." Ruth was stunned. "I am a very good cook," Zofia said. "I make a much better cheesecake than Walentyna."

"My father doesn't need cheesecake," Ruth said.

"He loves cheesecake," Zofia said. "And I make a special one with cottage cheese. It is not so fattening."

Ruth contemplated asking Zofia where you could buy cottage cheese in Poland. She had only seen full-fat cream cheese on sale anywhere. She hadn't seen any skim milk or nonfat yogurt either. She decided against inquiring about the cottage cheese.

"I will make your father happy," Zofia said.

"I don't think so," said Ruth. She was about to explain her seemingly harsh attitude. To explain Edek's past and the traumas he had suffered in Poland, when Zofia interrupted her.

"You don't know," Zofia said.

"Yes, I do," Ruth said, before she could stop herself.

"No, you do not," Zofia said. "I know what Edek needs in order to be happy. He needs me. He is a wonderful man," Zofia said. "He has more life in him than men one quarter of his age. I have been looking for a man with life. I have much life, myself."

"I can see that you are a very lively person," Ruth said. She meant it kindly, and hoped it hadn't appeared as a censorious comment on Zofia's sexual activities the night before.

"I have said no to many men," Zofia said. There it was again, Ruth thought. To many men. But it was the wrong "to." The gypsy woman had definitely meant "too," not "to." You have too many men in your life, the gypsy had said. It really must have been Zofia's life the gypsy woman had been thinking of, Ruth thought.

"I have said no to men of thirty," Zofia said.

"Really?" Ruth said. She was impressed. No men of thirty were running after her.

"My word of honor," Zofia said. "On the grave of my mother, I am telling you the truth."

"I believe you," Ruth said.

"I would like to be your friend," Zofia said. She leaned over and put her hand on Ruth's hand.

"You can be," Ruth said. "But you can't have my father."

Zofia removed her hand. "I think I can," she said.

"I've got nothing against you," Ruth said to Zofia. "But you are too young." Where had she come up with that notion from? Ruth thought. That was a stupid thing to say. She must be feeling more anxious about Zofia than she knew.

"I am sixty-three," Zofia said.

"That's too young for my father," Ruth said. She was stunned at herself. She couldn't believe the stern and judgmental attitude she was taking.

"Your father needs someone young," Zofia said. "He is very young." Ruth didn't say anything. She didn't want to let any more disapproving, disparaging, or vituperative sentences loose. "You will see," Zofia said. "Your father will be very happy."

Ruth kept quiet. She was torn between admiring Zofia's audacity and feeling annoyed at her certainty. "I can move anywhere," Zofia said. "I can pack up in a minute. I don't have children. I don't even have a cat."

"Do you like cats?" Ruth said.

"No, not at all," Zofia said. "And I do not like dogs." Zofia said this with no hint of apology. Few people would admit so directly to an indifference to or a dislike of pets. It was an admission that almost guaranteed hostility.

"My father likes dogs," Ruth said.

"That is fine with me," Zofia said.

Ruth was tired. She wished her father would come back. She wondered how she could end this conversation. She wanted to end it on a conciliatory note, to erase the tensions and frictions. To eliminate the discord that seemed so unnecessary. She and Edek were leaving tomorrow. They would never see Zofia again. Why not leave on a harmonious note?

"I don't like cats myself," Ruth said. "Or dogs. It's definitely not a popular attitude to have in America."

"Even in New York?" Zofia said.

"Even in New York," Ruth said.

"I always wanted to go to New York," Zofia said.

Ruth knew she had to veer the conversation straight back to animals. "They have acupuncture for dogs and cats in America," she said to Zofia.

"No," Zofia said.

"And chiropractors for dogs and cats, too," Ruth said. "Do you know what a chiropractor is?"

"Of course," Zofia said. "I swim every day. I know very much about the body."

Why did every sentence seem to be heading in a dangerous direction? Ruth wondered.

"You are not interested in having children are you?" Zofia said to Ruth.

"No," said Ruth.

"I was the same," Zofia said. Ruth wanted to put some distance into this togetherness, this shared view on parenthood.

"Lots of people feel the same way," Ruth said to Zofia.

"Not too many women feel like this," Zofia said.

"More and more women do," said Ruth.

"Maybe," said Zofia.

Ruth couldn't believe her own argumentativeness. Would she argue with Zofia about anything at all? Couldn't she allow some accord between them?

"I would have had children if I could have been assured of having identical twins," Ruth said. "I've had a fascination for identical twins all my life. Triplets would have been even better."

Zofia laughed. "I would have liked twins, too," she said.

Ruth stared at Zofia in disbelief. She was sure Zofia was making this up. Making it up in an effort to align herself with Ruth. "My sister had twins," Zofia said.

"Identical twins?" said Ruth.

"Yes," said Zofia.

"Lucky woman," Ruth said.

"My sister did feel very lucky to have her twins," Zofia said.

So Zofia was telling the truth, Ruth thought. Or was she? She could be making up the whole sister story. She might not have a sister, let alone a sister with identical twins. Ruth knew there was something very unpleasant about her own suspicions, but she couldn't discard them. She had to get out of Poland, she thought. Poland was turning her into someone else. Someone she didn't like much. Maybe being in Poland was revelatory.

Maybe she was seeing aspects of herself she should know about. She didn't like that thought, either.

"Identical twins are not hereditary," Ruth said to Zofia.

"I know that," Zofia said. "Otherwise I would have tried." Ruth wondered why Zofia had wanted twins. She thought her own desire for multiple units of the same person was a desire to replicate those who had been lost. She corrected herself. The word "lost" was too amorphous. Those who had been killed. She had wanted twins or triplets to make duplicates. Duplicates of people with similar traits and faces. It was lucky that it hadn't been possible. Lucky that technology could induce only fraternal twins. She thought she would have gone to any lengths to have identical children. It was such an intense longing. She really was lucky it wasn't possible, she thought. She couldn't imagine herself as the mother of twins or triplets or quadruplets.

She had to veer this conversation back to more subdued ground, she thought. To animals. Animals were always a safe subject. "Do you know," she said to Zofia, "that in Australia they have invented a protein injection for sheep that makes the wool come off by itself?"

Zofia laughed. "I don't believe this," she said.

"It's true," Ruth said. "It was developed by government scientists."

"What happens?" Zofia said.

"They inject the sheep with this protein," Ruth said, "and a week later the fleece falls off."

"Exactly a week," Zofia said. "This is very well planned."

Ruth laughed. She hadn't thought about the precise timing. The precision of the procedure made her laugh. "It would not be good," Zofia said, "if the wool fell off at the wrong moment." Images of sheep losing their fleece while shopping or strolling in the street or having their hair done came into Ruth's head. She fell about laughing. Tears ran down Ruth's face at the thought of groups of sheep losing their fleece at inopportune moments. Zofia was laughing hard, too.

The two women were still laughing when Edek arrived. Ruth saw her father. She sat up in mid-laugh. Edek was beaming. "I was just telling Zofia about a new invention by the Australian government," she said to Edek, and told Edek about the self-shearing sheep.

"I did not know anything about this," Edek said to Ruth. "My daughter does know everything," he said to Zofia.

"Maybe not everything," Zofia said, with a broad smile. She stood up and kissed Edek on the cheek. "I will see you later," she said.

"I am very glad you did get on well with Zofia," Edek said to Ruth as they were walking in the Market Square.

"I was being polite," Ruth said. "Because she's your friend." She waited for Edek to deny that he was Zofia's friend. She had expected him to brush off the suggestion that theirs was a real friendship. Edek said nothing. Ruth began to feel nervous that her father had made plans she was unaware of.

"We are going tomorrow, aren't we?" she said.

"Of course," Edek said. Ruth felt her tension dissipate. "Maybe we will go even a little earlier than what we did plan," Edek said.

"Okay," she said. "But why?"

"I will explain to you while we have a cup of coffee," Edek said.

Ruth felt relieved. They were definitely leaving. Possibly leaving for Warsaw even earlier than they had planned. An earlier departure for Edek was definitely not on Zofia's itinerary. Maybe Edek was trying to get away from Zofia. Ruth could feel herself relaxing. She would be home very soon. She would be going home to New York. Home to her apartment. To her office. To her routines. Life would be back to normal, very soon.

"This café does look good," Edek said, pointing to a café with a large display of *pontshkes* in the window. They went inside.

"I'm glad to be in a café," Ruth said. "If I see one more of those anti-Semitic carved wooden caricatures of Jews, I'll scream."

"Do you want a *pontshke*, Ruthie?" Edek said.

"No thanks," she said. "You have one."

"I will have just one," he said.

"Excuse me," a man sitting at the next table said to Ruth and Edek. "I heard you saying that the Polish people are anti-Semitic," he said. "Please forgive me but I had to say something." Ruth looked at the man. He was in his mid-thirties, with an intelligent, well-defined face. "There is a reason why Polish people are hostile to Jews," he said. Ruth turned around to face him.

"Yes?" she said.

"Ruthie darling, please," Edek said.

"Polish people did suffer greatly at the hands of the Jews after the war," the man said. Ruth could feel her blood pressure rising. She knew that the elevation of one's blood pressure was supposed to be indiscernible, but she knew that hers was rising. She could feel it.

"Really?" she said to the man.

"Ruthie," Edek said. She ignored him.

"Yes?" she said to the man again.

"Yes," he said. "Before and during the war, the Jews, who were Communists, ran off to Russia to save their necks when the Nazis arrived."

"You think all the Jews escaped to Russia when the Nazis arrived?" Ruth said.

"Not all of them, but quite a few," the man said. "After the war they all came back and occupied top positions in the Communist government, and persecuted the Polish people."

Ruth was speechless. This man looked so presentable, so reasonable, so intelligent. His English was immaculate. He was clearly educated. How could he have gotten things so wrong? And what hope was there for other less educated Poles?

"They all came back after the war?" she said. "No one came back. Two and a half Jews came back. The only Jews in Poland are the imaginary Jews, and the carved wooden Jews. Do you understand me?" she shouted. "No one came back. Maybe a few lucky Jews did manage to get away from the Nazis, and survive, in the Soviet Union. And maybe they were Communists. But you can't translate that into Communist Jews persecuting the Polish people."

"Ruthie, Ruthie, please column down," Edek said.

The man looked at Ruth. "I did not expect you to agree with me," he said. "But I did not expect you to be rude."

"Rude?" Ruth shouted. "You people are the rudest people on earth. Vulgar, coarse, bigoted, obscene assholes." Ruth looked at him. "If you stay here any longer, I'll slug you," she said. She was in a sweat. How could this man say what he had just said? The country was full of ignorant imbeciles and every one of them was hooked up to an intravenous anti-Semitic drip. The man stood up and began to walk out. "I wish you every misfortune in the world," Ruth shouted out after him.

"Ruthie darling, you got to take it more easy," Edek said.

"He's an asshole," Ruth said.

"I know," Edek said. "But you cannot take it all so hard. It is not good for you."

"I'm all right," Ruth said. "Maybe I will have a *pontshke*."

"Good," said Edek. "I will go and get us a couple of *pontshkes*. Do you want also a hot chocolate?"

"No, thanks," Ruth said. "I'll have chamomile tea."

"With lemon?" Edek said.

"With lemon," she said.

She took off her jacket. She was still hot. Edek was right, she had to calm down. She took a couple of deep breaths. She was pleased she had shouted at the man. It felt good to say what she wanted to say. Or rather to shout it. In New York, she never shouted at anyone. In New York there was little cause to shout. The city wasn't populated by Poles.

She couldn't wait to be out of Poland. She decided she would call Max and ask Max to put some fresh fruit in her apartment. It would be nice to come home to some fresh strawberries and mangoes and kiwi fruit. You could get the best fruit in the world in New York. She made a vow to herself. She would never criticize New York again.

Edek came back with four *pontshkes*. "Four?" Ruth said.

"You need to eat," Edek said. Ruth laughed.

"I'll have one," she said. She wanted to mention Zofia. To see Edek's reaction. She really wanted to ask him how he felt about Zofia, but she didn't want to imbue the issue of Zofia with any more importance than it already had. If, in fact, it was important at all. She wished she knew what Edek felt about Zofia. It couldn't be much. He seemed to be leaving Kraków without any evident regret.

She decided to bring up Zofia's name. "Zofia doesn't like dogs," she said. Edek looked puzzled. Ruth thought she should have introduced the subject of Zofia more languorously. This fact about Zofia and dogs obviously seemed out of context to Edek. As out of context as it was, she thought.

"I was just thinking about it because I saw a dog go by," she lied.

"Where?" said Edek.

"It's gone," she said. Why was she behaving in this adolescent, juvenile manner? Why didn't she just ask her father how he felt about Zofia? "She doesn't like cats either," Ruth said. Edek looked at her again.

"You do not like dogs, too," he said. "It looks like there are many people what do not like dogs or cats."

Well, she hadn't got very far with that opening gambit, Ruth thought. She had learned nothing at all. She cut her *pontshke* into quarters. Edek had already finished his first *pontshke*. He took a bite out of a second *pontshke*. "Ruthie darling," he said. "I want to tell you something and I want you to promise not to be angry with me." Oh no, Ruth thought. She stiffened. Here was the news that she didn't want to hear about Zofia. What was Edek going to tell her? That he was madly in love with Zofia? That he wanted to run off with her and live in Sopot? That he was going to live in Poland, surrounded by Poles? She prepared herself to respond to the news with moderation, reasonableness, and understanding.

"Okay," Ruth said. "What is it? I hope it's not something terrible."

"What could be terrible next to what we been seeing and thinking about in Poland?" Edek said. Ruth wondered if Edek was bringing in the anti-Semitism and the absence of Jews and the horror of the past in order to make the news of Zofia seem less disastrous. No, she decided. That was unfair of her. Edek was not that manipulative.

"I want to tell you," Edek said, "that I did see Garth just before I came to Poland." Ruth felt a flood of relief. The news was not about Zofia.

"That's fine," she said to Edek. "You can see him as often as you want to. It's no big deal to me."

"I saw him in Sydney," Edek said.

"When were you in Sydney?" said Ruth.

"I was there on my way to Bangkok," said Edek.

"But that was only a two-hour stopover," Ruth said.

"Yes," said Edek. "It was such a big rush. I never did anything like this in my life before."

"What did you do?" said Ruth. She couldn't see what Edek was worried she would be angry about. She had often told him she had no objection to his seeing Garth. It was extreme though, she thought, of Edek to try and fit in a visit to Garth while he was in transit on his way to Poland. But she wasn't annoyed.

"I did catch a taxi and go to Garth's place," Edek said. "I do not have to tell you how this did make me nervous. I was frightened I would miss the plane and you would be annoyed."

"If you had missed the plane I would have been worried, not annoyed," Ruth said. "Anyway, you didn't, so it's all okay."

"I was frightened," said Edek. "I never been to Sydney before. I did not know how far was Garth's place from the airport. I did just get a taxi and I did give the driver the address." Edek shook his head, still surprised at his own boldness. "I did ask the driver to go very fast," Edek said.

"I can't believe this," Ruth said. "You were speeding through Sydney, endangering your life to see Garth?"

"It was lucky he was home," Edek said. "I did ask the driver what did drive me to wait for me in case there was no one home. If there was no one home he could take me straight back to the airport. As it was, Garth did take me back to the airport."

"Why did you do all of that rushing around when you were about to begin a long plane flight?" Ruth said.

"I did want to ask Garth something," Edek said.

"Couldn't you have just called him?" Ruth said.

"No," said Edek. "This I did have to ask him in person." Ruth felt apprehensive.

"What did you want to ask him?" she said.

"You promise me you will be column," Edek said.

"I'll try," she said.

"I did ask Garth to meet me in New York," Edek said. He looked at Ruth as though he was expecting an explosion.

"What?" said Ruth. "How could Garth meet you in New York? You're not going to New York."

"Maybe I am," Edek said.

Ruth's head started to spin. Was everything in her life not what it seemed? Not what she thought it was? Why was so much up-ended? Unraveled and unfastened? "What's happening?" Ruth said to Edek. "What do you mean you may be going to New York?" She looked at Edek. "Tell me, clearly, what's going on," she said. "I can't take too many more unexpected and unexplained things. This trip has been difficult enough as it is for me."

"This trip is difficult for you?" Edek said. "This trip was your big idea.

You was the one who did want so very much to come to Poland. Do you think I did want so very much to be in Poland? No."

"Okay," she said. "Let's not argue about that. Tell me the rest of the something you don't want me to be angry about." She tried to calm down. In the context of other possible occurrences, seeing Garth wouldn't be all that terrible. She would keep herself in check. She would be friendly and cheerful. She would make sure the subject of their past together was kept at bay. It wouldn't be too bad. Nothing seemed too bad as long as it was out of Poland.

"I can invite Garth to New York if I do want to," Edek said.

"Of course you can," Ruth said. "But as he was part of my life, it would have been a good idea to discuss it with me first."

"You would say you did not want to see him," Edek said.

"Well, I would be saying it for a reason," Ruth said.

"This reason is not a reason I can understand," Edek said. He looked at Ruth. "Garth is like a son-in-law to me," he said.

"Great," Ruth said. "You've married him to me despite any participation on my part."

"He can be a son-in-law to me even if he is not married to my daughter," Edek said. "He is like a son to me."

There was a silence between them. Ruth looked up, and to her horror saw that Edek was on the verge of tears. She felt terrible.

"I understand, Dad," she said. "I understand how you feel about Garth." Edek started to cry.

"He is like a son to me," he said. "Garth is the only company what I feel very happy with since Mum did die. Except for you, Ruthie. With other people I do feel okay, but with Garth I feel comfortable. He does know me and I do know him."

"Don't cry, Dad," she said. "I'm sorry I sounded upset. I do understand." She did understand, she thought. Garth loved Edek. Garth lit up with love when he was with Edek and Edek was all right, in Garth's company. She was glad Edek had Garth. She realized she had been holding her breath. She breathed out. Well, at least Zofia seemed to be out of the picture, she thought.

"I'm not angry," Ruth said to Edek. "You can see Garth. But in New York? You're not going to New York."

"I am going to New York," Edek said.

"When?" said Ruth.

"With you," said Edek.

"With me?" Ruth said. "What do you mean?"

"That is what I was doing in the airport in Warsaw," Edek said.

"What?" she said. She was finding it hard to follow what her father was saying.

"In the airport, in Warsaw, I did change my ticket," Edek said. He looked at Ruth expectantly and nervously. She still didn't understand what he was saying. "I did change my ticket to go via New York from Warsaw," he said. "Now my ticket is from Warsaw to New York, then from New York to Sydney and then Melbourne." Ruth was speechless. "I will stay with you a few days in New York," Edek said.

"When did you change your ticket?" Ruth said.

"You did see me," Edek said. "At the airport."

"When you were getting upgraded?" Ruth said.

"I did not get such an upgrade," Edek said. "There was nothing wrong with my seat. I did tell you this about the rest for the feet so you would understand why I had to go to get something fixed up."

Ruth shook her head. She couldn't believe what she was hearing. Her father had tricked her. He had invented a whole dialogue of detailed explanations for his actions, which was fraudulent. Not true. How could he have done this to her? How could he have carried out that charade so masterfully? She hadn't suspected a thing.

"You did believe me?" Edek said.

"Of course I believed you," Ruth said.

"You should be more suspicious," Edek said with a smile. Ruth was glad to see him smiling.

"Suspicious of you?" she said.

"Yes," said Edek. "It was such a stupid story about the rest for the feet, and the chair what did not go back. Who has a chair what is broken like that, in a plane? Not even Polish Airlines."

"I must be an idiot," Ruth said. "I didn't suspect a thing."

"I love you, Ruthie," Edek said. He looked much happier. He was clearly relieved that she had not gone ballistic about the news. "Gone ballistic." That was a very contemporary expression, she thought. On the

whole she preferred more traditional expressions. She could have used
"exploded with anger" or "lost her temper." She shook herself back to the
present. She couldn't afford to get lost, at this moment, in a welter of words.

"I did tell Garth what day we will be back in New York," Edek said.
"And he will be there two days later."

Ruth shook her head again. She wouldn't have believed this of Edek.
She wouldn't have thought him capable of orchestrating a deception and
keeping it to himself for the entire trip. She hadn't had a hint of his intention to accompany her back to New York. She had thought they would be
saying good-bye in Warsaw. At the airport. She had managed to get flights
that left more or less at the same time. Hers bound for New York, and
Edek's for Australia.

Her father had constructed a pantomime. A spectacle. He had run
backward and forward to her at the airport, improvising explanations for
his bizarre activity. She wouldn't have thought him capable of this, or
capable of keeping it to himself for the bulk of the trip. It was not easy to
act out a lie. And she wouldn't have thought it was in Edek's nature to do
it so well.

Edek was now looking quite pleased with himself. He bit into another
pontshke. "I did ask Garth to come to New York two days after us because
I did want to give you a chance to not have a jet lag still," he said.

"Thank you," Ruth said.

"Have your *pontshke,*" Edek said. "You did not eat one piece of it yet.
I am going to take you and Garth to a beautiful dinner in New York,"
Edek said.

"With my American Express card?" Ruth said, with a smile.

"With your American Express card," Edek said. "You did say I should
use it as often as I want to. And I want to take you and Garth out to a beautiful dinner."

"I'm surprised you haven't already made a booking at a restaurant,"
Ruth said. She picked up a piece of her *pontshke.* She put it in her mouth.
It tasted good. The sweetness of the doughnut soothed her. "This *pontshke*
is very good," she said to Edek.

"What did I tell you?" he said. "In Poland they got the best *pontshkes.*"
Ruth took another bite of *pontshke.* She thought of her father at Warsaw
airport. She thought of him running from one side of the airport to the

other. Appearing and disappearing. She thought of the details he had provided her with.

"Seat 2B?" she said to Edek. "That's what you told me you had arranged for yourself. Seat 2B."

"Not bad, eh?" said Edek. "I did learn a lot about clues from my detective books. I did learn how to make sure people are not suspecting what is happening."

"You did a good job," Ruth said.

"I did learn all this from my books," Edek said. "You put in such a clue. Like what I did with the seat 2B, and then no one is suspecting anything. It is called a herring."

"A herring?" Ruth said.

"Yes," said Edek. "A herring."

"Oh, you mean a red herring," Ruth said.

"That's it," Edek said. "A red herring." He looked very pleased with himself.

"You certainly know a lot about herring," Ruth said. "Red herrings and pickled herrings and smoked herrings."

Edek laughed. "I do not like so much the smoked herrings," he said.

"I know," said Ruth. "You prefer pickled herrings. Especially roll-mops."

"*Oy*, a rollmop is very good," Edek said. "We did not have a rollmop in Poland."

"I think that's because rollmops are Jewish," Ruth said. She herself quite liked rollmops.

"You do like a rollmop yourself, Ruthie," Edek said.

"That's true, I do," she said.

"I did not do such a bad job," Edek said, wiping the last of the icing sugar off his plate. "You are not so easy to tell a lie to. You are not stupid, and you do notice everything what I do."

"Really?" she said.

"I do watch you," Edek said. "I see that you do watch everything. You are watching me and other people what are next to us. You are watching everything."

"You're probably right," she said. Edek was right, she had spent her whole life watching and observing.

"And you know things, Ruthie," Edek said. "Things what you did not even see."

Ruth felt alarmed. Jolted. What did Edek mean?

"I see what you feel about the Jews who used to be in Łódź," Edek said. "I can see how you do feel them even though there is no more any Jews in Łódź." Ruth was relieved. It was sensitivity and sympathy her father was talking about. "You can feel the Jews, Ruthie," he said. "I did watch you in the cemetery. In the ghetto. In Kamedulska Street. It is like you was there yourself when the Jews was there. Sometimes I think that you do understand too much, Ruthie."

"I'm not sure you can ever understand too much, Dad," she said. She felt that her life had too much in it that she was still trying to understand.

"Why don't you understand about Garth?" Edek said. There it was, the trick question. Why didn't she understand about Garth? What was there to understand? They had a relationship once, and it ended. That was it.

"What is there to understand, Dad?" she said, wearily. "That you love him?"

"What you do need to understand," Edek said. "Which is not such a hard thing to see is that Garth does love you. You will see that in New York when we are all together."

"Thanks, Dad," she said. "I'm going back to a mountain of work and you've arranged for me to see Garth."

"You did already too much work in your life," Edek said. "You did not have enough of other things."

"I've had more than enough of everything that I have needed," Ruth said. She felt annoyed. She had worked so hard to have a balanced life, and here was Edek flippantly suggesting a lack of balance. She had thought long and hard about balance. Her life was balanced.

"You didn't have a man what was your husband for a long time," Edek said.

"You can live without husbands, you know," Ruth said, with what she hoped was obvious sarcasm. "Not every woman needs a husband. I don't need a husband. I don't need a man in my life."

"Column down, Ruthie, column down," Edek said.

"I'm calm," she said. "The world is a different place, now, Dad. Women don't need a man in order to be happy and fulfilled." She felt distressed.

"I'm happy," she shouted at Edek in case he hadn't understood. She was close to tears. Why was it such a difficult concept to grasp? Nobody thought men were unfulfilled or unhappy if they didn't have wives. On the contrary, many men who didn't have wives were seen as lucky. Happy bachelors. Envied by other men. And attractive to women. A tear ran down the side of her face. She wiped it away.

"If you are so happy why do you cry?" Edek said.

"They're tears of frustration," Ruth said.

"If you are so happy," Edek said. "Why do you move your leg so up and down, and do such funny things with your eye?" Ruth felt exhausted.

"Don't pick on me, Dad," she said.

"I am not doing a picking," he said.

"You did have many men what did want to marry you," Edek said. Ruth kept quiet. She didn't have the energy to explain again that times had changed. That being married was no longer a top priority for quite a few women.

"You did have many men what did want to marry you," Edek said again. "Too many men." What had he just said? Too many men. She was beginning to feel haunted by that phrase.

"Who wanted to marry me?" she said to Edek.

"The two husbands for a start," he said. "And maybe even the green card man."

"That's a joke, Dad. I had to pay him," Ruth said.

"You had to pay him?" Edek said.

"I had to pay him four thousand dollars," Ruth said. "Two when we got married and two after the final interview."

"Oh, brother," Edek said. "Four thousand dollars. You did not tell me this."

"It was just another detail of what I needed to do to live in New York," she said. "Anyway, I was worried that you would be bothered by husband number three. The first two divorces were difficult enough for you. I didn't want to burden you with divorce number three."

"You are right," Edek said. "Your divorces was more difficult for me than they was for you."

"I don't know if I'd go that far," Ruth said. "I didn't breeze through them."

"Well, they was definitely not breezes for me," Edek said.

Ruth was glad the conversation had veered away from the men who had wanted to marry her. There had been so few of them, anyway.

"Shall we go back to the hotel?" Ruth said. "I want to see if there are any faxes."

"Okay," Edek said. He looked at his watch. "It is nearly lunchtime," he said.

"I saw a small vegetarian restaurant," Ruth said. "We could have lunch there, after I check the faxes."

"Vegetarian?" Edek said. "You can eat such vegetables when you go back to New York. Why do we not have some *pierogi* today? In New York you cannot get such good *pierogi*."

"That's true," she said. "The *pierogi* in New York are good, but not as good as the ones in Poland."

"You can say that, again, brother," Edek said.

Ruth was looking for her purse to pay the bill, when she felt Edek staring at her. "That John and that Allan did want to marry you," he said. Ruth groaned. "I went out with John what's-his-name for about four weeks and Allan never wanted to marry me," she said. "And I definitely didn't want to marry him."

"That Allan did tell me he did want to marry you," Edek said.

"He was nuts," Ruth said. "And so what if he wanted to marry me. You can't measure a woman's worth by the number of men who have wanted to marry her."

"No?" Edek said.

"No," she shouted.

"What's the difference?" Edek said. "The main thing is that you could not see that from all of these men Garth was the one who did love you."

"I could see that," Ruth said.

They were both quiet. "We will be in New York on the thirteenth, yes?" Edek said.

"Yes," Ruth said. Suddenly the number thirteen seemed an ominous number. "Do you think thirteen is an unlucky number?" Ruth asked Edek.

"Unlucky? A number? Are you crazy?" Edek said. Ruth felt better. Believing in superstitions was just a way of burdening yourself, she decided.

She tried to think about the news of Garth's visit, and what it would mean. But she was tired. She realized that she could have dispensed with all of her worries about Zofia. Zofia didn't seem to be at the center of Edek's universe. Zofia didn't seem a problem anymore. There was a problem though. Edek's plans to reunite her with Garth. But that problem seemed surmountable, soluble. Not anywhere near as big a problem as Zofia had seemed to be, earlier in the day.

The word "big," in the same sentence as Zofia, reminded Ruth of Zofia's breasts. Why did Zofia's breasts fixate her? Big breasts were not that desirable. Many big-breasted women had problems managing their big breasts. Problems with bras, problems with men, problems with other women. Why was she making Zofia's breasts a problem for herself?

"I'll see Garth in New York," she said to Edek. "But nothing will happen."

"We will see," Edek said.

"Garth is in the past, for me," Ruth said. "What's in the past is in the past." If only that was true, she thought, after she had said it.

Walentyna was sitting in the lounge of the Hotel Mimoza when they got back. She jumped up when she saw Ruth and Edek.

"Could I speak for a moment with Ruth alone?" she said to Ruth and Edek.

"Of course," Edek said.

"Excuse me," Walentyna said to Edek. "I hope it is not rude for me to ask this."

"Of course not," Edek said.

Ruth was puzzled by Walentyna's request to talk privately with her.

"I will go to my room," Edek said to Walentyna, "to get ready for lunch." He looked at his hands. "I have to wash my hands," he said. "They are sticky from the *pontshkes*. I will see you two ladies later."

Ruth sat down next to Walentyna. "Zofia is a very good woman," Walentyna said. So, this was what the talk was about, Ruth thought. Walentyna was making a pitch on Zofia's behalf. She was surprised that she hadn't guessed. She wondered whether Zofia had asked Walentyna to intercede. Somehow Ruth couldn't imagine Zofia needing Walentyna's help. She was annoyed at herself. Why did she have to view Walentyna's actions so cynically? Why couldn't she just see them as sensitive acts of friendship? As a sign of a deep bond between two deeply dissimilar women. She hated herself for being cynical.

"I'm sure Zofia is a very good woman," Ruth said.

"I know that she is," Walentyna said. Walentyna looked at Ruth. "Zofia did not ask me to talk to you," she said.

"Zofia doesn't seem to be the sort who asks for help," Ruth said. Walentyna laughed.

"You are right," she said. "Zofia is very independent. But she is a good person. You do not need to be nervous of her."

"I'm not nervous," Ruth said.

"You are nervous," Walentyna said. "I can see this."

Everyone, apparently, could see her nerves. Could see that she, Ruth Rothwax, was a nervous person, Ruth thought. "I did see that you were nervous about me and Zofia on the first day," Walentyna said. "There is no need to be nervous. There is no need to be nervous of me. There is no need to be nervous of Zofia."

Ruth wished Walentyna would use a different word. She was becoming sick of the word "nervous." What other words could Walentyna have used? She could have used anxious, apprehensive, troubled. She could have used fearful, agitated, skittish. No, that was unfair of her. You couldn't expect a Polish-speaking person to know the word "skittish." Ruth was settling into her reverie about the word "nervous," when Walentyna spoke again. "Zofia is a good person. A very good person," Walentyna said. "And a very good friend."

A good friend? Was the face that Zofia had made about Walentyna's cheesecake the act of a good friend? Ruth thought. It could have been if Walentyna's cheesecake was terrible, she decided.

"I know Zofia is sometimes not easy," Walentyna said. "Sometimes she does say too strongly what she does think. She doesn't know how strong she is. It is hard for me to speak sometimes when I am with her. But she is a good friend and a good person."

"I'm sure she is," Ruth said. Walentyna hadn't finished, Ruth realized. She had only paused to draw breath.

"And she does adore Edek," Walentyna said, a bit flushed and a bit breathless from her speech. "Who would not adore Edek?" Walentyna added quickly. "I think he is wonderful, myself, but Zofia did get to him first." Zofia got to him first, Ruth thought. What was Edek? A prize to be divided out or delivered to the earliest arrival? Ruth decided Walentyna had intended this remark as a compliment. As a sincere declaration of Edek's worth. Not as a sexist statement.

"In any case," Walentyna said, "I am too quiet for Edek." She put her hand on Ruth's arm. "Give Zofia a chance," she said.

"I don't think Zofia needs my help," said Ruth. "She's doing quite well on her own."

"She does need your help," Walentyna said.

"There is nothing to help her about," Ruth said. "We are going tomorrow. We won't see you or Zofia for a long time."

She stopped herself from adding, if ever. She didn't want to be too harsh to either woman. "I don't think we'll be making another trip to Poland in the near future," she said to Walentyna. That was a reasonable compromise, she thought.

"We will see," Walentyna said.

"Yes," said Ruth. "We will see."

"I hear that you will have an old boyfriend visiting you in New York," Walentyna said. Ruth was startled. How did Walentyna know that? Had Zofia told her? Zofia must have told her. Edek must have told Zofia. Before he told Ruth. Ruth felt uneasy. This was not a good sign. She took a deep breath. She was being silly, she thought. There was nothing to worry about. Edek had kept quiet about the news of Garth's visit for a long time. Obviously he had had trouble containing himself and had leaked the news to Zofia.

Ruth shuddered. Why had she had to use the term "containing himself"? It was too sexual a metaphor for that sentence. And then the words "leaked" to Zofia. She didn't want to think of her father not being able to contain himself or leaking anything, with Zofia. She shuddered again.

Edek was back. "Are you ready for lunch?" he said to Ruth.

"Yes," she said quickly. She didn't want to give Edek the opportunity of inviting Zofia or Walentyna to lunch.

"I must go and find Zofia," Walentyna said. "We are going to visit the site of Schindler's factory."

"Don't take a guide," Ruth said. "Unless you want to hear about Steven Spielberg."

"Why do you have to say such things?" Edek said to Ruth, after Walentyna had left. "Maybe Walentyna does want to hear about Steven Spielberg."

"That's probably exactly what she wants to hear about," Ruth said.

"There is nothing wrong with that," Edek said.

"I want people to hear about the Jews or about Oskar Schindler before they hear about Steven Spielberg."

"What does it matter?" Edek said.

"It matters," Ruth said.

"It does not change anything what did happen to the Jews," Edek said.

A couple, a man and woman, in their sixties, were standing next to Ruth and Edek.

"I couldn't help overhearing your conversation," the woman said. "I'm Sylvia Rosenzweig and this is my husband Tommy," she said. "We want to go to the Jewish cabaret at the Samson Restaurant tonight. Do you know if we have to book tickets?"

"Don't bother going," Ruth said to Tom and Sylvia Rosenzweig. "It's just a lot of anti-Semitic drivel. There's nothing Jewish about this cabaret." Both Rosenzweigs looked shocked.

"I heard it was a Jewish cabaret," Sylvia Rosenzweig said.

"That's what they advertise," Ruth said.

"Why?" said Tommy.

"I don't know," said Ruth. The Rosenzweigs left, shaking their heads.

"Why did you say this?" Edek said. "You are upsetting every Jewish person what is traveling in Poland, and every Polish person what you do meet."

"There is a lot to be upset about," Ruth said.

Edek looked happier when they were having lunch. His irritation with her seemed to have diminished. Eating often made him happy. Ruth thought about that sentence. It was incorrect. Eating always made her father happy. It seemed to be an obvious consequence of years of starvation. Or maybe he had been that way before the war. There had been so many maybes in Ruth's thoughts about Edek's and Rooshka's lives.

Ruth and Edek were in a small restaurant in Mikołájska Street, just off the Rynek Główny. The restaurant specialized in *pierogi*. Edek had chosen a selection of beef *pierogi*, veal *pierogi*, and potato and cheese *pierogi*. Ruth was eating chicken soup again. Her stomach was unsettled. Feeling ill had its advantages, she thought. She had never had so little trouble resisting food.

Edek was eating unusually fast. He always ate speedily, but something about today's speed alarmed Ruth. She looked at him. He had nearly finished the *pierogi*. His good mood seemed to have vanished with the beef, veal, and potato and cheese *pierogi*. Suddenly he put down his knife and fork. He banged the table with his right hand. "I have made a decision," he said.

Ruth's heart sank. What was she going to hear now? She put down her spoon. She tried to steady herself in preparation for what she was about to hear. What was Edek's decision? It sounded more decisive than a decision to order more *pierogi* or have a slice of cake.

"I have something to tell you, Ruthie," Edek said.

Ruth shook her head. Whatever it was, she didn't want to know about it. "Why do you shake your head?" Edek said.

"I know more than I need to know about a number of things," Ruth said. "I don't need to hear anything else. I'm already overloaded."

"But you do always want to know things," Edek said.

"Not now," Ruth said. "I don't want to know about Zofia, I don't want to know about Garth. I don't want to know about anything. I just want to go home."

"This is not to do with Zofia," Edek said, "and it is not to do with Garth. I did tell you everything what there was to tell about Garth."

"It's not?" Ruth said. "Then, what is it?"

"I do need to go back to Łódź," he said.

"You want to go back to Łódź?" Ruth said. "But you couldn't wait to get out of the place. You hated being there."

"I did not hate it," Edek said.

"You weren't happy there," said Ruth.

"What person in my position would be happy to be in Łódź?" Edek said.

"Exactly," said Ruth. "So why do you want to go back?"

"I want to go only for one hour or two hours," Edek said.

Ruth felt frightened. They had spent three days in Łódź. Why hadn't

Edek done whatever it was that he wanted to do then? What was different now? She started to tremble.

"What is wrong, Ruthie?" Edek said.

"I'm just cold," she said.

She wondered where the chill in her bones had arrived from. Her teeth started chattering. She wanted to put on her coat, but she couldn't move. She could feel her lips turning blue. "I'm frightened," she said to Edek.

"There is nothing to be frightened of, Ruthie," he said. It didn't reassure her. If she became any more immobile, she thought, her blood would halt. It would just stop in whatever artery or vein it happened to be coursing through. And she would be frozen stiff. "This is not something to be frightened about," Edek said.

"Could you help me put my coat on?" Ruth said. Edek got up and helped Ruth on with the coat.

"I do only want to go for one hour or two hours maximum," he said. One or two hours, she thought. What could they discover in one or two hours that could be so bad? Why did she think it would be a discovery? Maybe Edek wanted one last look at Kamedulska Street. She held her teeth together to stop her jaw from making its involuntary movements.

"There is probably nothing there," Edek said.

"I thought we had established that," said Ruth.

"I have to dig a little bit," Edek said. Dig, Ruth thought. Dig where? Why did her father always speak in such cryptic, clipped sentences?

"Dig where?" said Ruth.

"In Kamedulska Street, of course," Edek said. Ruth was startled. "My cousin Herschel did bury something there," Edek said.

"So the old man was right," Ruth said. "There is something buried there."

"There was something buried there," Edek said. "I do not know if it is still there."

"It is still there," she said suddenly. Edek looked at her. He looked disturbed. She was disturbed herself. Why did she have to say things like that? It had come out of her mouth, with no warning. It is still there. The words had been uttered before she had even known about them.

"How do you know this?" Edek said.

"I don't know," she said quietly. "I'm probably just guessing."

"I did never tell you about this," Edek said.

"It was just a guess," Ruth said. Edek looked at her suspiciously. "It was a guess," she said, "and I had a fifty percent chance of being right. Whatever it is is going to be there or not be there."

"Do you know what it is?" Edek said.

"It's something small," Ruth said. Edek shook his head. He looked a bit pale. "I don't know why I said that," Ruth said.

"It is something very small, Ruthie," Edek said quietly.

"It was just a good guess, Dad," she said. "I've always been good at guessing." Edek looked carefully at her. He looked unnerved.

"I do not think it is a guess," he said.

"Of course it is," she said. "It's a logical guess. If it had been something big, those Poles would have found it in a flash." Ruth felt the back of her neck. It was damp. She was in a cold sweat. "It was an intelligent guess, Dad," she said, and laughed in order to lighten the atmosphere.

"Maybe you are right," Edek said.

"It wasn't gold?" Ruth said. Edek laughed. "No, Ruthie darling, it was not gold."

"I thought we'd never go to Łódź again," she said.

"What do you think?" Edek said. "That I did think I would go many times more? I did think I was finished with Łódź."

"We might as well stay at the Grand Victoria again," Ruth said. She cheered up. If they were going to go back to Łódź, there were things to be organized. Travel arrangements. A hotel. The organization required for the trip to Łódź revitalized her. There was a normality to arrangements. To schedules and bookings and dates and appointments. She loved to know hotel rates and airline prices and train schedules. She used to read train schedules, sometimes, for relaxation.

She had a copy of the Long Island Railroad timetable in her desk at work. She loved the precision of the schedules, the destinations, and the times. A train scheduled to leave Penn Station at 7:03 A.M. was scheduled to arrive at its destination at 9:07 A.M. It was a wonderful world of order and certainty. Max had decimated Ruth's pleasure in the Long Island Railroad schedule one day by telling her that that particular railroad company was never on time.

"Why do we need to go to a hotel?" Edek said.

"Because we need a base. We need to get a shovel. We need to organize ourselves."

"Okay," said Edek. "There is probably nothing there," he said after a couple of minutes. Ruth didn't say anything. She knew that whatever was there, was there. The knowledge frightened her.

"What is it, Dad?" she said. "What's buried there?"

"I will tell you, Ruthie," he said, "I will tell you, in Łódź. It is not such an easy story." Ruth felt sick again.

"It is nothing to do with you, Ruthie," Edek said "It is nothing to do with you."

"I'll get the doorman to get us a shovel," Ruth said. "Maybe I'll ask him to come with us. He'll keep that old couple at bay."

"You was not so nice to this doorman," Edek said. "I, myself, was always nice to him. It can never hurt to be on someone's good side."

"You're right, Dad," she said. She was glad they had tipped the doorman well.

She couldn't believe that they were going back to Łódź. And for what? For something that was buried in the ground, fifty-two years ago. If it was in the ground, it couldn't be too frightening. That was a ludicrous thought, she thought. She had spent half of her life tormented by buried beings. This was something very small, though. Too small to be a being. How big did a being have to be to be a being?

Ruth shook her head. She had to stop driving herself crazy with abstract riddles. She thought of a distraction. What was it that Edek had said before? He had said that what he wanted to tell her was not about Zofia, and not about Garth. He said he had told her all there was to tell about Garth. He didn't say the same about Zofia. Was that an ominous omission? Did it mean there was something he was not revealing about Zofia?

"Should we look for a driver with a Mercedes to drive us to Łódź?" Edek said.

"Drive us to Łódź?" Ruth said. "I don't want to drive to Łódź. We've got no time, anyway. I want to go home. We'll fly to Łódź."

"Are you sure?" said Edek. "We been very comfortable in the cars."

"I want to fly," Ruth said. "I want to get there and I want to leave. I don't want to hang around Poland. I've had enough of Poles, and enough of the Polish countryside. I've had enough shrines and crosses and Virgin

Marys and Christs on crosses. I've had enough pastel Madonnas to last me a lifetime. I've seen more sweet-faced donkeys and their sour-expressioned owners than I ever needed to see." Edek looked alarmed. Ruth's voice had been rising and rising. People were staring at them.

"Column down, Ruthie," Edek said. "Column down."

"It's calm, not column," she shouted.

"Okay, colm," Edek said. "Colm down."

"I'm sorry," she said.

"It got too much for you, Ruthie, the whole trip," Edek said.

"It sure did," she said.

Several people in the restaurant were still staring at her. One of them was a priest. Ruth stared back at him. "Don't look so sanctimonious," she said to him. "Your crowd doesn't have a wonderful war record." She hoped that he understood English.

"Ruthie, Ruthie, what has got into you?" Edek said. There was that question, again. Nothing had got into her. All of this had been inside her for a long time.

"I hate them," she said.

"Who?" he said.

"The Polish priests," Ruth said. "Especially the older ones. They pretend to be so pious."

"You cannot hate everybody," Edek said.

"I didn't, before I came to Poland," she said. What was happening to her? Where was her compassion? Her humanity? She hated who she was turning into more than she hated the Poles. She had to get out of this spiral of hatred.

"Can we leave this afternoon?" she said to Edek.

"You want to leave today?" Edek said.

"Yes," she said.

"Why not tomorrow?" he said.

"I need to get out of Poland," Ruth said.

"You was the one who did want to come to Poland," Edek said.

"Well, I've had enough," she said. "I want to go home."

"Okay, okay," Edek said. "We can go to Łódź today."

"Thanks, Dad," she said. "I'll make the airline and hotel reservations. I'll see if I can get a flight around six o'clock."

"That is fine with me," Edek said.

Ruth worried briefly that she had wanted to leave Kraków early in order to leave Edek little time for Zofia. She dismissed the worry. Edek hadn't mentioned Zofia. There were far bigger things on Edek's mind. Bigger things. Like Zofia's breasts. She had to stop thinking about Zofia's breasts. Up until now, she had considered smaller breasts to be superior.

"I will have to say good-bye to Zofia and Walentyna," Edek said. Had she telegraphed her thoughts about Zofia's breasts to Edek? How absurd, she thought. Thoughts couldn't be telegraphed. Zofia's breasts had probably been in Edek's thoughts all morning. They didn't need telegraphing.

"That's a good idea," Ruth said.

Zofia and Walentyna were both agitated. Ruth could see their agitation, as soon as she stepped out of the elevator. The two women were standing in a tense huddle in the lounge with Edek. Ruth could see the turbulence in the air. Zofia was waving her arms and shaking her shoulders. Walentyna was nodding. Ruth could see the exclamations and declarations.

Zofia saw Ruth. "You are going so soon?" she called out to Ruth. Ruth walked over to the group. "You are going so soon?" Zofia said again. Zofia looked hurt. Wounded. As though Ruth had somehow plotted this departure.

"We have to go," Ruth said. "My father discovered something he needed to do in Łódź."

"You could go tomorrow," Zofia said. Walentyna nodded.

"I have to get back to New York," Ruth said.

"She does," Edek said. "She does have a big business what she must look after."

"A small business," Ruth said. "But a business that needs my attention." Zofia still looked wounded. "If you are ever in New York," Ruth said to Zofia, "please feel welcome to call me." Ruth looked at Walentyna, to make sure she knew she, too, was included in the invitation. Neither of the women answered.

"It is time that we have to go," Edek said to the two women. "Poland is not so good for my daughter. It is not so good for me, too, to tell you the truth."

"Of course, dear Edek, of course," Zofia said.

"Of course," Walentyna said.

"It's been nice meeting you," Ruth said to Walentyna.

"For me it has been a pleasure to get to know you and to get to know Edek," Walentyna said. "I think you are a brave girl."

"I'm not a girl," Ruth said. "I'm a rapidly aging woman. I'm exhausted. But thank you anyway."

"You are a brave girl," Walentyna said.

Zofia had taken Edek to one side, and was saying something in a low voice to him. Ruth strained to hear her. "My darling Edek," Zofia was saying, "I will call you every day until you come to Sopot." Edek laughed.

"We have to go," Ruth said loudly, and walked over to where Zofia and Edek were standing.

"What is Melbourne like?" Zofia said to Ruth.

"Damp and gray," Ruth said.

"Like Poland," Zofia said, nodding her head. "Maybe I will come to Melbourne," Zofia said to Edek.

"We have to go," Ruth said again. Zofia threw her arms around Edek. "I will see you very soon, dear Edek." Edek laughed. Zofia turned to Ruth. "Good-bye, Ruthie," she said. She put her arms around Ruth and gave her a hug. Ruth stiffened in mid-hug. She wished she hadn't. She didn't want to hurt Zofia. She was leaving. She was sure they would never see Zofia again.

Ruth gave Walentyna a hug. "Good-bye," she said to Walentyna. Walentyna kissed Edek on the cheek. "You are two brave people," she said to Edek.

"Who?" Zofia said. "Me and Edek?"

"No," Walentyna said. "Edek and Ruthie." Zofia glared at Walentyna, then she turned back to Edek. "Bye bye, dear Edek," she said.

Ruth and Edek got into the taxi. Zofia stood in the street and blew kisses to Edek. Walentyna stood beside her. In the car, Ruth could hear Zofia's kisses. Mwah, mwah, mwah was the sound Zofia's kisses were making. Zofia stood in the street and blew kisses until Ruth and Edek were out of sight.

The Polish Airlines flight from Kraków to Łódź was almost empty. There were only two other people in first class, and ten or fifteen people in economy. Ruth had booked first-class seats to give her and Edek some breathing space. "I don't want Poles breathing down my neck," she had said to Edek.

She looked at Edek. He looked bright-eyed and buoyant, but he must be tired. She was exhausted and she hadn't had a late night. The image of Zofia blowing kisses to them all the way down the street came into her head. It had been a sweet image. The two women, one blowing kisses wildly, and the other standing primly beside her.

"You must be tired, Dad," she said to Edek.

"I am not tired," he said. He looked at Ruth. "Who would imagine I would go back to Łódź? What would Rooshka say?" Ruth was glad that Edek was thinking about her mother. "Don't be frightened, Ruthie," Edek said. Ruth felt worried. Edek had reassured her one time too many. He must be reassuring himself, she thought. She tried to allay her worry. Whatever it was that was or wasn't in Łódź, they would be out of there, very promptly, and on their way to New York.

"Why don't you have a short nap?" Ruth said to Edek.

"I do not need to have a nap," Edek said. "I am fine. I got my book." He held up the book he was just starting. *As Blood Goes By*.

"Oh, Dad," she said. "You choose the worst-sounding titles."

"This is very good," Edek said. "I can see already it is a good book. It is about a man what one day finds—"

"Don't tell me any more," Ruth said. "Please."

"We are flying at an altitude of twenty-three thousand feet," the pilot said, in Polish and English. "You can move about the cabin if necessary but we recommend that you remain in your seat with your seat belt fastened." Ruth checked her seat belt. She checked Edek's seat belt. They were both securely fastened.

She looked back at Edek. He had fallen asleep. Ruth was surprised. Edek never slept during the day. *As Blood Goes By* had dropped to the floor. Edek must be exhausted, she thought. She looked at him again. He was out of it. It must have been some night he had last night, she thought.

⟡ *Chapter Sixteen* ⟡

*R*uth felt a change in the plane's atmosphere. It startled her. She had been daydreaming. Thinking about the Union Square farmer's market, and what she would buy there. She looked around. Everything looked normal. There had been no announcements from the flight deck. No turbulence. No series of beeps from the captain to the crew. It had been a smooth, uneventful flight. Still, she felt bothered. She felt sure she could sense a movement in the air. The usually still, artificial air of airplanes was moving. The normally dormant, stiff air of all flights definitely had a ripple. She could even hear a flurry, a flicker of wind. She listened carefully. There was definitely a stirring, a ruffling.

She looked at Edek. He was still asleep. *As Blood Goes By* was still on the floor. The two other passengers in first class were sitting, motionless, in their seats. Neither of them looked worried. She listened again. She could hear breathing. Labored breathing. She could also feel jerking and twitching. "I can hear you," she said suddenly. "I can hear your mouth opening and closing. I can hear saliva sticking to your gums. Semidry suction noises. Are you not well?" There was no answer. "I can hear your bones," Ruth said. "I can hear creaks and clicks. Are your bones giving you trouble?" There was no reply. The air was still shuddering. Still unsteady. "I know you can hear me," she said.

She remembered how unnerved she had been when she had first heard those words. Now, the words were coming from her. She wasn't unnerved now. She was not even nervous. "I know you can hear me," she said again. There was no answer. She felt uneasy. Why was she summoning him? Why was she calling out to him? She wanted to let him know, she thought, that she had the upper hand. That he couldn't surprise her anymore. That she could detect his presence.

"I know you hear me," she said with more force. Neither of the other two passengers looked up. Edek stayed asleep. "I know you can hear me," she shouted. "Why are you hiding? What are you frightened of?"

"I am not hiding," said Höss.

"You were hiding from me," Ruth said. "Why have you turned into a wallflower? You're not known for being shy and retiring. A shrinking violet is not what people think of when they think of you."

"You think people do still think of me?" Höss said.

"I hope so," said Ruth. She thought Höss was pleased with this answer. She could feel his pleasure. It displeased her. She wanted to needle him, not please him.

"I know you did not intend your previous remark as a compliment," Höss said.

"It isn't a compliment," Ruth said.

"You and I have a different understanding of where history will place me," Höss said.

"History has already placed you," said Ruth.

"This is recent history you are speaking about," said Höss. "This will change."

"I don't think you'll ever be seen as a hero," Ruth said.

"We will see," Höss said.

"If you're such a big hero, why were you hiding?" Ruth said. Höss snorted. "You think you can hide from me?" Ruth said. "I can sense your presence. I can detect the smell that accompanies you, too."

"The smell is faint, no?" Höss said.

"So you know what smell I'm talking about," Ruth said.

"Of course," said Höss.

"The smell of burning flesh," Ruth said. "It still adheres to you. It's still stuck to your skin."

"I thought it was still possible to smell it," Höss said. He sounded glum.

"I couldn't identify it at first," Ruth said. "I thought it was just your presence that was making me feel bilious."

"I cannot remove this smell," Höss said. "Day and night, awake and asleep, I am surrounded by it. I am drenched and steeped and congested with that stench."

"It must have seeped into your soul," Ruth said. "Burning flesh can do that."

"This is why you do not eat meat, yes?" said Höss.

"Meat being grilled or fried or seared reminds me of burning flesh," Ruth said. How could she be reminded of something she'd never seen, never witnessed, never smelled? she thought.

"It is not necessary to have experienced something directly in order for it to be part of your memory," Höss said. It was easy for him to give her a flip answer.

"What do you know?" she said.

"If I knew so little you would not bother with me," Höss said.

"You think it's my choice?" Ruth said.

"I know it is your choice," said Höss. He made a blowing noise. "The smell is very strong today," he said.

"Why are you bothered by the smell of burning flesh?" Ruth said. "It should remind you of happier times."

"It is not so strong, the smell, where you are," Höss said. "If I could come closer, you would be overwhelmed. Sick to your stomach."

"You're absolutely right," Ruth said. "If you could come any closer, I would be sick to my stomach. So you can't come any closer?" Ruth said. "That's interesting. I'm glad there's a limit imposed on how close you can get. I'm glad the distance isn't arbitrary."

"Nobody from Zweites Himmel's Lager is able to come closer than this," Höss said.

"Thank God," Ruth said. Höss breathed out in exasperation. "Why do you insist on thanking God?" he said.

"I have to thank somebody for the fact that you can't close the gap between us," Ruth said. Ruth was startled by what she had just said. How could she even imagine that the gap between her and Höss was so small it could be closed? The thought shocked her. She and Höss were miles apart. Physically, morally, temperamentally. She had to stop speaking as though they were close. The thought of being close to Höss made her feel sick. Clogged and blocked. As though Höss had invaded her. She wished she could go for a walk. Get some fresh air.

She opened her mouth. A loud burp came out. And then a fart. A large fart. She felt better, but embarrassed. The passenger in the seat closest to her had looked up. He looked surprised. "Excuse me," Ruth said to him. He nodded. She felt uncomfortable. Uncouth. People traveling in first class rarely burped or farted. She looked at Edek. He was sound asleep. She hoped her fart didn't smell.

"You can't smell anything in Auschwitz now," she said to Höss. "That stench of bodies burning that spread for miles has all gone." Höss didn't say anything. Ruth could feel Höss's reluctance to discuss her visit to his old stamping ground. His former place of employment. His former home. "I thought you would be interested in my trip," she said. There was silence. "Is this not something that you want to discuss?" she said. Höss remained silent.

"There is no sign near the gallows, where you were hanged," Ruth said. "I thought there might be a plaque that said: 'Rudolf Franz Ferdinand Höss, commandant of Auschwitz, was hanged here.' But there wasn't." Ruth thought she heard the sound of someone gagging. "The gallows were quite close to the kitchens, weren't they?" she said.

A choking noise came from Höss. It had a liquid sound. Like a gurgle or ripple.

"Is this painful for you?" Ruth said.

Höss swallowed. "It is not an easy memory," he said.

"The hanging?" she said. Höss started coughing.

"Yes, yes, yes," he said, through a series of coughs.

"You have a sore throat?" Ruth said.

"I am fine," Höss said, and coughed again.

"Something else that surprised me, in Auschwitz, was the sign, ARBEIT MACHT FREI," Ruth said. "The sign was small. In photographs it always looks so big. I think the sign should have been bigger," Ruth said. "It was out of scale with its intentions."

"The intention was to appear harmless," Höss said, "and in this regard the size was appropriate."

"I guess so," said Ruth.

"Auschwitz today is not what it once was," Höss said. His voice had a renewed buoyancy. Almost as though he was amused at what Auschwitz had become.

"It's almost a circus today," Ruth said. "There's a cafeteria, tourist buses, Polish schoolchildren thrilled to be getting a day off school. They should have built a separate museum and left Auschwitz as it was. Like Birkenau. The tourists who go there are kept busy reading the literature around the exhibits. They go from one room to another reading. The reading takes the place of feeling. They can't feel the place."

"And they are warm," Höss shouted. "They have put in heating." He roared with laughter. Ruth lifted her heel. Höss stopped laughing. What was she doing talking to Höss? Part of her couldn't believe she was talking to Rudolf Höss again. She couldn't believe she had encountered him on a plane. On a Polski Airways flight between Kraków and Łódź.

She wanted to ask Höss where he had been since she had last heard from him. But she was reluctant to appear curious about his patterns and habits. She assumed that he could move around the world.

"I went to Baden-Baden for a few days," Höss said. So he did know what she was thinking.

"To your birthplace," she said. "You've probably still got relatives there."

"Possibly," said Höss.

"Did any of your children settle there?" Ruth said.

"I will not discuss my children," Höss said.

"I think they must have changed their names," Ruth said. "Whether they were in Baden-Baden or another part of Germany."

"Please leave my children out of this," Höss said, his voice rising.

"So you went to Baden-Baden for old times' sake?" she said to Höss.

"Yes," Höss said. "My movements are restricted compared to the residents of Himmel," Höss said. "But compared to you, I can move anywhere. You are restricted."

"It's a restriction I can live with," Ruth said. Höss shrieked.

"This is a pun, is it not?" he shouted. "You are restricted because you live, still." He roared with laughter. Ruth put her hands over her ears. It didn't dim the laughter.

"I really have got you hooked on language, haven't I?" she said to Höss.

"Yes, yes," he squealed.

"It's better than being hooked on many other things," Ruth said. "It's better than being hooked up to the gallows."

Höss's squeal stiffened. It turned into a different squeal altogether. It became a shrill, pointed squeal. The squeal of a rodent. You could feel the long thin tail and sharp, whiskered nose of something verminous behind that squeal. The squeal gave Ruth goose bumps. She rubbed her arms.

"You are not comfortable?" Höss said. She detected a pleasure in his voice at her discomfort.

"How do you get to the different places?" Ruth said.

"You merely will yourself to be there," he said.

"Really?" said Ruth.

"I can go almost anywhere I wish," Höss said. "With the exception of Himmel. Of course. For example, I traveled to Łódź to be with you."

"To *be* with me?" Ruth said. "You meant to *meet* with me. Not to *be* with me. I may *meet* you, but you are never with me. Do you understand that?" She raised the heel of her foot.

"I understand," Höss said. "My purpose on that particular journey was to meet with you. After all, who in his right mind would go to Łódź for no particular reason?" Höss emitted a conspiratorial guffaw. It made Ruth feel queasy. A shared view of Łódź didn't make her and Höss bosom buddies. Why had she used the word "bosom"? Bosom conjured up images of Zofia. She and Zofia certainly weren't bosom buddies either.

Why was she thinking about Zofia? She was sure they wouldn't see Zofia again. Why was she so hostile to Zofia? she thought. What did she have against her? That she was Polish? If that was the reason, it was extremely unfair of her. Was she annoyed at Zofia for leaping into bed with her father? Leaping? Why use the word "leap"? It was so judgmental. And how did she know who was doing the leaping? It could have been Edek. Although, she decided, it was more likely to be Zofia.

She had to cut these thoughts about leaps. Too many visions of Edek and Zofia in various stages of leap were creeping into her head. It didn't matter who initiated the leap. It was not something that she should hold against Zofia. Young people leaped into bed with strangers all the time. Young people had one-night stands. Why shouldn't Edek and Zofia have a

one-night stand? She felt ashamed of her hostility toward Zofia. It was definitely out of line.

"I am on a journey at the moment," Höss said, interrupting her
thoughts. Ruth was annoyed. She would much rather be thinking about
Zofia than Höss. "This is a journey with a higher end in mind," Höss said.
"A good cause."

"What do you mean?" she said.

"I think you know," Höss said.

"I have no idea what you are talking about," Ruth said.

A stewardess came by with a basket of oranges. She gave Ruth an
orange. The stewardess looked at Edek. "I'll take an orange for my father,
for when he wakes up," Ruth said. The orange came nestled in a napkin.
Why were they passing out oranges? Fifteen years ago when she had flown
with Polski, they had passed out oranges. She had assumed the food shortage, then, had contributed to the small scale of the snack. An orange was an
absurd thing to serve on a plane. It was impossible to peel an orange or
prize apart the segments without a mess, when you were sitting in an air-
plane seat. And this was first class. An orange must be the standard refresh-
ment served on this flight, she decided. Unless the caviar and the petit fours
were coming later.

"Why do you not eat your orange?" Höss said.

"Because I can't peel it without making a mess," she said.

"You should eat it," he said. Ruth was astonished. Now, Höss *and* her
father were ordering her to eat. "You like fruit," Höss said. "I noticed that
you prepared bananas and pears for yourself for your trip to Auschwitz."
So, he could see her even when she couldn't detect his presence.

"I am everywhere," Höss said.

"That's what I feared," Ruth said.

"I was in Auschwitz myself, the day you and your father were there,"
Höss said.

"I'm sure you were," she said. "Did it make you homesick?"

"I do think about my time there much of the time," Höss said.

"Good," Ruth said.

"I was reluctant to leave Auschwitz," Höss said. "Reluctant to leave my
job as camp commandant. But in November 1943, I was offered a promo-

tion. The move did not appeal to me. I had become totally absorbed with Auschwitz because of the very difficult complications of the job. But one cannot refuse a promotion. So I accepted the job of head of Department D1 in the Economic Administration Head Office."

"That made you Inspector of Concentration Camps, didn't it?" Ruth said.

"Yes," Höss said. He sighed. "I really would have preferred to go to the front," he said. "But the Reichsführer had most firmly forbidden me to do this. Not once did he forbid me, but twice."

"Himmler thwarted you?" said Ruth.

"The Reichsführer was doing what was best for the country," Höss said.

"I think it was definitely best for the prisoners that you left Auschwitz," Ruth said. "Things improved, minimally, for the prisoners after you left."

Höss laughed. "Yes, I heard this," he said. "They say things were never quite as harsh after I left."

"It was a minimal difference," Ruth said. "But the most minuscule difference in Auschwitz could make a difference."

"I do not believe there was much difference," Höss said. "Liebehenschel, who replaced me, was a short man, a pudgy type. He had particularly protruding eyes. He was a weak type."

"Short? Pudgy? Protruding eyes?" Ruth said. "Where were all the Aryan prototypes?" Höss ignored her.

"I was discussing my new job as Inspector of Concentration Camps," Höss said. "In my new job, I was now able, thanks to the aid of an efficient office, to follow the development and progress of all of the concentration camps. I was able to obtain an overview, which was essential for us."

"You were like a time and motion expert, an efficiency expert," Ruth said. "Your job was to make sure that the death camps were working at full capacity, with a healthy production line and maximum profits."

"That is correct," said Höss. "It was quite a challenge. Maurer, the deputy director, and I were able to correct much of what was wrong. But by 1944, it was really too late to make extreme changes."

"What a shame," Ruth said. "If you had been given another year on the job Europe could have been truly *Judenrein*. Free of Jews. There could have been not even one Jew left."

"I think so," Höss said, quite matter-of-factly.

"You had barely been in the job for a year when things began to decline for you, didn't they?" Ruth said.

"This is absolutely correct," Höss said. "From the beginning of the intensified air offensive in 1944 not a single day passed without reports of casualties."

"The poor Germans," Ruth said.

"Yes," said Höss. "These persistent air attacks placed great difficulty and stress on the civilian population. Especially on women."

"I nearly forgot your sensitivity to women," Ruth said. "Were all Germans as sensitive about this as you were?"

"No," Höss said. He didn't notice her sarcasm. He was too immersed in his recollections, Ruth realized. "Even Berliners, whose spirits are not so easily brought down, were in the end exhausted," Höss said. "Worn out by the endlessness of the attacks. Having to spend days and nights in cellars and shelters, their nerves came under strain. The psychological torment suffered by the German people could not have gone on for much longer without severe psychological repercussions."

"You think it was too much for the Germans trying to dodge bombs in cellars and shelters?" Ruth said.

"Yes," said Höss. "Absolutely."

"It's hard for me to feel sorry for them," Ruth said. Höss didn't say anything.

"Our new jet fighters could not keep back the enemy," Höss said. "The offensive continued and increased. Despite this the Führer gave orders to continue to hold firmly to our mission and our principles. Goebbels wrote about the necessity to believe in miracles and he made several speeches to that effect."

"They didn't seem like desperate men to you?" Ruth said. "After all, you were being trounced."

"I had serious and grave misgivings about whether it was possible for us to win the war," Höss said.

"I should hope so," Ruth said. "The war was nearly over."

"But I refused to let myself doubt our final victory," Höss said.

"Well, you knew you had won," Ruth said. "You knew how many Jews you had gotten rid of, how many gypsies, how many others you didn't approve of you had murdered. You knew the world was already a different place. And it would never be the same. You knew you had definitely won."

"We had not yet won," Höss said sternly. "Our mission was to be in power. To purify Europe and give the German people a world free of disease, and distrust. My heart stayed with the Führer and his ideals. I knew that we must not let these ideals perish.

"I am certain that others had similar thoughts to my own. Thoughts that we might lose the war. But none of us dared to voice this possibility. Each of us worked with a grim dedication, as though if we as individuals worked as hard as possible we could achieve victory. We made sure that the prisoners who were working in our war factories that had not yet been destroyed, were kept working at full pitch. We shared the same attitude to those defeatists among us who said that our efforts no longer mattered. We dealt with them immediately."

"When you were getting rid of colleagues who were voicing doubts about a victory, you really knew it was all over. You knew the enemy was surrounding you. You knew it would all be over fairly soon," Ruth said.

"I knew that I had to do everything I could to support the Führer," Höss said.

"You drove to Auschwitz, didn't you?" Ruth said. "You left your office, and you drove to Auschwitz. You were desperate to do whatever you could to cover your tracks, and the tracks of your fellow Nazis."

"Of course," Höss said, with pride in his voice. "Of course. I hoped to reach Auschwitz in time to ensure that the orders to destroy everything in the camp were being correctly carried out."

"You didn't want any evidence left behind, did you?" Ruth said. "Why? If you were so proud of your ideals, why were you worried about others uncovering your actions?"

Höss snorted. "That is a stupid question," he said. "Please do not interrupt me. I tried to get to Auschwitz but I was only able to get as far as the Oder River, quite close to Ratibor, because the Russians and their tanks were already spreading out in great numbers across the other side of the river." He paused for a moment. "The scenes that I encountered on that chaotic journey will never leave me," he said. "It was complete chaos everywhere. A chaos that was a result of the orders to evacuate all concentration camps."

"There were Nazis marching streams of half-dead Jews all over Poland and into parts of Germany and Czechoslovakia," Ruth said.

"Yes," said Höss. "On every road, and even on tracks, I encountered columns and columns of prisoners. These miserable, wretched, abject prisoners were struggling to walk in snow that was often, particularly west of the Oder, very deep. They had no food."

"You noticed?" said Ruth. "The lack of food didn't bother you in Auschwitz."

"I gave very strict orders to the men who were in charge of the columns of prisoners," Höss said. "I told them in no uncertain terms and with the full status of the SS ranking, that they were not, under any circumstances, to shoot those prisoners who were not capable of marching farther."

"Really?" said Ruth. "Why would you bother to do that? They were helping you by shooting Jews. They were keeping up your good work. I don't think Hitler or the Reichsführer would have approved of that attitude."

"In one instance," Höss said, "just as I had stopped my car next to a dead body, I heard the sound of revolver shots very close to where I was. I ran in the direction of the shots and saw a soldier who was about to shoot a prisoner who had slumped against a tree.

"The soldier had barely gotten off his motorcycle and already had his revolver drawn. I called out quickly to this soldier. He ignored me. I shouted at him. 'What on earth do you think you are doing?' I shouted. 'Has this prisoner caused you any harm?' The soldier laughed out loud, at me. 'What do you think you can do about it?' the soldier said to me in the most impertinent manner."

"The soldier obviously didn't know who he was dealing with," Ruth said.

"I drew my pistol and shot him with no further delay," Höss said. "He was a sergeant major in the air force." Höss breathed out heavily. Ruth could feel that he was still flushed. That he was still experiencing the adrenaline rush of that memory. That swift response with his pistol.

"I know why you were trying to show some compassion, some concern for the prisoner," Ruth said.

"Why?" said Höss.

"You were trying to save your neck," Ruth said. "You knew it was about to snap, about to break." A gurgling noise, followed by a semisuppressed wet cough, came from Höss. Ruth flinched. It sounded disgusting. "It still hurts, doesn't it?" she said to Höss. "The memory of the hanging. The memory of that pull on the neck. The memory of the snap. The memory of the fracture and the rupture." She paused. "That was rupture, not rapture," she said.

Höss was quiet. Ruth thought she could hear him trying to swallow. "Really, Rudolf," she said. She stopped, in surprise. She had never addressed Höss by his name. It felt strange. She looked around the cabin of the plane. No one was taking any notice of her. Edek was still asleep. "Really, Rudolf," she said again. "I don't see why you were bothering to appear concerned. It was a bit late in the day for you to be trying to save your neck. Do you know this expression, a 'bit late in the day'?"

Höss didn't answer. "It doesn't refer to the time of day," Ruth said. "It refers to your life. It was too late for you. You had murdered too many. It was too late to defend a Jew. Too late to save a Jew. Too late to shoot a Nazi or an air force officer. Or any other German. It was just plain too late. You had murdered too many."

"When I saw this chaos on the road, at the end, I tried with all of my power, until the very end, to bring a sort of order to the madness," Höss said. "But it was no use, nothing I could do could make any difference. And then we ourselves had to flee."

"There were people looking for you, weren't there?" said Ruth. "You had to grab Hedwig and run." Höss didn't answer her. "You don't want to talk about it, do you?" she said. "Okay, we can drop the subject." She felt magnanimous. She was nearly in Łódź. They would be in Łódź briefly, and then she would be on her way home. Höss cleared his throat. Ruth wondered if he was clearing lingering fragments of the hanging out of his esophagus.

"You will be angry with your father very soon," Höss said.

"I've been angry with him lots of times," Ruth said. "Don't try to sound like a prophet. I know you see yourself as a visionary, but your prophecies don't frighten me. They don't even faze me." She thought Höss was probably not fooled by her air of bravado. But, really, what did he know? He was just an old Nazi. "What do you know, anyway?" she said to Höss. "You're still stuck in Zweites Himmel's Lager."

"I am not so stuck. I am going on a journey. Quite a journey," Höss said, and he laughed. It was an eerie laugh. A weird laugh. More like a cackle or a hoarse screech. The laugh rang out. Ruth was sure that it could be heard throughout the plane. She looked at the stewardess, who was offering her some canapés—a pat of liverwurst on a rye biscuit. The stewardess didn't look as though she was hearing anything abnormal. Ruth declined the canapés.

She looked at Edek. He was snoring quietly. He looked peaceful. She wondered why she and Edek were going back to Łódź. What did Edek expect to find there? Something small. Why hadn't he looked for it when they were there? Was it something he didn't want to face? Something troubling? Something he thought he didn't want? It couldn't be anything essential. He had lived without it for fifty-two years. He had lived without even mentioning it.

Edek could have asked her to look for it when she was in Łódź, fifteen years ago, if it had been that important to him, she thought. She sighed. She really didn't have enough energy to muster up too much anxiety about the buried object. That's what she did, she realized. She mustered up anxiety for herself. Conjured it up. Wished for it. Searched for it. Sought it out. And when the anxiety hit her, she was finally able to relax. To relax in the fear, the dread, the tension, and the sense of foreboding. It was all so familiar to her. The tension, the apprehension, the uneasiness. It put her in the same hemisphere as her mother. The same orbit. It put her in the world of those who suffer.

"The bite on your face is still very enlarged," Höss said.

"It was a very large fly," Ruth said.

"I know," said Höss.

"I guess you do," Ruth said.

"By a very strange coincidence," Höss said. "I myself was circled by a large fly."

"There are flies everywhere," Ruth said. "Even, I presume, in Zweites Himmel's Lager."

"The fly I was referring to did not circle me in Zweites Himmel's Lager, but in Auschwitz," Höss said.

"My mother said there were no flies in Auschwitz," Ruth said.

"That was correct during my time there," Höss said. "But this fly appeared later in my life."

"So what?" said Ruth.

"Everyone was surprised to see a fly in April," Höss said. "It was not even late April. It was mid-April. This black fly circled me and circled me." Ruth suddenly realized what day Höss was talking about.

"It was April 16, wasn't it?" she said. "The day you were hanged." She heard Höss wince. The word clearly hurt him.

"It was April 16," Höss said. "The day on which I was h-h-h-" He couldn't get more than the *h* to come out of him. Ruth started to laugh.

"The day on which you were hanged," she said. "It's not such a hard word to enunciate."

"Yes, that day," Höss said quietly.

"The day you were hanged in the very gallows in Auschwitz where errant prisoners were hanged," Ruth said. Höss winced again. A small, piercing wince. Almost a squeak. "You were hanged on your own home ground. Your own turf. Your own territory. Your former kingdom," Ruth said. She could hear Höss trying to keep his mouth shut. "You were hanged on that day in April," she said. Höss let out a bleat. "Hanged, hanged, hanged," Ruth said. Höss yelped. "If I had known this word caused you such difficulties, I would have used it earlier," Ruth said.

"Are you interested in the coincidence of the fly?" Höss said. His voice was hoarse and raspy. He cleared his throat several times. "Why do you think the fly bit you?" Höss said.

Ruth stiffened. "No reason," she said. "There are no reasons why flies bite you. The fact that there was a large black fly buzzing around you the day you were executed is just coincidence. And not a very notable coincidence."

"I would not agree," Höss said.

"The fly that bit you has flown closer and closer to me recently. It was circling me that day. My face was next to your face. I was watching you, when the fly flew between us. It bit you and you moved away. The fly was warning you to move out of my orbit."

Ruth felt sick. A wave of biliousness rose up in her throat. She wished Höss would go back to his conversation about himself and his wife fleeing the Allies.

"As you wish," Höss said. "In Wismar, my wife and I heard, by chance, in a farmhouse, that the Führer was dead. When we heard this news," Höss said, "my wife and I knew exactly what we must do. We must go. With the Führer gone, our world would be gone, too. It didn't seem possible to go on living. We knew we would be hounded and persecuted wherever we went.

"I had a supply of poison for myself and my wife," Höss said. "We prepared to take the poison. But then, we decided for the sake of the children, we should try to stay alive."

"Good parents to the end," Ruth said.

"It was a big mistake," Höss said. "One which I regret to this day. We all would have been spared a large amount of suffering and grief and distress. The pain and misery my wife and the children had to endure could have been avoided.

"The Reichsführer was, together with other members of the government, in hiding, in Flensburg. I reported there. It was a disheartening meeting. All talk of continuing to fight for our ideals was gone. It was truly now every man for himself.

" 'Well, gentlemen, this is the end,' the Reichsführer said to us," Höss said. "And then he gave us our final directive. 'Hide in the army,' he said. Hide in the army. Can you believe that? Hide like a coward. To this day I am still filled with disgust at the Reichsführer's directive."

"I sent my son back to his mother, together with my driver and my car," he said.

"A family man to the very end," Ruth said.

"I am not quite at the end," Höss said. "By sheer chance I heard on the radio that Himmler had been arrested and had taken his own life, with poison. I had my vial of poison on me, also. I made the decision not to take the poison. I would wait and see what eventuated. The departmental staff were given false papers. The papers which would enable them to disappear into the navy.

"I was fortunate in that I had a certain knowledge about naval life, and I was able to blend in well. But my profession was stated as farmer, I was soon released," Höss said. "I worked on a farm near Flensburg for eight months. It was a peaceful time. My wife's brother worked in Flensburg. He helped me to stay in touch with my wife."

"You were a close family, obviously," Ruth said.

"Very close," Höss said. "It was through my brother-in-law that I heard that the British Field Security Police were searching for me. I learned that they were keeping my family under surveillance. I knew I could not remain free for much longer."

"And you were right," Ruth said. "You were arrested on March 11, 1946."

"My vial of poison had broken two days earlier," Höss said.

"That was very bad timing," Ruth said.

"It was very bad luck," Höss said. He sounded morose.

"You believe in luck?" Ruth said.

"Of course," said Höss, in a flat voice.

"So luck is one of the genuinely random elements?" Ruth said.

"As is bad luck," said Höss. "It was my bad luck to be captured."

"Of course," Ruth said.

"It was necessary for me to be destroyed," he said. "The world demanded it. Without knowing it, I was a cog in the wheel of a large piece of extermination machinery. When the machinery was smashed to pieces and all its parts disassembled, it was necessary for me, too, to be destroyed."

"How can you say that with a straight face?" Ruth said.

"Let the public continue to regard me as a cruel, pitiless, heartless persecutor," Höss said. "Let them see me as a mass murderer. An inhuman, barbarous, bestial being. They could never understand that I, too, had a heart, and I was not evil.

"I can see, now that I have had much time to reflect upon the facts," Höss said, "that the leaders of the Third Reich, because of a policy of force, must bear the guilt of causing this vast war and all the consequences thereof."

He cleared his throat. "I see, also, now, from a perspective of time," he said, "that the extermination of Jews was fundamentally wrong."

"Really?" said Ruth, sitting up.

"Of course," said Höss. "Precisely because of these mass exterminations, Germany drew upon herself the ire and anger of the whole world." Ruth slumped back into her seat. "There was a hatred of Germany for many years," Höss said. "It took quite a few years for the hostility toward Germany to evaporate."

"Do you think it has completely disappeared?" Ruth said.

"Of course," Höss said. "Don't you?"

"Yes," she said.

"You are approaching your death again, aren't you?" she said to Höss suddenly. He didn't reply. "You have to live through it all again, don't you?" Ruth said. "They're trying to make you get it right, aren't they?" she said.

"Who?" Höss said.

"I don't know," she said. "But I'm right, aren't I? They're going to make you relive every unpleasant moment, every unsavory aspect of your existence, every ill, until you get it right?"

"Only those moments I myself find difficult to endure," Höss said quietly.

She was right, she thought. Höss was about to die again. He had said he was going on a journey. A journey with a higher end in mind. Höss had thought she had known where he was heading. "Heading" was a tasteless choice of a word to use in the case of someone who was about to be hanged, Ruth thought to herself.

Ruth heard Höss clearing his throat. She knew he was preparing himself. She knew that Höss knew that his death was close. She heard another sound. A quiet sound. It was the sound of a noose being slipped around Höss's neck. Höss swallowed a few times. She could feel his nervousness. She could feel the tension in the air.

"Mein Gott," Höss cried.

Ruth looked in the direction of the cry. "Please do not watch," Höss said.

"I can't see," Ruth said.

"Yes, you can," Höss said. "If you look, you will be a witness to this. I would very much prefer it if I could be on my own."

"It's out of my control," Ruth said.

"Go away," Höss pleaded.

"I don't know how to," she said. It was true, she thought. She would have left if she could. Or would she? Was she staying voluntarily? She didn't know.

Some bubbles of air escaped from somewhere. Ruth realized with horror that Höss was losing control of his bowels. She felt sick. She was sure she could smell the shit. She could hear Höss panting. She could hear his shame. She could hear him trying to retain control. Trying to tighten his grip on his sphincter. He groaned as he failed. The groan was followed by the sound of flooding. Ruth gripped the sides of her seat. Höss seemed to have let go. *"Mein Gott,"* Höss cried out again.

He was calling to God, Ruth thought. He wasn't calling out to his wife. Ruth wondered if Höss was going to have to start at the very beginning again. To live through his adolescence and his early adulthood. And how many times did you have to die before you were finally dead? Ruth thought. Before you ceased to exist? Did that time ever arrive?

"I thought you could help me to avoid this," Höss said in a strained voice.

"Me?" she said.

"Yes," he said. "I thought you would be my salvation."

"Me, your salvation?" Ruth said. She was stunned. She could still smell Höss. The smell was terrible. She put her hand over her nose.

Ruth's body suddenly felt very hot. She could feel Höss tense himself. She could feel that he was holding his breath. Something was moving. She knew what it was. The noose was tightening. There was a brisk sound. A snap. Ruth had thought that it would be a louder sound. The sound of a man being hanged. She could feel him twitching. A gurgling noise came from Höss.

Ruth dug her heel into the floor of the plane. Höss spluttered. She dug her heel in again. His body began to twitch again. Small involuntary jerks. There were some more trickles and several gulping sounds. Ruth kept her heel on the ground. She could feel she was covered in sweat. She heard a thud. A loud thud. She knew that Höss was gone.

She picked up her bag and got out her lipstick. She felt much much better. Almost refreshed. Clearheaded. She lifted her heel up. It had remained pressed into the floor. She crossed her legs. She knew Höss was gone. She smiled. She didn't think she would be hearing from him again. She hoped she was right.

∽ *Chapter Seventeen* ∽

Ruth and Edek had been standing in the baggage collection area for twenty minutes. There was no luggage in sight. The carousel hadn't even begun to move. The other passengers were just standing there. Mute. Resigned. There was no movement among the people waiting for luggage. No agitation. In America, Ruth thought, there would have been consternation, irritation, complaints, and accusations. Here in Łódź, the passengers stood and waited. In silence.

"What is happening?" Edek said.

"Nothing is happening," Ruth said. "The baggage isn't arriving," Ruth said.

"What is wrong with them?" Edek said. "Everything does take two times as long as necessary." He asked a couple of passengers, in Polish, if they knew why the luggage was delayed. Both men shrugged their shoulders.

"I hope the luggage isn't lost," Ruth said. Edek asked another passenger if it was common for luggage to be lost. "Not common, but not unheard of," the man said.

"Great," said Ruth. "I'll have to live in these clothes and use the shit shampoo at the hotel."

"It is not necessary to speak like this, Ruthie," Edek said. Ruth wondered why he was so bothered by the word "shit," or any other of the mild obscenities she occasionally used. They must sound more profound to him than they did to native English speakers.

"If the luggage is lost we will buy new everything," Edek said. "We can afford it."

"I'm not that bothered," Ruth said. It was true, she thought. She would be home soon. She could replace everything. She could buy new face creams, new cleansers, a new running outfit. She could buy another pedometer, another cassette recorder, another headset with a microphone attachment. There was no need to panic. Everything could be replaced.

The lost luggage really didn't bother her. She didn't care, she thought, if the airline employees or someone else had stolen the luggage. Then, she thought of the coat. Israel Rothwax's coat was in her suitcase.

"The coat," she said to Edek.

"You will buy another coat," Edek said.

"No, it's your father's coat," Ruth said. Edek was quiet for a minute.

"This coat, to tell you the truth, was going to look a bit funny on you, Ruthie," he said.

"I want the coat," she said. "I'm not going to lose the coat."

"The luggage will come," Edek said.

They stood and waited. It was lucky she had kept the photographs in her bag, Ruth thought. She opened her bag. The photographs were still there. After ten minutes Edek turned to Ruth. "You stay here and watch for the suitcases. I will be back in a couple of minutes."

"Where are you going?" Ruth said. But he was already off. "I'll be back," he called out to Ruth as he ran toward the exit.

I'll be back, Ruth thought. Did Edek think he was Arnold Schwarzenegger in *The Terminator*? Edek had used exactly the same intonation as Arnold, and an almost identical accent. An intonation of urgency. And remedy. What was Edek up to? Ruth wondered. What was he going to do? Rush out onto the tarmac? Talk to the ground staff? Ruth felt agitated. Why did Edek always have to do something unexpected? Why couldn't he have waited quietly? Like the Poles. Not one of the assembled passengers had moved. No one was looking at their watch, or speaking into mobile phones. They were all immobile.

There was the sound of machinery starting up. And a loud series of shudders. The carousel began moving. The crowd remained static. Ruth moved closer to the carousel. A few pieces of luggage came out. After several circuits, Ruth's suitcase emerged. It was followed by Edek's. Ruth pulled both cases off the carousel. The bright yellow masking tape was still wound around Edek's case. But he had added some more tape. Now, bright yellow tape was taped along the length of the case as well as across the middle. Ruth had meant to ask Edek in the taxi, in Kraków, when he had added the extra tape. But Zofia's kisses had sidetracked her.

Ruth could still hear the sound of those kisses Zofia had begun blowing as they were getting into the car. Mwah, mwah, mwah. She remembered Edek smiling at the kisses. Ruth looked at Edek's suitcase. What was the purpose of the second round of bright yellow masking tape? The suitcase was already easily identifiable with the initial strips. Who knew what was behind Edek's thinking? And where was Edek?

She looked around the airport. Was he calling Garth? she thought. No, why would he call Garth from the airport? He could call Garth from his room at the hotel. She had no idea what Edek could be doing. His movements and thoughts were impossible to track or predict. She looked at her own suitcase. It was so subdued. All black, with black leather, neatly filled-in luggage labels. She didn't think she could travel with wild yellow bands of plastic tape wound around her case. Although she wasn't sure why she had to be so pristine and prissy.

"Ruthie," she heard. She looked up. It was Edek. He was running across the baggage collection area toward her. She wished he didn't have to run everywhere. As far as she could see, most of the emergencies in Edek's life were over with. He didn't have to run. It was dangerous to run at his age. He could easily slip.

"I did get a driver to take us to the hotel," Edek said, puffing a bit. Ruth was relieved. Edek had only been getting a taxi.

"That's good," she said. "Is it a Mercedes?"

"Yes," said Edek. "Of course."

"Why not?" Ruth said. "When I go back to New York I'll probably have Mercedes withdrawal."

Edek laughed. "You could buy a Mercedes for yourself," he said.

"I don't need a car," said Ruth.

"You can afford a car," Edek said.

"The parking in New York is exorbitant," Ruth said.

"What is the good of earning big money," Edek said, "if you worry about parking?"

"I've told you before," Ruth said. "I don't need a car in New York."

She wished she had never mentioned the subject of Mercedes withdrawal. It was meant to be a joke. A throwaway line. And Edek had laughed. "I thought we weren't buying German, anyway," she said to Edek.

"Ach," he said. "I do not care anymore. It is not such a big deal. Who cares if we buy some German things or we don't buy German things? The Germans do not care. And I do not care, anymore."

"Neither do I," said Ruth. "I'm too tired to boycott anything German."

"Maybe we will look together at a Mercedes, in New York," Edek said.

"Dad," she said. "Drop it."

"Maybe I will come to live in New York," Edek said. "With Garth."

"You're going to move to New York and live with Garth?" Ruth said.

"Are you crazy?" Edek said. "I am thinking of moving to New York to live next to you. You will be the one what lives with Garth."

"Oh," she said. "Thanks for letting me in on the decision."

"A car would be good for me, in New York," Edek said.

Ruth was speechless. What was this new plan Edek was hatching? At least it didn't seem to involve Zofia, she thought. They were almost at the entrance of the terminal.

"The Mercedes cars are cheaper in America," Edek said. "In Australia they cost a fortune."

"They're not that cheap in America," Ruth said.

"I did not say they were cheap," Edek said. "I did say they was cheaper than the Mercedes cars in Australia. A Mercedes is a very expensive car. Everybody knows that." He paused. "Why should I not have a Mercedes if I live in New York?" he said. "I cannot walk so much like I used to. I am getting old."

"You can walk faster than I can," Ruth said. "I'm not buying you a Mercedes until you're much older." Edek started to laugh. His laughter almost unbalanced him. He put his suitcase down for a moment.

"Sometimes, Ruthie, you are a very funny girl."

"You mean sometimes I am very funny," she said. "I'm not really a girl anymore."

"I mean sometimes you are a very funny girl," he said.

They had reached the front entrance of the airport. Ruth could see the Mercedes waiting outside. It was a large Mercedes. The driver, when he saw Edek, leaped out of the car to help them with their luggage. He opened the trunk of the car. Ruth lifted her suitcase up and put it in the trunk. The driver looked appalled. "Please, madam," he said. "I am here to help you."

"I'm fine," she said to the driver. She liked showing Poles, particularly the men, that she had muscles and strength. Edek was annoyed. "Why not to let him put in the suitcase in the car?" he said to Ruth.

"I like lifting suitcases," Ruth said.

"You are crazy," said Edek.

Ruth got into the backseat. "I will sit in front with the driver," Edek said. "Sit in the back with me, for a change," Ruth said. Edek looked at her. "It is not such a bad feeling," he said, "to have a daughter what still wants to sit next to her father." Ruth moved over in the seat. Edek got in. "I'll always want to sit next to you," she said to him. The remark took Edek by surprise. Tears came into his eyes. "We'll soon be out of here, Dad," she said. "We'll soon be in my apartment, in New York."

Ruth looked around at the interior of the car. Everything was a subdued shade of brown. A tasteful, elegant yet comfortable color.

"By the time we leave Poland," Ruth said to Edek, "we will have seen every model of Mercedes on the market." Edek laughed.

"Can I escort you anywhere in the coming days?" the driver said. Ruth wondered where he had learned his English. It was almost Etonian. Ruth was about to say no, when Edek said, "Yes, as a matter of fact."

"Where would you like to go, sir?" the driver said.

"Tomorrow morning, is it possible for you to take us to Kamedulska Street," Edek said. "And then to wait there for us maybe a half an hour, maybe a bit more?"

"Certainly sir," the driver said. "What time would you like me to pick you up?"

Edek looked at Ruth. "What do you think?" she said to Edek. "Ten o'clock? It will be Sunday morning and it's probably not a good idea to wake the old couple up by arriving too early."

"What for do we need to see this couple at all?" Edek said.

"Because we can't just turn up with a spade and start digging in somebody's yard," Ruth said.

"It is not somebody's yard," Edek said. "It is my yard."

"The old couple could call the police," Ruth said, "and it would be hard to explain, then and there on the spot, that this is really your yard."

"Maybe," Edek said. "But why should they call the police?"

"How do I know?" said Ruth. "In the old couple's eyes we're trespassers. Trespassing on their property."

"We are very profitable trespassers," Edek said.

Ruth laughed. "I think it's a good idea to tell the old couple what we plan to do," she said. "I think I'll pay them, too."

"Pay them, so I can dig in my own yard?" Edek said. "What for?"

"So things will go as smoothly as possible," Ruth said.

"You did already pay them a lot of money," Edek said.

"It's not a lot for what I got," Ruth said.

"I would like to say something to this old couple," Edek said.

"There's no point," said Ruth. "Anyway, they have to live with their own miserable selves. I can't think of a worse punishment."

"This old couple is not so old," Edek said. "I think this old couple is much younger than what I am."

"You're probably right," Ruth said.

"Let us go at nine o'clock and get it over with," Edek said.

"Okay," she said.

"Could you pick us up, please, at nine o'clock?" Edek said to the driver.

"Certainly, sir," he said.

"Nine o'clock is a good idea," Ruth said to Edek. "That way we'll catch them before they go to church."

"You think these people do go to church?" Edek said.

"Probably," said Ruth. "Most Poles seem to."

"I will pick you up at nine o'clock sharp," the driver said.

At least this driver hadn't offered to drive them to a death camp disguised as a museum, Ruth thought. There wasn't one close by, she realized. They passed some graffiti painted, in white, on a large brown wall. *Juden Raus!* the graffiti screamed. Whoever had painted it knew enough German to paint in an exclamation mark. Ruth pointed out the graffiti to Edek. The driver looked at what they were looking at. "It is just children," Edek said, quickly to the driver. Edek looked at Ruth and raised his eyebrows. Ruth understood that Edek had wanted to preempt the driver's response. "It's just children," Ruth said. Edek laughed. "It is just children," Edek repeated. "Just children," said the driver.

Edek looked at Ruth, again. "You do look much better," he said to her.

"Better?" she said. "Better than what?"

"Better than you did look since you did come to Poland," Edek said. "You was not looking so good. Now, you do look much better."

"I think it's because we're on our way home," Ruth said. "I've had enough of Poland."

"More than enough," I think," said Edek.

"More than enough," she said.

She was glad she was looking better. She felt better. More alert, more optimistic. She couldn't wait to be in her own apartment.

"So it is not such a bad thing I did what I did arrange with Garth?" Edek said.

"Next to a lot of other bad things, inviting Garth to New York doesn't seem so bad," Ruth said.

"You will try?" Edek said.

"Try what?" said Ruth.

"Try to get together with Garth," Edek said.

"Dad," Ruth said, "I've only just agreed that inviting Garth to New York without asking me was not an evil act. Can't we leave it at that?"

"My daughter is very stubborn," Edek said to Ruth, and shook his head.

Łódź didn't look any better. It was still grim. Still smoke-ridden. What had she expected, Ruth thought, a transformation? It was exactly a week since she and Edek had last arrived in the city. A week since they had arrived in the city of Edek's birth and youth together. The taxi turned into Piotrkowska Street. This Saturday night in Piotrkowska was no different from the previous Saturday night. There was the same sparse crowd out for the evening. Ruth looked out of the car window. Surely there had to be more people who went out on a Saturday night? There had to be lots of people in Łódź who were relaxing and celebrating. Or maybe there weren't? Maybe there was not much to celebrate in Łódź, Ruth thought.

"This is a far cry from the old Saturday nights in Piotrkowska Street, isn't it?" she said to Edek.

Edek shook his head. "It is not the same place," he said.

"You can say that, again," Ruth said. She looked at the few people who were walking along the street. "They got what they wanted," she said to Edek. "They got rid of the Jews. You would think they would look happier."

"Shsh, shsh," Edek said. "Do not speak like this, Ruthie. Why do you have to speak like this? It upsets people," he said, nodding in the direction of the driver.

"Okay," Ruth said. "I'll try not to upset anyone in the very short time we've got left."

"Thank you very much," Edek said, in an exaggerated tone of graciousness, at her agreement to try to be more civilized.

Ruth looked away. She felt Edek's gaze still on her. "You do not look so bad," Edek said. "For the first time since we did come to Poland you look like you did used to look."

"I look like I used to look?" said Ruth.

"Like you was normally," Edek said. "Not always tired with such black near your eyes."

"I feel less tired," she said.

"You do look like your old self," Edek said.

"Oh, good," Ruth said. She was pleased that Edek thought she looked like her old self. Her old self, she thought. Which self was that? The self that ran a business? The self that updated files at night, after everyone had left the office? Would she ever be that old self again? Or was she someone else? Someone who knew that no amount of order could clear or clarify certain uncertainties?

"I'm glad I look better," Ruth said. She looked at Edek. He looked tired. "You look tired, Dad," she said.

"I am a bit tired to tell you the truth," he said. Ruth knew that if Edek was admitting to tiredness, he must be very tired. It must have been quite a night he had had with Zofia.

"You'll be able to have an early night tonight," Ruth said to him. "And you'll feel better tomorrow."

"Of course I will," Edek said.

They had arrived at the Grand Victoria. Ruth watched the doorman and the porter and the driver rush to open the car doors. The taxi driver and the doorman almost collided. It was almost comic. And almost predictable. This is how she and Edek had arrived at the hotel last week. At the center of several collisions. Taxi drivers, doormen, and porters in Łódź must be covered in bruises, Ruth thought. These jobs were obviously more dangerous than they seemed.

The doorman beamed at Ruth. Ruth smiled at him. He beamed even more broadly. "Please welcome back," he announced loudly. "I have plenty of strong boxes if you need boxes," he said.

"No thank you," Ruth said to the doorman. "But thank you for offering." She tipped the doorman lavishly. "I do need to speak to you later," she said to him. "I have a business request." She stressed the word "business."

"I will be here till ten P.M.," the doorman said in a businesslike manner. Maybe he wasn't quite as revolting as she had originally thought, Ruth thought. Maybe she had been a bit harsh in her judgment.

Edek greeted the doorman with gusto. You would have thought they were old friends. Ruth looked away. Edek's ease with Poles still made her uncomfortable. She noticed that Edek had slipped the doorman what she was sure was a large tip.

The next time Ruth looked, the porter was embracing Edek. The two men were embracing and conversing rapidly in Polish. It looked like a jovial conversation. Ruth shook her head. She knew she would never understand a fraction of the complexity that existed between Edek and all the Polish men he got on so well with. What history were they sharing? What understanding? What strange bonds gave them their ease with each other? She couldn't even begin to understand.

Ruth put her own and Edek's passports down on the front desk. The clerk looked up and recognized her. "I will give you the very best rooms," he said to Ruth. "Thank you," she said, "I really appreciate that." Edek was waiting for her in the lobby. He looked a bit lost. As though he had run out of people to embrace and tip and was feeling mildly bereft. She would be so glad to be leaving Poland, she thought, as she walked over to her father.

"They said they've given us the best rooms in the hotel," she said to Edek.

"Very good," he said.

"Shall we unpack and meet downstairs in ten minutes?" Ruth said.

"Where is your room?" Edek said.

"Two doors from yours," Ruth said.

Edek looked relieved. "Good," he said. They walked to the elevator. "Are we going to have a dinner?" Edek said.

"Of course," Ruth said.

Edek looked more cheerful. "See you in ten minutes," he said.

Ruth looked around her room. This room looked as unprepossessing as her last room. So much for being given the best rooms in the hotel. She hoped that this bed was not as lumpy as the last bed. She pulled back the bedding. Three overlapping single sheets had been used as a substitute for a double sheet. She knew that her arms and legs were going to get twisted and tangled tonight in all the edges. She turned on the shower. It dripped and spurted. She had really wanted to have a shower. She would have to stand under this one for hours to wash herself. She would shower tomorrow when she got to Warsaw, she decided.

Edek called. "You was the one what did get the best room?" he said.

"No," she said. "Not me."

"It was not me, too," he said, and started to laugh. Ruth was glad to hear him laugh. You needed to laugh in a place like Łódź.

Edek was still laughing when they met in the lobby. "My room is even worse than the room what I did have last time," he said.

"Oh no," said Ruth.

"This bed has got one leg missing," Edek said. He started to laugh even harder. "Where is supposed to be the leg," he said, "is six bricks."

"Six bricks?" Ruth said, laughing.

Edek nodded. He was trying to stop laughing. "I did count them, myself," he said eventually.

"You have to laugh, don't you?" Ruth said, wiping her eyes.

"Ruthie, you do have to laugh," he said.

"If you can't sleep tonight," Ruth said to Edek, "call me and I'll ask them to move you to another room."

"I did try the bed, already," Edek said. "I did lie down. It was not too bad."

"One night here is all we need, and then we can leave," Ruth said. "I've booked us into the Bristol in Warsaw, for our last night in Poland," Ruth said. "I'm ready for some luxury."

"I think I am, too, Ruthie," Edek said.

"Do you want a big dinner, or something small?" Ruth said. As soon as the words came out of her mouth, Ruth knew she shouldn't have phrased the question that way. Edek could never admit to being hungry or to wanting a large meal. "Let's eat somewhere where we can have more if we're hungry, and less if we're not so hungry," she said.

"I am not so hungry," Edek said.

"There's a café across the road," Ruth said. "They serve light meals."

"I did not get anything to eat on the plane," Edek said.

"You didn't miss much," Ruth said. "Liverwurst on a biscuit, and an orange."

"I do not like so much an orange," Edek said.

"I know," said Ruth. "So let's choose a restaurant."

"What about Chinee?" Edek said.

"That Chinese restaurant we went to last time?" Ruth said.

"Yes," said Edek.

"I'm not going back there," Ruth said.

"That was not such a bad Chinee," Edek said.

"That was a very Polish Chinese," Ruth said.

"You did like the worms," Edek said.

"Not enough to go back," she said. "What about a French restaurant?"

"What about the McDonald's?" Edek said.

"Dad, I don't eat hamburgers in America," she said. "Why would I eat a hamburger in Łódź?"

"Okay," he said, looking flat.

"Let's compromise," Ruth said. "I'll go to McDonald's with you and then you can keep me company while I have a bowl of soup in the hotel."

"Okay, that is a deal," Edek said.

At McDonald's Edek ordered two cheeseburgers, two servings of french fries, and two chocolate thickshakes. "The McDonald's make a very good hamburger," he said, midway through the second hamburger. He looked less tired, Ruth thought. The hamburgers had revitalized him.

"Have another one," Ruth said. "They're not very big." Edek ordered another cheeseburger. By the time Edek had eaten the last french fry, his color had improved. His cheeks looked rosy. His eyes were shining. "That was a very good dinner," he said to Ruth. They walked back to the hotel.

"I think I'll have the soup in my room," Ruth said. "I'm feeling tired."

"Okey dokey," Edek said.

"You go upstairs," she said to Edek. "I'll order my soup, and check to see if there are any faxes for me."

"Good night, Ruthie," Edek said.

There were no faxes. Ruth was relieved. She didn't want to think about work at the moment. She'd be happy to deal with whatever was happening in the office as soon as she got back. The doorman waved to her. She went up to him. "Are you ready to ask your business request?" he said.

"Yes," she said.

She wished he would clip the clumps of hair protruding from his nose. They were making her feel sick. This man needed a nose- and ear-hair clipper. Maybe she would send him one from New York. She tried to focus on his eyes. She explained that she wanted to know if he could accompany her and her father on an expedition they had to make to Kamedulska Street in the morning.

The doorman looked bewildered. "A taxi can take you there," he said.

"My father needs to dig something up in the backyard of a house, in Kamedulska Street," Ruth said to the doorman. "What he is looking for was buried over fifty years ago."

"Ah, gold," said the doorman.

"No," said Ruth. "What is buried there has no financial value, only emotional value."

"So what is the problem?" the doorman said, stepping closer. Ruth stepped back from him.

"The problem is that this object is buried on property that belonged to my father before the war," she said. "The current residents are disturbed by my father's presence. I just want to make sure that my father can look for what is buried and then leave, peacefully."

"I see," the doorman said. "You want me for protection."

"Yes," Ruth said.

"With pleasure," the doorman said. "It will be my pleasure to protect you."

"To protect me and my father," Ruth said.

"Of course," the doorman said. Ruth was pleased. She smiled at the doorman. "I'll pay you well," she said. He nodded. She was glad that he was so thickset. Glad that he had such a thick neck and a thick body. His presence would show the old couple that she meant business. She hoped that the door-man would leave all of his gold chains on. They added a degree of menace.

"Is it possible for you to bring a spade and some plastic gloves?" Ruth said to the doorman. He hesitated.

"I'll pay well for them, of course," she said.

"A large spade?" he said.

"A medium spade," Ruth said. "The object we are looking for is small."

"I will have a spade and gloves with me," the doorman said.

"I've got a car booked to pick us up at nine o'clock," Ruth said.

"You will see me here at nine A.M. sharp," the doorman said.

"Thank you," said Ruth.

She went up to her room. She rang Tadeusz, the interpreter. She asked him if he was free to accompany them to Kamedulska Street. Tadeusz was pleased to hear from her. "Of course I will accompany you," he said. She told him the doorman would also be joining them. Tadeusz laughed. "I am pleased to see that you will be more prepared this time," he said.

Ruth felt as though she had assembled a swat team. A guard, an inter-preter, a driver. What would they be presiding over? What was it that was buried? And was it still there? She would know very soon. She would know tomorrow. She thought about ordering some soup to be brought up to her room. She decided against it. She wasn't really hungry.

She looked in the mirror. Her father was right. She looked much better. Her features weren't flattened and dampened with fatigue and tension. Her complexion was clear. She no longer looked pallid. The circles under her eyes had disappeared. She fidgeted with her hair. Even her hair seemed revitalized. The curls were curling themselves into more aesthetically pleas-ing loops and rings.

She went to her suitcase and got out a small candle in a filigree silver container. She opened the lid. The candle was a gift someone had given her years ago. She had traveled with it for years. Ostensibly in case of a power shortage. After she had learned that most hotels had their own generators, she had continued to take the candle with her on trips. The candle was intact. It was not chipped or cracked. She placed the candle, in its holder, on a plate. She got out the matches she always packed with the candle. She lit the candle. The flame cast a large shadow for such a small candle. Ruth switched the lights in the room off. She felt peaceful sitting there with the candle. Very peaceful.

In Jewish tradition, a candle was a symbol of the body and soul. The flame was the soul. Always reaching upward. Jews believed that the burning of a candle aided the soul of the departed in a journey toward heaven. Centuries ago, Ruth had read, it had been a custom to place a towel and a glass of water near a memorial candle. This was in order to appease the Angel of Death. To allow him to wash his sword in the water and dry it with a towel. Other scholars, at the time, believed that a man's soul returned to cleanse itself in the water. Ruth filled a glass with water. She put the glass next to the candle, along with a neatly folded hand towel. She sat in a chair in front of the candle.

Jewish people lit candles on the Sabbath, on holidays, at weddings and bar mitzvahs. Candles also celebrated joy and life. Ruth watched the candle. The flame seemed to have a calm flicker. Some candles were erratic. This candle was very steady. Ruth breathed in and out deeply. A line from an old school prayer came into her head. It was a Christian prayer, the only sort they had had at Ruth's primary school. *"If I should die before I wake, I pray the Lord my soul to take,"* Ruth said.

That night she slept soundly. She dreamed about the gypsy woman in Warsaw. In Ruth's dream, the gypsy woman's baby was clean and well nourished. Ruth woke up feeling peaceful. She showered slowly and got dressed. She put on a pair of earrings. They were small gold hearts she had had since she was a child.

Edek was waiting for her at breakfast. He was sitting at a table in the far corner of the room. His shoulders were slumped. He was staring down at the table. He looked forlorn. Lonely. Alone. Ruth ran up to him. "Hi, Dad," she said, and kissed him on the cheek. "How are you?" she said.

"I am okay, as usual," Edek said.

"You don't look quite okay," Ruth said.

"There is nothing wrong with me," Edek said. "I am always okay." Edek looked at Ruth. "You do look very nice, today, Ruthie," he said.

"Thanks," she said. "It's been a big trip, hasn't it?"

"You can say that again, brother," Edek said.

"It's almost over," Ruth said. "We'll be out of here, out of Łódź, and out of Poland, very soon."

"Yes," said Edek. He still looked flat.

"I'm so grateful you came to Poland with me," Ruth said. "So grateful." Edek seemed surprised.

"I did think you was not so happy you did come to Poland," he said.

"You're right," she said. "It hasn't been a picnic. It hasn't been one fun-filled event after another." Edek laughed. "But I'm glad I came," she said. "I needed to do this."

"You did want to do this for a long time," Edek said.

"I've wanted to do this for a very long time," she said. "Let's eat."

"Okay," said Edek. Ruth got up to go to the buffet. Edek stayed seated. "I am not so hungry to tell you the truth," he said. Ruth looked at him.

"You're always hungry in the morning," Ruth said. "You always eat a good breakfast."

"Today I am not so hungry," Edek said.

"Come on, Dad," she said. "It's important to eat breakfast."

"Ruthie darling," Edek said. "A girl what eats birdseeds for a breakfast shouldn't talk about it is important to eat breakfast to an old man like me who does know what is a breakfast."

"I don't eat birdseed," Ruth said. "And you are definitely not an old man."

"You go to the buffet, Ruthie," Edek said. "I will wait here." Ruth felt alarmed. Edek never lost his appetite. This was not a good sign.

"Are you worried about this morning?" Ruth said.

"Maybe," said Edek.

"Whatever is buried there or not buried there," Ruth said, "it's in the past. Whatever it is we will deal with it. You and me." She looked at Edek. "There is nothing that we can't deal with, Dad," she said. "As long as we've got each other." She put her arm around him. "Do you understand that?" she said. Edek looked as though he was about to cry. "Please have something to eat, Dad," Ruth said. "What about a hot chocolate?" Edek straightened his shoulders.

"Okay, I will have a hot chocolate," he said. "Just for my daughter." Ruth ordered the hot chocolate. She brought Edek a slice of sponge cake from the buffet.

"This will be good with the hot chocolate," she said.

"You is still going to eat the birdseeds?" Edek said.

"What can I do?" she said. "I just happen to like birdseed." Edek laughed.

Ruth was relieved to hear him laugh. Anything that bothered him enough to take away his appetite was serious. What was bothering him? The prospect of what were they going to find this morning? There was probably nothing there, she thought. The Poles would have raked through that earth pretty thoroughly. She wondered what it was that Edek was looking for. She had no idea. She also wondered why she was so calm. The thought of seeing the old man or his wife was not exactly a pleasing prospect. The calm she felt was probably because she knew that this trip was almost over, she thought. She knew that she was on her way home.

"They got compote on the buffet," Edek said. "You want me to get you some compote?"

"Oh, thanks, Dad," she said. "I feel like a bit of compote." Edek got up. He ran to the buffet. The buffet was ten feet away. "A small bowl," she called out after him. The portion of compote Edek brought back was enough to feed six people.

"I did ring the lawyer, in Melbourne," Edek said.

"When?" said Ruth.

"Last night," Edek said. He shook his head. "Before I did come to Poland I did want very much to get back what did belong to us," he said. "But now it does not seem so important, to me."

"Now, you just want to get out of Poland," Ruth said.

"That is the truth, Ruthie," he said. "I am ready to leave Poland."

"What did the lawyer say?" Ruth said.

"He did say that because they was successful with the Swiss banks what agreed to give the Jews back their money, they are now going to sue some big companies," Edek said. "Big companies who did use slave labor."

"That's good," said Ruth.

"The lawyer did tell me that, also that a few big insurance companies in Europe did agree that an international commission will work out the details of what should be paid to Jewish people whose insurance policies was never paid," said Edek.

"You want some of my compote?" Ruth said. "Maybe a little bit," said Edek. Ruth spooned a few spoonfuls onto a plate. Edek took a mouthful.

"This compote is very good," he said. Ruth was very relieved that Edek looked better. Relieved he had had something to eat.

"I've hired the interpreter I used before, Tadeusz, to come to Kamedulska Street with us," she said.

"You did hire an interpreter?" Edek said. "What for?"

"Because I thought that we needed someone who was not emotionally involved," Ruth said, "in case we have to negotiate anything."

"For what would we need to negotiate?" Edek said.

"For the right to dig," said Ruth.

"We do not need an interpreter," Edek said. "I speak a perfect Polish. I can speak for myself."

"Of course you can," said Ruth. "But I wanted things to go as smoothly as possible. You can't underestimate that old Polish couple."

"All right, all right," Edek said. "But it is a bit crazy. You are spending money for nothing."

"It won't be the first time in my life," Ruth said.

"That is right," said Edek. "Look what you do pay for shoes and for dresses. This interpreter will probably cost you less than one sleeve of the dress what you are wearing."

"Possibly," said Ruth. She laughed. "My clothes aren't that expensive," she said. "Not for New York."

"I do not care," Edek said. "You do deserve what dresses and shoes you do buy."

"I've hired the doorman, too," Ruth said. Edek opened his mouth to reply. "Don't say anything," Ruth said. "I've hired him to intimidate the old couple and any other neighbors who happen to be present."

Edek closed his mouth. "That," he said, "is a good idea. This doorman is a big man."

"And he looks like he means business," Ruth said. Edek laughed.

"I did tell you not to be rude to this doorman," Edek said. "It is always good to be on the good side of a doorman like this."

Edek finished his compote. Ruth had already eaten hers. She felt full. This was the biggest breakfast she had had since they had been in Poland.

"Are you ready, Dad?" she said.

"Okay," he said. "Let us get it over with." He stood up.

"*Oy a broch,*" said Edek, suddenly.

"What's wrong?" said Ruth.

"We have not got with what to dig," Edek said. "It is Sunday. All the shops in Łódź will be for sure closed."

"The doorman is getting a spade for me," Ruth said.

"Thank God," Edek said. "It is a very good thing, Ruthie, that you do think of such things."

"I'm going to go to the bathroom before we leave," Ruth said.

"I will go to see if the doorman is here," said Edek.

Ruth found Edek, and the doorman, and Tadeusz, and the taxi driver standing in a huddle near the front door of the hotel. The sight of them almost made Ruth laugh. The doorman was holding a collection of spades and shovels. Out of his doorman's uniform, he looked even bigger. More like a thug. More threatening. The assembled men with their assorted equipment, Ruth thought, looked like a gathering who were preparing to leave for a war zone. Even Tadeusz had tried to look rugged. He was wearing a plastic jacket and had his hair slicked back.

"I have a very strong box," the doorman said, when he saw Ruth.

"Thank you," she said. "But we won't need it. The object we're looking for is small."

"I will bring the box in case it is necessary," the doorman said.

"Okay," said Ruth. She introduced Tadeusz formally to Edek. They shook hands. Tadeusz introduced himself to the doorman. There was more handshaking. Edek introduced the driver. "And this is the driver," he said, with a flourish. "I am Robert," the driver said. There was a final round of handshakes.

"Robert is not such a Polish name," Edek said.

"It is also not such an unusual name in Poland," the driver said.

"That is correct," said Tadeusz. "I myself know two Polish Roberts."

"I also know a Robert," the doorman said.

Ruth's head began to spin at the surreal turn the conversation had taken. She wanted to laugh. There was something utterly Polish about the situation, but she wasn't sure what. There was a brief silence. All the men looked at each other. The doorman looked at his watch. "It is 9:01 A.M." he said. "Are we ready?"

"We're ready," Ruth said, trying not to laugh. This really was no time for laughter, she told herself sternly. She smiled at the doorman. The comedy of this gathering had removed her anxiety. She felt worryingly carefree. She had better sober up, she told herself. A degree of tension in these circumstances was probably not a bad thing. Edek looked cheerful. He was obviously feeling better, Ruth thought.

"I will sit in the front with Robert," Edek said.

"Where would you like to sit?" the doorman said to Ruth. Not next to you, would not be the right reply, Ruth decided. "Tadeusz," she said. "You sit in the middle."

"Tadeusz is smaller than you," Ruth said to the doorman, in an effort to explain the seating arrangements. "I need to sit by a window, so it's best if Tadeusz sits in the middle," she added.

"Of course," the doorman said.

Ruth was relieved. She really hadn't wanted to sit next to the doorman. And she hadn't wanted to offend him. She was surprised that she hadn't anticipated a need for a seating strategy. Oh well, she thought, she couldn't think of everything.

"I think," Ruth said to the doorman, "it will be better if, when we get there, you wait in the car."

"As you wish," he said.

"I'll call you when we need you," Ruth said.

"I will be ready for your call," he said.

Ruth settled back into the seat. She tried to prepare herself for the sight of the old man and, possibly, his wife. She looked out of the car window. Every street looked bleak. Bleak and gray. She was glad that she and Edek were only here briefly. She couldn't imagine ever wanting to come back to this city. She thought that she had finally grasped that what was gone from Łódź was gone. Completely gone.

"I know two Roberts, not one," the doorman said.

"Then I am wrong," Edek said, from the front seat. "Robert is not such an unusual name in Poland. But I myself did know not one Polish Robert."

"I know one Polish Robert, too," Ruth said. "But there probably weren't that many Jewish Polish Roberts, Dad, which would explain why you didn't know any."

"Probably not," Robert, the driver, said.

They were in Kamedulska Street. The conversation about the Polish Roberts had distracted her. She started to feel nervous. "Are you all right, Dad?" she said.

"Of course," said Edek. The car pulled up outside number 23.

"Who would think we would once again be here," Edek said.

"Not me," said Ruth.

"Not me, too," said Edek.

Ruth, Edek, and Tadeusz got out of the car and walked to the front door of the apartment block. "I will for sure not come back here again," Edek said to Ruth.

"That makes two of us, Dad," Ruth said. Edek walked up the stairs in front of her. Ruth looked at her father, putting one foot after another, on the stairs he must have walked up and down so many times. He was the lone survivor of so many people who had walked up and down these stairs. And here he was, at eighty-one, needing a guard and an interpreter to be in his own building. It was enough to make you cry.

"Are you all right?" Ruth said to Edek again. Edek stopped for a moment.

"I am all right, Ruthie," he said.

Edek and Ruth stood in front of the door to his old apartment. Tadeusz stood behind them.

"Shall we get it over with?" she said.

"Let us get it over with," Edek said. He knocked loudly on the door.

"I hope they're home," Ruth said.

Almost before she had finished the sentence, the door opened. The old woman stood behind the half-open door and stared at Ruth and Edek. Ruth stared back at her. It was hard not to stare. The old woman was wearing a blond wig. A very big blond wig. Ruth looked more closely. The old woman was wearing two wigs. The top wig, which covered the top half of her head, was a different color and texture from the blond synthetic hair that circled the woman's neck.

"I am very surprised to see you," the old woman said to Edek and Ruth.

"She says she is surprised to see you," Tadeusz said.

"I can understand perfectly what she does say," Edek said.

"I was translating for your daughter," said Tadeusz.

"I'll ask you to interpret when I need it, Tadeusz," Ruth said.

"Very good," said Tadeusz.

"My husband told me about the interpreter," the old woman said. She looked at Tadeusz. "Not a bad-looking young man," she said to Ruth. "Does he do anything else for you?"

"She said—" Edek said.

"I understood," Ruth said. "She is as repulsive as her husband."

"Ruthie, are you starting already?" Edek said.

"It's okay," Ruth said. "She can't understand."

"It is not so okay," Edek said to Ruth. "Please behave yourself."

"Good morning, madam," Edek said to the old woman.

"Good morning, sir," she said. "Come look who is here," she called out into the apartment. "It was lucky you caught us," she said, turning back toward Edek. The old man came to the door.

"What a surprise," he said. "We didn't expect you."

Looking at the old man made Ruth feel sick. She tried to take some deep breaths to counter her nausea.

"It was lucky you caught us," the old woman said again. "We were on our way to church."

"I knew the two of you would be churchgoers," Ruth said.

"Ruthie," said Edek.

"They really can't understand what I am saying," Ruth said to Edek.

"Your father is right," Tadeusz said. "It is better not to speak like this. The tone of your voice suggests what you are saying."

"I don't care," she said.

"Do you wish to accomplish what you came here for?" Tadeusz said.

"Yes," she said.

"Thank you, Tadeusz," Edek said.

"To what do we owe this pleasure?" the old woman said.

"Gold," the old man cried out. "They came here for the gold."

"Shut up," the old woman said to her husband.

"It's not gold," Ruth said. "Tell, them, Tadeusz, that it's not gold."

"I can tell them," Edek said.

"Dear, kind people," Edek said. "We have not come here to look for gold." Dear, kind people, Ruth thought. What a joke. Why was Edek addressing the old couple so politely? She wanted to say something. She looked at Tadeusz. He shook his head.

Ruth decided to hold her tongue. She and Edek were on a mission. Why shouldn't Edek address the old couple in whatever form would best get this mission accomplished? Mission accomplished. This whole thing was sounding more and more like a military maneuver.

"We have come here to look for something small," Edek said. "Something of no value to anyone."

"Something of value to you," said the old man.

"That is right," said Edek. "We need to dig a small hole in the backyard."

The old man slapped his thigh and grinned. Ruth had to look away. She couldn't bear another viewing of those stained, rotted teeth. "I told you they buried something," the old man said excitedly to his wife. He slapped his thigh again. The slap made a thin reedy sound.

"So you want to do some digging on our property?" the old woman said.

"Yes, madam," Edek said. Ruth kept her mouth shut. They hadn't flown all the way back to Łódź for her to argue about who owned the property.

"We are going to pay you for the privilege," Ruth said. She looked at Tadeusz. He translated what she had said.

"Oh," said the old man.

"Very good," said his wife.

"Come outside," Ruth said. "We'll show you where we think it is buried."

"My daughter would like you to accompany us outside to the backyard, where we will show you where we think the small item is buried," Edek said.

"I think we should discuss the price," the old man said.

"We can talk outside," Ruth said. "I don't feel well. I need some air." Tadeusz relayed this to the old couple.

"She is still not well," the old man said to his wife.

"She doesn't look the sickly sort," the old woman said.

"Trust me," said the old man, "she is a sickly type."

"Anyone would feel sick in his presence," Ruth said to Edek.

"Ruthie," Edek said. "Please. You don't feel so well?"

"I think I'll feel unwell until we're out of the country," Ruth said. Edek looked at Tadeusz.

"She does not mean this as an insult to you, Tadeusz," he said.

"Tadeusz knows that," Ruth said.

"You must calm down," Tadeusz said to Ruth.

"Yes," said Edek. "This is what I am always telling her. Column down, Ruthie. Column down." Tadeusz nodded.

"Your daughter is not such a calm person," Tadeusz said to Edek.

"You can say that again, brother," Edek said. He turned to the old couple. "Are we going to go downstairs?" The old man looked at his wife. His wife nodded.

"We will talk downstairs," she said.

The large brown dog was at the bottom of the stairs. The dog saw Ruth. He looked at Ruth, and then turned and walked in the opposite direction. Ruth felt hurt by the dog's rejection. She didn't want to be rebuffed by an old Polish dog. She felt peculiarly deserted by this dog. The dog must be remembering the kick, she thought. The dog was clearly brighter than it looked, she thought.

Edek walked to the far corner of the yard.

"I think it is buried approximately here," he said.

"We did look here," the old man said.

"We found nothing in this area," the old woman said.

"We looked here first, because that is where we saw the Jew digging," the old man said.

"The sight of a Jew digging probably electrified the neighborhood," Ruth said to Edek. "Every second Pole was probably in here with a shovel."

"You want to make this more hard for me, Ruthie?" Edek said.

"No," she said.

"Then do not say stupid things," he said.

"They're not stupid things," she said.

"Your father means that it is not wise to voice these opinions at the moment," Tadeusz said.

"I know what he means," Ruth said sullenly. It all felt too much to her. She could feel her heart pounding. She just wanted to slug the Polish couple and leave.

"There is nothing buried here," the old woman said.

"Well, let's try anyway," Ruth said to Edek.

"We will try ourselves," Edek said to the old couple.

"How much is it worth?" the old man said.

"A hundred dollars," Ruth said. Edek translated.

"It's not enough," the old woman said.

"Two hundred," said Ruth.

"Not enough," the old woman said.

"I'll pay you more, if we find something," Ruth said. "If we find something, I'll pay you an extra five hundred dollars."

Edek turned to Ruth. "What for do you offer them more money if we do find something?" he said.

"It's expedient," she said.

"We want more money than that," the old man said. "What's a few dollars to rich Jews?" He laughed. All of the brown stumps in his mouth were on display in the laugh. Ruth felt queasy.

"I can stop you from digging," the old woman said. "After all, this is not your property."

"Tadeusz, can you get our companion from the car?" Ruth said quietly. "Tell him that this couple are making threats."

"Certainly," Tadeusz said. The old man and the old woman looked at Tadeusz walking away.

"Are we going to deal directly with each other?" the old man said to Edek. "Just us and you. We can do business together. I did some very good business with your daughter."

"Don't bother answering him," Ruth said to Edek.

"We will accept five thousand dollars," the old woman said. Ruth gasped. She thought she mustn't have heard the number correctly. She looked at Edek. He looked numb.

"How much did she say, Dad?" Ruth said.

"Five thousand dollars," Edek said, shaking his head.

"What's a few more dollars to you?" the old man said.

"A few more dollars is nothing to her," the old woman said.

"Tell her I said I'd pay an extra five hundred dollars if we found anything," Ruth said.

"If you really want me to say this, Ruthie, I will say it," Edek said. "But I do not want to give them any more of our money." Edek told the couple.

"That is not good enough for us," the old woman said. "You Jews need to learn to treat Poles with respect." Ruth could see Edek's face clenching. She felt sorry for him.

"Don't let them get to you," she said. "We can't let them upset us."

"I am okay," Edek said. "We have a companion with us," Edek said to the couple.

"A relative?" the old man said. "The cousin who buried this?"

"The cousin is no longer alive," Edek said.

"I am very sorry," said the old woman.

"Our companion is Polish," Edek said. "I think we should let him negotiate on our behalf."

"Negotiation is the right attitude," the old man said, and grinned.

Tadeusz arrived back with the doorman. The doorman was carrying the spades and shovels. He nodded to Ruth and Edek. He walked over to the old couple.

"Good morning, good people," he said in a very loud voice. "Are we having any trouble this morning?" The old man and woman looked at the doorman.

"All of a sudden they're mute," Ruth said to Edek.

"We are not really having trouble," Edek said to the doorman. "This kind couple are merely trying to establish a price for allowing us to dig up a small part of their yard."

"A price?" the doorman said. "Just to dig in a dirty old yard?" He moved closer to the old couple. He was three or four times their size, Ruth thought.

"It's okay, it's okay," the old man said, trying to edge away from the doorman. "We have negotiated a price, the rich Jewess and I have agreed on a price."

"The rich Jewess, did you hear that?" Ruth said to Edek.

"You do understand what he says?" Edek said to Ruth.

"Unfortunately, yes," said Ruth.

"What is the price?" the doorman said to Ruth.

"Two hundred dollars now and five hundred when the digging is finished," the old man answered.

"Five hundred if we find anything," Ruth said to the doorman.

"That is very expensive," the doorman said to Ruth. "Shall we try to lower the price?" he said, in Polish.

"An agreement is an agreement," the old woman said vehemently. Both of her wigs shook.

"I'm happy to stick to that," Ruth said to the doorman. She got out her purse.

"Your money is in American dollars, I hope," the old man said.

"Yes," said Ruth. She handed the money to the doorman. "Give it to him, please," she said. The old man counted the money and grinned.

"Do you want to dig?" Ruth said to Edek. "Or should we ask the doorman to help?"

"I will dig myself," Edek said. He took one of the spades and looked at the ground. He started to push the spade into the earth. No one spoke. The ground was hard. Edek pushed and pushed. He was hardly making a dent.

"Let me help you, sir," Tadeusz said.

"Why should you help?" the doorman said to Tadeusz. "I can help."

"Dad, would you like me to try?" Ruth said.

"No," said Edek. He kept digging. He managed to get through the top layer of frozen earth.

"Please," said the doorman. "Let me assist you."

"I am okay," Edek said. He bent down and ran his fingers through the uncovered earth. The old man and his wife peered at Edek's hands fingering the black earth he had brought up.

"Anything there?" the old man said, in a high-pitched voice. Ruth looked at the old man. His face was stretched and pulled into a large leer. His wife, who was next to him, was shriveled and creased in concentration.

"I cannot see anything," Edek said. He wiped his brow. Digging had made him hot. Ruth could see the sweat on his brow.

"Please, sir, let me," the doorman said to Edek.

"No, thank you," Edek said. He took off his jacket and handed it to Ruth.

Edek dug the spade into the ground and pushed it in farther with his foot. He brought out several more spadefuls of earth. Ruth watched her father. He was in the middle of a ritual. He didn't want anyone's help. This was his own ritual. His own upending and bringing up of something long buried. Something long swallowed and covered. It seemed like a funeral in reverse, Ruth thought. What would that be? A funeral in reverse? Rebirth, renewal, redemption? A small object, buried in the ground, couldn't possibly cause rebirth, renewal, or redemption.

Edek kept digging. He was opening the earth. The earth that his mother and father and brothers and sister and nephews and nieces had all walked on. Ruth looked at the earth. It was very black. Ruth wanted to dig, too.

"Can I do some digging?" she said to Edek.

"No, Ruthie," Edek said, standing up. "There is nothing there." He had dug a large, deep hole. "There is nothing there," Edek said again.

"You're still going to pay for this," the old man said. "You have dug a very big hole on our property."

"You've spoiled our garden," the old woman said. Both of them looked pinched and tense.

"Your garden?" Ruth said and laughed.

"Let me fix the hole up," the doorman said. "There will be no mess left," he said to the old couple. They looked grim. Ruth looked at her father. He looked flat. Deflated.

"I am sorry, Ruthie," he said. "It is not here."

"It's okay, Dad," she said. "We tried our best."

"I am sorry to bring you here again," Edek said to Ruth. "I did drag you all the way from Kraków for what? For nothing."

"I'm fine," said Ruth. "And it was good that we looked for whatever it was. Now at least you'll know it's not there."

"Nothing is here," Edek said. He looked as though he might cry. Ruth walked over to her father. She put her arm around him.

"We'll be in New York, soon," she said. "We can go to the Carnegie Deli and we can take Garth with us." Edek tried to smile. Ruth felt flat herself. What had she been hoping for? She didn't know. She just knew she had been hoping for something.

"We feel we are entitled to more money," the old woman said, adjusting the upper wig. "We waited for you to do this, and now we have missed church."

"You had a long list of confessions prepared, did you?" Ruth said.

"Do not translate this," Edek said to Tadeusz.

"These people are the assholes of the earth," Ruth said.

"Do not translate this, too," Edek said.

The doorman laughed. Ruth saw that every one of his back teeth, upper and lower, was covered in gold.

"I like your language," he said. "Assholes of the earth."

"Please," said Edek. "Do not speak like this."

"Forgive me," the doorman said to Edek. "You will not pay them any extra?" the doorman said to Ruth.

"No," she said.

"I will fill in the digging," the doorman said to Edek. "And I will speak to the old couple." He rolled up his sleeves.

Suddenly, Edek spun around. "I did just remember something what Herschel did say," he said to Ruth. "Herschel did say he did bury it very close to the wall of the toilet, nearly under the wall." Edek picked up the spade and walked to the wall of the outhouse. He began to dig. Everyone moved closer. Ruth, Tadeusz, the doorman, and the old couple were all now standing only a few feet from Edek.

"You will have to pay for this destruction," the old man said. He was staring at Edek. Following the movements of the spade with his eyes. He looked almost mesmerized, Ruth thought.

"Destruction?" Ruth said. "In this place? This is landscaping we're doing. Tadeusz, tell them we're doing them a favor." The old woman glared at Ruth. She had clearly understood the tone of the comment if not the content. Ruth smiled at her.

"This is not a helpful attitude," Tadeusz said to Ruth.

"I don't care," she said.

She looked at Edek. He was still digging. He was glistening with sweat. She felt worried about the effect of the stress and the physical exertion on him. But she knew that she had to let him dig. He dug for several minutes in silence. No one spoke. Edek had uncovered part of the foundation of one wall of the outhouse. What were they doing, she and Edek? Ruth thought. Here they were, in Łódź in this miserable, wretched, industrial city, with coal smoke in the air and soot in the souls of its inhabitants. What were they doing? Two Jews surrounded by four Poles, all of whom they were shelling out money to.

Ruth looked at the old man. A grimace of excitement filled his face. He was hopping from one of his skinny legs to the other. He seemed unable to keep still. His wife was scowling. Both of her feet were planted firmly on the ground. They were both staring at the spot Edek had now uncovered. Edek kept digging. Ruth wished that she could stop looking at the old man. His face was shiny. Every now and then a big grin slipped from his grimace.

"I think we are going to find something," the old man said to his wife.

"Maybe we will," she said. "Our luck has been with us lately." The old man roared with laughter. He clutched his crotch in excitement. Ruth felt sick. The old woman looked at her husband clutching his crotch, and grinned. A wide, sly grin. Ruth felt furious. She wanted to blotch that grin. To muddy it. To smudge it right off the old woman's face. The old woman looked at Ruth and gestured with her head in the direction of the old man's hand firmly gripped around his crotch. She grinned at Ruth. Ruth felt sick.

Ruth looked at the doorman. "Would it be possible for you to come back later?" she said to him.

"Yes," he said.

"Good," she said. "Could you come back and beat up this old couple for me?" The doorman looked at her. "I would pay you very well," she said.

"I understand," the doorman said.

"This is not a wise idea," Tadeusz said.

"I wasn't asking you," said Ruth. She felt better. She smiled at the doorman. The doorman moved closer to Edek.

"Do you know what your daughter has requested of me?" he said to Edek. The doorman lowered his voice. Ruth couldn't hear the rest of what was being said. Edek stopped digging.

"What has got into you, Ruthie?" he said. Why did Edek keep asking her what had got into her?

"Nothing has got into me," she said. "I'm still me. The same me. I just want to kill the old couple."

"Ruthie, Ruthie," Edek said.

"It's okay, I won't do anything," she said.

Edek resumed his digging. He dug and dug. Half of the outhouse's foundations now seemed to be exposed. Edek got down on his knees, and dug a hole at the base of the foundations. Suddenly he stiffened.

"I think I did find something." Everyone crowded in.

"Step back please," the doorman said to the old couple.

"I thought you looked in this spot," the old woman said to her husband.

"I did," the old man said. "But I didn't look under the wall."

"Idiot," she said, and cuffed him on the back of the head. He cringed.

"We still get five hundred dollars from this," he said to her.

"But who knows what he's got hidden under that wall," she said, in disgust.

"Hit him again," Ruth said to the old woman. The old woman spat in Ruth's direction.

"Ruthie, Ruthie, column down," said Edek. "I think I got something." He reached under the foundation and dug around with his fingers. He was lying stretched out on the ground.

"Could I help you?" the doorman said.

"I got it," Edek said breathlessly. He pulled out a small object, and began removing the dirt from its surface. The old man and woman tried to get closer.

"What has he got? What has he got?" the old woman said.

"Step back please," the doorman said. The old couple stepped back in unison. Like two schoolchildren who had been ordered to move by the headmaster. Ruth wanted to hug the doorman.

Edek got up. He had cleaned up the object. Ruth could see it. It was a small, rusty, flat tin. "I did find it," Edek said, and smiled. He looked pleased with himself. Ruth looked up. Two strange men had arrived. They were standing there watching Edek.

"Who are you?" the doorman said to the men.

"Neighbors," one of the men replied.

"Did they find gold?" one of the men said to the old woman. She shook her head.

"There was no gold," she said.

"The Jews took it with them," the neighbor said. The old woman nodded in agreement.

Edek put the tin in his pocket. "We can fix up the hole and go now," he said to the doorman.

"I will return later and fix this up," the doorman said. Ruth looked at him. She felt hopeful. What did he mean? Was this his way of saying he was accepting her invitation to rough up the old couple? The doorman laughed. "I mean that I will come back and replace this earth," he said.

"Oh," she said.

"I like you very much," the doorman said to Ruth.

"Thank you," she said. He must think that she was a thug, like him, she thought. Maybe she was.

"Are you going to open the tin?" Ruth said to Edek.

"Not here," he said. "We will wait till we are in the hotel."

"Where's our money?" the old man said. "You said five hundred dollars if you found something." Ruth opened her purse.

"You are going to pay him?" the doorman said.

"I like being honorable," Ruth said.

"She said that she would pay them," Edek said.

"Anyhow, what's another few dollars?" Ruth said to Edek. Ruth handed the doorman the money.

"Tell her to wait for a minute," the old woman said to the doorman after taking the money from him. "I have something else I think she will want." The old woman ran inside. Ruth felt sick. What was she going to come up with now?

"We do not need anything more," Edek said. "Those bestids did take enough from us. I do not want you to give them any more money."

"Let's see what she's got," Ruth said. She needed a Mylanta. She wished she hadn't run out. The old man smiled at her. The smile made Ruth feel worse. What were the old couple doing? What did they have in store for her? What had they kept in reserve? What was the old woman going to unearth now?

The old woman came back. She was out of breath. She was carrying a vase. A bright green vase, with a crack down one side.

"I think this might interest you," she said. Edek looked at the vase.

"This was not ours," he said to Ruth. Ruth shook her head at the old woman. "We are not interested in this vase," Edek said in Polish to the doorman. Ruth wanted to grab the vase and break it over the old couple's heads. Instead, she walked away. She turned, after a couple of steps, and spat in their direction. Edek looked at her.

"What has got into you, Ruthie?" he said.

They drove back to the hotel in silence. Ruth felt exhausted. Edek must be very tired, she thought. He sat in the back of the car with her. He didn't speak for the whole trip. At the hotel, Edek thanked Robert, the driver. Then he thanked Tadeusz and the doorman, lavishly. "We could not have done this without you," he said to the doorman. Ruth paid Tadeusz and the doorman. She paid them an excessive amount. She didn't care. She was so glad to be out of the old couple's orbit. To be away from Kamedulska Street. She knew that the street and the building were no longer part of anything that belonged to her or to Edek. She knew that she would never be back.

"Give the doorman a bit extra," Edek said.

"Okay," said Ruth. The doorman smiled.

"It is a pleasure to do business with you," he said to Ruth.

"My daughter is a businesswoman," Edek said. Everybody shook hands.

"Thank you, thank you, thank you," Edek said again.

"I'm going to tell the front desk that we're checking out at four o'clock," Ruth said to Edek. I'll meet you in the lobby."

"Shall I order something to eat?" Edek said. Ruth looked at him. He must be feeling okay if he was thinking about food. Maybe the contents of the tin weren't too troubling.

"Order whatever you want," Ruth said. "And get me some soup. Chicken soup."

"You want some rye bread, too?" Edek said.

"Okay," she said.

Ruth ordered a taxi to pick them up at 3:55 P.M. "I'll have a Mercedes," she said to the man at the front desk. "A big Mercedes." She went to the bathroom. She wanted to wash her face. She needed to wash some of the grime of this morning away. In the bathroom, she looked in the mirror. She was surprised when she saw that she looked quite clean. Her face was clear. Her eyes were bright. The curls in her hair were jutting out at joyful angles. She looked at herself again. There was no sign of any grubbiness.

Edek was sitting in an armchair, next to a small table, in the lobby. He looked quite calm, Ruth thought, when she saw him. She pulled up another chair.

"What a morning," she said to Edek, as she sat down.

"What a morning," Edek said.

"Have you opened the tin?" Ruth said.

"Yes," said Edek. "I seen already what is inside."

"Is it what you wanted to find?" Ruth said.

"It is what I did want to find," Edek said.

"Can I see?" Ruth said.

"Let us eat something first," Edek said. "It is good to eat after a morning like this."

"Okay," Ruth said. "Anyway, you need something to eat. You did a lot of digging. And it was pretty awful being there."

"It was not so nice," Edek said. He rubbed his hands together. "The soup will be here soon," he said. "And I did order for myself a ham sandwich."

Ruth laughed. "You might as well enjoy that Polish ham while you're here. We won't be here much longer."

"I do like the Polish ham very much," Edek said.

"Weren't that old couple the most revolting people in the world?" Ruth said.

Edek looked at her. "You was not so wonderful yourself," he said. "I did not know that my daughter was a criminal."

"I'm not a criminal," Ruth said.

"Maybe you would not go through with this idea that the doorman should beat them up," Edek said. "Maybe you would not do it if the doorman did say yes to your suggestion."

"And maybe I would," Ruth said.

The food arrived. "This is very good service," Edek said to the waiter. "Give him a tip," Edek said to Ruth. Ruth gave the waiter twenty zlotys.

"Our tips have come to more than our hotel bills and airfares, I think," Ruth said.

"So what?" said Edek.

Ruth took a sip of her soup. "At least the soup is very good," she said. They ate in silence. Ruth felt warmed and nourished by the soup. She decided to make some chicken soup when she got home to New York. She had her mother's recipe.

Edek's ham sandwich had come with potato salad, dill pickles, and pickled cabbage. Edek was eating mouthful after mouthful. "I did not eat so much for breakfast," he said eventually, when he took a break.

"I've never wanted to go home to New York so badly in my life," she said to Edek. "You must be looking forward to leaving Poland, too."

"That is the truth, Ruthie," he said. "I am ready to leave." He finished off the last of the pickled cabbage. He let out a large sigh, and mopped his mouth with a napkin. He moved all of the dishes out of the way, and reached into his pocket. Ruth felt scared.

"Are you sure you want to show me?" she said.

"I am happy that you will see this," Edek said.

Ruth felt more fearful. A sense of dread was mounting up inside her. She could feel the dread in her mouth, in her throat, in her lungs, and in her stomach. The dread was fueled by a feeling of imminent change. Big change. A change that had been traveling in her direction for years. A change that was part of something inevitable. Part of a destiny that had been mapped out long ago. Why was she thinking about destiny? She didn't believe in destiny. Was she destined to see the contents of this small tin? She didn't think so. Destiny was composed of much bigger moments. If, indeed, there was any destiny. There were destinations, Ruth decided. Not destinies. She could deal with destinations. She believed in destinations. She took a deep breath. There was no need to feel scared, she told herself.

Edek opened the tin. There was no rust on the inside of the lid. It was silver and shiny. Ruth marveled at the condition of the inside of the tin. How could it have remained so clean after fifty-two years in the earth? Fifty-two years of being buried in Polish earth. Surrounded by Poles looking for Jewish gold. And it was still there. Still in pristine condition. Ruth was glad that the tin was now with its rightful owner. She realized that she was avoiding looking at what was in the tin. The tin held only one thing. Edek removed the object from the tin. It was a photograph. A small photograph. He held the small sepia-toned photograph in his hand. Ruth looked at the tin. There was definitely nothing else in the tin. Was this what they had come to Łódź for?

Edek handed Ruth the photograph. She looked at it. It was a photograph of her mother. Rooshka's hair was very short in the photograph. And her face was thicker than Ruth had ever seen it. Rooshka was holding a small baby. The small baby was Ruth. "It's a photograph of Mum and me," she said to Edek. "No, it couldn't be," she corrected herself with a start. "I wasn't born yet. I wasn't born when this tin was buried."

"It does look like you," Edek said. "But it is not you." Ruth felt sick. She wished she hadn't eaten the soup. What was this? Who was this?

"It's one of the babies that she lost, isn't it?" Ruth said. "It's one of the babies Mum grieved for all of her life."

"That is right," Edek said. He swallowed hard. Ruth could see that this was not easy for him.

She looked at the baby in the photograph. It looked just like her. Just like all the baby photographs of her. Large hooded eyes. Fine face. You could see the baby's face so clearly in this small photograph. Ruth felt chilled. Was this the baby of her dreams, too? The baby she couldn't look after? The baby she always lost? Who was this little boy?

"His name was Israel," Edek said.

"After your father?" said Ruth.

"Yes," said Edek. "After my father." Ruth started crying. "Do not cry yet, Ruthie," Edek said. "I want to tell you the whole story." She looked at Edek. He was holding a napkin. His hand was trembling.

"You know when Mum and me did find each other after the war they put us in Feldafing," Edek said.

"The DP camp," she said.

"Yes," said Edek. "We was still without enough food. We was living in barracks. We did have armed guards and barbed wire around us."

"The American general," Ruth said, "General George S. Patton Jr., insisted that every one of the Displaced Persons camps in Germany that were under the jurisdiction of the United States was manned by armed guards and enclosed by barbed wire. He was treating the displaced people as though they were prisoners."

"We was like prisoners again," Edek said, "but not so bad like before."

"Few things would rival what you and Mum had just experienced," Ruth said.

"That is true," Edek said. "And we was grateful for a place to sleep, and grateful to have something to eat."

"I think the great American general enjoyed the extra difficulties he created," Ruth said. "He wrote in his diary that others 'believe that the Displaced Person is a human being, which he is not, and this applies particularly to the Jews, who are lower than animals.' "

"*Oy a broch,*" Edek said. "A big American general did say that?" He looked at Ruth. "And you, Ruthie, poor *kindeleh,* do have to remember every word."

Tears came into Ruth's eyes, again. Her father had not called her *kindeleh*, the affectionate diminutive of child, in Yiddish, for years, for decades.

"I was trying to get Mum extra food, in Feldafing," Edek said. "We was both hungry. It was not so easy in Feldafing. People what was prisoners for so many years, and treated worse than dogs, sometimes did act like animals. They did not want to wash, or to flush the toilet. It was not easy. Mum always did say that we did not stay alive to act like animals. She used to wash the whole bathroom at Feldafing before she did use it. Many people in Feldafing did also hide food. They did hide it so that they would have something to eat when they was starving again." Edek paused. "Poor Mum," he said. "She did hide bread. She did put bread in our coats and in our shoes. She was sure every day that it was our last bread. We lived like this for a long time." He looked at Ruth. "Sometimes I would look at Mum and me and ask myself, did I live through everything what I lived through, in order to watch poor Rooshka hiding pieces of bread."

"It must have been so awful," Ruth said, "because by then you knew that your parents, Mum's parents, and all your brothers and sisters were dead."

Edek nodded. "Mum did not even know she was pregnant," he said. "She was eating a lot of bread, and slowly, like quite a few of the women there, she was getting a bit fat. If you been starving for six years it is not so easy to stop eating. Mum went one day to a doctor what was looking after some of the women in the camp and he did tell her she was pregnant. She was not happy, Ruthie. What mother does want to bring a baby into a bar-racks, that has mud and policemen and guards. I did make a promise to Rooshka that we would get out of the camp." Edek heaved a big sigh. "It was not so easy," he said.

"Poor Mum," Ruth said.

"Poor Mum," said Edek. "I was myself happy to have a child. I did think we would get out of the camp and make a life together. I did say to Rooshka, 'Rooshka this child will be a wonderful child.' And Mum did feel better. She did make some clothes for the baby. One of the officers did give Mum some parachute silk. And she did sit and cut out and stitch, by hand, very beautiful things for the baby." Edek started to cry. Ruth took his hand. "I am sorry," he said. Ruth started to cry, too.

"It's okay to cry, Dad," she said.

"The doctor did arrange with Mum that a midwife would come for the birth," Edek said. "But Mum did want the doctor himself to be with her. He did say he would try." Edek sniffed, and wiped his eyes with the back of his hand. "It was lucky that the doctor did come," he said. "As soon as the doctor did see the baby, he did see that something was wrong. The midwife could see it also. When Mum did ask what was wrong, the midwife did say the baby was not such a good color. The doctor did say the baby must go to a hospital."

Edek stopped speaking. He turned away from Ruth. Ruth could see his shoulders heaving. He was weeping. She put her arm around him.

"Dad, you don't have to tell me this," she said. Edek got a handkerchief out of his pocket. He blew his nose.

"I want to tell you, Ruthie," he said. He wiped his eyes. "Mum did scream and scream when they did take the baby away from her," Edek said. "Ruthie, she did scream like an animal, like a dying person, it was a terrible, terrible scream. Nobody could stop her. 'Where is my baby?' she did scream, in German, until they did give her something to make her go to sleep. Even the midwife was crying."

Ruth was trembling. She didn't want to hear any more of this story. She didn't want to think of her mother screaming. Screaming for a baby that had been taken from her again.

"The midwife did say to me when Mum was asleep that she did think there was something wrong with the baby's heart," Edek said, and started weeping, again.

"You can tell me the rest of the story later," Ruth said. "You don't have to tell me right now, Dad." She was freezing. Her teeth were almost knocking into each other. She couldn't bear to see Edek cry like this.

"The midwife did say it was a tragedy," Edek said. "The midwife did look at Mum and say, 'She did bury, already, too many.' I said to the midwife, 'She did not bury any,' " Edek said. "The midwife said she did understand what I was saying."

Ruth felt exhausted. Her legs were shaking. She tried to keep them pinned onto the floor.

"Mum was still crying when she did wake up," Edek said. "The doctor did bring the baby back the next day. Mum was so happy. He was a beautiful little baby. The doctor did explain to me what he did think was wrong. And I did have to explain it to Mum."

Edek shook his head and blew his nose again. Ruth looked at him. His eyes were red. His features were in disarray. He looked broken. Heartbroken. "The doctor did explain to me," Edek said, "that there was something wrong with the baby's heart. He did explain to me that the job of the heart is to pump the blood through the body. The blood does carry the oxygen from the lungs to the body. He did explain to me that there is two sides to the heart. The left side and the right side. The left side is bigger and does get the blood from the lungs, which does have a lot of oxygen, and does pump it to the body. The right side is smaller and does take the blood which is coming back from the body and does pump it to the lungs. Do you understand what I am saying, Ruthie?"

"I'm following you," she said.

"The doctor was a nice man," Edek said. "He did explain to me that he was not sure but he did think that this baby did have a small hole between two places what are smaller pumps on the left and the right. He did say the baby would not die straightaway, but babies with this small hole did not usually live to be adults. He did say it did depend on how big was the hole. He did say this baby was not so blue, so maybe the hole was small."

Edek put his face in his hands. "The doctor did say to me," he said, "that this baby should not be living in barracks. Especially as it would be soon winter. He said this baby needed to have the best doctors." Edek stopped. "Ruthie, I did never cry so much in my life. I did cry and cry. And then I did have to tell Mum. Before I did tell Mum, the doctor did say to me that he did know about a couple who did want to adopt a child. He did say that this couple was very rich. He did say the couple was neighbors of his. They did want children for a long time. The doctor did say to go to a couple like this was the only chance for the baby."

Edek started weeping again. Ruth felt as though every part of her body was shaking. Her brain, her heart, her fingers, her feet. She couldn't stop shaking. "Mum did already breast-feed the baby," Edek said. "She was so happy with him. 'He is a beautiful baby, Edek,' she did say to me." Edek's voice broke, again.

"Do you want to have a break, Dad?" Ruth said. "Would you like to go for a walk or get some fresh air?" Edek shook his head.

"Mum and me we did make the decision together," Edek said. "Mum did feel that what was wrong with the baby was because of her."

"How?" said Ruth.

"Because of the things what they did do to her, in the camps," Edek said. "She did say her insides was not clean."

"That is terrible," Ruth said. Tears ran down her face. "Mum felt it was her fault."

"They did terrible things to your mum," Edek said.

"I know," said Ruth.

"Ruthie, no one, not even me, can know how terrible," Edek said.

"I know," she said.

"The doctor did tell us he would organize the adoption," Edek said. Edek looked as though he was unable to continue. He looked down at his lap, and swallowed several times. "Your mum, Ruthie," he said, "did say that we have to give this baby the best chance to have a life. And she did say that the baby's best chance was not to stay with us." Tears were running down Edek's face.

"The doctor did say it was for the best for the baby if Mum did breast-feed the baby for two weeks," Edek said. "Mum did say she would do everything what was best for the baby. The doctor did move us to a little house, in the town of Feldafing, for two weeks. Mum did cry for the whole two weeks." Edek looked at Ruth. "Are you all right, Ruthie?" he said.

"I'm all right," she said. Her chest felt tight. She tried to undo her bra through her shirt. It finally opened. Maybe undoing her bra would help her to breathe, she thought.

"We did organize a circumcision," Edek said. "There was a *mohel* in the DP camp who was from Poland. On the night before the circumcision we did have a *vachnacht*, a night of watching. It was such a custom among some Jews to watch the baby the night before the circumcision. Mum did want this. She did say we did have to do everything what we could. So we did ask people from the camp to come and pray for the baby. All night we did sit around the baby and pray. People did do this to make sure that no evil spirits did get to the baby on the night before the circumcision. My cousin Herschel was there. He did pray all night, too."

Edek looked at Ruth. "You do not look so good, Ruthie," he said.

"I'm fine," she said.

"Do you want me to finish the story?" Edek said. Ruth nodded. "The doctor did bring us all the papers for the adoption," Edek said. "Mum and me did sign them and Mum did say to the doctor that she would give the baby to him the next day. Mum did want to have one last ceremony for her beautiful baby boy," Edek said. He stopped speaking and started to weep again.

"We did have a name-changing ceremony for our little boy," he said, after a couple of minutes. "Some Jews did believe that it was necessary to change the name of a sick person. They did believe that if you did change the name, any evil spirits what did want to do the sick person harm, would be confused. Herschel did organize a *minyan*. Ten men to pray for the baby. They did come and pray. They did tell God that this sick baby was no longer called Israel. He was now to be known as Chaim." Edek paused. "It did make Mum feel better. She did say she did not know if there was a God or not, but it was for the best to do everything possible for the baby. Of course, the German couple would give the baby straightaway another name. I do not think a German couple would want a son what is called Chaim."

Edek breathed out deeply. He looked exhausted. Collapsed. "There are some things, Ruthie, it is for the best not to think about," he said. "I been trying not to think about this, for many years. I been trying not to think about too many things for too many years."

"I know, Dad," she said. "I know." She felt numb. Numbed by the pain of Edek's and Rooshka's lives. Why had it been necessary for them to experience so much pain? She shook her head. That was a stupid question. There was no answer to that question.

"I know Rooshka did never forget," Edek said. "Every time she did look at me I did know that she was thinking about it. I did ask her once when she was looking very miserable if she think of the baby. She did say that if I did say one word to her about the baby, she would do something that she would regret. This was when we was already in Australia. I did not know what she did mean, but I did never mention it to her again."

Ruth looked around her. She was glad that the lobby was empty. This was not a time to be shared with anybody else.

"I did take a photograph of the baby," Edek said. "Mum was angry. She did say that if we are going to give him away, he will be out of our lives, so why should we pretend with a photograph that he is part of us."

"He would always be part of you," Ruth said. She picked up the photograph and looked at it. "He is a very beautiful baby," she said.

"He was a very beautiful baby," Edek said. "Not he is."

"He had a lot of hair," she said.

"Yes," said Edek. "Like you, he did have a lot of hair."

Her own birth, Ruth thought, must have been a nightmare for her mother. Another baby. Another baby to lose. She wished Rooshka was here, so she could tell her that she understood. Understood how difficult Rooshka's life had been. She wanted her mother to know that she, Ruth, held nothing against Rooskha. Not the haircut, not the diets, not anything.

"Mum did say it would be harder if we did have a photograph of the baby," Edek said. "Mum did tell me to throw away the photograph. But I did not want to throw it away. I had nowhere, in the barracks, to hide it from Mum, so I did give it to Herschel. Herschel did want to go back to Kamedulska Street. He did live there, too, on the top floor."

"So, he went back?" Ruth said.

"Herschel did say Kamedulska Street was still more his home than the barracks. When he did get there, he did see it was no more his home. He did not know what to do with the photograph, so he did bury it there. He did tell me when he did get back to Feldafing." Edek started to cry again. Ruth put her arm around him. She had stopped trembling. She was still numb. Still in a daze. She hugged Edek.

"I'm sorry you had to relive all of this, for me," she said.

"It did live with me all the time anyway, Ruthie," Edek said. "This is not something what a person does forget." He took another deep breath. "Mum did blame me," he said. "I always did feel this. She did blame me. We all do need to blame someone. Mum had no one to blame for so many things. So, she did blame me for this." He put his head in his hands. "I did understand," he said. "She did have too many people to blame for too many things. But it is too hard to blame hundreds of people. It is impossible to blame hundreds of people, so she did blame me for this one thing. That we did give our baby away. And to tell you the truth, I did blame myself, too." Tears ran down his face.

"It wasn't your fault, Dad," Ruth said.

"I think we did make the wrong decision," Edek said. "I did feel ashamed my whole life."

"You did nothing wrong," Ruth said. "You were trying to do your best for a child who would require a lot of care. You did nothing wrong. You gave him a chance. You couldn't look after him. You and Mum were so battered, so powerless, so bereaved, so homeless. You loved the baby. You wanted to do the best for him."

"Me and Rooshka did cry for a long time for this baby," Edek said. "In a way this decision to give the baby away did build such a brick between us. Do you understand what I mean?"

"You mean the decision created a wedge between you," Ruth said.

"That is it," Edek said. "A wedge. It did build a wedge between us. We did know always that we did do this. And it was not a good feeling. Mum did see the love she did have for me as a good thing, the only good thing in her life, before this. After that, the love she did feel for me was mixed up with the decision about the baby. Her love for me did never look so good to Mum again."

Edek and Ruth were both weeping now. "But Mum loved you," Ruth said.

"She did love me," Edek said. "But it was never again in the same way." Edek stopped for a moment. "I did know, Ruthie," he said, "that when I did sign the adoption papers, I did sign away part of the rest of all of my time on this earth. And I did know," he said through his tears, "that for Mum it was the same."

"You did nothing wrong, Dad," Ruth said. "And neither did Mum. Nothing wrong at all."

"I did read many years later that there was an operation to fix up this thing in the heart," Edek said. "In the newspapers they did call it a hole-in-the-heart operation. But I think this operation came too late for our baby."

"Maybe he managed to grow up, and then have the operation," Ruth said.

"I do not think so," said Edek.

"Why didn't you tell me about the baby?" Ruth said. "It would have been good for me to know."

"If I could not speak even with your mum about the baby," Edek said, "it would have been too hard to speak with you. Some things are too much."

"I understand," Ruth said. "But so much of what happened in your life became part of my life. It was impossible to grow up unaffected. The things that happened to you and to Mum became part of my life. Not the original experiences, but the effects of the experiences."

"I understand, Ruthie," Edek said.

"It's easier for people to think that children born after the war were not affected," Ruth said. "But they were. They had to be affected. Enormously affected. No matter how much everyone wanted to protect them from what happened, and to separate them from what happened, they couldn't. It was impossible."

"I can see this now," said Edek.

"You said that what was buried had nothing to do with me," Ruth said. "You said that in Kraków."

"This did happen years before you was born," Edek said.

"But it does have something to do with me," she said.

"It is just a picture," Edek said. "A photograph."

"It is still a brother," she said. "My brother." Saying those two words made her feel breathless. "My brother." What extraordinary words. She started gasping for air.

"Are you okay, Ruthie?" Edek said.

"I'm okay," she said. "It was just saying those words, 'my brother,' made me very tense. Made me unable to breathe." She took a deep breath.

"This is not your brother," Edek said. "This is a picture of your brother. You have to column down, Ruthie. This is a picture of a person what is probably not alive."

"I think he is," Ruth said. As soon as she said the words, a sense of calm descended on her. Her heart stopped pounding. She felt curiously still. Edek looked shocked.

"You do not know what you are saying, Ruthie," he said. "You are too upset. You do need a rest."

"Maybe," she said. "Maybe."

She shouldn't have said that, she thought. The words had flown out of her. Propelled by a strange force. A force that seemed separate from the rest of her. She had uttered the words without knowing where they had come from. Suddenly she thought about Gerhard Schmidt, Martina's husband. Could it be possible that Gerhard was the baby Edek and Rooshka gave away? That was absurd, she thought. She was clutching at straws. She remembered Martina saying that Gerhard had written a play about German parents who adopt a Jewish baby. Adoption was a common enough fantasy, Ruth thought. Many children had fantasies about being adopted. And Gerhard was a writer. Writers wrote out their fantasies. She thought of Martina saying that Gerhard's mother had cried at the play. Any mother would cry at that theme, Ruth thought. Gerhard couldn't possibly be the baby. It was too far-fetched.

Gerhard tapped his foot, she thought. That was a ridiculous link, Ruth thought. Foot tapping couldn't possibly be hereditary. "His parents treated him like glass," Martina had said. That could be a clue. A clue to what? she thought. A clue to something that was not possible. In order to placate herself, she decided, she would call Martina Schmidt. With a start, she remembered she didn't have Martina's phone number or her address. She would ring the Łódź Film School, she thought. Surely the Łódź Film School would have a forwarding address.

"What date was the baby born?" Ruth said to Edek.

"He was born on the seventh day of September, 1946," Edek said. Ruth added up the dates. They came to eight. Gerhard Schmidt was told by a numerologist that he was looking for a number eight, she remembered Martina Schmidt saying. But was Gerhard himself an eight? Why was she even thinking about this? Ruth thought. She didn't believe in numerology.

"So my birthday was a day before the baby's birthday, a decade later," she said.

"Yes," said Edek. "Rooshka did not want to have you born on the same day. She did walk up and down the house all day. All day, she did say, 'This baby will be born today.' Finally, five minutes before twelve o'clock at night, you was born. Mum was so happy. She did think it would bring you bad luck to be born on the same day. I did say to her, 'Rooshka, days and numbers do not bring bad luck.' But she would not listen."

"I'm tired, Dad," Ruth said. "I'm going to go to my room for a while."

"Me, too," said Edek. "Maybe I will read a book."

"Is *As Blood Goes By* good?" Ruth said.

"It was not bad," Edek said. "I did finish it last night."

"I can't believe you've already finished it," Ruth said.

"I got a new one," Edek said. "It is my last one what I brought with me to Poland."

"What is it called?" said Ruth.

"The Cross-Eyed Stranger," Edek said.

"I hope it's good," Ruth said.

"It does look good, already," Edek said. "It is lucky that we are going to New York, I can buy some more books."

"You'll be able to buy plenty more in New York," Ruth said.

Ruth sat in her room. She felt worn out. She had to stop thinking about numbers and babies and heart operations. She thought about the fortune-teller at the circus. The one who had told her, when she was sixteen, that a man with a scar would play a large part in her life. She shook her head. She had to stop thinking like this. She didn't believe in fortune-tellers. She didn't believe in predictions of any sort. Anyway, if that fortune-teller was so good, Ruth thought, why had she had to sell soft drinks as well as predict the future?

The scar was large, the fortune-teller had said. A large scar that ran vertically from the top of the rib cage to the waist. Ruth was suddenly seized with a need to know what sort of scar a hole-in-the-heart operation would leave. She wanted to ring a doctor. She looked at her watch. It was already after office hours in New York.

Of course cardiac surgery would leave a chest scar. Any layperson could work that out. What did it prove? Nothing. It proved nothing. It suggested that there were many coincidences in life, Ruth thought. And this was something that she already knew. And even if some people had the ability to predict things, it still didn't mean much. It didn't mean that the baby had survived. It certainly didn't mean that the baby was Martina's husband. It probably meant very little.

Ruth felt frightened. What did it all mean? she thought. Did it mean there was a destiny? A guiding force? There couldn't be a guiding force. If there was a guiding force, all of the Jews who suffered and died wouldn't have died and suffered like that. Did some people know what the future held? Did they know bits and pieces of the future? Was there a grand plan? She didn't think so.

She decided to write herself a list. Writing a list would help her to calm down. She would list the avenues that she could investigate when she was safely at home in New York. When she was back on familiar territory, familiar terrain. Back in a place where not everything seemed tilted. She got out a pen and paper. She headed the list "Things to Investigate in New York." Underneath the heading she wrote:

> Doctors who worked with DPs in Feldafing.
> Midwives who worked in the Feldafing area.
> Adoption agencies in southern Germany.
> Ring Łódź Film School.
> Place ads in German papers.

The list made her feel much better. There was a knock on her door. She answered the door. It was Edek.

"I did just want to see if you was all right," he said.

"Come in, Dad," she said. "I'm okay. I actually feel better than I did before."

"I do feel much better myself," Edek said. "I am happy that I did come back to Łódź and get the photograph," he said. "I am happy I did tell you the whole story."

"I'm glad, too, Dad," she said.

Edek looked around the room. "This room is as bad as mine room," he said.

"It's pretty awful, isn't it?" Ruth said.

"It is a shocking room," Edek said. Ruth pulled back the bedding on the bed.

"Look at this, Dad," she said. "Three sheets to cover one double bed." Edek looked at the sheets.

"This is really something special. I never seen anything like this."

"Special to Łódź," Ruth said.

"Very special to Łódź," he said. Edek started to laugh. "This is a very funny way to make a bed," he said. He clutched his stomach, and laughed harder. "I did never see a bed what was made like this," he said.

Ruth started laughing. "You have to laugh," she said.

The phone in the room rang. "Who could that be?" Ruth said.

"I think it could be for me," Edek said. He ran toward the phone. He picked it up. "It is for me," he said to Ruth. He turned away from her. "Hello, hello," he said into the phone. Ruth wondered who it could be.

Maybe it was Edek's lawyer. The lawyer from Melbourne. Edek had lowered his voice. She heard him say he was in his daughter's room. Ruth stared at him. "I do not have time to call you back," Edek said in Polish, into the phone.

Ruth was bewildered. Who was her father talking to? She looked at Edek. "Yes, yes, yes," he was saying. "Yes, of course. My daughter did take it fine," he said. She tapped Edek on the shoulder.

"Who is it?" she whispered.

"My daughter does send you her warmest regards," Edek said.

"Who is it?" Ruth said.

"Yes," Edek said. "She does send you her most warm regards."

"Who is it?" Ruth said, again.

"Yes, yes," Edek said into the phone. He laughed. "I do not have time to talk now, my sweetheart," Edek said. My sweetheart, Ruth thought. Is that what he said? My sweetheart. "My sweetheart, we are leaving very soon for New York," Edek said, into the phone. *Moje ukochanie.* My sweetheart. My love. Was that what Edek had said? The words spun around Ruth's head. My sweetheart. That was definitely what Edek had said.

Ruth shook her head. She sat down on the bed. "I will call you as soon as I get to New York," Edek said into the phone. Ruth was still shaking her head. "Bye bye, my sweetheart," Edek said. "I will call you the second I do get to New York." He hung up the phone. "That was Zofia," Edek said.